HAN

A TALE OF IRISH LIFE

HANDY ANDY

A TALE OF IRISH LIFE

Samuel Lover

NONSUCH

First published 1842
Copyright © in this edition 2006
Nonsuch Publishing Ltd

Nonsuch Publishing Limited
The Mill, Brimscombe Port, Stroud, Gloucestershire, GL5 2QG
www.nonsuch-publishing.com

For comments or suggestions, please email the editor of this series at:
classics@tempus-publishing.com

Nonsuch Publishing Ltd is an imprint of Tempus Publishing Group

British Library Cataloguing in Publication Data.
A catalogue record for this book is available from the British Library.

ISBN 1-84588-198-2

Typesetting and origination by Nonsuch Publishing Limited
Printed in Great Britain by Oaklands Book Services Limited

CONTENTS

Introduction to the Modern Edition   7
Address   11
Notice   13

Handy Andy   15

INTRODUCTION TO THE
MODERN EDITION

Here's a health to you, my darlin'
Though I'm not worth a farthin';
For when I'm drunk I think I'm rich,
I've a feather-bed in every ditch.

Paddy's Pastoral Rhapsody,
Samuel Lover (1797–1868)

IT IS OFTEN REMARKED THAT an unfortunate trait of many writers is that their characters persist in emerging and re-emerging as thinly disguised variations of the writers themselves. This is a charge that has never been laid at the door of Samuel Lover. As a successful artist, musician, novelist and entertainer, he was worth substantially more than a farthing, and during the second half of his life, in London, he tended to spend more time at the centre of Lady Blessington's social and artistic coterie than asleep in a ditch.

An accusation that has, with some justification, been levelled at Lover is that he painted a picture of the Irish character with very broad strokes, creating clownish rogues and cunning rascals, witty knaves and noble fools. And all of them fond of a drink. If one was inclined to lend the weight of their opinion to this school, than one need look for no more exemplary a text than *Handy Andy*.

'Andy Rooney' begins this novel, 'was a fellow who had the most singularly ingenious knack of doing everything the wrong way; disappointment waited on all affairs in which he bore a part, and destruction was at his finger's ends.' The hero of the piece is, clearly, being set up as a fool, if a happy one. He is the *amadán* of Irish culture, the poor unfortunate to whom everything seems simple and nothing ever works. Maureen Waters in *The Comic Irishman* compares this character to the *schlemiel* of Yiddish folk culture, who struggles through a world which baffles him, reliant only on the goodness of his heart. This is the case for Andy.

Accompanying our hero through his simple trials and catastrophic failings are a host of friends and enemies that, were one of such a mind, could be damned as stock characters. There is the good Squire Egan, whose fierce temper is reined in by a stronger sense of the good; there is Murtough Murphy, the lawyer, sharp of mind and tongue, and proud of his talents; there is Squire O'Grady, sometimes cruel and often mean. Battling with these men for the reader's attention are the acerbic Doctor, whose shambling manner belies a mind and wit sharper than any so far, the beautiful Oonah, and the wise Father Blake. It is easy to imagine why *Handy Andy* could be accused of being simply a burlesque, a parody of a culture, in which Lover is exploiting the notion of the 'stage-Irishman' for his own ends.

This, however, is only one school of thought. Running contrary to this is the fact that Lover saw himself as something of a patriot. There is no doubt he was exploring a comfortably-worn track, and he was clearly not seeking to explode his reader's preconceptions and literary expectations. But his portrayal is a kind one. It is sympathetic within its confines. His characters are recognisable, certainly, but not to the point where they could be dismissed without consideration. They have a very great vitality, which is created to no little extent by Lover's ear for dialogue. Although, unlike Lady Gregory, he is not thought to have become an Irish-speaker for his art, the musical ability for which he was famous allowed him to pick up the nuances and inflections of the speech. This accuracy of tenor and cadence gives *Handy Andy* a colour, a musicality that brings it to life. The result, and this is Lover's greatest defence, is that the novel is really very good.

Handy Andy is structured in a series of episodic segments, with richly coloured strands of plot woven around the affairs of the central character. Lover seems to be a writer bursting at the seams with stories to tell, and there is a sense of the author's exuberance running through all his dramatic asides. Essentially, however, the tale of Andy Rooney is a relatively simple one. He is a character for whom things go wrong. From the very beginning he is pitched into a forest of misunderstandings, of half-truths and mistakes. Again and again, the reader is caught in the almost unbearably tense position of knowing more than the characters and seeing before they do how a fall is looming. There is a sense of Michael Crawford's portrayal of Frank Spencer in recent times, or of the convolutions of *The Comedy of Errors*. A simple formula, perhaps, but terribly easy for the author to be the one to get it wrong, and for the work to be flat and listless, no more than a litany of mishaps. It is only if the author gets the tone and pace correct that he can hold his readers' attention. And *Handy Andy* is compelling. It is also wonderfully funny.

Much of this was the author's skill, but more of it seems to be the care with which he crafted this novel. If he was famous for his ballads, including 'Rory O'More', which was later to be turned into a much-fêted novel, and 'The Low-back-d Car', quoted within James Joyce's *Ulysses*, he was even better regarded as a painter. Miniature portraits were his speciality, and of those Paganini was his most famous. There is a lovely story about how Lover drew the best out of the violinist as he sat for him, reminding him of a *capriccio motivo* that he played in accompaniment to the great soprano Giuditta Pasta. Paganini was flattered to be reminded of this moment and, in the reminiscence, became aglow. Lover captured the violinist's satisfaction in his painting and the portrait was widely lauded. It is a similar level of care and attention to the minutiae of his writing that imbues *Handy Andy* with such a warmth and vibrancy.

First published in *Bentley's Miscellany* in 1837, while under the editorial control of Charles Dickens, *Handy Andy* was extended and published in novel form in 1842. It was the novel which announced Lover the musician's arrival on the literary scene. He had published shorter stories before, notably 'The Gridiron', in *Dublin University*

Magazine, and *Legends & Stories of Ireland* (1832). His early writing, in the author's own words, was for glory; after that he would always get paid.

ADDRESS

I HAVE BEEN ACCUSED, IN certain quarters, of giving flattering portraits of my countrymen. Against this charge, I may plead that, being a portrait-painter by profession, the habit of taking the best view of my subject, so long prevalent in my eye, has gone deeper, and influenced my mind:—and if to paint one's country in its gracious aspect has been a weakness, at least, to use the words of an illustrious compatriot,

"——the failing leans to virtue's side."

I am disinclined, however, to believe myself an offender in this particular. That I love my country dearly, I acknowledge, and I am sure every Englishman will respect me the more for loving *mine*, when he is, with justice, so proud of *his*—but I repeat my disbelief that I overrate my own.

The present volume, I hope, will disarm any cavil from old quarters on the score of national prejudice. The hero is a blundering servant. No English or any other gentleman would like him in his service; but still he has some redeeming natural traits: he is not made either a brute or a villain, yet his "twelve months' character," given in successive numbers of this volume, would not get him a place upon advertisement, either in "The Times" or "The Chronicle." So far am I clear of the charge of national prejudice as regards the hero of the following pages.

In the subordinate personages, the reader will see two "Squires" of a different type—good and bad: there are such in all countries. And, as a tale cannot get on without villains, I have given some touches of villainy, quite sufficient to prove my belief in Irish villains, though I do not wish it to be believed the Irish are *all villains*.

I confess I have attempted a slight sketch, in one of the persons represented, of a gentleman and a patriot;—and I conceive there is a strong relationship between the two. He loves the land that bore him—and so did most of the great spirits recorded in history. His own mental cultivation, while it yields him personal enjoyment, teaches him not to treat with contumely inferior men. Though he has courage to protect his honour, he is not deficient in conscience to feel for the consequences; and when opportunity offers the means of *amende*, it is embraced. In a word, I wish it to be believed that, while there are knaves, and fools, and villains in Ireland, as in other parts of the world, honest, intelligent, and noble spirits are there as well.

I cannot conclude without offering my sincere thanks for the cordial manner in which my serial offering has been received by the public and noticed by the critical press, whose valuable columns have been so often opened to it in quotation; and, when it is considered how large an amount of intellect is employed in this particular department of literature, the highest names might be proud of such recognition.

SAMUEL LOVER

Charles Street, Berners Street, London,
December 1st, 1842.

NOTICE

K IND READER,

A FEW SHORT papers, under the title of this little venture, appeared, at intervals, in Bentley's Miscellany.

Frequent inquiries, have been made

"Why Handy Andy was not continued?"

and, indeed, I myself regretted the abandonment of what I thought a fruitful subject for fun and whimsicality, though, from various causes, needless to particularize here, the papers were discontinued; still, from time to time, recurred the question, "why Handy Andy was not continued?" and the frequency of the demand has produced the supply.

Ancient custom declares "we should begin at the beginning," therefore, a short reprint is unavoidable in the first number; but, while fairness to the public demands this acknowledgment, justice to myself requires me to state, that much revision and the introduction of fresh matter has taken place, with a view to the development of story and character necessary to a sustained work; for the first paper of *Handy Andy* was written without any intention of continuation, and required the amendments and additions I have mentioned. The reprint cannot affect those who have not read the beginning of Andy's adventures; and those who have, and wish to know more, will, it is hoped, skim over the first number to refresh their memories, and lead them well into the second. If, after all this explanation, there be any who object to the partial reprint, I answer, in the words of the well-known old saying,

"Sure hasn't an Irishman lave to spake twice?"

SAMUEL LOVER

I

A NDY ROONEY WAS A FELLOW who had the most singularly ingenious knack of doing everything the wrong way; disappointment waited on all affairs in which he bore a part, and destruction was at his fingers' ends: so the nickname the neighbours stuck upon him was Handy Andy, and the jeering jingle pleased them.

Andy's entrance into this world was quite in character with his after achievements, for he was nearly the death of his mother. She survived, however, to have herself clawed almost to death while her darling babby was in arms, for he would not take his nourishment from the parent fount unless he had one of his little red fists twisted into his mother's hair, which he dragged till he made her roar; while he diverted the pain by scratching her till the blood came, with the other. Nevertheless she swore he was "the loveliest and sweetest craythur the sun ever shined upon;" and when he was able to run about and wield a little stick, and smash everything breakable belonging to her, she only praised his precocious powers, and used to ask, "Did ever any one see a darlin' of his age handle a stick so bowld as he did?"

Andy grew up in mischief and the admiration of his mammy; but, to do him justice, he never meant harm in the course of his life, and was most anxious to offer his services on all occasions to those who would accept them; but they were only the persons who had not already proved Andy's peculiar powers.

There was a farmer hard by in this happy state of ignorance, named Owen Doyle, or, as he was familiarly called, *Owny na Coppal*, or, "Owen of the Horses," because he bred many of these animals, and sold them at the neighbouring fairs; and Andy one day offered his services to Owny when he was in want of some one to drive up a horse to his house from a distant "bottom," as low grounds by a river side are always called in Ireland.

"Oh, he's wild, Andy, and you'd never be able to ketch him," said Owny.

"Throth, an' I'll engage I'll ketch him if you'll let me go. I never seen the horse I couldn't ketch, sir," said Andy.

"Why, you little spridhogue, if he took to runnin' over the long bottom, it 'ud be more than a day's work for you to folly him."

"Oh, but he won't run."

"Why won't he run?"

"Bekaze I won't make him run."

"How can you help it?"

"I'll soother him."

"Well, you're a willin' brat, anyhow; and so go, and God speed you!" said Owny.

"Just gi' me a wisp o' hay an' a han'ful iv oats," said Andy, "if I should have to coax him."

"Sartinly," said Owny, who entered the stable and came forth with the articles required by Andy, and a halter for the horse also.

"Now, take care," said Owny, "that you're able to ride that horse if you get on him."

"Oh never fear, sir. I can ride owld Lanty Gubbins's mule betther nor any o' the other boys on the common, and he couldn't throw me th' other day, though he kicked the shoes av him."

"After that you may ride anything," said Owny: and indeed it was true; for Lanty's mule, which fed on the common, being ridden slily by all the young vagabonds in the neighbourhood, had become such an adept in the art of getting rid of his troublesome customers, that it might be well considered a feat to stick on him.

"Now, take grate care of him, Andy, my boy," said the farmer.

"Don't be afeard, sir," said Andy, who started on his errand in that peculiar pace which is elegantly called a "sweep's trot;" and as the river lay between Owny Doyle's and the bottom, and was too deep for Andy to ford at that season, he went round by Dinny Dowling's mill, where a small wooden bridge crossed the stream.

Here he thought he might as well secure the assistance of Paudeen, the miller's son, to help him in catching the horse; so he looked about the place until he found him, and, telling him the errand on which he was going, said,

"If you like to come wid me, we can both have a ride." This was temptation sufficient for Paudeen, and the boys proceeded together to the bottom, and they were not long in securing the horse. When they had got the halter over his head, "Now," said Andy, "give me a lift on him;" and accordingly, by Paudeen's catching Andy's left foot in both his hands clasped together in the fashion of a stirrup, he hoisted his friend on the horse's back; and, as soon as he was secure there, Master Paudeen, by the aid of Andy's hand, contrived to scramble up after him; upon which Andy applied his heels to the horse's side with many vigorous kicks, and crying "hurrup!" at the same time, endeavoured to stimulate Owny's steed into something of a pace as he turned his head towards the mill.

"Sure aren't you going to crass the river?" said Paudeen.

"No, I'm going to lave you at home."

"Oh, I'd rather go up to Owny's, and it's the shortest way acrass the river."

"Yes, but I don't like."

"Is it afeard you are?" said Paudeen.

"Not I, indeed," said Andy; though it was really the fact, for the width of the stream startled him; "but Owny towld me to take grate care o' the baste, and I'm loth to wet his feet."

"Go 'long wid you, you fool! what harm would it do him? Sure he's neither sugar nor salt, that he'd melt."

"Well, I won't anyhow," said Andy, who by this time had got the horse into a good high trot, that shook every word of argument out of Paudeen's body; besides, it was as much as the boys could do to keep their seats on Owny's Bucephalus, who was not long in reaching the miller's bridge. Here voice and halter were employed to pull him in, that he might cross the narrow wooden structure at a quiet pace. But whether his double load had given him the idea of double exertion, or that the pair of legs on each side sticking into his flanks, (and perhaps the horse was ticklish) made him go the faster, we know not; but the horse charged the bridge as if an Enniskilliner were on his back, and an enemy before him; and in two minutes his hoofs clattered like thunder on the bridge, that did not bend beneath him. No, it did *not* bend, but, it broke; proving the falsehood of the boast, "I may break, but I won't bend;" for, after all, the really strong may bend, and be as strong as ever: it is the unsound, that has only the seeming of strength, which breaks at last when it resists too long.

Surprising was the spin the young equestrians took over the ears of the horse, enough to make all the artists of Astley's envious; and plump they went into the river, where each formed his own ring, and executed some comical "scenes in the circle," which were suddenly changed to evolutions on the "flying cord" that Dinny Dowling threw the performers, which became suddenly converted into a "tight rope" as he dragged the *voltigeurs* out of the water; and for fear their blood might be chilled by the accident, he gave them both an enormous thrashing with the dry end of the rope, just to restore circulation; and his exertions, had they been witnessed, would have charmed the Humane Society.

As for the horse, his legs stuck through the bridge, as though he had been put in a *chiroplast*, and he went playing away on the water with considerable execution, as if he were accompanying himself in the song which he was squealing at the top of his voice. Half the saws, hatchets, ropes, and poles in the parish were put in requisition immediately; and the horse's first lesson in *chiroplastic* exercise was performed with no other loss than some skin and a good deal of hair. Of course Andy did not venture on taking Owny's horse home; so the miller sent him to his owner with an account of the accident. Andy for years kept out of Owny na Coppal's way; and at any time that his presence was troublesome, the inconvenienced party had only to say, "Isn't that Owny na Coppal coming this way?" and Andy fled for his life.

When Andy grew up to be what in country parlance is called "a brave lump of a boy," his mother thought he was old enough to do something for himself; so she took him one day along with her to the squire's, and waited outside the door, loitering up and down the yard behind the house, among a crowd of beggars and great lazy dogs that were thrusting their heads into every iron pot that stood outside the kitchen door, until chance might give her "a sight o' the squire afore he wint out or afore he wint in;" and, after spending her entire day in this idle way, at last the squire made his appearance and Judy presented her son, who kept scraping his foot, and pulling his forelock, that stuck out like a piece of ragged thatch from his forehead, making his obeisance to the squire, while his mother was sounding his praises for being the "handiest craythur alive—and so willin'—nothin' comes wrong to him."

"I suppose the English of all this is, you want me to take him?" said the squire.

"Throth, an' your honour, that's just it—if your honour would be plazed."

"What can he do?"

"Anything, your honour."

"That means *nothing*, I suppose," said the squire.

"Oh, no, sir. Everything, I mane, that you would desire him to do."

To every one of these assurances on his mother's part, Andy made a bow and a scrape.

"Can he take care of horses?"

"The best of care, sir," said the mother; while the miller, who was standing behind the squire waiting for orders, made a grimace at Andy, who was obliged to cram his face into his hat to hide the laugh, which he could hardly smother from being heard, as well as seen.

"Let him come, then, and help in the stables, and we'll see what he can do."

"May the Lord—"

"That'll do—there, now go."

"Oh, sure but I'll pray for you, and—"

"Will you go?"

"And may angels make your honour's bed this blessed night, I pray!"

"If you don't go, your son shan't come."

Judy and her hopeful boy turned to the right about in double-quick time, and hurried down the avenue.

The next day Andy was duly installed into his office of stable-helper; and, as he was a good rider, he was soon made whipper-in to the hounds, as there was a want of such a functionary in the establishment; and Andy's boldness in this capacity made him soon a favourite with the squire, who was one of those rollicking boys on the pattern of the old school, who scorned the attentions of a regular valet, and let any one that chance threw in his way bring him his boots, or his hot water for shaving, or his coat, whenever it was brushed. One morning, Andy, who was very often the attendant on such occasions, came to his room with hot water. He tapped at the door.

"Who's that?" said the squire, who was but just risen, and did not know but it might be one of the women servants.

"It's me, sir."

"Oh—Andy! Come in."

"Here's the hot wather, sir," said Andy, bearing an enormous tin can.

"Why, what the d—l brings that tin can here? You might as well bring the stable-bucket."

"I beg your pardon, sir," said Andy, retreating. In two minutes more Andy came back, and, tapping at the door, put in his head cautiously, and said, "the maids in the kitchen, your honour, says there's not so much hot wather ready."

"Did I not see it a moment since in your hands?"

"Yes, sir; but that's not nigh the full o' the stable-bucket."

"Go along, you stupid thief! and get me some hot water directly."

"Will the can do, sir?"

"Ay, anything, so you make haste."

Off posted Andy, and back he came with the can.

"Where'll I put it, sir?"

"Throw this out," said the squire, handing Andy a jug containing some cold water, meaning the jug to be replenished with the hot.

Andy took the jug, and the window of the room being open, he very deliberately threw the jug out. The squire stared with wonder, and at last said,

"What did you do that for?"

"Sure you *towld* me to throw it out, sir."

"Go out of this, you thick-headed villain!" said the squire, throwing his boots at Andy's head, along with some very neat curses. Andy retreated, and thought himself a very ill-used person.

Though Andy's regular business was "whipper-in," yet he was liable to be called on for the performance of various other duties:

he sometimes attended at table when the number of guests required that all the subs should be put in requisition, or rode on some distant errand, for "the mistress," or drove out the nurse and children on the jaunting-car; and many were the mistakes, delays, or accidents arising from Handy Andy's interference in such matters;—but, as they were seldom serious, and generally laughable, they never cost him the loss of his place, or the squire's favour, who rather enjoyed Andy's blunders.

The first time Andy was admitted into the mysteries of the dining-room, great was his wonder. The butler took him in to give him some previous instructions, and Andy was so lost in admiration at the sight of the assembled glass and plate, that he stood with his mouth and eyes wide open, and scarcely heard a word that was said to him. After the head man had been dinning his instructions into him for some time, he said he might go, until his attendance was required. But Andy moved not; he stood with his eyes fixed by a sort of fascination on some object that seemed to rivet them with the same unaccountable influence which the rattle-snake exercises over its victim.

"What are you looking at?" said the butler.

"Them things, sir," said Andy, pointing to some silver forks.

"Is it the forks?" said the butler.

"Oh no, sir! I know what forks is very well; but I never seen them things afore."

"What things do you mean?"

"These things, sir," said Andy, taking up one of the silver forks, an turning it round and round in his hand in utter astonishment while the butler grinned at his ignorance, and enjoyed his own superior knowledge.

"Well!" said Andy, after a long pause, "the divil be from me if ever I seen a silver spoon split that way before!"

The butler laughed a horse-laugh, and made a standing joke of Andy's split spoon; but time and experience made Andy less impressed with wonder at the show of plate and glass, and the split spoons became familiar as 'household words' to him; yet still there were things in the duties of table attendance beyond Andy's comprehension,—he used to hand cold plates for fish, and hot plates for jelly, &c. But 'one day,' as

Zanga says,—'one day' he was thrown off his centre in a remarkable degree by a bottle of soda-water.

It was when that combustible was first introduced into Ireland as a dinner beverage that the occurrence took place, and Andy had the luck to be the person to whom a gentleman applied for some soda-water.

"Sir?" said Andy.

"Soda-water," said the guest, in that subdued tone in which people are apt to name their wants at a dinner-table.

Andy went to the butler. "Mr. Morgan, there's a gintleman—"

"Let me alone, will you?" said Mr. Morgan.

Andy manoeuvred round him a little longer, and again essayed to be heard.

"Mr. Morgan!"

"Don't you see I'm as busy as I can be! Can't you do it yourself!"

"I dunna what he wants."

"Well, go an ax him," said Mr. Morgan.

Andy went off as he was bidden, and came behind the thirsty gentleman's chair, with "I beg your pardon, sir."

"Well!" said the gentleman.

"I beg your pardon, sir; but what's this you ax'd me for?"

"Soda-water."

"What, sir?"

"Soda-water: but, perhaps, you have not any."

"Oh, there's plenty in the house, sir! Would you like it hot, sir!"

The gentleman laughed, and supposing the new fashion was not understood in the present company, said, "Never mind."

But Andy was too anxious to please, to be so satisfied, and again applied to Mr. Morgan.

"Sir!" said he.

"Bad luck to you! can't you let me alone?"

"There's a gintleman wants some soap and wather."

"Some what?"

"Soap and wather, sir."

"Divil sweep you!—Soda-wather, you mane. You'll get it under the sideboard."

"Is it in the can, sir?

"The curse o' Crum'll on you!—in the bottles."

"Is this it, sir?" said Andy, producing a bottle of ale.

"No, bad cess to you!—the little bottles."

"Is it the little bottles with no bottoms, sir?"

"I wish *you* wor in the bottom o' the say!" said Mr. Morgan, who was fuming and puffing, and rubbing down his face with a napkin, as he was hurrying to all quarters of the room, or, as Andy said, in praising his activity, that he was "like bad luck,—everywhere."

"There they are! " said Morgan, at last.

"Oh! them bottles that won't stand," said Andy; "sure them's what I said, with no bottoms to them. How'll I open it?—it's tied down."

"Cut the cord, you fool!

Andy did as he was desired; and he happened at the time to hold the bottle of soda-water on a level with the candles that shed light over the festive board from a large silver branch, and the moment he made the incision, bang went the bottle of soda, knocking out two of the lights with the projected cork, which, performing its parabola the length of the room, struck the squire himself in the eye at the foot of the table, while the hostess at the head had a cold-bath down her back. Andy, when he saw the soda-water jumping out of the bottle, held it from him at arm's length; every fizz it made, exclaiming "Ow!—ow!—ow!" and, at last, when the bottle was empty, he roared out, "Oh, Lord!—it's all gone!'

Great was the commotion;—few could resist laughter except the ladies, who all looked at their gowns, not liking the mixture of satin and soda-water. The extinguished candles were relighted,—the squire got his eye open again,—and, the next time he perceived the butler sufficiently near to speak to him, he said in a low and hurried tone of deep anger, while he knit his brow, "Send that fellow out of the room!" but, within the same instant, resumed the former smile, that beamed on all around as if nothing had happened.

Andy was expelled the *salle à manger* in disgrace, and for days kept out of his master's and mistress's way: in the mean time the butler made a good story of the thing in the servants' hall; and, when he held up Andy's ignorance to ridicule, by telling how he asked for "soap and water," Andy was given the name of "Suds," and was called by no other for months after.

But, though Andy's functions in the interior were suspended, his services in out-of-doors affairs were occasionally put in requisition. But here his evil genius still haunted him, and he put his foot in a piece of business his master sent him upon one day, which was so simple as to defy almost the chance of Andy making any mistake about it; but Andy was very ingenious in his own particular line.

"Ride into the town, and see if there's a letter for me," said the squire one day to our hero.

"Yis, sir."

"You know where to go?"

"To the town, sir."

"But do you know where to go in the town?"

"No, sir."

"And why don't you ask, you stupid thief?"

"Sure I'd find out, sir."

"Didn't I often tell you to ask what you're to do, when you don't know?"

"Yis, sir."

"And why don't you?"

"I don't like to be throublesome, sir."

"Confound you!" said the squire; though he could not help laughing at Andy's excuse for remaining in ignorance.

"Well," continued he, "go to the post-office. You know the post-office, I suppose?"

"Yis, sir, where they sell gunpowdher."

"You're right for once," said the squire; for his Majesty's postmaster was the person who had the privilege of dealing in the aforesaid combustible. "Go then to the post-office, and ask for a letter for me. Remember,—not gunpowder, but a letter."

"Yis, sir," said Andy, who got astride of his hack, and trotted away to the post-office. On arriving at the shop of the postmaster, (for that person carried on a brisk trade in groceries, gimlets, broad-cloth, and linen-drapery,) Andy presented himself at the counter, and said,

"I want a letther, sir, if you plaze."

"Who do you want it for?" said the postmaster, in a tone which Andy considered an aggression upon the sacredness of private life: so

Andy thought the coolest contempt he could throw upon the prying impertinence of the postmaster was to repeat his question.

"I want a letther, sir, if you plaze."

"And who do you want it for?" repeated the post master.

"What's that to you?" said Andy.

The postmaster, laughing at his simplicity, told him he could not tell what letter to give him unless he told him the direction.

"The directions I got was to get a letther here,—that's the directions."

"Who gave you those directions?"

"The masther."

"And who's your master?"

"What consarn is that o' yours?"

"Why, you stupid rascal! If you don't tell me his name, how can I give you a letter?"

"You could give it, if you liked; but you're fond of axin' impidint questions, bekaze you think I'm simple."

"Go along out o' this! Your master must be as great a goose as yourself, to send such a messenger."

"Bad luck to your impidince," said Andy; "is it Squire Egan you dar to say goose to?"

"Oh, Squire Egan's your master, then?"

"Yis; have you anything to say agin it?"

"Only that I never saw you before."

"Faith, then you'll never see me agin if I have my own consint."

"I won't give you any letter for the squire, unless I know you're his servant. Is there any one in the town knows you?"

"Plenty," said Andy, "it's not every one is as ignorant as you."

Just at this moment a person to whom Andy was known entered the house, who vouched to the post master that he might give Andy the squire's letter. "Have you one for me?"

"Yes, sir," said the postmaster, producing one,—"fourpence."

The gentleman paid the fourpence postage, and left the shop with, his letter.

"Here's a letter for the squire," said the postmaster, "you've to pay me elevenpence postage."

"What 'ud I pay elevenpence for?"

"For postage."

"To the divil wid you! Didn't I see you give Mr. Durfy a letther for fourpence this minit, and a bigger letther than this? and now you want me to pay elevenpence for this scrap of a thing. Do you think I'm a fool?"

"No; but I'm sure of it," said the postmaster.

"Well, you're welkim to be sure, sure;—but don't be delayin' me now; here's fourpence for you, and gi' me the letther."

"Go along, you stupid thief," said the postmaster, taking up the letter, and going to serve a customer with a mousetrap.

While this person and many others were served, Andy lounged up and down the shop, every now and then putting in his head in the middle of the customers, and saying, "Will you gi' me the letther?"

He waited for above half an hour, in defiance of the anathemas of the postmaster, and at last left, when he found it impossible to get common justice for his master, which he thought he deserved as well as another man; for, under this impression, Andy determined to give no more than the fourpence.

The squire in the meantime was getting impatient for his return, and when Andy made his appearance, asked if there was a letter for him.

"There is, sir," said Andy.

"Then give it to me."

"I haven't it, sir."

"What do you mean?"

"He wouldn't give it to me, sir."

"Who wouldn't give it to you?"

"That owld chate beyant in the town,—wanting to charge double for it."

"Maybe it's a double letter. Why the devil didn't you pay what he asked, sir?"

"Arrah, sir, why would I let you be chated? It's not a double letther at all: not above half the size o' one Mr. Durfy got before my face for fourpence."

"You'll provoke me to break your neck some day, you vagabond! Ride back for your life, you omadhaun! and pay whatever he asks, and get me the letter."

"Why, sir, I tell you he was sellin' them before my face for fourpence a-piece."

"Go back, you scoundrel! or I'll horsewhip you; if you're longer than an hour, I'll have you ducked in the horsepond!"

Andy vanished and made a second visit to the post-office. When he arrived, two other persons were getting letters, and the postmaster was selecting the epistles for each, from a large parcel that lay before him on the counter; at the same time many shop customers were waiting to be served.

"I'm come for that letther," said Andy.

"I'll attend to you by-and-by."

"The masther's in a hurry."

"Let him wait till his hurry's over."

"He'll murther me if I'm not back soon."

"I'm glad to hear it."

While the postmaster went on with such provoking answers to these appeals for despatch, Andy's eye caught the heap of letters which lay on the counter; so while certain weighing of soap and tobacco was going forward, he contrived to become possessed of two letters from the heap, and, having effected that, waited patiently enough till it was the great man's pleasure to give him the missive directed to his master.

Then did Andy bestride his hack, and, in triumph at his trick on the postmaster, rattle along the road homeward as fast as the beast could carry him. He came into the squire's presence, his face beaming with delight, and an air of self-satisfied superiority in his manner, quite unaccountable to his master, until he pulled forth his hand, which had been grubbing up his prizes from the bottom of his pocket; and holding three letters over his head, while he said, " Look at that! " he next slapped them down under his broad fist on the table before the squire, saying,

"Well! if he did make me pay elevenpence, by gor, I brought your honour the worth o' your money any how!"

II

ANDY WALKED OUT OF THE room with an air of supreme triumph, having laid the letters on the table, and left the squire staring after him in perfect amazement.

"Well, by the powers! that's the most extraordinary genius I ever came across," was the soliloquy the master uttered as the servant closed the door after him; and the squire broke the seal of the letter that Andy's blundering had so long delayed. It was from his law agent, on the subject of an expected election in the county which would occur in the case of the demise of the then-sitting member;—it ran thus:

> *"Dublin, Thursday.*
> "My dear Squire,—I am making all possible exertions to have every and the earliest information on the subject of the election. I say the election,—because though the seat for the county is not yet vacant, it is impossible but that it must soon be so. Any other man than the present member must have died long ago; but Sir Timothy Trimmer has been so undecided all his life that he cannot at present make up his mind to die; and it is only by Death himself giving the casting vote that the question can be decided. The writ for the vacant county is expected to arrive by every mail, and in the meantime I am on the alert for information. You know we are sure of the barony of Ballysloughgutthery, and the boys of Killanmaul will murder any one that dares to give a vote against you. We are sure of Knockdoughty also, and the

very pigs in Glanamuck would return you; but I must put
you on your guard in one point where you least expected
to be betrayed. You told me you were sure of Neck-or-
nothing Hall; but I can tell you you're out there; for the
master of the aforesaid is working heaven, earth, ocean, and
all the little fishes, in the other interest; for he is so over head
and ears in debt, that he is looking out for a pension, and
hopes to get one by giving his interest to the honourable
Sackville Scatterbrain, who sits for the borough of Old
Gooseberry at present, but whose friends think his talents
are worthy of a county. If Sack wins, Neck-or-nothing gets
a pension,—that's *poz*. I had it from the best authority. I
lodge at a milliner's here:—no matter; more when I see
you. But don't be afraid; we'll bag Sack, and distance Neck-
or-nothing. But seriously speaking, it's too good a joke that
O'Grady should use you in this manner, who have been
so kind to him in money matters: but, as the old song says,
'Poverty parts good company;' and he is so cursed poor that
he can't afford to know you any longer, now that you have
lent him all the money you had, and the pension *in prospectu*
is too much for his feelings. I'll be down with you again as
soon as I can, for I hate the diabolical town as I do poison.
They have altered Stephen's Green—*ruined* it, I should
say. They have taken away the big ditch that was round
it, where I used to hunt water-rats when a boy. They are
destroying the place with their d—d improvements. All the
dogs are well, I hope, and my favourite bitch. Remember
me to Mrs. Egan, Whom all admire.

> My dear squire,
> Yours per quire,
> MURTOUGH MURPHY.

"To Edward Egan, Esq. Merryvale."

Murtough Murphy was a great character, as may be guessed from his
letter. He was a country attorney of good practice because he could
not help it,—for, he was a clever, ready-witted fellow, up to all sorts of

trap, and one in whose hands a cause was very safe; therefore he had plenty of clients without his seeking them. For, if Murtough's practice had depended on his looking for it, he might have made broth of his own parchment; for, though to all intents and purposes a good attorney, he was so full of fun and fond of amusement, that it was only by dint of the business being thrust upon him he was so extensive a practitioner. He loved a good bottle, a good hunt, a good joke, and a good song, as well as any fellow in Ireland; and even when he was obliged in the way of business to press a gentleman hard,—to hunt his man to the death,—he did it so good-humouredly that his very victim could not be angry with him. As for those he served, he was their prime favourite; there was nothing they *could* want to be done in the parchment line that Murtough would not find out some way of doing; and he was so pleasant a fellow, that he shared in the hospitality of all the best tables in the county. He kept good horses, was on every race-ground within twenty miles, and a steeple chase was no steeple-chase without him. Then he betted freely, and, what's more, won his bets very generally; but no one found fault with him for that, and he took your money with such a good grace, and mostly gave you a *bon-mot* in exchange for it,—so that, next to winning the money yourself, you were glad it was won by Murtough Murphy.

The squire read his letter two or three times, and made his comments as he proceeded. "'Working heaven and earth to,'—ha—So, that's the work O'Grady's at—that's old friendship,—foul—foul; and after all the money I lent him too;—he'd better take care—I'll be down on him if he plays false;—not that I'd like that much either:—but—Let's see who's this is coming down to oppose me?—Sack Scatterbrain—the biggest fool from this to himself;—the fellow can't ride a bit,—a pretty member for a sporting county! 'I lodge at a milliner's'—divil doubt you, Murtough; I'll engage you do.—Bad luck to him!—he'd rather be fooling away his time in a back-parlour, behind a bonnet-shop, than minding the interests of the county. 'Pension'—ha!—wants it, sure enough;—take care, O'Grady, or by the powers I'll be at you.—You may baulk all the bailiffs, and defy any other man to serve you with a writ; but, by jingo! if I take the matter in hand, I'll be bound I'll get it done. 'Stephen's Green—big ditch—where I used to hunt water-rats.'

Divil sweep you, Murphy, you'd rather be hunting water-rats any day than minding your business.—He's a clever fellow, for all that. 'Favourite bitch—Mrs. Egan.' Ay! there's the end of it—with his bit o' po'thry too! The divil!"

The squire threw down the letter, and then his eye caught the other two that Andy had purloined.

"More of that stupid blackguard's work!—robbing the mail—no less—that fellow will be hanged some time or other. Egad, maybe they'll hang him for this! What's best to be done?—Maybe it will be the safest way to see who they are for, and send them to the parties, and request they will say nothing: that's it."

The squire here took up the letters that lay before him, to read their superscriptions; and the first he turned over was directed to Gustavus Granby O'Grady, Esq., Neck-or-Nothing Hall, Knockbotherum. This was what is called a curious coincidence. Just as he had been reading all about O'Grady's intended treachery to him, here was a letter to that individual, and with the Dublin post-mark too, and a very grand seal.

The squire examined the arms, and, though not versed in the mysteries of heraldry, he thought he remembered enough of most of the arms he had seen to say that this armorial bearing was a strange one to him. He turned the letter over and over again, and looked at it, back and front, with an expression in his face that said, as plain as countenance could speak, "I'd give a trifle to know what is inside of this." He looked at the seal again: "Here's a—goose, I think it is, sitting in a bowl, with cross-bars on it, and a spoon in its mouth; like the fellow that owns it, maybe. A goose with a silver spoon in its mouth! Well, here's the gable-end of a house, and a bird sitting on the top of it. Could it be Sparrow? There's a fellow called Sparrow, an under secretary at the Castle. D—n it! I wish I knew what it's about."

The squire threw down the letter as he said, "D—n it," but took it up again in a few seconds, and catching it edgewise between his forefinger and thumb, gave a gentle pressure that made the letter gape at its extremities, and then, exercising that sidelong glance which is peculiar to postmasters, waiting-maids, and magpies who inspect marrow-bones, peeped into the interior of the epistle, saying to himself as he did so, "All's fair in war, and why not in electioneering?" His face, which

was screwed up to the scrutinizing pucker, gradually lengthened as he
caught some words that were on the last turn over of the sheet, and so
could be read thoroughly, and his brow darkened into the deepest frown
as he scanned these lines: "As you very properly and pungently remark,
poor Egan is a spoon—a mere spoon." "Am I a spoon, you rascal?" said
the squire, tearing the letter into pieces, and throwing it into the fire.
"And so, *Misther* O'Grady, you say I'm a spoon!" and the blood of the
Egans rose as the head of that pugnacious family strode up and down
the room: "I'll spoon you, my buck,—I'll settle your hash! And maybe
I'm a spoon you'll sup sorrow with yet!"

Here he took up the poker, and make a very angry lunge at the fire,
that did not want stirring, and there he beheld the letter blazing merrily
away. He dropped the poker as if he had caught it by the hot end, as he
exclaimed, "What the d—l shall I do? I've burnt the letter!" This threw
the squire into a fit of what he was wont to call his "considering cap;"
and he sat with his feet on the fender for some minutes, occasionally
muttering to himself what he began with,—"What the d—l shall I
do? It's all owing to that infernal Andy— I'll murder that fellow some
time or other. If he hadn't brought it, I shouldn't have seen it—to be
sure, if I hadn't looked; but then the temptation—a saint couldn't have
withstood it. Confound it! what a stupid trick to burn it. Another here,
too—must burn that as well, and say nothing about either of them;"
and he took up the second letter, and, merely looking at the address,
threw it into the fire. He then rang the bell, and desired Andy to be sent
to him. As soon as that ingenious individual made his appearance, the
squire desired him with peculiar emphasis to shut the door, and then
opened upon him with,

"You unfortunate rascal!"

"Yis, your honour."

"Do you know that you might be hanged for what you did to-
day?"

"What did I do, sir?"

"You robbed the post-office."

"How did I rob it, sir?"

"You took two letters you had no right to."

"It's no robbery for a man to get the worth of his money."

"Will you hold your tongue, you stupid villain! I'm not joking: you absolutely might be hanged for robbing the post-office."

"Sure I didn't know there was any harm in what I done; and for that matther, sure, if they're sitch wonderful value, can't I go back again wid 'em?"

"No, you thief. I hope you have not said a word to any one about it."

"Not the sign of a word passed my lips about it."

"You're sure?"

"Sartin."

"Take care, then, that you never open your mouth to mortal about it, or you'll be hanged, as sure as your name is Andy Rooney."

"Oh, at that rate, I never will. But maybe your honour thinks I ought to be hanged?"

"No,—because you did not intend to do a wrong thing: but, only I have pity on you, I could hang you to-morrow for what you've done."

"Thank you, sir."

"I've burnt the letters, so no one can know anything about the business unless you tell on yourself: so remember,—not a word."

"Faith, I'll be as dumb as the dumb baste."

"Go, now; and, once for all, remember you'll be hanged so sure as you ever mention one word about this affair."

Andy made a bow and a scrape, and left the squire, who hoped the secret was safe. He then took a ruminating walk round the pleasure grounds, revolving plans of retaliation upon his false friend O'Grady; and having determined to put the most severe and sudden measure of the law in force against him for the monies in which he was indebted to him, he only awaited the arrival of Murtough Murphy from Dublin to execute his vengeance. Having settled this in his own mind, he became more contented, and said, with a self-satisfied nod of the head, "We'll see who's the spoon."

In a few days Murtough Murphy returned from Dublin, and to Merryvale he immediately proceeded. The squire opened to him directly his intention of commencing hostile law proceedings against O'Grady, and asked what most summary measures could be put in practice against him.

"Oh! various, various, my dear squire," said Murphy; "but I don't see any great use in doing so *yet*,—he has not openly avowed himself."

"But does he not intend to coalesce with the other party?"

"I believe so, that is, if he's to get the pension."

"Well, and that's as good as done, you know; for if they want him, the pension is easily managed."

"I'm not so sure of that."

"Why, they're as plenty as blackberries."

"Very true; but, you see, Lord Gobblestown swallows all the pensions for his own family; and there are a great many complaints in the market against him for plucking that blackberry-bush very bare indeed; and unless Sack Scatterbrain has swingeing interest, the pension may not be such an easy thing."

"But still O'Grady has shown himself not my friend."

"My dear squire, don't be so hot: he has not *shown* himself yet—"

"Well, but he means it."

"My dear squire, you oughtn't to jump a conclusion like a twelve-foot drain or a five-bar gate."

"Well, he's a blackguard."

"No denying it; and therefore keep him on your side, if you can, or he'll be a troublesome customer on the other."

"I'll keep no terms with him. I'll slap at him directly. What can you do that's wickedest?—latitat, capias—fee-faw-fum, or whatever you call it?"

"Hollo! squire, you're overrunning your game: may be, after all, he *won't* join the Scatterbrains, and—"

"I tell you it's no matter; he intended doing it, and that's all the same. I'll slap at him,—I'll blister him!"

Murtough Murphy wondered at this blind fury of the squire, who, being a good-humoured and good-natured fellow in general, puzzled the attorney the more by his present manifest malignity against O'Grady. But *he* had not seen the turn-over of the letter; he had not seen "spoon,"—the real secret and cause of the "war to the knife" spirit which was kindled in the squire's breast.

"Of course you can do what you please; but, if you'd take a friend's advice—"

"I tell you I'll blister him."

"He certainly *bled* you very freely."

"I'll blister him, I tell you, and that smart. Lose no time, Murphy, my boy: let loose the dogs of law on him, and harass him till he'd wish the d—l had him."

"Just as you like; but—"

"I'll have it my own way, I tell you; so say no more."

"I'll commence against him at once, then, as you wish it; but it's no use, for you know very well that it will be impossible to serve him."

"Let me alone for that! I'll be bound I'll find fellows to get the inside of him."

"Why, his house is barricaded like a jail, and he has dogs enough to bait all the bulls in the country."

"No matter; just send me the blister for him, and I'll engage I'll stick it on him."

"Very well, squire; you shall have the blister as soon as it can be got ready. I'll tell you whenever you may send over to me for it, and your messenger shall have it hot and warm for him. Good-b'ye, squire!"

"Good-b'ye, Murphy!—lose no time."

"In the twinkling of a bed-post. Are you going to Tom Durfy's steeple-chase?"

"I'm not sure."

"I've a bet on it. Did you see the Widow Flanagan lately? You didn't? They say Tom's pushing it strong there. The widow has money, you know, and Tom does it all for the love o' God; for you know, squire, there are two things God hates,—a coward and a poor man. Now, Tom's no coward; and, that he may be sure of the love o' God on the other score, he's making up to the widow; and, as he's a slashing fellow, she's nothing loth, and, for fear of any one cutting him out, Tom keeps as sharp a look-out after her as she does after him. He's fierce on it, and looks pistols at any one that attempts putting his *comether* on the widow, while she looks "as soon as you plaze," as plain as an optical lecture can enlighten the heart of man: in short, Tom's all ram's horns, and the widow all sheep's eyes. Good-b'ye, squire!" And Murtough put spurs to his horse and cantered down the avenue, whistling the last popular tune.

Andy was sent over to Murtough Murphy's for the law process at the appointed time; and, as he had to pass through the village, Mrs. Egan desired him to call at the apothecary's for some medicine that was prescribed for one of the children.

"What'll I ax for, ma'am?"

"I'd be sorry to trust to you, Andy, for remembering. Here's the prescription; take great care of it, and Mr. M'Garry will give you something to bring back; and mind, if it's a powder,—"

"Is it gunpowdher, ma'am?"

"No—you stupid—will you listen—I say, if it's a powder, don't let it get wet, as you did the sugar the other day."

"No, ma'am."

"And if it's a bottle, don't break it as you did the last."

"No, ma'am."

"And make haste."

"Yis, ma'am" and off went Andy.

In going through the village he forgot to leave the prescription at the apothecary's, and pushed on for the attorney's: there he saw Murtough Murphy, who handed him the law process, enclosed in a cover, with a note to the squire.

"Have you been doing anything very clever lately, Andy?" said Murtough.

"I don't know, sir," said Andy.

"Did you shoot any one with soda-water since I saw you last?"

Andy grinned.

"Did you kill any more dogs lately, Andy?"

"Faix, you're too hard on me, sir: sure I never killed but one dog, and that was an accident——"

"An accident!—Curse your impudence, you thief! Do you think, if you killed one of the pack on purpose, we wouldn't cut the very heart out o' you with our hunting whips?"

"Faith, I wouldn't doubt you, sir: but, sure, how could I help that divil of a mare runnin' away wid me and thramplin' the dogs?"

"Why didn't you hold her, you thief?"

"Hould her, indeed!—you just might as well expect to stop fire among flax as that one."

"Well, be off with you now, Andy, and take care of what I gave you for the squire."

"Oh, never fear, sir," said Andy, as he turned his horse's head homeward. He stopped at the apothecary's in the village, to execute his commission for the "misthis". On telling the son of Galen that he wanted some physic "for one o' the children up at the big house," the dispenser of the healing art asked *what* physic he wanted.

"Faith, I dunna what physic."

"What's the matter with the child?"

"He's sick, sir."

"I suppose so, indeed, or you wouldn't be sent for medicine.—You're always making some blunder. You come here, and don't know what description of medicine is wanted."

"Don't I?" said Andy with a great air.

"No, you don't, you omadhaun!" said the apothecary.

Andy fumbled in his pockets, and could not lay hold of the paper his mistress entrusted him with until he had emptied them thoroughly of their contents upon the counter of the shop; and then taking the prescription from the collection, he said, " So you tell me I don't know the description of the physic I'm to get. Now, you see you're out; for *that's the description*." And he slapped the counter impressively with his hand as he threw down the recipe before the apothecary.

While the medicine was in the course of preparation for Andy, he commenced restoring to his pockets the various parcels he had taken from them in hunting for the recipe. Now, it happened that he had laid them down close beside some articles that were compounded, and sealed up for going out, on the apothecary's counter; and as the law process which Andy had received from Murtough Murphy chanced to resemble in form another enclosure that lay beside it, containing a blister, Andy, under the influence of his peculiar genius, popped the blister into his pocket instead of the packet which had been confided to him by the attorney, and having obtained the necessary medicine from M'Garry, rode home with great self-complacency that he had not forgot to do a single thing that had been entrusted to him. "I'm all right this time," said Andy to himself.

Scarcely had he left the apothecary's shop when another messenger alighted at his door, and asked "If Squire O'Grady's things *was* ready?"

"There they are," said the innocent M'Garry, pointing to the bottles, boxes, and *blister*, he had made up and set aside, little dreaming that the blister had been exchanged for a law process: and Squire O'Grady's own messenger popped into his pocket the legal instrument, that it was as much as any seven men's lives were worth to bring within gun-shot of Neck-or-Nothing Hall.

Home he went, and the sound of the old gate creaking on its hinges at the entrance to the avenue awoke the deep-mouthed dogs around the house, who rushed infuriate to the spot to devour the unholy intruder on the peace and privacy of the patrician O'Grady; but they recognised the old grey hack and his rider, and quietly wagged their tails and trotted back, and licked their lips at the thoughts of the bailiff they had hoped to eat. The door of Neck-or-Nothing Hall was carefully unbarred and unchained, and the nurse-tender was handed the parcel from the apothecary's, and re-ascended to the sick-room with slippered foot as quietly as she could; for the renowned O'Grady was, according to her account, "as cross as two sticks;" and she protested, further more, "that her heart was grey with him."

Whenever O'Grady was in a bad humour, he had a strange fashion of catching at some word that either he himself, or those with whom he spoke, had uttered, and after often repeating it, or rather mumbling it over in his mouth as if he were chewing it, off he started into a canter of ridiculous rhymes to the aforesaid word, and sometimes one of these rhymes would suggest a new idea, or some strange association, which had the oddest effect possible; and to increase the absurdity, the jingle was gone through with as much solemnity as if he were indulging in a deep and interesting reverie, so that it was difficult to listen without laughing, which might prove a serious matter, when O'Grady was in one of his *tantarums*, as his wife used to call them.

Mrs. O'Grady was near the bed of the sick man as the nurse-tender entered.

"Here's the things for your honour now," said she in her most soothing tone.

"I wish the d—l had you and them!" said O'Grady.

"Gusty, dear!" said his wife. (She might have said stormy instead of gusty.)

"Oh! they'll do you good, your honour," said the nurse-tender, curtsying, and uncorking bottles, and opening a pill-box.

O'Grady made a face at the pill-box, and repeated the word "pills," several times, with an expression of extreme disgust—"Pills—pills—kills—wills—aye—make your wills—make them—take them—shake them. When taken—to be well shaken—show me that bottle."

The nurse tender handed a phial, which O'Grady shook violently.

"Curse them all," said the squire. "A pretty thing to have a gentleman's body made a perfect sink, for these blackguard doctors and apothecaries to pour their dirty drugs into—faugh!—drugs—mugs—jugs;"—he shook the phial again and looked through it.

"Isn't it nice and pink, darlin'?" said the nurse-tender.

"Pink!"—O'Grady, eyeing her askance, as if he could have eaten her. "Pink—you old besom—pink—" he uncorked the phial and put it to his nose. "Pink—phew!" and he repeated a rhyme to pink which would not look well in print.

"Now, sir, dear, there's a little blisther just to go on your chest—if you plaze—"

"A *what!*"

"A warm plasther, dear."

"A *blister* you said, you old *divil!*"

"Well, sure, it's something to relieve you."

The squire gave a deep growl, and his wife put in the usual appeal of "Gusty, dear!"

"Hold your tongue, will you? how would you like it? I wish you had it on your—"

"'Deed-an-deed, dear,—" said the nurse-tender.

"By the 'ternal war! if you say another word, I'll throw the jug at you!"

"And there's a nice dhrop o' gruel I have on the fire for you," said the nurse, pretending not to mind the rising anger of the squire, as she stirred the gruel with one hand, while with the other she marked herself with the sign of the cross, and said in a mumbling manner,

"God preserve us! he's the most cantankerous Christian I ever kem across!"

"Show me that infernal thing!" said the squire.

"What thing, dear?

"You know well enough, you old hag!—that blackguard blister!"

"Here it is, dear. Now, just open the *brust* o' your shirt, and let me put it an you."

"Give it into my hand here, and let me see it."

"Sartinly, sir;—but I think, if you'd let me just —"

"Give it to me, I tell you!" said the squire, in a tone so fierce that the nurse paused in her unfolding of the packet, and handed it with fear and trembling to the already indignant O'Grady. But it is only imagination can figure the outrageous fury of the squire, when, on opening the envelope with his own hand, he beheld the law process before him. There, in the heart of his castle, with his bars, and bolts, and bull-dogs, and blunderbusses around him, he was served,— absolutely served,—and he had no doubt the nurse-tender was bribed to betray him.

A roar and a jump up in bed, first startled his wife into terror, and put the nurse on the defensive.

"You infernal old strap!" shouted he, as he clutched up a handful of bottles on the table near him and flung them at the nurse, who was near the fire at the time; and she whipped the pot of gruel from the grate, and converted it into a means of defence against the phial pelting storm.

Mrs. O'Grady rolled herself up in the bed-curtains, while the nurse screeched "murther!" and at last, when O'Grady saw that bottles were of no avail, he scrambled out of bed, shouting, "Where's my blunderbuss!" and the nurse-tender, while he endeavoured to get it down from the rack, where it was suspended over the mantel-piece, bolted out of the door, which she locked on the outside, and ran to the most remote corner of the house for shelter.

In the mean time, how fared it at Merryvale? Andy returned with his parcel for the squire, and his note from Murtough Murphy, which ran thus:

"MY DEAR SQUIRE.—I send you the *blister* for O'Grady, as
you insist on it; but I think you won't find it easy to serve
him with it.

"Your obedient and obliged,
"MURTOUGH MURPHY."
"*To Edward Egan, Esq. Merryvale.*"

The squire opened the cover, and when he saw a real instead of a
figurative blister, grew crimson with rage. He could not speak for some
minutes, his indignation was so excessive. "So!" said he, at last, "Mr.
Murtough Murphy—you think to cut your jokes with me, do you? By
all that's sacred! I'll cut such a joke on you with the biggest horsewhip
I can find, that you'll remember it. '*Dear squire, I send you the blister.*' Bad
luck to your impidence! Wait till awhile ago—that's all. By this and that
you'll get such a blistering from me that all the spermaceti in M'Garry's
shop won't cure you.'

III

SQUIRE EGAN WAS AS GOOD as his word. He picked out the most suitable horsewhip for chastising the fancied impertinence of Murtough Murphy; and as he switched it up and down with a powerful arm, to try its weight and pliancy, the whistling of the instrument through the air was music to his ears, and whispered of promised joy in the flagellation of the jocular attorney.

"We'll see who can make the sorest blister," said the squire. "I'll back whalebone against Spanish flies any day. Will you bet, Dick?" said he to his brother-in-law, who was a wild helter-skelter sort of fellow, better known over the country as Dick the Devil than Dick Dawson.

"I'll back your bet, Ned."

"There's no fun in that, Dick, as there is nobody to take it up."

"Maybe Murtough will. Ask him before you thrash him; you'd better."

"As for *him*," said the squire, "I'll be bound he'll back my bet after he gets a taste o' this;" and the horsewhip whistled as he spoke.

"I think he had better take care of his back than his bet," said Dick, as he followed the squire to the hall door, where his horse was in waiting for him, under the care of the renowned Andy, who little dreamed of the extensive harvest of mischief which was ripening in futurity, all from his sowing.

"Don't kill him quite, Ned," said Dick, as the squire mounted to his saddle.

"Why, if I went to horsewhip a gentleman, of course I should only shake my whip at him; but an attorney is another affair. And, as I'm sure he'll have an action against me for assault, I think I may as well get the worth o' my money out of him, to say nothing of teaching him better manners for the future than to play off his jokes on his employers." With these words off he rode in search of the devoted Murtough, who was not at home when the squire reached his house; but as he was returning through the village, he espied him coming down the street in company with Tom Durfy and the widow, who were laughing heartily at some joke Murtough was telling them, which seemed to amuse him as much as his hearers.

"I'll make him laugh at the wrong side of his mouth," thought the squire, alighting and giving his horse to the care of one of the little ragged boys who were idling in the street. He approached Murphy with a very threatening aspect, and confronting him and his party so as to produce a halt, he said, as distinctly as his rage would permit him to speak, "You little insignificant blackguard, I'll teach you how you'll cut your jokes on *me* again; *I'll* blister you, my buck!" and, laying hands on the astonished Murtough with the last word, he began a very smart horsewhipping of the attorney. The widow screamed, Tom Durfy swore, and Murtough roared, with some interjectional curses. At last he escaped from the squire's grip, leaving the lappel of his coat in his possession; and Tom Durfy interposed his person between them when he saw an intention on the part of the flagellator to repeat his dose of horsewhip.

"Let me at him, sir; or by——"

"Fie, fie, squire—to horsewhip a gentleman like a cart-horse."

"A gentleman!—an attorney, you mean."

"I say, a gentleman, Squire Egan," cried Murtough fiercely, roused to gallantry by the presence of a lady, and smarting under a sense of injury and whalebone. "I'm a gentleman, sir, and demand the satisfaction of a gentleman. I put my honour into your hands, Mr. Durfy."

"Between his finger and thumb, you mean, for there's not a handful of it," said the squire.

"Well, sir," replied Tom Durfy, "little or much, I'll take charge of it.—That's right, my cock," said he to Murtough, who, notwithstanding his desire to assume a warlike air, could not resist the natural impulse of rubbing his back and shoulders, which tingled with pain, while he exclaimed, "Satisfaction! Satisfaction!"

"Very well," said the squire: "you name yourself as Mr. Murphy's friend?" added he to Durfy.

"The same, sir," said Tom. "Who do you name as yours?"

"I suppose you know one Dick the Divil,"

"A very proper person, sir;—no better: I'll go to him directly."

The widow clung to Tom's arm, and looking tenderly at him, cried, "Oh, Tom, Tom, take care of your precious life!"

"Bother!" said Tom.

"Ah, Squire Egan, don't be so bloodthirsty!"

"Fudge, woman!" said the squire.

"Ah, Mr. Murphy, I'm sure the squire's very sorry for beating you."

"Divil a bit," said the squire.

"There, ma'am," said Murphy; "you see he'll make no apology."

"Apology!" said Durfy;—"apology for a horse-whipping, indeed!—Nothing but handing a horsewhip (which I wouldn't ask any gentleman to do), or a shot, can settle the matter."

"Oh, Tom! Tom! Tom!" said the widow.

"Ba! ba! ba!" shouted Tom, making a crying face at her. "Arrah, woman, don't be makin' a fool o' yourself. Go in there to the 'pothecary's, and get something under your nose to revive you; and let *us* mind *our* business."

The widow, with her eyes turned up, and an exclamation to Heaven, was retiring to M'Garry's shop, wringing her hands, when she was nearly knocked down by M'Garry himself, who rushed from his own door, at the same moment that an awful smash of his shop-window, and the demolition of his blue and red bottles alarmed the ears of the bystanders, while their eyes were drawn from the late belligerent parties to a chase which took place down the street of the apothecary, roaring "Murder!" followed by Squire O'Grady with an enormous cudgel.

O'Grady, believing that M'Garry and the nurse-tender had combined to serve him with a writ, determined to wreak double vengeance on the apothecary, as the nurse had escaped him; and, notwithstanding all his illness and the appeals of his wife, he left his bed and rode to the village to break every bone in M'Garry's skin. When he entered his shop, the pharmacopolist was much surprised, and said, with a congratulatory grin at the great man, "Dear me, Squire O'Grady, I'm delighted to see you."

"Are you, you scoundrel!" said the squire, making a blow of his cudgel at him, which was fended by an iron pestle the apothecary fortunately had in his hand. The enraged O'Grady made a rush behind the counter, which the apothecary nimbly jumped over, crying "Murder;" as he made for the door, followed by his pursuer, who gave a back-handed slap at the window-bottles *en passant*, and produced the crash which astonished the widow, who now joined her screams to the general hue-and-cry; for an indiscriminate chase of all the ragamuffins in the town, with barking curs and screeching children, followed the flight of M'Garry and the pursuing squire.

"What the divil is all this about?" said Tom Durfy, laughing. "By the powers! I suppose there's something in the weather, to produce all this fun,—though it's early in the year to begin thrashing, for the harvest isn't in yet. But, however, let us manage our little affair, now that we're left in peace and quietness, for the blackguards are all over the bridge afther the hunt. I'll go to Dick the Divil immediately, squire, and arrange time and place."

"There's nothing like saving time and trouble on these occasions," said the squire. "Dick is at my house, I can arrange time and place with you this minute, and he will be on the ground with me."

"Very well," said Tom; "where is it to be?"

"Suppose we say the cross-roads, halfway between this and Merryvale? There's very pretty ground there, and we shall be able to get our pistols, and all that, ready in the mean time between this and four o'clock,— and it will be pleasanter to have it all over before dinner."

"Certainly, squire," said Tom Durfy; "we'll be there at four—Till then, good morning, squire;" and he and his man walked off.

The widow, in the mean time, had been left to the care of the apothecary's boy, whose tender attentions were now, for the first time in his life, demanded towards a fainting lady; for the poor raw country lad, having to do with a sturdy peasantry in every day matters, had never before seen the capers cut by a lady who thinks it proper, and delicate, and becoming, to display her sensibility in a swoon; and truly her sobs, and small screeches, and little stampings and kickings, amazed young gallipot.—Smelling salts were applied—they were rather weak, so the widow inhaled the pleasing odour with a sigh, but did not recover.—Sal Volatile was next put in requisition—this was somewhat stronger, and made her wriggle on her chair, and throw her head about with sundry ohs! and ahs!—The boy, beginning to be alarmed at the extent of the widow's syncope, bethought him of asafoetida, and, taking down a goodly bottle of that sweet smelling stimulant, gave the widow the benefit of the whole jar under her nose.—Scarcely had the stopper been withdrawn, when she gave a louder screech than she had yet executed, and, exclaiming "faugh!" with an expression, of the most concentrated disgust, opened her eyes fiercely upon the offender, and shut up her nose between her fore-finger and thumb against the offence, and snuffled forth at the astonished boy, "Get out o' that, you dirty cur!—Can't you let a lady faint in peace and quietness?—Gracious: heavens! would you smother me, you nasty brute?—Oh, Tom, where are you?"—and she took to sobbing forth, "Tom! Tom!" and put her handkerchief to her eyes, to hide the tears that were not there, while from behind the corner of the cambrick she kept a sharp eye on the street, and observed what was going on. She went on acting her part very becomingly, until the moment Tom Durfy walked off with Murphy; but then she could feign no longer, and jumping up from her seat, with an exclamation of "The brute!" she ran to the door, and looked down the street after them. "The savage!" sobbed the widow—"the hard-hearted monster, to abandon me here to die—oh! to use me so—to leave me like a—like a—(the widow was fond of similes) like an old shoe—like a dirty glove—like a—like I don't know what!" (the usual fate of similes.) "Mister Durfy, I'll punish you for this—I will!" said the widow, with an energetic emphasis on the last word; and she marched out of the shop, boiling over with indignation, through which, nevertheless, a little bubble of love now and then rose to the surface; and by the time she reached her own door, love predominated, and she sighed as she laid her hand on the knocker: "After all, if the dear fellow should be killed, what would become of me!—oh!—and that wretch, Dick Dawson, too—*two* of them.—The worst of these merry devils is, they are always fighting!"

The squire had ridden immediately homewards, and told Dick Dawson the piece of work that was before them.

"And so he'll have a shot at you, instead of an action?" said Dick. "Well, there's pluck in that: I wish he was more of a gentleman, for your sake. It's dirty work, shooting attorneys."

"He's enough of a gentleman, Dick, to make it impossible for me to refuse him."

"Certainly, Ned," said Dick.

"Do you know, is he anything of a shot?"

"Faith, he makes very pretty snipe-shooting; but I don't know if he has experience of the grass before breakfast."

"You must try and find out from any one on the ground; because, if the poor devil isn't a good shot, I wouldn't like to kill him, and I'll let him off easy—I'll give it to him in the pistol-arm, or so."

"Very well, Ned. Where are the flutes? I must look over them."

"Here," said the squire, producing a very handsome mahogany case of Rigby's best. Dick opened the case with the utmost care, and took up one of the pistols tenderly, handling it as delicately as if it were a young child or a lady's hand. He clicked the lock back and forwards a few times; and, his ear not being satisfied at the music it produced, he said he should like to examine them: "At all events, they want a touch of oil."

"Well, keep them out of the misthriss's sight, Dick, for she might be alarmed."

"Divil a taste," says Dick; "she's a Dawson, and there never was a Dawson yet that did not know men must be men."

"That's true, Dick. I wouldn't mind so much if she wasn't in a delicate situation just now, when it couldn't be expected of the woman to be so stout: so go, like a good fellow, into your own room, and Andy will bring you anything you want."

Five minutes after, Dick was engaged in cleaning the duelling-pistols, and Andy at his elbow, with his mouth wide open, wondering at the interior of the locks which Dick had just taken off.

"Oh, my heavens! but that's a quare thing, Misther Dick, sir," said Andy, going to take it up.

"Keep your fingers off it, you thief, do!" roared Dick, making a rap of the turnscrew at Andy's knuckles.

"Sure I'll save you the throuble o' rubbin' that, Misther Dick, if you let me; here's the shabby leather."

"I wouldn't let your clumsy fist near it, Andy, nor your *shabby* leather, you villain, for the world. Go get me some oil."

Andy went on his errand, and returned with a can of lamp-oil to Dick, who swore at him for his stupidity "The divil fly away with you; you never do anything right; you bring me lamp-oil for a pistol."

"Well, sure I thought lamp-oil was the right thing for burnin'."

"And who wants to burn it, you savage?"

"Aren't you goin' to fire it, sir?"

"Choke you, you vagabond!" said Dick, who could not resist laughing nevertheless; "be off, and get me some sweet oil, but don't tell any one what it's for."

Andy retired, and Dick pursued his polishing of the locks. Why he used such a blundering fellow as Andy for a messenger might be wondered at, only that Dick was fond of fun, and Andy's mistakes were a particular source of amusement to him, and on all occasions when he could have Andy in his company he made him his attendant. When the sweet oil was produced, Dick looked about for a feather; but, not finding one, desired Andy to fetch him a pen. Andy went on his errand, and returned, after some delay, with an inkbottle.

"I brought you the ink, sir, but I can't find a pin."

"Confound your numskull! I didn't say a word about ink; I asked for a pen."

"And what use would a pin be without ink, now I ax yourself, Misther Dick?"

"I'd knock your brains out if you had any, you *omadhaun!* Go along and get me a feather, and make haste."

Andy went off, and, having obtained a feather, returned to Dick, who began to tip certain portions of the lock very delicately with oil.

"What's that for, Misther Dick, sir, if you plaze?"

"To make it work smooth."

"And what's that thing you're grazin' now, sir?"

"That's the tumbler."

"O Lord! a tumbler—what a quare name for it. I thought there was no tumbler but a tumbler for punch."

"That's the tumbler you would like to be cleaning the inside of, Andy."

"Thrue for you, sir.—And what's that little thing you have your hand on now, sir?"

"That's the cock."

"Oh dear, a cock!—Is there e'er a hin in it, sir?"

"No, nor a chicken either, though there *is* a feather."

"The one in your hand, sir, that you're grazin' it with."

"No: but this little thing—that is called the feather-spring."

"It's the feather, I suppose, makes it let fly."

"No doubt of it, Andy."

"Well, there's some sinse in that name, then; but who'd think of sitch a thing as a tumbler and a cock in a pistle? And what's that place that opens and shuts, sir?"

"The pan."

"Well, there's sinse in that name too, bekaze there's fire in the thing; and it's as nath'ral to say pan to that as to a fryin'-pan—isn't it, Misther Dick?"

"Oh! there was a great gunmaker lost in you, Andy," said Dick, as he screwed on the locks, which he had regulated to his mind, and began to examine the various departments of the pistol case, to see that it was properly provided. He took the instrument to cut some circles of thin leather, and Andy again asked him for the name "o' *that*" thing."

"This is called the punch, Andy."

"So there *is* the punch as well as the tumbler, sir?"

"Ay, and very strong punch it is, you see, Andy;" and Dick struck it with his little mahogany mallet, and cut his patches of leather.

"And what's that for, sir?—the leather, I mane."

"That's for putting round the ball."

"Is it for fear 'twould hurt him too much when you shot him?"

"You're a queer customer, Andy," said Dick, smiling.

"And what weeshee little balls thim is, sir."

"They are always small for duelling-pistols."

"Oh, then thim is jewellin' pistles. Why, musha, Misther Dick, is it goin' to fight a jule you are?" said Andy, looking at him with earnestness.

"No, Andy,—but the master is: but don't say a word about it."

"Not a word for the world. The masther goin' to fight!—God send him safe out iv it!—Amin. And who is he going to fight, Misther Dick?"

"Murphy the attorney, Andy."

"Oh, won't the masther disgrace himself by fightin' the 'torney?"

"How dare you say such a thing of your master?"

"I ax your pard'n, Misther Dick; but sure you know what I mane. I hope he'll shoot him."

"Why, Andy, Murtough was always very good to you, and now you wish him to be shot."

"Sure, why wouldn't I rather have him kilt more than the masther?"

"But neither may be killed."

"Misther Dick," said Andy, lowering his voice, "wouldn't it be an iligant thing to put two balls into the pistle instead o' one, and give the masther a chance over the 'torney?

"Oh, you murderous villain!"

"Arrah, why shouldn't the masther have a chance over him? Sure he has childre, and 'Torney Murphy has none."

"At that rate, Andy, I suppose you'd give the masther a ball additional for every child he has, and that would make eight. So you might as well give him a blunder-buss and slugs at once."

Dick locked the pistol-case, having made all right; and desired Andy to mount a horse, carry it by a back road out of the domain, and wait at a certain gate he named until he should be joined there by himself and the squire, who proceeded at the appointed time to the ground.

Andy was all ready, and followed his master and Dick with great pride, bearing the pistol-case after them, to the ground where Murphy and Tom Durfy were ready to receive them; and a great number of spectators were assembled; for the noise of the business had gone abroad, and the ground was in consequence crowded.

Tom Durfy had warned Murtough Murphy, who had no experience as a pistol-man, that the squire was a capital shot, and that his only chance was to fire as quickly, as he could.—"Slap at him, Morty, my boy, the minute you get the word; and, if you don't hit him itself, it will prevent his dwelling on his aim."

Tom Durfy and Dick the Devil soon settled the preliminaries of the ground and mode of firing; and twelve paces having been marked, both the seconds opened their pistol-cases, and prepared to load. Andy was close to Dick all the time, kneeling beside the pistol-case, which lay on the sod; and, as Dick turned round to settle some other point on which Tom Durfy questioned him, Andy thought he might snatch the opportunity of giving his master "the chance" he suggested to his second.—"Sure, if Misther Dick wouldn't like to do it, that's no raison I wouldn't," said Andy to himself; "and, by the powers! I'll pop in a ball *onknownst* to him." And, sure enough, Andy contrived, while the seconds were engaged with each other, to put a ball into each pistol before the barrel was loaded with powder, so that, when Dick took up his pistols to load, a bullet lay between the powder and the touch-hole. Now this must have been discovered by Dick, had he been cool; but he and Tom Durfy had wrangled very much about the point they had been discussing, and Dick, at no time the quietest person in the world, was in such a rage, that the pistols were loaded by him without noticing Andy's ingenious interference, and he handed a harmless weapon to his brother-in-law when he placed him on his ground.

The word was given. Murtough, following his friend's advice, fired instantly: bang he went, while the squire returned but a flash in the pan. He turned a look of reproach upon Dick, who took the pistol silently from him, and handed him the other, having carefully looked to the priming, after the accident which happened to the first.

Durfy handed his man another pistol also; and, before he left his side, said in a whisper, " Don't forget; have the first fire,"

Again the word was given: Murphy blazed away a rapid and harmless shot; for his hurry was the squire's safety, while Andy's murderous intentions were his salvation.

"D—n the pistol! " said the squire, throwing it down in a rage. Dick took it up with manifest indignation, and d—d the powder.

"Your powder's damp, Ned."

"No, it's not," said the squire; "it's you who have bungled the loading.

"Me!" said Dick, with a look of mingled rage and astonishment: "*I* bungle the loading of pistols!—*I*, that have stepped more ground and arranged more affairs than any man in the country!—Arrah, be aisy, Ned!"

Tom Durfy now interfered, and said, for the present it was no matter as, on the part of his friend, he begged to express himself satisfied.

"But it's very hard *we*'re not to have a shot," said Dick, poking the touch-hole of the pistol with a pricker which he had just taken from the case which Andy was holding before him.

"Why, my dear Dick," said Durfy, "as Murphy has had two shots, and the squire has not had the return of either, he declares he will not fire at him again; and, under these circumstances, I must take my man off the ground."

"Very well," said Dick, still poking the touch-hole, and examining the point of the pricker as he withdrew it.

"And now Murphy wants to know, since the affair is all over and his honour satisfied, what was your brother-in-law's motive in assaulting him this morning, for he himself cannot conceive a cause for it."

"Oh, be *aisy*, Tom."

"'Pon my soul, it's true."

"Why, he sent him a blister,—a regular apothecary's blister,—instead of some law process, by way of a joke, and Ned wouldn't stand it."

Durfy held a moment's conversation with Murphy, who now advanced to the squire, and begged to assure him there must be some mistake in the business, for that he had never committed the impertinence of which he was accused.

"All I know is," said the squire, "that I got a blister, which my messenger said you gave him."

"By virtue of my oath, squire, I never did it! I gave Andy an enclosure of the law process."

"Then it's some mistake that vagabond has made," said the squire. "Come here, you sir!" he shouted to Andy, who was trembling under the angry eye of Dick the Devil, who, having detected a bit of lead on the point of the pricker, guessed in a moment Andy had been at work; and the unfortunate rascal had a misgiving that he had made some blunder, from the furious look of Dick.

"Why don't you come here when I call you?" said the squire.—Andy laid down the pistol-case and sneaked up to the squire.—"What did you do with the letter Mr. Murphy gave you for me yesterday?"

"I brought it to your honour."

"No, you didn't," said Murphy. "You've made some mistake."

"Divil a mistake I made," answered Andy very stoutly; "I wint home the minit you gev it to me."

"Did you go home direct from my house to the squire's?"

"Yis, sir, I did: I wint direct home, and called at Mr. M'Garry's by the way for some physic for the childre'."

"That's it!" said Murtough; "he changed my enclosure for a blister there; and if M'Garry has only had the luck to send the bit o' parchment to O'Grady, it will be the best joke I've heard this month of Sundays."

"He did! he did!" shouted Tom Durfy; "for don't you remember how O'Grady was after M'Garry this morning?"

"Sure enough," said Murtough, enjoying the double mistake. "By dad! Andy, you've made a mistake this time that I'll forgive you."

"By the powers o' war! " roared Dick the Devil, "I won't forgive him what he did now, though! What do you think?" said he, holding out the pistols, and growing crimson with rage: "may I never fire another shot if he hasn't crammed a brace of bullets down the pistols before I loaded them: so no wonder you burned prime, Ned."

There was a universal laugh at Dick's expense, whose pride in being considered the most accomplished regulator of the duello was well known.

"Oh, Dick, Dick! you're a pretty second," was shouted by all.

Dick, stung by the laughter, and feeling keenly the ridiculous position in which he was placed, made a rush at Andy, who, seeing the storm brewing, gradually sneaked away from the group, and when he perceived the sudden movement of Dick the Devil, took to his heels, with Dick after him.

"Hurra!" cried Murphy; "a race—a race! I'll bet on Andy—five pounds on Andy."

"Done!" said the squire; "I'll back Dick the Divil."

"Tare an' ouns!" roared Murphy; "how Andy runs! Fear's a fine spur."

"So is rage," said the squire. "Dick's hot-foot after him. Will you double the bet?"

"Done!" said Murphy.

The infection of betting caught the bystanders, and various gages were thrown down and taken up upon the speed of the runners, who were getting rapidly into the distance, flying over hedge and ditch with surprising velocity, and, from the level nature of the ground an extensive view could not be obtained; therefore Tom Durfy, the steeplechaser, cried, "Mount, mount! or we'll lose the fun: into our saddles, and after them.

Those who had steeds took the hint, and a numerous field of horsemen joined in the chase of Handy Andy and Dick the Devil, who still maintained great speed. The horsemen made for a neighbouring hill, whence they could command a wider view; and the betting went on briskly, varying according to the vicissitudes of the race.

"Two to one on Dick—he's closing."

"Done!—Andy will wind him yet."

"Well done!—there's a leap! Hurra!—Dick's down! Well done, Dick!—up again and going."

"Mind the next quickset hedge—that's a rasper, it's a wide gripe, and the hedge is as thick as a wall—Andy'll stick in it—Mind him!—Well leap'd, by the powers!—Ha! he's sticking in the hedge—Dick'll catch him now.—No, by jingo! he has pushed his way through—there, he's going again at the other side.—Ha! ha! ha! ha! look at him—he's in tatthers!—he has left half of his breeches in the hedge."

"Dick is over now.—Hurra!—he has lost the skirt of his coat—Andy is gaining on him.—Two to one on Andy!"

"Down he goes!" was shouted, as Andy's foot slipped in making a dash at another ditch, into which he went head over heels, and Dick followed fast, and disappeared after him.

"Ride! ride!" shouted Tom Durfy; and the horsemen put their spurs in the flanks of their steeds, and were soon up to the scene of action. There was Andy, roaring murder, rolling over and over in the muddy bottom of a deep ditch, floundering in rank weeds and duck's meat, with Dick fastened on him, pummelling away most unmercifully, but not able to kill him altogether, for want of breath.

The horsemen, in a universal *screech* of laughter, dismounted, and disengaged the unfortunate Andy from the fangs of Dick the Devil, who was dragged from out of the ditch much more like a scavenger than a gentleman.

The moment Andy got loose, away he ran again, with a rattling "Tally ho!" after him, and he never cried stop till he earthed himself under his mother's bed in the parent cabin.

Murtough Murphy characteristically remarked, that the affair of the day had taken a very whimsical turn:—"Here are you and I, squire, who went out to shoot each other, safe and well, while one of the seconds has come off rather worse for the wear; and a poor devil, who had nothing to say to the matter in hand, good, bad, or indifferent, is nearly killed."

The squire and Murtough then shook hands, and parted friends in half an hour after they had met as foes; and even Dick contrived to forget his annoyance in an extra stoup of claret that day after dinner,— filling more than one bumper in drinking *confusion* to Handy Andy, which seemed a rather unnecessary malediction.

IV

A FTER THE FRIENDLY PARTING OF the foes (*pro tempore*), there was a general scatter of the party who had come to see the duel; and how strange is the fact, that, much as human nature is prone to shudder at death under the gentlest circumstances, yet men will congregate to be its witnesses, when violence aggravates the calamity! A public execution or a duel is a focus where burning curiosity concentrates: in the latter case, Ireland bears the palm, for a crowd; in the former, the annals of the Old Bailey can *amply* testify. Ireland has its own interest, too, in a place of execution, but not in the same degree as England. They have been too used to hanging in Ireland, to make it piquant: "*toujours perdrix*" is a saying which applies in this, as in many other cases. The gallows, in its palmy days, was shorn of its terrors; it became rather a pastime. For the victim, it was a pastime, with a vengeance;—for, through it, all time was past with him. For the rabble who beheld his agony, the frequency of the sight had blunted the edge of horror, and only sharpened that of unnatural excitement. The great school, where law should be the respected master, failed to inspire its intended awe;—the legislative lesson became a mockery; and death, instead of frowning with terror, grinned in a fool's cap from the scaffold.

This may be doubted now, when a milder spirit presides in the councils of the nation and on the bench; but those who remember Ireland not very long ago, can bear witness how lightly life was valued or death regarded.—Illustrative of this, one may refer to the story of the two basket-women, in Dublin, who held gentle converse on the subject of an approaching execution.

"Won't you go see de man die to-morrow, Judy?"

"Oh no, darlin'," said Judy;—by the bye, Judy pronounced the *n* through her nose, and said "*do.*"

"Ah do, jewel," said her friend.

Judy again responded,—"*do.*"

"And why won't you go, dear?" inquired her friend again.

"I've to wash de child," said Judy.

"Sure, didn't you wash it last week?" said her friend in an expostulatory tone.

"Oh, well, I *won't* go," said Judy.

"Throth, Judy, you're ruinin' your health," said this soft-hearted acquaintance; "dere's a man to die to-morrow, and you won't come—augh!—you *d*ever take *d*o divarshin!"

And wherefore is it thus? Why should tears bedew the couch of him who dies in the bosom of his family, surrounded by those who love him, whose pillow is smoothed by the hand of filial piety, whose past is without reproach, and whose future is bright with hope;—and why should dry eyes behold the duellist or the culprit, in whom folly or guilt may he the cause of a death on which the seal of censure or infamy may be set, and whose futurity we must tremble to consider? With more reason might we weep for the fate of either of the latter than the former, and yet we *do* not. And why is it so?—If I may venture an opinion, it is that nature is violated: a natural death demands and receives the natural tribute of tears; but a death of violence falls with a stunning force upon the nerves, and the fountain of pity stagnates and will not flow.

Though there was a general scattering of the persons who came to see the duel, still a good many rode homeward with Murphy, who with his second, Tom Durfy, beside him, headed the party, as they rode gaily towards the town, and laughed over the adventure of Andy and Dick.

"No one can tell how anything is to finish," said Tom Durfy; "here we came out to have a duel, and, in the end, it turned out a hunt."

"I'm glad you were not in at *my* death, however," said Murphy, who seemed particularly happy at not being killed.

"You lost no time in firing, Murtough," said one of his friends.

"And, small blame to me, Billy," answered Murphy; "Egan is a capital shot, and how did I know but he might take it into his head to shoot me? for he's very hot, when roused, though as good-natured a fellow, in the main, as ever broke bread; and yet I don't think, after all, he'd have liked to do me much mischief either; but you see he couldn't stand the joke he thought I played him."

"Will you tell us what it was?" cried another of the party, pressing forward, "for we can't make it out exactly, though we've heard something of it:—wasn't it leeches you sent to him, telling him he was a blood sucking villain?"

A roar of laughter from Murtough followed this question. "Lord, how a story gets mangled and twisted," said he, as soon as he could speak. "Leeches!—what an absurdity!—no—it was—"

"A bottle of castor oil, wasn't it, by way of a present of noyau?" said another of the party, hurrying to the front to put forward *his* version of the matter.

A second shout of laughter from Murphy greeted this third edition of the story. "If you will listen to me, I'll give you the genuine version," said Murtough, "which is better, I promise you, than any which invention could supply. The fact is, Squire Egan is engaged against O'Grady, and applied to me to harass him in the parchment line, swearing he would blister him; and this phrase of blistering occurred so often, that when I sent him over a bit o' parchment, which he engaged to have served on my bold O'Grady, I wrote to him, "Dear Squire, I send you the blister;" and that most ingenious of all blunderers, Handy Andy, being the bearer, and calling at M'Garry's shop on his way home, picked up from the counter a *real* blister, which was folded up in an enclosure, something like the process, and left the law-stinger behind him."

"That's grate," cried Doyle.

"Oh, but you have not heard the best of it yet," added Murphy. "I am certain the bit of parchment was sent to O'Grady, for he was hunting M'Garry this morning through the town, with a cudgel of portentous dimension—put that and that together."

"No mistake!" cried Doyle; "and divil pity O'Grady, for he's a blustering, swaggering, overbearing, ill-tempered"—

"Hillo, hillo, Bill," interrupted Murphy, "you are too hard on the adjectives; besides, you'll spoil your appetite if you ruffle your temper; and that would fret me, for I intend you to dine with me to-day."

"Faith, an' I'll do that same, Murtough, my boy, and glad to be asked, as the old maid said."

"I'll tell you all what it is," said Murphy. "Boys, you must all dine with me to-day, and drink long life to me since I'm not killed."

"There are seventeen of us," said Durfy; "the little parlour won't hold us all."

"But isn't there a big room at the inn, Tom?" returned Murphy, "and not better drink in Ireland than Mrs. Fay's. What do you say, lads, one and all—will you dine with me?"

"Will a duck swim?" chuckled out Jack Horan, an oily veteran, who seldom opened his mouth but to put some thing into it, and spared his words, as if they were of value; and to make them appear so, he spoke in apophthegms.

"What say you, James Reddy?" said Murtough.

"Ready, sure enough, and willing too!" answered James, who was a small wit, and made the aforesaid play upon his name, at least three hundred and sixty-five times every year.

"Oh, we'll all come," was uttered right and left.

"Good men and true!" shouted Murphy; "won't we make the rafters shake, and turn the cellar inside out!—whoo! I'm in great heart to-day. But who is this powdhering up the road? by the powers, 'tis the doctor, I think; 'tis—I know his bandy hat over the cloud of dust."

The individual, thus designated as *the* doctor, now emerged from the obscurity in which he had been enveloped, and was received with a loud shout by the whole cavalcade as he approached them. Both parties drew rein; and the doctor, lifting from his head the aforesaid bandy hat, which was slouched over one eye, with a sinister droop, made a low obeisance to Murphy, and said with a mock solemnity, "Your servant, sir—and so you're not killed?"

"No," said Murphy; "and you've lost a job, which I see you came to look for; but you're not to have the carving of me yet."

"Considering it's so near Michaelmas, I think you've had a great escape, signor," returned the doctor.

"Sure enough," said Murphy, laughing; "but you're late, this time; so you must turn back, and content yourself with carving something more innocent than an attorney, to-day—though at an attorney's cost. You must dine with me."

"Willingly, signor," said the doctor; "but pray don't make use of the word 'cost.' I hate to hear it out of an attorney's mouth—or *bill*, I should say."

A laugh followed the doctor's pleasantry, but no smile appeared upon *his* countenance; for though uttering quaint, and often very good, but oftener very bitter things, he never moved a muscle of his face, while others were shaking their sides at his sallies. He was, in more ways than one, a remarkable man. A massive head, large and rather protruding eyes, lank hair, slouching ears, a short neck and broad shoulders, rather inclined to stooping; a long body, and short legs slightly bowed, constituted his outward man; and a lemon-coloured complexion, which a residence of some years in the East Indies had produced, did not tend to increase his beauty. His mind displayed a superior intelligence, original views, contempt of received opinions, with a power of satire and ridicule, which rendered him a pleasing friend or a dangerous enemy, as the case might be; though, to say the truth, friend and foe were treated with nearly equal severity, if a joke or a sarcasm tempted the assault. His own profession hated him; for he unsparingly ridiculed all stale practice, which his conviction led him to believe was inefficient, and he daringly introduced fresh, to the no small indignation of the more cut and dry portion of the faculty, for whose hate he returned contempt, of which he made no secret. From an extreme coarseness of manner, even those who believed in his skill were afraid to trust to his humour; and the dislike of his brother practitioners to meet him, superadded to this, damaged his interest considerably, and prevented his being called in until extreme danger frightened patients, or their friends, into sending for Doctor Growling. His carelessness in dress, too, inspired disgust in the fair portion of the creation; and "snuffy," and "dirty," and "savage," and "brute," were among the sweet words they applied to him.

Nevertheless those who loved a joke more than they feared a hit, would run the risk of an occasional thrust of the doctor's stiletto, for the sake of enjoying the mangling he gave other people; and such rollicking fellows as Murphy, and Durfy, and Dawson, and Squire Egan, petted this social hedgehog.

The doctor now turned his horse's head, and joined the cavalcade to the town. "I have blown my Rozinante," said he, "I was in such a hurry to see the fun."

"Yes," said Murphy, "he smokes."

"And his master takes snuff," said the doctor, suiting the action to the word. "I suppose, signor, you were thinking a little while ago that the squire might serve an ejectment on your vitality?"

"Or that in the trial between us I might get damages," said Murphy.

"There is a difference, in such case," said the doctor, "between a court of law, and the court of honour; for, in the former, the man is plaintiff, before he gets his damages, while in the latter, it is after he gets his damages that he complains."

"I'm glad my term is not ended, however," said Murphy.

"If it had been," said the doctor, "I think you'd have had a long vacation in limbo."

"And suppose I had been hit," said Murphy, "you would have been late on the ground. You're a pretty friend!"

"It's my luck, sir," said the doctor. "I'm always late for a job. By the bye, I'll tell you an amusing fact of that musty piece of humanity, Miss Jenkins. Her niece was dangerously ill, and she had that licensed slaughterer from Killanmaul, trying to tinker her up, till the poor girl was past all hope, and then she sends for me. She swore, some time ago, I should never darken her doors, but when she began to apprehend that death was rather a darker gentleman than me, she tolerated my person. The old crocodile met me in the hall;—by the bye, did you ever remark she's *like* a crocodile—only not with so pleasing an expression?—and wringing her hands, she cried, 'Oh, doctor, I'll be bound to you for ever;'—I hope not, thought I to myself,—'Save my Jemima, doctor, and there's nothing I won't do to prove my gratitude.' 'Is she long ill, ma'am?' said I. 'A fortnight, doctor.'—'I wish I had been called in sooner, ma'am,' says I,—for, 'pon my conscience, Murphy, it is too ridiculous the way people go on about me. I verily believe they think I can raise people out of their graves; and they call me in to repair the damages disease *and* the doctors have been making; and while the gentlemen in black silk stockings, with gold-headed canes, have been fobbing fees for three weeks, perhaps, they call in poor Jack Growling, who scorns jack-a-dandyism, and *he* gets a solitary guinea for mending the bungling that cost something to the tune of twenty or thirty, perhaps. And when I have plucked them from the jaws of death,—regularly cheated the sexton out of them,—the best word they have for me is to call me a pig, or abuse my boots; or wonder the doctor is not more particular about his linen—the fools! But to return to my gentle crocodile. I was shown up stairs to the sick room, and there, sir, I saw the unfortunate girl, speechless, at the last gasp, absolutely. The Killanmaul dandy had left her to die—absolutely given her up; and *then*, indeed, I'm sent for! Well, I was in a rage, and was rushing out of the house, when the crocodile waylaid me in the hall. 'Oh, doctor, won't you do something for my Jemima?' 'I can't, ma'am,' says I; 'but Mister Fogarty can.' 'Mister Fogarty!' says she. 'Yes, ma'am,' says I. 'You have mistaken my profession, Miss Jenkins—I'm a doctor, ma'am; but I suppose *you took me for the undertaker.*'"

"Well you hit her hard, doctor," said Murphy.

"Sir, you might as well hit a rhinoceros," returned the doctor.

"When shall we dine?" asked Jack Horan.

"As soon as Mrs. Fay can let us have the eatables," answered Murphy; "and, by the bye, Jack, I leave the ordering of the dinner to you; for no man understands better how to do that same; besides, I want to leave my horse in my own stable, and I'll be up at the inn, after you, in a brace of shakes."

The troop now approached the town. Those who lived there rode to their own stables, and returned to the party at Mrs. Fay's; while they who resided at a distance dismounted at the door of the inn, which soon became a scene of bustle in all its departments, from this large influx of guests and the preparation for the dinner, exceeding in scale what Mrs. Fay was generally called upon to provide, except when the assizes, or races, or other such cause of commotion, demanded all the resources of her establishment, and more, if she had them. So the Dinnys, and the Tims, and the Mickeys, were rubbing down horses, cleaning knives, or drawing forth extra tables from their dusty repose; and the Biddys, and Judys, and Nellys, were washing up plates, scouring pans, and brightening up extra candlesticks, or doing deeds of doom in the poultry yard, where an audible commotion gave token of the premature deaths of sundry supernumerary chickens.

Murphy soon joined his guests, grinning from ear to ear, and rubbing his hands as he entered.

"Great news, boys," said he,—"who do you think was at my house when I got home, but M'Garry, with his head bandaged up, and his whole body, as he declares, bearing black and blue testimony to the merciless attack of the bold O'Grady, against whom he swears he'll bring an action for assault and battery. Now, boys, I thought it would be great fun to have him here to dinner,—it's as good as a play to hear him describe the thrashing,—so I asked him to come. He said he was not in a fit state to dine out, but I egged him on, by saying that a sight of him in his present plight would excite sympathy for him, and stir up public feeling against O'Grady, and that all would tell in the action, as most likely some of the present company might be on the jury, and would be the better able to judge how far he was entitled to damages, from witnessing the severity of the injury he had received. So he's coming; and mind, you must all be deeply affected at his sufferings, and impressed with the *powerful* description he gives of the same."

"Very scientific, of course," said old Growling.

"Extensively so," returned Murphy; "he laid on the Latin, *heavy*."

"Yes—the fool," growled the doctor; "he can't help sporting it, even on me; I went into his shop one day, and asked for some opium wine; and he could not resist calling it *vinum opii* as he handed it to me."

"We'll make him a martyr!" cried Durfy.

"We'll make him dhrunk," said Jack Horan, "and that will be better— he brags that he never was what he calls 'inebriated' in his life; and it will be great fun to send him home on a door, with a note to his wife, who is proud of his propriety."

As they spoke, M'Garry entered, his head freshly bound up, to look as genteel as possible amongst the gentlemen with whom he was to have the honour of dining. His wife had suggested a pink ribbon, but M'Garry, while he acknowledged his wife's superior taste, said black would look more professional. The odd fellows, to whom he had now committed himself, crowded round him, and in the most exaggerated phrases, implied the high sense they entertained of his wrongs and O'Grady's aggression.

"Unprovoked attack!" cried one.

"Savage ruffian!" ejaculated another.

"What atrocity!" said a third.

"What dignified composure!" added a fourth, in an audible whisper meant for M'Garry's ear.

"Gentlemen!" said the apothecary, flurried at the extreme attention of which he became the object, "I beg to assure you I am deeply—that is this proof of—of—of—of symptoms—gentlemen—I mean sympathy, gentlemen—in short, I really—"

"The fact is," said Growling, " I see Mr. M'Garry is rather shaken in nerve—whether from loss of blood, or—"

"I have lost a quantity of blood, doctor," said M'Garry; "much vascular,—to say nothing of extravasated."

"Which I'll state in my case," said Murphy—"Murphy, don't interrupt," said Growling; who, with a very grave face, recommenced,— "Gentlemen, from the cause already stated, I see Mr. M'Garry is not prepared to answer the out-pouring of feeling with which you have greeted him, and if I might be permitted—"

Every one shouted, "Certainly—certainly."

"Then, as I am permitted, I *will* venture to respond *for* Mr. M'Garry, and address you, as he *would* address you. In the, words of Mister M'Garry, I would say,—Gentlemen—unaccustomed as I am—"

Some smothered laughter followed this beginning—upon which the doctor, with a mock gravity proceeded—

"Gentlemen, this interruption I conceive to be an infringement on the liberty of the subject. I recommence, there in the words of my honourable and wounded friend, and our honourable and wounded feelings, and say—as my friend would say, or, to speak classically, M'Garry *loquitur*—"

The apothecary bowed his head to the bit of Latin, and the doctor continued.

"Gentlemen—unaccustomed as I am to public thrashing, you can conceive what my feelings are at the present moment, in mind and body. [*Bravo*]. You behold an outrage [*much confusion*]; shall an exaggerated savagery like this escape punishment, and 'the calm sequestered vale' (as the poet calls it) of private life, be ravaged with impunity? [*Bravo! bravo!*] Are the learned professions to be trampled under-foot by barbarian ignorance and brutality? No; I read in the indignant looks of my auditory their high-souled answers. Gentlemen, your sympathy is better than dyachylon to my wounds, and this is the proudest day of my life."

Thunders of applause followed the doctor's address, and every one shook M'Garry's hand, till his bruised bones ached again. Questions poured upon him from all sides as to the nature and quantity of his drubbing, to all which M'Garry innocently answered in terms of exaggeration, spiced with scientific phrases. Muscles, tendons, bones, and sinews, were particularized with the precision of an anatomical demonstration; he swore he was pulverized, and paralyzed, and all the other lies he could think of.

"A large stick, you say?" said Murphy.

"Sir! I never saw such a stick—'twas like a weaver's beam."

"I'll make a note of that," said Murphy, "a weaver's beam—'twill tell well with a jury."

"And beat you all over?" said Durfy.

"From shoulder to flank, sir, I am one mass of welts and weals; the abrasures are extensive, the bruises terrific, particularly in the lumbar region."

"Where's that?" asked Jack Horan.

"The lumbar region is what is commonly called the loins, sir."

"Not always," said the doctor. "It varies in different subjects: I have known some people whose *lumber* region lay in the head."

"You laugh, gentlemen," said M'Garry, with a mournful smile, "but you *know* the doctor—he *will* be jocular." He then continued to describe the various other regions of his injuries, amidst the well-acted pity and indignation of the queer fellows who drew him out, until they were saturated, so far, with the fun of the subject. After which, Murphy, whose restless temperament could never let him be quiet for a moment, suggested that they should divert themselves before dinner with a badger fight.

"Isn't one fight a day enough for you, signor?" said the doctor.

"It is not every day we get a badger, you know," said Murphy; "and I heard just now from Tim the waiter that there is a horse dealer lately arrived at the stables here, who has a famous one with him, and I know Reilly the butcher has two or three capital dogs, and there's a wicked

mastiff below stairs, and I'll send for my 'buffer,' and we'll have some
spanking sport."

He led his guests then to the inn yard, and the horse dealer, for a
consideration, allowed his badger to wage battle; the noise of the affair
spread through the town, while they were making their arrangements,
and sending right and left for dogs for the contest; and a pretty
considerable crowd soon assembled at the place of action, where the
before dinner was spent in the intellectual amusement of a badger-
fight.

V

THE FIERCE YELLS OF THE badger fight, ringing far and wide, soon attracted a crowd, which continued to increase every minute by instalments of men and boys, who might be seen running across a small field by the road side, close to the scene of action, which lay at the back of the inn; and heavy-caped and skirted frieze coats streamed behind the full grown, while the rags of the gossoons (boys) fluttered in the race. Attracted by this evidence of "something going on," a horseman who was approaching the town, urged his horse to speed, and turning his head towards a yawning double ditch that divided the road from the field, he gracefully rode the noble animal over the spanking leap.

The rider was Edward O'Connor; and he was worthy of his name— the pure blood of that royal race was in his heart, which never harboured a sentiment that could do it dishonour, and overflowed with feelings which ennoble human nature, and make us proud of our kind. He was young and handsome; and as he sat his mettled horse, no lady could deny that Edward O'Connor was the very type of the gallant cavalier. Though attached to every manly sport and exercise, his mind was of a refined order; and a youth passed amidst books and some of the loveliest scenery of Ireland had nurtured the poetic feeling with which his mind was gifted, and which found its vent in many a love-taught lyric, or touching ballad, or spirit-stirring song whose theme was national glory. To him the bygone days of his country's history were dear, made more familiar by many an antique relic which hung around his own room, in his father's house. Celt, and sword, and spear-head of Phoenician bronze, and golden gorget, and silver bodkin, and ancient harp, and studded crozier, were there; and these time-worn evidences of arts, and arms, and letters, flattered the affection with which he looked back on the ancient history of Ireland, and kept alive the ardent love of his country with which he glowed,—a love too deep, too pure, to be likely to expire, even without the aid of such poetic sources of excitement. To him the names of Fitzgerald, and Desmond, and Tyrone, were dear; and there was no romantic legend of the humbler outlaws with which he was not familiar; and "Charley of the Horses," and "Ned of the Hill," but headed the list of names he loved to recall; and the daring deeds of bold spirits who held the hill side for liberty were often given in words of poetic fire from the lips of Edward O'Connor.

And yet Edward O'Connor went to see the badger fight.

There is something inherent in man's nature, urging him to familiarize himself with cruelty; and perhaps, without such a power of witnessing savage deeds, he would be unequal to the dominion for which he was designed. Men of the highest order of intellect the world has known have loved the chase. How admirable Scott displays this tendency of noble minds, in the meeting of Helen with her father, when Douglas says—

> "The chase I followed far;
> 'Tis mimicry of noble war."

And the effect of this touch of character is heightened by Douglas, in a subsequent scene—Douglas, who could enjoy the sport which ends in death, bending over his gentle child, and dropping tears of the tenderest affection; tears, which

> "Would not stain an angel's cheek."

Superadded to this natural tendency, Edward O'Connor had an additional motive. He lived amongst a society of sporting men, less cultivated than he was, whose self-esteem would have easily ignited to the spark of jealousy, if he had seemed to scorn the things which made their principal enjoyment, and formed the chief occupation of their lives; and his good sense and good heart (and there is an intimate

connexion between them) pointed out to him, that wherever your lot
is cast, duty to yourself and others suggests the propriety of adapting
your conduct to the circumstances in which you are placed (so long
as morality and decency are not violated), and that the manifestation
of one's own superiority may render the purchase too dear, by being
bought at the terrible price of our neighbour's dislike. He therefore
did not tell every body he wrote verses; he kept the gift as secret as
he could. If an error, however gross, on any subject, were made in his
presence, he never took willing notice of it; or if circumstances obliged
him to touch upon it, it was always done with a politeness and tact
that afforded the blunderer the means of retreat. If some gross historical
error, for instance, happened to be committed in a conversation *with
himself* (and then only), he would set the mistake right, as a matter of
conscience, but he would do so by saying there was a great similarity
between the event spoken of and some other event. "I know what you
are thinking of," he would say, "but you make a slight mistake in the
dates; the two stories are very similar, and likely to mislead one."

But with all this modest reserve, did the least among his companions
think him less clever? No. It was shrewdly suspected he was a poet; it
was well known he was highly educated and accomplished; and yet
Edward O'Connor was a universal favourite, bore the character of being
a "real fine fellow," and was loved and respected by the most illiterate of
the young men of the country; who, in allusion to his extensive lore on
the subject of the legendary heroes of the *romantic* history of Ireland, his
own christian name, and his immediate place of residence, which was
near a wild mountain pass, christened him "Ned of the Hill."

His appearance amidst the crowd assembled to witness the rude sport
was hailed with pleasure,—varying from the humble, but affectionate
respect of the peasant, who cried   "Long life to you, Misther
O'Connor," to the hearty burst of equality, which welcomed him as
"Ned of the Hill."

The fortune of the fight favoured the badger, who proved himself
a trump; and Murphy appreciated his worth so highly, that, when the
battle was over, he would not quit the ground until he became his
owner at a high price to the horse dealer. His next move was to *insist*
on Edward O'Connor dining with him and Edward, after many excuses

to avoid the party he foresaw would be a drinking bout (of which he had a special horror, notwithstanding all his toleration), yielded to the entreaties of Murphy, and consented to be his guest, just as Tim, the waiter, ran up, steaming from every pore, to announce that the dinner was "ready to be sarved."

"Then sarve it, sir," said Murphy, "and sarve it right."

Off cantered Tim, steaming and snorting like a locomotive engine, and the party followed to the inn, where a long procession of dish bearers was ascending the stairs to the big room, as Murphy and his friends entered.

The dinner it is needless to describe. One dinner is the same as another in the most essential point, namely, to satisfy hunger and slake consequent thirst; and whether beef and cabbage, and heavy wet, are to conquer the dragon of appetite, or your stomach is to sustain the more elaborate attack fired from the *batterie de cuisine* of a finished *artiste*, and moistened with champagne, the difference is only of degree in the fashion of the thing and the tickling of the palate: hunger is as thoroughly satisfied with the one as the other; and head-aches as well manufactured out of the beautiful bright and taper glasses which bear the foam of France to the lip, as from the coarse flat-bottomed tumblers of an inn that reek with punch. At the diner, there was the same tender solicitude on the part of the carvers as to "Where would you like it ?" and the same carelessness on the part of those whom they questioned, who declared they had no choice, "but, if there *was* a bit near the shank," &c., or, "if there was a liver wing to *spare*." By the way, some carvers there are who push an aspirant's patience too far. I have seen some, who, after giving away both wings, and all the breast, two sidebones, and the short legs, meet the eager look of the fifth man on their left with a smile, and ask him, with an effrontery worthy of the Old Bailey, "has he any choice?" and, at the same time, toss a drum-stick on the destined plate, or boldly attempt to divert his melancholy with a merry-thought. All this and more, was there at Murtough Murphy's dinner, long memorable in the country from a frolic that wound up the evening, which soon began to warm, after the cloth was removed, into the sort of thing commonly known by the name of a jollification. But before the dinner was over, poor M'Garry was nearly pickled: Jack

Horan, having determined to make him drunk, arranged a system of attack on M'Garry's sobriety which bade defiance to his prudence to withstand. It was agreed that every one should ask the apothecary to take wine; and he, poor innocent man, when gentlemen, whom he had never had the honour to meet at dinner before addressed him with a winning smile, and said, "Mr. M'Garry—will you do me the *honour?*" to use Jack Horan's own phrase, the apothecary was "sewed up" before he had any suspicion of the fact; and, unused to the indications of approaching vinous excitement, he supposed it was the delightful society made him so hilarious, and he began to launch forth after dinner in a manner quite at variance with the reserve he usually maintained in the presence of his superiors, and talked largely. Now, M'Garry's principal failing was to endeavour to make himself appear very learned in his profession; and every new discovery in chemistry, operation in surgery, or scientific experiment he heard of, he was prone to shove in, head and shoulders in his soberest moments: but now that he was half-drunk, he launched forth on the subject of galvanism, having read of some recent wonderful effect produced on the body of a certain murderer who was hanged and given over to the College of Surgeons in Dublin. To impress the company still more with a sense of his learning, he addressed Growling on the subject, and the doctor played him off to advantage.

"Don't you consider it very wonderful, doctor?" inquired M'Garry, speaking somewhat thickly.

"Very!" answered the doctor drily.

"They say, sir, the man—that is, the subject, when under the influence of the battery—absolutely twiddled his left foot, and raised his right arm."

"And raised it to some purpose, too," said the doctor, "for he raised a contusion on the Surgeon-General's eye, having hit him over the same."

"Dear me!—I did not hear that."

"It is true, however," said the doctor; "and that gives you an idea of the power of the galvanic influence, for you know the Surgeon-General is a powerful man, and yet he could not hold him down."

"Wonderful!" hiccupped M'Garry.

"But that's nothing to what happened in London. They experimented there, the other day, with a battery of such power, that the man who was hanged absolutely jumped up, seized a scalpel from the table, and making a rush on the assembled Faculty of London, cleared the theatre in less than no time—dashed into the hall, stabbed the porter who attempted to stop him, made a chevy down the south side of Leicester-square and as he reached the corner, a woman, who was carrying tracts published by the Society for the Suppression of Vice, shrieked at beholding a man in so startling a condition, and fainted;—he, with a presence of mind perfectly admirable, whipped the cloak from her back, and threw it round him; and scudding through the tortuous alleys which abound in that neighbourhood, he made his way to the house where the learned Society of the Noviomagians hold their convivial meetings, and telling the landlord he was invited there to dinner as a curiosity, he gained admittance, and, it is supposed, took his opportunity for escaping, for he has not since been heard of."

"Good heavens!" gasped M'Garry; "and do you believe that, doctor?"

"Most firmly, sir! My belief is that galvanism is, in fact, the original principle of vitality."

"Should we not rejoice, doctor," cried M'Garry, "at this triumph of science?"

"I don't think you should, Mister M'Garry," said the doctor, gravely, "for it would utterly destroy *your* branch of the profession:—pharma-copolists, instead of compounding medicine, must compound with their creditors; they are utterly ruined. Mercury is no longer in the ascendant;—all doctors have to do now is to carry a small battery about them, a sort of galvanic pocket pistol, I may say, and restore the vital principle by its application."

"You are not serious, doctor," said M'Garry, becoming *very* serious, with that wise look so peculiar to drunken men.

"Never more serious in my life, sir."

"That would be dreadful!" said M'Garry.

"*Shocking*, you mean," said the doctor.

"Leave off your confounded scientifics, there," shouted Murphy from the head of the table, "and let us have a song."

"I can't sing, indeed, Mister Murphy," said, M'Garry, who became more intoxicated every moment; for he continued to drink, having once overstepped the boundary which custom had prescribed to him.

"I didn't ask you, man," said Murphy; "but my darling fellow, Ned here, will gladden our hearts and ears with a stave."

"Bravo!" was shouted round the table, trembling under the "thunders of applause," with which heavy hands made it ring again:—and "Ned of the Hill!"—"Ned of the Hill!" was vociferated with many a hearty cheer about the board that might indeed be called "festive."

"Well," said O'Connor, "since you call upon me in the name of Ned of the Hill, I'll give you a song under that very title. Here's, Ned of the Hill's own shout;" and in a rich, manly voice, he sang, with the fire of a bard, these lines:—

THE SHOUT OF NED OF THE HILL

I

The hill! the hill! with its sparkling rill,
   And its dawning air so light and pure,
Where the morning's eye scorns the mists that lie
   On the drowsy valley and the moor.
Here, with the eagle I rise betimes
   Here, with the eagle my state I keep;
The first we see of the morning sun,
   And his last as he sets o'er the deep;
And there, while strife is rife below,
   Here from the tyrant I am free:
Let shepherd slaves the valley praise,
   But the hill!—the hill for me!

II

The baron below in his castle dwells,
   And his garden boasts the costly rose;
But mine is the keep of the mountain steep,
   Where the matchless wild flower freely blows!
Let him fold his sheep, and his harvest reap,—

I look down from my mountain throne;
And I choose and pick of the flock and the rick,
    And what is his I can make my own!
Let the valley grow in its wealth below,
    And the lord keep his high degree;
But higher am I in my liberty—
    The hill!—the hill for me!

O'Connor's song was greeted with what the music publishers are
pleased to designate, on their title-pages, "distinguished applause;" and
his "health and song" were filled to and drunk with enthusiasm.

"Whose lines are these?" asked the doctor.

"I don't know," said O'Connor.

"That's as much as to say they are your own," said Growling. "Ned,
don't be too modest; it is the worst fault a man can have who wants to
get on in this world."

"The call is with you, Ned," shouted Murphy from the head of the
table; "knock some one down for a song."

"Mr. Reddy, I hope, will favour us," said Edward, with a courteous
inclination of his head towards the gentleman he named, who returned
a very low bow, with many protestations that he would "do his best,"
&c. : "but after Mr. O'Connor, really;"—and this was said with a certain
self-complacent smile, indicative of his being on very good terms with
himself. Now, James Reddy wrote rhymes, bless the mark! and was
tolerably well convinced that, except Tom Moore, (if he *did* except
even him,) there was not a man in the British dominions his equal at a
lyric:—he sang, too, with a kill-me-quite air, as if no lady could resist his
strains; and to "give effect," as he called it, he began every stanza as loud
as he could, and finished it in a gentle murmur—tailed it off very taper
indeed; in short, it seemed as if a shout had been suddenly smitten with
consumption, and died in a whisper. And this, his style, never varied,
whatever the nature or expression of the song might be, or the sense
to be expressed; but as he very often sang his own, there was seldom
any to consider. This rubbish he had set to music by the country music
master, who believed himself to be a better composer than Sir John
Stevenson, to whom the prejudices of the world gave the palm; and he

eagerly caught at the opportunity which the verses and vanity of Reddy afforded him, of stringing his crotchets and quavers on the same hank with the abortive fruits of Reddy's muse, and the wretched productions hung worthily together.

Reddy, with the proper quantity of "hems and haws," and rubbing down his upper lip and chin with his forefinger and thumb, cleared his throat, tossed his nose into the air, and said, he was going to give them "a little *classic* thing."

"Just look at the puppy!" snarled out old Growling to his neighbour, "he's going to measure us out some yards of his own fustian, I'm sure,—he looks so pleased."

Reddy gave his last "a-hem!" and sang what he called

THE LAMENT OF ARIADNE

> The graceful Greek with gem-bright hair
> Her garments rent, and rent the air.

"What a tearing rage she was in!" said old Growling in an undertone.

> With sobs and sighs
> And tearful eyes,
> Like fountain fair of Helicon!

"Oh, thunder and lightning!" growled the doctor, who pulled a letter out of his pocket, and began to scribble on the blank portions of it, with the stump of a blunt pencil, which he very audibly sucked, to enable it to make a mark.

> For ah, her lover false was gone!
> The fickle brave,
> And fickle wave,

"And pickled cabbage," said the doctor—

Combined to cheat the fickle fair.
   Oh, fickle! fickle! fickle!
But the brave should be true,
And the fair ones too— True, true,
   As the ocean's blue!
And Ariadne had not been,
Deserted there, like beauty's queen.
Oh, Ariadne!—adne!—adne!

"Beautiful!" said the doctor, with an approving nod at Reddy, who continued his song, while the doctor continued to write.

The sea-nymphs round the sea-girt shore
   Mock'd the maiden's sighs,
And the ocean's savage roar
   Replies—
Replies—Replies—replies, replies, replies
(*After the manner of "Tell me where is Fancy bred."*)

"Very original," said the doctor.

   With willow wand
   Upon the strand
She wrote with trembling heart and hand,
   "The brave should ne'er
   Desert the fair."
But the wave the moral washed away,
   Ah, well-a-day!—well-a-day!
   A-day!—a-day!—a-day!

Reddy smiled and bowed, and thunders of applause followed;—the doctor shouted—"Splendid!" several times, and continued to write and take snuff voraciously, by which those who knew him could comprehend he was bent on mischief.

"What a beautiful thing that is!" said one.

"Whose is it?" said another.

"A little thing of my own," answered Reddy with a smile.

"I thought so," said Murphy: "by Jove, James, you *are* a genius!"

"Nonsense!" smiled the poet; "just a little classic trifle—I think *them* little classic allusions is pleasing in general—Tommy Moore is very happy in his classic allusions, you *may* remark; not that I, of course, mean to institute a comparison between so humble an individual as myself, and Tommy Moore, who has so well been called 'the poet of all circles, and the idol of his own;' and if you will permit me, in a kindred spirit,—I hope I may say the kindred spirit of a song,—in that kindred spirit I propose *his* health—the health of Tommy Moore!"

"Don't say, *Tommy!*" said the doctor, in an irascible tone; "call the man TOM, sir;—with all my heart, TOM MOORE!"

The table took the word from Jack Growling, and "Tom Moore," with all the honours of "hip and hurra," rang round the walls of the village inn;—and where is the village in Ireland, *that* health has not been hailed with the fiery enthusiasm of the land whose lays he hath "wedded to immortal verse," that land which is proud of his birth, and holds his name in honour.

There is a magic in a great name; and in this instance, that of Tom Moore turned the current from where it was setting, and instead of quizzing the nonsense of the fool who had excited their mirth, every one launched forth in praise of their native bard, and couplets from his favourite songs ran from lip to lip.

"Come, Ned of the Hill," said Murphy, "sing us one of *his* songs—I know you have them all as pat as your prayers"—

"And say them oftener," said the doctor, who still continued scribbling over the letter.

Edward, at the urgent request of many, sang that most exquisite of the Melodies, "And doth not a meeting like this make amends?" and long ran the plaudits, and rapidly circulated the bottle, at its conclusion.

"We'll be the 'Alps in the sun-set,' my boys," said Murphy, "and here's the wine to enlighten us!—But what are *you* about there, doctor? is it a prescription you are writing?"

"No. Prescriptions are written in Latin, and this is a bit of Greek I'm doing. Mr. Reddy has inspired me with a classic spirit, and if you will permit me, I'll volunteer a song, [*Bravo! Bravo!*] and give you another

version of the subject he has so beautifully treated; only mine is not so
heart-breaking."

The doctor's proposition was received with cheers, and after he had
gone through the mockery of clearing his throat, and pitching his voice
after the usual manner of your would-be-fine singers, he gave out, to
the tune of a well-known rollicking Irish lilt, the following burlesque
version of the subject of Reddy's song:—

LOVE AND LIQUOR

A GREEK ALLEGORY

I

Oh sure 'twould amaze yiz
How one Misther Theseus
Desarted a lovely young lady of owld,
On a dissolute island,
All lonely and silent,
She sobb'd herself sick as she sat in the cowld.
Oh you'd think she was kilt,
As she roar'd with the quilt
Wrapp'd round her in haste as she jump'd out of bed,
And ran down to the coast
Where she look'd like a ghost,
Though 'twas *he* was departed—the vagabone fled.
And she cried, "Well-a-day!
Sure my heart it is grey;
They're deceivers, them sojers that goes on half-pay!"

II

While abusing the villain,
Came riding postilion,
A nate little boy on the back of a baste,
Big enough, faith, to ate him,
But he lather'd and bate him,

And the baste to unsate him ne'er struggled the laste;
    And an iligant car
    He was dhrawing—by gar!
It was finer by far than a Lord Mayor's state coach;
    And the chap that was in it,
    He sang like a linnet,
With a nate kag of whisky beside him to broach.
    And he tipp'd, now and then,
    Just a matter o' ten
Or twelve tumblers o' punch to his bowld sarving men.

III

    They were dress'd in green livery,
    But seem'd rather shivery,
For 'twas only a thrifle o' leaves that they wore,
    But they caper'd away,
    Like the sweeps on May-day,
And shouted and tippled the tumblers galore!
    A print of their masther
    Is often in plasther-
o' Paris, put over the door of a tap;
    A fine chubby fellow,
    Ripe, rosy, and mellow,
Like a peach that is ready to drop in your lap.
    Hurrah! for Brave Bacchus,
    A bottle to crack us,
He's a friend of the people, like bowld Caius Gracchus

IV

    Now Bacchus perceiving
    The lady was grieving,
He spoke to her civil, and tipp'd her a wink;
    And the more that she fretted,
    He soother'd and petted,

And gave her a glass her own health just to dhrink;
  Her pulse it beat quicker,
  The thrifle o' liquor
Enlivend her sinking heart's cockles, I think;
  So the MORAL is plain,
  That if love gives you pain,
There's nothing can cure it like taking to dhrink!

Uproarious were the "bravos" which followed the doctor's impromptu; the glasses overflowed, and were emptied to his health and song, as laughing faces nodded to him round the table. The doctor sat seriously rocking himself in his chair backwards and forwards, to meet the various duckings of the beaming faces about him; for every face beamed, but one—and that was the unfortunate M'Garry's. He was most deplorably drunk, and began to hold on by the table. At last he contrived to shove back his chair and get on his legs; and making a sloping stagger towards the wall, contrived by its support to scramble his way to the door. There he balanced himself as well as he could by the handle of the lock, which chance, rather than design, enabled him to turn, and the door suddenly opening, poor M'Garry made a rush across the landing-place, and stumbling against an opposite door would have fallen, had he not supported himself by the lock of that also, which again yielding to his heavy tugs, opened, and the miserable wretch making another plunge forward, his shins came in contact with the rail of a very low bed, and into it he fell head foremost, totally unable to rise, and after some heavy grunts, he sank into a profound sleep.

In this state he was discovered soon after by Murphy, whose inventive faculty for frolic instantly suggested how the apothecary's mishap might be made the foundation of a good practical joke. Murtough went down stairs, and procuring some blacking and red pickled cabbage, by stealth, returned to the chamber where M'Garry now lay in a state of stupor, and dragging off his clothes, he made long dabs across his back with the purple juice of the pickle, and Warren's paste, till poor M'Garry was as regularly striped as a tiger, from his shoulder to his flank. He then returned to the dinner-room, where the drinking bout had assumed a formidable character, and others, as well as the apothecary, began to feel the influence of their potations. Murphy confided to the doctor what he had done, and said, that when the men were drunk enough, he would contrive that M'Garry should be discovered, and then they would take their measures accordingly. It was not very long before his company were ripe enough for his designs, and then ringing the bell, he demanded of the waiter, when he entered, what had become of Mr. M'Garry? The waiter, not having any knowledge on the subject, was desired to inquire, and a search being instituted, M'Garry was discovered by Mrs. Fay in the state Murphy had left him in. On seeing him, she was so terrified that she screamed, and ran into the dinner-room, wringing her hands, and shouting "Murder!" A great commotion ensued, and a general rush to the bed-room took place, and exclamations of wonder and horror flew round the room, not only from the gentlemen of the dinner-party, but from the servants of the house, who crowded to the chamber on the first alarm, and helped not a little to increase the confusion.

"Oh, who ever see the like of it!" shouted Mrs. Fay. "He's kilt with the batin' he got! Oh, look at him!—black and blue all over!—Oh, the murther it is! Oh, I wouldn't be Squire O'Grady for all his fort'n."

"Gad, I believe he's killed, sure enough," said Murphy.

"What a splendid action the widow will have!" said Jack Horan.

"You forget, man," said Murphy, "this is not a case for action of damages, but a felony—hanging matter."

"Sure enough," said Jack.

"Doctor, will you feel his pulse?" said Murphy.

The doctor did as he was required, and assumed a very serious countenance. "'Tis a bad business, sir:—his wounds are mortifying already."

Upon this announcement, there was a general retreat from the bed round which they had been crowding too close for the carrying on of the joke; and Mrs. Fay ran for a shovel of hot cinders, and poured vinegar over them, to fumigate the room.

"A very proper precaution, Mrs. Fay," said the doctor, with imperturbable gravity.

"That villanous smoke is choking me," said Jack Horan.

"Better that, sir, than have a pestilence in the house," said Growling.

"I'll leave the place," said Jack Horan.

"And I, too," said Doyle.

"And I," said Reddy— "'tis disgusting to a sensitive mind."

"Gentlemen!" said Murphy, shutting the door, "you must not quit the house. I must have an inquest on the body."

"An inquest!" they all exclaimed.

"Yes—an inquest."

"But there's no coroner here," said Reddy.

"No matter for that," said Murphy. "I, as the under-sheriff of the county, can preside at this inquiry. Gentlemen, take your places;—bring in more light, Mrs. Fay. Stand round the bed, gentlemen."

"Not too close," said the doctor. "Mrs. Fay, bring more vinegar."

Mrs. Fay had additional candles and more vinegar introduced, and the drunken fellows were standing as straight as they could, each with a candle in his hand, round the still prostrate M'Garry.

Murphy then opened on them with a speech, and called in every one in the house to ask did they know any thing about the matter; and it was not long before it was spread all over the town, that Squire O'Grady had killed M'Garry, and that the coroner's inquest brought in a verdict of murder, and that the Squire was going to be sent to jail.

This almost incredible humbug of Murphy's had gone on for nearly half an hour, when the cold arising from his want of clothes, and the riot about him, and the fumes of the vinegar, roused M'Garry, who turned on the bed and opened his eyes. There he saw a parcel of people standing round him, with candles in their hands, and countenances of drunken wonder and horror. He uttered a hollow groan and cried,—

"Save us and keep us! where am I?"

"Retire, gentlemen!" said the doctor, waving his hand authoritatively; "retire—all but the under-sheriff."

Murphy cleared the room, and shut the door, while M'Garry still kept exclaiming,—"Save us and keep us! Where am I? What's this? O Lord!"

"You're dead!" says Murphy, "and the coroner's inquest has just sat on you!"

"Dead!" cried M'Garry, with a horrified stare.

"Dead!" repeated the doctor solemnly.

"Are not you Doctor Growling?"

"You see the effect, Mr. Murphy," said the doctor, not noticing M'Garry's question— "you see the effect of the process."

"Wonderful!" said Murphy.

"Preserve us!" cried the bewildered apothecary. "How could I know you, if I was dead, doctor? Oh! doctor dear, sure I am not dead!"

"As a herring," said the doctor.

"Lord have mercy on me!—Oh, Mister Murphy, sure I'm not dead."

"You're dead, sir," said Murphy; "the doctor has only galvanised you for a few moments."

"Oh Lord!" groaned M'Garry. "Doctor—indeed, doctor?"

"You are in a state of temporary animation," said the doctor.

"I do feel very odd, indeed," said the terrified man, putting his hands to his throbbing temples. "How long am I dead?"

"A week next Tuesday," said the doctor. "Galvanism has preserved you from decomposition."

M'Garry uttered a heavy groan, and looked up piteously at his two tormentors. Murphy, fearful the shock might drive him out of his mind, said, "Perhaps, doctor, you can preserve his life altogether; you have kept him alive so long."

"I'll try," said Growling; "hand me that tumbler."

Murphy handed him a tumbler full of water, and the doctor gave it to M'Garry, and desired him to try and drink it;—he put it to his lips and swallowed a little drop.

"Can you taste it?" asked the doctor.

"Isn't it water?" said M'Garry.

"You see how dull the nerves are yet," said Growling to Murphy; "that's aquafortis and assafoetida, and he can't taste it; we must give him another touch of the battery. Hold him up while I go into the next room and immerse the plates."

The doctor left the bed-room, and came back with a hot poker, and some lemon-juice and water.

"Turn him gently round," said he to Murphy, "while I conduct the wires."

His order was obeyed; and giving M'Garry a touch of the hot poker, the apothecary roared like a bull.

"That did him good!" said Growling. "Now try, can you taste anything?" and he gave him the lemon-juice and water.

"I taste a slight acid, doctor, dear!" said M'Garry, hopefully.

"You see what that last touch did," said Growling, gravely; "but the palate is still feeble; that's nearly pure nitric."

"Oh, dear!" said M'Garry, "is it nitric?"

"You see his hearing is coming back too," said the doctor to Murphy; "try, can he put his legs under him?"

They raised the apothecary from the bed; and when he staggered and fell forward, he looked horrified—"Oh dear, I can't walk.—I'm afraid I am—I am no more!"

"Don't despair," said the doctor; "I pledge my professional reputation to save you now, since you can stand at all, and your senses are partly restored; let him lie down again; try, could he sleep—"

"Sleep!"—said M'Garry with horror,—"perhaps never to awaken."

"I'll keep up the galvanic influence—don't be afraid; depend upon me—there lie down, can you shut your eyes? Yes I see you can;—don't open them so fast. Try, can you keep them shut? Don't open them till I tell you—wait till I count two hundred and fifty:—that's right; turn a little more round—keep your eyes fast;—that's it—One—two—three—four—five—six—seven;" and so he went on, making a longer interval between every number, till the monotonous sound, and the closed eye of the helplessly-drunken man, produced the effect desired by the doctor; and the heavy snoring of the apothecary soon bore witness that he slept.

We hope it is not necessary to assure our fair readers that Edward O'Connor had nothing to do with this scene of drunken absurdity:— no. Long before the evening's proceedings had assumed the character of a regular drinking bout, he had contrived to make his escape, his head only sufficiently excited to increase his sentimentality; so instead of riding home direct, he took a round of some eight miles, to have a look at Merryvale; for there dwelt Fanny Dawson—the Darling Fanny Dawson, sister to Dick, whose devilry was more than redeemed in the family by the angelic sweetness of his lovely and sportive sister. For the present, however, poor Edward O'Connor was not allowed to address Fanny; but his love for her knew no abatement, not withstanding; and to see the place where she dwelt had for him a charm. There he sat in his saddle, at the gate, looking up the long line of old trees through which the cold moonlight was streaming; and he fancied that Fanny's foot had trodden that avenue perhaps a few hours before, and even *that* gave him pleasure: for to those who love with the fond enthusiasm of Edward O'Connor, the very vacancy where the loved one has been is sacred.

The horse pawed impatiently to be gone, and Edward reined him up with a chiding voice; but the animal continuing restless, Edward's apostrophes to his mistress, and warnings to his horse, made an odd mixture; and we would recommend gentlemen, after their second bottle, not to let themselves be overheard in their love fits: for even as fine a fellow as Edward O'Connor is likely to be ridiculous under such circumstances.

"O, Fanny!" cried Edward,—"My adored Fanny!"—then to his horse, "*Be quiet, you brute!*"—"My love—my angel—*you devil, I'll thrash you, if you don't be quiet*—though separated from me, you are always present to my mind; your bright eyes, your raven locks—*your mouth's as hard as a paving-stone, you brute!*—Oh, Fanny, if fate be ever propitious; should I be blessed with the divine possession of your charms; you should then know—*what a devil you are*—you should then know the tenderest care. I'll guard you, caress you, fondle you—*I'll bury my spurs in you, you devil*. Oh, Fanny!—beloved one!—farewell—good night—a thousand blessings on you!—*and now go and be d—d to you!*" said he, bitterly, putting spurs to his horse and galloping home.

When the doctor was satisfied that M'Garry was fast asleep, he and Murphy left the room, and locked the door. They were encountered on the lobby by several curious people, who wanted to know "was the man dead?" The doctor shook his head very gravely, and said, "Not quite;" while Murphy, with a serious nod, said, "All over, I'm afraid, Mrs. Fay;" for he perceived among the persons on the lobby a servant of O'Grady's, who chanced to be in the town, and was all wonder and fright at the news of his master having committed murder. Murphy and the doctor proceeded to the dinner-room, where they found the drunken men wrangling about what verdict they should bring in, and a discursive dispute touching "murder," and "manslaughter," and "accidental death," and "the visitation of God," mingled with noisy toasts and flowing cups, until any sagacity the company ever possessed was sacrificed to the rosy god.

The lateness of the hour, and the state of the company, rendered riding home impossible to most of them; so Mrs. Fay was called upon to prepare beds. The inn did not afford a sufficiency to accommodate every gentleman with a single one, so a toss up was resorted to, to decide who should sleep double. The fortune of war cast the unfortunate James Reddy upon the doctor, who, though one of the few who were capable of self-protection, preferred remaining at the inn to riding home some miles. Now James Reddy, though very drunk indeed, had sense enough left to dislike the lot that fate had cast him. To sleep with such a slovenly man as the doctor shocked James, who was a bit of a dandy. The doctor seemed perfectly contented with the arrangement; and as he bade Murphy good night, there was a lurking devilment hung about his huge mouth. All the men staggered off, or were supported to their various beds, but one, he could not stir from the floor, where he lay hugging the leg of the table. To every effort to disturb him, he replied, with an imploring grunt, to "let him alone," and he hugged the leg of the table closer, exclaiming "I won't leave you, Mrs. Fay—my darling Mrs. Fay; rowl your arms round me, Mrs. Fay."

"Ah, get up and go to bed, Misther Doyle," said Tim. "Sure the misthress is not here at all."

"I know she's not," said Doyle. "Who says a word against her?"

"Sure you're talkin' to her yourself, sir."

"Pooh, pooh, man—you're dhrunk."

"Ah, come to bed, Misther Doyle!" said Tim, in an imploring tone: "Och sure, my heart's broke with you!"

"Don't say your heart's broke, my sweet landlady—my darling Mrs. Fay; the apple of my eye you are!"

"Nonsense! Misther Doyle."

"True as the sun, moon, and stars. Apple of my eye, did I say? I'd give you the apples of my eyes to make sauce for the cockles of your heart: Mrs. Fay, darling—don't be coy: ha! I have you fast!" and he gripped the table closer.

"Well, you *are* dhrunk, Misther Doyle!" said Tim.

"I hope my breath is not offensive from drink, Mrs. Fay," said Doyle, in an amatory whisper to the leg of the table.

"Ah, get out o' that, Misther Doyle," said Tim, accompanying the exclamation with a good shake, which somewhat roused the prostrate swain.

"Who's there?"

"I want you to come to bed, sir;—ah, don't be so foolish, Misther Doyle. Sure you don't think the Misthis would be rowlin' on the flure there wid you, as dhrunk as a pig—"

"Dare not to wound her fame!—Who says a word of Mrs. Fay?"

"Arrah, sure, you're talkin' there about her this half hour."

"False, villain!—Whisht, my darling," said he to the leg of the table: "I'll never betray you. Hug me tight, Mrs. Fay!"

"Bad luck to the care I'll take any more about you," says Tim. "Sleep an the flure, if you like." And Doyle was left to pass the night in the soft imaginary delights of Mrs. Fay's mahogany embraces.

How fared it with James Reddy?—Alas, poor James was doomed to a night of torment, the effects of which he remembered for many days after. In fact, had James been left to his choice, he would rather have slept with the house-dog than the doctor; but he dreaded the consequences of letting old Jack perceive his antipathy; and visions of future chastisement from the doctor's satirical tongue awed him into submission to the present punishment.—He sneaked into bed, therefore, and his deep potations ensured him immediate sleep, from which he woke, however, in the middle of the night in torture, from the deep scratches inflicted upon him by every kick of old Growling. At last, poor Reddy could stand it no longer and the earliest hour of dawn revealed him to the doctor, putting on his clothes, swearing like a trooper at one moment, and at the next apostrophising the genius of gentility. "What it is to have to do with a person that is not a gentleman!" he exclaimed, as he pulled on one leg of his trousers.

"What's the matter with you?" asked old Jack, from the bed.

"The matter, sir, is that I'm going."

"Is it at this hour! Tut, man, don't be a fool. Get into bed again."

"Never, sir, with *you* at least. I have seldom slept two in a bed, Doctor Growling, for my gentlemanly habits forbid it; but when circumstances have obliged me, it has been with gentlemen—*gentlemen,* doctor;"—and he laid a strong stress on the word—"Gentlemen, sir—who cut their toe nails. Sir, I am a serious sufferer by your coarse habits; you have scratched me, sir, nearly to death. I am one gore of blood"—

"Tut, man, 'twas not my nails scratched you; it was only my spurs I put on going to bed, to keep you at a distance from me; you were so disgustingly drunk, my *gentleman!*—look there;" and he poked his leg out of bed, and there, sure enough, Reddy saw a spur buckled: and, dumb-foundered at this evidence of the doctor's atrocity, he snatched up his clothes, and rushed from the room, as from the den of a bear.

Murphy twisted a beneficial result to M'Garry out of the night's riotous frolic at his expense; for, in the morning, taking advantage of the report of the inquest which he knew must have reached Neck-or-Nothing-Hall, he made a communication to O'Grady, so equivocally worded that the Squire fell into the trap.

The note ran as follows:—

"Sir,—You must he aware that your act of yesterday has raised a strong feeling in the country against you, and that so flagrant a violation of the laws cannot fail to be visited with terrible severity upon you: for though your position in rank places you far above the condition of the unfortunate man on whom you wreaked your vengeance, you know, sir, that in the eye of the law you are equal, and the shield of justice protects the peasant as well as the prince. Under these circumstances, sir, considering the *awful consequences* of your ungoverned rage (which, I doubt not, now, you deplore), I would suggest to you, by a timely offer of compromise, in the shape of a handsome sum of money—say two hundred pounds—to lull the storm which must otherwise burst on your devoted head, and save your name from dishonour. I anxiously await your answer, as proceedings must instantly commence, and the law take its course, unless Mrs. M'Garry can be pacified.

"I have the honour to be, Sir,

"Your most obedient Servant,

"MURTOUGH MURPHY."

To Gustavus Granby O'Grady, Esq.

Neck-or-Nothing Hall.

O'Grady was thoroughly frightened; and, strange as it may appear, did believe he could compromise for killing only a plebeian; and actually sent Murphy his note of hand for the sum demanded. Murtough posted off to M'Garry: he and his wife received him with shouts of indignation, and heaped reproaches on his head, for the trick he had played on the apothecary.

"Oh! Mister Murphy—never look me in the face again!" said Mrs. M'Garry, who was ugly enough to make the request quite unnecessary. "To send my husband home to me a beast!"

"Striped like a tiger!" said M'Garry.

"Blacking and pickled cabbage, Misther Murphy!" said the wife. "Oh, fie, sir!—I did not think you could be so low."

"Galvanism!" said M'Garry, furiously. "My professional honour —wounded!"

"Whisht, whisht, man!" said Murphy; "there's a finer plaister than any in your shop for the cure of wounded honour. Look at that!"—and he handed him the note for two hundred,—"There's galvanism for you!"

"What *is* this?" said M'Garry, in amazement.

"The result of last night's inquest," said Murphy. "You have got your damages without a trial; so pocket your money, and be thankful."

The two hundred pounds at once changed the aspect of affairs. M'Garry vowed eternal gratitude, with protestations that Murphy was the cleverest attorney alive, and ought to be chief justice. The wife was equally vociferous in her acknowledgments, until Murtough, who, when he entered the house, was near falling a sacrifice to the claws of the apothecary's wife, was obliged to rush from the premises, to shun the more terrible consequences of her embraces.

VI

WE HAVE SAT SO LONG at our dinner, that we have almost lost sight of poor Andy, to whom we must now return. When he ran to his mother's cabin to escape from the fangs of Dick Dawson, there was no one within; his mother being digging a few potatoes for supper from the little ridge behind her house, and Oonah Riley, her niece,—an orphan girl who lived with her,—being up to Squire Egan's to sell some eggs; for round the poorest cabins in Ireland you scarcely ever fail to see some ragged hens, whose eggs are never consumed by their proprietors, except, perhaps, on Easter Sunday, but sold to the neighbouring gentry at a trifling price.

Andy cared not who was out or who was in, provided he could only escape from Dick; so, without asking any questions, he crawled under the wretched bed in the dark corner, where his mother and Oonah slept, and where the latter, through the blessed influence of health and youth and an innocent heart, had brighter dreams than attend many a couch whose downy pillows and silken hangings would more than purchase the fee-simple of any cabin in Ireland. There Andy, in a state of utter exhaustion from his fears, his race, and his thrashing, soon fell asleep, and the terrors of Dick the Devil gave place to the blessing of the profoundest slumber.

Quite unconscious of the presence of her darling Andy was the widow Rooney, as she returned from the potato ridge into her cabin; depositing a *skeough* of the newly dug esculent at the door, and replacing the spade in its own corner of the cabin. At the same moment Oonah returned, after disposing of her eggs, and handed the threepence she had received for them to her aunt, who dropped them into the deep pocket of blue striped tick which hung at her side.

"Take the pail; Oonah, *ma chree*, and run to the well for some wather to wash the pratees, while I get the pot ready for bilin' them; it wants scowrin', for the pig was atin' his dinner out iv it, the craythur!"

Off went Oonah with her pail, which she soon filled from the clear spring; and placing the vessel on her head, walked back to the cabin with that beautifully erect form, free step, and graceful swaying of the figure, so peculiar to the women of Ireland and the East, from their habit of carrying weights upon the head. The potatoes were soon washed; and as they got their last dash of water in the *skeough,* whose open wicker-work let the moisture drain from them, up came Larry Hogan, who, being what is called "a civil-spoken man," addressed Mrs. Rooney in the following agreeable manner:— "Them's purty pratees, Mrs. Rooney; God save you, ma'am!"

"'Deed an' they are,—thank you kindly, Mr. Hogan; God save you and your's too! And how would the woman that owns you be?"

"Hearty, thank you."

"Will you step in?

"No—I'm obleeged to you—I must be aff home wid me; but I'll just get a coal for my pipe, for it wint out on me awhile agone with the fright."

"Well, I've heer'd quare things, Larry Hogan," said Oonah, laughing and showing her white teeth; "but I never heer'd so quare a thing as a pipe goin' out with the fright."

"Oh, how sharp you are!—takin' one up afore they're down."

"Not afore they're down, Larry, for you said it."

"Well, if I was down, you were down *on* me, so you are down too, you see. Ha, ha! And afther all now, ponah, a pipe is like a Christian in many ways:—sure it's made o' clay like a Christian, and has the spark o' life in it, and while the breath is in it the spark is alive; but when the breath is out of it, the spark dies, and then it grows cowld like a Christian; and isn't it a pleasant companion like a Christian?"

"Faix, some Christians isn't pleasant companions at all!" chimed in Mrs. Rooney, sententiously.

"Well, but they ought to be," said Larry; "and isn't a pipe sometimes cracked like a Christian, and isn't it sometimes choked like a Christian?"

"Oh, choke you and your pipe together, Larry! will you never have done?" said the widow.

"The most improvinist thing in the world is smokin'," said Larry, who had now relit his pipe, and squatted himself on a three-legged stool beside the widow's fire. "The most improvinist thing in the world"—(paugh!)— and a parenthetical whiff of tobacco smoke curled out of the corner of Larry's mouth—"is smokin': for the smoke shows you, as it were, the life a' man passin' away like a puff,—(paugh!)—just like that; and the tibakky turns to ashes like his poor perishable body: for, as the song says,—

> Tibakky is an Indian weed,
> Alive at morn, and dead at eve;
> It lives but an hour,
> Is cut down like a flower.
> Think o' this when you're smoking tiba-akky!"

And Larry sung the ditty as he crammed some of the weed into the bowl of his pipe with his little finger.

"Why, you're as good as a sarmint this evenin', Larry," said the widow, as she lifted the iron pot on the fire.

"There's worse sarmints nor that, I can tell you," rejoined Larry, who took up the old song again—

> "A pipe it larns us all this thing,—
> 'Tis fair without and foul within,
> Just like the sowl begrim'd with sin.
> Think o' this when you're smoking tiba-akky!"

Larry puffed away silently for a few minutes, and when Oonah had placed a few sods of turf round the pot in an upright position, that the flame might curl upward round them, and so hasten the boiling, she drew a stool near the fire, and asked Larry to explain about the fright.

"Why, I was coming up by the cross road there, when what should I see but a ghost—"

"A ghost!!!" exclaimed the widow and Oonah, with suppressed voices, and distended mouth and eyes.

"To all appearance," said Larry; "but it was only a thing was stuck in the hedge to freken whoever was passin' by; and as I kem up to it there was a groan, so I started, and looked at it for a minit, or thereaway; but I seen what it was, and threwn a stone at it, for fear I'd be mistaken; and I heer'd tittherin' inside the hedge, and then I knew 'twas only divilment of some one."

"And what was it?" asked Oonah.

"'Twas a horse's head, in throth, with an owld hat on the top of it, and two buck-briars stuck out at each side, and some rags hanging on them, and an owld breeches shakin' undher the head; 'twas just altogether like a long pale-faced man with high shouldhers and no body, and very long arms and short legs:—faith, it frightened me at first."

"And no wondher," said Oonah. "Dear, but I think I'd lose my life if I seen the like!"

"But sure," said the widow, "wouldn't you know that ghosts never appears by day?"

"Ay, but I hadn't time to think o' that, bein' taken short wid the fright,—more betoken, 'twas the place the murdher happened in long ago."

"Sure enough," said the widow. "God betune us and harm!" and she marked herself with the sign of the cross as she spoke:—"and a terrible murdher it was," added she.

"How was it?" inquired Oonah, drawing her seat closer to her aunt and Larry.

"'Twas a schoolmaster, dear, that was found dead on the road one mornin', with his head full of fractions," said the widow.

"All in jommethry,"[1] said Larry.

"And some said he fell off the horse," said the widow.

"And more say the horse fell on him," said Larry.

"And again, there was some said the horse kicked him in the head," said the widow.

"And there was talk of shoe-aside," said Larry.

"The horse's shoe was it?" asked Oonah.

"No, *alanna*," said Larry: "shoe-aside is Latin for cutting your throat."

"But he didn't cut his throat," said the widow.

"But sure it's all one whether he done it wid a razhir on his throat, or a hammer on his head; it's shoe-aside all the same."

"But there was no hammer found, was there?" said the widow.

"No," said Larry. "But some people thought he might have had the hammer afther he done it, to take off the disgrace of the shoe-aside."

"But wasn't there any life in him when he was found?"

"Not a taste. The crowner's jury sot on him, and he never said a word agin it, and if he was alive he would."

"And didn't they find anything at all?" asked Oonah.

"Nothing but the vardick," said Larry.

"And was that what killed him?" said Oonah.

"No, my dear; 'twas the crack in the head that killed him, however he kem by it; but the vardick o' the crowne was, that it was done, and that some one did it, and that they wor blackguards, whoever they wor, and persons onknown; and sure if they wor unknown then, they'd always stay so, for who'd know them afther doing the like?"

"Thrue for you, Larry," said the widow: "but what was that to the murdher over at the green hills beyant?"

"Oh! that was the terriblest murdher ever was in the place, or nigh it: that was the murdher in earnest!"

With that eagerness which always attends the relation of horrible stories, Larry and the old woman raked up every murder and robbery that had occurred within their recollection, while Oonah listened with mixed curiosity and fear. The boiling over of the pot at length recalled them to a sense of the business that ought to be attended to at the moment, and Larry was invited to take share of the potatoes. This he declined; declaring, as he had done some time previously, that he must "be off home," and to the door he went accordingly; but as the evening shades had closed into the darkness of night, he paused on opening it with a sensation he would not have liked to own. The fact was, that after the discussion of numerous nightly murders, he would rather have had daylight on the outside of the cabin; for the horrid stories that had been revived round the blazing hearth were not the best preparation for going a lonely road on a dark night. But go he should, and go he did; and it is not improbable that the widow, from sympathy, had a notion why Larry paused upon the threshold; for the moment he had crossed it, and that they had exchanged their "Good night, and God speed you," the door was rapidly closed and bolted. The widow returned to the fireside and was silent, while Oonah looked by the light of a candle into the boiling pot, to ascertain if the potatoes were yet done, and cast a fearful glance up the wide chimney as she withdrew from the inspection.

"I wish Larry did not tell us such horrid stories," said she, as she laid the rushlight on the table; "I'll be dhramin' all night o' them."

"'Deed an' that's thrue," said the widow; "I wish he hadn't."

"Sure you was as bad yourself," said Oonah.

"Throth, an' I b'lieve I was, child, and I'm sorry for it now; but let us ate our supper, and go to bed, in God's name."

"I'm afeard o' my life to go to bed!" said Oonah. "Wisha! but I'd give the world it was mornin'."

"Ate your supper, child, ate your supper," said her aunt, giving the example, which was followed by Oonah; and after the light meal, their prayers were said, and perchance with a little extra devotion, from their peculiar state of mind; then to bed they went. The rushlight being extinguished, the only light remaining was that shed from the red embers of the decaying fire, which cast so uncertain a glimmer within the cabin that its effect was almost worse than utter darkness to a timid person, for any object within its range assumed a form unlike its own, and presented some fantastic image to the eye; and as Oonah, contrary to her usual habit, could not fall asleep the moment she went to bed, she could not resist peering forth from under the bed-clothes through the uncertain gloom, in a painful state of watchfulness, which became gradually relaxed into an uneasy sleep.

The night was about half spent when Andy began to awake; and as he stretched his arms, and rolled his whole body round, he struck the bottom of the bed above him, in the action, and woke his mother. "Dear me," thought the widow, " I can't sleep at all to-night." Andy gave another turn soon after, which roused Oonah. She started, and shaking her aunt, asked her, in a low voice, if it was she who kicked her, though she scarcely hoped an answer in the affirmative, and yet dared not believe what her fears whispered.

"No, *a cushla,*" whispered the aunt.

"Did *you* feel anything?" asked Oonah, trembling violently.

"What do you mane, *alanna?*" said the aunt.

Andy gave another roll. "There it is again!" gasped Oonah: and in a whisper, scarcely above her breath, she added, "Aunt,—there's some one under, the bed!"

The aunt did not answer; but the two women drew closer together, and held each other in their arms, as if their proximity afforded protection. Thus they lay in breathless fear for some minutes, while Andy began to be influenced by a vision, in which the duel, and the chase, and the thrashing, were all enacted over again, and soon an odd word began to escape from the dreamer:—"Gi' me the pist'l, Dick—the pist'l!"

"There are two of them!" whispered Oonah. "God be merciful to us!—Do you hear him asking for the pistol?"

"Screech!" said her aunt.

"I can't," said Oonah.

Andy was quiet for some time, while the women scarcely breathed.

"Suppose we get up, and make for the door?" said the aunt.

"I wouldn't put my foot out of the bed for the world," said Oonah. "I'm afeard one o' them would catch me by the leg."

"Howld him! howld him!" grumbled Andy.

"I'll die with the fright, aunt! I feel I'm dyin'! Let us say our prayers, aunt, for we're goin' to be murdered!" The two women began to repeat with fervour their aves and paternosters, while at this immediate juncture Andy's dream having borne him to the dirty ditch where Dick Dawson had pommelled him, he began to vociferate, " Murder, murder!" so fiercely, that the women screamed together in an agony of terror, and "Murder! murder!" was shouted by the whole party; for once the widow and Oonah found their voices, they made good use of them. The noise awoke Andy, who had, be it remembered, a tolerably long sleep by this time; and he having quite forgotten where he had lain down, and finding himself confined by the bed above him, and smothering for want of air, with the fierce shouts of murder ringing in his ears, woke in as great a fright as the women in the bed, and became a party in the terror he himself had produced; every plunge he gave under the bed inflicted a poke or a kick on his mother and cousin, which was answered by the cry of "Murder!"

"Let me out! Let me out, Misther Dick!" roared Andy. "Where am I at all? Let me out!"

"Help, help! murdher!" roared the women.

"I'll never shoot any one again, Misther Dick!—let me up!"

Andy scrambled from under the bed, half awake, and whole frightened by the darkness and the noise, which was now increased by the barking of the cur-dog.

"High! at him, Coaly!" roared Mrs. Rooney; "howld him! howld him!"

Now as this address was often made to the cur respecting the pig, when Mrs. Rooney sometimes wanted a quiet moment in the day, and the pig didn't like quitting the premises, the dog ran to the corner of the cabin where the pig habitually lodged, and laid hold of his ear with the strongest testimonials of affection, which polite attention the pig acknowledged by a prolonged squealing, that drowned the voices of the women and Andy together; and now the cocks and hens that were roosting on the rafters of the cabin, were startled by the din, and the crowing and cackling, and the flapping of the frightened fowls as they flew about in the dark, added to the general uproar and confusion.

"A—h!" screamed Oonah, "take your hands off me!" as Andy, getting from under the bed, laid his hand upon it to assist him, and caught a grip of his cousin.

"Who are you at all?" cried Andy, making another claw, and catching hold of his mother's nose.

"Oonah, they're murdhering me!" shouted the widow.

The name of Oonah, and the voice of his mother, recalled his senses to Andy, who shouted, "Mother, mother! what's the matter?" A frightened hen flew in his face, and nearly knocked Andy down. "Bad cess to you," cried Andy, "what do you hit me for?"

"Who are you at all?" cried the widow.

"Don't you know me?" said Andy.

"No, I don't know you; by the vartue o' my oath, I don't; and I'll never swear again' you, jintlemen, if you lave the place, and spare our lives!"

Here the hens flew against the dresser, and smash went the plates and dishes.

"Oh, jintlemen, dear, don't rack and ruin me that way: don't desthroy a lone woman!"

"Mother, mother, what's this at all? Don't you know your own Andy?"

"Is it you that's there?" cried the widow, catching hold of him.

"To be sure it's me," said Andy.

"You won't let us be murdhered, will you?"

"Who'd murdher you?"

"Them people that's with you." Smash went another plate. "Do you hear that? they're rackin' my place, the villains!"

"Divil a one's wid me at all!" said Andy.

"I'll take my oath there was three or four under the bed," said Oonah.

"Not one but myself," said Andy.

"Are you sure?" said his mother.

"Cock sure!" said Andy; and a loud crowing gave evidence in favour of his assertion.

"The fowls is going mad," said the widow. "And the pig's distracted," said Oonah.

"No wonder; the dog's murdherin' him," said Andy.

"Get up and light the rushlight, Oonah," said the widow; "you'll get a spark out o' the turf cendhers."

"Some o' them will catch me, maybe!" said Oonah.

"Get up, I tell you," said the widow.

Oonah now arose, and groped her way to the fire place, where by dint of blowing upon the embers, and poking the rushlight among the turf ashes, a light was at length obtained. She then returned to the bed, and threw her petticoat over her shoulders.

"What's this at all?" said the widow rising, and wrapping a blanket round her.

"Bad cess to the know I know!" said Andy.

"Look under the bed, Oonah," said the aunt.

Oonah obeyed, and screamed, and ran behind Andy. "There's another here yet!" said she.

Andy seized the poker, and standing on the defensive, desired the villain to come out: the demand was not complied with.

"There's nobody there," said Andy.

"I'll take my oath there is," said Oonah; "a dirty blackguard without any clothes on him."

"Come out, you robber!" said Andy, making a lunge under the truckle.

A grunt ensued, and out rushed the pig, who had escaped from the dog, the dog having discovered a greater attraction in some fat that was knocked from the dresser, which the widow intended for the dipping of rushes in; but the dog being enlightened to his own interest without rushlights, and preferring mutton fat to pig's ear, had suffered the grunter to go at large, while he was captivated by the fat. The clink of a three-legged stool the widow seized to the rescue, was a stronger argument against the dog than he was prepared to answer, and a remnant of fat was preserved from the rapacious Coaly.

"Where's the rest o' the robbers?" said Oonah: "there's three o' them, I know."

"You're dhramin'," said Andy. "Divil a robber is here but myself."

"And what brought you here?" said his mother.

"I was afeard they'd murdher me," said Andy.

"Murdher!" exclaimed the widow and Oonah together, still startled by the very sound of the word. "Who do you mane?"

"Misther Dick," said Andy.

"Aunt, I tell you," said Oonah, "this is some more of Andy's blundhers. Sure Misther Dawson wouldn't be goin' to murdher any one; let us look round the cabin, and find out who's in it, for I won't be aisy ontil I look into every corner, to see there's no robbers in the place; for I tell you again, there was three o' them undher the bed."

The search was made, and the widow and Oonah at length satisfied that there were no midnight assassins there with long knives to cut their throats; and then they began to thank God that their lives were safe.

"But, oh! look at my chaynee!" said the widow, clapping her hands, and casting a look of despair at the shattered delf that lay around her; "look at my chaynee!"

"And what *was* it brought you here?" said Oonah, facing round on Andy with a dangerous look, rather, in her bright eye. "Will you tell us that?—what was it?"

"I came to save my life, I tell you," said Andy.

"To put us in dhread of ours, you mane," said Oonah. Just look at the *omadhawn* there," said she to her aunt, "standin' with his mouth open, just as if nothin' happened, and he after frightenin' the lives of us."

"Thrue for you, *alanna*," said her aunt.

"And would no place sarve you, indeed, but undher our bed, you vagabone?" said his mother, roused to a sense of his delinquency; "to come in like a morodin' villain, as you are, and hide under the bed, and frighten the lives out of us, and rack and ruin my place!"

"'Twas Misther Dick, I tell you," said Andy.

"Bad scran to you, you unlooky hangin' bone thief!" cried the widow, seizing him by the hair, and giving him a hearty cuff on the ear, which would have knocked him down, only that Oonah kept him up by an equally well applied box on the other.

"Would you murdher me?" shouted Andy, as he saw his mother lay hold of the broom.

"Ar'n't you after frightenin' the lives out of us, you dirty, good-for-nothing, mischief-making!—"

On poured the torrent of abuse, rendered more impressive by a whack at every word. Andy roared, and the more he roared the more did Oonah and his mother thrash him. So great, indeed, was their zeal in the cause, that the widow's blanket and Oonah's petticoat fell off in the *mêlée* which compels us to put our hands to our eyes, and close the chapter.

1.   Anything very badly broken is said by the Irish peasantry to be in jommethry.

VII

"Love rules the camp, the court, the grove,
And men on earth and saints above;
For Love is Heaven, and Heaven is Love.

So sang Scott. Quite agreeing with the antithesis of the last line, perhaps in the second, where he talks of men and saints, another view of the subject, or turn of the phrase, might have introduced sinners quite as successfully. This is said without the smallest intention of using the word *sinners* in a questionable manner. Love, in its purest shape, may lead to sinning on the part of persons least interested in the question; for is it not a sin, when the folly, or caprice, or selfishness of a third party or fourth, makes a trio or quartette of that which nature undoubtedly intended for a duet, and so spoils it?

Fathers, mothers, sisters, brothers, uncles, aunts,—ay, and even cousins,—sometimes put in their oar to disturb that stream which is troubled enough without their interference, and, as the bard of Avon says,

"never did run smooth."

And so it was in the case of Fanny Dawson and Edward O'Connor. A piece of innocent fun on the part of her brother, and blind pertinacity—indeed, downright absurdity—on her father's side, interrupted the intercourse of affection, which had subsisted silently for many a long day between the lovers, but was acknowledged at last, with delight to the two whom it most concerned, and satisfaction to all who knew or held them dear. Yet the harmony of this sweet concordance of spirits was marred by youthful frolic and doting absurdity. This welding together of hearts in the purest fire of nature's own contriving, was broken at a blow by a weak old man. Is it too much to call this a *sin?* Less mischievous things are branded with the name in the common-place parlance of the world. The cold and phlegmatic may not understand this; but they who *can* love know how bitterly every after-hour of life may be poisoned with the taint which hapless love has infused into the current of future years, and can believe how many a heart, equal to the highest enterprise, has been palsied by the touch of despair. Sweet and holy is the duty of child to parent; but sacred also is the obligation of those who govern in so hallowed a position. Their rule should be guided by justice; they should pray for judgment in their mastery.

Fanny Dawson's father was an odd sort of person. His ancestors were settlers in Ireland of the time of William the Third, and having won their lands by the sword, it is quite natural the love of arms should have been hereditary in the family. Mr. Dawson, therefore, had served many years as a soldier, and was a bit of a martinet, not only in military but all other affairs. His mind was of so tenacious a character, that an impression once received there, became indelible; and if the Major once made up his mind, or indulged the belief, that such and such things were so and so, the waters of truth could never wash out the mistake; stubbornness had written them there with her own indelible marking ink.

Now, one of the old gentleman's weak points was a museum of the most heterogeneous nature, consisting of odds and ends from all parts of the world, and appertaining to all subjects. Nothing was too high or too low:—a bronze helmet from the plain of Marathon, which, to the classic eye of an artist, conveyed the idea of a Minerva's head beneath it, would not have been more prized by the Major than a cavalry cap with some bullet mark of which *he could tell an anecdote.* A certain skin of a tiger he prized much, because the animal had dined on his dearest friend in one of the jungles of Bengal; also a pistol, which he vouched for as being the one with which Hatfield fired at George the Third; the hammer with which Crawley (of Hessianboot memory) murdered his landlady; the string which was on Viotti's violin, when he played before Queen Charlotte; the horn which was *supposed* to be in the lantern of Guy Fawkes; a small piece of the coat worn by the Prince of Orange on his landing in England, and other such relics. But far above these the Major prized the skeleton of a horse's head, which occupied the principal place in his museum. This he declared to be part of the identical horse which bore Duke Shonberg when he crossed the Boyne in the celebrated battle so called; and with whimsical ingenuity he had contrived to string some wires upon the bony fabric, which yielded a sort of hurdy-gurdy vibration to the strings when touched; and the Major's most favourite feat was to play the tune of the Boyne Water on the head of Duke Shonberg's horse. In short, his collection was composed of trifles from north, south, east, and west. Some leaf from the prodigal verdure of India, or gorgeous shell from the Pacific, or paw of bear, or tooth of walrus; but beyond all teeth, one pre-eminently was valued,—it was one of his own, which he had lost the use of by a wound in the jaw, received in action; and no one ever entered his house and escaped without hearing all about it, from the first shot fired in the affair by the skirmishers, to the last charge of the victorious cavalry. The tooth was always produced along with the story, together with the declaration, that every dentist who ever saw it protested it was the largest human tooth ever seen. Now some little sparring was not unfrequent between old Mr. Dawson and Edward, on the subject of their respective museums; the old gentleman "poo-pooing" Edward's "rotten, rusty rubbish," as he called it, and Edward defending, as gently as he could, his patriotic partiality for national antiquities. This little war never led to any evil results; for Edward not only loved Fanny too well, but respected age too much, to lean hard on the old gentleman's weakness, or seek to reduce his fancied superiority as a collector; but the tooth, the ill-omened tooth, at last gnawed asunder the bond of friendship and affection which had subsisted between two families for so many years.

The Major had paraded his tooth so often, that Dick Dawson began to tire of it, and for the purpose of making it a source of amusement to himself, he stole his father's keys one day, and opening the cabinet in which his tooth was enshrined, he abstracted the grinder which Nature had bestowed on the Major, and substituted in its stead a horse's tooth, of no contemptible dimensions. A party some days after dined with the old gentleman, and after dinner the story of the skirmish turned up, as a matter of course, and the enormous size of the tooth wound up the tedious tale.

"Hadn't you better show it to them, sir?" said Dick from the foot of the table.

"Indeed, then, I will," said the Major; "for it really is a curiosity."

"Let me go for it, sir," said Dick, well knowing he would be refused.

"No, no," answered his father, rising; "I never let any one go to my pet cabinet but myself;" and so saying he left the room, and proceeded to his museum. It has been already said that the Major's mind was of that character, which once being satisfied of anything, could never be convinced to the contrary; and having for years been in the habit of drawing his own tooth out of his own cabinet, the increased size never struck him of the one which he now extracted from it; so he returned to the dining-room, and presented with great exultation to the company the tooth Dick had substituted. It may be imagined how the people stared, when an old gentleman, and moreover a Major, declared upon his honour, that a great horse's tooth was his own; but having done so, politeness forbade they should contradict him, more particularly at the head of his own table, so they smothered their smiles, as well as they could, and declared it was the most wonderful tooth they ever beheld; and instead of attempting to question the fact, they launched forth in expressions of admiration and surprise, and the fable, instead of being questioned, was received with welcome, and made food for mirth. The difficulty was not to laugh; and in the midst of twisted mouths, affected sneezing, and applications of pocket handkerchiefs to rebellious cachinations, Dick, the maker of the joke, sat unmoved, sipping his claret with a serenity which might have roused the envy of a red Indian.

"I think that's something like a tooth!" said Dick.

"Prodigious—wonderful—tremendous!" ran round the board.

"Give it to me again," said one.

"Let me look at it once more," said another.

"Colossal!" exclaimed a third.

"Gigantic!" shouted all, as the tooth made the circuit of the table.

The Major was delighted, and never remembered his tooth to have created such a sensation; and when at last it was returned to him, he turned it about in his own hand, and cast many fond glances at the monstrosity, before it was finally deposited in his waistcoat pocket. This was the most ridiculous part of the exhibition: to see a gentleman, with the use of his eyes, looking affectionately at a thumping horse's tooth; and believing it to be his own. Yet this was the key to the Major's whole character. A received opinion was with him unchangeable; no alteration of circumstances could shake it: *it was his tooth*. A belief or a doubt was equally sacred with him; and though his senses in the present case should have shown him it was a horse's tooth,—no, it was a piece of himself his own dear tooth.

After this party, the success which crowned his anecdote and its attendant relic, made him fonder of showing it off; and many a day did Dick the Devil enjoy the astonishment of visitors as his father exhibited the enormous tooth as his own. Fonder and fonder grew the Major of his tooth and his story, until the unlucky day Edward O'Connor happened to be in the museum with a party of ladies, to whom the old gentleman was showing off his treasures with great effect, and some pains; for the Major, like most old soldiers, was very attentive to the fair sex. At last the pet cabinet was opened, and out came the tooth. One universal exclamation of surprise arose on its appearance: "What a wonderful man the Major was to have such a tooth!" Just then, by an unlucky chance, Edward, who had not seen the Major produce the wonder from his cabinet, perceived the relic in the hand of one of the ladies at the extremity of the group, and fancying it had dropped from the horse's head, he said—"I suppose that is one of the teeth out of old Shonberg's skull."

The Major thought this an impertinent allusion to his political bias, and said, very sharply, "What do you mean by old Shonberg?"

"The horse's head, sir," replied Edward, pointing to the musical relic.

"It was of *my* tooth you spoke, sir, when you said old Shonberg," returned the Major, still more offended at what he considered Edward's evasion.

"I assure you," said Edward, with the strongest evidence of a desire to be reconciled in his voice and manner,—"I assure, you, sir, it was of *this* tooth I spoke;" and he held up the one the Major had produced as his own.

"I know it was, sir," said the Major, "and therefore I didn't relish your allusions to my tooth."

"*Your* tooth, sir?" exclaimed Edward, in surprise.

"Yes, sir,—mine!"

"My dear sir," said Edward, "there is some mistake here; this is a horse's tooth."

"Give it to me, sir!" said the Major, snatching it from Edward. "You may think this very witty, Mr O'Connor, but *I* don't; if my tooth is of superhuman size, I'm not to be called a horse for it, sir!—nor Shonberg, sir!—horse—a-hem!—better than ass, however!"

While this brief but angry outbreak took place, the bystanders, of course, felt excessively uncomfortable; and poor Edward knew not what to do. The Major he knew to be of too violent a temper to attempt explanation for the present; so, bowing to the ladies, he left the room, with that flushed look of silent vexation to which courteous youth is sometimes obliged to submit at the hands of intemperate age.

Neither Fanny nor Dick was at home when this occurred, so Edward quitted the house, and was forbidden to enter it afterwards. The Major suddenly entertained a violent dislike to Edward O'Connor, and hated even to hear his name mentioned. It was in vain that explanation was attempted, his self-love had received a violent shock, of which Edward had been the innocent means. In vain did Dick endeavour to make himself the peace-offering to his father's wounded consequence; in vain was it manifest that Fanny was grieved: the old Major persisted in declaring that Edward O'Connor was a self-sufficient jackanapes, and forbade most peremptorily that further intercourse should take place between him and his daughter; and she had too high a sense of duty, and he of honour, to seek to violate the command. But though they never met, they loved not the less fondly and truly; and Dick, grieved that a frolic of his should have interrupted the happiness of a sister he loved and a friend he valued, kept up a sort of communion between them by talking to Edward about Fanny, and to Fanny about Edward, whose last song was sure, through the good offices of the brother, to find its way into the sister's album, already stored with many a tribute from her lover's muse.

Fanny was a sweet creature—one of those choice and piquant bits of Nature's creation which she sometimes vouchsafes to treat the world with, just to show what she *can* do. Her person I shall not attempt to describe; for however one may endeavour to make words play the part of colour, lineament, voice, and expression—and however successfully,—still a verbal description can never convey a true notion of personal charms; and personal charms Fanny had, decidedly; not that she was strictly beautiful, but, at times, nevertheless, eclipsing beauty far more regular, and throwing symmetry into the shade, by some charm which even they whom it fascinated could not define.

Her mind was as clear and pure as a mountain stream; and if at times it chafed and was troubled from the course it which it ran, the temporary turbulence only made its limpid depths and quietness more beautiful. Her heart was the very temple of generosity, the throne of honour, and the seat of tenderness. The gentlest sympathies dwelt in her soul, and answered to the slightest call of another's grief; while mirth was dancing in her eye, a word that implied the sorrow of another would bring a tear there. She was the sweetest creature in the world!

The old Major, used to roving habits from his profession, would often go on a ramble somewhere for weeks together, at which times Fanny went to Merryvale to her sister, Mistress Egan, who was also a fine-hearted creature, but less soft and sentimental than Fanny. She was of the dashing school rather, and before she became the mother of so large a family, thought very little of riding over a gate or a fence. Indeed it was her high mettle that won her the squire's heart. The story is not long, and it may as well be told here—though a little out of place, perhaps; but it's an Irish story, and may therefore be gently irregular.

The squire had admired Letitia Dawson as most of the young men of her acquaintance did—appreciated her round waist and well-turned ankle, her spirited eyes and cheerful laugh, and danced with her at every ball as much as any other fine girl in the country; but never seriously thought of her as a wife, until one day a party visited the parish church, whose old tower was often ascended for the fine view it commanded. At this time the tower was under repair, and the masons were drawing up materials in a basket, which, worked by rope and pulley, swung on a beam protruding from the top of the tower. The basket had just been lowered for a fresh load of stones, when Letitia exclaimed, "Wouldn't it be fine fun to get into the basket and be hauled up to the top of the tower?—how astonished the workmen would be to see a lady get out of it!"

"I would be more astonished to see a lady get into it," said a gentleman present.

"Then here goes to astonish you," said Letitia, laying hold of the rope and jumping into the basket. In vain did her friends and the workmen below endeavour to dissuade her; up she would, go, and up she did go; and it was during her ascent that Egan and a friend were riding towards the church. Their attention was attracted by so strange a sight; and, spurring onward, Egan exclaimed, "By the powers, 'tis Letty Dawson!—Well done, Letty!—you're the right girl for my money!—by Jove, if ever I marry, Letty's the woman!" And sure enough she *was* the woman, in another month.

Now, Fanny would not have done the basket feat, but she had plenty of fun in her, notwithstanding; her spirits were light; and though, for some time, she felt deeply the separation from Edward, she rallied after a while, felt that unavailing sorrow but impaired the health of the mind, and, supported by her good sense, she waited in hopefulness for the time that Edward might claim and win her.

At Merryvale now, all was expectation about the anticipated election. The ladies were making up bows of ribbon, for their partizans, and Fanny had been so employed all the morning atone in the drawing-room; her pretty fingers pinching, and pressing, and stitching the silken favours, while now and then her hand wandered to a wicker basket which lay beside her, to draw forth a scissors or a needlecase. As she worked, a shade of thought crossed her sweet face, like a passing cloud across the sun; the pretty fingers stopped—the work was laid down—and a small album gently drawn from the neighbouring basket. She opened the book and read; they were lines of Edward O'Connor's, which she drank into her heart; they were the last he had written, which her brother had heard him sing and had brought her.

THE SNOW

I

An old man sadly said,
  "Where's the snow
That fell the year that's fled?—
  Where's the snow?"
As fruitless were the task
Of many a joy to ask,
  As the snow!

II

The hope of airy birth,
  Like the snow,
Is stain'd on reaching earth,
  Like the snow:
While 'tis sparkling in the ray
'Tis melting fast away,
  Like the snow.

III

A cold deceitful thing
  Is the snow,
Though it come on dove-like wing,—
  The false snow!
'Tis but rain disguis'd appears;
And our hopes are frozen tears,
  Like the snow.

A tear *did* course down Fanny's cheek as she, read the last couplet; and, closing the book and replacing it, in the little basket, she sighed, and said, "Poor, fellow!—I wish he were not so sad!"

VIII

LOVE IS OF AS MANY patterns, cuts, shapes, and colours, as people's garments; and the loves of Edward O'Connor and Fanny Dawson had very little resemblance to the tender passion which agitated the breast of the widow Flanagan, and made Tom Durfy her slave. Yet the widow and Tom demand the offices of the chronicler as well as the more elevated pair, and this our veracious history could never get on if we exhausted all our energies upon the more engaging personages, to the neglect of the rest; your plated handles, scrolls, and mountings, are all very well on your carriage, but it could not move without its plain iron bolts.

Now the reader must know something of the fair Mistress Flanagan, who was left in very comfortable circumstances by a niggardly husband, who did her the favour to die suddenly one day, to the no small satisfaction of the pleasure-loving widow, who married him in an odd sort of a hurry, and got rid of him as quickly. Mr. Flanagan was engaged in supplying the export provision trade, which, every one knows, is considerable in Ireland; and his dealings in beef and butter were extensive. This brought him into contact with the farmers for many miles round, whom he met, not only every market day at every market town in the county, but at their own houses, where a knife and fork were always at the service of the rich buyer. One of these was a certain Mat Riley, who, on small means, managed to live, and rear a son and three bouncing, good-looking girls, who helped to make butter, feed calves, and superintend the education of pigs; and on these active and comely lasses Mr. Flanagan often cast an eye of admiration, with a view to making one of them his wife; for though he might have had his pick and choice of many fine girls in the town he dealt in, he thought the simple, thrifty, and industrious habits of a plain farmer's daughter more likely to conduce to his happiness and *profit*,—for in that, principally, lay the aforesaid happiness of Mr. Flanagan. Now this intention of honouring one of the three Miss Rileys with promotion, he never hinted at in the remotest degree, and even in his own, mind the thought was mixed up with fat cattle and prices current; and it was not until a leisure moment, one day, when he was paying Mat Riley for some of his farming produce, that he broached the subject, thus:—

"Mat."

"Sir."

"I'm thinkin' o' marrying."

"Well, she'll have a snug house, whoever she is, Misther Flanagan."

"Them's fine girls o' your's."

Poor Mat opened his eyes with delight at the prospect of such a match for one of his daughters, and said they were "comely lumps o' girls, sure enough; but what was betther, they wor good."

"That's what I'm thinking," says Flanagan.—"There's two ten-poun' notes, and a five, and one is six; and one is seven; and three tenpinnies is two and sixpence; that's twenty-seven poun' two and sixpence; eightpence ha'penny is the lot; but I haven't copper in my company, Mat."

"Oh, no matther, Misther Flanagan. And is it one o' my colleens you've been throwin' the eye at, sir?"

"Yes, Mat, it is. You're askin' too much for them firkins."

"Oh, Misther Flanagan, consider it's prime butther. I'll back my girls for making up a bit o' butther agen any girls in Ireland; and my cows is good, and the pasture prime."

"'Tis a farthin' a pound too high, Mat; and the market not lively."

"The butther is good, Misther Flanagan; and not decenther girls in Ireland than the same girls, though I am their father."

"I'm thinkin' I'll marry one o' them, Mat."

"Sure an' it's proud I'll be, sir;—and which o' them is it, maybe?"

"Faith I don't know myself, Mat. Which do you think, yourself?"

"Troth, myself doesn't know,—they're all good. Nance is nice, and Biddy's biddable, and Kitty's cute."

"You're a snug man, Mat; you ought to be able to give a husband a thrifle with them."

"Nothing worth *your* while, anyhow, Misther Flanagan. But sure one o' my girls without a rag to her back, or a tack to her feet, would be betther help to an honest industherin' man, than one o' your showy lantherumswash divils out of a town, that would spend more than she'd bring with her."

"That's thrue, Mat. I'll marry one o' your girls, I think."

"You'll have my blessin', sir; and proud I'll be—and proud the girl ought to be—*that* I'll say. And suppose now you'd come over on Sunday, and take share of a plain man's dinner, and take your pick o' the girls;—there's a fine bull goose that Nance towld me she'd have ready afther last mass; for Father Ulick said he'd come and dine with us."

"I can't, Mat; I must be in the canal boat on Sunday; but I'll go and breakfast with you to on my way to Billy Mooney's, who has a fine lot of pigs to sell—remarkable fine pigs."

"Well, we'll expect you to breakfast, sir."

"Mat; there must be no nonsense about the wedding."

"As you plase, sir."

"Just marry her off, and take her home. Short reckonings make long friends."

"Thrue for you, sir."

"Nothing to give with the girl, you say?"

"My blessin' only, sir."

"Well, you must throw in that butther, Mat, and take the farthin' off."

"It's yours, sir," said Mat, delighted, loading Flanagan with "good byes" and "God save yous," until they should meet next morning at breakfast.

Mat rode home in great glee at the prospect of providing so well for one of his girls, and told them a man would be there the next morning to make choice of one of them for his wife. The girls, very naturally, inquired who the man was; to which Mat, in the plenitude of patriarchal power, replied, "that was nothing to them;" and his daughters had sufficient experience of his temper to know there was no use in asking more questions after such an answer. He only added, she would be "well off that should get him." Now, their father being such a bug-a-boo, it is no wonder the girls were willing to take the chance of a good-humoured husband instead of an iron-handed father; so they set to work to make themselves as smart as possible for the approaching trial of their charms, and a battle royal ensued between the sisters as to the right and title to certain pieces of dress which were hitherto considered a sort of common property amongst them, and which the occasion of a fair, or a pattern,[1] or market-day, was enough to establish the possession of, by whichever of the girls went to the public place; but now, when a husband was to be won, privilege of all sorts was pleaded, in which discussion there was more noise than sound reason, and so many violent measures to secure the envied *morceaux,* that some destruction of finery took place, where there was none to spare; and, at last, seniority was agreed upon to decide the question of possession; so that, when Nance had the first plunder of the chest which held all their clothes in common, and Biddy made the second grab, poor Kitty had little left but her ordinary rags to appear in. But as in the famous judgment on Ida's mount, it is hinted that Venus carried the day by her scarcity of drapery, so did Kitty conquer by want of clothes; not that Love sat in judgment; it was Plutus turned the scale. But, to leave metaphor and classic illustration, and go back to Mat Riley's cabin; the girls were washing, and starching, and ironing all night, and the morning saw them arrayed for conquest; Flanagan came, and breakfasted, and saw the three girls. A flashy silk handkerchief which Nancy wore, put her *hors de combat* very soon; she was set down at once, in his mind, as extravagant. Biddy might have had a chance if she had made anything like a fair division with her younger sister; but Kitty had been so plundered that her shabbiness won an easy victory over the niggard's heart; he saw in her "the making of a thrifty wife;" besides which, she was possibly the best looking, and certainly the youngest of the three; and there is no knowing how far old Flanagan might have been influenced by these considerations.

He spoke very little to any of girls; but when he was leaving the house he said to the father, as he was shaking hands with him, "Mat, I'll do it:" and pointing at Kitty, he added, "That's the one I'll have."

Great was the rage of the elder sisters, for Flanagan was notoriously
a wealthy man, and when he quitted the house, Kitty set up such a
shout of laughter, that her father and sisters told her several times "not
to make a fool of herself." Still she laughed, and through out the day
sometimes broke out into sudden roars; and while her sides shook
with merriment, she would throw herself into a chair, or lean against
the wall, to rest herself after the fatigue of her uproarious mirth. Now
Kitty, while she laughed at the discomfiture of her greedy sisters, also
laughed at the mistake into which Mr. Flanagan had fallen; for, as
her father said of her, she was "cute," and she more than suspected
the cause of Flanagan's choice, and enjoyed the anticipation of his
disappointment, for she was fonder of dress than either Nancy or
Biddy, and revelled in the notion of astonishing "the old niggard," as
she called him; and this she did "many a time and oft." In vain did
Flanagan try to keep her extravagance within bounds. She would
either wheedle, or reason, or bully, or shame him into doing what
she said "was right and proper for a snug man like him." His house
was soon well furnished: she made him get her a jaunting car. She
sometimes *would* go to parties, and no one was better dressed than
the woman he chose for her rags. He got enraged now and then; but
Kitty pacified him by soft words or daring inventions of her fertile
fancy. Once, when he caught her in the fact of wearing a costly
crimson silk gown, and stormed,—she soothed him by telling him
it was her old black one she had dyed; and this bouncer, to the great
amusement of her female friends, he loved to repeat, as a proof of
what a careful contriving creature he had in Kitty. She was naturally
quick-witted. She managed him admirably, deceived him into being
more comfortable than ever he had been before, and had the laudable
ambition of endeavouring to improve both his and her own condition
in every way. She set about educating herself, too, as far as her
notions of education went; and in a few years after her marriage, by
judiciously using the means which her husband's wealth afforded her
of advancing her position in society, no one could have recognised in
the lively and well-dressed Mrs. Flanagan, the gawky daughter of a
middling farmer. She was very good-natured, too, towards her sisters,
whose condition she took care to improve with her own; and a very

fair match for the eldest was made through her means. The younger one was often staying in her house, dividing her time nearly between the town and her father's farm, and no party which Mrs. Flanagan gave or appeared at, went off without giving Biddy a chance to "settle herself in the world." This was not done without a battle now and then with old Flanagan, whose stinginess would exhibit itself upon occasion; but at last all let and hindrance to the merry lady ceased, by the sudden death of her old husband, who left her the entire of his property, so that, for the first time, his will was her pleasure.

After the funeral of the old man, the "disconsolate widow" was withdrawn from her own house by her brother and sister to the farm, which grew to be a much more comfortable place than when Kitty left it, for to have remained in her own house after the loss of "her good man," would have been too hard on "the lone woman." So said her sister and her brother, though, to judge from the widow's eyes, she was not very heart-broken: she cried as much, no doubt, as young widows generally do after old husbands,—and could Kitty be expected to do more?

She had not been many days in her widowhood, when Biddy asked her to drive her into the town, where Biddy had to do a little shopping,—that great business of ladies' lives.

"Oh, Biddy, dear, I must not go out so soon."

"'Twill do you good, Kitty."

"I mustn't be seen, you know—'twouldn't be right, and poor dear Flanagan not buried a week!"

"Sure, who'll see you? We'll go in the covered car, and draw the curtains close, and who'll be the wiser?"

"If I thought no one would see me," said the widow.

"Ah, who'll see you?" exclaimed Biddy. "Come along; the drive will do you good."

The widow agreed; but when Biddy asked for a horse to put to the car, her brother refused, for the only horse not at work he was going to yoke in a cart that moment, to send a lamb to the town. Biddy vowed she would have a horse, and her brother swore the lamb should be served first, till Biddy made a compromise, and agreed to take the lamb under the seat of the car, and thus accommodate all parties.

Matters being thus accommodated, off the ladies set, the lamb tied neck and heels, and crammed under the seat, and the curtains of the car ready to be drawn at a moment's notice, in case they should meet any one on the road; for "why should not the poor widow enjoy the fresh air as they drove along?" About half way to the town, however, the widow suddenly exclaimed,

"Biddy, draw the curtains!"

"What's the matter?" says Biddy.

"I see him coming after us round the turn o' the road!" and the widow looked so horrified, and plucked at the curtains so furiously, that Biddy, who was superstitious, thought nothing but old Flanagan's ghost could have produced such an effect; and began to scream and utter holy ejaculations, until the sight of Tom Durfy riding after them showed her the cause of her sister's alarm.

If that divil, Tom Durfy, sees me, he'll tell it all over the country, he's such a quiz; shove yourself well before the door there, Biddy, that he can't peep into the car. Oh, why did I come out this day!—I wish your tongue was cut out, Biddy, that asked me!"

In the meantime Tom Durfy closed on them fast, and began telegraphing Biddy, who, according to the widow's desire, had shoved herself well before the door.

"Pull up, Tim, pull up," said the widow, from the inside of the car, to the driver, whom she thumped in the back at the same time, to impress upon him her meaning,—"turn about, and pretend to drive back!—We'll let that fellow ride on," said she quietly to Biddy.

Just as this manoeuvre was executed, up came Tom Durfy.

"How are you, Miss Riley?" said he, as he drew rein.

"Pretty well, thank you," said Biddy, putting her head and shoulders through the window, while the widow shrunk back into the corner of the car.

"How very sudden poor Mr. Flanagan's death was! I was quite surprised."

"Yes, indeed," says Biddy, "I was just taking a little drive; good bye."

"I was very much shocked to hear of it," said Tom.

"'Twas dreadful," said Biddy.

"How is poor Mrs. Flanagan?" said Tom.

"As well as can be expected, poor thing!—good bye!" said Biddy, manifestly anxious to cut short the conference.

This anxiety was so obvious to Tom, who, for the sake of fun, loved cross-purposes dearly, that he determined to push his conversation further, just because he saw it was unwelcome.

"To be sure," continued he, "at his time of life—"

"Very true," said Biddy. "Good morning!"

"And the season has been very unhealthy."

"Doctor Growling told me so yesterday," said Biddy;—"I wonder you're not afraid of stopping in this east wind: colds are very prevalent.—Good bye!"

Just now, the Genius of farce, who presides so particularly over all Irish affairs, put it into the lamb's head to bleat. The sound at first did not strike Tom Durfy as singular, they being near a high hedge, within which it was likely enough a lamb might bleat; but Biddy, shocked at the thought of being discovered in the fact of making her jaunting car a market car, reddened up to the eyes, while the widow squeezed herself closer into the corner.

Tom seeing the increasing embarrassment of Biddy, and her desire to be off, still *would* talk to her, for the love of mischief.

"I beg your pardon," he continued, "just one moment more,—I wanted to ask was it not apoplexy, for I heard an odd report about the death."

"Oh, yes," says Biddy,—"apoplexy—good bye."

"Did he speak at all?" asked Tom.

"*Baa!*" says the lamb.

Tom cocked his ears, Biddy grew redder, and the widow crammed her handkerchief into her mouth to endeavour to smother her laughter.

"I hope poor Mrs. Flanagan bears it well," says Tom.

"Poor thing!" says Biddy, "she's inconsolable."

"*Baa-a!*" says the lamb.

Biddy spoke louder and faster, the widow kicked with laughing, and Tom then suspected whence the sound proceeded.

"She does nothing but cry all day!" says Biddy.

"*Baa-a-a!*" says the lamb.

The widow could stand it no longer, and a peal of laughter followed the lamb's bleat.

"What is all this?" said Tom, laying hold of the curtains with relentless hand, and spite of Biddy's screams, rudely unveiling the sanctuary of sorrowing widowhood. Oh! what a sight for the rising—I beg their pardon—the sinking generation of old gentlemen who take young wives, did Tom behold!—There was the widow, lying back in the corner,—she who was represented as inconsolable and crying all day, shaking with laughter, and tears, not of sorrow, but irrepressible mirth rolling down a cheek rosy enough for a bride.

Biddy, of course, joined the shout. Tom roared in an agony of delight. The very driver's risibility rebelled against the habits of respect, and strengthened the chorus, while the lamb, as if conscious of the author ship of the joke, put in a longer and louder *baa-a-a-a!!!*

Tom, with all his devilment, had good taste enough to feel it was not a scene to linger on; so merely giving a merry nod to each of the ladies, he turned about his horse as fast as he could, and rode away in roars of laughter.

When, in due course of time, the widow again appeared in company, she and Tom Durfy could never meet without smiling at each other. What a pleasant influence lies in mutual smiles;—we love the lips which welcome us without words! Such sympathetic influence it was that led the widow and Tom to get better and better acquainted, and like each other more and, more, until she thought him the pleasantest fellow in the county, and he thought her the handsomest woman:—besides, she had a good fortune.

The widow, conscious of her charms and her money, did not let Tom, however, lead the quietest life in the world. She liked, with the unfailing propensity of her sex, to vex the man she loved, now and then, and assert her sway over so good-looking a fellow. He, in his turn, played off the widow very well; and one unfailing source of a mirthful reconciliation on Tom's part, whenever the widow was angry, and that he wanted to bring her back to good humour, was to steal behind her chair, and coaxingly putting his head over her fair shoulder, to pat her gently on her peachy cheek; and cry "*Baa!*"

1.   A half-holy half-merry meeting held at some certain place on the day dedicated to the Saint who is supposed to be the *patron* of the ˙ spot:—hence the name "*pattern*."

IX

ANDY WAS IN SAD DISGRACE for some days with his mother; but, like all mothers, she soon forgave the blunders of her son,—and indeed mothers are well off who have not more than blunders to forgive. Andy did all in his power to make himself useful at home, now that he was out of place and dependent on his mother, and got a day's work here and there when he could. Fortunately the season afforded him more employment than winter months would have done. But the farmers had soon all their crops made up, and when Andy could find no work to be paid for, he set-to to cut the "scrap o' meadow," as he called it, on a small field of his mother's. Indeed, it was but a "scrap," for the place where it grew was one of those broken bits of ground, so common in the vicinity of mountain ranges, where rocks, protruding through the soil, give the notion of a very fine crop of stones. Now, this locality gave to Andy the opportunity of exercising a bit of his characteristic ingenuity; for when the hay was ready for "cocking," he selected a good thumping rock as the foundation for his haystack, and the super-structure consequently cut a more respectable figure than one could have anticipated from the appearance of the little crop as it lay on the ground; and as no vestige of the rock was visible, the widow, when she came out to see the work completed, wondered and rejoiced at the size of her haystack, and said, "God bless you, Andy, but you're the natest hand for puttin' up a bit o' hay I ever seen: throth, I didn't think there was the half of it in it!" Little did the widow know that the cock of hay was as great a cheat as a bottle of champagne—more than half bottom. It was all very well for the widow to admire her hay; but at last she came to sell it, and such sales are generally effected in Ireland by the purchaser buying "in the lump," as it is called, that is, calculating the value of the hay from the appearance of the stack, as it stands, and drawing it away upon his own cars. Now, as luck would have it, it was Andy's early acquaintance, Owny na Coppal, bought the hay; and in consideration of the *lone woman*, gave her as good a price as he could afford, for Owny was an honest, open-hearted fellow, though he *was* a horse-dealer; so he paid the widow the price of her hay on the spot, and said he would draw it away at his convenience.

In a few days Owny's cars and men were sent for this purpose; but when they came to take the hay stack to pieces, the solidity of its centre rather astonished them,—and instead of the cars going back loaded, two had their journey for nothing, and went home empty. Previously to his men leaving the widow's field they spoke to her on the subject, and said,

"'Pon my conscience, ma'am, the centre o' your hay stack was mighty heavy."

"Oh, indeed, it's powerful hay," said she.

"Maybe so," said they; "but there's not much nourishment in that part of it."

"Not finer hay in Ireland," said she.

"What's of it, ma'am," said they. "Faix, we think Mr. Doyle will be talkin' to you about it." And they were quite right; for Owny became indignant at being overreached, as he thought, and lost no time in going to the widow to tell her so. When he arrived at her cabin, Andy happened to be in the house; and when the widow raised her voice through the storm of Owny's rage, in protestations that she knew nothing about it, but that "Andy, the darlin', put the cock up with his own hands," then did Owny's passion gather strength.

"Oh! it's you, you vagabone, is it?" said he, shaking his whip at Andy, with whom he never had had the honour of a conversation since the memorable day when his horse was nearly killed. "So this is more o' your purty work! Bad cess to you! wasn't it enough for you to nighhand kill one o' my horses, without plottin' to chate the rest o' them?"

"Is it *me* chate them?" said Andy. "Throth, I wouldn't wrong a dumb baste for the world."

"Not he, indeed, Misther Doyle," said the widow.

"Arrah, woman, don't be talkin' your balderdash to me," said Doyle; "sure, you took my good money for your hay?"

"And sure I gave all I had to you,—what more could I do?"

"Tare an ounty, woman! who ever heerd of sich a thing as coverin' up a rock wid hay, and sellin' it as the rale thing."

"'Twas Andy done it, Mr. Doyle; hand, act, or part, I hadn't in it."

"Why, then, arn't you ashamed o' yourself?" said Owny Doyle, addressing Andy.

"Why would I be ashamed?" said Andy.

"For chatin'—that's the word, sinse you provoke me."

"What I done is no chatin'," said Andy; "I had a blessed example for it."

"Oh! do you hear this?" shouted Owny, nearly provoked to take the worth of his money out of Andy's ribs.

"Yes, I say a blessed example," said Andy. "Sure didn't the blessed St. Peter build his church upon a rock, and why shouldn't I build my cock o' hay on a rock?"

Owny, with all his rage, could not help laughing at the ridiculous conceit. "By this and that, Andy," said he, "you're always sayin' or doin' the quarest things in the counthry, bad cess to you!" So he laid his whip upon his little hack instead of Andy, and galloped off.

Andy went over next day to the neighbouring town, where Owny Doyle kept a little inn and a couple of post-chaises (such as they were), and expressed much sorrow that Owny had been deceived by the appearance of the hay,—"But I'll pay you the differ out o' my wages, Misther Doyle,—in troth I will,—that is, whenever I have any wages to get, for the Squire turned me off, you see, and I'm out of place at this present."

"Oh, never mind it," said Owny. "Sure it was the widow woman got the money, and I don't begrudge it; and now that it's all past and gone, I forgive you. But tell me, Andy, what put sich a quare thing in your head?"

"Why, you see," said Andy, "I didn't like the poor mother's pride should be let down in the eyes o' the neighbours; and so I made the weeshy bit o' hay look as dacent as I could,—but at the same time I wouldn't chate any one for the world, Misther Doyle."

"Throth, I b'lieve you wouldn't, Andy; but, 'pon my sowl, the next time I go buy hay I'll take care that Saint Pether hasn't any hand in it."

Owny turned on his heel, and was walking away with that air of satisfaction which men so commonly assume after fancying they have said a good thing, when Andy interrupted his retreat by an interjectional "Misther Doyle."

"Well," said Owny, looking over his shoulder.

"I was thinkin', sir," said Andy.

"For the first time in your life, I b'lieve," said Owny; "and what was it you wor thinkin'?"

"I was thinkin' o' dhrivin' a chay, sir."

"And what's that to me?" said Owny.

"Sure, I might dhrive one o' your chaises."

"And kill more o' my horses, Andy,—eh? No, no, faix; I'm afeerd o' you, Andy."

"Not a boy in Ireland knows dhrivin' betther nor me, any way," said Andy.

"Faix, it's any way and every way but the way you ought, you'd dhrive, sure enough, I b'lieve: but at all events, I don't want a post-boy, Andy,—I have Micky Doolin, and his brother Pether, and them's enough for me."

"Maybe you'd be wantin' a helper in the stable, Misther Doyle?"

"No, Andy; but the first time I want to make hay to advantage I'll send for you," said Owny, laughing as he entered his house, and nodding at Andy, who returned a capacious grin to Owny's shrewd smile, like the exaggerated reflection of a concave mirror. But the grin soon subsided, for men seldom prolong the laugh that is raised at their expense; and the corners of Andy's mouth turned down as his hand turned up to the back of his head, which he rubbed as he sauntered down the street from Owny Doyle's.

It was some miles to Andy's home, and night overtook him on the way. As he trudged along in the middle of the road, he was looking up at a waning moon and some few, stars twinkling through the gloom, absorbed in many sublime thoughts as to their existence, and wondering what they were made of, when his cogitations were cut

short by tumbling over something which lay in the middle of the
highway; and on scrambling to his legs again, and seeking to investigate
the cause of his fall, he was rather surprised to find a man lying in such
a state of insensibility that all Andy's efforts could not rouse him. While
he was standing over him, undecided as to what he should do, the
sound of approaching wheels, and the rapid steps of galloping horses,
attracted his attention; and it became evident that unless the chaise and
pair which he now saw in advance were brought to a pull up, the cares
of the man in the middle of the road would be very soon over. Andy
shouted lustily, but to every "Halloo there!" he gave, the crack of a whip
replied, and accelerated speed, instead of a halt, was the consequence;
at last, in desperation, Andy planted himself in the middle of the road,
and with outspread arms before the horses, succeeded in arresting their
progress, while he shouted "Stop!" at the top of his voice.

A pistol shot from the chaise was the consequence of Andy's summons,
for a certain Mr. Furlong, a foppish young gentleman, travelling from
the castle of Dublin, never dreamed that a humane purpose could
produce the cry of "Stop" on a *horrid Irish* road; and as he was reared
in the ridiculous belief that every man ran a great risk of his life who
ventured outside the city of Dublin, he travelled with a brace of loaded
pistols beside him; and as he had been anticipating murder and robbery
ever since nightfall, he did not await the demand for his "money or his
life" to defend both, but fired away the instant he heard the word "Stop;"
and fortunate it was for Andy that the traveller's hurry impaired his aim.
Before he could discharge a second pistol, Andy had screened himself
under the horses' heads, and recognising in the postilion his friend Micky
Doolin, he shouted out, "Micky, jewel, don't let them be shootin' me!"

Now Micky's cares were quite enough engaged on his own account;
for the first pistol shot made the horses plunge violently, and the second
time Furlong blazed away, set the saddle-horse kicking at such a rate
that all Micky's horsemanship was required to preserve his seat. Added
to which, the dread of being shot came over him; and he crouched
low on the grey's neck, holding fast by the mane, and shouting for
mercy as well as Andy, who still kept roaring to Mick, "not to let them
be shootin' him," while he held his hat above him, in the fashion of a
shield, as if that would have proved any protection against a bullet.

"Who are you at all?" said Mick.

"Andy Rooney, sure."

"And what do you want?"

"To save the man's life."

The last words only caught the ear of the frightened Furlong; and as the phrase "his life" seemed a personal threat to himself, he swore a trembling oath at the postilion that he would shoot him if he did not *dwive* on, for he abjured the use of that rough letter, R, which the Irish so much rejoice in.

"Dwive on, you wascal, dwive on!" exclaimed Mr. Furlong.

"There's no fear o' you, sir," said Micky, " it's a friend o' my own."

Mr. Furlong was not quite satisfied that he was therefore the safer.

"And what is it at all, Andy?" continued Mick.

"I tell you there's a man lying dead in the road there, and sure you'll kill him if you dhrive over him; 'light, will you, and help me to rise him."

Mick dismounted and assisted Andy in lifting the prostrate man from the centre of the road to the slope of turf which bordered its side. They judged he was not dead, from the warmth of the body, but that he should still sleep seemed astonishing, considering the quantity of shaking and kicking they gave him.

"I b'lieve it's dhrunk he is," said Mick.

"He gave a grunt that time," said Andy,—"shake him again and he'll spake."

To a fresh shaking the drunken man at last gave some tokens of returning consciousness by making several winding blows at his benefactors, and uttering some half intelligent maledictions.

"Bad luck to you, do you know where you are?" said Mick.

"Well!" was the drunken ejaculation.

"By this and that it's my brother Pether!" said Mick. "We wondhered what had kept him so late with the return shay, and this is the way, is it? he tumbled off his horses, dhrunk: and where's the shay, I wonder? Oh, murdher! What will Misther Doyle say?"

"What's the weason you don't dwive on?" said Mr. Furlong, putting his head out of the chaise.

"It's one on the road here, your honour, a'most killed."

"Was it wobbers?" asked Mr. Furlong.

"Maybe you'd take him into the shay wid you, sir."

"What a wequest!—dwive on, sir!"

"Sure I can't leave my brother on the road, sir."

"*Your* bwother!—and you pwesume to put your bwother to wide with me? You'll put me in the debdest wage if you don't dwive on."

"Faith, then, I won't dhrive on and lave my brother here on the road."

"You wascally wappawee!" exclaimed Furlong.

"See, Andy," said Micky Doolin, "will you get up and dhrive him, while I stay with Pether?

"To be sure I will," said Andy. "Where is he goin'?

"To the Squire's," said Mick; "and when you lave him there, make haste back, and I'll dhrive Pether home."

Andy mounted into Mick's saddle; and although the traveller "pwotested" against it, and threatened "pwoceedings" and "magistwates," Mick was unmoved in his brotherly love. As a last remonstrance, Furlong exclaimed, "And pwehaps this fellow can't wide, and don't know the woad."

"Is it not know the road to the Squire's?—wow! wow!" said Andy. "It's I that'll rattle you there in no time, your honour."

"Well, wattle away then!" said the enraged traveller, as he threw himself back in the chaise, cursing all the postilions in Ireland.

Now it was to Squire O'Grady's that Mr. Furlong wanted to go; but in the confusion of the moment the name of O'Grady never once was mentioned; and with the title of "Squire" Andy never associated another idea than that of his late master, Mr. Egan.

Mr. Furlong, it has been stated, was an official of Dublin Castle, and had been despatched on electioneering business, to the county. He was related to a gentleman of the same name, who held a lucrative post under government, and was well known as an active agent in all affairs requiring what in Ireland was called "Castle influence;" and this, his relative, was now despatched, for the first time, on a similar employment. By the way, while his name is before one, a little anecdote may be appropriately introduced, illustrative of the wild waggery prevailing in the streets of Dublin in those days.

Those days were the good old days of true virtue!—When a bishop who had daughters to marry, would advance a deserving young curate to a good living; and, not content with *that* manifestation of his regard, would give him *one of his own children* for a wife! those were the days, when, the country being in danger, fathers were willing to sacrifice, not only their sons, but their daughters, on the altar of patriotism! Do you doubt it?—unbelieving and selfish creatures of these degenerate times! Listen! A certain father waited upon the Irish Secretary one fine morning, and in that peculiar strain which secretaries of state must be pretty well used to, descanted at some length on the devotion he had always shown to the government, and yet they had given him no *proof of their confidence.* The Secretary declared they had the highest sense of his merits, and that they had given him their entire confidence.

"But you have given me nothing else, my lord," was the answer.

"My dear sir, of late we have not had any proof of sufficient weight in our gift to convince you."

"Oh, I beg your pardon, my lord; there's a majority of the — Dragoons vacant."

"Very true, my dear sir; and if you *had* a child to devote to the service of your country, no one should have it sooner."

"Thank you, my lord!!!" said the worthy man, with a low bow,— "then I *have* a child."

"Bless me, sir! I never heard you had a son."

"No, my lord; but I have a daughter."

"A daughter!" said my Lord Secretary, with a look of surprise; "but you forget, sir,—this is a regiment;—a *dragoon* regiment."

"Oh, she rides elegant!" said her father.

"But, my dear sir, a woman?"

"Why shouldn't a woman do her duty, my lord, as well as a man, when the country is in danger? I'm ready to sacrifice my daughter," said the heroic man, with an air wortby of Virginius.

"My dear sir, this is really impossible; you *know* it's impossible."

"I know no such thing, my lord. But I'll tell you what I know: there's a bill coming on next week,—and there are *ten friends of mine* who have not made up their minds yet."

"My dear sir," said the Lord Secretary, squeezing his hand with vehement friendship, "why place us in this dreadful difficulty? It would be impossible even to draw up the commission;—fancy 'Major *Maria*,' or 'Major *Margery*!'"

"Oh, my lord," said the father, quickly; "I have fancied all that long ago, and got a cure ready for it. My wife, not having been blessed with boys, we thought it wise to make the girls ready for any chance that might turn up, and so we christened the eldest George, the second Jack, and the third Tom; which enables us to call them Georgina, Jacqueline, and Thomasine, in company, while the secret of their real names rests between ourselves and the parish register. Now, my lord, what do you say? I have George, Jack, and Tom;—think of your *bill*." The, argument was conclusive, and the patriotic man got the majority of a cavalry corps, with perpetual leave of absence for his daughter Jack, who would much rather have joined the regiment.

Such were the days in which our Furlong flourished; and in such days it will not be wondered at that a secretary, when he had no place to give away—invented one. The old saying has it, that "Necessity is the mother of invention;" but an Irish Secretary can beat Necessity hollow. For example:

A commission was issued, with a handsome salary to the commissioner, to make a measurement through all the streets of Dublin, ascertaining exact distances from the Castle, from a furlong upwards; and for many a year did the commission work, inserting handsome stone slabs into the walls of most ignorant houses, till then unconscious of their precise proximity or remoteness from the seat of government. Ever after that, if you saw some portly building, blushing in the pride of red brick, and perfumed with fresh paint, and saw the tablet recording the interesting fact, thus:

> FROM THE CASTLE,
> ONE FURLONG.

Fancy might suggest that the house rejoiced, as it were, in its honoured position, and did

———"look so fine and smell so sweet,"

because it was under the nose of Viceroyalty, while the suburbs revealed poor tatterdemalion tenements, dropping their slates like tears, and uttering their hollow sighs through empty casements, merely because they were "one mile two furlongs from the Castle." But the new stone tablet which told you so seemed to mock their misery, and looked like a fresh stab into their poor old sides; as if the rapier of a king had killed a beggar.

This very original measure of measurement was provocative of ridicule, or indignation, as the impatient might happen to be infected; but while the affair was in full blow, Mr. Furlong, who was the commissioner, while walking in Sackville-street one day, had a goodly sheet of paper pinned to his back by some

———"delicate Roman hand,"

bearing in large letters the inversion of one of his own tablets:

> ## ONE FURLONG
> ## FROM THE CASTLE.

And as he swaggered along in conscious dignity, he wondered at the shouts of laughter ringing behind him, and turned round occasionally to see the cause; but ever as he turned, faces were screwed up into seriousness, while the laughter rang again in his rear. Furlong was bewildered; and much as he was used to the mirthfulness of an Irish populace, he certainly did wonder what fiend of fun possessed them that day, until the hall-porter of the Secretary's Office solved the enigma by respectfully asking would he not take the placard from his back before he presented himself. The Mister Furlong who is engaged in our story was the nephew of the man of measurement memory; and his mother, a vulgar woman, sent her son to England to be educated, that he might "pick up the ax'nt; 'twas so jinteel, the Inglish ax'nt!" And accordingly, the youth endeavoured all he could to become *un*-Irish in every thing, and was taught to believe that all the virtue and wisdom in Ireland was vested in the Castle and hangers on thereof, and that the mere people were worse than savages.

With such feelings it was that this English Irishman, employed to open negotiations between the government and Squire O'Grady, visited the wilds of Ireland; and the circumstances attendant on the stopping of the chaise, afforded the peculiar genius of Handy Andy an opportunity of making a glorious confusion, by driving the political enemy of the sitting member into his house, where, by a curious coincidence, a strange gentleman was expected every day, on a short visit. After Andy had driven some time, he turned round and spoke to Mr. Furlong through the pane of glass with which the front window-frame of the chaise was *not* furnished.

"Faix, you wor nigh shootin' me, your honour," said Andy.

"I should not wepwoach myself, if I had," said Mr. Furlong, "when you quied stop on the woad: wobbers always qui stop, and I took you for a wobber."

"Faix, the robbers here, your honour, never axes you to stop at all, but they stop you without axin', or by your lave, or wid your lave. Sure was only afeerd you'd dhrive over the man in the road."

"What was that man in the woad doing?"

"Nothin' at all, faith, for he wasn't able; he was dhrunk, sir."

"The postilion said he was his bwother."

"Yis, your honour, and he's a postilion himself—only he lost his horses and then got dhrunk, and fell off."

"Those wascally postilions often get dwunk, I suppose."

"Oh, common enough, sir, particlar now about the 'lection time; for the gintlemin is dhrivin' over the counthry like mad, right and left, and gives the boys money to dhrink their health, till they are killed a'most with the falls they get."

"Then postilions often fall on the woads here?"

"Throth the roads is covered with them sometimes, when the 'lections comes' an."

"What howwid immowality! I hope you're not dwunk?"

"Faix, I wish I was," said Andy. "It's a great while since I had a dhrop; but it won't be long so, when your honour gives me something to dhrink your health."

"Well, don't talk, but dwive on."

All Andy's further endeavours to get "his honour" into conversation were unavailing; so he whipped on in silence till his arrival at the gate-house of Merryvale demanded his call for entrance.

"What are you shouting there for?" said the traveller; "cawn't you wing?"

"Oh; they undhershtand the *shilloo* as well, sir:" and in confirmation of Andy's assurance, the bars of the entrance gate were withdrawn, and the post-chaise rattled up the avenue to the house.

Andy alighted and gave a thundering tantara-ra at the door. The servant who opened it was surprised at the sight of Andy, and could not repress a shout of wonder.

Here Dick Dawson came into the hall, and seeing Andy at the door, gave a loud halloo, and clapped his hands in delight—for he had not seen him since the day of the chase. "An' is it there you are again, you unlucky vagabone?" said Dick; "and what brings you. here?"

"I come with a jintleman to the masther, misther Dick."

"Oh! it's the visitor, I suppose," said Dick, as he himself went out with that unceremonious readiness, so characteristic of the wild fellow he was, to open the door of the chaise for his brother-in-law's guest. "You're, welcome," said Dick;—"come, step in,—the servants will look to your luggage. James, get in Mr — I beg your pardon, but 'pon my soul I forgot your name, though Moriarty told me."

"Mr. Furlong," gently uttered the youth.

"Get in the luggage, James. Come, sir, walk into the dinner-room; we haven't finished our wine yet." With these words Dick ushered in Furlong to the apartment where Squire Egan sat, who rose as they entered.

"Mr. Furlong, Ned," said Dick.

"Happy to see you, Mr. Furlong," said the hearty Squire, who shook Furlong's hand in what Furlong considered a most savage manner. "You seem fatigued."

"Vewy," was the languid reply of the traveller, as he threw himself into a chair.

"Ring the bell for more claret, Dick," said Squire Egan.

"I neveh dwink."

Dick and the Squire both looked at him with amazement, for in the friend of Moriarty they expected to find a hearty fellow.

"A cool bottle wouldn't do a child any harm," said the Squire. "Ring, Dick. And now, Mr. Furlong, tell us how you like the country."

"Not much, I pwotest."

"What do you think of the people?"

"Oh, I don't know: you'll pawdon me, but—a—in short, there are so many wags."

"Oh, there are wags enough, I grant; not funnier d—ls in the world."

"But I mean *wags*—tatters, I mean."

"Oh, rags. Oh, yes—why indeed they've not much clothes to spare."

"And yet these wetches, are fweeholders, I'm told."

"Ay, and stout voters too."

"Well, that's all we wequire. By the by, how goes on the canvass, Squire?"

"Famously."

"Oh, wait till I explain to you our plan of opewations from headqwaters. You'll see how famously we shall wally at the hustings. These *Iwish* have no idea of tactics: we'll intwoduce the English mode—take them by supwise. We *must* unseat him."

"Unseat who?" said the Squire.

"That—a—Egan, I think you call him."

The Squire opened his eyes; but Dick, with the ready devilment that was always about him, saw how the land lay in an instant, and making a signal to his brother-in-law, chimed in with an immediate assent to Furlong's assertion, and swore that Egan would be unseated to a certainty. "Come, sir," added Dick, "fill one bumper at least to a toast I propose.—Here's 'Confusion to Egan, and success to O'Grady.'"

"Success to O'Gwady," faintly echoed Furlong, as he sipped his claret. "These *Iwish* are so wild—so uncultivated," continued he; "you'll see how I'll supwise them with some of my plans."

"Oh, they're poor ignorant brutes," said Dick, "that know nothing: a man of the world like you would buy and sell them."

"You see they've no finesse; they have a certain degwee of weadiness, but no depth—no weal finesse."

"Not as much as would physic a snipe," said Dick, who swallowed a glass of claret to conceal a smile.

"What's that you say about snipes and physic?" said Furlong; "what queer things you *Iwish* do say."

"Oh, we've plenty o' queer fellows here," said Dick;—"but you are not taking your claret."

"The twuth is, I am fatigued—vewy—and if you'd allow me, Mr. O'Gwady, I should like to go to my woom; we'll talk over business to-mowwow."

"Certainly," said the Squire, who was glad to get rid of him, for the scene was becoming too much for his gravity. So Dick Dawson lighted Furlong to his room, and after heaping civilities upon him left him to sleep in the camp of his enemies, and then returned to the dining-room to enjoy with the Squire the laugh they were so long obliged to repress, and to drink another bottle of claret on the strength of the joke.

"What shall we do with him, Dick?" said the Squire.

"Pump him as dry as a lime kiln," said Dick, "and then send him off to O'Grady—all's fair in war."

"To be sure," said the Squire. "Unseat me, indeed! he was near it, sure enough, for I thought I'd have dropped off my chair with surprise when he said it."

"And the conceit and impudence of the fellow," said Dick. "The ignorant *Iwish*—nothing will serve him but abusin' his own countrymen!—'The ignorant Irish'—Oh, is that all you learned in Oxford, my boy?—just wait, my buck—if I don't astonish your weak mind, it's no matter!"

"Faith he has brought his pigs to a pretty market here," said the Squire; "but how did he come here? how was the mistake made?"

"The way every mistake in the country is made," said Dick; "Handy Andy drove him here."

"More power to you, Andy," said the Squire. "Come, Dick, we'll drink Andy's health—this is a mistake on the right side."

And Andy's health was drunk, as well as several other healths. In short, the Squire and Dick the Devil were in high glee—the dining-room rang with laughter to a late hour; and the next morning a great many empty claret bottles were on the table—and a few on the floor.

X

NOTWITHSTANDING THE DEEP POTATIONS OF the Squire and Dick Dawson the night before, both were too much excited by the arrival of Furlong to permit their being laggards in the morning; they were up and in consultation at an early hour, for the purpose of carrying on prosperously the mystification so well begun on the Castle agent.

"Now, first of all, Dick," said the Squire, "is it fair, do you think?"

"Fair!" said Dick, opening his eyes in astonishment. "Why, who ever heard of any one questioning anything being fair in love, war, or electioneering;—to be sure, it's fair—and more particularly when the conceited coxcomb has been telling us how he'll astonish with his plans the poor ignorant Irish, whom he holds in such contempt. Now let me alone, and I'll get all his plans out of him—turn him inside out like a glove, pump him as dry as a pond in the summer, squeeze him like a lemon—and, let him see whether the poor ignorant *Iwish,* as he softly calls us, are not an overmatch for him, at the finesse upon which he seems so much to pride himself."

"Egad! I believe you're right, Dick," said the Squire, whose qualms were quite overcome by the argument last advanced; for if one thing more than another provoked him, it was the impertinent self-conceit of presuming and shallow strangers, who fancied their hackneyed and cut-and-dry knowledge of the common places of the world gave them a mental elevation above an intelligent people of primitive habits, whose simplicity of life is so often down to stupidity, whose contentment under privation is frequently attributed to laziness, and whose poverty is constantly coupled with the epithet "ignorant." "A *poor* ignorant

HANDY ANDY   135

creature," indeed is a common term of reproach, as if poverty and
ignorance must be inseparable. If a list could be obtained of the *rich*
ignorant people, it would be no flattering document to stick on the
doors of the temple of Mammon.

"Well, Ned," said Dick, "as you agree to *do* the Englishman, Murphy
will be a grand help to us; it is the very thing he will have his heart in.
Murtough will be worth his weight in gold to us: I will ride over to
him and bring him back with me to spend the day here; and you in the
mean time can put every one about the house on their guard not to
spoil the fun by letting the cat out of the bag too soon; we'll *shake her*
ourselves in good time, and maybe we won't have, fun in the hunt!"

"You're right, Dick. Murphy is the very man for our money. Do
you be off for him, and I will take care that all shall be right at home
here."

In ten minutes more Dick was in his saddle, and riding hard for
Murtough Murphy's. A good horse and a sharp pair of spurs were not
long in placing him *vis-à-vis* with the merry attorney, whom he found
in his stable-yard up to his eyes in business with some ragged country
fellows, the majority of whom were loud in vociferating their praises
of certain dogs; while Murtough drew from one of them, from time
to time, a solemn assurance, given with many significant shakes of the
head, and uplifting of hands and eyes, "that it was the finest badger in
the world!" Murtough turned his head on hearing the rattle of the
horse's feet, as Dick the Devil dashed into the stable-yard, and with a
view-halloo welcomed him.

"You're just in, time, Dick. By the powers, we'll have the finest day's
sport you've seen for some time."

"I think we will," said Dick, "if you will come with me."

"No; but you come with me," said Murtough. "The grandest badger-
fight, sir."

"Pooh!" returned Dick; "I've better fun for you."—He then told him
of the accident that conveyed their political enemy into their toils. "And
the beauty of it is," said Dick, "that he has not the remotest suspicion
of the condition he's in, and fancies himself able to buy and sell all
Ireland—horse-dealers and attorneys included."

"That's elegant," said Murphy.

"He's come to enlighten us, Murtough," said Dick.

"And maybe we won't return the compliment," said Murtough: "just let me put on my boots. Hilloa, you Larry! saddle the grey. Don't cut the pup's ears till I come home; and if Mr. Ferguson sends over for the draft of the lease, tell him it won't be ready till tomorrow. Molly! Molly!—where are you, you old divil? Sew, on that button for me,—I forgot to tell you yesterday,—make haste! I won't delay you a moment, Dick. Stop a minute, though. I say, Lanty Houligan,—mind, on your peril, you old vagabone, don't let them fight that badger without me. Now, Dick, I'll be with you in the twinkling of a bedpost, and *do* the Englishman, and that smart! Bad luck to their conceit!—they think we can do nothing regular in Ireland."

On his arrival, and hearing how matters stood, Murtough Murphy was in a perfect agony of delight in anticipating the mystification of the kidnapped agent. Dick's intention had been to take him along with them on their canvass, and openly engage him in all their electioneering movements; but to this Murphy objected, as running too great a risk of discovery. He recommended rather to engage Furlong in amusements which would detain him from O'Grady and his party, and gain time for their side; to get out of him all the electioneering plot of the other party, *indirectly*; but to have as little *real* electioneering business as possible. "If you do, Dick," said Murphy, "take my word we shall betray ourselves somehow or other.—he could not be so soft as not to see it; but let us be content to amuse him with all sorts of absurd stories of Ireland and the Irish—tell him magnificent lies—astonish him with grand materials for a note book, and work him up to publish—that's the plan, sir!"

The three conspirators now joined the family party, which had just sat down to breakfast. Dick, in his own jolly way, hoped Furlong had slept well.

"Vewy," said Furlong, as he sipped his tea with an air of peculiar *nonchalance* which was meant to fascinate Fanny Dawson, who, when Furlong addressed to her his first silly commonplace, with his peculiar *non*-pronunciation of the letter R, established a lisp directly, and it was as much as her sister Mrs. Egan could do to keep her countenance as Fanny went on slaughtering S's as fast as Furlong ruined R's.

"I'll twouble you for a little mo' queam," said he, holding forth his cup and saucer with an affected air.

"Perhaps you'd like thum more thougar," lisped Fanny, lifting the sugar-tongs with an exquisite curl of her little finger.

"I'm glad to hear you slept well," said Dick to Furlong.

"To be sure he slept well," said Murphy; "this is the sleepiest air in the world."

"The sleepiest air?" returned Furlong somewhat surprised. "That's vewy odd."

"Not at all, sir," said Murphy,—"well-known fact. When I first came to this part of the country, I used to sleep for two days together sometimes. Whenever I wanted to rise early I was always obliged to get up the night before."

This was said by the brazen attorney, from his seat at a side table, which was amply provided with a large dish of boiled potatoes, capacious jugs of milk, a quantity of cold meat and game. Murphy had his mouth half filled with potatoes as he spoke, and swallowed a large draught of milk as the stranger swallowed Murphy's lie.

"You don't eat potatoes, I perceive, sir," said Murphy.

"Not for bweakfast," said Furlong.

"Do you for thupper?" lisped Fanny.

"Never in England," he replied.

"Finest things in the world, sir, for the intellect," said Murphy. "I attribute the natural intelligence of the Irish entirely to their eating potatoes."

"That's a singular theowy," said Furlong; "for it is genewally atwibuted to the potatoe, that it detewiowates the wace of man. Cobbett said that any nation feeding exclusively on the potatoe, must inevitably be fools in thwee genewations."

"By the powers, sir!" said Murphy, "they'd be fools if they *didn't* eat them in Ireland; for they've nothing else to eat. Why, sir, the very pigs that we feed on potatoes are as superior—"

"I beg your pawdon," smiled Furlong; "daiwy-fed po'ke is vewy superior."

"Oh, as far as the eating of it goes, I grant you!" said Murphy; "but I'm talking of the intelligence of the animal. Now, I have seen them in England killing your dairy-fed pork, as you call it, and to see the simplicity—the sucking simplicity, I will call it—of your milk-fed pigs,—sir, the fellow lets himself be killed with the greatest ease,—whereas, look to the potatoe-fed pig. He makes a struggle for his life;—he shouts, he kicks, he plunges,—squeals murder to the last gasp, as if he were sensible of the blessings of existence and potatoes!"

This was pronounced by Murphy with a certain degree of energy and oratorical style that made Furlong stare: he turned to Dick Dawson, and said, in an undertone, "How vewy odd your fwiend is!"

"Very," said Dick; "but that's only on the surface: he's a prodigiously clever fellow: you'll be delighted with him when you know more of him,—he's our solicitor, and as an electioneering agent his talent is tremendous, as you'll find out when you come to talk with him about business."

"Well, I should neve' ha' thought it," said Furlong; "I'm glad you told me."

"Are you fond of sporting, Mr. Furlong?" said the Squire.

"Vewy," said Furlong.

"I'll give you some capital hunting."

"I pwefer fishing."

"Oh!" returned the Squire, rather contemptuously.

"Have you good twout stweams here?" asked the exquisite.

"Yeth," said Fanny, "and *thuch* a thamon fithshery!"

"Indeed!

"Finest salmon in the world, sir," said Murphy. "I'll show you some sport, if you like."

"I've seen some famous spo't in Scotland," said Furlong.

"Nothing to what we can show you here," said Murphy. "Why, sir, I remember once at the mouth of our river here, when the salmon were coming up one morning before the tide was in, there was such a crowd of them, that they were obliged to wait till there was water enough to cross the bar, and an English sloop that had not a pilot aboard, whose captain did not know the peculiar nature of the river, struck on the bank of salmon and went down."

"You don't mean to say," said Furlong, in astonishment, " that—a—"

"I mean to say, sir," said Murphy, with an unruffled countenance, "that the river was so thick with salmon the vessel was wrecked upon them. By the by, she was loaded with salt, and several of the salmon were pickled in consequence, and saved by the poor people for the next winter. "But I'll show you such fishing!" said Murphy,—"you'll say you never saw the like."

"Well, that *is* the *wichest* thing I've heard for some time," said the dandy confidentially to Dick.

"I assure you," said Dick, with great gravity, "Murphy swears he saw it himself. But here's the post, let's see what's the news."

The post-bag was opened, and letters and newspapers delivered. "Here's one for you, Fan," said Dick, throwing the letter across the table to his sister.

"I thee by the theal ith from my couthin Thophy," said Fanny, who invented the entire sentence, cousinship and all, for the sake of the lisp.

"None fo' me?" asked Furlong.

"Not one," said Dick.

"I welied on weceiving some fwom the Ca-astle."

"Oh, they are thometimes tho thleepy at the Cathtle," said Fanny.

"Weally!" said the exquisite, with the utmost simplicity.

"Fanny is very provoking, Mr. Furlong," said Mrs. Egan, who was obliged to say something with a smile, to avoid the laugh which continued silence would have forced upon her.

"Oh; no!" said the dandy, looking tenderly at Fanny; "only vewy agweable,—fond of a little wepa'tee."

"They call me thatirical here," said Fanny; "only fanthy;" and she cast down her eyes with an exquisite affectation of innocence.

"By the by, when does your post awwive here—the mail, I mean?" said Furlong.

"About nine in the morning," said the Squire.

"And when does it go out?"

"About one in the afternoon."

"And how far is the post-town fwom your house?"

"About eight or nine miles."

"Then you can answer your letters by wetu'n of post."

"Oh dear; no!" said the Squire, "the boy takes any letters that may be for the post the following morning; as he goes to the town to look for letters."

"But you lose a post by that," said Furlong.

"And what matter?" said the Squire. The official's notions of regularity were somewhat startled by the Squire's answer; so he pushed him with a few more questions. In reply to one of the last, the Squire represented that the post-boy was saved going twice a day by the present arrangement.

"Ay, but you lose a post, my dear sir," said Furlong, who still clung with pertinacity to the fitness of saving a post. "Don't you see that you might weceive your letter at half-past ten; well, then you'll have a full hour to wite you' answer; that's quite enough time, I should think, for you' wetu'ning an answer."

"But, my dear sir," said Murtough Murphy, "our grand object in Ireland is *not* to answer letters."

"Oh!—ah!—hum!—indeed!—well, that's odd;—how *vewy* odd you Iwish are!"

"Sure that's what makes us such pleasant fellows," said Murtough. "If we were like the rest of the world, there would be nothing remarkable about us; and who'd care for us?"

"Well, Mr. Muffy, you say such queer things— weally."

"Ay, and I *do* queer things sometimes,—don't I, Squire?"

"There's no denying it, Murphy."

"Now, Mr. O'Gwady," said Furlong, "had we not better talk over our election business?

"Oh! hang business to-day," said Murphy; "let's have some fishing: I'll show you such a salmon fishing as you never saw in your life."

"What do *you* say, Mr. O'Gwady?" said Furlong.

"'Faith, I think we might as well amuse ourselves."

"But the election is weally of such consequence; I should think it would be a wema'kbly close contest, and we have no time to lose: I should think—with submission—"

"My dear sir," said Murphy, "we'll beat them hollow; our canvass has been most prosperous; there's only one thing I am afraid of—"

"What's that?" said Furlong.

"That Egan has money; and I'm afraid he'll bribe high."

"As for bwibewy, neve' mind that," said Furlong, with a very wise nod of his head and a sagacious wink. "*We'll spend money too.* We're pwepared for that; plenty of money will be advanced, for the gov'nment is weally anxious that Mr. Scatte'bwain should come in."

"Oh, then, all's right!" said Murphy. "But—whisper—Mr. Furlong— be cautious how you mention *money*, for there are sharp fellows about here, and there's no knowing how the wind of the word might put the other party on their guard, and maybe, help to unseat our man upon a petition."

"Oh, let me alone," said Furlong. "I know a twick too many for that: let them catch me betwaying a secwet! No, no,—*wather* too sharp for that."

"Oh! don't suppose, my dear sir," said Murphy, "that I doubt your caution for a moment. I see, sir, in the twinkling of an eye, a man's character—always did—always could, since I was the height o' that,"—and Murphy stooped down and extended his hand about two feet above the floor, while he looked up in the face of the man he was humbugging with the most unblushing impudence,—"since I was the height o' that, sir, I had a natural quickness for discerning character; and I see you're a young gentleman of superior acuteness and discretion; but at the same time, don't be angry with me for just hinting to you that some of these Irish chaps are d——d rogues. I beg your pardon, Mrs. O'Grady, for saying d——n before a lady,"—and he made a low bow to Mrs. Egan, who was obliged to leave the room to hide her laughter.

"Now," said Furlong, "suppose befo'e the opening of the poll we should pwopose, as it were, with a view to save time, that the bwibewy oath should not be administe'd on either side."

"That's an eligant idea," said Murphy. "By the wig o' the chief justice—and that's a big oath—you're a janius, Misther Furlong, and I admire you. Sir, you're worth your weight in gold to us!"

"Oh, you flatte' me!—weally," said Furlong, with affected modesty, while he ran his fingers through his Macassar-oiled ringlets.

"Well, now for a start to the river, and won't we have sport! You English-taught gentlemen have only one fault on the face of the earth,—you're too fond of business;—you make yourselves slaves to propriety,—there's no fun in you."

"I beg pawdon—there," said Furlong, "we like fun in good time."

"Ah! but there's where we beat you," said Murphy, triumphantly; "the genuine home-bred Paddy makes time for fun sooner than anything else,—we take our own way, and live the longer."

"Ah! you lose your time—though—excuse me; you lose your time, indeed."

"Well, 'divil may care,' as Punch said when he lost mass, 'there's more churches nor one,' says he,—and that's the way with us," said Murphy. "Come, Dick, get the fishing-lines ready; heigh for the salmon fishery! You must know, Mr. Furlong, we fish for salmon with line here."

"I don't see how you could fish any other way," said the dandy, smiling at Murphy as if he had caught him in saying something absurd.

"Ah, you rogue," said Murphy, affecting to be hit; "you're too sharp for us poor Irish fellows; but you know the old saying, 'An Irishman has leave to speak twice;' and after all, it's no great mistake I've made; for, when I say we fish for salmon with a line, I mean we don't use a rod, but a leaded line, the same as in sea-fishing."

"How vewy extwaordinary! why, I should think that impossible."

"And why should it be impossible?" said Murphy, with the most unabashed impudence. "Have not all nations habits and customs peculiar to themselves? Don't the Indians catch their fish by striking them under water with a long rough stick, and a little curwhibble of a bone at the end of it?"

"Speawing them, you mean," said Furlong.

"Ah, you know the right name, of course : but isn't that quite as odd, or more so, than our way here?"

"That's vewy twue indeed; but your sea line-fishing in a wiver, and for salmon, strikes me as vewy singular."

"Well, sir, the older we grow the more we learn. You'll see what fine sport it is; but don't lose any more time; let us be off to the river at once."

"I'll make a slight change in my dress, if you please,—I'll be down immediately;" and Furlong left the room. During his absence, the Squire, Dick, and Murphy, enjoyed a hearty laugh, and ran over the future proceedings of the day.

"But what do you mean by this salmon-fishing, Murphy?" said Dick, "you know there never was a salmon in the river."

"But there will be to-day," said Murphy; "and a magnificent Gudgeon shall see him caught. What a spoon that fellow is! we've got the bribery out of him already."

"You did that well, Murphy," said the Squire.

"Be at him again when he comes down," said Dick.

"No, no," said Murphy, "let him alone; he is so conceited about his talent for business, that he will be talking of it without our pushing him: just give him rope enough, and he'll hang himself; we'll have the whole plan of their campaign out before the day's over."

XI

A LL MEN LOVE TO GAIN their ends; most men are contented with the shortest road to them, while others like by-paths. Some carry an innate love of triumph to a pitch of epicurism, and are not content unless the triumph be achieved in a certain way, making collateral passions accessories before or after the fact; and Murphy was of the number. To him, a triumph without *fun* was beef without mustard, lamb without salad, turbot without lobster sauce. Now, to entangle Furlong in their meshes was not sufficient for him; to detain him from his friends, every moment betraying something of their electioneering movements, though sufficiently ludicrous in itself, was not enough for Murtough;—he would make his captive a source of ridicule as well as profit, and while plenty of real amusements might have served his end, to divert the stranger for the day, this mock fishing party was planned to brighten with fresh beams the halo of the ridiculous which already encircled the magnanimous Furlong.

"I'm still in the dark," said Dick, "about the salmon. As I said before, there never was a salmon in the river."

"But, as I said before," replied Murphy, "there will be to-day; and you must help me in playing off the trick."

"But what *is* this trick? Confound you, you're as mysterious as a chancery suit."

"I wish I was likely to last half as long," said Murphy.

"The trick!" said Dick. "Bad luck to you, tell me the trick, and don't keep me waiting, like a poor relation."

"You have two boats on the river," said Murphy.

"Yes."

"Well, you must get into one with our victim: and I will get into the other with the salmon."

"But where's the salmon, Murphy?"

"In the house, for I sent one over this morning, a present to Mrs. Egan. You must keep away about thirty yards or so, when we get afloat, that our dear friend may not perceive the trick,—and in proper time I will hook my dead salmon on one of my lines, drop him over the off side of the boat, pass him round to the gunwale within view of our intelligent castle customer, make a great outcry, swear I have a noble bite, haul up my fish with an enormous splash, and after affecting to kill him in the boat, hold up my salmon in triumph."

"It's a capital notion, Murphy, if he doesn't smoke the trick."

"He'll smoke the salmon sooner. Never mind, if I don't hoax him: I'll bet you what you like he's done."

"I hear him coming down stairs," said the squire.

"Then send off the salmon in a basket by one of the boys, Dick," said Murphy; "and you, Squire, may go about your canvass, and leave us in care of the enemy."

All was done as Murphy proposed, and in something less than an hour, Furlong and Dick in one boat, and Murphy and his attendant *gossoon* in another, were afloat on the river, to initiate the Dublin citizen into the mysteries of this new mode of salmon fishing.

The sport at first was slack, and no wonder; and Furlong began to grow tired, when Murphy hooked on his salmon, and gently brought it round under the water within range of his victim's observation.

"This is wather dull work," said Furlong.

"Wait awhile, my dear sir; they are never lively in biting so early as this—they're not set about feeding in earnest yet. Hilloa! by the Hokey I have him!" shouted Murphy. Furlong looked on with great anxiety as Murphy made a well-feigned struggle with a heavy fish.

"By this and that he's a whopper!" cried Murphy in ecstasy. "He's kicking like a two-year-old. I have him, though, as fast as the rock o' Dunamase. Come up, you thief!" cried he, with an exulting shout, as he pulled up the salmon with all the splash he could produce; and suddenly whipping the fish over the side into the boat, he began flopping it about as if it were plunging in the death struggle. As soon as he had affected to kill it, he held it up in triumph before the castle conjuror, who was quite taken in by the feint, and protested his surprise loudly.

"Oh! that's nothing to what we'll do yet. If the day should become a little more overcast, we'd have a splendid sport, sir."

"Well, I could not have believed it, if I hadn't seen it," said Furlong.

"Oh! you'll see more than that, my boy, before we've done with them."

"But I haven't got even a bite yet."

"Nor I either," said Dick : "you're not worse off than I am."

"But how extwaordinawy it is that I have not seen a fish wise since I have been on the wiver."

"That's because they see us watching them," said Dick. "The d—l such cunning brutes I ever met with as the fish in this river: now, if you were at a distance from the bank you'd see them jumping as lively as grasshoppers. Whisht! I think I had a nibble."

"You don't seem to have good sport there," shouted Murphy.

"Vewy poo' indeed," said Furlong, dolefully.

"Play your line a little," said Murphy; "keep the bait lively—you're not up to the way of fascinating them yet."

"Why no; it's rather *noo* to me."

"Faith!" said Murphy to himself, "it's new to all of us. It's a bran new invention in the fishing line. Billy," said he to the *gossoon*, who was in the boat with him, "we must catch a salmon again to *divart* that strange gentleman; hook him on, my buck."

"Yis, sir," said Billy with delighted eagerness; for the boy entered into the fun of the thing heart and soul, and as he hooked on the salmon for a second haul, he interlarded his labours with such ejaculations as, "Oh, Misther Murphy, sir, but you're the funny jintleman. Oh, Misther Murphy, sir, how soft the stranger is, sir. The salmon's ready for ketchin' now, sir. Will you ketch him yet, sir?"

"Coax him round, Billy," said Murphy.

The young imp executed the manoeuvre with adroitness; and Murphy was preparing for another haul, as Furlong's weariness began to manifest itself.

"Do you intend wemaining here all day?—do you know, I think I've no chance of any spo't."

"Oh, wait till you hook *one* fish, at all events," said Murphy; just have it to say you killed a salmon in the new style, The day is promising better. I'm sure we'll have sport yet. Hilloa! I've another!" and Murphy began hauling in the salmon. "Billy, you rascal, get ready: watch him—that's it—mind him now!" Billy put out his gaff to seize the prize, and, making a grand swoop, affected to miss the fish.

"Gaff him, you thief, gaff him!" shouted Murphy; "gaff him, or he'll be off."

"Oh, he's so lively, sir!" roared Billy; "he's a rogue, sir—he won't let me put the gaff undher him, sir—ow, he slipp'd away agin."

"Make haste, Billy, or I can't hold him."

"Oh, the thief!" said Billy; "one would think he was cotcht before, he's so up to it. Ha!—hurroo!—I have him now, sir!"

Billy made all the splash he could in the water as Murphy lifted the fish to the surface and swung him into the boat. Again there was the flopping and the riot, and Billy screeching, "Kill him, sir!—kill him, sir! or he'll be off out o' my hands!" In proper time the fish *was* killed, and shown up in triumph, and the imposture completed.

And now Furlong began to experience that peculiar longing for catching a fish, which always possesses men who see fish taken by others; and the desire to have a salmon of his own killing induced him to remain on the river. In the long intervals of idleness which occurred between the occasional hooking up of the salmon, which Murphy *did* every now and then, Furlong *would be talking* about business to Dick Dawson, so that they had not been very long on the water until Dick became enlightened on some more very important points connected with the election. Murphy now pushed his boat towards the shore.

"You're not going yet?" said the anxious fisherman; "*do* wait till I catch a fish."

"Certainly," said Murphy; "I'm only going to put Billy ashore and send home what we've already caught. Mrs. O'Grady is passionately fond of salmon."

Billy was landed, and a large basket in which the salmon had been brought down to the boat was landed also—*empty*; and Murphy, lifting the basket as if it contained a considerable weight, placed it on Billy's head, and the sly young rascal bent beneath it, as if all the fish Murphy had pretended to take were really in it; and he went on his homeward way, with a tottering step, as if the load were too much for him.

"That boy," said Furlong, "will never be able to cawwy all those fish to the house."

"Oh, they won't be too much for him," said Dick. "Curse the fish! I wish they'd bite. That thief, Murphy, has had all the sport; but he's the best fisherman in the county, I'll own that."

The two boats all this time had been drifting down the river, and on opening a new reach of the stream, a somewhat extraordinary scene of fishing presented itself. It was not like Murphy's fishing, the result of a fertile invention, but the consequence of the evil destiny which presided over all the proceedings of Handy Andy.

The fishing party in the boats beheld another fishing party on shore, with this difference in the nature of what they sought to catch, that, while they in the boats were looking for salmon, those on the shore were seeking for a post-chaise, and as about a third part of a vehicle so called was apparent above the water, Furlong exclaimed with extreme surprise,

"Well! if it ain't a post-chaise!"

"Oh! that's nothing extraordinary," said Dick;— "common enough here."

"How do you mean?"

"We've a custom here of running steeple-chases in post-chaises."

"Oh, thank you," said Furlong; "come, that's *too* good."

"You don't believe it, I see," said Dick; "but you did not believe the salmon fishing till you saw it."

"Oh, come now! How the deuce could you leap a ditch in a post-chaise?"

"I never said we leaped ditches; I only said we rode steeple-chases. The system is this: you go for a given point, taking high-road, by-road, plain, or lane, as the case may be, making the best of your way how you can. Now, our horses in this country are celebrated for being good swimmers, so it's a favourite plan to shirk a bridge sometimes by swimming a river."

"But no post-chaise will float," said Furlong, regularly arguing against Dick's mendacious absurdity.

"Oh! we're prepared for that here. The chaises are made light, have cork bottoms, and all the solid work is made hollow; the doors are made water-tight, and if the stream runs strong the passenger jumps out and swims."

"But that's not fair," said Furlong; "it alters the weight."

"Oh! it's allowed on both sides," said Dick, "so it's all the same. It's as good for the goose as the gander."

"I wather imagine it is much fitter for geese and ganders than human beings. I know I should wather be a goose on the occasion."

All this time they were nearing the party on shore, and as the post-chaise became more developed, so did the personages on the bank of the river; and amongst these Dick Dawson saw Handy Andy in the custody of two men, and Squire O'Grady shaking his fist in his face and storming at him. How all this party came there, it is necessary to explain. When Handy Andy had deposited Furlong at Merryvale, he drove back to pick up the fallen postilion and his brother on the road; but before he reached them he had to pass a public house—I say, *had* to pass—but he didn't. Andy stopped, as every honourable postilion is bound to do, to drink the health of the gentleman who gives him the last half-crown; and he was so intent on "doing that same," as they say in Ireland, that Andy's driving be came very equivocal afterwards. In short, he drove the post-chaise into the river; the horses got disentangled by kicking the traces, which were very willing to break into pieces; and Andy, by sticking to the neck of the horse he rode, got out of the water. The horses got home without the post-chaise, and the other post-chaise and pair got home without a postilion, so that Owny Doyle was roused from his bed by the neighing of the horses at the gate of the inn. Great was his surprise at the event, as, half clad and a candle in his hand, he saw two pair of horses, one chaise, and no driver, at his door. The next morning the plot thickened; Squire O'Grady came to know if a gentleman had arrived at the town on his way to Neck-or-Nothing Hall. The answer was in the affirmative. Then "where was he?" became the question. Then the report arrived of the post-chaise being upset in the river. Then came stories of postilions falling off, of postilions being changed, of Handy Andy being employed to take the gentleman to the place; and out of these materials the story became current that "an English gentleman was dhrownded in the river in a post-chaise." O'Grady set off directly with a party to have the river dragged, and near the spot, encountering Handy Andy, he ordered him to be seized, and accused him of murdering his friend.

It was in this state of things that the boats approached the party on the land, and the moment Dick Dawson saw Handy Andy, he put out his oars, and pulled away as hard as he could. At the moment he did so, Andy caught sight of him, and pointing out Furlong and Dick to O'Grady, he shouted, "There he is!—there he is!—I never murdhered him! There he is!—stop him!—Misther Dick, stop, for the love o' God!"

"What is all this about?" said Furlong, in great amazement.

"Oh, he's a process-server," said Dick; "the people are going to drown him, maybe."

"To dwown him!" said Furlong in horror.

"If he has luck," said Dick, "they'll only give him a good ducking; but we had better have nothing to do with it. I would not like you to be engaged in one of these popular riots."

"I shouldn't wellish it, myself," said Furlong.

"Pull away, Dick!" said Murphy; "let them kill the blackguard, if they like."

"But will they kill him weally?" inquired Furlong, somewhat horrified.

"'Faith, it's just as the whim takes them," said Murphy; "but as we wish to be popular in the hustings, we must let them kill as many as they please."

Andy still shouted loud enough to be heard. "Misther Dick, they're goin' to murdher me!"

"Poor wretch!" said Furlong, with a very uneasy shudder.

"Maybe you'd think it right for us to land and rescue him," said Murphy, affecting to put about the boat.

"Oh, by no means," said Furlong. "You're better acquainted with the customs of the countwy than I am."

"Then we'll row back to dinner as fast as we can," said Murphy. "Pull away, my hearties!" and, as he bent to his oars, he began bellowing the Canadian Boat-Song, to drown Andy's roars; and when he howled,

"Our voices keep tune—"

there never was a more practical burlesque upon the words; but as he added—

"Our oars keep time,"

he seemed to have such a pleasure in pulling, and looked so lively and florid, that Furlong, chilled by his inactivity on the water, and whose subsequent horror at the thought of seeing a real, regular Irish drowning of a process-server before his face, had produced a shivering fit, requested Murtough to let him have an oar, to restore circulation by exercise. Murtough complied; but the novice had not pulled many strokes, before his awkward handling of the oar produced that peculiar effect called "catching a crab," and a smart blow upon his chest sent him heels over head under the thwarts of the boat.

"Wha-wha-a-t's that?" gasped Furlong, as he scrambled up again.

"You only caught a crab," said Murtough.

"Good heaven!" said Furlong, "you don't mean to say there are crabs as well as salmon in the river."

"Just as many crabs as salmon," said Murtough; "pull away, my hearty."

"Row, brothers, row—the stream runs fast—
The rapids are near, and the daylight's past!"

XII

THE BOATS DOUBLED ROUND AN angle in the river, and Andy was left in the hands of Squire O'Grady, still threatening vengeance; but Andy, as long, as the boats remained in sight, heard nothing but his own sweet voice, shouting at the top of its pitch, "They're going to murdher me!—Misther Dick, Misther Dick, come back for the love o' God!"

"What are you roaring like a bull for?" said the Squire.

"Why wouldn't I roar, sir? A bull would roar if he had as much rayson."

"A bull has more reason than ever you had, you calf," said the Squire.

"Sure there he is, and can explain it all to you," said Andy, pointing after the boats.

"Who is there?" asked the Squire.

"Misther Dick, and the jintleman himself that I dhruv there."

"Drove where?"

"To the Squire's."

"What Squire's?

"Squire Egan's, to be sure."

"Hold your tongue, you rascal; you're either drunk still, or telling lies. The gentleman I mean wouldn't go to Mister Egan's: he was coming to me."

"That's the jintleman I dhruv—that's all I know. He was in the shay, and was nigh shootin' me; and Micky Doolin stopped on the road, when his brother was nigh killed, and towld me to get up, for he wouldn't go no farther, when the jintleman objected—"

"What did the gentleman object to?"

"He objected to Pether goin' into the shay."

"Who is Peter?

"Pether Doolin, to be sure."

"And what brought Peter Doolin there?"

"He fell off the horse's—"

"Wasn't it Mick Doolin you said was driving, but a moment ago?"

"Ay, sir; but that was th'other shay."

"What other chaise, you vagabond?"

"Th'other shay, your honour, that I never seen at all, good or bad—
only Pether."

"What diabolical confusion you are making of the story, to be sure!—
there's no use in talking to you here, I see. Bring him after me," said the
Squire to some of his people standing by. "I must keep him in custody
till something more satisfactory is made out about the matter."

"Sure it's not makin' a presner of me you'd be?" said Andy.

"You shall be kept in confinement, you scoundrel, till something is
heard of this strange gentleman. I'm afraid he's drowned."

"D—l a dhrown'd. I dhruv him to Squire Egan's, I'll take my book
oath."

"That's downright nonsense, sir. He would as soon go into Squire
Egan's house as go to Fiddler's Green."

"Faith, then, there's worse places than Fiddler's Green," said Andy, "as
some people may find out one o' these days."

"I think, boys," said O'Grady to the surrounding countrymen, "we
must drag the river."

"Dhrag the river, if you plase," said Andy; "but, for the tender mercy
o' heaven, don't dhrag me to jail! By all the crosses in a yard o' check, I
dhruv the jintleman to Squire Egan's!—and there he was in that boat I
showed you five minutes agone."

"Bring him after me," said O'Grady. "The fellow is drunk still, or
forgets all about it; I must examine him again. Take him over to the hall,
and lock him up in the justice-room till I go home."

"Arrah, sure, your honour—" said Andy, commencing an appeal.

"If you say another word, you scoundrel," said the Squire, shaking
his whip at him, "I'll commit you to jail this minute. Keep a sharp eye

after him, Molloy," were the last words of the Squire to a stout-built peasant who took Andy in charge as the Squire mounted his horse and rode away.

Andy was marched off to Neck-or-Nothing Hall; and, in compliance with the Squire's orders, locked up in the justice-room. This was an apartment where the Squire in his magisterial capacity dispensed what he called justice, and what he possibly meant to be such; but poor Justice, coming out of Squire O'Grady's hands, was something like the little woman in the song, who, having her petticoats cut short while she was asleep, exclaimed on her waking,

"As sure as I'm a little woman, this is none of I."

Only that Justice in the present instance doubted her identity, not from her nakedness, but from the peculiar dressing Squire O'Grady bestowed upon her. She was so muffled up in O'Gradyism, that her own mother, who by the same token was Themis, wouldn't know her. Indeed, if I remember, Justice is worse off than mortals respecting her parentage; for while there are many people who do not know who were their fathers, poets are uncertain who was Justice's mother:—some say Aurora, some say Themis. Now, if I might indulge at this moment in a bit of reverie, it would not be unreasonable to suppose that it is the classic disposition of Ireland, which is known to be a very ancient country, that tends to make the operations of Justice assimilate with the uncertainty of her birth; for her dispensations there are as distinct as if they were the offspring of two different influences. One man's justice is not another man's justice;—which I suppose must arise from the difference of opinion as to who or what Justice is. Perhaps the rich people, who incline to power, may venerate Justice more as the child of Jupiter and Themis; while the unruly worship her as the daughter of Titan and Aurora; for undoubtedly the offspring of *Aurora* must be most welcome to "*Peep-o'-day boys.*"

Well,—not to indulge further in reverie,—Andy, I say, was locked up in the justice-room; and as I have been making all these observations about Justice, a few words will not be thrown away about the room which she was supposed to inhabit. Then I must say Squire O'Grady did not use her well. The room was a cold, comfortless apartment, with a plastered wall and an earthen floor, save at one end, where a raised platform of boards sustained a desk and one high office-chair. No other seat was in the room, nor was there any lateral window, the room being lighted from the top, so that Justice could be no way interested with the country outside—she could only contemplate her native heaven through the sky-light. Behind the desk were placed a rude shelf, where some "modern instances," and old ones too, were lying covered with dust—and a gunrack, where some carbines with fixed bayonets were paraded in show of authority; so that, to an imaginative mind, the aspect of the books and the fire-arms gave the notion of JUSTICE on the shelf, and LAW on the rack.

But Andy thought not of those things; he had not the imagination which sometimes gives a prisoner a passing pleasure in catching a whimsical conceit from his situation, and, in the midst of his anxiety, anticipating the satisfaction he shall have in saying a good thing, even at the expense of his own suffering. Andy only knew that he was locked up in the justice-room for something he never did. He had only sense enough to feel that he was wronged, without the spirit to wish himself righted; and he sauntered up and down the cold, miserable room, anxiously awaiting the arrival of "his honour, Squire O'Grady," to know what would be done with him, and wondering if they could hang him for upsetting a post-chaise in which a gentleman *had been* riding, rather than brooding future means of redress for his false imprisonment.

There was no window to look out of—he had not the comfort of seeing a passing fellow-creature; for the sight of one's kind is a comfort. He could not even see the green earth and the freshness of nature, which, though all unconsciously, has still a soothing influence on the most uncultivated mind; he had nothing but the walls to look at, which were blank, save here and there that a burnt stick, in the hand of one of the young O'Grady's, emulated the art of a Sandwich islander, and sketched faces as grotesque as any pagan could desire for his idol; or figures, after the old well-established schoolboy manner, which in the present day is called Persian painting, "warranted to be taught in three lessons." Now, this bespeaks degeneracy in the arts; for in the time we write of, boys and girls acquired the art without any lessons at all, and abundant proofs of this intuitive talent existed on the aforesaid walls. Napoleon and Wellington were fighting a duel, while Nelson stood by to see fair play, he having nothing better to do, as the battle of Trafalgar, represented in the distance, could, of course, go on without him. The anachronism of jumbling Bonaparte, Wellington, and Nelson together, was a trifle amongst the O'Gradys, as they were nearly as great proficients in history, ancient and modern, as in the fine arts. Amidst these efforts of genius appeared many an old rhyme, scratched with rusty nails by rustier policemen, while lounging in the justice-room during the legal decisions of the great O'Grady; and all these were gone over again and again by Andy, till they were worn out, all but one,—a rough representation of a man hanging.

This possessed a sort of fascination for poor Andy; for at last, relinquishing all others, he stood riveted before it, and muttered to himself, "I wondher can they hang me—sure it's no murdher I done—but who knows what witnesses they might get? and these times they sware mighty hard; and Squire O'Grady has such a pack o' blackguards about him, sure he could get any thing swore he liked. Oh! wirra! wirra! what'll I do at all, at all—faix! I wouldn't like to be hanged—oh! look at him there—just the last kick in him—and a disgrace to my poor mother into the bargain. Augh!—but it's a dirty death to die—to be hung up, like a dog over a gate, or an ould hat on a peg, just that-a-way;"—and he extended his arm as he spoke, suspending his *caubeen*, while he looked with disgust at the effigy. "But sure they *can't* hang me—though now I remember, Squire Egan towl me long ago I'd be hanged some day or other—I wondher does my mother know I'm tuk away— and Oonah too: the craythur would be sorry for me.—Maybe if the mother spoke to Squire Egan, his honour would say a good word for me. Though that wouldn't do; for him and Squire O'Grady's bitther inimies now, though they wor once good frinds.—Och hone!—sure that's the way o' the world; and a cruel hard world it is—so it is. Sure 'twould be well to be out of it a'most, and in a betther world. I hope there's no po'-chaises in heaven!"

The soliloquy of poor Andy was interrupted by a low measured sound of thumping, which his accustomed ear at once distinguished to be the result of churning; the room in which he was confined being one of a range of offices stretching backward from the principal building, and next door to the dairy. Andy had grown tired by this time of his repeated contemplation of the rhymes and the sketches, his own thoughts thereon, and his long confinement; and now the monotonous sound of the churn-dash falling on his ear, acted as a sort of *husho*,[1] and the worried and wearied Andy at last lay down on the platform, and fell asleep to the bumping lullaby.

1.   The nurses' song for setting a child to sleep, which they pronounce softly, *huzzho*."

XIII

THE SPORTSMEN HAVING RETURNED FROM their fishing excursion to dinner, were seated round the hospitable board of Squire Egan; Murphy and Dick in high glee, at still successfully hoodwinking Furlong, and carrying on their mystification with infinite frolic.

The soup had been removed, and they were in the act of enjoying the salmon, which had already given so much enjoyment, when a loud knocking at the door announced the arrival of some fresh guest.

"Did you ask any one to dinner, my dear?" inquired Mrs. Egan of her good-humoured lord, who was the very man to invite any friend he met in the course of the day, and forget it after.

"No, my dear," answered the Squire. "Did you, Dick?" said he.

Dick replied in the negative, and said he had better go and see who it was; for looks of alarm had been exchanged between him, the Squire, and Murphy, lest any stranger should enter the room without being apprised of the hoax going forward; and Dawson had just reached the door, on his cautionary mission, when it was suddenly thrown wide open, and in walked, with a rapid step and bustling air, an active little gentleman dressed in black, who was at Mrs. Egan's side in a moment, exclaiming with a very audible voice and much *empressement* of manner,

"My dear Mrs. Egan, how do you do? I'm delighted to see you. Took a friend's privilege, you see, and have come unbidden to claim the hospitality of your table. The fact is, I was making a sick visit to this side of my parish; and, finding it impossible to get home in time to my own dinner, I had no scruple in laying yours under contribution."

Now this was the Protestant clergyman of the parish, whose political views were in opposition to those of Mr. Egan; but the good hearts of both men prevented political feeling from interfering, as in Ireland it too often does, with the social intercourse of life. Still, however, even if Dick Dawson had got out of the room in time, this was not the man to assist them in covering their hoax on Furlong, and the scene became excessively ludicrous the moment the reverend gentleman made his appearance. Dick, the Squire, and Murphy, opened their eyes at each other, while Mrs. Egan grew as red as scarlet when Furlong stared at her in astonishment as the new-comer mentioned her name,—she stammered out welcome as well as she could, and called for a chair for Mr. Bermingham, with all sorts of kind inquiries for Mrs. Bermingham and the little Berminghams,—for the Bermingham manufactory in that line was extensive.

While the reverend doctor was taking his seat, spreading his napkin, and addressing a word to each round the table, Furlong turned to Fanny Dawson, beside whom he was sitting, (and who, by the by, could not resist a fit of laughter on the occasion,) and said, with a bewildered look,

"Did he not addwess *Madame* as Mistwess Egan?"

"Yeth," said Fanny, with admirable readiness; "but whithper." And as Furlong inclined his head towards her, she whispered in his ear—"You muthn't mind him—he's mad, poor man!—that is, a little inthane,—and thinks every lady is Mrs. Egan.—An unhappy patshion, poor fellow!— but *quite harmleth*."

Furlong uttered a very prolonged "Oh!" at Fanny's answer to his inquiry, and looked sharply round the table; for there was an indefinable something in the conduct of every one at the moment of Mr. Bermingham's entrance that attracted his attention; and the name "Egan," and everybody's *fidgityness*, (which is the only word I can apply,) roused his suspicion. Fanny's answer only half satisfied him; and looking at Mrs. Egan, who could not conquer her confusion, he remarked,— "How *vewy* wed Mistress O'Gwady gwew!"

"Oh, tshe can't help blutching, poor thoul! when he thays 'Egan' to her, and thinks her his *furth* love."

"How *vewy* widiculous, to be sure," said Furlong.

"Haven't you innothent mad people thumtimes in England?" said Fanny.

"Oh, vewy," said Furlong; "but this appea's to me so wema'kably stwange an abbewation."

"Oh," returned Fanny with quickness, "I thuppose people go mad on their ruling patshion, and the ruling patshion of the Irish, you know, is love."

The conversation all this time was going on in other quarters, and Furlong heard Mr. Bermingham talking of his having preached last Sunday in his new church.

"Suwely," said he to Fanny, "they would not pe'mit an insane cle'gyman to pweach?"

"Oh," said Fanny, almost suffocating with laughter, "he only *thinkth* he's a clergyman."

"How vewy dwoll you are!" said Furlong.

"Now you're only quithing me," said Fanny, looking with affected innocence in the face of the unfortunate young gentleman she had been quizzing most unmercifully the whole day.

"Oh, Miste' O'Gwady," said Furlong, "we saw them going to dwown a man to-day."

"Indeed!" said the Squire, reddening, as he saw Mr. Bermingham stare at his being called O'Grady; so, to cover the blot, and stop Furlong, he asked him to take wine.

"Do they often dwown people here?" continued Furlong, after he had bowed.

"Not that I know of," said the Squire.

"But are not the lowe' o'ders wather given to what Lo'd Bacon calls—"

"Who cares about Lord Bacon?" said Murphy.

"My dear sir, you supwise me!" said Furlong, in utter amazement. "Lo'd Bacon's sayings—"

"By my sowl," said Murphy, "both himself and his sayings are very *rusty* by this time."

"Oh, I see, Miste' Muffy.—You neve' will be sewious."

"God forbid!" said Murphy,—"at dinner, at least,—or after. Seriousness is only a morning amusement;—it makes a very poor figure in the evening."

"By the by," said Mr. Bermingham, "talking of drowning, I heard a very odd story to-day from O'Grady. You and he, I believe," said the clergyman, addressing Egan, "are not on as good terms as you were."

At this speech Furlong did *rather* open his eyes, the Squire hummed and hawed, Murphy coughed, Mrs. Egan looked into her plate, and Dick, making a desperate dash to the rescue, asked Furlong which he preferred, a single or a double-barrelled gun.

Mr. Bermingham, perceiving the sensation his question created, thought he had touched upon forbidden ground, and therefore did not repeat his question, and Fanny whispered Furlong that one of the stranger's mad peculiarities was mistaking one person for another; but all this did not satisfy Furlong, whose misgivings as to the real name of his host, were growing stronger every moment. At last Mr. Bermingham, without alluding to the broken friendship between Egan and O'Grady, returned to the "odd story" he had heard that morning about drowning.

"'Tis a very strange affair," said he, "and our side of the country is all alive about it. A gentleman who was expected from Dublin last night at Neck-or-Nothing Hall, arrived, as it is ascertained, at the village, and thence took a post-chaise, since which time he has not been heard of; and as a post-chaise was discovered this morning, sunk in the river close by Ballysloughgutthery bridge, it is suspected the gentleman has been drowned either by accident or design. The postilion is in confinement, on suspicion; and O'Grady has written to the Castle about it to-day, for the gentleman was a government officer."

"Why, sir," said Furlong, "that must be me!"

"*You*, sir!" said Mr. Bermingham, whose turn it was to be surprised now.

"Yes, sir," said Furlong "I took a post-chaise at the village last night,—and I'm an office' of the gove'ment."

"But you're not drowned, sir,—and he was." said Bermingham.

"To be su'e I'm not dwowned; but I'm the pe'son."

"Quite impossible, sir," said Mr. Bermingham. "You can't be the person."

"Why, sir, do you expect to pe'swade me out of my own identity?"

"Oh," said Murphy, "there will be no occasion to prove identity till the body is found, and the coroner's inquest sits;—that's the law, sir,—at least, in Ireland."

Furlong's bewildered look at the unblushing impudence of Murphy was worth anything. While he was dumb from astonishment, Mr. Bermingham, with marked politeness, said,

"Allow me, sir, for a moment to explain to you. You see, it could not be you, for the gentleman was going to Mr. O'Grady's."

"Well, sir," said Furlong, "and here I am."

The wide stare of the two men as they looked at each other was killing; and while Furlong's face was turned towards Mr. Bermingham, Fanny caught the clergyman's eye, tapped her forehead with the forefinger of her right hand, shook her head, and turned up her eye with an expression of pity, to indicate that Furlong was not quite right in his mind.

"Oh, I beg, pardon, sir," said Mr. Berrningham. "I see it's a mistake of mine."

"There certainly is a vewy gweat mistake somewhere," said Furlong, who was now bent on a very direct question. "Pway, Miste' O'Gwady," said he, addressing Egan,—"that is, if you *are* Miste' O'Gwady,—will you tell me, *are* you Miste' O'Gwady?"

"Sir," said the Squire, "you have chosen to call me O'Grady ever since you came here,—but my name is Egan."

"What!—the member for the county?" cried Furlong, horrified.

"Yes," said the Squire, laughing, "do you want a frank?"

"'Twill save your friends postage," said Dick, "when you write to them to say you're safe."

"Miste' Wegan," said Furlong, with an attempt at offended dignity, "I conside' myself vewy ill used."

"You're the first man I ever heard of being ill used in Merryvale House," said Murphy.

"Sir, it is a gwievous w'ong!"

"What *is* all this about?" asked Mr. Bermingham.

"My dear friend," said the Squire, laughing, though, indeed, that was not peculiar to *him*, for every one round the table, save the victim, was doing the same thing, (as for Fanny, she *shouted*,)—"My dear friend, this gentleman came to my house last night, and I took him for a friend of Moriarty's, whom I have been expecting for some days. *He* thought, it appears, this was Neck Hall, and thus a mutual mistake has arisen. All I can say is that you are most welcome, Mr. Furlong, to the hospitality of this house as long as you please."

"But, sir, you should not have allowed me to wemain in you' house," said Furlong.

"That's a doctrine," said the Squire, "in which you will find it difficult to make an Irish host coincide."

"But you must have known, sir, that it was not my intention to come to your house."

"How could I know that, sir?" said the Squire jocularly.

"Why, Miste' Wegan—you know—that is—in fact—d—n it, sir," said Furlong at last, losing his temper, "you know I told you all about our electioneering tactics."

A loud laugh was all the response Furlong received to this outbreak.

"Well, sir," repeated he, "I pwotest it is extremely unfair!"

"You know, my dear sir," said Dick, "we Irish are such *poor ignorant creatures*, according to your own account, that we can make no use of the knowledge with which you have so generously supplied us."

"You know," said the Squire, "we have no *real* finesse."

"Sir," said Furlong, growing sulky, "there is a certain finesse that is *fair*, and another that is *unfair*—and I pwotest against—"

"Pooh! pooh!" said Murphy. "Never mind trifles. Just wait till to-morrow, and I'll show you even better salmon-fishing than you had to-day."

"Sir, no considewation would make me wemain anothe' wower in this house."

Murphy, screwing his lips together, puffed out something between a whistle and the blowing out of a candle, and ventured to suggest to Furlong he had better wait even a couple of hours, till he had got his allowance of claret. "Remember the adage, sir—'*In vino veritas*,' and we'll tell you all *our* electioneering secrets after we've had enough wine."

"As soon, Miste' Wegan," said Furlong, quite chap-fallen, "as you can tell me how I can get to the house to which I *intended* to go, I will be weady to bid you good evening."

"If you are determined, Mr. Furlong, to remain here no longer, I shall not press my hospitality upon you: whenever you decide on going, my carriage shall be at your service."

"The soone' the bette', sir," said Furlong, retreating still further into a cold and sulky manner.

The Squire made no further attempt to conciliate him; he merely said, "Dick, ring the bell. Pass the claret, Murphy."

The bell was rung—the claret passed—a servant entered, and orders were given by the Squire that the carriage should be at the door as soon as possible. In the interim, Dick Dawson, the Squire, and Murphy, laughed as if nothing had happened, and Mrs. Egan conversed in an under-tone with Mr. Bermingham. Fanny looked mischievous, and Furlong kept his hand on the foot of his glass, and shoved it about something in the fashion of an uncertain chess-player, who does not know where to put the piece on which he has laid his finger.

The carriage was soon announced, and Mrs. Egan, as Furlong seemed so anxious to go, rose from table; and as she retired he made her a cold and formal bow. He attempted a tender look, and soft word, to Fanny,— for Furlong, who thought himself a *beau garçon,* had been playing off his attractions upon her all day, but the mischievously merry Fanny Dawson, when she caught the sheepish eye, and heard the mumbled gallantry of the Castle Adonis, could not resist a titter, which obliged her to hide her dimpling cheek and pearly teeth in her handkerchief as she passed to the door. The ladies being gone, the Squire asked Furlong, would he not have some more wine before he went.

"No, thank you, Miste' Wegan," replied he, "after being twicked in the manner that a—"

"Mr. Furlong," said the Squire, "you have said quite enough about that. When you came into my house last night, sir, I had no intention of practising any joke upon you. You should have had the hospitality of an Irishman's house, without the consequence that has followed, had you not indulged in sneering at the Irishman's country, which, to your shame be it spoken, is *your own.* You vaunted your own superior intelligence and finesse over us, sir; and told us you came down to overthrow poor Pat in the trickery of electioneering movements. Under those circumstances, sir, I think what we have done is quite fair. We have shown you that you are no match for us in the finesse upon which you pride yourself so much; and the next time you talk of your countrymen, and attempt to undervalue them, just remember how you have been outwitted at Merryvale House. Good evening, Mr. Furlong. I hope we part without owing each other any ill-will." The Squire offered his hand, but Furlong drew up, and amidst such expletives as "weally," and "I must say," he at last made use of the word "atwocious."

"What's that you say?" said Dick. "You don't speak very plain, and I'd like to be sure of the last word you used."

"I mean to say that a—" and Furlong, not much liking the *tone* of Dick's question, was humming and hawing a sort of explanation of what "he meant to say," when Dick thus interrupted him,—

"I tell you this, Mr. Furlong,—all that has been done is my doing—I've humbugged you, sir—*humbugged*. I've sold you—dead. I've pump'd you, sir—your electioneering bag of tricks, *bribery*, and all, exposed; and, now go off to O'Grady, and tell him how the poor ignorant Irish have *done* you; and, see, Mr. Furlong," added Dick in a quiet under-tone, "if there's anything that either he or you don't like about the business, you shall have any satisfaction you like, and as often as you please."

"I shall *conside'* of that, sir," said Furlong, as he left the house, and entered the carriage, where he threw himself back in offended dignity, and soliloquized vow of vengeance. But the bumping of the carriage over a rough road disturbed the pleasing reveries of revenge, to awaken him to the more probable and less agreeable consequences likely to occur to himself for the blunder he had made; for, with all the puppy's self-sufficiency and conceit, he could not by any process of mental delusion conceal from himself the fact that he had been most tremendously *done,* and how his party would take it was a serious consideration. O'Grady, another horrid Irish squire—how should he face him? For a moment he thought it better to go back to Dublin, and he pulled the check-string—the carriage stopped—down went the front glass. "I say, coachman."

"I'm not the coachman, sir."

"Well, whoever you are—"

"I'm the groom only, sir; for the coachman was—"

"D—n it, I don't want to know who you are, or about your affairs. I
want you to listen to me—*cawn't* you listen."

"Yes, sir."

"Well, then—dwive to the village."

"I thought it was to the Hall I was to dhrive, sir."

"Do what you're told, sir,—the village!"

"What village, sir?" asked Mat, the groom—who knew well enough,
but from Furlong's impertinence did not choose to understand anything
gratuitously.

"Why the village I came fwom yeste'day."

"What village was that, sir?"

"How stoopid you are!—the village the mail goes to."

"Sure, the mail goes to all the villages in Ireland, sir."

"You pwovoking blockhead!—Good heavens, how *stoopid* you Iwish
are!—the village that leads to Dublin."

"Faith, they all lead to Dublin, sir."

"Confound you—you must know!—the posting village, you know—
that is, not the post town, if you know what a post town is."

"To be sure I do, sir—where they sell blankets, you mane."

"No!—no!—no!—I want to go to the village where they keep
postchaises—now you know."

"Faix, they have po'chayses in all the villages here; there's no betther
accommodation for man or baste in the world than here, sir."

Furlong was mute from downright vexation, till his rage got vent in
an oath, another denunciation of Irish stupidity, and at last a declaration
that the driver *must* know the village.

"How would I know it, sir, when you don't know it yourself?" asked
the groom; "I suppose it has a name to it, and if you tell me that, I'll
dhrive you there fast enough."

"I cannot wemember your howwid names here—it is a Bal, or Bally,
or some such gibbewish—"

Mat would not be enlightened.

"Is there not Bal or Bally something?"

"Oh a power o' Ballies, sir; there's Ballygash, and Ballyslash, and
Ballysmish, and Ballysmash, and"—so went on Mat, inventing a string
of Ballies till he was stopped by the enraged Furlong.

"None o' them! none o' them!" exclaimed he in a fury; "'tis something about 'dirt,' or 'mud.'"

"Maybe 'twould be *gutther*, sir," said Mat, who saw Furlong was near the mark and he thought he might as well make a virtue of telling him.

"I believe you're right" said Furlong.

"Then it is Ballysloughgutthery you want to go to, sir."

"That's the name!" said Furlong, snappishly; "dwive *there!*" and, hastily pulling up the glass, he threw himself back again in the carriage. Another troubled vision of what the secretary would say came across him, and, after ten minutes' balancing the question, and trembling at the thoughts of an official blowing up, he thought he had better even venture on an Irish squire; so the check-string was again pulled, and the glass hastily let down.

Mat halted. "Yis, sir," said Mat.

"I think I've changed my mind—dwive to the Hall!"

"I wish you towld me, sir, before I took the last turn—we're nigh a mile towards the village now."

"No matte', sir!" said Furlong; "dwive where I tell you."

Up went the glass again, and Mat turned round the horses and carriage with some difficulty in a narrow by-road.

Another vision came across the bewildered fancy of Furlong—the certainty of the fury of O'Grady—the immediate contempt, as well as anger, attendant on his being bamboozled; and the result, at last, being the same, in drawing down the secretary's anger. This produced another change of intention, and he let down the glass for the third time,—once more changed his orders as concisely as possible, and pulled it up again. All this time Mat was laughing internally at the bewilderment of the stranger, and as he turned round the carriage again he exclaimed, "By this and that, you're as hard to dhrive as a pig; for you'll neither go one road nor th'other." He had not proceeded far, when Furlong determined to face O'Grady instead of the castle, and the last and final order for another turnabout was given. Mat hardly suppressed an oath; but respect for his master's carriage and horses stopped him. The glass of the carriage was not pulled up this time, and Mat was asked a few questions about the Hall, and at last about the Squire. Now Mat had acuteness enough to fathom the cause of Furlong's indecision, and determined to make him as unhappy as he could; therefore, to the question of "What sort of a man the Squire was," Mat, reechoing the question, replied—"What sort of a man, sir?—faith, not a man at all, sir; he's the divil."

Furlong pulled up the glass, and employed the interval between Mat's answer and reaching the Hall in making up his mind as to how he should "face the devil."

The carriage, after skirting a high and ruinous wall for some time, stopped before a gateway that had once been handsome; and Furlong was startled by the sound of a most thundering bell, which the vigorous pull of Mat stimulated to its utmost pitch; the baying of dogs which followed was terrific. A savage-looking gatekeeper made his appearance with a light—not in a lantern, but shaded with his tattered hat: many questions and answers ensued, and at last the gate was opened. The carriage proceeded up a very rough avenue, and stopped before a large, rambling sort of building, which even moonlight could exhibit to be very much out of repair. After repeated knocking at the door, (for Mat knew *his* squire and the other squire were not friends now, and that he might be impudent,) the door was unchained and unbarred, and Furlong deposited in Neck-or-Nothing Hall.

XIV

"Such is the custom of Branksome hall."—*Lay of the Last Minstrel*.

NECK-OR-NOTHING HALL

CANTO I

Ten good nights and ten good days
It would take to tell the ways,
Various, many, and amazing,
Neck-or-nothing bangs all praising;
Wonders great and wonders small
Are found in Neck-or-Nothing Hall.

Racing rascals, of ten a twain,
Who care not a rush for hall nor rain,
Messages swiftly to go or to come,
Or duck a taxman or harry a bum,[1]
Or "clip a server,"[2] did blithely lie
In the stable parlour next to the sky.[3]
Dinners, save chance ones, seldom had they,
Unless they could nibble their beds of hay,
But the less they got, they were hardier all—
'Twas the custom of Neck-or-Nothing Hall.

One lord there sat in that terrible hall;
Two ladies came at his terrible call,—
One his mother, and one his wife,
Each afraid of her separate life;
Three girls who trembled—Four boys who shook
Five times a-day at his lowering look;
Six blunderbusses in goodly show,
Seven horse-pistols were ranged below;
Eight domestics, great and small,
In idleness, did nothing but curse them all;
Nine state-beds, where no one slept—
Ten for family use were kept;
Dogs Eleven with bums to make free,
With a bold Thirteen[4] in the treasury!
Such its numerical strength, I guess;
It can't be more, but it may be less.

Tar-barrels new, and feathers old,
Are ready, I trow, for the caitiff bold
    Who dares to invade
    The stormy shade
    Of the grim O'Grade,
    In his hunting hold.

When the iron-tongue of the old gate bell
Summons the growling groom from his cell,
    Through cranny and crook,
    They peer and they look,
With guns to send the intruders to heaven.[5]
But when passwords pass
That might "sarve a mass,"[6]
Then bars are drawn and chains let fall,
And you get into Neck-or-Nothing Hall.

Canto II

And never a doubt
   But when your are in,
   If you love a whole skin,
   I'll wager and win,
You'll be glad to get out.

Doctor Growling's Metrical Romance.

The bird's-eye view which the doctor's peep from Parnassus has afforded, may furnish the imagination of the reader with materials to create in his own mind a vague, yet not unjust, notion of Neck-or-Nothing Hall; but certain details of the hall itself, its inmates, and its customs, may be desired by the matter-of-fact reader or the more minutely curious, and as an author has the difficult task before him of trying to please all tastes, something more definite is required.

The hall itself was, as we have said, a rambling sort of structure. Ramifying from a solid centre, which gave the notion of a founder well to do in the world, additions, without any architectural pretensions to fitness, were *stuck* on here and there, as whim or necessity suggested or demanded, and a most incongruous mass of gables, roofs, and chimneys, odd windows and blank walls, was the consequence. According to the circumstances of the occupants who inherited the property, the building was either increased or neglected. A certain old bachelor, for example, who in the course of events inherited the property, had no necessity for nurses, nursery-maids, and their consequent suite of apartments; and as he never aspired to the honour of matrimony, the ball-room, the drawing-room, and extra bed-chambers were neglected: while, he being a fox-hunter, a new kennel and range of stables were built, the dining-room enlarged, and all the ready-money he could get at spent in augmenting the plate, to keep pace with the racing-cups he won, and proudly displayed at his drinking bouts; and when he died suddenly (broke his neck), the plate was seized at the suit of his wine-merchant; and as the heir next in succession got the property in a ruinous condition, it was impossible to keep a stud of horses along with a wife and a large family, so the stables and kennel went to decay, while the lady's and family apartments could only be patched up. When the house was dilapidated, the grounds about it, of course, were ill kept. Fine old trees were there, originally intended to afford shade to walks which were so neglected as to be no more walkable than any other part of the grounds—the vista of aspiring stems indicated where an avenue had been, but neither hoe nor rolling-stone had, for many a year, checked the growth of grass or weed.—So much for the outside of the house: now for the inside.

That had witnessed many a thoughtless, expensive, headlong, and irascible master, but never one more so than the present owner; added to which, he had the misfortune of being unpopular. Other men, thoughtless, and headlong, and irritable as he, have lived and had friends, but there was something about O'Grady that was felt, perhaps, more than it could be defined, which made him unpleasing:—perhaps the homely phrase "cross-grained" may best express it, and O'Grady was, essentially, a cross-grained man. The estate, when he got it, was pretty heavily saddled, and the "galled jade" did not "wince" the less for his riding.

A good jointure to his mother was chargeable on the property, and this was an excuse on all occasions for the Squire's dilatory payment in other quarters.

"Sir," he would say, "my mother's jointure is sacred—it is more than the estate can well bear, it is true—but it is a sacred claim, and I would sooner sacrifice my life—my, *honour,* sir, than see that claim neglected!—" Now all this sounded mighty fine, but his mother could never get her jointure regularly paid, and was obliged to live in the house with him: she was some what of *an oddity*, and had apartments to herself, and, as long as she was let alone, and allowed to read romances in quiet, did not complain; and whenever a stray ten pound note *did* fall into her hands, she gave the greater part of it to her younger grand-daughter, who was fond of flowers and plants, and supported a little conservatory on her grandmother's bounty, she paying the tribute of a bouquet to the old lady when the state of her botanical prosperity could afford it. The eldest girl was a favourite of an uncle, and her passion being dogs, all the presents her uncle made her in money were converted into canine curiosities; while the youngest girl took an interest in the rearing of poultry. Now the boys, varying in age from eight to

fourteen, had their separate favourites too:—one loved bull dogs and
terriers, another game cocks, the third ferrets, and the fourth rabbits
and pigeons. These multifarious tastes produced strange results.—In the
house, flowers and plants, indicating refinement of taste and costliness,
were strongly contrasted with broken plaster, soil hangings, and faded
paint; an expensive dog might be seen lapping cream out of a shabby
broken plate; a never-ending sequence of wars raged among the
dependant favourites; the bull dogs and terriers chopping up the ferrets,
the ferrets killing the game cocks, the game cocks killing the tame
poultry and rabbits, and the rabbits destroying the garden, assisted by the
flying reserve of pigeons. It was a sort of Irish retaliation, so amusingly
exemplified in the nursery jingle:

> The water began to quench the fire,
> The fire began to burn the stick,
> The stick began to beat the dog,
> The dog began to bite the kid.

In the midst of all these distinct and clashing tastes, that of Mrs.
O'Grady (the wife) must not be forgotten; her weak point was a feather
bed. Good soul! anxious that whoever slept under her roof should lie
softly, she would go to the farthest corner of the county to secure an
accession to her favourite property—and such a collection of luxurious
feather-beds never was seen in company with such rickety bedsteads,
and tattered and mildewed curtains, in rooms uncarpeted, whose paper
was dropping off the wall: well might it be called paper-hanging,
indeed!—whose washing-tables were of deal, and whose delft was of
the plainest ware, and even that minus sundry handles and spouts. Nor
was the renowned O'Grady without his hobby, too. While the various
members of his family were thwarting each other, his master mischief
was thwarting them all; like some wicked giant looking down on a
squabble of dwarfs, and ending the fight by kicking them all right and
left. Then *he* had *his* troop of pets, too—idle blackguards who were
slingeing[7] about the place eternally, keeping up a sort of *cordon sanitaire*
to prevent the pestilential presence of a bailiff, which is so catching,
and turns to jail fever:—a disease which had been fatal in the family.

O'Grady never ventured beyond his domain, except on the back of a fleet horse—there he felt secure: indeed, the place he most dreaded legal assault in, was his own house, where he apprehended trickery might invade him: a carriage might be but a feint, and hence the great circumspection in the opening of doors.

From the nature of the establishment, thus hastily sketched, the reader will see what an ill-regulated jumble it was. The master, in difficulties, had disorderly people hanging about his place for his personal security; from these very people his boys picked up the love of dog-fights, cock-fights, &c.; and they, from the fights of their pets, fought amongst themselves, and were always fighting with their sisters; so the reader will see the "metrical romance" was not overcharged in its rhymes on Neck-or-Nothing Hall.

When Furlong entered the hall he gave his name to a queer-looking servant, with wild scrubby hair, a dirty face, a tawdry livery, worse for wear, which had manifestly been made for a larger man, and hung upon its present possessor like a coat upon a clothes-horse; his cotton stockings, meant to be white, and clumsy shoes, meant to be black, met each other half-way, and split the difference in a pleasing neutral tint. Leaving Furlong standing in the hall, he clattered up stairs, and a dialogue ensued between master and man, so loud that Furlong could hear the half of it, and his own name in a tone of doubt, with that of "Egan" in a tone of surprise, and that of his "sable majesty" in a tone of anger, rapidly succeeded one another; then such broken words and sentences as these ensued,—"fudge!—humbug!—rascally trick!—eh!—by the hokey, they'd better take care!—put the scoundrel under the pump!"

Furlong more than half suspected it was to him this delicate attention was intended, and began to feel uncomfortable; he sharpened his ears to their keenest hearing, but there was a lull in the conversation, and he could ascertain one of the gentler sex was engaged in it, by 'the ogre-like voice uttering,—"Fudge, woman!—fiddle-de-dee!" Then he caught the words, "perhaps" and "gentleman," in a lady's voice,—then out thundered "that rascal's carriage!—why come in that?—friend!—humbug!—rascal's carriage!—tar and feather him, by this and that!"

Furlong began to feel very uncomfortable; the conversation ended; down came the servant, to whom Furlong was about to address himself, when the man said, "he would be with him in a minit," and vanished; a sort of reconnoitering party, one by one, then passed through the hall, eyeing the stranger very suspiciously, any of them to whom Furlong ventured a word, scurrying off in double quick time. For an instant, he meditated a retreat, and looking to the door saw a heavy chain across it, the pattern of which must have been had from Newgate. He attempted to unfasten it, and as it clanked heavily, the ogre's voice from up stairs bellowed "Who the d—l's that opening the door?" Furlong's hand dropped from the chain, and a low growling went on up the stair-case. The servant whom he first saw returned.

"I fear," said Furlong, "there is some misappwehension."

"A what, sir?

"A misappwehension."

"Oh no, sir! it's only a mistake the master thought you might be making; he thinks you mistuk the house, may be, sir."

"Oh, no—I *wather* think he mistakes me; will you do me the favo',"—and he produced a packet of papers as he spoke,—"the favo' to take my cwedentials to Mr. O'Gwady, and if he thwows his eye over these pape's—"

At the word "papers," there was a shout from above, "Don't touch them, you thief, don't touch them!—another blister,—ha, ha!—by the 'ternal this and that, I'll have him in the horse-pond!" A heavy stamping overhead ensued, and furious ringing of bells; in the midst of the din a very pale lady came down stairs, and, pointing the way to a small room, beckoned Furlong to follow her. For a moment he hesitated, for his heart misgave him; but shame at the thought of doubting or refusing the summons of a lady overcame his fear, and he followed to a little parlour, where mutual explanations between Mrs. O'Grady and himself, and many messages, questions, and answers, which she carried up and down stairs, at length set Furlong's mind at ease respecting his personal safety, and finally admitted him into the presence of the truculent lord of the castle,—who, when he heard that Furlong had been staying in the enemy's camp, was not, it may be supposed, in a sweet state of temper to receive him. O'Grady looked thunder as Furlong entered: and eyeing him keenly for some seconds, as if he were taking a mental as well as an ocular measurement of him, he saluted him with,

"Well, sir,—a pretty kettle of fish you've made of this. I hope you have not blabbed much about our affairs."

"Why, I weally don't know—I'm not sure—that is, I won't be positive, because when one is thwown off his guard, you know—"

"Pooh, sir! a man should never be off his guard in an election. But, how the d—l, sir, could you make such a thundering mistake as to go to the wrong house?"

"It was the howwid postilion, Miste' O'Grady."

"The scoundrel," exclaimed O'Grady, stamping up and down the room.

At this moment a tremendous crash was heard; the ladies jumped from their seats; O'Grady paused in his rage, and his poor pale wife exclaimed, "'Tis in the conservatory."

A universal rush was now made to the spot, and there was Handy Andy buried in the ruins of flower-pots and exotics, directly under an enormous breach in the glass-roof of the building. How this occurred, a few words will explain. Andy, when he went to sleep in the justice-room slept soundly for some hours, but awoke in the horrors of a dream, in which he fancied he was about to be hanged. So impressed was he by the vision, that he determined on making his escape if he could, and to this end piled the chair upon the desk, and the volumes of law books on the chair; and being an active fellow, contrived to scramble up high enough to lay his hand on the frame of the sky-light, and thus make his way out on the roof. Then walking, as well as the darkness would permit him, along the coping of the wall, he approached, as it chanced, the conservatory, but the coping being loose, one of the flags turned under Andy's foot, and bang he went through the glass-roof, carrying down in his fall some score of flower-pots, and finally stuck in a tub, with his legs upwards, and embowered in the branches of crushed geraniums and hydrangias.

He was dragged out of the tub, amidst a shower of curses from O'Grady; but the moment Andy recovered the few senses he had, and saw Furlong, regardless of the anathemas of the Squire, he shouted out, "There he is!—there he is!" and, rushing towards him, exclaimed, "Now, did I dhrowned you, sir,—did I? Sure, I never murdhered you!"

'Twas as much as could be done to keep O'Grady's hands off Andy, for smashing the conservatory, when Furlong's presence made him no longer liable to imprisonment.

"Maybe he has a vote?" said Furlong, anxious to display how much he was on the *qui vive* in election matters.

"*Have* you a vote, you rascal?" said O'Grady.

"You may sarche me, if you like, your honour," said Andy, who thought a vote was some sort of property he was suspected of stealing.

"You are either the biggest rogue, or the biggest fool, I ever met," said O'Grady. "Which are you now?"

"Whichever your honour plazes," said Andy.

"If I forgive you, will you stand by me at the election?"

"I'll stand anywhere your honour bids me," said Andy, humbly.

"That's a thoroughgoing rogue, I'm inclined to think," said O'Grady aside, to Furlong.

"He looks more like a fool, in my appwehension," was the reply.

"Oh, these fellows conceal the deepest roguery some times under an assumed simplicity. You don't understand the Irish."

"Unde'stand!" exclaimed Furlong; "I pwonounce the whole countwy quite incompwehensible!"

"Well!" growled O'Grady to Andy, after a moment's consideration, "go down to the kitchen, you house breaking-vagabond, and get your supper!"

Now, considering the "fee, faw, fum," qualities of O'Grady, the reader may be surprised at the easy manner in which Andy slipped through his fingers, after having slipped through the roof of his conservatory; but as between two stools folks fall to the ground, so between two rages people sometimes tumble into safety. O'Grady was in a divided passion—first, his wrath was excited against Furlong for *his* blunder, and just as that was about to explode, the crash of Andy's sudden appearance amidst the flower-pots (like a practical parody on "Love among the roses") called off the gathering storm in a new direction, and the fury sufficient to annihilate one, was, by dispersion, harmless to two. But on the return of the party from the conservatory, after Andy's descent to the kitchen, O'Grady's rage against Furlong, though moderated, had settled down into a very substantial dissatisfaction, which he evinced by poking his nose between his forefinger and thumb, as if he meditated the abstraction of that salient feature from his face, shuffling his feet about, throwing his right leg over his left knee, and then suddenly, as if that were a mistake, throwing his left over the right, thrumming on the arm of his chair with his clenched hand, inhaling the air very audibly through his protruded lips, as if he were supping hot soup, and all the time fixing his eyes on the fire with a portentous gaze, as if he would have evoked from it a salamander.

Mrs. O'Grady, in such a state of affairs, wishing to speak to the stranger, yet anxious she should say nothing that could bear upon immediate circumstances, lest she might rouse her awful lord and master, racked her invention for what she should say; and at last, with "bated breath" and a very worn-out smile, faltered forth—"Pray, Mr. Furlong, are you fond of shuttle cock?"

Furlong stared, and began a reply of "Weally, I *cawnt* say that—"

When O'Grady gruffly broke in with "You'd better ask him, does he love teetotum."

"I thought you could recommend me the best establishment in the metropolis, Mr. Furlong, for buying shuttlecocks," continued the lady, unmindful of the interruption.

"You had better ask him where you could get mousetraps," growled O'Grady.

Mrs. O'Grady was silent, and O'Grady, whose rage had now assumed its absurd form of tagging changes, continued, increasing his growl, like a *crescendo* on the double-bass, as he proceeded: "You'd better ask, I think—mouse-traps—steel-traps—clap-traps—rat-traps—rattle-traps—rattle-snakes!"

Furlong stared,—Mrs. O'Grady was silent,—and the Misses O'Grady cast fearful sidelong glances at "Pa," whose strange iteration always bespoke his not being in what good people call a "sweet state of mind;" he laid hold of a tea-spoon, and began beating a tattoo on the mantelpiece to a low smothered whistle of some very obscure tune, which was suddenly stopped to say to Furlong, very abruptly,

"So, Egan diddled you?"

"Why, he certainly, as I conceive, pwactised, or I might say, in short—he—a—in fact—"

"Oh, yes," said O'Grady, cutting short Furlong's humming and hawing; "oh yes, I know,—diddled you."

Bang went the spoon again, keeping time with another string of nonsense.—"diddled you—diddle, diddle, the cat and the fiddle, the cow jumped over the moon,—who was there?"

"A Mister Dawson."

"Phew!" ejaculated O'Grady, with a doleful whistle;

"Dick the Divil! You were in nice hands! All up with us,—up with us,—

> Up, up, up,
> And here we go down, down, down, Derry down!

Oh, murther!" and the spoon went faster than before. "Any one else?"

"Mister Bermingham."

"Bermingham!" exclaimed O'Grady.

"A clergyman, I think," drawled Furlong.

"Bermingham!" reiterated O'Grady. "What business has he there, and be—!" O'Grady swallowed a curse when he remembered he was a clergyman. "The enemy's camp—not his principles! Oh, Bermingham, Bermingham—Brimmagem, Brummagem, Sheffield, Wolverhampton—Murther! Any one else? Was Durfy there?"

"No," said Furlong; "but there was an odd pe'son, whose name wymes to his—as you seem fond of wymes, Mister O'Gwady."

"What!" said O'Grady, quickly, and fixing his eye on Furlong; "Murphy?"

"Yes. Miste' Muffy."

O'Grady gave a more doleful whistle than before, and, banging the spoon faster than ever, exclaimed again, "Murphy!—then I'll tell you what it is; do you see that?" and he held up the spoon before Furlong, who, being asked the same question several times, confessed he *did* see the spoon. "Then I'll tell you what it is," said O'Grady again; "I wouldn't give you *that* for the election;" and with a disdainful jerk, he threw the spoon into the fire. After which he threw himself back in his chair, with an appearance of repose, while he glanced fiercely up at the ceiling and indulged in a very low whistle indeed. One of the girls stole softly round to the fire, and gently took up the tongs to recover the spoon; it made a slight rattle, and her father turned smartly round, and said, "Can't you let the fire alone?—there's coal enough on it;—the devil burn 'em all,—Egan, Murphy, and all o' them! What do you stand there for, with the tongs in your hands, like a hairdresser or a stuck pig? I tell you I'm as hot as a lime kiln; go out o' that!"

The daughter retired, and the spoon was left to its fate; the ladies did not dare to utter a word; O'Grady continued his gaze on the ceiling, and his whistle; and Furlong, very uncomfortable and much more astonished, after sitting in silence for some time, thought a retreat the best move he could make, and intimated his wish to retire.

Mrs. O'Grady gently suggested it was yet early; which Furlong acknowledged, but pleaded his extreme fatigue after a day of great exertion.

"I suppose you were canvassing," said O'Grady, with a wicked grin.

"Ce'tainly not; they could hardly pwesume on such a twick as that, I should think, in *my* pwesence."

"Then what fatigued you?—eh?"

"Salmon fishing, sir."

"What!" exclaimed O'Grady, opening his fierce eyes and turning suddenly round. "Salmon fishing! Where the d—l were you salmon-fishing?"

"In the wiver, close by here."

The ladies now all stared; but Furlong advanced a vehement assurance, in answer to their looks of wonder that he had taken some very fine salmon indeed.

The girls could not suppress their laughter; and O'Grady, casting a look of mingled rage and contempt on the fisherman, merely uttered the ejaculation, "Oh Moses!" and threw himself back in his chair; but starting up a moment after, he rang the bell violently. "What do you want, my dear?" said his poor wife, venturing to lift her eyes, and speaking in the humblest tone—"what do you want?"

"Some broiled bones!" said O'Grady, very much like an ogre; "I want something to settle my stomach after what I've heard, for by the powers of ipecacuanha, 'tis enough to make a horse sick—sick, by the powers!—shivering all over like a dog in a wet sack. I must have broiled bones and hot punch!"

The servant entered, and O'Grady swore at him for not coming sooner, though he was really expeditious in his answer to the bell.

"Confound your lazy bones; you're never in time."

"'Deed, sir; I came the minit I heerd the bell."

"Hold your tongue! who bid you talk? The devil fly away with you! and you'll never go fast till he does. Make haste now—go to the cook—"

"Yes, sir—"

"Curse you, can't you wait till you get your message—go to the devil with you!—get some broiled bones—hot water and tumblers—don't forget the whisky—and pepper them well. Mind, hot—every thing hot—screeching hot. Be off, now, and make haste—mind!—make haste!—"

"Yes, sir," said the servant, whipping out of the room with celerity, and thanking Heaven when he had the door between him and his savage master. When he got to the kitchen, he told the cook to make haste, if ever she made haste in her life, "for there's owld Danger, up stairs, in the divil's timper, God bless us!" said Mick.

"Faix, he's always that," said the cook, scurrying across the kitchen for the gridiron.

"Oh, but he's beyant all, to-night," said Mick; "I think he'll murther that chap up stairs, before he stops."

"Oh, wirra! Wirra!" cried the cook; "there's the fire not bright, bad luck to it, and he wantin' a brile!"

"Bright or not bright," said Mick, "make haste, I'd advise you, or he'll have your life."

The bell rang violently.

"There, do you here him tattherin!" said Mick, rushing up stairs—"I thought it was tay they wor takin'," said Larry

Hogan, who was sitting in the chimney corner, smoking. "So they are," said the cook.

"Then I suppose briled bones is ginteel with tay!" said Larry.

"Oh no! it's not for tay, at all, they want them; it's only owld Danger himself. Whenever he's in a rage, he ates briled bones."

"Faith, they're a brave cure for anger," said Larry; "I wouldn't be angry myself, if I had one."

Down rushed Mick, to hurry the cook—bang, twang! went the bell, as he spoke. "Oh, listen to him!" said Mick; "for the tendher mercy o' Heaven, make haste!"

The cook transferred the bones from the gridiron to a hot dish.

"Oh, murther, but they're smoked!" said Mick.

"No matther," said the cook, shaking her red elbow furiously; "I'll smother the smoke with the pepper—there!—give them a good dab o' musthard now, and serve them hot!"

Away rushed Mick, as the bell was rattled into fits again.

While the cook had been broiling bones for O'Grady, below, he had been grilling Furlong for himself, above. In one of the pauses of the storm, the victim ventured to suggest to his tormentor that all the mischances that had arisen might have been avoided, if O'Grady had met him at the village, as he requested of him in one of his letters. O'Grady denied all knowledge of such a request, and after some queries about certain portions of the letter, it became manifest it had miscarried.

"There!" said O'Grady—"there's a second letter astray; I'm certain they put my letters astray on purpose. There's a plot in the post-office against me; by this and that, I'll have an inquiry. I wish all the post-offices in the world were blown up; and all the postmasters hanged, postmaster-general and all—I do—by the 'ternal war, I do—and all the mail coaches in the world ground to powder, and the roads they go on, into the bargain—devil a use in them, but to carry bad news over the universe—for all the letters with any good in them, are lost; and if there's a money enclosure in one, that's sure to be robbed. Blow the post-office! say I—blow it, and sink it!"

It was at this moment Mick entered with the broiled bones, and while he was in the room, placing glasses on the table and making the necessary arrangements for making "screeching hot punch," he heard O'Grady and Furlong talking about the two lost letters. On his descent to the kitchen, the cook was spreading a bit of supper there, in which Andy was to join, Andy having just completed some applications of brown paper and vinegar to the bruises received in his fall. Larry Hogan, too, was invited to share in the repast; and it was not the first time, by many, that Larry quartered on the Squire. Indeed, many a good larder was open to Larry Hogan; he held a very deep interest in the regards of all the female domestics over the country, not, on the strength of his personal charms, for Larry had a hanging lip, a snub nose, a low forehead, a large ugly head, whose scrubby grizzled hair grew round the crown some what in the form of a priest's tonsure. Not on the strength of his gallantry, for Larry was always talking morality and making sage reflections while he supplied the womankind with bits of lace, rolls of ribbon and now and then silk stockings. He always had some plausible story of how they happened to come in his way, for Larry was not a regular pedlar;—carrying no box, he drew his chance treasures from the recesses of very deep pockets, contrived in various parts of his attire. No one asked Larry how he came by such a continued supply of natty articles, and if they had, Larry would not have told them, for he was a very "close" man, as well as a "civil spoken," under which character he was first introduced to the reader on the memorable night of Andy's destructive adventure in his mother's cabin. Larry Hogan was about as shrewd a fellow as any in the whole country, and while no one could exactly make out what *he* was, or how he made the two ends of his year meet, he knew nearly as much of every one's affairs as they did themselves; in the phrase of the country, he was "as cute as a fox, as close as wax, and as deep as a draw-well."

The supper party sat down in the kitchen, and between every three mouthfuls poor Mick could get, he was obliged to canter up stairs at the call of the fiercely-rung bell. Ever and anon, as be returned, he bolted his allowance with an ejaculation, sometimes pious, and sometimes the reverse, on the hard fate of attending such a "born divil," as he called the Squire.

"Why, he's worse nor ever, to-night," says the cook.

"What ails him, at all—what is it all about?"

"Oh, he's blowin' and blastin' away, about that quare slink-lookin' chap, up stairs, goin' to Squire Egan's instead of comin' here."

"That was a bit o' your handy work," said Larry, with a grim smile at Andy.

"And then," said Mick, "he's swarin' all the murthers in the world agen the whole counthry, about some letthers was stole out of the post-office by somebody."

Andy's hand was in the act of raising a mouthful to his lips, when these words were uttered; his hand fell, and his mouth remained open. Larry Hogan had his eye on him at the moment.

"He swares he'll have some one in the body o' the jail," said Mick; "and he'll never stop till he sees them swing."

Andy thought of the effigy on the wall, and his dream, and grew pale.

"By the hokey," said Mick, "I never see him in sitch a tattherin rage!—bang went the bell again—"Ow! ow!" cried Mick, bolting a piece of fat bacon, wiping his mouth in the sleeve of his livery, and running up stairs.

"Missis Cook, ma'am," said Andy, shoving back his chair from the table; "thank you, ma'am, for your good supper. I think I'll be goin' now."

"Sure, you're not done yet, man alive."

"Enough is as good as a feast, ma'am," replied Andy.

"Augh! sure the morsel you took is more like a fast than a feast," said the cook; "and it's not Lent."

"It's not lent, sure enough," said Larry Hogan, with a sly grin; "it's not *lent*, for you *gave* it to him."

"Ah, Misther Hogan, you're always goin' on with your conundherums," said the cook; "sure, that's not the lent I mane, at all—I mane, Good Friday Lent."

"Faix, every Friday is good Friday that a man gets his supper," said Larry.

"Well, you *will* be goin' on, Misther Hogan," said the cook. "Oh, but you're a witty man, but I'd rather have a yard of your lace, any day, than a mile o' your discourse."

"Sure, you oughtn't to mind my goin' *on*, when you're lettin' another man go off that-a-way," said Larry, pointing to Andy, who, hat in hand, was quitting the kitchen.

"Faix, an' he mustn't go," said the cook; "there's two words to that bargain," and she closed the door and put her back against it.

"My mother's expectin' me, ma'am," said Andy.

"Throth, if it was your wife was expectin' you, she must wait a bit," said the cook; "sure you wouldn't leave the thirsty curse on my kitchen?—you must take a dhrop before you go; besides, the dogs about the place would ate you, onless there was some one they knew along wid you; and sure, if a dog bit you, you couldn't dhrink wather afther, let alone a dhrop o' beer, or a thrifle o' sper'ts: isn't that thrue, Misther Hogan?"

"Indeed, an' it is, ma'am," answered Larry; "no one can dhrink afther a dog bites them, and that's the rayson that the larn'd fackleties calls the disaise high-*dhry*—"

"High-dhry what?" asked the cook.

"That's what I'm thinkin' of," said Larry. "High-dhry—high-dhry—something."

"There's high-dhry snuff," said the cook.

"Oh, no—no, no, ma'am!" said Larry, hand and shaking his head, as if unwilling interrupted in endeavouring to recall

Some fleeting remembrance,

"high-dhry—po—po—something about po; faith, it's not unlike popery," said Larry.

"Don't say popery," cried the cook; "it's a dirty word! Say Roman Catholic, when you spake of the faith."

"Do you think *I* would undhervalue the faith?" sad Larry, casting up his eyes. "Oh, Missis Mulligan, you know little of me; d'you think *I* would undhervalue what is my hope past, present, and to come?—*what* makes our hearts light when our lot is heavy?—*what* makes us love our neighbour as ourselves?—"

"Indeed, Misther Hogan," broke in the cook—"I never knew any one fonder of calling in on a neighbour than yourself, particularly about dinner-time—"

"What makes us," said Larry, who would *not* let the cook interrupt his outpouring of pious eloquence; "what makes us fierce in prosperity to our friends, and meek in adversity to our inimies?"

"Oh! Misther Hogan!" said the cook, blessing herself.

"What puts the leg undher you when you are in throuble? why, your faith: what makes you below deceit, and above reproach, and on neither side of nothin'?" Larry slapped the table like a prime minister, and there was no opposition. "Oh, Missis Mulligan, do you think I would desaive or bethray my fellow-crayture? Oh, no—I would not wrong the child unborn,"—and this favourite phrase of Larry (and other rascals)—was and is, unconsciously, true:—for people, most generally, must be born before they *can* be much wronged.

"Oh, Missis Mulligan," said Larry, with a devotional appeal of his eyes to the ceiling, "be at war with sin, and you'll be at paice with yourself!"

Just as Larry wound up his pious peroration, Mick shoved in the door against which the cook supported herself, and told Andy the Squire said he should not leave the hall that night.

Andy looked aghast.

Again Larry Hogan's eye was on him.

"Sure I can come back here in the mornin'," said Andy, who at the moment he spoke was conscious of the intention of being some forty miles out of the place before dawn, if he could get away.

"When the squire says a thing, it must be done," said Mick. "You must sleep here."

"And pleasant dhrames to you," said Larry, who saw Andy wince under his kindly-worded stab.

"And where must I sleep?" asked Andy, dolefully.

"Out in the big loft," said Mick.

"I'll show you the way," said Larry; "I'm goin' to sleep there myself to-night, for it would be too far to go home. Good night, Mrs. Mulligan—good night, Micky—come along, Andy."

Andy followed Hogan; they had to cross a yard to reach the stables; the night was clear, and the waning moon shed a steady though not a bright light on the enclosure. Hogan cast a lynx eye around him to see if the coast were clear; and satisfying himself it was, he laid his hand impressively on Andy's arm as they reached the middle of the yard, and setting Andy's face right against the moonlight, so that he might watch the slightest expression, he paused for a moment before he spoke; and when he spoke, it was in a low mysterious whisper,—low, as if he feared the night breeze might hear:—and the words were few, but potent, which he uttered; they were these,—"*Who robbed the post office?*"

The result quite satisfied Hogan; and he knew how to turn his knowledge to account.—O'Grady and Egan were no longer friends; a political contest was pending; letters were missing; Andy had been Egan's servant; and Larry Hogan had enough of that mental chemical power, which, from a few raw facts, unimportant separately, could make a combination of great value.

Soon after breakfast at Merryvale the following morning, Mrs. Egan wanted to see the squire. She went to his sitting-room—it was bolted. He told her, from the inside, he was engaged just then, but would see her by and by. She retired to the drawing-room, where Fanny was singing. "Oh, Fanny," said her sister, "sing me that dear new song of 'the voices'—'tis so sweet, and must be felt by those who, like me, have a happy home."

Fanny struck a few notes of a wild and peculiar symphony, and sang her sister's favourite.

THE VOICE WITHIN

I

You ask the dearest place on earth,
   Whose simple joys can never die;
'Tis the holy pale of the happy hearth,
   Where love doth light each beaming eye!
     With snowy shroud
     Let tempests loud
Around my old tower raise their din;—
     What boots the shout
     Of storms without,
While voices sweet resound within?
     O! dearer sound
     For the tempest round,
      The voices sweet within!

II

I ask not wealth, I ask not power;
   But, gracious Heaven, oh, grant to me
That, when the storms of Fate may lower,
   My heart just like my home may be!
     When in the gale
     Poor Hope's white sail
No haven can for shelter win,
    Fate's darkest skies
    The heart defies
Whose still small voice is sweet within!
     Oh heavenly sound!
     'Mid the tempest round,
      That voice so sweet within!

Egan had entered as Fanny was singing the second verse; he wore a troubled air, which his wife, at first, did not remark. "Is not that a sweet song, Edward?" said she. "No one ought to like it more than you, for your home is your happiness, and no one has a clearer conscience."

Egan kissed her gently, and thanked her for her good opinion—and asked what she wished to say to him: they left the room.

Fanny remarked Egan's unusually troubled air, and it marred her music: leaving the piano, and walking to the window, she saw Larry Hogan walking from the house, down the avenue.

1.   A facetious phrase for bailiff; so often kicked.
2.   Cutting off the ears of a process-server.
3.   Hayloft.
4.   A shilling, so called from its being worth thirteen pence in those days.
5.   This is not the word in the MS.
6.   Serving mass occupies about twenty-five minutes.
7.   An Hibernicism, expressive of lounging laziness.

XV

I F THE MORNING BROUGHT UNEASINESS and distrust to Merryvale, it dawned not more brightly on Neck-or-Nothing Hall. The discord of the former night was not preparatory to a harmony on the morrow, and the parties separating in ill-humour from the drawing-room, were not likely to look forward with much pleasure to the breakfast-parlour. But before breakfast, sleep was to intervene—that is, for those who could get it, and the unfortunate Furlong was not amongst the number. Despite the very best feather-bed Mrs. O'Grady had selected for him from amongst her treasures, it was long before slumber weighed down his feverish eyelids; and even then, it was only to have them opened again in some convulsive start of a troubled dream. All his adventures of the last four-and-twenty hours were jumbled together in strange confusion:—now on a lonely road, while dreading the assaults of robbers, his course was interrupted not by a highwayman, but a river, whereon embarking, he began to catch salmon in a most surprisingly rapid manner, but just as he was about to haul in his fish, it escaped from the hook, and the salmon, making wry faces at him, very impertinently exclaimed, "Sure, you wouldn't catch a poor ignorant Irish salmon?"—he then snapped his pistols at the insolent fish, and then his carriage breaks down, and he is suddenly transferred from the river to the road;—thieves seize upon him and bind his hands, but a charming young lady with pearly teeth cuts his bonds and conducts him to a castle where a party are engaged in playing cards;—he is invited to join, and as his cards are dealt to him, he anticipates triumph in the game, but by some malicious fortune his trumps are transformed into things of no value, as they touch the board;—he loses his money, and is kicked out when his purse has been emptied, and he escapes along a dark road, pursued by his spoilers, who would take his life, and a horrid cry of "broiled bones" rings in his ears as he flies;—he is seized and thrown into a river, where, as he sinks, the salmon raise a chorus of rejoicing, and he wakes, in the agonies of drowning, to find himself nearly suffocated by sinking into the feathery depths of Mrs. O'Grady's pet bed. After a night passed in such troubled visions, poor Furlong awoke unrefreshed, and, with bitter recollections of the past and mournful anticipations of the future, arose, and prepared to descend to the parlour, where a servant told him breakfast was ready.

His morning greeting by the family was not of that hearty and cheerful character which generally distinguishes the house of an Irish squire; for though O'Grady was not so savage as on the preceding evening, he was rather gruff, and the ladies dreaded being agreeable when the master's temper blew from a stormy point. Furlong could not help regretting at this moment the lively breakfast-table of Merryvale, nor avoid contrasting to disadvantage the two Miss O'Gradys with Fanny Dawson. Augusta, the eldest, inherited the prominent nose of her father, and something of his upper lip, too, beard included; and these, unfortunately, were all she was ever likely to inherit from him; and Charlotte, the younger, had the same traits in a moderated degree. Altogether, he thought the girls the plainest he had ever seen, and the house more horrible, than anything that was ever imagined; and he sighed a faint fashionable sigh, to think his political duties had expelled him from a paradise to send him

"The other way—the other way!"

Four boys and a little girl sat at a side-table, where a capacious jug of milk, large bowls, and a lusty loaf, were laid under contribution amidst a suppressed but continuous wrangle, which was going forward amongst the juniors; and a snappish "I will," or "I won't," and "Let me alone," or a "Behave yourself," occasionally was distinguishable above the murmur of dissatisfaction. A little squall from the little girl at last made O'Grady turn round and swear that if they did not *behave* themselves, he'd turn them all out.

"It is all Goggy, sir," said the girl.

"No, it's not, you dirty little thing," cried George, whose name was thus euphoniously abbreviated.

"He's putting—" said the girl with excitement.

"Ah, you dirty little—" interrupted Goggy, in a low contemptuous tone.

"He's putting, sir,"—

"Whisht! you young devils, will you!" cried O'Grady, and a momentary silence prevailed; but the little girl snivelled, and put up her bib (pinafore) to wipe her eyes, while Goggy put out his tongue at her. Many minutes had not elapsed when the girl again whimpered:

"Call to Goggy, papa; he's putting some mouses' tails into my milk, sir."

"Ah, you dirty little tell-tale!" cried Goggy reproachfully; "a tell-tale is worse than a mouse's-tail."

O'Grady jumped up, gave Master Goggy a box on the ear, and then caught him by the aforesaid appendage to his head, and as he led him to the door by the same, Goggy bellowed lustily, and when ejected from the room howled down the passage more like a dog than a human being. O'Grady, on resuming his seat, told Polshee (Mary, the little girl) she was always getting Goggy a beating, and she *was* a little cantankerous cat and a dirty tell-tale, as Goggy said. Amongst the ladies and Furlong the breakfast went forward with coldness and constraint, and all were glad when it was nearly over. At this period, Mrs. O'Grady half filled a large bowl from the tea-urn, and then added to it some weak tea, and Miss O'Grady collected all the broken bread about the table on a plate. Just then Furlong ventured to "twouble" Mrs. O'Grady for a *leetle* more tea, and before he handed her his cup, he would have emptied the sediment in the slop-basin, but by mistake he popped it into the large bowl of *miserable* Mrs. O'Grady had prepared. Furlong begged a thousand apologies, but Mrs. O'Grady assured him it was of no consequence, *as it was only for the tutor.*

O'Grady having swallowed his breakfast as fast as possible, left the room; the whole party soon followed, and on arriving in the drawing-room, the young ladies became more agreeable when no longer under the constraint of their ogre father. Furlong talked slip-slop common-places with them; they spoke of the country and the weather, and he of the city; they assured him that the dews were heavy in the evening, and that the grass was so green in that part of the country; he obliged them with the interesting information that the Liffy ran through Dublin, but that the two sides of the city communicated by means of bridges—that the houses were built of red brick generally, and that the hall-doors were painted in imitation of mahogany; to which the young ladies responded, "La, how odd!" and added, that in the country people mostly painted their hall-doors green to match the grass. Furlong admitted the propriety of the proceeding, and said he liked uniformity. The young ladies quite coincided in his opinion, declared they all were so fond of uniformity! and added, that one of their carriage horses was blind.

Furlong admitted the excellence of the observation, and said, in a very soft voice, that Love was blind also.

"Exactly," said Miss O'Grady, "and that's the reason we call our horse 'Cupid!'"

"How clever!" replied Furlong.

"And the mare that goes in harness with him—she's an ugly creature, to be sure—but we call her 'Venus.'"

"How dwoll!" said Furlong.

"That's for uniformity," said Miss O'Grady.

"How good!" was the rejoinder.

Mrs. O'Grady, who had left the room for a few minutes, now returned, and told Furlong she would show him over the house, if he pleased. He assented, of course, and under her guidance went through many apartments:—those on the basement story were hurried through rapidly, but when Mrs. O'Grady got him up stairs, amongst the bed-rooms, she dwelt on the excellence of every apartment. "This I need not show you, Mr. Furlong,—'tis your own; I hope you slept well last night."—This was the twentieth time the question had been asked. "Now, here is another, Mr. Furlong; the window looks out on the lawn;—so nice to look out on a lawn, I think, in the morning, when one gets up!—so refreshing and wholesome! Oh! you are looking at the stain in the ceiling, but we couldn't get the roof repaired in time before the winter set in last year, and Mr. O'Grady thought we might as well have the painters and slaters together in the summer—and the house does want paint indeed—but we all hate the smell of paint. See here, Mister Furlong," and she turned up a quilt as she spoke, "just put your hand into that bed; did you ever feel a finer bed?"

Furlong declared he never did.

"Oh, you don't know how to feel a bed!—put your hand into it—well, that way;"—and Mrs. O'Grady plunged her arm up to the elbow into the object of her admiration.

Furlong poked the bed, and was all admiration.

"Isn't it beautiful?

"Cha'ming!" replied Furlong, trying to pick off the bits of down which clung to his coat.

"Oh, never mind the down,—you shall be brushed after; I always show my beds, Mr. Furlong. Now, here's another;"—and so she went on, dragging poor Furlong up and down the house, and he did not get out of her clutches till he had poked all the beds in the establishment.

As soon as that ceremony was over, and that his coat had undergone the process of brushing, he wished to take a stroll, and was going forth, when Mrs. O'Grady interrupted him, with the assurance that it would not be safe unless some one of the family became his escort, for the dogs were so fierce—Mr. O'Grady was *so* fond of dogs, and *so* proud of a particular breed of dogs he had, so remarkable for their courage,—he had better wait till the boys had done their Latin lesson. So Furlong was marched back to the drawing-room.

There the younger daughter addressed him with a message from her grandmama, who wished to have the pleasure of making his acquaintance, and hoped he would pay her a visit. Furlong, of course, was "quite delighted" and "too happy," and the young lady, thereupon, led him to the old lady's apartment.

The old dowager had been a beauty in her youth, and one of the belles of the Irish court, and when she heard "a gentleman from Dublin Castle" was in the house, she desired to see him. To see any one from that seat of her juvenile joys and triumphs would have given her delight, were it only the coachman that had driven a carriage to a levee or a drawing-room; she could ask him about the sentinels at the gate, the entrance-porch, and if the long range of windows yet glittered with lights on St. Patrick's night; but to have a conversation with an

official from that seat of government and courtly pleasure, was, indeed,
something to make her happy.

On Furlong being introduced, the old lady received him very
courteously, at the same time with a certain air that betokened she
was accustomed to deference. Her commanding figure was habited in
a loose morning wrapper, made of grey flannel; but while, this gave
evidence she studied her personal comfort rather than appearance, a bit
of pretty silk handkerchief about the neck, very knowingly displayed,
and a becoming ribbon in her cap, showed she did not quite neglect her
good looks; it did not require a very quick eye to see, besides, a small
touch of rouge on the cheek which age had depressed, and the assistance
of Indian ink to the eye-brow which time had thinned and faded. A
glass filled with flowers stood on the table before her, and a quantity
of books lay scattered about; a guitar—not the Spanish instrument
now in fashion, but the English one of some eighty years ago, strung
with wire and tuned in thirds—hung, by a *blue ribbon*, beside her; a
corner-cupboard, fantastically carved, bore some curious specimens of
China, on one side of the room; while, in strange discord with what
was really scarce and beautiful, the commonest Dutch cuckoo-clock
was suspended on the opposite wall; close beside her chair stood a very
pretty little Japan table, bearing a looking-glass with numerous drawers,
framed in the same material; and while Furlong seated himself, the old
lady cast a sidelong glance at the mirror, and her withered fingers played
with the fresh ribbon.

"You have recently arrived from the Castle, sir, I understand."

"Quite wecently, madam,—awived last night."

"I hope his Excellency is well—not that I have the honour of his
acquaintance, but I love the Lord Lieutenant—and the aides-de-camps
are so nice, and the little pages!—put a marker in that book," said she,
in an undertone, to her granddaughter, "page seventy-four;—ah," she
resumed in a higher tone, "that reminds, me of the Honourable Captain
Wriggle, who commanded a seventy-four, and danced with me at the
Castle the evening Lady Legge sprained her ankle.—By the bye, are
there any seventy-fours in Dublin now?"

"I wather think," said Furlong, "the bay is not sufficiently deep for
line-of-battle ships."

"Oh dear, yes! I have seen quantities of seventy-fours there—though, indeed, I am not quite sure if it wasn't at *Splithead*. Give me the smelling-salts, Charlotte, love; mine does ache indeed! How subject the dear duchess of Rutland was to headaches; you did not know the duchess of Rutland?—no, to be sure, what am I thinking of—you're too young; but those were the charming days! You have heard, of course, the duchess's *bon mot* in reply to the compliment of Lord—, but I must not mention his name, because there was some scandal about them; but the gentleman said to the duchess—I must tell you she was Isabella, duchess of Rutland—and he said, 'Isabelle is a *belle*,' to which the duchess replied, 'Isabelle *was* a *belle*.'"

"Vewy neat, indeed!" said Furlong.

"Ah! poor thing," said the dowager, with a sigh, "she was beginning to be a little *passée*, then;"—she looked in the glass herself, and added,—"Dear me, how pale I am this morning!" and pulling out one of the little drawers from the Japan looking-glass, she took out a pot of rouge and heightened the colour on her cheek. The old lady not only heightened her own colour, but that of the witnesses—of Furlong, particularly, who was *quite* surprised. "Why am I so very pale this morning, Charlotte, love?" continued the old lady.

"You sit up so late reading, grandmama."

"Ah, who can resist the fascination of the muses? You are fond of literature, I hope, Sir?"

"Extwemely," replied Furlong.

"As a statesman," continued the old lady,—to whom Furlong made a deep obeisance, at the word 'statesman,'—"as a statesman, of course your reading lies in the more solid department; but if you ever *do* condescend to read a romance, there is the sweetest thing I ever met, I am just now engaged in;—it is called 'The Blue Robber of the Pink Mountain.' I have not come to the pink mountain yet, but the blue robber is the most perfect character. The author, however, is guilty of a strange forgetfulness—he begins by speaking of the robber as of the middle age, and soon after describes him as a young man. Now, how could a young man be of the middle age?"

"It seems a stwange inaccuwacy," lisped Furlong. "But poets sometimes pwesume on the pwivelege they have of doing what they please with their hewoes."

"Quite true, sir. And talking of heroes; I hope the knights of St. Patrick are well—I do admire them so much!—'tis so interesting to see their banners and helmets hanging up in St. Patrick's Cathedral, that venerable pile!—with the loud peal of the organ—sublime—isn't it?—the banners almost tremble in the vibration of the air to the loud swell of the— 'A-a-a-men!'—the very banners seem to wave 'Amen.' Oh, that swell is so fine!—I think they are fond of swells in the quire; they have a good effect, and some of the young men are so good-looking!—and the little boys, too—I suppose they are the choristers' children?"

The old lady made a halt, and Furlong filled up the pause by declaring, "he weally couldn't say."

"I hope you admire the service at St. Patrick's," continued the old lady.

"Ye-s—I think St. Paytwick's a vewy amusing place of wo'ship."

"Amusing!" said the old lady, half-offended. "Inspiring, you mean; not that I think the sermon interesting, but the anthem!—oh! the anthem, it is so fine!—and the old banners, those are my delight—the dear banners, covered with dust."

"Oh, as far as that goes," said Furlong, "they have impwoved the cathedwal vewy much, for they have whitewashed it inside, and put up *noo* banners."

"Whitewash and new banners!" exclaimed the indignant dowager, "the Goths! to remove an atom of the romantic dust! I would not have let a housemaid into the place for the world! But they have left the anthem, I hope?"

"Oh, yes the anthem is continued, but with a small diffewence;—they used to sing the anthem befo' the se'mon, but the people used to go away after the anthem and neve' waited for the se'mon, and the Bishop, who is pwoud of his pweaching, orde'ed the anthem to be postponed till afte' the se'mon."

"Oh, yes," said the old lady, "I remember now hearing of that, and some of the wags in Dublin saying the Bishop was jealous of old Spray,[1] and didn't some body write something called 'Pulpit versus Organ-loft?'"

"I cawnt say."

"Well, I am glad you like the cathedral, sir; but I wish they had not dusted the banners; I used to look at them all the time the service went on—they were so romantic! I suppose you go there every Sunday?"

"I go in the summe'," said Furlong, "the place is *so* cold in the winter."

"That's true, indeed," responded the Dowager "and it's quite funny, when your teeth are chattering with cold, to hear Spray singing, 'Comfort ye, my people;' but, to be sure, *that* almost is enough to warm you. You are fond of music, I perceive?"

"Vewy."

"*I* play the guitar—citra—cithra, or lute, as it is called by the poets. I sometimes sing, too. Do you know 'The lass with the delicate air?' a sweet ballad of the old school—my instrument once belonged to Dolly Bland, the celebrated Mrs. Jordan now—ah, there, sir, is a brilliant specimen of Irish mirthfulness—what a creature she is! Hand me my lute, child," she said to her granddaughter, and having adjusted the blue ribbon over her shoulder, and twisted the tuning-pegs, and thrummed upon the wires for some time, she made a prelude, and cleared her throat to sing "The lass with the delicate air," when the loud whirring of the clock-wheels interrupted her, and she looked up with great delight at a little door in the top of the clock, which suddenly sprang open, and out popped a wooden bird.

"Listen to my bird, sir," said the old lady.

The sound of "cuckoo" was repeated twelve times, the bird popped in again, the little door closed, and the monotonous tick of the clock continued.

"That's my little bird, sir, that tells me secrets; and now, sir, you must leave me; I never receive visits after twelve. I can't sing you 'The lass with the delicate air' to-day, for who would compete with the feathered songsters of the grove? and after my sweet warblers there I dare not venture; but I will sing it for you to-morrow. Good morning, sir. I am happy to have had the honour of making your acquaintance." She bowed Furlong out very politely, and as her granddaughter was following, she said, "My love, you must not forget some seeds for my little bird." Furlong looked *rather* surprised, for he saw no bird but the one in the clock; the young lady marked his expression, and as she closed the door, she said, "You must not mind grandmama, you know; she is sometimes a little queer."

Furlong was now handed over to the boys, to show him over the domain; and they, young imps as they were, knowing he was in no favour with their father, felt they might treat him as ill as they pleased, and quiz him with impunity. The first portion of Furlong's penance consisted in being dragged through dirty stable-yards and out-houses, and shown the various pets of all the parties; dogs, pigeons, rabbits, weasels, &c. were paraded, and their qualities expatiated upon, till Furlong was quite weary of them, and expressed a desire to see the domain. Horatio, the second boy, whose name was abbreviated to Ratty, told him they must wait for Gusty, who was mending his spear. "We're going to spear for eels," said the boy; "did you ever spear for eels?"

"I should think not," said Furlong, with a knowing smile, who suspected this was intended to be a second edition of quizzing *à la mode de saumon.*

"You think I'm joking," said the boy, "but it's famous sport, I can tell you; but if you're tired of waiting here, come along with me to the milliner's, and we can wait for Gusty there."

While following the boy, who jumped along to the tune of a jig he was whistling, now and then changing the whistle into a song to the same tune, with very odd words indeed, and a burden of gibberish ending, with "riddle-diddle-dow," Furlong wondered what a milliner could have to do in such an establishment, and his wonder was not lessened when his guide added, "The milliner is a queer chap, and maybe he'll tell us something funny."

"Then the milline' is a man?" said Furlong.

"Yes," said the boy, laughing, "and he does not work with needle and thread, either."

They approached a small out-house as he spoke, and the sharp clinking of a hammer fell on their ears. Shoving open a rickety door, the boy cried, "Well, Fogy, I've brought a gentleman to see you. This is Fogy, the milliner, sir," said he to Furlong, whose surprise was further increased, when, in the person of the man called the milliner, he beheld a tinker. "What a strange pack of people I have got amongst," thought Furlong.

The old tinker saw his surprise, and grinned at him. "I suppose it was a nate young woman you thought you'd see when he towld you he'd bring you to the milliner—ha! ha! ha! Oh, they're nate lads, the Masther O'Gradys; divil a thing they call by the proper name, at all."

"Yes, we do," said the boy, sharply, "we call ourselves by our proper name—ha, Fogy, I have you there!"

"Divil a taste, as smart as you think yourself, Masther Ratty; you call yourselves gentlemen, and that's not your proper name."

Ratty, who was scraping triangles on the door with a bit of broken brick, at once converted his pencil into a missile, and let fly at the head of the tinker, who seemed quite prepared for such a result, for, raising the kettle he was mending, he caught the shot adroitly, and the brick rattled harmlessly on the tin.

"Ha!" said the tinker, mockingly, "you missed me, like your mammy's blessin';" and he pursued his work.

"What a very odd name he calls you," said Furlong, addressing young O'Grady.

"Ratty," said the boy. "Oh, yes, they call me Ratty, short for Horatio. I was called Horatio after Lord Nelson, because Lord Nelson's father was a clergyman, and papa intends me for the Church."

"And a nate clargy you'll make," said the tinker.

"And why do they call you milline'?" inquired Furlong.

The old man looked up and grinned, but said nothing. "You'll know before long, I'll engage," said Ratty,—"won't he, Fogy? You were with old Gran' to-day, weren't you?"

"Yes."

"Did she sing you 'The lass with the delicate air'?" said the boy, putting himself in the attitude of a person playing the guitar, throwing up his eyes, and mimicking the voice of an old woman,—

> So they call'd her, they call her,
>   The lass—the lass
>   With a delicate air,
>   De—lick-it—lick-it—lick-it,
> The lass with a de—lick-it air!"

The young rascal made frightful mouths, and put out his tongue every time he said "lick it," and when he had finished, asked Furlong, "wasn't that the thing?" Furlong told him his grandmama had been going to sing it, but his pleasure had been deferred till to-morrow.

"Then you did not hear it?" said Ratty.

Furlong answered in the negative.

"Oh, murder! murder! I'm sorry I told you," said the boy.

"Is it so *vewy* pa'ticula' then?" inquired Furlong.

"Oh, you'll find that out, and more, if you live long enough," was the answer. Then turning to the tinker, he said, "Have you any milliner work in hand, Fogy?"

"To be sure I have," answered the tinker; "who has so good a right to know that as yourself?—throth, you've little to do, I'm thinkin', when you ax that idle question.—Oh, you're nate lads! And would nothin' sarve you but breakin' the weather-cock?"

"Oh, 'twas such a nice cock-shot, 'twas impossible not to have a shy at it," said Ratty, chuckling.

"Oh, you're nice lads!" still chimed in the tinker.

"Besides," said Ratty, "Gusty bet me a bull-dog pup against a rabbit, I could not smash it in three goes."

"Faix, an' he ought to know you betther than that," said the tinker; "for you'd make a fair offer² at anything, I think, but an answer to your schoolmaster. Oh, a nate lad you are—a nate lad!—a nice clargy you'll be, your *rivirince*. Oh, if you hit off the tin commandments as fast as you hit off the tin weather-cock, it's a good man you'll be—an' if I never had a head-ache 'till then, sure it's happy I'd be!"

"Hold your prate, old Growly," said Ratty; "and why don't you mend the weather-cock?"

"I must mend the kittle first,—and a purtty kittle you made of it!—and would nothing sarve you but the best kittle in the house to tie to the dog's tail? Ah, masther Ratty, you're terrible boys, so yiz are!"

"Hold your prate, you old thief!—why wouldn't we amuse ourselves?"

"And huntin' the poor dog, too."

"Well, what matter?—he was a strange dog."

"That makes no differ in the *crulety*."

"Ah, bother! you old humbug!—who was it blackened the rag-woman's eye?—ha! Fogy—ha! Fogy—dirty Fogy!"

"Go away, Masther Ratty, you're too good, so you are, your Rivirince. Faix, I wondher his honour, the Squire, doesn't murther you sometimes."

"He would, if he could catch us," replied Ratty, "but we run too fast for him, so divil thank him!—and you, too, Fogy—ha! old Growly! Come along, Mr. Furlong, here's Gusty;—bad scran to you, Fogy!" and he slapped the door as he quitted the tinker.

Gustavus, followed by two younger brothers, Theodore and Godfrey, (for O'Grady loved high-sounding names in baptism, though they got twisted into such queer shapes in family use,) now led the way over the park towards the river. Some fine timber they passed occasionally, but the axe had manifestly been busy, and the wood seemed thinned rather from necessity than for improvement; the paths were choked with weeds and fallen leaves, and the rank moss added its evidence of neglect. The boys pointed out anything *they* thought worthy of observation, by the way, such as the best places to find a hare, the most covered approach to the river to get a shot at wild ducks, or where the best young wood was to be found from whence to cut a stick. On reaching their point of destination, which was where the river was less rapid, and its banks sedgy and thickly grown with flaggers and bullrushes, the sport of spearing for eels commenced. Gusty first undertook the task, and after some vigorous plunges of his implement into the water, he brought up the prey wriggling between its barbed prongs. Furlong was amazed, for he thought this, like salmon fishing, was intended as a quiz, and after a few more examples of Gusty' prowess, he undertook the sport; a short time however fatigued his unpractised arm, and he relinquished the spear to Theodore or Tay, as they called him, and Tay shortly brought up his fish, and thus, one after another, the boys, successful in their sport, soon made the basket heavy.

Then, and not till then, they desired Furlong to carry it; he declared he had no curiosity whatever in that line, but the boys would not let him off so easy, and told him the practice there was, that every one should take his share in the day's sport, and as he could not catch the fish, he should carry it. He attempted a parley, and suggested he was only a visitor, but they only laughed at him,—said that might be a very good Dublin joke, but it would not pass in the country. He then attempted laughingly to decline the honour, but Ratty, turning round to a monstrous dog, which hitherto had followed them quietly, said, "Here! Bloody-bones; here! boy! at him, sir!—make him do his work, boy!" The bristling savage gave a low growl, and fixed his fierce eyes on Furlong, who attempted to remonstrate, but he very soon gave *that* up, for another word from the boys urged the dog to a howl and a crouch, preparatory to a spring, and Furlong made no further resistance, but took up the basket amid the uproarious laughter of the boys, who continued their sport, adding every now and then to the weight of Furlong's load, and whenever he lagged behind, they cried out, "Come along, man-jack!" which was the complimentary name they called him by for the rest of the day. Furlong thought spearing for eels worse sport than fishing for salmon, and was rejoiced when a turn homeward was taken by the party; but his annoyances were not yet ended. On their return, their route lay across a plank of considerable length, which spanned a small branch of the river; it had no central support, and consequently sprang considerably to the foot of the passenger, who was afforded no protection from hand rail or even a swinging rope, and this rendered its passage difficult to an unpractised person. When Furlong was told to make his way across, he hesitated, and after many assurances on his part that he could not attempt it, Gusty said he would lead him over in security, and took his hand for the purpose; but when he had him just in the centre, he loosed himself from Furlong's hold, and ran to the opposite side. While Furlong was praying him to return, Ratty stole behind him sufficiently far to have purchase enough on the plank, and began jumping till he made it spring too high for poor Furlong to hold his footing any longer; so squatting on the plank, he got astride upon it, and held on with his hands, every descending vibration of the board dipping his dandy boots in the water.

"Well done, Ratty!" shouted all the boys.

"Splash him, Tay!" cried Gusty. "Pull away, Goggy."

The three boys now began pelting large stones into the river close beside Furlong, splashing him so thoroughly, that he was wringing wet in five minutes. In vain Furlong shouted, "Young gentlemen! young gentlemen!" and, at last, when he threatened to complain to their father, they recommenced worse than before, and vowed they'd throw him into the stream if he did not promise to be silent on the subject, for, to use their own words, if they *were* to be beaten, they might as well duck him at once, and have the "worth of their licking." At last, a compromise being effected, Furlong stood up to walk off the plank. "Remember," said Ratty, "you won't tell we hoised you."

"I won't, indeed," said Furlong; and he got safe to land.

"But I will!" cried a voice from the neighbouring wood; and Miss O'Grady appeared, surrounded by a crowd of little pet-dogs. She shook her hand in a threatening manner at the offenders, and all the little dogs set up a yelping bark, as if to enforce their mistress's anger.

The snappish barking of the pets was returned by one hoarse bay from Bloody-bones, which silenced the little dogs, as a broadside from a seventy-four would scatter a flock of privateers, and the boys returned the sister's threat by a universal shout of "Tell-tale!"

"Go home, tell-tale!" they cried, all at once; and with an action equally simultaneous, they stooped one and all for pebbles, and pelted Miss Augusta so vigorously, that she and her dogs were obliged to run for it.

1.   The first tenor of the last century.
2.   A "fair offer," is a phrase amongst the Irish peasantry, meaning a successful aim.

XVI

HAVING RECOUNTED FURLONG'S OUT-DOOR adventures, it is necessary to say something of what was passing at Neck-or-Nothing Hall in his absence.

O'Grady, on leaving the breakfast-table, retired to his justice-room to transact business, a principal feature in which was the examination of Handy Andy touching the occurrences of the evening he drove Furlong to Merryvale; for though Andy was clear of the charge for which he had been taken into custody, namely, the murder of Furlong, O'Grady thought he might have been a party to some conspiracy to drive the stranger to the enemy's camp, and therefore put him to the question very sharply. This examination he had set his heart upon; and reserving it as a *bon bouche*, dismissed all preliminary cases in a very off-hand manner, just as men carelessly swallow a few oysters preparatory to dinner.

As for Andy, when he was summoned to the justice-room, he made sure it was for the purpose of being charged with robbing the post-office, and cast a side long glance at the effigy of the man hanging on the wall, as he was marched up to the desk where O'Grady sat in magisterial dignity; and, therefore, when he found it was only for driving a gentleman to a wrong house all the pother was made, his heart was lightened of a heavy load, and he answered briskly enough. The string of question and reply was certainly an entangled one, and left O'Grady as much puzzled as before, whether Andy was stupid and innocent, or too knowing to let himself be caught,—and to this opinion he clung at last. In the course of the inquiry he found Andy had been in service at Merryvale; and Andy, telling him he knew all about waiting at table, and so forth, and O'Grady being in want of an additional man-servant in the house, while his honourable guest Sackville Scatterbrain should be on a visit with him, Andy was told he should be taken on trial for a month. Indeed, a month was as long as most servants could stay in the house—they came and went as fast as figures in a magic lanthorn.

Andy was installed in his new place, and set to work immediately scrubbing up extras of all sorts to make the reception of the honourable candidate for the county as brilliant as possible, not only for the honour of the house, but to make a favourable impression on the coming guest; for Augusta, the eldest girl, was marriageable, and, to her father's ears, "The Honourable Mrs. Sackville Scatterbrain" would have sounded much more agreeably than "Miss O'Grady."

"Well—who knows?" said O'Grady to his wife; "such things have come to pass. Furbish her up, and make her look smart at dinner—he has a good fortune, and will be a peer one of these days—worth catching. Tell her so."

Leaving these laconic observations and directions behind him, he set off to the neighbouring town to meet Scatterbrain, and to make a blow-up at the post-office about the letters; this he was the more anxious to do, as the post-office was kept by the brother of M'Garry, the apothecary; and since O'Grady had been made to pay so dearly for thrashing him, he swore eternal vengeance against the whole family. The postmaster could give no satisfactory answer to the charge made against him, and O'Grady threatened a complaint to head-quarters, and prophesied the postmaster's dismissal. Satisfied, for the present, with this piece of prospective vengeance, he proceeded to the inn, and awaited the arrival of his guest.

In the interim, at the hall, Mrs. O'Grady gave Augusta the necessary hints, and recommended a short walk to improve her colour; and it was in the execution of this order that Miss O'Grady's perambulation was cut short by the pelting her sweet brothers gave her.

The internal bustle of the establishment caught the attention of the dowager, who contrived to become acquainted with its cause, and set about making herself as fascinating as possible; for though, in the ordinary routine of the family affairs, she kept herself generally

secluded in her own apartments, whenever any affair of an interesting
nature was pending, nothing could make her refrain from joining any
company which might be in the house;—nothing;—not even O'Grady
himself. At such times, too, she became strangely excited, and invariably
executed one piece of farcical absurdity, of which, however, the family
contrived to confine the exercise to her own room. It was wearing on
her head a tin concern, something like a chimney-pot, ornamented
by a small weather-cock, after the fashion of those which surmounted
church-steeples; this, she declared, influenced her health wonderfully,
by indicating the variation of the wind in her stomach, which she
maintained to be the grand ruling principle of human existence.
She would have worn this head-dress in any company, had she been
permitted, but the terrors of her son had sufficient influence over her
to have this laid aside for a more seemly *coiffure* when she appeared at
dinner, or in the drawing-room; but while she yielded really through
fear, she affected to be influenced through tenderness to her son's
infirmity of temper.

"It is very absurd," she would say, "that Gustavus should interfere with
my toilette; but, poor fellow, he's very queer, you know, and I *humour*
him."

This at once explains why Master Ratty called the tinker "the
milliner."

It will not be wondered at, that the family carefully excluded the old
lady from the knowledge of any exciting subject; but those who know
what a talkative race children and servants are, will not be surprised that
the dowager sometimes got scent of proceedings which were meant to
be kept secret. The pending election, and the approaching visit of the
candidate, somehow or other, came to her knowledge, and of course she
put on her tin chimney-pot. Thus attired, she sat watching the avenue
all day; and when she saw O'Grady return in a handsome travelling
carriage with a stranger, she was quite happy, and began to attire herself
in some ancient finery, rather the worse for wear, and which might have
been interesting to an antiquary.

The house soon rang with bustle—bells rang, and footsteps rapidly
paced passages, and pattered up and down stairs. Andy was the nimblest
at the hall-door at the first summons of the bell; and, in a livery too

short in the arms, and too wide in the shoulders, he bustled here and there, his anxiety to be useful only putting him in every body's way, and ending in getting him a hearty cursing from O'Grady.

The carriage was unpacked, and letter-boxes, parcels, and portmanteaus, strewed the hall. Andy was desired to carry the latter to "the gentleman's room;" and, throwing it over his shoulder, he ran up stairs.

It was just after the commotion created by the arrival of the *Honourable* Mr. Scatterbrain, that Furlong returned to the house, wet and weary.

He retired to his room to change his clothes, and fancied he was now safe from further molestation, with an inward protestation that the next time the Master O'Gradys caught him in their company they might bless themselves; when he heard a loud sound of hustling near his door, and Miss Augusta's voice audibly exclaiming, "Behave yourself, Ratty!—Gusty, let me go!" when, a the words were uttered, the door of his room was sho'ved open, and Miss Augusta thrust in, and the door locked outside.

Furlong had not half his clothes on. Augusta exclaimed, "Gracious me!"—first put up her hands to her eyes, and then turned her face to the door.

Furlong hid himself in the bed-curtains, while Ratty, the vicious little rascal, with a malicious laugh, said, "Now, promise you'll not tell papa, or I'll bring him up here—and then how will you be?"

"Ratty, you wretch!" cried Augusta, kicking at the door, "let me out!"

"Not a bit, till you promise."

"Oh, fie, Maste' O'Gwady!" said Furlong.

"I'll scream, Ratty, if you don't let me out!" cried Augusta.

"If you screech, papa will hear you, and then he'll come up, and kill that fellow there."

"Oh, don't squeam, Miss O'Gwady!" said Furlong, very vivaciously, from the bed-curtains; "Don't squeam, pway!"

"I'm not squeamish, sir," said Miss Augusta; "but it's dreadful to be shut up with a man who has no clothes on him. Let me out, Ratty! let me out!"

"Well, will you tell on us?"

"No."

"'Pon your honour."

"'Pon my honour, no!—Make haste!—Oh, if papa knew of this!"

Scarcely had the words been uttered, when the heavy tramp and gruff voice of O'Grady resounded in the passage, and the boys scampered off in a fright, leaving the door locked.

"Oh, what will become of me!" said the poor girl, with the extremity of terror in her look—a terror so excessive, that she was quite heedless of the *dishabille* of Furlong, who jumped from the curtains when he heard O'Grady coming.

"Don't be fwightened, Miss O'Grady," said Furlong, half frightened to death himself. "When we explain the affair——"

"Explain!" said the girl, gasping. "Oh, you don't know papa!"

As she spoke, the heavy tramp ceased at the door—a sharp tap succeeded, and Furlong's name was called in the gruff voice of the squire.

Furlong could scarcely articulate a response.

"Let me in," said O'Grady.

"I'm not dwess'd, sir," answered Furlong.

"No matter," said the squire; "you're not a woman."

Augusta wrung her hands.

"I'll be down with you as soon as I'm dress'd, sir," replied Furlong.

"I want to speak to you immediately—and here are letters for you—open the door."

Augusta signified by signs, to Furlong, that resistance would be vain; and hid herself under the bed.

"Come in, sir," said Furlong, when she was secreted.

"The door is fastened," said O'Grady.

"Turn the key, sir," said Furlong.

O'Grady unlocked the door, and was so inconsequent a person, that he never thought of the impossibility of Furlong's having locked it, but, in the richest spirit of bulls, asked him if he always fastened his door on the outside.

Furlong said he always did.

"What's the matter with you?" inquired O'Grady. "You're as white as the sheet there." And he pointed to the bed as he spoke.

Furlong grew whiter as he pointed to that quarter.

"What ails you, man?—Ar'n't you well?"

"Wather fatigued—but I'll be bette' pwesently. What do you wish with me, sir?"

"Here are letters for you—I want to know what's in them—Scatterbrain's come—do you know that?"

"No—I did not."

"Don't stand there in the cold—go on dressing yourself; I'll sit down here till you can open your letters I want to tell you something besides." O'Grady took a chair as he spoke.

Furlong assumed all the composure he could, and the girl began to hope she should remain undiscovered, and most likely she would have been so lucky, had not the Genius of Disaster, with aspect malign, waved her sable wand and called her chosen servant Handy Andy to her aid. He, her faithful and unfailing minister, obeyed the call, and at that critical juncture of time gave a loud knock at the chamber door.

"Come in," said O'Grady.

Andy opened the door and popped in his head.—"I beg your pardon, sir, but I kem for the jintleman's port-mantle."

"What gentleman?" asked O'Grady.

"The Honourable, Sir; I tuk his portmantle to the wrong room, sir, and I'm come for it now bekase he wants it."

"There's no po'tmanteau here," said Furlong.

"O yis, sir," said Andy; "I put it undher the bed."

"Well, take it and be off," said O'Grady.

"No—no—no" said Furlong, "don't distu'b my woom, if you please, till I have done dwessing."

"But the Honourable is dhressing too, sir; and that's why he wants the portmantle."

"Take it, then," said the Squire.

Furlong was paralyzed, and could offer no further resistance: Andy stooped, and lifting the valance of the bed to withdraw the portmanteau, dropped it suddenly and exclaimed, "O Lord!"

"What's the matter?" said the Squire. "Nothin', sir," said Andy, looking scared. "Then take the portmanteau and be hanged to you."

"Oh, I'll wait till the jintleman's done, sir," said Andy, retiring.

"What the devil is all this about?" said the Squire, seeing the bewilderment of Furlong and Andy; "what is it, at all?" and he stooped as he spoke and lifted the valance. But here description must end, and imagination supply the scene of fury and confusion which succeeded. At the first fierce folly of imprecation O'Grady gave vent to, Andy ran off and alarmed the family, Augusta screamed, and Furlong held for support by the bed post, while, between every hurricane of oaths, O'Grady ran to the door and shouted for his pistols, and anon returned to the chamber to vent every abusive epithet which could be showered on man and woman. The prodigious uproar soon brought the whole house to the spot; Mrs. O'Grady and the two spare girls amongst the first; Mat, and the cook, and the scullion, and all the housemaids in rapid succession; and Scatterbrain himself at last; O'Grady all the time foaming at the mouth, and stamping up and down the room, shaking his fist at Furlong, and, after a volley of names impossible to remember or print, always concluding with the phrase, "Wait till I get my pistols!"

"Gusty, dear," said his trembling wife, " what is it all about?"

He glared upon her with his flashing eyes, and said, "Fine education you give your children, ma'am. Where have you brought up your daughters to go to, eh?"

"To church, my dear," said Mrs. O'Grady, meekly; for she being a Roman catholic, O'Grady was very jealous of his daughters being reared staunch Protestants, and she, poor simple woman, thought that was the drift of his question.

"Church, my eye! woman!—Church, indeed!—'faith, she ought to have gone there before she came where I found her. Thunderanouns! where are my pistols?"

"Where *has* she gone to, my love?" asked the wife in a tremor.

"To the divil, ma'am.—Is that all you know about it?" said O'Grady; "And you'd wish to know where she is?"

"Yes, love," said his wife.

"Then look under that bed, ma'am, and you'll see her without spectacles."

Mrs. O'Grady now gave a scream, and the girls and the housemaids joined in the chorus. Augusta bellowed from under the bed, "Mama! mama! indeed it's all Ratty—I never did it."

At this moment, to help the confusion, a fresh appearance made its way into the room; it was that of the Dowager O'Grady—arrayed in all the by-gone finery of faded full dress, and the tin chimney-pot on her head.

"What is all this about?" she exclaimed, with an air of authority; "though my weathercock tells me the wind is Nor'west, I did not expect such a storm. Is any one killed?"

"No," said O'Grady, "but somebody will be soon. Where are my pistols? Blood and fire, will nobody bring me pistols?"

"Here they are, sir," said Handy Andy, running in.

O'Grady made a rush for the pistols, but his mother and his wife threw themselves before him, and Scatterbrain shoved Andy outside the room.

"Confound you, you numscull, would you give pistols to the hands of a frantic man?"

"Sure, he ax'd for them, sir!"

"Go out o' this, you blockhead! go and hide them somewhere, where your master won't find them."

Andy retired, muttering something about the hardness of a servant's case in being scolded and called names for doing his master's bidding. Scatterbrain returned to the room where the confusion was still in full bloom; O'Grady swearing between his mother and wife, while Furlong endeavoured to explain how the young lady happened to be in his room; and she kicking in hysterics amidst the maids and her sisters, while Scatterbrain ran to and fro between all the parties, giving an ear to Furlong, an eye to O'Grady, and smelling salts to his daughter.

The case was a hard one to a milder man than O'Grady, his speculation about Scatterbrain all knocked on the head, for it could not be expected he would marry the lady who had been found under another man's bed. To hush the thing up would be impossible, after the publicity his own fury had given to the affair. "Would she ever be married after such an affair was *éclaté*?" The question rushed into his head at one side, and the answer rushed in at the other, and met it with a plump "No,"—the question and answer then joined hands in O'Grady's mind, and danced down the middle to the tune of "Haste to the wedding."

"Yes," he said, slapping his forehead, "she must be married at once." Then, turning to Furlong, he said, "You're not married, I hope?"

Furlong acknowledged he was not, though he regretted the moment he made the admission.

"'Tis well for you," said O'Grady, "for it has saved your life. You shall marry her then!"—

He never thought of asking Furlong's acquiescence in the measure.

"Come here! you baggage!" he cried to Augusta, as he laid hold of her hand and pulled her up from her chair; "come here! I intended you for a better man, but since you have such a hang-dog taste, why go to him!"—and he shoved her over to Furlong.

"There!" he said, addressing *him*, "take her, since you *will* have her. We'll speak of her fortune after."

The poor girl stood abashed, sobbing aloud, and tears pouring from her downcast eyes. Furlong was so utterly taken by surprise, that he was rivetted to the spot where he stood, and could not advance a step towards his drooping intended. At this awkward moment, the glorious old dowager came to the rescue; she advanced, tin chimney-pot and all, and taking a hand of each of the principals in hers, she joined them together in a theatrical manner, and ejaculated with a benignant air, "Bless you, my children!"

In the midst of the mingled rage, confusion, fright, and astonishment of the various parties present, there was something so exquisitely absurd in the old woman's proceeding, that nearly every one felt inclined to laugh, but the terror of O'Grady kept their risible faculties in check. Fate, however, decreed the finale should be comic; for the cook, suddenly recollecting herself, exclaimed, "Oh, murther! the goose will be burned," and ran out of the room; a smothered burst of laughter succeeded, which roused the ire of O'Grady, who, making a charge right and left amongst the delinquents, the room was soon cleared, and the party dispersed in various directions, O'Grady's voice rising loud above the general confusion, as he swore his way down stairs, kicking his mother's tin turban before him.

XVII

CANVASSING BEFORE AN ELECTION RESEMBLES skirmishing before
a battle;—the skirmishing was over, and the arrival of the
Honourable Sackville Scatterbrain was like the first gun that commences
an engagement;—and now both parties were to enter on the final
struggle.

A jolly group sat in Murphy's dining parlour on the eve of the day
fixed for the nomination. Hitting points of speeches were discussed—
plans for bringing up voters—tricks to interrupt the business of the
opposite party—certain allusions on the hustings that would make the
enemy lose temper; and, above all, every thing that could cheer and
amuse the people, and make them rejoice in their cause.

"Oh, let me alone for *that* much," said Murtough. "I have engaged
every piper and fiddler within twenty miles round, and divil a screech
of a chanter,[1] or a scrape of catgut, Scatterbrain can have for love or
money—that's one grand point."

"But," said Tom Durfy, "he has engaged the yeomanry band."

"What of that?" asked Dick Dawson; "a band is all very well for
making a splash in the first procession to the hustings, but what good is
it in working out the details?"

"What do you call details?" said Durfy.

"Why the popular tunes in the public houses, and in the tally
rooms, while the fellows are waiting to go up. Then the dances in the
evening—Wow!—won't Scatterbrain's lads look mighty shy when they
know the Eganites are kicking their heels to 'Moll in the Wad,' while
they hav'n't a lilt to shake their bones to?"

"To be sure," said Murphy; "we'll have deserters to our cause from the enemy's camp before the first night is over;[2] till the girls know where the fiddles are—and won't they make the lads join us!"

"I believe a woman would do a great deal for a dance," said Doctor Growling; "they are immensely fond of saltatory motion: I remember, once in my life, I used to flirt with a little actress who was a great favourite in a provincial town where I lived, and she was invited to a ball there, and confided to me she had no silk stockings to appear in, and without them, her presence at the ball was out of the question."

"That was a hint to you to buy the stockings," said Dick.

"No—you're out," said Growling. "She knew I was as poor as herself; but though she could not rely on my purse, she had every confidence in my taste and judgment, and consulted me on a plan she formed for going to the ball in proper twig. Now, what do you think it was?"

"To go in cotton, I suppose," returned Dick.

"Out again, sir—you'd never guess it; and only a woman could have hit on the expedient: it was the fashion in those days for ladies in full dress to wear pink stockings, and she proposed *painting her legs!*"

"Painting her legs!" they all exclaimed.

"Fact sir," said the doctor; "and she relied on me for telling her if the cheat was successful——"

"And was it?" asked Durfy.

"Don't be in a hurry, Tom.—I complied on one condition— namely—that *I* should be the painter."

"Oh, you old rascal!" cried Dick.

"A capital bargain," said Tom Durfy.

"But not a safe covenant," added the attorney.

"Don't interrupt me, gentlemen," said the doctor: "I got some rose-pink accordingly; and I defy all the hosiers in Nottingham to make a tighter fit than I did on little Jinney; and a prettier pair of stockings I never saw."

"And she went to the ball?" said Dick.

"She did."

"And the trick succeeded?" added Durfy.

"So completely," said the doctor, "that several ladies asked her to recommend her dyer to them—so you see what a woman will do to go to a dance. Poor little Jinney!—she was a merry minx:—she boxed my ears that night for a joke I made about the stockings. 'Jinney,' said I, 'for fear your stockings should fall down when you're dancing, hadn't you better let me paint a pair of garters on them?'"

The fellows laughed at the doctor's quaint conceit about the garters, but Murphy called them back to the business of the election.

"What next?" he said; "public-houses and tally-rooms to have pipers and fiddlers—ay—and we'll get up as good a march, too, as Scatterbrain, with all his yeomanry band:—I think a cart-full of fiddlers would have a fine effect!"

"If we could only get a double-bass amongst them!" said Dick.

"Talking of double-basses," said the doctor, "did you ever hear the story of the sailor in an admiral's ship, who, when some fine concert was to be given on board—"

"Hang your concerts and stories!" said Murphy; "let us get on with the election!"

"Oh, the doctor's story!" cried Tom Durfy and Dick Dawson together.

"Well, sir," continued the doctor; "a sailor was handing in, over the side, from a boat, which bore the instruments from shore, a great lot of fiddles. When some tenors came into his hand, he said, those were real good-sized fiddles; and when a violoncello appeared, Jack, supposing it was to be held between the hand and the shoulder, like a violin, declared, 'He must be a strapping chap that fiddle belonged to!' But when the double-bass made its appearance,—'My eyes and limbs!' cried Jack, 'I *would* like to see the chap as plays that!!!'"

"Well, doctor, are you done?" cried Murphy; "for, if you are, now for the election.—You say, Dick, Major Dawson is to propose your brother-in-law?"

"Yes."

"And he'll do it well, too: the Major makes a very good straight-forward speech."

"Yes," said Dick; "the old cock is not a bad hand at it; but I have a suspicion he's going to make a greater oration than usual, and read some long rigmarolish old records."

"That will never do," said Murphy; "as long as a man looks Pat in the face, and makes a good rattling speech 'out o' the face,' Pat will listen to him; but when a lad takes to heavy readings, Pat grows tired:—we must persuade the Major to give up the reading."

"Persuade my father," cried Dick,—"when did you ever hear of his giving up his own opinion?"

"If he could be prevailed on even to shorten," said Murphy.

"Oh, leave him to me," said Dick, laughing; "I'll take care he'll not read a word."

"Manage that, Dick, and you're a jewel!"

"I will," said Dick; "I'll take the glasses out of his spectacles the morning of the nomination, and then let him read, if he can."

"Capital, Dick; and now the next point of discussion is—"

"Supper, ready to come up, sir," said a servant, opening the door.

"Then, that's the best thing we could discuss, boys," said Murphy to his friends—"so up with the supper, Dan. Up with the supper!—Up with the Egans! Down with the Scatterbrains—hurra!—we'll beat them gaily."

"Hollow!" said Durfy.

"Not hollow," said Dick; "we'll have a tussle for it."

"So much the better," cried Murphy: "I would not give a fig for an easy victory—there's no fun in it. Give me the election that is like a race—now one a-head, and then the other; the closeness calling out all the energies of both parties, and developing their tact and invention, and at last, the return secured by a small majority."

"But think of the glory of a large one," said Dick.

"Ay," added Durfy, "besides crushing the hope of a petition on the part of your enemy, to pull down the majority."

"But think of Murphy's enjoyment," said the doctor, "in defending the seat, to say nothing of the bill of costs."

"You have me there, doctor," said Murphy, "a fair hit, I grant you; but see, the supper is on the table. To it, my lads; to it! and then a jolly glass to drink success to our friend Egan."

And glass after glass they did drink in all sorts and shapes of well-wishing toasts:—in short, to have seen the deep interest those men took in the success of their friend, might have gladdened the heart of a philanthropist; though there is no knowing what Father Mathew, had he flourished in those times, might have said to their overflowing benevolence.

1.   The principal tube of a bag-pipe.
2.   In those times elections often lasted many days.

XVIII

THE MORNING OF THE NOMINATION which dawned on Neck-or-Nothing Hall saw a motley group of O'Grady's retainers assembling in the stable-yard, and the out-offices rang to laugh and joke over a rude, but plentiful breakfast,—tea and coffee, there, had no place,—but meat, potatoes, milk, beer, and whisky, were at the option of the body-guard, which was selected for the honour of escorting the wild chief and his friend, the candidate, into the town. Of this party was the yeomanry-band, of which Tom Durfy spoke, though, to say the truth, considering Tom's apprehensions on the subject, it was of slender force. One trumpet, one clarionet, a fife, a big drum, and a pair of cymbals, with a "*real* nigger" to play them, were all they could muster.

After clearing off every thing in the shape of breakfast, the "musicianers" amused the retainers, from time to time, with a tune on the clarionet, fife, or trumpet, while they waited the appearance of the party from the house. Uproarious mirth and noisy joking rang round the dwelling, to which none contributed more largely than the trumpeter, who fancied himself an immensely clever fellow, and had a heap of cut and dry jokes at his command, and practical drolleries, in which he indulged to the great entertainment of all, but of none more than Andy, who was in the thick of the row, and in a divided ecstasy between the "*blackymoor's*" turban and cymbals and the trumpeter's jokes and music, the latter articles having a certain resemblance, by-the-bye, to the former in clumsiness and noise, and therefore suited to Andy's taste. Whenever occasion offered, Andy got near the big drum, too, and gave it a thump, delighted with the result of his ambitious achievement.

Andy was not lost on the trumpeter:—"Arrah, may be you'd like to have a touch at these?" said the joker, holding up the cymbals.

"Is it hard to play them, sir?" inquired Andy.

"Hard!" said the trumpeter; "sure they're not hard at all—but as soft and smooth as satin inside—just feel them—rub your finger inside."

Andy obeyed; and his finger was chopped between the two brazen plates. Andy roared, the by-standers laughed, and the trumpeter triumphed in his wit; sometimes he would come behind an unsuspecting boor, and give, close to his ear, a discordant bray from his trumpet, like the note of a jackass, which made him jump, and the crowd roar with merriment;—or, perhaps, when the clarionet or the fife was engaged in giving the people a tune, he would drown either, or both of them in a wild yell of his instrument. As they could not make reprisals upon him, he had his own way in playing whatever he liked for his audience; and in doing so indulged in all the airs of a great artist—pulling out one crook from another—blowing through them softly, and shaking the moisture from them in tasty style—rearranging them with a fastidious nicety—then, after the final adjustment of the mouthpiece, lipping the instrument with an affectation exquisitely grotesque; but, before he began, he always asked for another drink.

"It's not for myself," he would say, "but for the thrumpet, the crayther, the divil a note she can blow without a dhrop."

Then taking a mug of drink, he would present it to the bell of the trumpet, and afterwards transfer it to his own lips, always bowing to the instrument first, and saying, "Your health, ma'am!"

This was another piece of delight to the mob, and Andy thought him the funniest fellow he ever met, though he *did* chop his finger.

"Faix, sir, an' it is dhry work I'm sure, playing the thing."

"Dhry!" said the trumpeter, "'pon my ruffles and tuckers, and that's a cambric oath, it's worse nor lime burnin', so it is—it makes a man's throat as parched as pays."

"Who dar say pays?" cried the drummer.

"Howld your prate!" said the trumpeter elegantly, and silenced all reply by playing a tune. As soon as it was ended, he turned to Andy and asked for a cork.

Andy gave it to him.

The man of jokes affected to put it into the trumpet.

"What's that for, sir?" asked Andy.

"To bottle up the music," said the trumpeter—"sure all the music would run about the place if I didn't do that."

Andy gave a vague sort of "ha, ha!" as if he were not quite sure whether the trumpeter was in jest or earnest, and thought at the moment that to play the trumpet and practical jokes must be the happiest life in the world. Filled with this idea, Andy was on the watch how he could possess himself of the trumpet, for could he get one blast on it, he would be happy: a chance at last opened to him; after some time, the lively owner of the treasure laid down his instrument to handle a handsome blackthorn which one of the retainers was displaying, and he made some flourishes with the weapon to show that music was not his only accomplishment. Andy seized the opportunity and the trumpet, and made off to one of the sheds where they had been regaling; and shutting the door to secure himself from observation, he put the trumpet to his mouth, and distended his cheeks near to bursting with the violence of his efforts to produce a sound; but all his puffing was unavailing for some minutes. At last a faint cracked squeak answered a more desperate blast than before, and Andy was delighted.—"Everything must have a beginning," thought Andy, "and maybe I'll get a tune out of it yet."—He tried again, and more in power; for a sort of strangled screech was the result. Andy was in ecstasy, and began to indulge visions of being one day a trumpeter;—he strutted up and down the shed like the original he so envied, and repeated some of the drolleries he heard him utter. He also imitated his action of giving a drink to the trumpet, and was more generous to the instrument than the owner, for he really poured about half a pint of beer down its throat: he then drank its health, and finished by "bottling up the music," absolutely cramming a cork into the trumpet. Now Andy, having no idea the trumpeter made a sham of the action, made a vigorous plunge of a goodly cork into the throat of the instrument, and in so doing, the, cork went farther than he intended:—he tried to withdraw it, but his clumsy fingers, instead of extracting only drove it in deeper—he became alarmed—and seizing a fork, strove with its assistance to remedy the mischief he had done, but the more he poked, the worse;—and in his fright, he thought the safest thing he could do was to cram the cork out of sight altogether, and having soon done that, he returned to the yard, and laid down the trumpet unobserved.

Immediately after, the procession to the town started. O'Grady gave orders that the party should not be throwing away their powder and shot, as he called it, in untimely huzzas and premature music. "Wait till you come to the town, boys;" said he, "and then you may smash away as hard as you can; blow your heads off and split the sky."

The party from Merryvale was in motion for the place of action about the same time, and a merrier pack of rascals never were on the march. Murphy, in accordance with his preconceived notion of a "fine effect," had literally "a cart full of fiddlers;"—but the fiddlers hadn't it all to themselves, for there was another cart full of pipers; and, by way of mockery to the grandeur of Scatterbrain's band, he had four or five boys with grid-irons, which they played upon with pokers, and half a dozen strapping fellows carrying large iron tea trays, which they whopped after the manner of a Chinese gong.

It so happened, that the two roads from Merryvale and Neck-or-Nothing Hall met at an acute angle, at the same end of the town, and it chanced that the rival candidates and their retinues arrived at this point about the same time.

"There they are!" said Murphy, who presided in the cart full of fiddlers like a leader in an orchestra, with a shilelah for his *baton,* which he flourished over his head as he shouted, "Now give it to them, your sowls!—rasp and lilt away, boys! slate the gridirons, Mick!—smaddher the tay-tray, Tom!"

The uproar of strange sounds that followed, shouting included, may be easier imagined than described; and O'Grady, answering the war cry, sung out to his band:

"What are you at there, you lazy rascals; don't you hear them blackguards beginning?—fire away and be hanged to you!"

His rascals shouted, bang went the drum, and clang went the cymbals; the clarinet squeaked, and the fife tootled, but the trumpet—ah!—the trumpet—their great reliance; where was the trumpet? O'Grady inquired in the precise words, with a diabolical addition of his own. "Where the d—— is the trumpet;" said he; he looked over the side of the carriage, as he spoke, and saw the trumpeter spitting out a mouthful of beer, which had ran from the instrument as he lifted it to his mouth.

"Bad luck to you, what are you wasting your time there for," thundered O'Grady in a rage; "why didn't you spit out when you were young, and you'd be a clean old man?—"Blow and be d— to you!"

The trumpeter filled his lungs for a great blast, and put the trumpet to his lips—but in vain; Andy had bottled his music for him. O'Grady, seeing the inflated cheeks and protruding eyes of the musician, whose visage was crimson with exertion, and yet no sound produced, thought the fellow was practising one of his jokes upon him, and became excessively indignant; he thundered anathemas at him, but his voice was drowned in the din of the drum and cymbals, which were plied so vigorously, that the clarionet and fife shared the same fate as O'Grady's voice. The trumpeter could judge of O'Grady's rage from the fierceness of his actions only, and answered him in pantomimic expression, holding up his trumpet and pointing into the bell, with a grin of vexation on his phiz, meant to express something was wrong; but this was all mistaken by the fierce O'Grady, who only saw in the trumpeter's grins the insolent intention of gibing him.

"Blow, you blackguard; blow!" shouted the Squire.

Bang went the drum.

"Blow—or I'll break your neck!"

Crash went the cymbals.

"Stop your banging there, you ruffians, and let me be heard!" roared the excited man; but as he was standing up on the seat of the carriage, and flung his arms about wildly as he spoke, the drummer thought his action was meant to stimulate him to further exertion, and he banged away louder than before.

"By the hokey, I'll murder some o' ye!" shouted the Squire, who, ordering the carriage to pull up, flung open the door and jumped out, made a rush at the drummer, seized his principal drumstick, and giving him a bang over the head with it, cursed him for a rascal, for not stopping when he told him: this silenced all the instruments together, and O'Grady, seizing the trumpeter by the back of the neck, shook him violently, while he denounced with fierce imprecations his insolence in daring to practise a joke on him. The trumpeter protested his innocence, and O'Grady called him a lying rascal, finishing his abuse by clenching his fist in a menacing attitude, and telling him to play.

"I can't, your honour!"

"You lie, you scoundrel."

"There's something in the thrumpet, sir."

"Yes, there's music in it; and if you don't blow it out of it—"

"I can't blow it out of it, sir."

"Hold your prate, your ruffian; blow, this minute."

"Arrah, thry it yourself, sir;" said the frightened man, handing the instrument to the Squire.

"D—n your impudence, you rascal; do you think I'd blow anything that was in your dirty mouth; blow, I tell you, or it will be worse for you."

"By the vartue o' my oath, your honour."

"Blow, I tell you!"

"By the seven blessed candles."

"Blow, I tell you!"

"The thrumpet is choked, sir."

"There will be a trumpeter choked, soon," said O'Grady gripping him by the neck-handkerchief with his knuckles ready to twist into his throat. "By this and that I'll strangle you, if you don't play this minute, you humbugger."

"By the blessed Vargin, I'm not humbuggin', your honour;" stammered the trumpeter with the little breath O'Grady left him.

Scatterbrain, seeing O'Grady's fury, and fearful of its consequences, had alighted from the carriage, and came to the rescue, suggesting to the infuriated Squire, that what the man said might be true. O'Grady said he knew better, that the blackguard was a notorious joker, and having indulged in a jest in the first instance, was now only lying to save himself from punishment; further more, swearing that if be did not play that minute, he'd throw him into the ditch.

With great difficulty O'Grady was prevailed upon to give up his grip of the trumpeter's throat; and the poor breathless wretch, handing his instrument to the clarionet player, appealed to him if it were possible to play on it. The clarionet player said he could not tell, for he did not understand the trumpet.

"You see there!" cried O'Grady. "You see he's humbugging, and the clarionet is an honest man."

"An honest man!" exclaimed the trumpeter, turning fiercely on the clarionet "He's the biggest *villian* unhanged, for sthrivin' to get me murthered, and refusin' the evidence for me!" The man's eyes flashed fury as he spoke; and throwing his trumpet down, he exclaimed, "Mooney!—by jakers, you're no man!" And clenching his fists, as he spoke, he made a rush on the clarionet and planted a hit on his mouth with such vigour, that he rolled in the dust; and when he rose, it was with such an upper lip that his clarionet was evidently finished for the next week certainly.

Now the fifer was the clarionet-player's brother; and he, turning on the trumpeter, roared—

"Bad luck to you!—you did not sthrek him fair!"

But while in the very act of reprobating the foul blow, he let fly a hit under the ear of the trumpeter, who was quite unprepared for it,—and he, too, measured his length on the road. On recovering his legs, he rushed on the fifer for revenge, and a regular scuffle ensued amongst "the musicianers," to the great delight of the crowd of retainers, who were so well primed with whisky that a fight was just the thing to their taste.

In vain O'Grady swore at them, and went amongst them, striving to restore order, but they would not be quiet till several black eyes and damaged noses bore evidence of a very busy five minutes having passed. In the course of "the scrimmage," Fate was unkind to the fifer, whose mouth-piece was considerably impaired; and "the boys" remarked, that the worst stick you could have in a crowd was a "whistling stick," by which name they designated the fifer's instrument.

At last, however, peace was restored, and the trumpeter again ordered to play by O'Grady.

He protested, again, it was impossible.

The fifer, in revenge, declared he was only humbugging the Squire.

Hereupon O'Grady, seizing the unfortunate trumpeter, gave him a more sublime kicking than ever fell to the lot even of a piper or fiddler, whose pay[1] is proverbially oftener in that article than the coin of the realm.

Having tired himself, and considerably rubbed down the toe of his boot with his gentlemanly exercise, O'Grady dragged the trumpeter to the ditch, and rolled him into it, there to cool the fever which burned in his seat of honour.

O'Grady then re-entered the carriage with Scatterbrain, and the party proceeded; but the clarionet-player could not blow a note, the fifer was not in good playing condition, and tootled with some difficulty; the drummer was obliged now and then to relax his efforts in making a noise, that he might lift his right arm to his nose, which had got damaged in the fray, and the process of wiping his face with his cuff changed the white facings of his jacket to red. The negro cymbal-player was the only one whose damages were not to be ascertained, as a black eye would not tell on him, and his lips could not be more swollen than nature had made them. On the procession went, however; but the rival mob, the Eganites, profiting by the delay caused by the row, got a-head, and entered the town first, with their pipers and fiddlers, hurrahing their way in good humour down the street, and occupying the best places in the court-house, before the arrival of the opposite party, whose band, instead of being a source of triumph, was only a thing of jeering merriment to the Eganites, who received them with mockery and laughter. All this by no means sweetened O'Grady's temper, who looked thunder as he entered the court-house with his candidate, who was, though a good fellow, a little put out by the accidents of the morning; and Furlong looked more sheepish than ever, as he followed his leaders.

The business of the day was opened by the high-sheriff, and Major Dawson lost no time in rising to propose, that Edward Egan, Esquire, of Merryvale, was a fit and proper person to represent the county in parliament.

The proposition was received with cheers by "the boys" in the body of the court-house; the Major proceeded, full sail, in his speech—his course aided by being on the popular current, and the "sweet voices" of the multitude blowing in his favour. On concluding (as "the boys" thought) his address, which was straightforward, and to the point, a voice in the crowd proposed, "Three cheers for the owld Major."

Three deafening peals followed the hint.

"And now," said the Major, "I will read a few extracts here from some documents, in support of what I have had the honour of addressing to you." And he pulled out a bundle of papers as he spoke, and laid them down before him.

The movement was not favoured by "the boys," as it indicated a tedious reference to facts, by no means to their taste, and the same voice which suggested the three cheers, now sung out—"Never mind, Major—sure, we'll take your word for it!"

Cries of "Order!" and "Silence!" ensued; and were followed by murmurs, coughs, and sneezes, in the crowd, with a considerable shuffling of hobnailed shoes on the pavement.

"Order!" cried a voice in authority.

"Order any thing you plaze, sir!" said the voice in the crowd.

"Whisky!" cried one.

"Porther!" shouted another.

"Tabakky!" roared a third.

"I must insist on silence!" cried the sheriff, in a very husky voice. "Silence—or I'll have the court-house cleared!"

"Faith, if you cleared your own throat it would be betther," said the wag in the crowd.

A laugh followed. The sheriff felt the hit, and was silent.

The Major all this time had been adjusting his spectacles on his nose, unconscious, poor old gentleman, that Dick, according to promise, had abstracted the glasses from them that morning. He took up his documents to read, made sundry wry faces, turned the papers up to the light,—now on this side, and now on that,—but could make out nothing; while Dick gave a knowing wink at Murphy. The old gentleman took off his spectacles to wipe the glasses.

The voice in the crowd cried, "Thank you, Major!"

The Major pulled out his handkerchief, and his fingers met where he expected to find a lens:—he looked very angry, cast a suspicious glance at Dick, who met it with the composure of an anchorite, and quietly asked what was the matter.

"I shall not trouble you, gentlemen, with the extracts," said the Major.

"Hear, hear," responded the genteel part of the auditory.

"I towld you we'd take your word, Major," cried the voice in the crowd.

Egan's seconder followed the Major, and the crowd shouted again. O'Grady now came forward to propose the Honourable Sackville Scatterbrain, as a fit and proper person to represent the county in parliament. He was received by his own set of vagabonds with uproarious cheers, and "O'Grady for ever!" made the walls ring. "Egan for ever!" and hurras were returned from the Merryvalians. O'Grady thus commenced his address:—

"In coming forward to support my honourable friend, the Honourable Sackville Scatterbrain, it is from the conviction—the conviction"—

"Who got the conviction agen the potteen last sishin?" the voice in the crowd.

Loud groans followed this allusion to the prosecution of a few little private stills, in which O'Grady had shown some unnecessary severity that made him unpopular. Cries of "Order" and "Silence" ensued.

"I say the conviction," repeated O'Grady fiercely, looking towards the quarter whence the interruption took place,—"and if there is any blackguard here who dares to interrupt me, I'll order him to be taken out by the ears. I say, I propose my honourable friend, the Honourable Sackville Scatterbrain, from the conviction that there is a necessity in this county—"

"Faith, there is plenty of necessity," said the tormentor in the crowd.

"Take that man out," said the sheriff.

"Don't hurry yourself, sir," returned the delinquent, amidst the laughter of "the boys," in proportion to whose merriment rose O'Grady's ill humour.

"I say there is a necessity for a vigorous member to represent this county in parliament, and support the laws, the constitution, the crown, and the—the—the interests of the county!"

"Who made the new road?" was a question that now rose from the crowd—a laugh followed—and some groans at this allusion to a bit of jobbing on the part of O'Grady, who got a grand jury presentment to make a road which served nobody's interest but his own.

"The frequent interruptions I meet here from the lawless and disaffected, show too plainly that we stand in need of men who will support the arm of the law in purging the country."—

"Who killed the 'pothecary?" said a fellow, in a voice so deep that it seemed suited to issue from the jaws of death.

The question, and the extraordinary voice in which it was uttered, produced one of those roars of laughter which sometimes shake public meetings in Ireland; and O'Grady grew furious.

"If I knew who that gentleman was, I'd pay him!" said he.

"You'd better pay *them you know*," was the answer; and this allusion to O'Grady's notorious character of a bad pay, was relished by the crowd, and again raised the laugh against him.

"Sir," said O'Grady, addressing the sheriff," I hold this ruffianism in contempt. I treat it, and the authors of it, those who no doubt have instructed them, with contempt." He looked over to where Egan and his friends stood, as he spoke of the crowd having had instruction to interrupt him.

"If you mean, sir," said Egan, "that I have given any such instruction, I deny, in the most unqualified terms, the truth of such an assertion."

"Keep yourself cool, Ned," said Dick Dawson, close to his ear.

"Never fear me," said Egan, "but I won't let him bully."

The two former friends now exchanged rather fierce looks at each other.

"Then why am I interrupted?" asked O'Grady.

"It is no business of mine to answer that," replied Egan; "but I repeat the unqualified denial of your assertion."

The crowd ceased its noise when the two Squires were seen engaged in exchanging smart words, in the hope of catching what they said.

"It is a disgraceful uproar," said the sheriff.

"Then it is your business, Mister Sheriff," returned Egan, "to suppress it—not mine; they are quiet enough now."

"Yes, but they'll make a wow again," said Furlong, "when Miste' O'Gwady begins."

"You seem to know all about it," said Dick; "maybe *you* have instructed them."

"No, sir, I didn't instwuct them," said Furlong, very angry at being twitted by Dick.

Dick laughed in his face, and said: "Maybe that's one of your electioneering tactics—eh?"

Furlong got very angry, while Dick and Murphy shouted with laughter at him.—"No, sir," said Furlong, "I don't welish the pwactice of such di'ty twicks."

"Do you apply the word 'dirty' to me, sir?" said Dick the Devil, ruffling up like a game-cock.—"I'll tell you what sir, if you make use of the word 'dirty' again, I'd think very little of kicking you—ay, or eight like you—I'd kick eight Furlongs one mile."

"Who's talking of kicking?" asked O'Grady.

"I am," said Dick, "do you want any?"

"Gentlemen! gentlemen!" cried the sheriff, "order! pray, order! do proceed with the business of the day."

"I'll talk to you after about this!" said O'Grady, in a threatening tone.

"Very well," said Dick, "we've time enough, the day's young yet."

O'Grady then proceeded to find fault with Egan, censuring his politics, and endeavouring to justify his defection from the same cause: he concluded thus, "Sir, I shall pursue my course of duty; I have chalked out my own line of conduct, sir, and I am convinced no other line is the right line. Our opponents are wrong, sir,—totally wrong—all wrong, and, as I have said, I have chalked out my own line, sir, and I propose the Honourable Sackville Scatterbrain as a fit and proper person to sit in parliament for the representation of this county."

The O'Gradyites shouted as their chief concluded; and the Merryvalians returned some groans, and a cry of "Go home, turncoat!"

Egan now presented himself, and was received with deafening and long-continued cheers, for he was really beloved by the people at large; his frank and easy nature, the amiable character he bore in all his social relations, the merciful and conciliatory tendency of his decisions and conduct as a magistrate, won him the solid respect as well as affection of the country.

He had been for some days in low spirits in consequence of Larry Hogan's visit and mysterious communication with him; but this, its cause, was unknown to all but himself, and therefore more difficult to support; for none but those whom sad experience has taught can tell the agony of enduring in secret and in silence the pang that gnaws a proud heart, which, Spartan like, will let the tooth destroy, without complaint or murmur.

His depression, however, was apparent, and Dick told Murphy he feared Ned would not be up to the mark at the election; but Murphy, with a better knowledge of human nature, and the excitement of such a cause, said, "Never fear him—ambition is a long spur, my boy, and will stir the blood of a thicker-skinned fellow than your brother-in-law. When he comes to stand up and assert his claims before the world, he'll be all right!"

Murphy was a true prophet, for Egan presented himself with confidence, brightness, and good-humour on his open countenance.

"The first thing I have to ask of you, boys," said Egan, addressing the assembled throng, "is a fair hearing for the other candidate."

"Hear, hear!" followed from the gentlemen in the gallery.

"And as he is a stranger amongst us, let him have the privilege of first addressing you."

With these words he bowed courteously to Scatterbrain, who thanked him very much like a gentleman, and accepting his offer, advanced to address the electors. O'Grady waved his hand in signal to his bodyguard, and Scatterbrain had three cheers from the ragamuffins.

He was no great things of a speaker, but he was a good-humoured fellow, and this won on the Paddies; and although coming before them under the disadvantage of being proposed by O'Grady, they heard him with good temper:—to this, however, Egan's good word considerably contributed.

He went very much over the ground his proposer had taken, so that, bating the bad temper, the pith of his speech was much the same, quite as much deprecating the political views of his opponent, and harping on O'Grady's worn-out catch-word of "Having chalked out a line for himself," &c., &c., &c.

Egan now stood forward, and was greeted with fresh cheers. He began in a very Irish fashion; for, being an unaffected, frank, and free-hearted fellow himself, he knew how to touch the feelings of those who possess such qualities themselves. He waited till the last echo of the uproarious greeting died away, and the first simple words he uttered were—

"Here I am, boys!"

Simple as the words were, they produced "one cheer more."

"Here I am, boys,—*the same I ever was.*"

Loud huzzas, and "Long life to you!" answered the last pithy words, which were sore ones to O'Grady; who, as a renegade, felt the hit.

"Fellow countrymen, I come forward to represent you, and, however I may be unequal to *that* task, at least, I will never *mis*represent you."

Another cheer followed.

"My past life is evidence enough on that point; God forbid I were of the mongrel breed of Irishmen, who speak ill of their own country. I never did it, boys, and I never will! Some think they get on by it, and so they do, indeed;—they get on as sweeps and shoe-blacks get on,—they drive a dirty trade, and find employment;—but are they respected?"

Shouts of "No—no."

"You're right!—No!—they are not respected,—even by their very employers. Your political sweep and, shoe-black is no more respected than he who cleans our chimneys or cleans our shoes. The honourable gentleman who has addressed you last, confesses he is a stranger amongst you; and is a stranger to be your representative? You may be civil to a stranger—it is a pleasing duty; but he is not the man to whom you would give your confidence. You might share a hearty glass with a stranger, but you would not enter into a joint lease of a farm without knowing a little more of him; and if you would not trust a single farm with a stranger, will you give a whole county into his hands? When a stranger comes to these parts, I'm sure he'll get a civil answer from every man I see here,—he will get a civil 'yes' or a civil 'no,' to his question,—and if he seeks his way, you will show him his road. And to the honourable gentleman, 'who has done you' the favour to come and ask you civilly, will you give him the county, you as civilly may answer 'No,' and *show him his road home again.* As for the gentleman who proposed him, he has chosen to make certain strictures upon my views, and, opinions, and conduct. As for views—there was a certain heathen god, the Romans worshipped, called Janus; he was a fellow with two heads—and, by-the-bye, boys, he would have been just the fellow to live amongst us; for when one of his heads was broken, he would have had the other for use. Well, this Janus was called 'double-face,' and could see before and behind him. Now, *I'm no double-face*, boys; and as for seeing before and behind me, I can look back on the past, and forward to the future, and *both* the roads are straight ones. (*Cheers.*) I wish every one could say as much. As for my opinions, all I shall say is, *I* never changed *mine; Mister* O'Grady can't say as much."

"Sure there's a weathercock in the family," said the voice in the crowd.

A loud laugh followed this sally, for the old dowager's eccentricity was not *quite* a secret.—O'Grady looked as if he could have eaten the whole crowd at a mouthful.

"Much has been said," continued Egan, "about gentlemen chalking out lines for themselves:—now, the plain English of this very determined chalking of *their own* line, is rubbing out every other man's line. Some of these chalking gentlemen have lines chalked up against them, and might find it difficult to pay the score if they were called to account. To such—*rubbing out other men's lines,* and their own, too, may be convenient; but I don't like the practice. Boys, I have no more to say than this, *We know and can trust each other!*"

Egan's address was received with acclamation, and when silence was restored, the sheriff demanded a show of hands; and a very fine show of hands there was, and every hand had a stick in it.

The show of hands was declared to be in favour of Egan, whereupon a poll was demanded on the part of Scatterbrain, after which every one began to move from the court-house.

O'Grady, in very ill-humour, was endeavouring to shove past a herculean fellow, rather ragged, and very saucy, who did not seem inclined to give place to the savage elbowing of the Squire.

"What brings such a ragged rascal as you here?" said O'Grady, brutally; "you're not an elector."

"Yis, I am!" replied the fellow, sturdily.

"Why, *you* can't have a lease, you beggar."

"No, but maybe I have an article."[2]

"What is your article?"

"What is it?" retorted the fellow, with a fierce look at O'Grady. "Faith, it's a fine brass blundherbuss; *and I'd like to see the man would dispute the title.*"

O'Grady had met his master, and could not reply; the crowd shouted for the ragamuffin, and all parties separated to gird up their loins for the next day's poll.

1.   Fiddlers' fare, or pipers' pay—more kicks than halfpence.
2.   A name given to a written engagement between landlord and tenant, promising to grant a lease, on which registration is allowed in Ireland.

XIX

AFTER THE ANGRY WORDS EXCHANGED at the nomination, the most peaceable reader must have anticipated the probability of a duel;—but when the inflammable stuff of which Irishmen are made is considered, together with the excitement and pugnacious spirit attendant upon elections in all places, the certainty of a hostile meeting must have been apparent.—The sheriff might have put the gentlemen under arrest, it is true, but that officer was a weak, thoughtless, and irresolute person, and took no such precaution; though, to do the poor man justice, it is only fair to say, that such an intervention of authority at such a time and place would have been considered on all hands as a very impertinent, unjustifiable and discourteous interference with the private pleasures and privileges of gentlemen.

Dick Dawson had a message conveyed to him from O'Grady, requesting the honour of his company the next morning to "grass before breakfast;" to which, of course, Dick returned an answer expressive of the utmost readiness to oblige the squire with his presence; and, as the business of the election was of importance, it was agreed they should meet at a given spot on the way to the town, and so lose as little time as possible.

The next morning, accordingly, the parties met at the appointed place, Dick attended by Edward O'Connor and Egan—the former in capacity of his friend; and O'Grady, with Scatterbrain for his second, and Furlong a looker-on: there were some straggling spectators besides, to witness the affair.

"O'Grady looks savage, Dick," said Edward.

"Yes," answered Dick, with a smile of as much unconcern as if he were going to lead off a country dance. "He looks as pleasant as a bull in a pound."

"Take care of yourself, my dear Dick," said Edward, seriously.

"My dear boy, don't make yourself uneasy," replied Dick, laughing.— "I'll bet you two to one he misses me."

Edward made no reply, but to his sensitive and more thoughtful nature, betting at such a moment savoured too much of levity, so, leaving his friend, he advanced to Scatterbrain, and they commenced making the preliminary preparations.

During the period which this required, O'Grady was looking down sulkily or looking up fiercely, and striking his heel with vehemence into the sod, while Dick Dawson was whistling a planxty and eyeing his man.

The arrangements were soon made, the men placed on their ground, and Dick saw by the intent look with which O'Grady marked him, that he meant mischief; they were handed their pistols—the seconds retired—the word was given, and as O'Grady raised his pistol, Dick saw he was completely covered, and suddenly exclaimed, throwing up his arm, "I beg your pardon for a moment."

O'Grady involuntarily lowered his weapon, and seeing Dick standing perfectly erect, and nothing following his sudden request for this suspension of hostilities, asked, in a very angry tone, why he had interrupted him. "Because I saw you had me covered," said Dick, "and you'd have hit me if you had fired that time: now fire away as soon as you like!" added he, at the same moment rapidly bringing up his own pistol to the level.

O'Grady was taken by surprise, and fancying Dick was going to blaze at him, fired hastily and missed his adversary.

Dick made him a low bow, and fired in the air.

O'Grady wanted another shot, saying Dawson had tricked him, but Scatterbrain felt the propriety of Edward O'Connor's objection to further fighting, after Dawson receiving O'Grady's fire; so the gentlemen were removed from the ground, and the affair terminated.

O'Grady, having fully intended to pink Dick, was excessively savage at being overreached, and went off to the election with a temper by

no means sweetened by the morning's adventure, while Dick roared
with laughing, exclaiming at intervals to Edward O'Connor, as he was
putting up the pistols, "Did not I *do* him neatly?"

Off they cantered gaily to the high road, exchanging merry and
cheering salutations with the electors, who were thronging towards the
town in great numbers and all variety of manner, group, and costume.
Some on foot, some on horseback, and some on cars; the gayest attire of
holiday costume, contrasting with the every-day rags of wretchedness;
the fresh cheek of health and beauty making gaunt misery look more
appalling, and the elastic step of vigorous youth outstripping the tardy
pace of feeble age. Pedestrians were hurrying on in detachments of five
or six—the equestrians in companies less numerous; sometimes the
cavalier who could boast a saddle carrying a woman on a pillion behind
him.—But saddle or pillion were not an indispensable accompaniment
to this equestrian duo, for many a "bare back" *garran* carried his couple,
his only harness being a halter made of a hay-rope, which in time of
need sometimes proves a substitute for rack and manger; for it is not
uncommon in Ireland to see the *garran* nibbling the end of his bridle
when opportunity offers.—The cars were in great variety: some bore
small kishes,[1] in which a woman and some children might be seen—
others had a shake down of clean straw to serve for cushions; while
the better sort spread a feather-bed for greater comfort, covered by a
patchwork quilt, the work of the "good woman" herself, whose own
quilted petticoat vied in brightness with the calico roses on which she
was sitting.—The most luxurious indulged still further in some arched
branches of hazel, which, bent above the car in the fashion of a booth,
bore another coverlid, by way of awning; and served for protection
against the weather; but few there were who could indulge in such a
luxury as this of the "*chaise marine*," which is the name the contrivance
bears, but why, Heaven only knows.

The street of the town had its centre occupied at the broadest place
with a long row of cars, covered in a similar manner to the *chaise marine*,
a door or a shutter laid across underneath the awning, after the fashion
of a counter, on which various articles were displayed for sale; for
the occasion of the election was as good as a fair to the small dealers,
and the public were therefore favoured with the usual opportunity of

purchasing uneatable gingerbread, knives that would not cut, spectacles to increase blindness, and other articles of equal usefulness.

While the dealers here displayed their ware, and were vociferous in declaring its excellence, noisy groups passed up and down on either side of these ambulatory shops, discussing the merits of the candidates, predicting the result of the election, or giving an occasional cheer for their respective parties, with a twirl of a stick or the throwing up of a hat; while from the houses on both sides of the street the scraping of fiddles, and the lilting of pipes increased the mingled din.

But the crowd was thickest and the uproar greatest in front of the inn where Scatterbrain's committee sat, and before the house of Murphy, who gave up all his establishment to the service of the election, and whose stable-yard made a capital place of mustering for the tallies of Egan's electors to assemble ere they marched to the poll.—At last the hour for opening the poll struck, the inn poured forth the Scatterbrains, and Murphy's stable-yard the Eganites, the two bodies of electors uttering thundering shouts of defiance, as, with rival banners flying, they joined in one common stream, rushing to give their votes,—for as for their *voices*, they were giving *them* most liberally and strenuously already. The dense crowd soon surrounded the hustings in front of the court-house, and the throes and heavings of this living mass resembled a turbulent sea lashed by a tempest:—but what sea is more unruly than an excited crowd?—what tempest fiercer than the breath of political excitement?

Conspicuous amongst those on the hustings were both the candidates and their aiders and abettors on either side; O'Grady and Furlong, Dick Dawson and Tom Durfy for work, and Growling to laugh at them all. Edward O'Connor was addressing the populace in a spirit-stirring appeal to their, pride and affections, stimulating them to support their tried and trusty friend, and not yield the honour of their county either to fear or favours of a stranger, nor copy the bad example which some (who ought to blush) had set them, of betraying old friends and abandoning old principles. Edward's address was cheered by those who heard it:—but being heard is not essential to the applause attendant on political addresses, for those who do not hear cheer quite as much as those who do. The old adage hath it, "Show me your company, and I'll

tell you who you are"—and, in the spirit of the adage, one might say,
"Let me see the speech-maker, and I'll tell you what he says." So, when
Edward O'Connor spoke, the boys welcomed him with the shout of
"Ned of the Hill for ever,"—and knowing to what tune his mouth
would be opened, they cheered accordingly when he concluded.—
O'Grady, on evincing a desire to address them, was not so successful;—
the moment he showed himself, taunts were flung at him; but in spite of
this, attempting to frown down their dissatisfaction, he began to speak;
but he had not uttered six words when his voice was drowned in the
discordant yells of a trumpet. It is scarcely necessary to tell the reader
that the performer was the identical trumpeter of the preceding day,
whom O'Grady had kicked so unmercifully, who, in indignation at his
wrongs, had gone over to the enemy; and having, after a night's hard
work, disengaged the cork which Andy had crammed into his trumpet,
appeared in the crowd ready to do battle in the popular cause.—"Wait,"
he cried, "till that savage of a baste of a squire dares for to go for to
spake!—won't I smother him!" Then he would put his instrument of
vengeance to his lips, and produce a yell that made his auditors put
their hands to their ears. Thus armed, he waited near the platform
for O'Grady's speech, and put, his threat effectually into execution.
O'Grady saw whence the annoyance proceeded, and shook his fist at
the delinquent, with protestations that the police should drag him from
the crowd, if he dared to continue—but every threat was blighted in the
bud by a withering blast of the trumpet, which was regularly followed
by a peal of laughter from the crowd. O'Grady stamped and swore with
rage, and calling Furlong, sent him to inform the sheriff how riotous the
crowd were, and requested him to have the trumpeter seized.

Furlong hurried off on his mission, and after a long search for the
potential functionary, saw him in a distant corner engaged in what
appeared to be an urgent discussion between him and Murtough
Murphy, who was talking in the most jocular manner to the sheriff,
who seemed any thing but amused with his argumentative merriment.
The fact was, Murphy, while pushing the interests of Egan with an
energy unsurpassed, did it all with the utmost mirthfulness, and gave his
opponents a laugh in exchange for the point gained against them, and
while he defeated, amused them. Furlong, after shoving and elbowing

his way through the crowd, suffering from heat and exertion, came
fussing up to the sheriff, wiping his face with a scented cambric pocket
handkerchief. The sheriff and Murphy were standing close beside one
of the polling desks, and on Furlong's lisping out "Miste' Shewiff,"
Murphy, recognising the voice and manner, turned suddenly round,
and with the most provoking cordiality addressed him thus with a smile
and a nod:

"Ah! Mister Furlong, how d'ye do? delighted to see you—here we
are at it, sir, hammer and tongs—of course you are come to vote for
Egan."

Furlong, who intended to annihilate Murphy with an indignant
repetition of the provoking question put to him, threw as much of
defiance as he could into his namby pamby manner, and exclaimed—

"*I* vote for Egan?"

"Thank you, sir," said Murphy. " Record the vote," added he to the
clerk.

There was loud laughter on one side, and anger as loud on the other,
at the way in which Murphy had entrapped Furlong, and cheated him
into voting against his own party. In vain the poor gull protested he
never *meant* to vote for Egan.

"But you did it," cried Murphy.

"What the deuce have you done?" cried Scatterbrain's agent, in a
rage.

"Of course, they know I wouldn't vote that way," said Furlong. "I
couldn't vote that way—it's a mistake, and I pwotest against the twick."

"We've got the trick, and we'll keep it, however," said Murphy.

Scatterbrain's agent said 'twas unfair, and desired the polling-clerk not
to record the vote.

"Didn't every one hear him say, '*I vote for Egan?*'" asked Murphy.

"But he didn't mean it, sir," said the agent.

"I don't care what he meant, but I know he said it," retorted Murphy;
"and every one round knows he said it; and as I mean what I say myself,
I suppose every other gentleman does the same—down with the vote,
Mister rolling-clerk."

A regular wrangle now took place between the two agents, amidst
the laughter of the bystanders, whose merriment was increased by

Furlong's vehement assurances he did not mean to vote as Murphy
wanted to make it appear he had; but the more he protested the more
the people laughed. This increased his energy in fighting out the point,
until Scatterbrain's agent recommended him to desist, for that he was
only interrupting their own voters from coming up. "Never mind now,
sir," said the agent, "I'll appeal to the assessor about that vote."

"Appeal as much as you like," said Murtough; "that vote is as dead as
a herring to you."

Furlong finding further remonstrance unavailing, as regarded his
vote, delivered to the sheriff the message of O'Grady, who was boiling
over with impatience, in the meantime, at the delay of his messenger,
and anxiously expecting the arrival of sheriff and police to coerce the
villanous trumpeter and chastise the applauding crowd, which became
worse and worse every minute.

They exhibited a new source of provocation to O'Grady, by exposing
a rat-trap hung at the end of a pole, with the caged vermin within,
and vociferated "Rat, rat," in the pauses of the trumpet. Scatterbrain,
remembering the hearing they gave him the previous day, hoped to
silence them, and begged O'Grady to permit *him* to address them; but
the whim of the mob was up, and could not be easily diverted, and
Scatterbrain himself was hailed with the name of "Rat-catcher."

"You cotch him—and I wish you joy of him!" cried one.

"How much did you give for him?" shouted another.

"What did you bait your thrap with?" roared a third.

"A bit o' *threasury bacon*," was the answer from a stentorian voice
amidst the multitude, who shouted with laughter at the apt rejoinder,
which they reiterated from one end of the crowd to the other, and the
cry of "threasury bacon" rang far and wide.

Scatterbrain and O'Grady consulted together on the hustings what
was to be done, while Dick the Devil was throwing jokes to the crowd,
and inflaming their mischievous merriment, and Growling looking on
with an expression of internal delight at the fun, uproar, and vexation
around him. It was just a dish to his taste, and he devoured it with silent
satisfaction.

"What the deuce keeps that sneaking dandy?" cried O'Grady to
Scatterbrain. "He should have returned long ago."—Oh! could he have

only known at that moment, that his sweet son-in-law elect was voting against him, what would have been the consequence!

Another exhibition, insulting to O'Grady, now appeared in the crowd,—a chimney-pot and weather-cock, after the fashion of his mother's, was stuck on a pole, and underneath was suspended an old coat turned inside out; this double indication of his change, so peculiarly insulting, was elevated before the hustings amidst the jeers and laughter of the people. O'Grady was nearly frantic—he rushed to the front of the platform, he shook his fist at the mockery, poured every abusive epithet on its perpetrators, and swore he would head the police himself and clear the crowd. In reply the crowd hooted, the rat-trap and weathercock were danced together after the fashion of Punch and Judy, to the music of the trumpet; and another pole made its appearance, with a piece of bacon on it, and a placard bearing the inscription of "Treasury bacon," all which Tom Durfy had run off to procure at a huckster's shop, the moment he heard the waggish answer which he thus turned to account.

"The military must be called out!" said O'Grady; and with these words he left the platform to seek the sheriff.

Edward O'Connor, the moment he heard O'Grady's threat, quitted the hustings also, in company with old Growling.

"What a savage and dangerous temper that man has!" said Edward; "calling for the military when the people have committed no outrage to require such interference."

"They have poked up the bear with their poles, sir, and it is likely he'll give them a hug before he's done with them," answered the doctor.

"But what need of military?" indignantly exclaimed Edward. "The people are only going on with the noise and disturbance common to any election, and the chances are, that savage man may influence the sheriff to provoke the people, by the presence of soldiers, to some act which would not have taken place but for their interference, and thus they themselves originate the offence which they are fore-armed with power to chastise. In England such extreme measures are never resorted to, until necessity compels them. How I have envied Englishmen, when on the occasion of assizes every soldier is marched from the town while the judge is sitting; in Ireland the place of trial bristles with bayonets!

How much more must a people respect and love the laws, whose own purity and justice are their best safeguard! whose inherent majesty is sufficient for their own protection! The sword of justice should never need the assistance of the swords of dragoons, and in the election of their representatives, as well as at judicial sittings, a people should be free from military despotism."

"But, as an historian, my dear young friend," said the doctor, "I need not remind you that dragoons have been considered good lookers-on in Ireland since the days of Strafford."

"Ay!" said Edward; "and scandalous it is, that the abuses of the seventeenth century should be perpetuated in the nineteenth.[2] While those who govern show, by the means they adopt for supporting their authority, that their rule requires undue force to uphold it, they tacitly teach resistance to the people, and their practices imply that the resistance is righteous."

"My dear Master Ned," said the doctor, "you're a patriot, and I'm sorry for you; you inherit the free opinions of your namesake 'of the hill' of blessed memory; with such sentiment you may make a very good Irish barrister, but you'll never be an Irish judge— and as for a silk gown, 'faith you may leave the wearing of that to your wife, for stuff is all that will ever adorn your shoulders."

"Well, I would rather have stuff there, than in my head," answered Edward.

"Very epigrammatic, indeed, Master Ned," said the doctor. "Let us make a distich of it," added he, with a chuckle; "for, of a verity, some of the K.C.'s of our times are but dunces.—Let's see—how will it go?"

Edward dashed off this couplet in a moment—

"Of modern king's counsel this truth may be said.
They have *silk* on their shoulders, but *stuff* in their head."

"Neat enough," said the doctor; "but you might contrive more sting in it;—something to the tune of the impossibility of making 'a silk purse out of a sow's ear,' but the facility of manufacturing silk gowns out of *bore's* heads."

"That's out of your bitter pill-box, Doctor," said Ned, smiling.

"Put it into rhyme, Ned—and set it to music—and dedicate it to the bar mess, and see how you'll rise in your profession!—Good-b'ye—I will be back again to see the fun as soon as I can, but I must go now and visit an old woman who is in doubt whether she stands most in need of me or the priest.—It's wonderful, how little people think of the other world till they are going to leave this; and with all their praises of heaven, how very anxious they are to stay out of it as long as they can!"

With this bit of characteristic sarcasm, the doctor and Edward separated. Edward had hardly left the hustings, when Murphy hurried on the platform and asked for him.

"He left a few minutes ago," said Tom Durfy.

"Well, I dare say he's doing good, wherever he is," said Murtough; "I wanted to speak to him, but when he comes back send him to me.—In the meantime, Tom, run down and bring up a good batch of voters—we're getting a little a-head, I think, with the bothering I'm giving them up there, and now I want to push them with good strong tallies—run down to the yard, like a good fellow, and march them up."

Off posted Tom Durfy on his mission, and Murphy returned to the court-house.

Tom, on reaching Murphy's house, found a strong posse of O'Grady's party hanging round the place, and one of the fellows had backed a car against the yard gate which opened on the street, and was the outlet for Egan's voters. By way of excuse for this, the car was piled with cabbages for sale, and a couple of very unruly pigs were tethered to the shafts, and the strapping fellow who owned all, kept guard over them. Tom immediately told him he should leave that place, and an altercation commenced; but even an electioneering dispute could not but savour of fun and repartee, between Paddies.

"Be off," said Tom.

"Sure I can't be off till the market's over," was the answer.

"Well, you must take your car out of this."

"Indeed now, you'll let me stay, Misther Durfy."

"Indeed I won't."

"Arrah! what harm?"

"You're stopping up the gate on purpose, and you must go."

"Sure your honour wouldn't spile my stand!"

"Faith, I'll spoil more than your stand, if you don't leave that."

"Not finer cabbage in the world."

"Go out o' that now, 'while your shoes are good,'³ said Tom, seeing he had none; for in speaking of shoes, Tom had no intention of alluding to the word *choux*, and thus making a French pun upon the *cabbage*,—for Tom did not understand French, but rather despised it as a jack-a-dandy acquirement.

"Sure, you wouldn't ruin my market, Misther Durfy!"

"None of your humbugging—but be off at once," said Tom, whose tone indicated he was *very much in earnest.*

"Not a nicer slip of a pig in the market than the same pigs—I'm expectin' thirty shillin's a piece for them."

"Faith, you'll get more than thirty shillings," cried Tom, "in less than thirty seconds, if you don't take your dirty cabbages and blackguard pigs out o' that!"

"Dirty cabbages!" echoed the fellow, in a tone of surprise.

The order to depart was renewed.

"Blackguard pigs!" cried Paddy, in affected wonder.—"Ah, Masther Tom, one would think it was after dinner you wor."

"What do you mean, you rap?—do you intend to say I'm drunk?"

"Oh no, sir!—But if it's not after dinner wid you, I think you wouldn't turn up your nose at bacon and greens."

"Oh; with all your joking," said Tom, laughing, "you won't find me a chicken to pluck for your bacon and greens, my boy; so, start!— vanish!—disperse!—my bacon merchant!—"

While this dialogue was going forward, several cars were gathered round the place, with a seeming view to hem in Egan's voters, and interrupt their progress to the poll; but the gate of the yard suddenly opened, and the fellows within soon upset the car which impeded their egress, gave freedom to the pigs, who used their liberty in eating the cabbages; while their owner was making cause with his party of O'Gradyites against the outbreak of Egan's men. The affair was not one of importance; the numbers were not sufficient to constitute a good row—it was but a hustling affair, after all, and a slight scrimmage enabled Tom Durfy to head his men in a rush to the poll.

The polling was now prosecuted vigorously on both sides, each party anxious to establish a majority on the first day; and of course the usual practices for facilitating their own, and retarding their opponent's progress, were resorted to.

Scatterbrain's party, to counteract the energetic movement of the enemy's voters, and Murphy's activity, got up a mode of interruption seldom made use of, but of which they availed themselves on the present occasion, It was determined to put the oath of allegiance to all the Roman Catholics, by which some loss of time to the Eganite party was effected.

This gave rise to odd scenes and answers, occasionally;—some of the fellows did not know what the oath of allegiance meant; some did not know whether there might not be a scruple of conscience against taking it; others, indignant at what they felt to be an insulting mode of address, on the part of the person who said to them, in a tone savouring of supremacy—"*You're* a Roman Catholic,"—would not answer immediately, and gave dogged looks, and sometimes dogged answers; and it required address on the part of Egan's agents to make them overcome such feelings, and expedite the work of voting. At last, the same herculean fellow who gave O'Grady the fierce answer about the *blunderbuss tenure* he enjoyed, came up to vote, and fairly bothered the querist with his ready replies, which, purposely, were never to the purpose;—the examination ran nearly thus:

"You're a Roman Catholic?"

"Am I?" said the fellow.

"Are you not?" demanded the agent.

"You say I am," was the answer. "Come, sir, answer—What's your religion?"

"The thrue religion."

"What religion is that?"

"My religion."

"And what's *your* religion?"

"My mother's religion."

"And what was your mother's religion?"

"*She tuk whisky in her tay.*"

"Come, now, I'll find you out, as cunning as you are," said the agent, piqued into an encounter of the wits with this fellow, whose baffling of every question pleased the crowd.

"You bless yourself, don't you?"

"When I'm done with you, I think I ought."

"What place of worship do you go to?"

"The most convaynient."

"But of what persuasion are you?"

"My persuasion is that you won't find it out."

"What is your belief?"

"My belief is that *you're* puzzled."

"Do you confess?"

"Not to you."

"Come! now I have you. Who would you send for if you were likely to die?"

"Docthor Growlin'."

"Not for the priest?"

"I must first get a messenger."

"Confound your quibbling!—tell me, then, what your opinions are—your conscientious opinions, I mean?"

"They are the same as my landlord's."

"And what are your landlord's opinions?"

"Faix, his opinion is, that I won't pay him the last half-year's rint; and I'm of the same opinion myself."

A roar of laughter followed this answer, and dumb-foundered the agent for a time; but, angered at the successful quibbling of the sturdy and wily fellow before him, he at last declared, with much severity of manner, that he *must* have a direct reply. "I insist, sir, on your answering, at once, *are* you a Roman Catholic?"

"I am," said the fellow.

"And could you not say so at once?" repeated the officer.

"You never axed me," returned the other.

"I did," said the officer.

"Indeed, you didn't. You said I was a great many things, but you never *axed* me—you wor dhrivin' *crass* words and *cruked* questions at me, and I gev you answers to match them, for sure I thought it was manners to cut out my *behavor* on your own patthern."

"Take the oath, sir!"

"Where am I to take it to, sir?" inquired the provoking blackguard.

The clerk was desired to "swear him" without further notice being taken of his impertinent answer.

"I hope the oath is not *woighty*, sir, for my conscience is tindher since the last *alibi* I swore."

The business of the interior was now suspended for a time by the sounds of fierce tumult which arose from without. Some rushed from the court-house to the platform outside, and beheld the crowd in a state of great excitement, beating back the police, who had been engaged in endeavouring to seize the persons and things which had offended O'Grady; and the police, falling back for support on a party of military which O'Grady had prevailed on the sheriff to call out. The sheriff was a weak, irresolute man, and was over-persuaded by such words as "mob" and "riot," and breaches of peace being *about to be* committed, if the ruffians were not checked before-hand. The wisdom of *preventive measures* was preached, and the rest of the hacknied phrases were paraded, which brazen-faced and iron-handed oppressors are only too familiar with.

The people were now roused, and thoroughly defeated the police, who were forced to fly to the lines of the military party for protection; having effected this object, the crowd retained their position, and did not attempt to assault the soldiers, though a very firm and lowering front was presented to them, and shouts of defiance against the "Peelers"[4] rose loud and long.

"A round of ball cartridge would cool their courage," said O'Grady.

The English officer in command of the party, looking with wonder and reproach upon him, asked if he had the command of the party.

"No, sir;—the sheriff, of course;—but if I were in his place, I'd soon disperse the rascals."

"Did you ever witness the *effect* of a fusilade, sir?" inquired the officer.

"No, sir," said O'Grady, gruffly; "but I suppose I know pretty well what it is."

"For the sake of humanity, sir, I hope you do not, or I am willing to believe you would not talk so lightly of it; but it is singular how much fonder civilians are of urging measures that end in blood, than those whose profession is arms, and who know how disastrous is their use."

The police were ordered to advance again and seize the "ringleaders:" they obeyed, unwillingly; but being saluted with some stones, their individual wrath was excited, and they advanced to chastise the mob, who again drove them back; and a nearer approach to the soldiers was made by the crowd in the scuffle which ensued.

"Now, will you fire?" said O'Grady to the sheriff.

The sheriff, who was a miserable coward, was filled with dread at the threatening aspect of the mob, and wished to have his precious person under shelter before hostilities commenced; so, with pallid lips, and his teeth chattering with fear, he exclaimed:

"No! no! no!—don't fire—don't fire—don't be precipitate: besides, I hav'n't read the Riot Act."

"There's no necessity for firing, sir, I should say," said the captain.

"I thought not, captain—I hope not, captain," said the sheriff, who now assumed a humane tone. "Think of the effusion of blood, my dear sir!" said he to O'Grady, who was grinning like a fiend all the time—"the sacrifice of human life—I couldn't, sir—I can't, sir—besides, the Riot Act—hav'n't it about me—must be read, you know, Mister O'Grady."

"Not always," said O'Grady, fiercely.

"But the inquiry is always very strict after, if it is not, sir—I should not like the effusion of human blood, sir, unless the Riot Act was read, and the thing done regularly—don't think I care for the d—d rascals, a button, sir,—only the regularity, you know; and the effusion of human blood is serious, and the inquiry, too, without the Riot Act.—Captain, would you oblige me to fall back a little closer round the court-house?"

"I'm in a better position here, sir," said the captain.

"I thought, sir, you were under my command, sir," said the sheriff.

"Under your command to fire, sir, but the choice of position rests with me; and we are stronger where we are, the court-house is completely covered, and while my men are under arms here you may rely on it the crowd is completely in check without firing a shot."

Off ran the sheriff to the court-house.

"You're saving of your gunpowder, I see, sir," said O'Grady to the captain, with a sardonic grin.

"You seem to be equally sparing of your humanity, sir," returned the captain.

"God forbid I should be afraid of a pack of ruffians," said O'Grady.

"Or I of a single one," returned the captain, with a look of stern contempt.

There is no knowing what this bitter bandying of hard words might have led to, had it not been interrupted by the appearance of the sheriff at one of the windows of the court-house; there, with the Riot Act in his hand, he called out:—

"Now I've read it—fire a'way, boys—fire away!" and all his compunction about the effusion of blood vanished the moment his own miserable carcase was safe from harm. Again he waved the Riot Act from the window, and vociferated, "Fire away, boys," as loud as his frog-like voice permitted.

"Now, sir, you're ordered to fire," said O'Grady to the captain.

"I'll not obey that order, sir," said the captain; "the man is out of his senses with fear, and I'll not obey such a serious command from a madman."

"Do you dare disobey the orders of the sheriff, sir?" thundered O'Grady.

"I am responsible for my act, sir," said the captain—"seriously responsible, but I will not slaughter unarmed people until I see further and fitter cause."

The sheriff had vanished—he was nowhere to be seen, and O'Grady, now he had the power, ordered a fresh advance of the police upon the people, and in this third affair matters assumed a more serious aspect; sticks and stones were used with more effect, and the two parties being nearer to each other, the missiles meant only for the police, overshot their mark and struck the soldiers, who bore their painful situation with admirable patience.

"Now will you fire, sir?" said O'Grady to the officer.

"If I fire now, sir, I am as likely to kill the police as the people; withdraw your police first, sir, and then I will fire."

This was but reasonable—so reasonable, that even O'Grady, enraged almost to madness, as he was, could not gainsay it; and he went forward himself to withdraw the police force.—O'Grady's presence increased the rage of the mob, whose blood was now thoroughly up, and as the police fell back they were pressed by the infuriated people, who now began almost to disregard the presence of the military, and poured down in a resistless stream upon them.

O'Grady repeated his command to the captain, who, finding matters thus driven to extremity, saw no longer the possibility of avoiding bloodshed; and the first preparatory word of the fatal order was given, the second on his lips, and the long file of bright muskets flashed in the sun ere they should quench his light for ever to some, and carry darkness to many a heart and hearth, when a young and handsome man, mounted on a noble horse, came plunging and ploughing his way through the crowd, and, rushing between the half-levelled muskets and those who in another instant would have fallen their victims, he shouted in a voice whose noble tone carried to its hearers involuntary obedience, "Stop!—for God's sake, stop!" Then wheeling his horse suddenly round, he charged along the advancing front of the people, plunging his horse fiercely upon them, and waving them back with his hand, enforcing his commands with words as well as actions. The crowd fell back as he pressed upon them with a fiery horsemanship unsurpassable by an Arab; and as his dark clustering hair streamed about his noble face, pale from excitement, and with flashing eyes, he was a model worthy of the best days of Grecian art—ay, and he had a soul worthy of the most glorious times of Grecian liberty!

It was Edward O'Connor.

"Fire!" cried O'Grady, again.

The gallant soldier, touched by the heroism of O'Connor, and roused by the brutality of O'Grady beyond his patience, in the excitement of the moment, was urged beyond the habitual parlance of a gentleman, and swore vehemently, "I'll be *damned* if I do! I wouldn't run the risk of shooting that noble fellow for all the magistrates in your county."

O'Connor had again turned round, and rode up to the military party, having heard the word 'fire!' repeated.

"For mercy's sake, sir, don't fire, and I pledge you my soul the crowd shall disperse."

"Ay!" cried O'Grady, "they won't obey the laws nor the magistrates; but they'll listen fast enough to a d—d rebel like you."

"Liar and ruffian!" exclaimed Edward, "I'm a better and more loyal subject than you, who provoke resistance to the laws you should make honoured."

At the word "liar," O'Grady, now quite frenzied, attempted to seize a musket from a soldier beside him; and had he succeeded in obtaining possession of it, Edward O'Connor's days had been numbered; but the soldier would not give up his firelock, and O'Grady, intent on immediate vengeance, then rushed upon Edward, and seizing him by the leg, attempted to unhorse him, but Edward was too firm in his seat for this, and a struggle ensued.

The crowd, fearing Edward was about to fall a victim, raised a fierce shout, and were about to advance, when the captain, with admirable presence of mind, seized O'Grady, dragged him away from his hold, and gave freedom to Edward, who instantly used it again to charge the advancing line of the mob, and drive them back.

"Back, boys, back!" he cried, "don't give your enemies a triumph by being disorderly. Disperse—retire into houses, let nothing tempt you to riot—collect round your tally rooms, and come up quietly to the polling—and you will yet have a peaceful triumph."

The crowd, obeying, gave three cheers for "Ned-o'-the-Hill," and the dense mass, which could not be awed, and dreaded not the engines of war, melted away before the breath of peace.

As they retired on one side, the soldiers were ordered to their quarters on the other, while their captain and Edward O'Connor stood in the midst; but ere they separated, these two, with charity in their souls, waved their hands towards each other in token of amity, and parted, verily, in friendship.

1.   A large basket of coarse wicker-work, used mostly for carrying turf, *Anglicè* peat.

2.   When Strafford's infamous project of the wholesale robbery of Connaught was put in practice, not being quite certain of his juries, he writes that he will send 300 horse to the province during the proceedings, "as *good lookers-on.*'

3.   A saying among the Irish peasantry,—meaning, there is danger in
        delay,

4.   The name given to the police by the people—the force being
        first established by Sir Robert Peei, then Mr. Peel, Secretary for
        Ireland.

XX

AFTER THE INCIDENTS JUST RECORDED, of course great confusion and excitement existed, during which O'Grady was forced back into the court-house in a state bordering on insanity. Inflamed as his furious passions had been to the top of their bent, and his thirst of revenge still remaining unslaked, foiled in all his movements, and flung back as it were into the seething cauldron of his own hellish temper, he was a pitiable sight, foaming at the mouth like a wild animal, and uttering the most horrid imprecations. On Edward O'Connor principally his curses fell, with denunciations of immediate vengeance, and the punishment of dismissal from the service was prophesied on oath for the English captain. The terrors of a court-martial gleamed fitfully through the frenzied mind of the raving squire for the soldier; and for O'Connor, instant death at his own hand was his momentary cry.

"Find the rascal for me," he exclaimed, "that I may call him out and shoot him like a dog—yes, by—, a dog—a dog: I'm disgraced while he lives—I wish the villain had three lives, that I might take them all at once—all—all!—"and he stretched out his hands as he spoke, and grasped at the air as if in imagination he clutched the visionary lives his bloodthirsty wishes conjured up.

Edward, as soon as he saw the crowd dispersed, returned to the hustings, and sought Dick Dawson, that he might be in readiness to undertake, on his part, the arrangement of the hostile meeting, to which he knew he should be immediately called. "Let it be over, my dear Dick, as soon as possible," said Edward; "it is not a case in which delay can be of any service; the insult was mortal between us, and the sooner expiated by a meeting the better."

"Don't be so agitated, Ned," said Dick; "fair and easy, man, fair and easy—keep yourself cool."

"Dear Dick—I'll be cool on the ground, but not till then,—I want the meeting over before my father hears of the quarrel—I'm his only child, Dick, and you know how he loves me!"

He wrung Dick's hand as he spoke, and his eye glistened with tenderness, but with the lightning quickness of thought all gentle feeling vanished, as he saw Scatterbrain struggling his way towards him, and read in his eye the purport of his approach. He communicated to Edward his object in seeking him, and was at once referred to Dawson, who instantly retired with him, and arranged an immediate meeting. This was easily done, as they had their pistols with them since the duel in the morning; and if there be those who think it a little too much of a good thing to have two duels in one day, pray let them remember it was election time, and even in sober England, that period often gives rise to personalities which call for the intervention of the code of honour. Only in Ireland, the thing is sooner over. We seldom have three columns of a newspaper filled with notes on the subject, numbered from 1 to 25. Gentlemen don't consider whether it is too soon or too late to fight, or whether a gentleman is perfectly entitled to call him out or not. The title in Ireland is generally considered sufficient in the *will* to do it, and few there would wait for the poising of a very delicately balanced scale of etiquette before going to the ground; they would be more likely to fight first, and leave the world to argue about the niceties after.

In the present instance, a duel was unavoidable, and it was to be feared a mortal one, for deadly insult had been given on both sides.

The rumour of the hostile meeting flew like wildfire through the town; and when the parties met in a field about a quarter of a mile beyond the bridge, an anxious crowd was present. The police were obliged to be in strong force on the ground, to keep back the people, who were not now, as an hour before, in the town, in uproarious noise and action, but still as death;—not a murmur was amongst them—the excitement of love for the noble young champion, whose life was in danger for his care of *them*, held them spell in a tranquillity almost fearful.

The aspect of the two principals was in singular contrast;—on the one side, a man burning for revenge, who, to use a common, but terrible parlance, desired to "wash out the dishonour put upon him in blood." The other was there, regretting that cause existed for the awful arbitrament, and only anxious to defend his own, not take another's life. To sensitive minds the reaction is always painful of having insulted another, when the excitement is over which prompted it: when the hot blood which inflamed the brain runs in cooler currents, the man of feeling always regrets, if he does not reproach himself, with having urged his fellow-man to break the commandments of the Most High, and deface, perhaps annihilate, the form that was moulded in His image. The words "liar and ruffian" haunted Edward's mind reproachfully;— but then the provocation—"Rebel!"—No gentleman could brook it. Because his commiseration for a people had endeared him to them, was he to be called "*rebel?*" Because, at the risk of his own life, he had preserved perhaps scores, and prevented an infraction of the law, was he to be called "*rebel?*" He stood acquitted before his own conscience— after all, the most terrible bar before which we can be called.

The men were placed upon their ground, and the word to fire given. O'Grady, in his desire for vengeance, raised his pistol deliberately, with deadly aim, and Edward was thus enabled to fire first, and with such cool precision that his shot took effect as he intended; O'Grady's pistol arm was ripped up from the wrist to the elbow; but so determined was his will, and so firm his aim, that the wound, severe as it was, produced but a slight twitch in his hand, which threw it up slightly, and saved Edward's life, for the ball passed through his hat *just* above his head.

O'Grady's arm instantly after dropped to his side, the pistol fell from his hand, and he staggered, for the pain of the wound was extreme. His second ran to his assistance.

"It is only in the arm," said O'Grady firmly, though his voice was changed by the agony he suffered; "give me another pistol."

Dick at the same moment was beside Edward.

"You're not touched," he said.

Edward coolly pointed to his hat.

"Too much powder," said Dick; "I thought so when his pistols were loaded."

"No," said Edward, "it was my shot; I saw his hand twitch."

Scatterbrain demanded of Dick another shot on the part of O'Grady.

"By all means," was the answer, and he handed a fresh pistol to Edward.—"To give the devil his due," said Dick, "he has great pluck, for you hit him hard—see how pale he looks—I don't think he can hurt you much this time—but watch him well, my dear Ned."

The seconds withdrew, but with all O'Grady's desperate courage, he could not lift the pistol with his right arm, which, though hastily bound in a handkerchief, was bleeding profusely, and racked with torture. On finding his right hand powerless, such was his unflinching courage, that he took the pistol in his left; this of course impaired his power of aim, and his nerve was so shattered by his bodily suffering, that his pistol was discharged before coming to the level, and Edward saw the sod torn up close beside his foot. He then, of course, fired in the air. O'Grady would have fallen but for the immediate assistance of his friends, he was led from the ground and placed in a carriage, and it was not until Edward O'Connor mounted his horse to ride away, that the crowd manifested their feelings. Then three tremendous cheers arose; and the shouts of their joy and triumph reached the wounded man as he was driven slowly from the ground.

XXI

THE WIDOW FLANAGAN HAD LONG ago determined that, whenever the election should take place, she would take advantage of the great influx of visitors that event would produce, and give a grand party. Her preparations were all made to secure a good muster of her country friends, when once the day of nomination was fixed; and after the election begun, she threw out all her hooks and lines in every direction to catch every straggler worth having whom the election brought into the town. It required some days to do this; and it was not until the eve of the fifth, that her house was turned upside down and inside out for the reception of the numerous guests whose company she expected.

The toil of the day's election was over: the gentlemen had dined and refreshed themselves with creature comforts; the vicissitudes, and tricks, and chances of the last twelve hours were canvassed,—when the striking of many a clock, or the consultation of the pocket-dial, warned those who were invited to Mrs. O'Flanagan's party, that it was time to wash off the dust of the battle-field from their faces, and mount fresh linen and cambric. Those who were pleased to call themselves "good fellows" declared for "another bottle;" the faint-hearted swore that an autograph invitation from Venus herself to the heathen Olympus, with nectar and ambrosia for tea and bread-and-butter, could not tempt them from the christian enjoyment of a feather-bed after the fag of such a day; but the *preux chevaliers*—those who did deserve to win a fair lady—shook off sloth and their morning trousers, and taking to tights and activity, hurried to the party of the buxom widow.

The widow was in her glory; hospitable, she enjoyed receiving her friends,—mirthful, she looked forward to a long night of downright sport,—coquettish, she would have good opportunity of letting Tom Durfy see how attractive she was to the men,—while from the women her love of gossip and scandal (was there ever a lady in her position without it?) would have ample gratification in the accumulated news of the county for twenty miles round. She had but one *large* room at her command, and *that* was given up to the dancing; and being cleared of tables, chairs, and carpet, could not be considered by Mrs. Flanagan as a proper reception-room for her guests, who were, therefore, received in a smaller apartment, where tea and coffee, toast and muffins, ladies and gentlemen, were all smoking hot together, and the candles on the mantel-piece trickling down rivulets of fat in the most sympathetic manner, under the influence of the gentle sighing of a broken pane of glass, which the head of an inquiring youth in the street had stove in, while flattening his nose against it, in hope of getting a glimpse of the company through the opening in the window curtain.

At last, when the room could hold no more, the company were drafted off to the dancing-room, which had only long deal forms placed against the wall to rest the weary after the exertions of the jig. The aforesaid forms, by-the-bye, were borrowed from the chapel: the old wigsby who had the care of them for some time doubted the propriety of the sacred property being put to such a profane use, until the widow's arguments convinced him it was quite right, after she had given him a tenpenny piece. As the dancing-room could not boast of a lustre, the deficiency was supplied by tin sconces hung against the wall; for ormolu branches are not expected to be plenty in county towns. But let the widow be heard for herself, as she bustled through her guests, and caught a critical glance at her arrangements: "What's that you're faulting now?—is it my deal seats without cushions? Ah! you're a *lazy Larry*, Bob Larkin. Cock you up with a cushion, indeed! if you sit the less, you'll dance the more. Ah! Matty, I see you're eyeing my tin sconces there; well, sure they have them at the county ball, when candlesticks are scarce, and what would you expect grander from a poor lone woman? besides, we must have plenty of lights, or how could the *beaux* see the girls?—though I see, Harry Cassidy, by your sly look, that *you* think they look as well in the dark—ah! you *divil!*"—and she slapped his shoulder as she ran past. "Ah! Mister Murphy, I'm delighted to see you; what kept you so late?—the election, to be sure. Well, we're beating them, ain't we? Ah! the old country for ever. I hope Edward O'Connor will be here. Come, begin the dance; there's the piper and the fiddler in the corner as idle as a milestone without a number. Tom Durfy, don't ask me to dance, for I'm engaged for the next four sets."

"Oh! but the first to me," said Tom.

"Ah! yis, Tom, I was; but then you know, I couldn't refuse the stranger from Dublin, and the English captain that will be here by-and-by;—he's a nice man too, and long life to him, wouldn't fire on the people the other day; I vow to the Virgin, all the women in the room ought to kiss him when he comes in. Ah, doctor! there you are; there's Mrs. Gubbins in the corner dying to have a chat with you; go over to her. Who's that *taazing* the piano there? Ah! James Reddy, it's *you* I see. I hope it's in tune; 'tis only four months since the tuner was here. I hope you've a new song for us, James. The tuner is so scarce, Mrs. Riley, in the country—not like Dublin; but we poor country people, you know, must put up with what we can get; not like you citizens, who has lashings of luxuries as easy as peas." Then, in a confidential whisper, she said: "I hope your daughter has practised the new piece well to-day, for I couldn't be looking after her, you know, to-day, being in such a bustle; with my party I was just like a dog in a fair, in and out everywhere; but I *hope* she's *perfect* in the piece;" then, still more confidentially, she added: "for *he's* here—ah! *I wish it was*, Mrs. Riley;" then, with a nod and a wink, off she rattled through the room with a word for every body.

The Mrs. Riley, to whom she was so confidential, was a friend from Dublin, an atrociously vulgar woman, with a more vulgar daughter, who were on a visit with Mrs. Flanagan. The widow and the mother thought Murtough Murphy would be a good speculation for the daughter to "cock her cap at," (to use their own phrase,) and with this view, the visit to the country was projected. But matters did not prosper; Murphy was not much of a marrying man; and if ever he might be caught in the toils of Hymen, some frank, joyous, unaffected, dashing girl would have been the only one likely to serve a writ on the jovial attorney's heart. Now Miss Riley was, to use Murtough Murphy's own phrase, "a batch of brass and a stack of affectation," and the airs she attempted to play off on the country folk, Murphy in particular, only made her an object for his mischievous merriment: as an example, we may as well touch on one little incident *en passant*.

The widow had planned one day a walking party to a picturesque ruin, not very far from the town, and determined that Murphy should give his arm to Miss Riley; for the party was arranged in couples, with a most deadly design on the liberty of the attorney. At the appointed hour, all had arrived but Murphy; the widow thought it a happy chance, so she hurried off the party, leaving Miss Riley to wait and follow under his escort. In about a quarter of an hour he came, having met the widow in the street, who sent him back for Miss Riley. Now Murtough saw the trap which was intended for him, and thought it fair to make what fun he could out of the affair, and, being already sickened by various disgusting exhibitions of the damsel's affectation, he had the less scruple of "taking her down a peg," as he said himself.

When Murtough reached the house and asked for Miss Riley, he was ushered into the little drawing-room; and there was that very full-blown young lady, on a chair before the fire, her left foot resting on the fender, her right crossed over it, and her body thrown back in a reclining attitude, with a sentimental droop of the head over a greasy novel: her figure was rather developed by her posture, indeed, more so than Miss Riley quite intended, for her ankles were not unexceptionable, and the position of her feet revealed rather more. A bonnet and green veil lay on the hearth-rug, and her shawl hung over the handle of the fire-shovel. When Murphy entered, he was received with a faint "How d' do?"

"Pretty well, I thank you; how are you?" said Murphy, in his rollicking tone.

"Oh! Miste' Murphy, you are so odd."

"Odd, am I, how am I odd?"

"Oh! so odd."

"Well, you'd better put on your bonnet and come walk, and we can talk of my oddity after."

"Oh, indeed, I *cawn't* walk."

"Can't walk!" exclaimed Murphy. "Why can't you walk? I was sent for you."

"'Deed I cawn't."

"Ah, now!" said Murphy, giving her a little tender poke of his forefinger on the shoulder.

"Don't, Mister Murphy, *pray* don't."

"But why won't you walk?"

"I'm too delicate."

Murphy uttered a very long 'Oh!!!!!'

"'Deed I am, Miste' Murphy, though you may disbelieve it."

"Well—a nice walk is the best thing in the world for the health.— Come along!"

"Cawn't indeed; a gentle walk on a terrace, or a shadowy avenue, is all very well—the Rotunda Gardens, for instance."

"Not forgetting the military bands that play there," said Murphy, "together with the officers of all the barracks in Dublin, clinking their sabres at their heels along the gravel walks, all for the small charge of a fi'penny bit."

Miss Riley gave a reproachful look and shrug at the vulgar mention of a "fi'penny bit," which Murphy purposely said to shock her "Brummagem gentility;" "How can you be so odd, Miste' Murphy?" she said. "I don't joke, indeed; a gentle walk—I repeat it—is all very well; but these horrid rough country walks—these *masculine* walks, I may say—are not consistent with a delicate frame like mine

"A delicate frame!" said Murtough. "Faith, I'll tell you what it is, Miss Riley," said he, standing bolt upright before her, plunging his hands into his pockets, and fixing his eyes on her feet, which still maintained their original position on the fender—"I'll tell you what it is, Miss Riley; by the *vartue* of my oath, if your *other* leg is a match for the one I see, the *divil* a harm a trot from this to Dublin would do you."

Miss Riley gave a faint scream, and popped her legs under her chair, while Murphy ran off in a shout of laughter and joined the party, to whom he made no secret of his joke.

But all this did not damp Miss Riley's hopes of winning him. She changed her plan; and seeing he did not bow to what she considered the supremacy of her very elegant manners, she set about feigning at once admiration and dread of him. She would sometimes lift her eyes to Murtough with a languishing expression, and declare she never knew any one she was so afraid of; but even this double attack on his vanity could not turn Murphy's flank, and so a very laughable flirtation went on between them, he letting her employ all the enginery of her sex against him, with a mischievous enjoyment in her blindness at not seeing she was throwing away her powder and shot.

But, to return to the party, a rattling country dance now called out at once the energies of the piper, the fiddler, and the ladies and gentlemen; and left those who had more activity in their heads than their heels, to sit on the forms in the background, and exercise their tongues in open scandal of their mutual friends and acquaintances under cover of the music; which prevented the most vigorous talker from being heard further than his or her next-door neighbour. Doctor Growling had gone over to Mrs. Gubbins's, as desired, and was buried deep in gossip.

"What an extraordinary affair that was about Miss O'Grady, doctor."

"Very, ma'am."

"In the man's bed she was, I hear."

"So the story goes, ma'am."

"And they tell me, doctor, that when her father—that *immaculate* madman, God keep us from harm!—said to poor Mrs. O'Grady in a great rage, 'Where have you brought up your daughters to go to, ma'am?' says he,—and she, poor woman, said, 'To church, my dear,' thinking it was the different religion the Saracen was after,—so says he, '*Church,* indeed! there's the church she is gone to, ma'am,' says he, turning down a quilted counterpane!"

"Are you sure it wasn't Marseilles, ma'am?" said the doctor.

"Well, whatever it was—'*There's* the church she is in,' says he, pulling her out of the bed."

"Out of the bed!" repeated the doctor.

"Out of the bed, sir."

"Then *her* church was in the diocese of *Down,*" said the doctor.

"That's good, docthor; indeed, that's good. She was caught in bed, says I—and it's the diocese of *Down,* says *you*; faith, that's good. I wish the diocese was your own—for you're funny enough to be a bishop, docthor—you lay howld of everything."

"That's a great qualification for a mitre, ma'am," said the doctor.

"And the poor young man that has got her is not worth a farthing, I hear, docthor."

"Then *he* must be the curate, ma'am—though I don't think it's a chapel of ease he has got into."

"Oh! what a tongue you have, docthor," said she, laughing; "faith, you'll kill me."

"That's my profession, ma'am. I'm a licentiate of the Royal College; but, unfortunately for me, my humanity is an overmatch for my science. Phrenologically speaking, my benevolence is large, and my destructiveness and acquisitiveness small."

"Ah, there you go off on another tack—and what a funny new thing that is you talk of!—that free-knowledge, or crow-knowledge, or whatever sort of knowledge you call it. And there's one thing I want to ask you about—there's a bump the ladies have, the gentlemen always laugh at, I remark."

"That's very rude of them, ma'am," said the doctor, drily. "Is it in the anterior region, or the—"

"Docthor, don't talk queer."

"I'm only speaking scientifically, ma'am."

"Well, I think your scientific discourse is only an excuse for saying impudent things; I mean the back of their heads."

"I thought so, ma'arn."

"They call it—dear me, I forget—something—motive—motive—it's Latin—but I'm no *scholard*, docthor."

"That's manifest, ma'am."

"But a lady is not bound to know Latin, docthor."

"Certainly not, ma'am—nor any other language, except that of the eyes."

Now, this was a wicked hit of the doctor's, for Mrs. Gubbins squinted frightfully; but Mrs. Gubbins did not know that,—so she went on.

"The bump, I mean, docthor—is motive something—motive—motive—I have it!—motive-*ness*."

"Now I know what you mean," said the doctor; "amativeness."

"That's it," said Mrs. Gubbins; "they call it number one, sometimes; I suppose amativeness is Latin for number one. Now, what does that bump mean?"

"Ah, madam," said the doctor, puzzled for a moment to give an explanation, but in a few seconds he answered, "That's a beautiful provision of nature. That ma'am, is the organ which makes your sex take compassion on ours."[1]

"Wonderful!" said Mrs. Gubbins; "but how good nature is in giving us provisions! and I don't think there is a finer provision county in Ireland than this."

"Certainly not, ma'am," said the doctor;—but the moment Mrs. Gubbins began to speak of provisions, he was sure she would get into a very solid discourse about her own farms; so he left his seat beside her and went over to Mrs. Riley, to see what fun could be had in that quarter.

Her daughter was cutting all sorts of bare-faced capers about the room, "astonishing the natives," as she was pleased to say; and Growling was looking on in amused wonder, at this specimen of vulgar effrontery, whom he had christened "The Brazen Baggage," the first time he saw her.

"You are looking at my daughter, sir," said the delighted mother.

"Yes, ma'am," said the doctor, profoundly.

"She's very young, sir."

"She'll mend of that, ma'am. We were young once ourselves."

This was not very agreeable to the mother, who dressed rather in a juvenile style.

"I mean, sir, that you must excuse any little awkwardness about her—that all rises out of timidity—she was lost with bashfulness till I roused her out of it—but now I think she is beginning to have a little self-possession."

The doctor was amused, and took a large pinch of snuff; he enjoyed the phrase "*beginning* to have a *little* self-possession" being applied to the most brazen baggage he ever saw.

"She's very accomplished, sir," continued the mother. "Misther Jew-val (Duval) taitches her dancin', and Musha Dunny-ai, (Mons. Du Noyer,[2]) French. Misther Low-jeer (Logier) hasn't the like of her in his academy on the pianya, and as for the harp, you'd think she wouldn't lave a sthring in it."

"She must be a treasure to her teachers, ma'am," said the doctor.

"Faith, you may well say *threasure*,—it costs handfuls o' money; but sure, while there's room for improvement, every apartment must be attended to, and the vocal apartment is filled by Sir John,—fifteen shillin's a lesson, no less."

"What silvery tones she ought to bring out, ma'am, at that rate."

"Faith, you may say that, sir. It's coining, so it is, with them tip-top men, and ruins one a'most to have a daughter: every shake I get out of her is to the tune of a ten-poun' note, at least. You shall hear her by-and-by; the minit the dancin' is over, she shall sing you the 'Bewildhered Maid.' Do you know the 'Bewildhered Maid,' sir?"

"I haven't the honour of her acquaintance, ma'am," said the doctor.

The dancing *was* soon over, and the mother's threat put into execution. Miss Riley was led over to the piano by the widow, with the usual protestations that she was hoarse. It took some time to get the piano ready, for an extensive clearance was to be made from it of cups and saucers, and half-empty glasses of negus, before it could be opened; then, after various thrummings, and hummings, and hawings, the 'Bewildered Maid' made her appearance in the wildest possible manner, and the final shriek was quite worthy of a maniac. Loud applause followed, and the wriggling Miss Riley was led from the piano by James Reddy, who had stood at the back of her chair, swaying backward and forward to the music, with a maudlin expression of sentiment on his face, and a suppressed exclamation of "B-û-tiful," after every extra shout from the young lady.

Growling listened with an expression of as much dissatisfaction as if he had been drinking weak punch.

"I see you don't like that," said the widow to him, under her breath; "ah, you're too hard, doctor—consider, she sung out of good-nature."

"I don't know if it was out of good-nature," said he, "but I'm sure it was out of tune."

James Reddy led back Miss Riley to her mama, who was much delighted with the open manifestations of "the poet's" admiration.

"She ought to be proud, sir, of your *conjunction*, I'm sure. A poet like you, sir!—what beautiful rhymes them wor you did on the 'lection."

"A trifle, ma'am—a mere trifle—a little occasional thing."

"Oh! but them two beautiful lines—

'We tread the land that bore us,
Our green flag glitters o'er us!'"

"*They* are only a quotation, ma'am," said Reddy.

"Oh, like every man of true genius, sir, you try and undervalue your own work; but call them lines what you like, to my taste they are the most beautiful lines in the thing you done."

Reddy did not know what to answer, and his confusion was increased by catching old Growling's eye, who was chuckling at the *mal-à-propos* speech of the flourishing Mrs. Riley.

"Don't you sing yourself, sir?" said that lady.

"To be sure he does," cried the widow Flanagan; "and he must give us one of his own."

"Oh!"

"No excuses; now, James!"

"Where's Duggan?" inquired the poetaster affectedly; "I told him to be here to accompany me."

"I attend your muse, sir," said a miserable structure of skin and bone, advancing with a low bow and obsequious smile;—this was the poor music-master, who set Reddy's rhymes to music as bad, and danced attendance on him everywhere.

The music-master fumbled over a hackneyed prelude, to show his command of the instrument.

Miss Riley whispered to her mama, that it was out of one of her first books of lessons.

Mrs. Flanagan, with a seductive smirk, asked, "what he was going to give them." The poet replied, "a little thing of his own,—'Rosalie; or, the Broken Heart,'—sentimental, but rather sad."

The musical skeleton rattled his bones against the ivory, in a very one, two, three, four, symphony; the poet ran his fingers through his hair, pulled up his collar, gave his head a jaunty nod, and commenced

ROSALIE
OR, THE BROKEN HEART

Fare thee—fare thee well—alas,
    Fare—farewell to thee!
On pleasure's wings, as dew-drops fade,
    Or honey stings the bee,
My heart is as sad as a black stone
    Under the blue sea.

                    Oh, Rosalie! Oh, Rosalie!

As ruder rocks with envy glow,
    Thy *coral* lips to see,
So the weeping waves more briny grow
    With my salt tears for thee!
My heart is as sad as a black stone
    Under the blue sea.

                    Oh, Rosalie! Oh, Rosalie

After this brilliant specimen of the mysteriously-sentimental and imaginative school was sufficiently applauded, dancing was recommenced, and Reddy seated himself beside Mrs. Riley, the incense of whose praise was sweet in his nostrils. "Oh, you *have* a soul for poetry indeed, sir," said the lady. "I was bewildered with all your beautiful *idays;* that 'honey stings the bee' is a beautiful *iday*—so expressive of the pains and pleasures of love. Ah! I was the most romantic creature myself once, Mister Reddy, though you wouldn't think it now; but the cares of the world and a family takes the shine out of us. I remember when the men used to be making hats in my father's establishment—for my father was the most extensive hatter in Dublin—I don't know if you knew my father was a hatter; but you know, sir, manufactures must be followed, and that's no reason why people shouldn't enjoy po'thry and refinement. Well, I was going to tell you how romantic I was, and when the men were making the hats—I don't know whether you ever saw them making hats—"

Reddy declared he never did.

"Well, it's like the witches round the iron-pot in Macbeth; did you ever see Kemble in Macbeth? Oh! he'd make your blood freeze, though the pit is so hot you wouldn't have a dwry rag on you. But to come to the hats. When they're making them, they have hardly any crown to them at all, and they are all with great sprawling wide flaps to them; well, the moment I clapt my eyes on one of them, I thought of a Spanish nobleman directly, with his slouched hat and black feathers like a hearse. Yes, I assure you, the broad hat always brought to my mind a Spanish noble or an Italian noble (that would do as well, you know), or a robber, or a murderer, which is all the same thing."

Reddy could not conceive a hat manufactory as a favourable nursery for romance, but as the lady praised *his* song, he listened complacently to her hatting.

"And that's another beautiful iday, sir," continued the lady, "where you make the rocks jealous of each other—that's so beautiful to bring in a bit of nature into a metaphysic that way."

"You flatter me, ma'am," said Reddy; "but if I might speak of my own work,—that is, if a man may *ever* speak of his own work,—"

"And why not, sir?" asked Mrs. Riley, with a business-like air; "who has so good a right to speak of the work as the man who *done* it, and knows what's in it?"

"That's a very sensible remark of yours, ma'am, and I will therefore take leave to say, that the idea *I* am proudest of, is, the *dark* and *heavy* grief of the heart being compared to a *black* stone, and its *depth* of misery implied by the *sea*."

"Thrue for you," said Mrs. Riley; "and the *blue* sea—ah! that didn't escape me; that's an elegant touch—the black stone and the blue sea; and black and blue, such a beautiful conthrast!"

"I own," said Reddy, "I attempted in that, the bold and daring style of expression which Byron has introduced."

"Oh, he's a fine *pote* certainly, but he's not moral, sir; and I'm afeared to let my daughther read such combustibles."

"But he's grand," said Reddy; "for instance:

'She walks in beauty like the night.'

How fine!"

"But how wicked!" said Mrs. Riley. "I don't like that night-walking style of poetry at all; so say no more about it; we'll talk of something else. You admire music, I'm sure."

"I adore it, ma'am."

"Do you like the piano?"

"Oh, ma'am! I could live under a piano."

"My daughther plays the piano beautiful."

"Charmingly."

"Oh, but if you heerd her play the harp, you'd think she wouldn't lave a sthring on it (this was Mrs. Riley's favourite bit of praise); and a beautiful harp it is; one of Egan's double action, all over goold, and cost eighty guineas; Miss Cheese chuse it for her. Do you know Miss Cheese? she's as plump as a partridge, with a voice like a lark; she sings elegant duets;—do you ever sing duets?"

"Not often."

"Ah! if you could hear Pether Dowling sing duets with my daughther! he'd make the hair stand straight on your head with the delight. Oh, he's a powerful singer! you never heerd the like; he runs up and down as fast as a lamplighter;—and the beautiful turns he gives; oh! I never heard any one sing a second like Pether. I declare he sings a *second* to that degree *that you'd think it was the first*, and never at a loss for a shake; and then off he goes in a run, that you'd think he'd never come back; but he *does* bring it back into the tune again with as nate a fit as a Limerick glove. Oh! I never heerd a singer like Pether!!!"

There is no knowing how much more Mrs. Riley would have said about "Pether," if the end of the dance had not cut her eloquence short, by permitting the groups of dancers as they promenaded to throw in their desultory discourse right and left, and so break up anything like a consecutive conversation.

But let it not be supposed that all Mrs. Flanagan's guests were of the Gubbins and Riley stamp. There were some of the better class of the country people present; intelligence and courtesy in the one sex, and gentleness and natural grace in the other, making a society not to be ridiculed in the mass, though individual instances of folly and ignorance and purse-proud effrontery were amongst it.

But to Growling every phase of society afforded gratification; and while no one had a keener relish for such scenes as the one in which we have just witnessed him, the learned and the courteous could be met with equal weapons by the doctor when he liked.

Quitting the dancing-room, he went into the little drawing-room, where a party of a very different stamp were engaged in conversation. Edward O'Connor and the "dear English captain," as Mrs. Flanagan called him, were deep in an interesting discussion about the relative practices in Ireland and England on the occasions of elections and trials, and most other public events; and O'Connor, and two or three listeners,—amongst whom was a Mr. Monk, whose daughters, remarkably nice girls, were of the party,—were delighted with the feeling tone in which the Englishman spoke of the poorer classes of Irish, and how often the excesses into which they sometimes fell were viewed through an exaggerated or distorted medium, and what was frequently mere exuberance of spirit pronounced and punished as riot.

"I never saw a people over whom those in authority require more good temper," remarked the captain.

"Gentleness goes a long way with them," said Edward.

"And violence never succeeds," added Mr. Monk.

"You are of opinion, then," said the soldier, "they are not to be forced."

"Except to do what they like," chimed in Growling.

"That's a very *Irish* sort of coercion," said the captain, smiling.

"And therefore fit for Irishmen," said Growling; "and I never knew an intelligent Englishman yet, who came to Ireland, who did not find it out. Paddy has a touch of the pig in him—he won't be *driven;* but you may *coax* him a long way; or if you appeal to his reason,—for he happens to *have* such a thing about him,—you may persuade him into what is right if you take the trouble."

"By Jove," said the captain, "it is not easy to argue with Paddy; the rascals are so ready with quip, and equivoque, and queer answers, that they generally get the best of it in talk, however fallacious may be their argument; and when you think you have Pat in a corner, and escape is inevitable, he's off without your knowing how he slipped through your fingers."

Wher the doctor joined the conversation, Edward, knowing his powers, gave up the captain into his hands, and sat down by the side of Miss Monk, who had just entered from the dancing-room, and threw herself into a chair in the corner.

She and Edward soon got engaged in a conversation particularly interesting to him. She spoke of having lately met Fanny Dawson, and was praising her in such terms of affectionate admiration, that Edward hung upon every word with delight. I know not if Miss Monk was aware of Edward's devotion in that quarter before, but she could not look upon the bland, though somewhat sad smile, which arched his expressive mouth, and the dilated eye which beamed as her praises were uttered, without being then conscious that Fanny Dawson had made him captive.

She was pleased, and continued the conversation with that inherent pleasure a woman has in touching a man's heart, even though it be not on her own account; and it was done with that tact and delicacy which only women possess, and which is so refined that the rougher nature of man is insensible of its drift and influence, and he is betrayed by a net whose meshes are too fine for his perception. Edward O'Connor never dreamt that Miss Monk saw he was in love with the subject of their discourse. While they were talking, the merry hostess entered, and the last words the captain uttered fell upon her ear, and then followed a reply from Growling, saying that Irishmen were as hard to catch as quicksilver. "Ay, and as hard to keep as other silver," said the widow; "don't believe what these wild Irish fellows tell you of themselves, they are all mad divils alike—you steady Englishmen are the safe men—and the girls know it. And faith, if you try them," added she, laughing, "I don't know any one more likely to have luck with them than yourself; for, 'pon my conscience, captain, we all doat on you since you would not shoot the people, the other day."

There was a titter among the girls at this open avowal.

"Ah, why wouldn't I say it?" exclaimed she, laughing. "I'm not a mealy-mouthed miss; sure, *I* may tell truth; and I wouldn't trust one o' ye," she added, with a very significant nod of the head at the gentlemen, "except the captain. Yes—I'd trust one more—I'd trust Mister O'Connor; I think he really could be true to a woman."

The words fell sweetly upon his ear: the expression of trust in his faith at that moment, even from the laughing widow, was pleasing; for his heart was full of the woman he adored, and it was only by long waiting and untiring fidelity she could ever become his.

He bowed courteously to the compliment the hostess paid him; and she, immediately taking advantage of his acknowledgment, said that, after having paid him such a pretty compliment, he couldn't refuse her to sing a song. Edward never liked to sing in mixed companies, and was about making some objection, when the widow interrupted him with one of those Irish "Ah, now's" so hard to resist. "Besides, all the noisy pack are in the dancing-room, or indeed I wouldn't ask you; and here there's not one won't be charmed with you. Ah, look at Miss Monk, there—I know she's dying to hear you; and see all the ladies *hanging on your lips*, absolutely.—Can you refuse me after that, now?"

It was true that, in the small room where they sat, there were only those who were worthy of better things than Edward would have ventured on to the many; and filled with the tender and passionate sentiment his conversation with Miss Monk had awakened, one of those effusions of deep, and earnest, and poetic feeling which love had prompted to his muse, rose to his lips, and he began to sing.

All were silent, for the poet singer was a favourite, and all knew with what touching expression he gave his compositions; but now the mellow tones of his voice seemed to vibrate with a feeling in more than common unison with the words, and his dark earnest eyes beamed with a devotion of which she who was the object might be proud.

A LEAF THAT REMINDS OF THEE

I

How Sweet is the hour we give,
When fancy may wander free,
To the friends who in memory live
For then I remember thee!
Then, wing'd, like the dove from the ark,

My heart, o'er a stormy sea,
Brings back to my lonely bark
A leaf that reminds of thee!

II

But still does the sky look dark,
The waters still deep and wide;
Oh! when may my lonely bark
In peace on the shore abide?
But through the future far,
Dark though my course may be,
Thou art my guiding star!
My heart still turns to thee!

III

When I see thy friends I smile,
I sigh when I hear thy name;
But they cannot tell the while
Whence the smile or the sadness came.
Vainly the world may deem
The cause of my sighs they know:
The breeze that ruffles the stream
Knows not the depth below.

Before the first verse of the song was over, the entrance to the room was filled with eager listeners, and at its conclusion, a large proportion of the company from the dancing-room had crowded round the door, attracted by the rich voice of the singer, and fascinated into silence by the charm of his song. Perhaps, after mental qualities, the most valuable gift a man can have is a fine voice; it at once commands attention, and may, therefore, be ranked in a man's possession as highly as beauty in a woman's.

In speaking thus of voice, I do not allude to the power of singing, but the mere physical quality of a fine voice, which, in the bare utterance of the simplest words, is pleasing, but, becoming the medium for the interchange of higher thoughts is irresistible. Super-added to this gift, which Edward possessed, the song he sang had meaning in it which could reach the hearts of all his auditory, though its poetry might be appreciated but by few: its imagery grew upon a stem whose root was in every bosom, and the song that possesses this quality, whatever may be its defects, contains not only the elements of future fame, but of immediate popularity. Startling was the contrast between the silence the song had produced and the simultaneous clapping of hands outside the door when it was over; not the poor plaudit of a fashionable assembly, whose "bravo" is an attenuated note of admiration, struggling into a sickly existence, and expiring in a sigh; applause of so suspicious a character, that no one seems desirous of owning it,—a feeble forgery of satisfaction which people think it disgraceful to be caught uttering. The clapping was not the plaudit of high-bred hands, whose sound is like the fluttering of small wings, just enough to stir gossamer,—but not the heart. No;—such was not the applause which followed Edward's song;—he had the outburst of heart-warm and unsophisticated satisfaction, unfettered by chilling convention. Most of his hearers did not know that it was disgraceful to admit being too well pleased, and the poor innocents really opened their mouths and clapped their hands. Oh, fie! tell it not in Grosvenor-square.

And now James Reddy contrived to be asked to sing; the coxcomb, not content with his luck in being listened to before, panted for such another burst of applause as greeted Edward, whose song he had no notion was any better than his own; the puppy fancied his rubbish of the "black stone under the blue sea" partook of a grander character of composition, and that while Edward's "breeze" but "ruffled the stream," he had fathomed the ocean. But a "heavy blow and great discouragement was in store for Master James, for as he commenced a love ditty which he called by the fascinating title of "The Rose of Silence," and verily believed, would have enraptured every woman in the room, a powerful voice, richly flavoured with the brogue, shouted forth outside the door, "*Ma'am, if you plaze, supper's sarved.*" The effect was magical; a rush was made to supper by the crowd in the doorway, and every gentleman in the little drawing-room offered his arm to a lady, and led her off without the smallest regard to Reddy's singing.

His look was worth anything, as he saw himself thus unceremoniously deserted, and likely soon to be left in sole possession of the room; the old doctor was enchanted with his vexation; and when James ceased to sing, as the last couple were going, the doctor interposed his request that the song should be finished.

"Don't stop, my dear fellow," said the doctor; "that's the best song I have heard a long time, and you must indulge me by finishing it—that's a gem."

"Why, you see, doctor, they have all gone to supper."

"Yes, and the devil choke them with it," said Growling, "for their want of taste; but never mind that; one judicious listener is worth a crowd of such fools, you'll admit; so sit down again, and sing for me."

The doctor seated himself as he spoke, and there he kept Reddy, whom he knew was very fond of a good supper, singing away for the bare life, with only one person for audience, and that one humbugging him. The scene was rich; the gravity with which the doctor carried on the quiz was admirable, and the gullibility of the coxcomb who was held captive by his affected admiration, exquisitely absurd, and almost past belief; even Growling himself was amazed as he threw in a rapturous "charming" or "bravissimo" at the egregious folly of his dupe, who still continued singing, while the laughter of the supper room, and the inviting clatter of its knives and forks, were ringing in his ear. When Reddy concluded, the doctor asked, might he venture to request the last verse again; "for," continued he, "there is a singular beauty of thought and felicity of expression in its numbers, leaving the mind unsatisfied with but one hearing;—once more, if you please."

Poor Reddy repeated the last verse.

"Very charming, indeed!" said the doctor.

"You really like it?" said Reddy.

"Like?" said the doctor—"sir, *like* is a faint expression of what I think of that song.—Moore had better look to his laurels, sir!"

"Oh, doctor!"

"Ah, you know yourself," said Growling.

"Then that last, doctor——?" said Reddy, inquiringly.

"Is your most successful achievement, sir; there is a mysterious shadowing forth of something in it which is very fine."

"You like it better than the 'Black Stone?'"

"Pooh! sir;—the 'Black Stone,' if I may be allowed an image, is but ordinary paving, while that 'Rose of Silence' of yours might strew the path to Parnassus."

"And is it not strange, doctor," said Reddy, in a reproachful tone, "that *them* people should be insensible to that song, and leave the room while I was singing it?"

"Too good for them, sir—above their comprehensions."

"Besides, so rude!" said Reddy.

"Oh, my dear friend," said the doctor, "when you know more of the world, you'll find out that an appeal from the lower house to the upper," and he changed his hand from the region of his waistcoat to his head as he spoke, "is most influential."

"True, doctor," said Reddy, with a smile; "and suppose *we* go to supper now."

"Wait a moment," said Growling, holding his button. "Did you ever try your hand at an epic?"

"No, I can't say that I did."

"I wish you would."

"You flatter me, doctor; but don't you think we had better go to supper?

"Ha!" said the doctor, "your own house of commons is sending up an appeal—eh?"

"Decidedly, doctor."

"Then you see, my dear friend, you can't wonder at those poor inferior beings hurrying off to indulge their gross appetites, when a man of genius like you is not insensible to the same call. Never wonder again at people leaving your song for supper, Master James," said the doctor, resting his arm on Reddy, and sauntering from the room. "Never wonder again at the triumph of supper over song, for the Swan of Avon himself would have no chance against roast ducks."

Reddy smacked his lips at the word ducks, and the savoury odour of the supper-room which they approached heightened his anticipation of an onslaught on one of the aforesaid tempting birds; but ah! when he entered the room, skeletons of ducks there were, but nothing more; the work of demolition had been in able hands, and the doctor's lachrymose exclamation of "the devil a duck!" found a hollow echo under Reddy's waistcoat. Round the room that deluded minstrel went, seeking what he might devour, but his voyage of discovery for any hot fowl was profitless; and Growling in silent delight witnessed his disappointment.

"Come, sir," said the doctor, "there's plenty of punch left, however—I'll take a glass with you, and drink success to your next song, for the last is all I could wish;" and so indeed it was, for it enabled him to laugh at the poetaster, and cheat him out of his supper.

"Ho, ho!" said Murtough Murphy, who approached the door; "you have found out the punch is good, eh? 'faith it is that same, and I'll take another glass of it with you before I go, for the night is cold."

"Are you going so soon?" asked Growling, as he clinked his glass against the attorney's.

"Whisht!" said Murphy; "not a word—I'm slipping away after Dick the Divil; we have a trifle of work in hand, quite in his line, and it is time to set about it. Good b'ye, you'll hear more of it to-morrow—snug's the word!"

Murphy stole away, for the open departure of so merry a blade would not have been permitted, and in the hall he found Dick mounting a large top-coat, and muffling up.

"Good people are scarce, you think, Dick," said Murphy.

"I'd recommend you to follow the example, for the night is bitter cold, I can tell you."

"And as dark as a coal-hole," said Murphy, as he opened the door and looked out.

"No matter, I have got a dark lanthorn," said Dick, "which we can use when required; make haste, the gig is round the corner, and the little black mare will roll us over in no time."

They left the house quietly, as he spoke, and started on a bit of mischief, which demands a separate chapter.

1.   This very ingenious answer was really given by an Irish professor to an over-inquisitive lady.

2.   My own worthy and excellent master,—the best in Ireland.

XXII

THE NIGHT WAS PITCH DARK, and on rounding the adjacent corner, no vehicle could be seen; but a peculiar whistle from Dick was answered by the sound of approaching wheels, and the rapid footfalls of a horse, mingled with the light rattle of a smart gig.—On the vehicle coming up, Dick took the little mare, that was blacker than the night, by the head, the apron of the gig was thrown down, and out jumped a smart servant boy.

"You have the horse ready too, Billy?"

"Yis, sir," said Billy, touching his hat.

"Then follow; and keep up with me, remember."

"Yis, sir."

"Come to her head, here," and he patted the little mare's neck as he spoke with a caressing 'whoa,' which was answered by a low neigh of satisfaction, while the impatient pawing of her fore foot showed the animal's desire to start. "What an impatient little devil she is," said Dick, as he mounted the gig; "I'll get in first, Murphy, as I'm going to drive,—now up with you—hook on the apron—that's it—are you all right?"

"Quite," said Murphy.

"Then you be into your saddle and after us, Billy," said Dick; "and now let her go."

Billy gave the little black mare her head, and away she went, at a slapping pace, the fire from the road answering the rapid strokes of her nimble feet. The servant then mounted a horse, which was tied to a neighbouring pallisade, and had to gallop for it to come up with his master, who was driving with a swiftness almost fearful, considering the darkness of the night and the narrowness of the roads he had to traverse, for he was making the best of his course by cross ways to an adjacent road-side inn, where some non-resident electors were expected to arrive that night by a coach from Dublin; for the county town had every nook and cranny occupied, and this inn was the nearest point where they could get any accommodation.

Now don't suppose that they were electors whom Murphy and Dick, in their zeal for their party, were going over to greet with hearty welcomes, and bring up to the poll the next day. By no means. They were the friends of the opposite party, and it was with the design of retarding their movements that this night's excursion was undertaken. These electors were a batch of plain citizens from Dublin, whom the Scatterbrain interest had induced to leave the peace and quiet of the city to tempt the wilds of the country at that wildest of times—during a contested election: and a night coach was freighted inside and out with the worthy cits, whose aggregate voices would be of immense importance the next day; for the contest was close, the county nearly polled out, and but two days more for the struggle. Now, to interrupt these plain unsuspecting men was the object of Murphy, whose well-supplied information had discovered to him this plan of the enemy, which he set about countermining. As they rattled over the rough bye-roads, many a laugh did the merry attorney and the untameable Dick the Devil exchange, as the probable success of their scheme was canvassed, and fresh expedients devised to meet the possible impediments which might interrupt them. As they topped a hill, Murphy pointed out to his companion a moving light in the plain beneath.

"That's the coach, Dick—there are the lamps, we're just in time—spin down the hill, my boy—let me get in as they're at supper, and faith they'll want it, after coming off a coach such a night as this, to say nothing of some of them being aldermen in expectancy, I suppose, and of course obliged to play trencher-men as often as they can, as a requisite rehearsal for the parts they must here after fill."

In fifteen minutes more, Dick pulled up before a small cabin within a quarter of a mile of the inn, and the mounted servant tapped at the door, which was immediately opened, and a peasant advancing to the gig, returned the civil salutation with which Dick greeted his approach.

"I wanted to be sure you were ready, Barny."

"Oh, do you think I'd fail you, misther Dick, your honour?"

"I thought you might be asleep, Barny."

"Not when you bid me wake, sir—and there's a nice fire ready for you, and as fine a dhrop o' potteen as ever tickled your tongue, sir."

"You're the lad, Barny!—good fellow—I'll be back with you by and by—" and off whipped Dick again.

After going about a quarter of a mile further, he pulled up, alighted with Murphy from the gig, unharnessed the little black mare, and then overturned the gig into the ditch.

"That's as natural as life," said Dick.

"What an escape of my neck I've had!" said Murphy.

"Are you much hurt?" said Dick.

"A trifle, lame only," said Murphy, laughing and limping.

"There was a great *boccagh*[1] lost in you, Murphy; wait; let me rub a handful of mud on your face—there—you have a very upset look, 'pon my soul," said Dick, as he flashed the light of his lantern on him for a moment, and laughed at Murphy scooping the thud out of his eye, where Dick had purposely planted it.

"Divil take you," said Murtough; "that's too natural."

"There's nothing like looking your part," said Dick.

"Well, I may as well complete my attire," said Murtough, so he lay down in the road and took a roll in the mud; "that will do," said he; "and now, Dick, go back to Barny and the mountain dew, while I storm the camp of the Philistines; I think in a couple of hours you may be on the look-out for me; I'll signal you from the window, so now good bye;" and Murphy, leading the mare, proceeded to the inn, while Dick, with a parting "Luck to you, my boy," turned back to the cottage of Barny.

The coach had set down six inside and ten out passengers (all voters) about ten minutes before Murphy marched up to the inn door, leading the black mare, and calling "ostler" most lustily. His call being answered for "the beast," "the man" next demanded attention; and the landlord wondered all the wonders he could cram into a short speech, at seeing Misther Murphy, sure, at such a time; and the soncy landlady, too, was

all lamentations for his iligant coat and his poor eye sure, all ruined with
the mud:—and what was it at all? an upset, was it? oh, wirra! and wasn't
it lucky he wasn't killed, and they without a spare bed to lay him out
dacent if he was,—sure, wouldn't it be horrid for his body to be only
on sthraw in the barn, instead of the best feather-bed in the house; and,
indeed, he'd be welcome to it, only the gintlemen from town had them
all engaged.

"Well, dead or alive, I must stay here to-night, Mrs. Kelly, at all
events."

"And what will you do for a bed?"

"A shake down in the parlour, or a stretch on a sofa will do; my gig
is stuck fast in a ditch—my mare tired—ten miles from home—cold
night, and my knee hurt." Murphy limped as he spoke.

"Oh! your poor knee," said Mrs. Kelly; "I'll put a dhrop o' whisky and
brown paper on it, sure—"

"And what gentlemen are these, Mrs. Kelly, who have so filled your
house?"

"Gentlemen that came by the coach a while agone, and supping in
the parlour now, sure."

"Would you give my compliments, and ask would they allow me,
under the present peculiar circumstances, to join them; and in the mean
time, send somebody down the road to take the cushions out of my gig;
for there is no use in attempting to get the gig out till morning."

"Sartinly, Misther Murphy, we'll send for the cushions, but as for the
gentlemen, they are all on the other side."

"What other side?

"The Honourable's voters, sure."

"Pooh! is that all?" said Murphy, I don't mind that, I've no objection
on that account; besides, they need not know who *I* am," and he gave
the landlord a knowing wink, to which the landlord as knowingly
returned another.

The message to the gentlemen was delivered, and Murphy was
immediately requested to join their party; this was all he wanted,
and he played off his powers of diversion on the innocent citizens so
successfully, that before supper was half over they thought themselves in
luck to have fallen in with such a chance acquaintance. Murphy fired

away jokes, repartees, anecdotes, and country gossip, to their delight; and when the eatables were disposed of, he started them on the punch-drinking tack afterwards so cleverly, that he hoped to see three parts of them tipsy before they retired to rest.

"Do you feel your knee better now, sir?" asked one of the party, of Murphy.

"Considerably, thank you; whisky punch, sir, is about the best cure for bruises or dislocations a man can take."

"I doubt that, sir," said a little matter-of-fact man, who had now interposed his reasonable doubts for the twentieth time during Murphy's various extravagant declarations, and the interruption only made Murphy romance the more.

"*You* speak of your fiery *Dublin* stuff, sir—but our country whisky is as mild as milk, and far more wholesome; then, sir, our fine air alone would cure half the complaints without a grain of physic."

"I doubt that, sir," said the little man.

"I assure you, sir, a friend of my own from town came down here last spring on crutches, and from merely following a light whisky diet, and sleeping with his window open, he was able to dance at the race ball in a fortnight; as for this knee of mine, it's a trifle, though it was a bad upset too."

"How did it happen, sir? Was it your horse—or your harness—or your gig—or—"

"None o' them, sir—it was a *Banshee*."

"A Banshee," said the little man, "what's that?"

"A peculiar sort of supernatural creatures, that are common here, sir; she was squatted down on one side of the road, and my mare shied at her, and being a spirited little thing, she attempted to jump the ditch, and missed it in the dark."

"Jump a ditch, with a gig after her, sir?" said the little man.

"Oh, common enough to do that here, sir—she'd have done it easy in the daylight, but she could not measure her distance in the dark, and bang she went into the ditch: but it's a trifle, after all. I am generally run over four or five times a year."

"And you alive to tell it!" said the little man, incredulously.

"It's hard to kill us here, sir; we are used to accidents."

"Well, the worst accident I ever heard of," said one of the citizens, "happened to a friend of mine, who went to visit a friend of his on a Sunday, and all the family happened to be at church; so on driving into the yard there was no one to take his horse, therefore he undertook the office of ostler himself; but being unused to the duty, he most incautiously took off the horse's bridle before unyoking him from his gig, and the animal, making a furious plunge forward—my friend being before him at the time—the shaft of the gig was driven through his body, and into the coach-house gate behind him, and stuck so fast that the horse could not drag it out after; and in this dreadful situation they remained until the family returned from church, and saw the awful occurrence. A servant was despatched for a doctor, and the shaft was disengaged, and drawn out of the man's body,—just at the pit of his stomach; he was laid on a bed, and every one thought of course he must die at once; but he didn't,—and the doctor came next day, and he wasn't dead—did what he could for him—and, to make a long story short, sir, the man recovered."

"Pooh! pooh!" said the diminutive doubter.

"It's true," said the narrator.

"I make no doubt of it, sir," said Murphy; "I know a more extraordinary case of recovery myself."

"I beg your pardon, sir," said the cit; "I have not finished my story yet, for the most extraordinary part of the story remains to be told: my friend, sir, was a *very* sickly man before the accident happened—a very sickly man, and after that accident he became a hale healthy rnan—what do you think of that, sir?"

"It does not surprise me in the least, sir," said Murphy—"I can account for it readily."

"Well, sir, I never heard it accounted for, though I know it to be true; I should like to hear how you account for it."

"Very simply, sir," said Murphy; "don't you perceive the man discovered a *mine* of health by a *shaft* being sunk in the *pit* of his stomach."

Murphy's punning solution of the cause of cure was merrily received by the company, whose critical taste was not of that affected nature which despises a *jeu de mots*, and *will not* be satisfied under a *jeu d'esprit*; the little doubting man alone refused to be pleased.

"I doubt the value of a pun always, sir. Dr. Johnson said, sir—"

"I know," said Murphy;—"that the man who would commit a pun would pick a pocket; that's old, sir,—but is dearly remembered by all those who cannot make puns themselves."

"Exactly," said one of the party they called Wiggins. "It is the old story of the fox and the grapes. Did you ever hear, sir, the story of the fox and the grapes? The fox one day was——"

"Yes, yes," said Murphy, who, fond of absurdity as he was, could *not* stand the fox and the grapes by way of something new.

"They're sour," said the fox.

"Yes," said Murphy, "a capital story."

"Oh, them fables is so good!" said Wiggins.

"All nonsense!" said the diminutive contradictor.—"Nonsense, nothing but nonsense; the ridiculous stuff of birds and beasts speaking! as if any one could believe such stuff."

"I do—firmly—for one," said Murphy.

"You do?" said the little man.

"I do—and do you know why?"

"I cannot indeed conceive," said the little man, with a bitter grin.

"It is, sir, because I myself know a case that occurred in this very country of a similar nature."

"Do you want to make me believe you knew a fox that spoke, sir?" said the mannekin, almost rising into anger.

"Many, sir," said Murphy, "many."

"Well! after that!" said the little man.

"But the case I immediately allude to is not of a fox, but a cat," said Murphy.

"A cat? Oh, yes—to be sure—a cat speak, indeed!" said the little gentleman.

"It is a fact, sir," said Murphy, "and if the company would not object to my relating the story, I will state the particulars."

The proposal was received with acclamation; and Murphy, in great enjoyment of the little man's annoyance, cleared his throat, and made all the preparatory demonstrations of a regular *raconteur*; but, before he began, he recommended the gentlemen to mix fresh tumblers all round, that they might have nothing to do but listen and drink silently. "For of all things in the world," said Murtough, "I hate a song or a story to be interrupted by the rattle of spoons."

They obeyed; and while they are mixing their punch, we will just turn over a fresh page, and devote a new Chapter to the following ...

Marvellous Legend

1.   Lame Beggar.

XXIII

𝔜𝔢 𝔐𝔞𝔯𝔳𝔢𝔩𝔩𝔬𝔲𝔰 𝔏𝔢𝔤𝔢𝔫𝔡 𝔬𝔣 𝔗𝔬𝔪 ℭ𝔬𝔫𝔫𝔬𝔯'𝔰 ℭ𝔞𝔱

"THERE WAS A MAN IN these parts, sir, you must know, called Tom Connor, and he had a cat that was equal to any dozen of rat-traps, and he was proud of the baste, and with rayson; for she was worth her weight in goold to him in saving his sacks of meal from the thievery of the rats and mice; for Tom was an extensive dealer in corn, and influenced the rise and fall of that article in the market, to the extent of a full dozen of sacks at a time, which he either kept or sold, as the spirit of free trade or monopoly came over him. Indeed, at one time, Tom had serious thoughts of applying to the government for a military force to protect his granary, when there was a threatened famine in the county."

"Pooh! pooh! sir," said the matter-of-fact little man, "as if a dozen sacks could be of the smallest consequence in a whole county—pooh!"

"Well, sir," said Murphy, "I can't help if you don't believe; but it's truth what I am telling you, and pray don't interrupt me, though you may not believe; by the time the story's done you'll have heard more wonderful things than that,—and besides, remember you're a stranger in these parts, and have no notion of the extraordinary things, physical, metaphysical, and magical, which constitute the idiosyncrasy of rural destiny."

The little man did not know the meaning of Murphy's last sentence—nor Murphy either; but having stopped the little man's throat with the big words, he proceeded.

"This cat, sir, you must know, was a great pet, and was so up to every thing, that Tom swore she was a'most like a Christian, only she couldn't speak and had so sensible a look in her eyes, he was sartin sure the cat knew every word that was said to her. Well, she used to sit by him at breakfast every morning, and the eloquent cock of her tail, as she used to rub against his leg, said, 'Give me some milk, Tom Connor,' as plain as print, and the plenitude of her purr afterwards spoke a gratitude beyond language.—Well, one morning, Tom was going to the neighbouring town to market, and he had promised the wife to bring home shoes to the childre', out o' the price of the corn; and sure enough, before he sat down to breakfast, there was Tom taking the measure of the children's feet, by cutting notches on a bit of stick; and the wife gave him so many cautions about getting a 'nate fit' for 'Billy's purty feet,' that Tom, in his anxiety to nick the closest possible measure, cut off the child's toe. That disturbed the harmony of the party, and Tom was obliged to breakfast alone, while the mother was endeavouring to cure Billy; in short, trying to make a *heal* of his *toe*. Well, sir, all the time Tom was taking measure for the shoes, the cat was observing him with that luminous peculiarity of eye for which her tribe is remarkable; and when Tom sat down to breakfast the cat rubbed up against him more vigorously than usual, but Tom, being bewildered between his expected gain in corn, and the positive loss of his child's toe, kept never minding her, until the cat, with a sort of caterwauling growl, gave Tom a dab of her claws, that went clean through his leathers, and a little further. 'Wow!' says Tom, with a jump, clapping his hand on the part, and rubbing it, 'by this and that, you drew the blood out o' me,' says Tom, 'you wicked divil—tish!—go along!' says he, making a kick at her. With that the cat gave a reproachful look at him, and her eyes glared just like a pair of mail-coach lamps in a fog. With that, sir, the cat, with a mysterious '*mi-ow*,' fixed a most penetrating glance on Tom, and distinctly uttered his name.

"Tom felt every hair on his head as stiff as a pump-handle—and scarcely crediting his ears, he returned a searching look at the cat, who very quietly proceeded with a sort of nasal twang—"'Tom Connor,' says she.

"'The Lord be good to me,' says Tom, 'if it isn't spakin', she is.'

"'Tom Connor,' says she, again.

"'Yes, ma'am,' says Tom.

"'Come here,' says she, 'whisper—I want to talk to you, Tom,' says she, 'the last taste in private,' says she—rising on her hams, and beckoning him with her paw out o' the door, with a wink and a toss o' the head aiqual to a milliner.

"Well, as you may suppose, Tom didn't know whether he was on his head or his heels, but he followed the cat, and off she went and squatted herself under the hedge of a little paddock at the back of Tom's house; and as he came round the corner, she held up her paw again, and laid it on her mouth, as much as to say, 'Be cautious, Tom.' Well, divil a word Tom could say at all, with the fright, so up he goes to the cat, and says she—

"'Tom,' says she, 'I have a great respect for you, and there's something I must tell you, bekase you're losing characther with your neighbours,' says she, 'by your goin's on,' says she; 'and it's out o' the respect that I have for you, that I must tell you,' says she.

"'Thank you, ma'am,' says Tom.

"'You're goin' off to the town,' says she, 'to buy shoes for the childhre',' says she, 'and never thought o' gettin' me a pair.'

"'You!' says Tom.

"'Yis, me, Tom Connor,' says she; 'and the neighbours wondhers that a respectable man like you allows your cat to go about the counthry barefutted,' says she.

"'Is it a cat to wear shoes?' says Tom.

"'Why not?' says she, 'doesn't horses ware shoes—and I have a prettier foot than a horse, I hope,' says she, with a toss of her head.

"'Faix, she spakes like a woman; so proud of her feet,' says Tom to himself, astonished, as you may suppose, but pretending never to think it remarkable all the time; and so he went discoursin', and says he, 'It's thrue for you, ma'am,' says he, 'that horses wares shoes—but that stands to rayson, ma'am, you see—seeing the hardship their feet has to go through on the hard roads.'

"'And how do you know what hardship my feet has to go through?' says the cat, mighty sharp.

"'But, ma'am,' says Tom, 'I don't well see how you could fasten a shoe on you,' says he.

"'Lave that to me,' says the cat.

"'Did any one ever stick walnut shells on you, pussey?' says Tom, with a grin.

"'Don't be disrespectful, Tom Connor,' says the cat, with a frown.

"'I ax your pard'n, ma'am,' says he, 'but as for the horses you wor spakin' about wearin' shoes, you know their shoes is fastened on with nails, and how would your shoes be fastened on?'

"'Ah, you stupid thief,' says she, 'haven't I iligant nails o' my own?'— and with that she gave him a dab of her claw, that made him roar.

"'Ow! murdher!' says he.

"'Now, no more of your palaver, Misther Connor,' says the cat, 'just be off and get me the shoes.'

"'Tare an ouns,' says Tom, 'what'll become o' me if I'm to get shoes for my cats?' says he, 'for you increase your family four times a year, and you have six or seven every time,' says he, 'and then you must all have two pair apiece—wirra! wirra!—I'll be ruined in shoe leather,' says Tom.

"'No more o' your stuff,' says the cat, 'don't be standin' here undher the hedge talkin', or we'll lose our karacthers—for I've remarked your wife is jealous, Tom.'

"''Pon my sowl, that's threw,' says Tom, with a smirk.

"'More fool she,' says the cat, 'for, 'pon my conscience, Tom, you're as ugly as if you wor bespoke.'

"Off ran the cat with these words, leaving Tom in amazement;—he said nothing to the family for fear of fright'ning them, and off he went to the *town*, as he *pretended*—for he saw the cat watching him through a hole in the hedge; but when he came to a turn at the end of the road, the dickins a mind he minded the market, good or bad, but went off to Squire Botherum's, the magisthrit, to sware examinations agen the cat."

"Pooh! pooh—nonsense!!"—broke in the little man, who had listened thus far to Murtough with an expression of mingled wonder and contempt, while the rest of the party willingly gave up the reins to nonsense, and enjoyed Murtough's legend, and their companion's more absurd common sense.

"Don't interrupt him, Goggins," said Mister Wiggins.

"How can you listen to such nonsense?" returned Goggins. "Swear examinations against a cat, indeed! pooh! pooh!"

"My dear sir," said Murtough, "remember this is a fairy story, and that the country all around here is full of enchantment. As I was telling you, Tom went off to swear examinations."

"Ay, ay!" shouted all but Goggins; "go on with the story."

"And when Tom was asked to relate the events of the morning, which brought him before Squire Botherum, his brain was so bewildered between his corn, and his cat, and his child's toe, that he made a very confused account of it".

"'Begin your story from the beginning,'—said the magistrate to Tom.

"'Well, your honour,' says Tom, 'I was goin' to market this mornin', to sell the child's corn,—I beg your pard'n—my own toes, I mane, sir.'

"'Sell your toes?' said the squire.

"'No, sir, takin' the cat to market, I mane—'

"'Take a cat to market?' said the squire—'You're drunk, man.'

"'No, your honour, only confused a little; for when the toes began to spake to me—the cat, I mane—I was bothered clane—'

"'The cat speak to you?'—said the squire; 'Phew!—worse than before; you're drunk, Tom!'

"'No, your honour; it's on the strength of the cat I come to spake to you—'

"'I think it's on the strength of a pint o' whisky, Tom—'

"'By the vartue o' my oath, your honour, it's nothin' but the cat.'

And so Tom then told him all about the affair, and the squire was regularly astonished. Just then the bishop of the diocese and the priest of the parish happened to call in, and heard the story, and the bishop and the priest had a tough argument for two hours on the subject; the former swearing she must be a witch—but the priest denying *that*, and maintaining she was *only* enchanted—and that part of the argument was afterwards referred to the primate, and subsequently to the conclave at Rome; but the pope declined interfering about cats, saying he had quite enough to do minding his own bulls.

"'In the mean time, what are to do with the cat?' says Botherum.

"'Burn her,' says the bishop; 'she's a witch.'

"'*Only* enchanted,' said the priest—'and the ecclesiastical court maintains that—'

"'Bother the ecclesiastical court!' said the Magistrate; 'I can only proceed on the statutes;' and with that he pulled down all the law-books in his library, and hunted the laws from Queen Elizabeth down, and he found that they made laws against every thing in Ireland, *except a cat.*—The devil a thing escaped them but a cat, which did *not* come within the meaning of any act of parliament:—*the cats only had escaped.*

"'There's the alien act, to be sure,' said the magistrate, 'and perhaps she's a French spy, in disguise.'

"'She spakes like a French spy, sure enough,' says Tom; 'and she was missin', I remember, all last Spy-Wednesday.'

"'That's suspicious,' says the squire—'but conviction might be difficult; and I have a fresh idea,' says Botherum.

"'Faith, it won't keep fresh long, this hot weather,' says Tom; 'so your honour had betther make use of it at wanst.'

"'Right,' says Botherum,—'we'll make her subject to the game laws; we'll hunt her,' says he.

"'Ow!—elegant!' says Tom;—'we'll have a brave run out of her.'

"'Meet me at the cross-roads,' says the squire, 'in the morning, and I'll have the hounds ready.'

"Well, off Tom went home; and he was racking his brain what excuse he could make to the cat for not bringing the shoes; and at last he hit one off just as he saw her cantering up to him, half a mile before he got home.

"'Where's the shoes, Tom?' says she.

"'I have not got them to-day, ma'am,' says he.

"'Is that the way you keep your promises, Tom?' says she;—'I'll tell you what it is, Tom—I'll tare the eyes out o' the children, if you don't get me shoes—'

"'Whisht! whisht!' says Tom, frightened out of his life for his children's eyes.—'Don't be in a passion, pussey. The shoemaker said he had not a shoe in his shop, nor a lass that would make one to fit you; and he says I must bring you into the town for him to take your measure.'

"'And when am I to go?' says the cat, looking savage.

"'To-morrow,' says Tom.

"'It's well you said that, Tom,' says the cat, 'or the divil an eye I'd lave in your family this night'—and off she hopped.

"Tom thrimbled at the wicked look she gave.

"'Remember!' says she, over the hedge, with a bitter caterwaul.

"'Never fear,' says Tom.

"Well, sure enough, the next mornin' there was the cat at cock-crow, licking herself as nate as a new pin, to go into the town, and out came Tom, with a bag undher his arm, and the cat afther him—

"'Now git into this, and I'll carry you into the town,' says Tom, opening the bag.

"'Sure I can walk with you,' says the, cat.

"'Oh, that wouldn't do,' says Tom; 'the people in the town is curious and slandherous people, and sure it would rise ugly remarks if I was seen with a cat afther me:—a dog is a man's companion by nature, but cats does not stand to rayson.'

"Well, the cat seeing there was no use in argument, got into the bag, and off Tom set to the cross-roads with the bag over his shoulder, and he came up, quite *innocent-like*, to the corner, where the squire and his huntsman, and the hounds, and a pack o' people were waitin'. Out came the squire on a sudden, just as if it was all by accident.

"'God save you, Tom,' says he.

"'God save you kindly, sir,' says Tom.

"'What's that bag you have at your back?' says the squire.

"'Oh, nothin' at all, sir,' says Tom—makin' a face all the time, as much as to say, I have her safe.

"'Oh, there's something in that bag, I think,' says the squire, 'and you must let me see it.'

"'If you bethray me, Tom Connor,' says the cat in a low voice, 'by this and that I'll never spake to you again!'

"''Pon my honour, sir,' says Tom, with a wink and a twitch of his thumb towards the bag—'I haven't any thing in it.'

"'I have been missing my praties of late,' says the squire, 'and I'd just like to examine that bag,' says he.

"'Is it doubtin' my charackther, you'd be, sir?' says Tom, pretending to be in a passion.

"'Tom, your sowl!' says the voice in the sack, '*if you let the cat out of the bag*, I'll murther you.'

"'An honest man would make no objection to be sarched,' said the squire, 'and I insist on it,' says he, laying hold o' the bag, and Tom purtending to fight all the time; but, my jewel! before two minutes, they shook the cat out o' the bag, sure enough, and off she went with her tail as big as a sweeping brush, and the squire, with a thundering view halloo, after her, clapt the dogs at her heels, and away they went for the bare life. Never was there seen such running as that day—the cat made for a shaking bog, the loneliest place in the whole counthry—and there the riders were all thrown out, barrin' the huntsman, who had a web-footed horse on purpose for soft places; and the priest, whose horse could go anywhere by rayson of the priest's blessing; and sure enough, the huntsman and his rivirence stuck to the hunt like wax; and just as the cat got on the border of the bog, they saw her give a twist as the foremost dog closed with her, for he gave her a nip in the flank. Still she went on, however, and headed them well, towards an old mud cabin in the middle of the bog, and there they saw her jump in at the window, and up came the dogs the next minit, and gathered round the house with the most horrid howling ever was heard.—The huntsman alighted, and went into the house to turn the cat out again—when what should he see but an old hag, lying in bed in the corner—

"'Did you see a cat come in here?' says he.

"'Oh, no—o—o—o!' squeeled out the old hag, in a trembling voice, 'there's no cat here,' says she.

"Yelp, yelp, yelp! went the dogs outside.

"'Oh, keep the dogs out o' this,' says the old hag—'oh—o—o—o!' and the huntsman saw her eyes glare under the blanket, just like a cat's.

"'Hillo' says the huntsman, pulling down the blanket—and what should he see but the old hag's flank, all in a gore of blood.

"'Ow, ow! you old divil—is it you? you owld cat!' says he, opening the door.

"In rushed the dogs—up jumped the old hag, and changing into a cat before their eyes, out she darted through the window again, and made another run for it; but she couldn't escape, and the dogs gobbled her while you could say 'Jack Robinson.' But the most remarkable part of this extraordinary story, gentlemen, is, that the pack was ruined from that day out; for after having eaten the enchanted cat, *the divil a thing they would ever hunt afterwards, but mice.*"

XXIV

Murphy's story was received with acclamation by all but the little man.

"That is all a pack of nonsense," said he.

"Well, you're welcome to it, sir," said Murphy, "and if I had greater nonsense, you should have it; but, seriously, sir, I again must beg you to remember, that the country all round here abounds in enchantment; scarcely a night passes without some fairy frolic: but however you may doubt the wonderful fact of the cat speaking, I wonder you are not impressed with the points of moral, in which the story abounds—"

"Fiddlestick!" said the miniature snarler.

"First, the little touch about the corn monopoly—then maternal vanity chastised by the loss of the child's toe—then Tom's familiarity with his cat, showing the danger arising from a man making too free with his female domestics—the historical point about the penal laws—the fatal results of letting the cat out o' the bag, with the curious final fact in natural history."

"It's all nonsense," said the little man, "and I am ashamed of myself for being such a fool as to sit a-listening to such stuff, instead of going to bed, after the fatigue of my journey, and the necessity of rising early to-morrow, to be in good time at the polling."

"Oh! then you're going to the election, sir?" said Murphy.

"Yes, sir—there's some sense in *that*—and *you*, gentlemen, remember we must be all up early—and I recommend you to follow my example."

The little man rang the bell—the bootjack and slippers were called for, and after some delay, a very sleepy-looking *gossoon* entered with a bootjack under his arm, but no slippers.

"Didn't I say slippers?" said the little man.

"You did, sir."

"And where are they, sir?"

"The masther says there isn't any, if you plaze, sir."

"No slippers—and you call this an inn? Oh!—well, 'what can't be cured must be endured'—hold me the bootjack, sir."

The gossoon obeyed—the little man inserted his heel in the cleft, but, on attempting to pull his foot from his boot, he nearly went heels over head backward.—Murphy caught him, and put him on his legs again.

"Heads up, soldiers," exclaimed Murtough—"I thought you were drinking too much."

"Sir, I'm not intoxicated," said the mannekin, snappishly—"It is the fault of that vile bootjack—What sort of a thing is that you have brought?" added he, in a rage, to the *gossoon*.

"It's the bootjack, sir; only one o' the horns is gone you see,"—and he held up to view a rough piece of board, with an angular slit in it, but one of 'the horns,' as he called it, had been broken off at the top, leaving the article useless.

"How dare you bring such a thing as *that?*" said the little man, in a great rage.

"Why, sir, you ax'd for a bootjack, sure, and I brought you the best I had—and it's not my fault it's bruk, so it is, for it wasn't me bruk it, but Biddy batin' the cock."

"Beating the cock!" repeated the little man, in surprise—"God bless me!—beat a cock with a bootjack! what savages!"

"Oh it's not the *hen* cock I mane, sir," said the gossoon, "but the beer cock—she was batin' the cock into the barrel, sir, wid the bootjack, sir."

"That was decidedly wrong," said Murphy; "a bootjack is better suited to a heel-tap than a full measure."

"She was tapping the beer, you mean," said the little man.

"Faix, she wasn't tappin' it at all, sir, but hittin' it very hard, she was, and that's the way she bruk it—"

"Barbarians!" exclaimed the little man, "using a bootjack instead of a hammer!"

"Sure the hammer was gone to the priest, sir, bekase he wanted it for the crucifixion."

"The crucifixion!" exclaimed the little man, horrified; "is it possible they crucify people?"

"Oh no, sir!" said the gossoon, grinning, "it's the picthur I mane, sir—an iligant picthur that is hung up in the chapel, and he wanted a hammer to dhrive the nails—"

"Oh, a *picture* of the crucifixion," said the little man.

"Yis, sure, sir—the alther piece, that was althered for to fit to the place, for it was too big when it came down from Dublin, so they cut off the sides where the sojers was, bekase it stop't out the windows, and wouldn't lave a bit o' light for his reverence to read mass; and sure the sojers was no loss out o' the alther piece, and was hung up afther in the Yesthrey, and sarve them right, the blackguards. But it was sore agen our will to cut off the ladies at the bottom, that was cryin' and roarin', only, by great good luck, the head o' the blessed Virgin was presarved in the corner, and sure it's beautiful to see the tears runnin' down her face, just over the hole in the wall for the holy wather—which is remarkable."

The gossoon was much offended by the laughter that followed his account of the altar-piece, which he had no intention of making irreverential, and suddenly became silent, with a muttered—"More shame for yiz;" and as his bootjack was impracticable, he was sent off with orders for the chambermaid to supply bed candles immediately.

The party soon separated for their various dormitories, the little man leaving sundry charges to call them early in the morning, and to be sure to have hot water ready for shaving, and, without fail, to have their boots polished in time, and left at their room doors;—to all of which injunctions he severally received the answer of—"Certainly, sir;" and as the bed-room doors were slapped to, one by one, the last sound of the retiring party was the snappish voice of the indefatigable little man, shouting, ere he shut his door,—"early—early—don't forget, Mistress Kelly—*early!*"

A shake-down for Murphy in the parlour was hastily prepared; and, after Mrs. Kelly was assured by Murtough that he was quite comfortable, and perfectly content with his accommodation, for which she made scores of apologies, with lamentations it was not better, &c. &c., the whole household retired to rest, and in about a quarter of an hour the inn was in perfect silence.

Then Murtough cautiously opened his door, and after listening for some minutes, and being satisfied he was the only watcher under the roof, he gently opened one of the parlour windows, and gave the preconcerted signal which he and Dick had agreed upon. Dick was under the window immediately, and after exchanging a few words with Murtough, the latter withdrew, and taking off his boots, and screening with his hand the light of a candle he carried, he cautiously ascended the stairs, and proceeded stealthily along the corridor of the dormitory, where, from the chambers on each side, a concert of snoring began to be executed, and at all the doors stood the boots and shoes of the inmates, awaiting the aid of Day and Martin in the morning. But, oh!—innocent calf-skins—destined to a far different fate—not Day and, Martin, but Dick the Devil and Company were in wait for you. Murphy collected as many as he could carry under his arms, and descended with them to the parlour window, where they were transferred to Dick, who carried them directly to the horse-pond, which lay behind the inn, and there committed them to the deep. After a few journeys up and down stairs, Murtough had left the electors without a morsel of sole or upper leather, and was satisfied that a considerable delay, if not prevention of their appearance at the poll on the morrow, would be the consequence.

"There, Dick," said Murphy, "is the last of them," as he handed the little man's shoes out of the window,—"and now, to save appearances, you must take mine too—for I must be without boots as well as the rest in the morning. What fun I shall have when the uproar begins—don't you envy me, Dick? There, be off now: I say—though; notwithstanding you take away my boots, you need not throw them into the horse-pond."

"Faith, an I will," said Dick, dragging them out of his hands; "'twould not be honourable, if I didn't—I'd give two pair of boots for the fun you'll have."

"Nonsense, Dick—Dick, I say—my boots."

"Honour!" cried Dick, as he vanished round the corner.

"That divil will keep his word," muttered Murphy, as he closed the window—"I may bid good-bye to that pair of boots—bad luck to him." And yet the merry attorney could not help laughing at Dick making him a sufferer by his own trick.

Dick *did* keep his word; and after, with particular delight, sinking Murphy's boots with the rest, he, as it was preconcerted, returned to the cottage of Barny, and with his assistance, drew the upset gig from the ditch, and with a second set of harness provided for the occasion, yoked the servant's horse to the vehicle, and drove home.

Murphy, meanwhile, was bent on more mischief at the Inn; and lest the loss of the boots and shoes might not be productive of sufficient impediment to the movements of the enemy, he determined on venturing a step further. The heavy sleeping of the weary and tipsy travellers enabled him to enter their chambers unobserved, and over the garments they had taken off, he poured the contents of the water-jug and water-bottle he found in each room, and then laying the empty bottle and a tumbler on a chair beside each sleeper's bed, he made it appear as if the drunken men had been dry in the night, and in their endeavours to cool their thirst, had upset the water over their own clothes. The clothes of the little man, in particular, Murphy took especial delight in sousing more profusely than his neighbours', and not content with taking his shoes, burnt his stockings, and left the ashes in the dish of his candlestick, with just as much unconsumed as would show what they had been. He then retired to the parlour, and with many an internal chuckle at the thought of the morning's hubbub, threw off his clothes, and flinging himself on the shake-down Mrs. Kelly had provided for him, was soon wrapped in the profoundest slumber, from which he never woke until the morning uproar of the inn aroused him. He jumped from his lair, and rushed to the scene of action, to soar in the storm of his own raising, and to make it more apparent that he had been as great a sufferer as the rest, he only threw a quilt over his shoulders, and did not draw on his stockings. In this plight he scaled the stairs and joined the storming party, where the little man was leading the forlorn hope, with his candlestick in one hand, and the remnant of his burnt stocking between the finger and thumb of the other—"Look at that, sir!" he cried, as he held it up to the landlord.

The landlord could only stare.

"Bless me!" cried Murphy, "how drunk you must have been, to mistake your stocking for an extinguisher!"

"Drunk, sir!—I wasn't drunk!"

"It looks very like it," said Murphy, who did not wait for an answer, but bustled off to another party, who was wringing out his inexpressibles at the door of his bedroom, and swearing at the gossoon, that he must have his boots.

"I never seen them, sir," said the boy.

"I left them at my door," said the man.

"So did I leave mine," said Murphy, "and here I am barefooted—it is most extraordinary."

"Has the house been robbed?" said the innocent elector.

"Not a one o' me knows, sir!" said the boy—"but how would it be robbed, and the doors all fast this mornin'?"

The landlady now appeared, and fired at the word "robbed!"

"Robbed, sir!" exclaimed Mrs. Kelly—"no, sir—no one was ever robbed in my house—my house is respectable and responsible, sir—a vartuous house—none o' your rantipole places, sir, I'd have you to know—but decent and well-behaved, and the house was as quiet as a lamb all night."

"Certainly, Mrs. Kelly," said Murphy—"not a more respectable house in Ireland—I'll vouch for that."

"You're a gentleman, Misther Murphy," said Mrs. Kelly, who turned down the passage, uttering indignant ejaculations in a sort of snorting manner, while her words of anger were returned by Murphy with expressions of soothing and condolence, as he followed her down stairs.

The storm still continued above, and while there they shouted, and swore, and complained, Murphy gave his notion of the catastrophe to the landlady below, inferring that the men were drunk, and poured the water over their own clothes. To repeat this idea to themselves, he re-ascended—but the men were incredulous. The little man he found buttoning on a pair of black gaiters, the only serviceable bit of decency he had at his command, which only rendered his denuded state more ludicrous.—To him Murphy asserted his belief that the whole affair was enchantment, and ventured to hope the small individual would have more faith in fairy machinations for the future; to which the little abortion only returned his usual "pho! pho!—nonsense!"

Through all this scene of uproar, as Murphy passed to and fro, whenever he encountered the landlord, that worthy individual threw him a knowing look; and the exclamation of "oh Misther Murphy—by dad!" given in a low chuckling tone, insinuated that the landlord not only smoked but enjoyed the joke.

"You must lend me a pair of boots, Kelly!" said Murtough.

"To be sure, sir—ha! ha! ha!—but you are the quare man, Misther Murphy—"

"Send down the road and get my gig out of the ditch."

"To be sure, sir—the poor divils.—Purty hands they got into—" and off went the landlord with a chuckle.

The messengers sent for the gig returned, declaring there was no gig to be seen anywhere.

Murphy affected great surprise at the intelligence—again went among the bamboozled electors, who were all obliged to go to bed for want of clothes; and his bitter lamentations over the loss of his gig almost reconciled them to their minor troubles.

To the fears they expressed that they should not be able to reach the town in time for polling that day, Murphy told them to set their minds at rest, for they would be in time on the next.

He then borrowed a saddle, as well as a pair of boots, from the landlord; and the little black mare bore Murphy triumphantly back to the town, after having securely impounded Scatterbrain's voters, who were anxiously and hourly expected by their friends.—Still they came not. At last Handy Andy, who happened to be in town with Scatterbrain, was dispatched to hurry them, and his orders were not to come back without them.

Handy, on his arrival at the inn, found the electors in bed, and all the fires in the house employed in drying their clothes. The little man, wrapped in a blanket, was superintending the cooking of his own before the kitchen grate;—there hung his garments on some cross sticks, suspended from a string, after the fashion of a roasting jack, which the small gentleman turned before a blazing turf fire; and beside this contrivance of his, swung a goodly joint of meat, which a bouncing kitchen wench came over to baste now and then.

Andy was answering some questions of the inquisitive little man, when the kitchen maid, handing the basting-ladle to Andy, begged him to do a good turn, and just to baste the beef for her, for that her heart was broke with all she had to do, cooking dinner for so many.

Andy, always ready to oblige, consented, and plied the ladle actively between the troublesome queries of the little man; but at last, getting confused with some very crabbed questions put to him, Andy became completely bothered, and lifting a brimming ladle of dripping, poured it over the little man's coat instead of the beef.

A roar from the proprietor of the clothes followed, and he implanted a kick at such advantage upon Andy, that he upset him into the dripping pan; and Andy, in his fall, endeavouring to support himself, caught at the suspended articles above him, and the clothes, and the beef, and Andy, all swam in gravy.

XXV

WHILE DISASTER AND HUBBUB WERE rife below, the electors up stairs were holding a council whether it would not be better to send back the 'Honourable's' messenger to the town, and request a supply of shoes, which the had no other means of getting. The debate was of an odd sort; they were all in their several beds at the time, and roared at each other through their doors, which were purposely left open, that they might enjoy each other's conversation; number seven replied to number three, and claimed respect to his arguments on the score of seniority; the blue room was completely controverted by the yellow; and the double room would, of course, have had superior weight in the argument, only that everything it said was lost by the two honourable members speaking together. The French king used to hold a council, called a "bed of justice," in which neither justice nor a bed had anything to do, so that this Irish conference better deserved the title than any council the Bourbon ever assembled. The debate having concluded, and the question being put and carried, the usher of the black counterpane was desired to get out of bed, and, wrapped in the robe of office, whence he derived his title, to go down stairs and call the 'Honourable's' messenger to the 'bar of the house,' and there order him a pint of porter, for refreshment after his ride; and forthwith to send him back again to the town for a supply of shoes.

The house was unanimous in voting the supplies. The usher reached the kitchen, and found Andy in his shirt sleeves, scraping the dripping from his livery with an old knife, whose hackled edge considerably assisted Andy's own ingenuity in the tearing of his coat in many places;

while the little man made no effort towards the repair of his garment, but held it up before him, and regarded it with a piteous look.

To the usher of the black counterpane's question, whether Andy was the Honourable's messenger; Andy replied in the affirmative; but to the desire expressed, that he would ride back to the town, Andy returned a decided negative.

"My ordhers is not to go back without you," said Andy.

"But we have no shoes," said the usher; "and cannot go until we get some."

"My ordher is, not to go back without you."

"But if we can't go."

"Well, then I can't go back, that's all," said Andy.

The usher, and the landlord, and the landlady, all hammered away at Andy for a long time, in vain trying to convince him he ought to return, as he was desired; still Andy stuck to the letter of his orders, and said he often got into trouble for not doing *exactly* what he was bid, and that he was bid 'not to go back without them; and he would not—so he wouldn't—devil a fut.'

At last, however, Andy was made to understand the propriety of riding back to the town; and was desired to go as fast as his horse could carry him—to gallop every foot of the way: but Andy did no such thing; he had received a good thrashing once for being caught galloping his master's horse on the road; and he had no intention of running the risk a second time, because '*the stranger*' told him to do so. "What does he know about it," said Andy to himself; "faith it's fair and aisy I'll go, and not disthress the horse, to plaze any one." So he went back his ten miles only at a reasonable pace; and when he appeared without the electors a storm burst on poor Andy.

"There!—I knew how it would be," said he; "and not my fault at all."

"Weren't you told not to return without them?"

"But wait till I tell you how it was, sure;" and then Andy began an account of the condition in which the voters lay at the inn; but between the impatience of those who heard and the confused manner of Andy's recital it was some time before matters were explained:—then Andy was desired to ride back to the inn again, to tell the electors shoes should be forwarded after him in a post-chaise, and requesting their utmost exertions in hastening over to the town, for that the election was going against them. Andy returned to the inn, and this time, under orders from head quarters, galloped in good earnest, and brought in his horse smoking hot, and indicating lameness. The day was wearing apace, and it was so late when the electors were enabled to start, that the polling booths were closed before they could reach the town; and in many of those booths the requisite number of electors had not been polled that day to keep them open, so that the next day nearly all these out electors, about whom there had been so much trouble and expense, would be of no avail. Thus, Murphy's trick was quite successful, and the poor pickled electors driven back to their inn in dudgeon.

Andy, when he went to the stable to saddle his steed, for a return to Neck-or-Nothing Hall, found him dead lame, so that to ride him better than twelve miles home was impossible. Andy was obliged to leave him where he was, and trudge it to the Hall; for all the horses in Kelly's stables were knocked up with their day's work.

As it was shorter by four miles across the country than by the road, Andy pursued the former course, and, as he knew the country well, the shades of evening, which were now closing round, did not deter him in the least. Andy was not very fresh for the journey, to be sure, for he had ridden upwards of thirty miles that day, so the merry whistle, which is so constantly heard from the lively Irish pedestrian, did not while away the tedium of his walk. It was night when Andy was breasting up a low ridge of hills which lay between him and the end of his journey; and when in silence and darkness he topped the ascent, he threw himself on some heather to rest and take breath. His attention was suddenly caught by a small blue flame, which flickered now and then upon the face of the hill, not very far from him; and Andy's fears of fairies and goblins came crowding upon him thick and fast. He wished to rise, but could not; his eye continued to be strained with the fascination of fear in the direction he saw the fire, and sought to pierce the gloom through which, at intervals, the small point of flame flashed brightly and sunk again, making the darkness seem deeper. Andy lay in perfect stillness, and in the silence which was unbroken, even by his own breathing, he thought he heard voices underground. He trembled from head to foot, for he was certain they were the voices of the fairies, whom he firmly believed to inhabit the hills.

"Oh murdher, what'll I do," thought Andy to himself; "sure I heerd often, if once you were within the sound of their voices you could never get out o' their power—Oh! if I could only say a *pather* and *ave*, but I forget my prayers, with the fright—Hail, Mary! The king o' the fairies lives in these hills, I know—and his house is undher me this minit, and I on the roof of it—I'll never get down again—they'll make me slater to the fairies; and sure enough, I remember me, the hill is all covered with flat stones they call fairy slates—Oh! I am ruined—God be praised." Here he blessed himself, and laid his head close to the earth. "Guardian angels—I hear their voices singin' a dhrinking song—Oh! if I had a dhrop o' wather myself, for my mouth is as dhry as a lime-burner's wig—and I on the top o' their house—see—there's the little blaze again—I wondher is their chimbley a-fire—Oh! murther, I'll die o' thirst—Oh! if I had only one dhrop o' wather—I wish it would rain or hall—Hail, Mary, full o' grace—whisht!—what's that?" Andy couched lower than before, as he saw a figure rise from the earth, and attain a height which Andy computed to be something about twenty feet; his heart shrank to the size of a nut-shell, as he beheld the monster expand to his full dimensions; and at the same moment, a second, equally large, emerged from the ground.

Now, as fairies are notoriously little people, Andy changed his opinion of the parties into whose power he had fallen, and saw clearly they were giants, not fairies, of whom he was about to become the victim. He would have ejaculated a prayer for mercy, had not terror rendered him speechless, as the remembrance of all the giants he had ever heard of from the days of Jack and the Bean-Stalk down, came into his head; but though his sense of speaking was gone, that of hearing was painfully acute, and he heard one of the giants say—

"That pot is not big enough."

"Oh! it howlds as much as we want," replied the other.

"O Lord," thought Andy; "they've got their pot ready for cooking."

"What keeps him?" said the first giant. "Oh! he's not far off," said the second. A clammy shivering came over Andy.

"I'm hungry," said the first; and he hiccupped as he spoke.

"It's only a false appetite you have," said the second; "you're drunk."

This was a new light to Andy, for he thought giants were too strong to get drunk.

"I could ate a young child, without parsley and butther," said the drunken giant.

Andy gave a faint spasmodic kick.

"And it's as hot as —— down there," said the giant.

Andy trembled at the horrid word he heard.

"No wonder," said the second giant; "for I can see the flame popping out of the top of the chimbley—that's bad—I hope no one will see it, or it might give them warning. Bad luck to that young divil for making the fire so sthrong."

What a dreadful hearing this was for Andy;—young devils to make their fires:—there was no doubt what place they were dwelling in. "Thunder and turf!" said the drunken giant; "I wish I had a slice of—"

Andy did not hear what he wished a slice of, for the night wind swept across the heath at the moment, and carried away the monster's disgusting words on its pure breath.

"Well, I'd rather have ——" said the other giant; and again Andy lost what his atrocious desires were—"than all the other slices in the world. What a lovely round shoulder she has—and the nice round ankle of her—"

The word 'ankle' showed at once it was a woman of whom they spoke, and Andy shuddered. "The monsters!—to eat a woman."

"What a fool you are to be in love," said the drunken giant, with several hiccups, showing the increase of his inebriation.

"Is that what the brutes call love," thought Andy; "to ate a woman?"

"I wish she was bone of my bone and flesh of my flesh," said the second giant.

Of this speech Andy heard only 'bone' and 'flesh,' and had great difficulty in maintaining the serenity of his diaphragm.

The conversation of the giants was now more frequently interrupted by the wind which was rising, and only broken sentences reached Andy, whose senses became clearer the longer he remained in a state of safety; at last he heard the name of Squire Egan distinctly pass between the giants.

"So they know Squire Egan," thought Andy.

The first giant gave a drunken laugh at the mention of Squire Egan's name, and exclaimed:—

"Don't be afraid of him (*hiccup*), I have him undher my thumb (*hiccup*). I can crush him when I plase."

"Oh! my poor owld masther," mentally ejaculated Andy.

Another break in their conversation occurred, and the next name Andy overheard was "O'Grady."

"The big bully!" said the second giant.

"They know the whole country," thought Andy.

"But tell me what was that you said to him at the election?" said the drunken one.

The word "election" recalled Andy to the business of this earth back again; and it struck upon his hitherto bewildered sensorium, that giants could have nothing to do with elections, and he knew he never saw them there; and, as the thought struck him, it seemed as if the giants diminished in size, and did not appear quite so big.

"Sure you know," said the second.

"Well, I'd like to hear it again," said the drunken one—(*hiccup*).

"The big bully says to me—'Have you a lease,' says he? 'no,' says I; 'but I have an article!' 'What article?' says he; 'It's a fine brass blundherbuss,' says I, 'and *I'd like to see the man would dispute the title!*'"

The drunken listener chuckled, and the words broke the spell of supernatural terror which had hung over Andy; he knew, by the words of the speaker, it was the bully joker of the election was present, who brow beat O'Grady and out-quibbled the agent about the oath of allegiance; and the voice of the other he soon recognised for that of Larry Hogan. So his giants were diminished into mortal men; the pot which had been mentioned to the terror of his soul was for the making of whisky instead of human broth, and the "hell" he thought his giants inhabited was but a private still. Andy felt as if a mountain had been lifted from his heart when he found it was but mortals he had to deal with; for Andy was not deficient in courage when it was but thews and sinews like his own he had to encounter. He still lay concealed, however, for smugglers might not wish their private haunt to be discovered, and it was possible Andy would be voted one too many in the company, should he announce himself; and with such odds as two to one against him, he thought he had better be quiet. Besides, his curiosity became excited, when he found them speaking of his old master Egan, and his present one O'Grady; and as a woman had been alluded to, and odd words caught up here and there, he became anxious to hear more of their conversation.

"So you're in love," said Larry, with a hiccup, to our friend of the blunderbuss; "ha! ha! ha! you big fool."

"Well, you old thief, don't you like a purty girl yourself?"

"Yis, when I was young and foolish."

"Faith then, you're young and foolish at that rate yet, for you're a rogue with the girls, Larry," said the other, giving him a slap on the back.

"Not I! not I!" said Larry, in a manner, expressive of his not being displeased with the charge of gallantry; "he! he! he!—how do you know? eh? (*hiccup*)."

"Sure I know myself, but as I was telling you, if I could only lay howld of," here his voice became inaudible to Andy, and the rest of the sentence was lost.

Andy's curiosity was great—"Who could the girl be?"

"And you'd carry her off," said Larry.

"I would," said the other, "I'm only afeard o' Squire Egan."

At this announcement of the intention of "carrying her off," coupled with the fear of "Squire Egan," Andy's anxiety to hear the name of the person became so intense, that he crawled cautiously a little nearer to the speakers.

"I tell you again," said Larry; "I can settle *him*, aisy (*hiccup*)—he's undher my thumb (*hiccup*)."

"Be aisy," said the other, contemptuously, who thought this was a mere drunken delusion of Larry's.

"I tell you I'm his masther!" said Larry, with a drunken flourish of his arm; and he continued bragging of his power over the squire in various ejaculations, the exact meaning of which our friend of the blunderbuss could not fathom, but Andy heard enough to show him that the discovery of the Post-office affair was what Larry alluded to.

That Larry, a close, cunning, circumventing rascal, should so far betray the source of his power over Egan, may seem strange, but be it remembered Larry was drunk—a state of weakness which his caution generally guarded him from falling into, but which being in, his foible was bragging of his influence, and so running the risk of losing it.

The men continued to talk together for some time, and the tenor of the conversation was that Larry assured his companion he might carry off the girl without fear of Egan, but her name Andy could not discover. His own name he heard more than once, and voluptuous raptures poured forth about lovely lips and hips and ankles from the herculean knight of the blunderbuss, amidst the maudlin admiration and hiccups of Larry, who continued to brag of his power, and profess his readiness to stand by his friend in carrying off the girl.

"Then," said the Hercules, with an oath, "I'll soon have you in my arms my lovely—"

The name was lost again.

Their colloquy was now interrupted by the approach of a man and woman, the former being the person for whose appearance Larry made so many inquiries when he first appeared to Andy as the hungry giant; the other was the sister of the knight of the blunderbuss. Larry having hiccupped his anger against the man for making them wait so long for the bacon, the woman said he should not wait longer without his supper now, for that she would go down and fry the rashers immediately. She then disappeared through the ground, and the men all followed.

Andy drew his breath freely once more, and with caution raised himself gradually from the ground with a careful circumspection, lest any of the subterranean community might be watchers on the hill; and when he was satisfied he was free from observation he stole away from the spot, with stealthy steps for about twenty paces, and there, as well as the darkness would permit, after taking such landmarks as would help him to retrace his way to the still, if requisite, he dashed down the hill at the top of his speed. This pace he did not moderate until he had placed nearly a mile between him and the scene of his adventure, he then paced slowly to regain his breath. His head was in a strange whirl;— mischief was threatened against some one of whose name he was ignorant;—Squire Egan was declared to be in the power of an old rascal; this grieved Andy most of all, for he felt he was the cause of his old master's dilemma.

"Oh! to think I should bring him into trouble," said Andy, "the kind and good masther he was to me ever, and I alive to tell it like a blackguard—throth I'd rather be hanged any day than the masther would come to throuble—maybe if I gave myself up and was hanged like a man at once, that would settle it; faith if I thought it would, I'd do it sooner than Squire Egan should come to throuble!" and poor Andy spoke but what he felt. Or would it do to kill that blackguard Hogan? *sure they could do no more than hang me afther,*[1] and that would save the masther, and be all one to me, for they often towld me I'd be hanged. But then there's my sowl," said Andy, and he paused at the thought: "if they hanged me for the letthers, it would be only for a mistake, and sure then I'd have a chance o' glory; for sure I might go to glory through a mistake; but if I killed a man on purpose, sure it would be slappin' the gates of heaven in my own face. Faix, I'll spake to Father Blake about it."[2]

1.   How often has the sanguinary penal code of past years suggested this reflection and provoked the guilt it was meant to awe! Happily now our laws are milder, and more protective from their mildness.

2.   In the foregoing passage, Andy stumbles on uttering a quaint pleasantry, for it is partly true as well as droll—the notion of a man gaining Paradise through a mistake. Our intentions too seldom lead us there, but rather tend the other way, for a certain place is said to be paved with good ones, and surely bad ones would not lead us upwards. Then the phrase of a man "slapping the gates of Heaven in his own face," is one of those wild poetic figures of speech in which the Irish peasantry often indulge: the phrase "slapping the door," is every day and common; but when applied to "the gates of heaven" and "in a man's own face," the common phrase becomes fine. But how often the commonest things become poetry by the fitness of their application, though poetasters and people of small minds think greatness of thought lies in big words.

XXVI

THE FOLLOWING DAY WAS THAT eventful one which should witness the return of either Edward Egan, Esq., or the Honourable Sackville Scatterbrain, as member for the county. There was no doubt, in any reasonable man's mind, as to the real majority of Egan, but the numbers were sufficiently close to give the sheriff an opportunity of doing a bit of business to oblige his friends, and therefore he declared the Honourable Sackville Scatterbrain duly elected. Great was the uproar; the people hissed and hooted and groaned, for which the Honourable Sackville very good-naturedly returned them his thanks. Murphy snapped his fingers in the sheriff's face, and told him his honourable friend should not long remain member, for that he must be unseated on petition, and that he would prove the return most corrupt, with which words he again snapped his fingers in the sheriff's face.

The sheriff threatened to read the riot act if such conduct were repeated.

Egan took off and thanked him for his *honourable, upright, and impartial* conduct, whereupon all Egan's friends took off their hats also, and made profound bows to the functionary, and then laughed most uproariously. Counter laughs were returned from the opposite party, who begged to remind the Eganites of the old saying, "that they might laugh who win." A cross fire of sarcasms was kept up amidst the two parties as they were crushing forward out of the courthouse; and at the door, before entering his carriage, Scatterbrain very politely addressed Egan, and trusted that though they had met as rivals on the hustings, they nevertheless parted friends, and expressing the highest respect for the squire, offered his hand in amity.

Egan, equally good-hearted as his opponent, shook his hand cordially, declaring he attributed to him none of the blame which attached to other persons. "Besides, my dear sir," said Egan, laughing, "I should be a very ill-natured person to grudge you so small an indulgence as being member of parliament *for a month or so.*"

Scatterbrain returned the laugh good-humouredly, and replied that, "at all events, he *had* the seat."

"Yes, my dear sir," said Egan, "and make the most of it *while* you have it. In short, I shall owe you an obligation when I go over to St. Stephen's, for you will have just *aired my seat* for me—good bye."

They parted with smiles, and drove to their respective homes; but as even doubtful possession is preferable to expectation for the time being, it is certain that Neck-or-Nothing Hall rang with more merriment that night on the reality of the present, than Merryvale did on the hope of the future.

Even O'Grady, as he lay with his wounded arm on the sofa, found more healing in the triumph of the hour than from all the medicaments of the foregoing week, and insisted on going down stairs and joining the party at supper.

"Gusty dear," said his wife, "you know the doctor said—"

"Hang the doctor!"

"Your arm, my love."

"I wish you'd lave off pitying my arm and have some compassion on my stomach."

"The doctor said—"

"There are oysters in house—I'll do myself more good by the use of an oyster knife than all the lancets in the College of Surgeons."

"But your wound, dear?"

"Are they Carlingford's or Poldoody?"

"So fresh, love."

"So much the better."

"Your wound I mean, dear."

"Nicely opened."

"Only dressed an hour ago?"

"With some mustard, pepper, and vinegar."

"Indeed Gusty, if you take my advice—"

"I'd rather have oysters any day."

O'Grady sat up on the sofa as he spoke, and requested his wife to say no more about the matter, but put on his cravat. While she was getting it from his wardrobe, his mind wandered from supper to the pension which he looked upon as secure now that Scatterbrain was returned; and oyster banks gave place to the Bank of Ireland which rose in a pleasing image before O'Grady's imagination. The wife now returned with the cravat, still dreading the result of eating, to her husband, and her mind occupied wholly with the thought of supper, while O'Grady was wrapped in visions of a pension.

"You won't take it, Gusty, dear," said his wife, with all the insinuation of manner she could command.

"Won't I faith," said O'Grady. "Maybe you think I don't want it?"

"Indeed I don't, dear."

"Are you mad, woman? Is it taking leave of the few senses you ever had you are?"

"'Twont agree with you."

"Won't it? just wait till I'm tried."

"Well, love—how much do you expect to be allowed?"

"Why I can't expect much just yet—we must begin gently—feel the pulse first; but I should hope by way of a start that six or seven hundred ——"

"Gracious heaven!" exclaimed the wife, dropping the cravat from her hands.

"What the devil is the woman shouting at?" said O'Grady.

"Six or seven hundred!!!" exclaimed Mrs. O'Grady; "my dear, there's not as much in the house."

"No, nor has not been for many a long day; I know that as well as you," said O'Grady; "but I hope we shall get as much for all that."

"My dear, where could you get them?" asked the wife, timidly, who began to think his head was a little light.

"From the treasury, to be sure."

"The treasury, my dear?" said the wife, still at fault; "how could you get oysters from the treasury?"

"Oysters?" exclaimed O'Grady, whose turn it was now to wonder, "who talks of oysters?"

"My dear, I thought you said you'd eat six or seven hundred of oysters."

"Pooh! pooh! woman; it is of the pension I'm talking—six or seven hundred pounds—pounds—cash—per annum; now I suppose you'll put on my cravat. I think a man may be allowed to eat his supper who expects six hundred a-year."

A great many people besides O'Grady order suppers, and dinners too, on the expectation of less than six hundred a-year. Perhaps there is no more active agent for sending people into the Insolvent Court than the aforesaid "*expectation*."

O'Grady went down stairs, and was heartily welcomed by Scatterbrain on his re-appearance from his sick-room; but Mrs. O'Grady suggested, that, for fear any excess would send him back there for a longer time, a very moderate indulgence at the table must suffice. She begged the honourable member to back her argument, which he did; and O'Grady promised temperance, but begged the immediate appearance of the oysters, for he expressed that longing desire which delicate health so often prompts for some particular food.

Andy was laying the table at the time, and was ordered to expedite matters as much as possible.

"Yis, ma'am."

"You're sure the oysters are all good, Andy?"

"Sartin, ma'am."

"Because the last oysters you know—"

"Oh yis, ma'am—were bad, ma'am—bekase they had their mouths all open. I remember, ma'am; but when I'm towld a thing once, I never forget it again; and you towld me when they opened their mouths once, they were no good. So you see, ma'am, I'll never bring up bad oysthers again, ma'am."

"Very good, Andy; and you have kept them in a cool place I hope."

"Faix they're cowld enough where I put them, ma'am."

"Very well; bring them up at once."

Off went Andy, and returned with all the haste he could with a large dish heaped with oysters.

O'Grady rubbed his hands with the impatience of a true lover of the crustaceous delicacy, and Scatterbrain, eager to help him, flourished his oyster-knife; but before he had time to commence operations, the olfactory nerves of the company gave evidence that the oysters were rather suspicious; every one began sniffing, and a universal "Oh dear!" ran round the table.

"Don't you smell it, Furlong?" said Scatterbrain, who was so lost in looking at Augusta's mustachios that he did not mind anything else.

"Isn't it horrid?" said O'Grady, with a look of disgust.

Furlong thought he alluded to the mustachio, and replied with an assurance that he 'liked it of all things.'

"Like it?" said O'Grady; "You've a queer taste—What do *you* think of it, Miss," added he to Augusta, "it's just under your nose?"

Furlong thought this rather personal, even from a father.

"I'll try my knife on one," said Scatterbrain, with a flourish of the oyster knife, which Furlong thought resembled the preliminary trial of the barber's razor.

Furlong thought this worse than O'Grady; but he hesitated to reply to his chief—and an *honourable* into the bargain.

In the mean time, Scatterbrain opened an oyster, which Furlong, in his embarrassment and annoyance, did not perceive.

"Cut off the beard," said O'Grady—"I don't like it."

This nearly made Furlong speak, but considering O'Grady's temper and ill health, he hesitated, till he saw Augusta rubbing her eye, in consequence of a small splinter of the oyster-shell having struck it from Scatterbrain's mismanagement of his knife; but Furlong thought she was crying, and then he could be silent no longer; he went over to where she sat, and with a very affectionate demonstration, in action, said—

"Never mind them, dear Gussy—never mind—don't cwy—I love her dear little moustachios—I do." He gave a gentle pat on the back of the neck, as he spoke, and it was returned by an uncommonly smart box on the ear from the young lady, and the whole party looked thunderstruck. 'Dear Gussy' cried for spite, and stamped her way out of the room, followed by Furlong.

"Let them go," said O'Grady; "they'll make it up outside."

"These oysters are all bad," said Scatterbrain.

O'Grady began to swear at his disappointment—he had set his heart on oysters. Mrs. O'Grady rang the bell—Andy appeared.

"How dare you bring up such oysters as these?" roared O'Grady.

"The misthris ordhered them, sir."

"I told you never to bring up bad oysters," said she.

"Them's not bad, ma'am," said Andy.

"Have you a nose?" cried O'Grady.

"Yis, sir."

"And can't you smell them, then?"

"Faix I smelt them for the last three days, sir."

"And how could you say they were good, then?" asked his mistress.

"Sure you tould me, ma'am, that if they didn't open their mouths they were good, and I'll be on my book oath them oysters never opened their mouths since I had them, for I laid them on a cool flag in the kitchen, and put the jack weight over them."

Notwithstanding O'Grady's rage, Scatterbrain could not help roaring with laughter at Andy's novel contrivance for keeping oysters fresh. Andy was desired to take the "ancient and fish-like smell" out of the room, amidst jeers and abuse; and, as he fumbled his way to the kitchen in the dark, lamenting the hard fate of servants, who can never give satisfaction, though they do everything they are bid, he went head over heels down stairs; which event was reported to the whole house as soon as it happened, by the enormous clatter of the broken dish, the oysters, and Andy, as they all rolled one over the other to the bottom.

O'Grady, having missed the cool supper he intended, and had longed for, was put into a rage by the disappointment; and as hunger with O'Grady was only to be appeased by broiled bones, accordingly, against all the endeavours of every body, the bells rang violently through the house, and the ogre-like cry of 'broiled bones,' resounded high and low.

The reader is sufficiently well acquainted with O'Grady by this time to know, that of course, when once he had determined to have his broiled bone, nothing on the face of the earth could prevent it but the want of any thing to broil, or the immediate loss of his teeth; and as his masticators were in order, and something in the house which could carry mustard and pepper, the invalid primed and loaded himself with as much combustible matter as exploded in a fever the next day.

The supper party, however, in the hope of getting him to bed, separated soon; and as Scatterbrain and Furlong were to start early in the morning for Dublin, the necessity of their retiring to rest was pleaded. The Honourable member had not been long in his room when he heard a tap at his door, and his order to 'come in,' was followed by the appearance of Handy Andy.

"I found somethin' on the road nigh the town to-day, sir, and I thought it might be yours, maybe," said Andy, producing a small pocket book.

The honourable member disavowed the ownership.

"Well, there's something else I want to spake to your honour about."

"What is it, Handy?"

"I want your honour to see the account of the money your honour gave me; I spint at the *shebeen*[1] upon the 'lecthors that couldn't be accommodated at Mrs. Fay's."

"Oh! never mind it, Andy—if there's anything over, keep it yourself."

"Thank your honour, but I must make the account all the same, if you plaze, for I'm goin' to Father Blake, to my duty[2] soon, and I must have my conscience as clear as I can, and I wouldn't like to be keepin' money back."

"But if I give you the money, what matter?"

"I'd rather you'd just look over this little bit of a count, if you plaze," said Andy, producing a dirty piece of paper, with some nearly inscrutable hieroglyphics upon it.

Scatterbrain commenced an examination of this literary phenomenon from sheer curiosity, asking Andy, at the same time, if *he* wrote it.

"Yis, sir," said Andy. "But you see the man wouldn't keep the count of the piper's dhrink at all, it was so confusin', and so I was obliged to pay him for that, every time the piper dhrunk, and keep it separate, and the 'lecthors that got their dinner afther the bill was made out, I put down myself too, and that's it you see, sir, both ating and dhrinkin'."

To Dhrinkin A blinD piper everry dai wan and tin Pens six dais	0 16 6	
To atein four Tin Illikthurs And Thare horses on Chewsdai	{1 8 8 {0 14 0	
Toe til	2 19 4	
Lan lord Bill For All Be four	7 17 8½	
	10 18 12½	

"Then I owe you money, instead of your having a balance in hand, Andy," said the member.

"Oh, no matther, your honour, it's not for that I showed you the account."

"It's very like it, though," said Scatterbrain, laughing; "here Andy, here are a couple of pounds for you, take them, Andy—take it and be off. Your bill is worth the money," and Scatterbrain closed the door on the great accountant.

Andy next went to Furlong's room, to know if the pocket-book belonged to him; it did not, but Furlong, though he disclaimed the ownership, had that small curiosity which prompts little minds to pry into what does not belong to them; and taking the pocket-book into his hands, he opened it, and fumbled over its leaves; in the doing of which a small piece of folded paper fell from one of the pockets unnoticed by the impertinent inquisitor or Andy, to whom he returned the book when he had gratified his senseless curiosity.

Andy withdrew, Furlong retired to rest, and as it was in the grey of an autumnal morning he dressed himself, the paper still remained unobserved; so that the housemaid, on setting the room to rights, found it, and fancying Miss Augusta was the proper person to confide Mister Furlong's stray papers to, she handed that young lady the manuscript which bore the following copy of verses:—

I CAN NE'ER FORGET THEE

I

It is the chime, the hour draws near
   When you and I must sever;
Alas, it must be many a year,
   And it *may* be for ever!
How long till we shall meet again:
   How short since first I met thee;
How brief the bliss—how long the pain—
   For I can ne'er forget thee.

II

You said my heart was cold and stern;
   You doubted love when strongest:
In future days you'll live to learn
   Proud hearts can love the longest.
Oh! sometimes think, when pressed to hear,
   When flippant tongues beset thee,
That *all* must love thee, when thou'rt near;
   But *one* will ne'er forget thee!

III

The changeful sand doth only know
   The shallow tide and latest;
The rocks have mark'd its highest flow,
   The deepest and the greatest;
And deeper still the flood-marks grow:—
   So, since the hour I've met thee,
The more the tide of time doth flow,
   The less can I forget thee!

When Augusta saw the lines she was charmed. She discovered her Furlong to be a poet! That the lines were his there was no doubt—they were *found in his room*, and of course they *must* be his, just as partial critics say certain ancient Irish airs must be English, because they are to be found in Queen Elizabeth's music book.

Augusta was so charmed with the lines, that she amused herself for a long time in hiding them under the sofa cushion, and making her pet dog find and fetch them. Her pleasure, however, was interrupted by her sister Charlotte remarking, when the lines were shown to her in triumph, that the writing was not Furlong's, but in a lady's hand.

Even as beer is suddenly soured by thunder, so the electric influence of Charlotte's words, converted all Augusta had been brewing, to acidity; jealousy stung her like a wasp, and she boxed her dog's ears as he was barking for another run with the verses.

"A *lady's* hand?" said Augusta, snapping the paper from her sister; "I declare if it a'nt! the wretch—so he receives lines from ladies."

"I think I know the hand too," said Charlotte.

"You do?" exclaimed Augusta, with flashing eyes.

"Yes—I'm certain it is Fanny Dawson's writing."

"So it is," said Augusta, looking at the paper as if her eyes could have burnt it; "to be sure—he was there before he came here."

"Only for two days," said Charlotte, trying to slake the flame she had raised.

"But I've heard that girl always makes conquests at first sight," returned Augusta, half-crying; "and what do I see here? some words in pencil."

The words were so faint as to be scarcely perceptible, but Augusta deciphered them; they were written on the margin, beside a circumflex which embraced the last four lines of the second verse, so that it stood thus:—

> Oh, sometimes think, when, press'd to hear,
>   When flippant tongues beset thee,
> That *all* must love thee when thou'rt near,
>   But *one* will ne'er forget thee.

Dearest,
I will.

"Will you indeed?" said Augusta, crushing the paper in her hand, and biting it; "but I must not destroy it—I must keep it to prove his treachery to his face." She threw herself on the sofa as she spoke, and gave vent to an outpour of spiteful tears.

1.   Low public-house.
2.   Confession.

XXVII

HOW MANY CHAPTERS HAVE BEEN written about love verses—and how many more might be written!—might, would, could, should, or ought to be written—I will venture to say, *will* be written! I have a mind to fulfil my own prophecy, and write one myself; but no—my story must go on. However, I *will* say, that it is quite curious in how many ways the same little bit of paper may influence different people: the poem whose literary merit may be small, becomes precious when some valued hand has transcribed the lines; and the verses, whose measure and meaning viewed in type might win favour and yield pleasure, shoot poison from their very sweetness, when read in some particular hand, and under particular circumstances. It was so with the copy of verses Augusta had just read—they were Fanny Dawson's manuscript—that was certain—and found in the room of Augusta's lover; therefore Augusta was wretched. But these same lines had given exquisite pleasure to another person, who was now nearly as miserable as Augusta in having lost them. It is possible the reader guesses that person to be Edward O'Connor, for it was he who had lost the pocket-book in which those (to him) precious lines were contained; and if the little case had held all the bank-notes he ever owned in his life, their loss would have been regarded less than that bit of manuscript, which had often yielded *him* the most exquisite pleasure, and was now inflicting on Augusta the bitterest anguish.

To make this intelligible to the reader, it is necessary to explain under what circumstances the lines were written. At one time, doubting the likelihood of making his way at home, was about to go to India, and push his fortunes there; and at that period, those lines, breathing of farewell—implying the dread of rivals during absence—and imploring remembrance of his eternal love, were written, and given to Fanny; and she, with that delicacy of contrivance, so peculiarly a woman's, hit upon the expedient of copying his own verses, and sending them to him in her writing, as an indication that the spirit of the lines was her own.

But Edward saw that his father, who was advanced in years, looked upon a separation from his son as an eternal one, and the thought gave so much pain, that Edward gave up the idea of expatriation. Shortly after, however, the misunderstanding with Major Dawson took place, and Fanny and Edward were as much severed as if dwelling in different zones. Under such circumstances, those lines were peculiarly precious, and many a kiss had Edward impressed upon them, though Augusta thought them fitter for the exercise of her teeth than her lips. In fact, Edward did little else than think of Fanny; and it is possible his passion might have degenerated into mere love-sickness, and enfeebled him, had not his desire of proving himself worthy of his mistress spurred him to exertion, in the hope of future distinction. But still the tone of tender lament pervaded all his poems, and the same pocket-book, whence the verses which caused so much commotion fell, contained the following also, showing how entirely Fanny possessed his heart and occupied his thoughts:—

WHEN THE SUN SINKS TO REST

I

When the sun sinks to rest,
And the star of the west
   Sheds its soft silver light o'er the sea,
What sweet thoughts arise,
As the dim twilight dies—
   For then I am thinking of thee!
Oh! then crowding fast
Come the joys of the past,
   Through the dimness of days long gone by,

Like the stars peeping out,
Through the darkness about,
   From the soft silent depth of the sky.

II

And thus, as the night
Grows more lovely and bright,
   With the clust'ring of planet and star,
So this darkness of mine
Wins a radiance divine
   From the light that still lingers afar.
Then welcome the night,
With its soft holy light!
   In its silence my heart is more free
The rude world to forget,
Where no pleasure I've met
   Since the hour that I parted from thee.

But we must leave love verses, and ask pardon for the few remarks into which the subject tempted us, and pursue our story.

The first prompting of Augusta's anger, when she had recovered her burst of passion, was to write "*such a letter*" to Furlong—and she spent half a day at the work, but she could not please herself—she tore twenty at least, and determined, at last, not to write at all, but just wait till he returned, and overwhelm him with reproaches. But though she could not compose a letter, she composed herself by the endeavour, which acted as a sort of safety-valve to let off the superabundant steam; and it is wonderful how general is this result of sitting down to write angry letters people vent themselves of their spleen on the uncomplaining paper, which silently receives words a listener would not. With a pen for our second, desperate satisfaction is obtained with only an effusion of ink, and, when once the pent-up bitterness has oozed out in all the blackness of that fluid—most appropriately made of the best galls—the time so spent, and the "letting of words," if I may use the phrase, has cooled our judgment

and our passion together—and the first letter is torn:—'tis *too* severe;
we write a second—we blot and interline, till it is nearly illegible; we
begin a third; till at last we are tired out with our own angry feelings,
and throw our scribbling by with a "pshaw! what's the use of it?" or
"It's not worth my notice;" or, still better, arrive at the conclusion, that
we preserve our own dignity best by writing with temper, though we
may be called upon to be severe.

Furlong at this time was on his road to Dublin, in happy
unconsciousness of Augusta's rage against him, and planning what
pretty little present he should send her specially, for his head was
naturally running on such matters, as he had quantities of commissions
to execute in the millinery line for Mrs. O'Grady, who thought it
high time to be getting up Augusta's wedding-dresses, and Andy was
to be despatched the following day to Dublin, to take charge of a
cargo of band-boxes from the city, to Neck-or-Nothing Hall. Furlong
had received a thousand charges from the ladies, "to be sure to lose
no time" in doing his devoir in their behalf, and he obeyed so strictly,
and was so active in laying milliners and mercers under contribution,
that Andy was enabled to start the day after his arrival, sorely against
Andy's will, for he would gladly have remained amidst the beauty and
grandeur and wonders of Dublin, which struck him dumb for the day
he was amongst them, but gave him food for conversation for many
a day after. Furlong, after racking his invention about the souvenir to
his "dear Gussy," at length fixed on a fan, as the most suitable gift; for
Gussy had been quizzed at home about "blushing" and all that sort
of thing, and the puerile perceptions of the *attaché* saw something
very smart in sending her wherewith "to hide her blushes." Then the
fan was the very pink of fans; it had quivers and arrows upon it, and
bunches of hearts looped up in azure festoons, and doves perched
upon them; though Augusta's little sister, who was too young to
know what hearts and doves were, when she saw them for the first
time, said they were pretty little birds picking at apples. The fan was
packed up in a nice case, and then on scented note paper did the dear
dandy indite a bit of namby-pamby badinage to his fair one, which he
thought excessively clever:—

"Dear Ducky Darling,

"You know how naughty they are in quizzing you about a little something, *I won't say what*; you will guess, I dare say—but I send you a little toy, *I won't say what,* on which Cupid might write this label after the doctor's fashion, 'To be used occasionally, when the patient is much troubled with the symptoms.'

"Ever, ever, ever,

Yours,

"J. F."

"P.S. Take care how you open it."

Such was the note that Handy Andy was given, with particular injunctions to deliver it the first thing on his arrival at the Hall to Miss Augusta, and to be sure to take most particular care of the little case; all which Andy faithfully promised to do. But Andy's usual destiny prevailed, and a slight turn of chance quite upset all Furlong's sweet little plan of his pretty present, and his ingenious note, for as Andy was just taking his departure, Furlong said he might as well leave something for him at Reade's the cutler, as he passed through College Green, and he handed him a case of razors which wanted setting, which Andy popped into his pocket, and as the fan case and that of the razors were much a size, and both folded up, Andy left the fan at the cutler's, and took the case of razors by way of present to Augusta. Fancy the rage of a young lady with a very fine pair of *moustaches*, getting such a souvenir from her lover, with a note too, every word of which applied to a beard and a razor, as patly as to a blush and a fan—and this too when her jealousy was aroused and his fidelity more than doubtful in her estimation.

Great was the row in Neck-or-Nothing Hall; and when, after three days Furlong came down, the nature of his reception may be better imagined than described. It was a difficult matter, through the storm which raged around him, to explain all the circumstances satisfactorily, but by dint of hard work, the verses were at length disclaimed, the razors disavowed, and Andy at last sent for to "clear matters up."

Andy was a hopeful subject for such a purpose, and, by his blundering answers, nearly set them all by the ears the upshot of the affair was,

that Andy, used as he was to good scoldings, never had such a torrent
of abuse poured on him in his life, and the affair ended in Andy being
dismissed from Neck-or-Nothing Hall on the instant; so he relinquished
his greasy livery for his own rags again, and trudged homewards to his
mother's cabin.

"She'll be as mad as a hatter with me," said Andy; "bad luck to them
for razhirs, they cut me out o' my place: but I often heard cowld steel
is unlucky, and sure I know it now.—Oh! but I'm always unfort'nate
in having cruked messages.—Well, it can't be helped—and one good
thing, at all events, is, I'll have time enough now to go and spake to
Father Blake;"—and with this sorry piece of satisfaction, poor Andy
contented himself.

XXVIII

THE FATHER BLAKE OF WHOM Andy spoke, was more familiarly known by the name of Father Phil, by which title Andy himself would have named him, had he been telling how Father Phil cleared a fair, or equally "leathered" both the belligerent parties in a faction-fight, or turned out the contents (or malcontents) of a public-house at an improper hour; but when he spoke of his Reverence respecting ghostly matters, the importance of the subject begot higher consideration for the man, and the familiar "Father Phil" was dropped for the more respectful title of Father Blake. By either title, or in whatever capacity, the worthy Father had great influence over his parish, and there was a free and easy way with him, even in doing the most solemn duties, which agreed wonderfully with the devil-may-care spirit of Paddy. Stiff and starched formality in any way is repugnant to the very nature of Irishmen; and I believe one of the surest ways of converting all Ireland from the Romish faith would be found, if we could only manage to have her mass celebrated with the dry coldness of the Reformation. This may seem ridiculous at first sight, and I grant it is a grotesque way of viewing the subject, but yet there may be truth in it, and to consider it for a moment seriously, look to the fact, that the north of Ireland is the stronghold of Protestantism, and that the north is the *least* Irish portion of the island:—there is a strong admixture of Scotch there, and all who know the country will admit that there is nearly as much difference between men from the north and south of Ireland, as from different countries. The Northerns retain much of the cold formality and unbending hardness of the stranger-settlers from whom they are descended, while the Southern exhibits that warm-hearted, lively, and poetical temperament for which the country is celebrated. The prevailing national characteristics of Ireland are not to be found in the north, where protestantism flourishes; they are to be found in the south and west, where it has never taken root. And though it has never seemed to strike theologians, that in their very natures some people are more adapted to receive one faith than another, yet I believe it to be true, and perhaps not quite unworthy of consideration. There are forms, it is true, and many in the Romish church, but they are not *cold* forms, but *attractive* rather, to a sensitive people; besides, I believe those very forms, when observed the least formally, are the most influential on the Irish; and perhaps the splendours of a high mass in the gorgeous temple of the holy city, would appeal less to the affections of an Irish peasant, than the service he witnesses in some half-thatched ruin by a lone hill side, familiarly hurried through by a priest who has sharpened his appetite by a mountain ride of some fifteen miles, and is saying mass for the third time, most likely, before breakfast, which consummation of his morning's exercise he is anxious to arrive at.

It was just in such a chapel, and under such circumstances, that Father Blake was celebrating the mass at which Andy was present, and after which he hoped to obtain a word of advice from the worthy Father, who was much more sought after on such occasions, than his more sedate superior who presided over the spiritual welfare of the parish—and whose solemn celebration of the mass was by no means so agreeable as the lighter service of Father Phil. The Rev. Dominick Dowling was austere and long-winded; *his* mass had an oppressive effect on his congregation, and from the kneeling multitude might be seen eyes fearfully looking up from under bent brows; and low breathings and subdued groans often rose above the silence of his congregation, who felt like sinners, and whose imaginations were filled with the thoughts of Heaven's anger; while the good humoured face of the light-hearted Father Phil produced a corresponding brightness on the looks of his hearers, who turned up their whole faces in trustfulness to the mercy of that Heaven, whose propitiatory offering their pastor was making for them in cheerful tones, which associated well with thoughts of pardon and salvation.

Father Dominick poured forth his spiritual influence like a strong dark stream, that swept down the hearer resistlessly, who struggled to keep his head above the torrent, and dreaded to be overwhelmed at the next word. Father Phil's religion bubbled out like a mountain rill,—bright, musical, and refreshing;—Father Dominick's people had decidedly need of cork jackets:—Father Phil's might drink and be refreshed.

But with all this intrinsic worth, he was, at the same time, a strange man in exterior manners; for with an abundance of real piety, he had an abruptness of delivery and a strange way of mixing up an occasional remark to his congregation in the midst of the celebration of the mass, which might well startle a stranger; but this very want of formality made him beloved by the people, and they would do ten times as much for Father Phil as for Father Dominick.

On the Sunday in question, when Andy attended the chapel, Father Phil intended delivering an address to his flock from the altar, urging them to the necessity of bestirring themselves in the repairs of the chapel, which was in a very dilapidated condition, and at one end let in the rain through its worn-out thatch. A subscription was necessary; and to raise this among a very impoverished people was no easy matter. The weather happened to be unfavourable, which was most favourable to Father Phil's purpose, for the rain dropped its arguments through the roof upon the kneeling people below, in the most convincing manner; and as they endeavoured to get out of the wet, they pressed round the altar as much as they could, for which they were reproved very smartly by his Reverence in the very midst of the mass, and these interruptions occurred sometimes in the most serious places, producing a ludicrous effect, of which the worthy Father was quite unconscious, in his great anxiety to make the people repair the chapel.

A big woman was elbowing her way towards the rails of the altar, and Father Phil, casting a sidelong glance at her, sent her to the right-about, while he interrupted his appeal to heaven to address her thus:

"*Agnus Dei*—you'd betther jump over the rails of the althar, I think.—Go along out o' that, there's plenty room in the chapel below there—."

Then he would turn to the altar, and proceed with the service, till turning again to the congregation, he perceived some fresh offender.

"*Orate, fratres!*—will you mind what I say to you, and go along out of that, there's room below there.—Thrue for you, Mrs. Finn—it's a shame for him to be thramplin' on you.—Go along, Darby Casey, down there, and kneel in the rain—it's a pity you haven't a dacent woman's cloak undher you, indeed!—*Orate, fratres!*"

Then would the service proceed again, and while he prayed in silence at the altar, the shuffling of feet edging out of the rain would disturb him, and casting a backward glance, he would say—

"I hear you there—can't you be quiet and not be disturbin' my mass, you haythens."

Again he proceeded in silence, till the crying of a child interrupted him. He looked round quickly—

"You'd betther kill the child, I think, thramplin' on him, Lavery.—Go out o' that—your conduct is scandalous—*Dominus vobiscum!*"

Again he turned to pray, and after some time he made an interval in the service to address his congregation on the subject of the repairs, and produced a paper containing the names of subscribers to that pious work who had already contributed, by way of example to those who had not.

"Here it is," said Father Phil, "here it is, and no denying it—down in black and white; but if they who give are down in black, how much blacker are those who have not given at all;—but I hope they will be ashamed of themselves, when I howld up those to honour who have contributed to the uphowlding of the house of God. And isn't it ashamed o' yourselves you ought to be, to lave His house in such a condition—and doesn't it rain a'most every Sunday, as if He wished to remind you of your duty—aren't you wet to the skin a'most every Sunday?—Oh, God is good to you! to put you in mind of your duty, giving you such bitther cowlds, that you are coughing and sneezin' every Sunday to that degree, that you can't hear the blessed mass for a comfort and a benefit to you, and so you'll go on sneezin' until you put a good thatch on the place, and prevent the appearance of the evidence from Heaven against you every Sunday, which is condemning you before your faces, and behind your backs too, for don't I see this minit a strame o' wather that might turn a mill running down Micky Mackavoy's back, between the collar of his coat and his shirt?"

Here a laugh ensued at the expense of Micky Mackavoy, who certainly *was* under a very heavy drip from the imperfect roof.

"And is it laughing you are, you haythens?" said Father Phil reproving the merriment which he himself had purposely created, *that he might reprove it.*—"Laughing is it you are—at your backslidings and insensibility to the honour of God—laughing, because when you come here to be saved, you are lost intirely with the wet; and how, I ask you, are my words of comfort to enter your hearts, when the rain is pouring down your backs at the same time? Sure I have no chance of turning your hearts while you are undher rain that might turn a mill—but once put a good roof on the house, and I will inundate you with piety!—Maybe it's Father Dominick you would like to have coming among you, who would grind your hearts to powdher with his heavy words."—(Here a low murmur of dissent ran through the throng.) "Ha! ha! so you wouldn't like it, I see—very well, very well—take care then, for if I find you insensible to my moderate reproofs, you hard-hearted haythens—you malefacthors and cruel persecuthors, that won't put your hands in your pockets, because your mild and quiet poor fool of a pasthor has no tongue in his head!—I say, your mild, quiet poor fool of a pasthor, (for I know my own faults, partly, God forgive me!) and I can't spake to you as you deserve, you hard-living vagabones, that are as insensible to your duties as you are to the weather.—I wish it was sugar or salt you were made of, and then the rain might melt you if I couldn't—but no—them naked rafthers grins in your face to no purpose—you chate the house of God—but take care, maybe you won't chate the divil so aisy;"—(here there was a sensation,) "Ha! ha! that makes you open your ears, does it?—More shame for you; you ought to despise that dirty enemy of man, and depend on something betther,—but I see I must call you to a sense of your situation with the bottomless pit undher you, and no roof over you. Oh dear! dear! dear!—I'm ashamed of you—troth, if I had time and sthraw enough, I'd rather thatch the place myself than lose my time talking to you; sure the place is more like a stable than a chapel. Oh, think of that!—the house of God to be like a stable!—for though our Redeemer was born in a stable, that is no reasonwhy you are to keep his house always like one.

"And now I will read you the list of subscribers, and it will make
you ashamed when you hear the name of several good and worthy
protestants in the parish, and out of it, too, who have given more than
the catholics."

He then proceeded to read the following list, which he interlarded
copiously with observations of his own; making *viva voce* marginal notes
as it were upon the subscribers, which were not unfrequently answered
by the persons so noticed, from the body of the chapel, and laughter
was often the consequence of these rejoinders, which Father Phil never
permitted to pass without a retort. Nor must all this be considered in
the least irreverent. A certain period is allowed between two particular
portions of the mass, when the priest may address his congregation on
any public matter: an approaching pattern, or fair, or the like; in which,
exhortations to propriety of conduct, or warnings against faction,
fights, &c. are his themes. Then they only listen in reverence. But when
a subscription for such an object as that already mentioned is under
discussion, the flock consider themselves entitled to "put in a word" in
case of necessity. This preliminary hint is given to the reader, that he
may better enter into the spirit of Father Phil's—

SUBSCRIPTION LIST

FOR THE REPAIRS AND ENLARGEMENT OF
BALLYSLOUGHGUTTHERY CHAPEL

PHILIP BLAKE, P.P.

	£ s. d.	
Micky Hicky	0 7 6	"He might as well have made it ten shillings; but half a loaf is betther than no bread." "Plase your reverence," says Mick from the body of the chapel, "sure seven and sixpence is more than half of ten shillins." (*a laugh*)

£ s. d.

"Oh! how witty you are.
Faith, if only you knew your
prayers as well as your
arithmetic, it
would be better for you, Micky."

Billy Riley   0 3 4

"Of course he manes to
subscribe again."

John Dwyer   0 15 0

"That's something like!" I'll be
bound he's only keeping back the
odd five shillings for a brush full
o' paint for the althar; it's as
black as a crow, instead o' being
as white as a dove."

He then hurried over rapidly
some small subscribers as
follows:—

Peter Hefferman   0 1 8
James Murphy   0 2 6
Mat Donovan   0 1 3
Luke Dannely   0 3 0
Jack Quigly   0 2 1
Pat Finnegan   0 2 2
EDWARD O'CONNOR,   2 0 0
ESQ.

"There's for you! Edward
O'Connor, Esq.—*a protestant in
the parish*—Two pounds."

"Long life to him," cried a voice
in the chapel.

"Amen," said Father Phil;
"I'm not ashamed to be clerk
to so good a prayer."

Nicholas Fagan   0 2 6
Young Nicholas Fagan   0 5 0

"Young Nick is better than
owld Nick, you see."

The congregation honoured the
Father's demand on their risibility.

Tim Doyle   0 7 6

	£ s. d.	
Owny Doyle	1 0 0	"Well done, Owny na Coppal— you deserve to prosper, for you make good use of your thrivings."
Simon Leary	0 2 6	"You ought to be ashamed o'
Bridget Murphy	0 10 0	yourself, Simon: a lone widow woman gives more than you."

Simon answered, "I have a large family, sir, and she has no childhre."

"That's not her fault," said the priest—"and maybe she'll mend o' that yet." This excited much merriment, for the widow was buxom, and had recently buried an old husband, and, by all accounts, was cocking her cap at a handsome young fellow in the parish.

| Jude Moylan | 0 5 0 | "Very good, Judy, the women are behaving like gentlemen, they'll have their reward in the next world." |
| Pat Finnerty | 0 8 4 | "I'm not sure if it is 8s. 4d. or 3s. 4d. for the figure is blotted— but I belive it is 8s. 4d." |

"It was three and four pince I gave your reverence," said Pat from the crowd.

"Well, Pat, as I said eight and four pence, you must not let me go back o' my word, so bring me five shillings next week."

"Sure you wouldn't have me pay for a blot, sir?"

"Yis, I would—that's the rule of backgammon, you know, Pat.

£   s.   d.

When I hit the blot, you pay for
it."

Here his reverence turned
round, as if looking for someone,
and called out, "Rafferty! Rafferty!
Rafferty! Where are you, Rafferty?"

An old grey-headed man
appeared, bearing a large plate, and
Father Phil continued—

'There now, be active—I'm
sending him among you, good
people, and such as cannot give
as much as you would like to be
read before your neighbours, give
what little you can towards the
repairs, and I will continue to read
out the names by way of
encouragement to you, and the
next name I see is that of Squire
Egan. Long life to him.

SQUIRE EGAN   5   0   0

"Squire Egan—five pounds—
listen to that—five pounds—*a
protestant in the parish*—five
pounds! Faith, the protestant will
make you ashamed of yourselves
if you don't take care!

Mrs. Flannagan   2   0   0

"Not her own parish, either—a
kind lady."

James Milligan of   1   0   0
Roundtown

"And here I must remark that
the people of Roundtown has not
been backward in coming forward
on this occasion. I have a long
list from Roundtown—I will read
it separate."—He then proceeded
at a great pace, jumbling the town

£   s.   d.

and the pounds and the people in a most extraordinary manner; "James Milligan of Roundtown, one pound; Darby Daly of Roundtown, one pound; Sam Finnigan of Roundtown, one pound. James Casey of Roundpound one town; Kit Dwyer of Town pound, one round—pound I mane; Pat Roundpound—Pounden, I mane—Pat Pounden a pound of Poundtown also—There's an example for you!—but what are you about, Rafferty? I don't like the sound of that plate of yours—you are not a good gleaner—go up first into the gallery there, where I see so many good-looking bonnets—I suppose they will give something to keep their bonnets out of the rain, for the wet will be into the gallery next Sunday if they don't. I think that is Kitty Crow I see, getting her bit of silver ready; them ribbons of yours cost a thrifle, Kitty—Well, good Christians, here is more of the subscriptions for you.

Matthew Lave   0   2   6

"*He* doesn't belong to Roundtown—Roundtown will be renowned in future ages for the support of the church.—mark my words—Roundtown will prosper from this day out—Roundtown

	£	s.	d.
Mark Hennessy	0	2	6
Luke Clancy	0	2	6
John Doolin	0	2	6

will be a rising place."

"One would think they all agreed only to give two and sixpence a piece. And they comfortable men, too. And look at their names, Matthew, Mark, Luke and John—the names of the blessed evangelists, and only ten shillings among them! Oh, they are apostles not worthy of the name— we'll call them the poor apostles from this, out," (here a low laugh ran through the chapel)—"Do you hear that, Matthew, Mark, Luke and John? Faith! I can tell you that name will stick to you."—(here the laugh was louder.)

A voice, when the laugh subsided, exclaimed, "I'll make it ten shilins, your reverence."

"Who's that?" said Father Phil.

"Hennessy, you reverence."

"Very well, Mark. I suppose Matthew, Luke and John will follow your example?"

"We will, your reverence."

"Ha! I thought you made a mistake; we'll call you now the faithful apostles—and I think the change in name is betther than seven and sixpence apiece to you."

"I see you in the gallery there, Rafferty—What do you pass that well-dressed woman for?—thry

£ s. d.

back—ha!—see that—she had her
money ready if you only asked for
it—don't go by that other woman
there—oh ho!—So you won't give
anything, ma'am.—You ought to
be ashamed of yourself.—There is
a woman with an elegant sthraw
bonnet, and she won't give a
farthing.—Well now,—afther that
—remember,—I give it from the
althar, that from this day out,
sthraw bonnets pay fi'penny
pieces."

Thomas Durfy, Esq.	1	0	0

"It's not his parish, and he's a
brave gentleman."

Miss Fanny Dawson	1	0	0

"A *protestant out of the parish*,
and a sweet young lady, God bless
Her!—Oh faith, the protestants is
shaming you!!!"

Dennis Fannin	0	7	6

"Very good indeed, for a
working mason."

Jemmy Riley	0	5	0

"Not bad, for a hedge
carpenther."

"I gave you ten, plaze your
reverence," shouted Jemmy; "and by
the same token, you may remember
it was on the Nativity of the
blessed Vargin, sir, I gave you the
second five shillins."

"So you did, Jemmy," cried
Father Phil—"I put a little cross
before it, to remind me of it; but I
was in a hurry to make a sick call
when you gave it to me, and forgot
it afther: and indeed myself doesn't

> know what I did with that same
> five shillings."

Here a pallid woman, who was kneeling near the rails of the altar, uttered an impassioned blessing, and exclaimed, "Oh, that was the very same five shillings, I'm sure, you gave to me that very day, to buy some comforts for my poor husband, who was dying in the fever!"—and the poor woman burst into loud sobs as she spoke.

A deep thrill of emotion ran through the flock as this accidental proof of their poor pastor's beneficence burst upon them; and as an affectionate murmur began to rise above the silence which that emotion produced, the burly Father Philip blushed like a girl at this publication of his charity, and even at the foot of that altar where he stood, felt something like shame in being discovered in the commission of that virtue so highly commended by the Providence to whose worship that altar was raised. He uttered a hasty "Whisht—whisht!" and waved with his outstretched hands his flock into silence.

In an instant one of those sudden changes so common to an Irish assembly, and scarcely credible to a stranger, took place. The multitude was hushed—the grotesque of the subscription list had passed away and was forgotten, and that same man and that same multitude stood in altered relations—*they* were again a reverent flock, and *he* once more a solemn pastor; the natural play of his nation's mirthful sarcasm was absorbed in a moment in the sacredness of his office; and with a solemnity befitting the highest occasion, he placed his hands together before his breast, and, raising his eyes to heaven he poured forth his sweet voice, with a tone of the deepest devotion, in that reverential call to prayer, "*Orate, fratres.*"

The sound of a multitude gently kneeling down followed, like the soft breaking of a quiet sea on a sandy beach; and when Father Philip turned to the altar to pray, his pent-up feelings found vent in tears, and while he prayed, he wept.

I believe such scenes as this are not of unfrequent occurrence in Ireland; that country so long suffering, so much maligned, and so little understood.

Suppose the foregoing scene to have been only described antecedent to the woman in the outbreak of her gratitude revealing the priest's charity, from which he recoiled—suppose the mirthfulness of the incidents arising from reading the subscription-list—a mirthfulness bordering on the ludicrous, to have been recorded, and nothing more—a stranger would be inclined to believe, and pardonable in the belief, that the Irish and their priesthood were rather prone to be irreverent; but observe, under this exterior, the deep sources of feeling that lie hidden, and wait but the wand of divination to be revealed. In a thousand similar ways are the actions and the motives of the Irish misunderstood by those who are careless of them; or worse, misrepresented by those whose interest, and too often *business*, it is to malign them.

Father Phil could proceed no further with the reading of the subscription-list, but finished the office of the mass with unusual solemnity. But if the incident just recorded abridged his address, and the publication of donors' names by way of stimulus to the less active, it produced a great effect on those who had but smaller donations to drop into the plate; and the grey-headed collector, who could have numbered the scanty coin before the bereaved widow had revealed the pastor's charity, had to struggle his way afterwards through the eagerly hands, that showered their hard-earned pence upon the plate, which was borne back to the altar heaped with contributions—heaped as it had not been seen for many a day. The studied excitement of their pride and their shame—and both are active agents in the Irish nature—was less successful than the accidental appeal to their affections.

Oh! rulers of Ireland, why have you not sooner learned to *lead* that people by love, whom all your severity has been unable to *drive*?

When the mass was over, Andy waited at the door of the chapel to catch "his reverence" coming out, and obtain his advice about what he overheard from Larry Hogan; and Father Phil was accordingly accosted by Andy just as he was going to get into his saddle to ride over to breakfast with one of the neighbouring farmers, who was holding the priest's stirrup at the moment. The extreme urgency of Andy's manner, as he pressed up to the pastor's side, made the latter pause and inquire what he wanted.

"I want to get some advice from your reverence," said Andy.

"Faith, then, the advice I give you is, never to stop a hungry man when he is going to refresh himself," said Father Phil, who had quite recovered his usual cheerfulness, and threw his leg over his little grey hack as he spoke. "How could you be so unreasonable as to expect me to stop here listening to your case, and giving you advice indeed, when I have said three masses[1] this morning, and rode fifteen miles;—how could you be so unreasonable, I say?"

"I ax your Rivirence's pardon," said Andy; "I wouldn't have taken the liberty, only the thing is mighty particular, intirely."

"Well, I tell you again, never ask a hungry man advice; for he is likely to cut his advice on the patthern of his stomach; and it's empty advice you'll get. Did you ever hear that a 'hungry stomach has no ears?'"

The farmer who was to have the honour of the priest's company to breakfast exhibited rather more impatience than the good-humoured Father Phil, and reproved Andy for his conduct.

"But it's so particular," said Andy.

"I wondher you would dar to stop his Rivirence, and he black fastin'. Go along wid you!"

"Come over to my house in the course of the week, and speak to me," said Father Phil, riding away.

Andy still persevered, and taking advantage of the absence of the farmer, who was mounting his own nag at the moment, said the matter of which he wished to speak involved the interests of Squire Egan, or he would not "make so bowld."—This altered the matter; and Father Phil desired Andy to follow him to the farmhouse of John Dwyer, where he would speak to him after he had breakfasted.

1.　　　The office of the mass must be performed fasting.

XXIX

JOHN DWYER'S HOUSE WAS A scene of activity that day, for not only was the priest to breakfast there,—which is always an affair of honour,—but a grand dinner also was preparing on a large scale; for a wedding feast was to be held in the house, in honour of Matty Dwyer's nuptials, which were to be celebrated that day with a neighbouring young farmer, rather well to do in the world. The match had been on and off for some time, for John Dwyer was what is commonly called a "close-fisted fellow," and his would be son-in-law could not bring him to what he considered proper terms, and though Matty liked young Casey, and he was fond of her, they both agreed not to let old Jack Dwyer have the best of the bargain in portioning off his daughter, who, having a spice of her father in her, was just as fond of *number one* as old Jack himself. And here it is worthy of remark, that, though the Irish are so prone in general to early and improvident marriages, no people are closer in their nuptial barter, when they are in a condition to make marriage a profitable contract. Repeated meetings between the elders of families take place, and acute arguments ensue, properly to equalize the worldly goods to be given on both sides. Pots and pans are balanced against pails and churns, cows against horses, a slip of bog against a gravel pit, or a patch of meadow against a bit of a quarry; a little lime-kiln sometimes burns stronger than the flame of Cupid—the doves of Venus herself are but crows in comparison with a good flock of geese—and a love-sick sigh less touching than the healthy grunt of a good pig; indeed, the last-named gentleman is a most useful agent in this traffic, for when matters are nearly poised, the balance is often adjusted by a grunter or two thrown into either scale. While matters are thus in a state of debate, quarrels sometimes occur between the lovers; the gentleman's caution sometimes takes alarm, and more frequently the lady's pride is aroused at the too obvious preference given to worldly gain over heavenly beauty; Cupid shies at Mammon, and Hymen is upset and left in the mire.

I remember hearing of an instance of this nature, when the lady gave her *ci-devant* lover an ingenious reproof, after they had been separated some time, when a marriage bargain was broken off, because the lover could not obtain from the girl's father a certain brown filly as part of her dowry. The damsel, after the lapse of some weeks, met her swain at a neighbouring fair, and the flame of love still smouldering in his heart, was reillumed by the sight of his charmer, who, on the contrary, had become quite disgusted with him, for his too obvious preference of profit to true affection.—He addressed her softly in a tent, and asked her to dance, but was much astonished at her returning him a look of vacant wonder, which tacitly implied, "*Who are you?*" as plain as looks could speak.

"Arrah, Mary?" exclaimed the youth.

"Sir!!!"—answered Mary, with what heroines call "ineffable disdain."

"Why one would think you didn't know me!"

"If I ever had the honour of your acquaintance, sir," answered Mary, "I forget you entirely."

"Forget me, Mary?—arrah be, aisy—is it forget the man that was courtin' and in love with you?"

"You're under a mistake, young man," said Mary, with a curl of her rosy lip, which displayed the pearly teeth to whose beauty her woman's nature rejoiced the recreant lover was not yet insensible—"You're under a mistake, young man," and her heightened colour made her eye flash more brightly, as she spoke—"You're quite under a mistake—no one was ever in love with *me*"—and she laid signal emphasis on the word—"There was a dirty mane blackguard, indeed, once *in love with my father's brown filly*, but I forget him intirely."

Mary tossed her head proudly, as she spoke, and her horse-fancying admirer reeled under the reproof she inflicted, and sneaked from the tent, while Mary stood up, and danced with a more open-hearted lover, whose earnest eye could see more charms in one lovely woman than all the horses of Arabia.

But no such result as this was likely to take place in Matty Dwyer's case; she and her lover agreed with one another on the settlement to be made, and Old Jack was not to be allowed an inch over what was considered an even bargain. At length all matters were agreed upon, the wedding day fixed and the guests invited; yet still both parties were not quite satisfied, for young Casey thought he should be put into absolute possession of a certain little farm and cottage, and have the lease looked over to see all was right, (for Jack Dwyer was considered rather slippery,) while old Jack thought it time enough to give him possession and the lease and his daughter altogether.

However, matters had gone so far, that, as the reader, has seen, the wedding feast was prepared, the guests invited, and Father Phil on the spot to help James and Matty, (in the facetious parlance of Paddy,) to "tie with their tongues what they couldn't undo with their teeth."

When the priest had done breakfast, the arrival of Andy was announced to him, and Andy was admitted to a private audience with Father Phil, the particulars. of which must not be disclosed, for in short, Andy made a regular confession before the Father, and, we know confessions must be held sacred;—but we may say that Andy confided the whole post-office affair to the pastor,—told him how Larry Hogan had contrived to worm that affair out of him, and by his devilish artifice had, as Andy feared, contrived to implicate Squire Egan in the transaction, and by threatening a disclosure, got the worthy squire into his villanous power. Andy, under the solemn queries of the priest, positively denied having said one word to Hogan to criminate the squire, and that Hogan could only *infer* the squire's guilt;—upon which Father Phil, having perfectly satisfied himself, told Andy to make his mind easy, for that he would secure the squire from any harm, and he moreover praised Andy for the fidelity he displayed to the interests of his old master, and declared he was so pleased with him, that he would desire Jack Dwyer to ask him to dinner.—"And that will be no blind nut, let me tell you," said Father Phil—"A wedding dinner, you lucky dog—lashings and lavings, and plenty of dancing afther!"

Andy was accordingly bidden to the bridal feast whither the guests began already to gather thick and fast.—They strolled about the field before the house, basked in groups in the sunshine, or lay in the shade under the hedges, where hints for future marriages were given to many a pretty girl, and nudges and pinches were returned by small screams suggestive of additional assault, and inviting denials of "Indeed I won't," and that crowning provocative to riotous conduct, "Behave yourself."

In the meantime, the barn was laid out with long planks supported on barrels or big stones, which, when covered with clean cloths, made a goodly board, that soon began to be covered with ample wooden dishes of corned beef, roasted geese, boiled chickens and bacon, and intermediate stacks of cabbage, and huge bowls of potatoes, all sending up their wreaths of smoke to the rafters of the barn, soon to become hotter from the crowd of guests, who, when the word was given, rushed to the onslaught with right good-will.

The dinner was later than the hour named, and the delay arose from the absence of one, who, of all others, ought to have been present— namely—the bridegroom. But James Casey was missing, and Jack Dwyer had been closeted from time to time with several long-headed grey beards, canvassing the occurrence, and wondering at the default on the bridegroom's part.—The person who might have been supposed to bear this default the worst, supported it better than any one.—Matty was all life and spirits, and helped in making the feast ready, as if nothing wrong happened, and she backed Father Phil's argument to sit down to dinner at once;—"that if James Casey was not there, that was no reason dinner should be spoiled—he'd be there soon enough—besides, if he didn't arrive in time, it was better he should have good meat cold, than every body have hot meat spoiled—the ducks would be done to cindhers—the beef boiled to rags, and the chickens be all in jommethry———"

So down they sat to dinner:—its heat, its mirth, its clatter, and its good cheer I will not attempt to describe; suffice it to say, the viands were good, the guests hungry, and the drink unexceptionable; and Father Phil no bad judge of such matters, declared he never pronounced grace over a better spread. But still, in the midst of the good cheer, neighbours (the women particularly) would suggest to each other the "wondher" where the bridegroom could be; and even within earshot of the bride elect, the low-voiced whisper ran, of "Where in the world is James Casey?"

Still the bride kept up her smiles, and cheerfully returned the healths that were drunk to her; but old Jack was not unmoved—a cloud hung on his brow, which grew darker and darker as the hour advanced and the bridegroom yet tarried.—The board was cleared of the eatables, and the copious jugs of punch going their round, but the usual toast of the united healths of the happy pair could not be given, for one of them was absent.—Father Phil hardly knew what to do, for even his overflowing cheerfulness began to forsake him, and a certain air of embarrassment began to pervade the whole assembly, till Jack Dwyer could bear it no longer, and standing up, he thus addressed the company:

"Friends and neighbours—you see the disgrace that's put on me and my child."

A murmur of "No, no," ran round the board.

"I say, yis."—

"He'll come yet, Sir," said a voice.

"No, he won't," said Jack, "I see he won't—I know he won't. He wanted to have every thing all his own way, and he thinks to disgrace me into doing what he likes, but he shan't!"—and he struck the table fiercely as he spoke, for Jack, when once his blood was up, was a man of desperate determination. "He's a greedy chap, the same James Casey, and he loves his bargain better than he loves you, Matty, so don't look glum abbut what I'm saying—I say he's greedy, he's just the fellow that if you gave him the roof aff your house, would ax you for the rails before your door—and he goes back on his bargain now, bekase I would not let him have it all his own way, and puts the disgrace on me, thinkin' I'll give in to him, through that same—but I won't. And I tell you what it is, friends and neighbours; there's the lease of the three-cornered field below there,"—and he held up a parchment as he spoke,—"and a snug cottage on it, and it's all ready for the girl to walk into with the man that will have her, and if there's a man among you here that's willing, let him say the word now, and I'll give her to him!"

The girl could not resist an exclamation of surprise, which her father hushed by a word and look so peremptory, that she saw remonstrance was in vain, and a silence of some moments ensued; for it was rather startling, this immediate offer of a girl who had been so strangely slighted, and the men were not quite prepared to make advances until they knew something more of the why and wherefore of her sweetheart's desertion.

"Are yiz all dumb?" exclaimed Jack in surprise. "Faix, it's not every day a snug little field and cottage, and a good-looking girl falls in a man's way;—I say again, I'll give her and the lase to the man that will say the word."

Still no one spoke, and Andy began to think they were using Jack Dwyer and his daughter very ill, but what business had *he* to think of offering himself—"a poor devil like him?" But the silence still continuing, Andy took heart of grace, and as the profit and pleasure of a snug match and a handsome wife flashed upon him, he got up and said, "Would I do, sir?"

Every one was taken by surprise—even old Jack himself; and Matty could not suppress a faint exclamation, which every one but Andy understood to mean "she didn't like it at all;" but which Andy interpreted quite the other way, and he grinned his loutish admiration at Matty, who turned away her head from him in sheer distaste, which action Andy took for mere coyness.

Jack was in a dilemma—for Andy was just the very last man he would have chosen as a husband for his daughter; but what could he do?—he was taken at his word, and even at the worst he was determined that some one should marry the girl out of hand, and show Casey the "disgrace should not be put on him;" but anxious to have another chance, he stammered something about the fairness of "letting the girl choose," and that "some one else might wish to spake;" but the end of all was, that no one rose to rival Andy, and Father Phil bore witness to the satisfaction he had that day in finding so much uprightness and fidelity in "the boy,"—that he had raised his character much in his estimation by his conduct that day—and if he was a little giddy betimes, there was nothing like a wife to steady him; and if he was rather poor, sure Jack Dwyer could mend that.

"Then come up here," says Jack; and Andy left his place at the very end of the board, and marched up to the head, amidst clapping of hands and thumping of the table, and laughing and shouting.

"Silence!" cried Father Phil, "this is no laughing matther, but a serious engagement—and John Dwyer, I tell you—and you, Andy Rooney, that girl must not be married against her own free will; but if she has no objection, well and good."

"My will is her pleasure, I know," said Jack, resolutely.

To the surprise of every one, Matty said, "Oh, I'll take the boy, with all my heart!"

Handy Andy threw his arms round her neck, and gave her a most vigorous salute which came smacking off, and thereupon arose a hilarious shout which made the old rafters of the barn ring again.

"There's the lase for you," said Jack, handing the parchment to Andy, who was now installed in the place of honour beside the bride elect, at the head of the table, and the punch circulated rapidly in filling to the double toast of health, happiness, and prosperity, to "the happy pair;" and after some few more circuits of the enlivening liquor had been performed, the women retired to the dwelling-house, whose sanded parlour was put in immediate readiness for the celebration of the nuptial knot between Matty and the adventurous Andy.

In half an hour the ceremony was performed, and the rites and blessings of the church dispensed between two people, who, an hour before, had never looked on each other with thoughts of matrimony.

Under such circumstances, it was wonderful with what lightness of spirit Matty went through the honours consequent on a peasant bridal in Ireland:—these, it is needless to detail; our limits would not permit; but suffice it to say, that a rattling country dance was led off by Andy and Matty in the barn, intermediate jigs were indulged in by the "picked dancers" of the parish, while the country dancers were resting and making love (if making love can be called rest) in the corners, and that the pipers and punch-makers had quite enough to do until the night was far spent, and it was considered time for the bride and bridegroom to be escorted by a chosen party of friends to the little cottage which was to be their future home. The pipers stood at the threshold of Jack Dwyer, and his daughter departed from under the "roof-tree" to the tune of "Joy be with you;" and then the lilters heading the body-guard of the bride, plied drone and chanter right merrily until she had entered her new home, thanked her old friends, (who did all the established civilities, and cracked all the usual jokes attendant on the occasion,) and Andy bolted the door of the snug cottage of which he had so suddenly become master, and placed a seat for the bride beside the fire, requesting "*Miss Dwyer*" to sit down—for Andy could not bring himself to call her "Matty" yet, and found himself in an awkward position in being "lord and master" of a girl he considered so far above him a few hours before: Matty sat quiet and looked at the fire.

"It's very quare, isn't it?" says Andy with a grin, looking at her tenderly, and twiddling his thumbs.

"What's quare?" inquired Matty, very drily.

"The estate," responded Andy.

"What estate?" asked Matty.

"Your estate and my estate," said Andy.

"Sure you don't call the three-cornered field my father gave us, an estate, you fool?" answered Matty.

"Oh no," said Andy. "I mane the blessed and holy estate of matrimony the priest put us in possession of;" and Andy drew a stool near the heiress, on the strength of the hit he thought he had made.

"Sit at the other side of the fire," said Matty, very coldly.

"Yes, Miss," responded Andy very respectfully; and in shoving his seat backwards, the legs of the stool caught in the earthen floor, and Andy tumbled heels over head.

Matty laughed, while Andy was picking himself up with increased confusion at his mishap; for even amidst rustics, there is nothing more humiliating than a lover placing himself in a ridiculous position at the moment he is doing his best to make himself agreeable.

"It is well your coat's not new," said Matty, with a contemptuous look at Andy's weather-beaten vestment.

"I hope I'll soon have a betther," said Andy, a little piqued, with all his reverence for the heiress, at this allusion to his poverty—"But sure, it wasn't the coat you married, but the man that's in it; and sure I'll take off my clothes as soon as you plase, Matty, my dear—Miss Dwyer, I mane—I beg your pardon."

"You had better wait till you get better," answered Matty, very drily—"You know the old saying, 'Don't throw out your dirty wather until you get in fresh.'"

"Ah darlin', don't be cruel to me," said Andy in a supplicating tone—"I know I'm not desarvin' of you, but sure I did not make so bowld as to make up to you, until I seen that nobody else would have you."

"Nobody else have me!" exclaimed Matty, as her eyes flashed with anger.

"I beg your pardon, Miss," said poor Andy, who in the extremity of his own humility had committed such an offence against Matty's pride. "I only meant that—"

"Say no more about it," said Matty, who recovered her equaniniity—"Didn't my father give you the lase of the field and house?"

"Yis, Miss."

"You had better let me keep it, then;—'twill be safer with me than you."

"Sartainly," said Andy—who drew the lease from his pocket and handed it to her, and as he was near her, he attempted a little familiarity, which Matty repelled very unequivocally.

"Arrah, is it jokes you are crackin'?" said Andy with a grin, advancing to renew his fondling.

"I tell you what it is," said Matty, jumping up, "I'll crack your head if you don't behave yourself!" and she seized the stool on which she had been sitting, and brandished it in a very Amazonian fashion.

"Oh wirra! wirra!" said Andy in amaze—"aren't you my wife?"

"*Your* wife!" retorted Matty, with a very devil in her eye—"*Your* wife, indeed, you great *omadhawn*; why then, had you the brass to think I'd put up with you?"

"Arrah, then, why did you marry me?" said Andy, in a pitiful argumentative whine.

"Why did I marry you?" retorted Matty—"Didn't I know better than to refuse you, when my father said the word *when the Divil was busy with him*?—Why did I marry you?—it's a pity I didn't refuse, and be murthered that night, maybe, as soon as the people's backs was turned.—Oh it's little you know of owld Jack Dwyer, or you wouldn't ask me that; but though I'm afraid of him, I'm not afraid of you—and stand off, I tell you!"

"Oh blessed Vargin!" cried Andy,—"and what will be the end of it?"

There was a tapping at the door as he spoke.

"You'll soon see what will be the end of it," said Matty, as she walked across the cabin and opened to the knock.

James Casey entered, and clasped Matty in his arms; and half a dozen athletic fellows, and one old and debauched looking man followed, and the door was immediately closed after their entry.

Andy stood in amazement while Casey and Matty caressed each other, and the old man said in a voice tremulous from intoxication, "A very pretty filly, by jingo!"

"I lost no time the minute I got your message, Matty," said Casey, "and here's the Father ready to join us."

"Aye, aye," cackled the old reprobate—"hammer and tongs!—strike while the iron's hot—I'm the boy for a short job"—and he pulled a greasy book from his pocket as he spoke.

This was a degraded clergyman, known in Ireland under the title of "couple beggar," who is ready to perform irregular marriages on such urgent occasions as the present.—And Matty had continued to inform James Casey of the strange turn affairs had taken at home, and recommended him to adopt the present course, and so defeat the violent measure of her father by one still more so.

A scene of uproar now ensued, for Andy did not take matters quietly, but made a pretty considerable row, which was speedily quelled, however, by Casey's bodyguard, who tied Andy neck and heels, and in that helpless state he witnessed the marriage ceremony performed by the "couple beggar," between Casey and the girl he looked upon as his own, five minutes before.

In vain did he raise his voice against the proceeding;—the "couple beggar" smothered his objections in ribald jests.

"You can't take her from me, I tell you," cried Andy.

"No—but we can take you from her," said the "couple beggar;" and at the words, Casey's friends dragged Andy from the cottage, bidding a rollicking adieu to their triumphant companion, who bolted the door after them, and became possessor of the wife and property poor Andy thought he had secured.

To guard against an immediate alarm being given, Andy was warned on pain of death to be silent, as his captors bore him along, and he took

them to be too much men of their word to doubt they would keep
their promise. They bore him along a lonely bye-lane for some time,
and on arriving at the stump of an old tree, they bound him securely
to it, and left him to pass his wedding night in the tight embraces of
hemp.

XXX

THE NEWS OF ANDY'S WEDDING, so strange in itself, and being celebrated before so many, spread over the country like wildfire, and made the talk of half the barony for the next day, and the question, "*Arrah, did you hear of the wondherful wedding?*" was asked in high road and bye-road, and scarcely a *boreen* whose hedges had not borne witness to this startling matrimonial intelligence. The story, like all other stories, of course got twisted into various strange shapes, and fanciful exaggerations became grafted on the original stem, sufficiently grotesque in itself; and one of the versions set forth how old Jack Dwyer, the more to vex Casey, had given his daughter the greatest fortune that had been ever heard of in the county.

Now one of the open-eared people, who had caught hold of the story by this end, happened to meet Andy's mother, and with a congratulatory grin, began with "The top o' the mornin' to you, Mrs. Rooney, and sure I wish you joy."

"Och hone, and for why, dear?" answered Mrs. Rooney, "sure it's nothin' but throuble and care I have, poor and in want, like me."

"But sure you'll never be in want more now."

"Arrah, who told you so, agra?"

"Sure the boy will take care of you now, won't he?"

"What boy?"

"Andy, sure!"

"Andy!" replied his mother in amazement. "Andy, indeed!—out o' place, and without a bawbee to bless himself with?—stayin' out all night, the blackguard!"

"By this and that, I don't think you know a word about it," cried the friend, whose turn it was for wonder now.

"Don't I, indeed?" says Mrs. Rooney, huffed at having her word doubted, as she thought. "I tell you, he never *was* at home last night, and maybe it's yourself was helping him, Micky Lavery, to keep his bad coorses—the slingein' dirty blackguard that he is."

Micky Lavery set up a shout of laughter, which increased the ire of Mrs. Rooney, who would have passed on in dignified silence, but that Micky held her fast, and when he recovered breath enough to speak, he proceeded to tell her about Andy's marriage, but in such a disjointed way, that it was some time before Mrs. Rooney could comprehend him—for his interjectional laughter at the capital joke it was, that she should be the last to know it, and that he should have the luck to tell it, sometimes broke the thread of his story—and then his collateral observations so disfigured the tale, that its incomprehensibility became very much increased, till at last Mrs. Rooney was driven to push him by direct questions.

"For the tendher mercy, Micky Lavery, make me sinsible, and don't disthract me—is the boy marri'd?"

"Yis, I tell you."

"To Jack Dwyer's daughter?"

"Yis."

"And gev him a fort'n'?"

"Gev him half his property, I tell you, and he'll have all when the owld man's dead."

"Oh, more power to you, Andy!" cried his mother in delight; "it's *you* that is the boy, and the best child that ever was! Half his property, you tell me, *Misther* Lavery," added she, getting distant and polite the moment she found herself mother to a rich man, and curtailing her familiarity with a poor one like Lavery.

"Yis, ma'am," said Lavery, touching his hat, "and the whole of it when the owld man dies."

"Then, indeed, I wish him a happy relase!" said Mrs. Rooney, piously,—"not that I owe the man spite—but sure he'd be no loss—and it's a good wish to any one, sure, to wish them in heaven. Good mornin', Misther Lavery,"—said Mrs. Rooney with a patronizing smile, and 'going the road with a dignified air.'

Mick Lavery looked after her with mingled wonder and indignation. "Bad luck to you, you owld sthrap!" he muttered between his teeth.—"How consaited you are, all of a sudden—by Jakers, I'm sorry I towld you—cock you up, indeed—put a beggar on horseback to be sure—humph!—the divil cut the tongue out o' me, if ever I give any one good news again—I've a mind to turn back and tell Tim Doolin his horse is in the pound."

Mrs. Rooney continued her dignified pace as long as she was within sight of Lavery, but the moment an angle of the road screened her from his observation, off she set, running as hard as she could, to embrace her darling Andy, and realize, with her own eyes and ears, all the good news she had heard. She puffed out by the way many set phrases about the goodness of Providence, and arranged, at the same time, sundry fine speeches to make to the bride; so that the old lady's piety and flattery ran a strange couple together along with herself; while mixed up with her prayers and her blarney, were certain speculations of how long Jack Dwyer could possibly live, and how much he would have to leave.

It was in this frame of mind she reached the hill which commanded a view of the three-cornered field and the snug cottage; and down she rushed to embrace her darling Andy, and his gentle bride. Puffing and blowing like a porpoise, bang she went into the cottage, and Matty being the first person she met, she flung herself upon her, and covered her with embraces and blessings.

Matty, being taken by surprise, was some time before she could shake off the old beldame's hateful caresses, but at last, getting free and tucking up her hair, which her imaginary mother-in-law had clawed about her ears, she exclaimed in no very gentle tones—

"Arrah, good woman, who axed for *your* company—who are you at all?"

"Your mother-in-law, jewel!" cried the widow Rooney, making another open-armed rush at her beloved daughter-in-law, who received the widow's protruding mouth on her clenched fist, instead of her lips; and the old woman's nose coming in for a share of Matty's knuckles, a ruby stream spurted forth, while all the colours of the rainbow danced before Mrs. Rooney's eyes as she reeled backwards on the floor.

"Take that, you owld faggot!" cried Matty, as she shook Mrs. Rooney's tributary claret from the knuckles which had so scientifically tapped it, and wiped her hand in her apron.

The old woman roared "millia' murther" on the floor, and snuffled out a deprecatory question, if that was the proper way to be received in her son's house.

"*Your* son's house, indeed!" cried Matty.—"Get out o' the place, you stack o' rags."

"Oh Andy! Andy!" cried the mother, gathering herself up.

"Oh—that's it, is it!" cried Matty; "so it's Andy you want?"

"To be sure: why wouldn't I want him, you hussy?—My boy! my darlin'! my beauty!"

"Well, go look for him!" cried Matty, giving her a shove towards the door.

"Well, now, do you think I'll be turned out of my son's house so quietly as that, you unnatural baggage?" cried Mrs. Rooney, facing round fiercely. Upon which, a bitter altercation ensued between the women; in the course of which the widow soon learned that Andy was not the possessor of Matty's charms: whereupon the old woman, no longer having the fear of damaging her daughter-in-law's beauty before her eyes, tackled to for a fight in right earnest; in the course of which some reprisals were made by the widow, in revenge for her broken nose; but Matty's youth and activity, joined to her Amazonian spirit, turned the tide in her favour, though, had not the old lady been blown by her long run, the victory would not have been so easy, for she was a tough customer, and left Matty certain marks of her favour that did not rub out in a hurry, while she took away as a keepsake, a handful of Matty's hair, by which she had held on, till a finishing kick from the gentle bride finally ejected Mrs. Rooney from the house.

Off she reeled, bleeding and roaring, and while on her approach she had been blessing Heaven, and inventing sweet speeches for Matty, on her retreat she was cursing fate, and heaping all sorts of hard names on the Amazon she came to flatter.

How fared it in the mean time with Andy? He, poor devil! had passed a cold night, tied up to the old tree, and as the morning dawned, every object appeared to him through the dim light in a distorted form;

the gaping hollow of the old trunk to which he was bound, seemed like a huge mouth, opening to swallow him, while the old knots looked like eyes, and the gnarled branches like claws, staring at, and ready to tear him in pieces.

A raven, perched above him on a lonely branch, croaked dismally, till Andy fancied he could hear words of reproach in the sounds, while a little tom-tit chattered and twittered on a neighbouring bough, as if he enjoyed and approved of all the severe things the raven uttered. The little tom-tit was the worse of the two, just as the solemn reproof of the wise can be better borne than the impertinent remark of some chattering fool. To these imaginary evils were added the real presence of some enormous water-rats, which issued from an adjacent pool, and began to eat Andy's hat and shoes, which had fallen off in his struggle with his captors; and all Andy's warning ejaculations could not make the vermin abstain from his shoes and his hat, which, to judge from their eager eating, must have been very high-flavoured. While Andy looked on at the demolition, and began to dread that they might transfer their favours from his attire to himself, the welcome sound of the approaching tramp of horses fell upon his ear, and in a few minutes two horsemen stood before him—they were Father Phil and Squire Egan.

Great was the surprise of the Father, to see the fellow he had married the night before, and whom he supposed to be in the enjoyment of his honeymoon, tied up to a tree, and looking more dead than alive; and his indignation knew no bounds when he heard that a "couple beggar" had dared to celebrate the marriage ceremony, which fact came out in the course of the explanation Andy made of the desperate misadventure which had befallen him; but all other grievances gave way in the eyes of Father Phil, to the "couple beggar."

"A 'couple beggar!'—the audacious vagabones!" he cried, while he and the Squire were engaged in loosing Andy's bonds. "A 'couple-beggar' in my parish!—How fast they have tied him up, Squire!" he added, as he endeavoured to undo a knot. "A 'couple-beggar' indeed!— I'll undo that marriage!—have you a knife about you, Squire?—the blessed and holy tie of matrimony—it's a black knot, bad luck to it, and must be cut— take your leg out o' that now—and wait till I lay my hands on them—a 'couple-beggar' indeed!"

"A desperate outrage this whole affair has been!" said the Squire.

"But a 'couple-beggar,' Squire."

"His house broken into—"

"But a 'couple-beggar'—"

"His wife taken from him!"—

"But a 'couple-beggar,'—"

"The laws violated—"

"But *my dues*, Squire,—think o' that!—what would become o' them, if 'couple-beggars' is allowed to show their audacious faces in the parish.—Oh wait till next Sunday, that's all—I'll have them up before the alther, and I'll make them beg God's pardon, and my pardon, and the congregation's pardon, the audacious pair!"[1]

"It's an assault on Andy," said the Squire.

"It's a robbery on me," said Father Phil.

"Could you identify the men?" said the Squire.

"Do you know the 'couple-beggar'?" said the priest. "Did James Casey lay his hands on you?" said the Squire; "for he's a good man to have a warrant against."

"Oh, Squire, Squire!" ejaculated Father Phil; "talking of laying hands on *him* is it you are?—didn't that blackguard 'couple-beggar' lay his dirty hands on a woman that my brand new benediction was upon! Sure they'd do anything after that!"

By this time Andy was free, and having received the Squire's directions to follow him to Merryvale, Father Phil and the worthy Squire were once more in their saddles, and proceeded quietly to the same place; the Squire silently considering the audacity of the coup-de-main which robbed Andy of his wife, and his Reverence puffing out his rosy cheeks, and muttering sundry angry sentences, the only intelligible words of which were "couple-beggar."

1.   A man and woman who had been united by a 'couple-beggar' were
       called up one Sunday by the priest in the face of the congregation,
       and summoned, as Father Phil threatens above, to beg God's
       pardon, and the priest's pardon, and the congregation's pardon;

but the woman stoutly refused the last condition: "I'll beg God's pardon and your Reverence's pardon," she said, "but I won't beg the congregation's pardon." "You won't?" said the priest. "I won't," says she. "Oh you conthrairy baggage," cried his Reverence, "take her home out o' that," said he to her husband, who *had* humbled himself—"take her home, and leather her well—for she wants it; and if you don't leather her, you'll be sorry—for if you don't make her afraid of you, she'll masther *you*, too—take her home and leather her." — *Fact*.

XXXI

THE READER HAS, NO DOUBT, anticipated that the presence of Father Phil in the company of the Squire at this immediate time, was on account of the communication made by Andy about the post-office affair. Father Phil had determined to set the Squire free from the stratagetic coil in which Larry Hogan had ensnared him, and lost no time in waiting upon him; and it was on his visit to Merryvale he met its hospitable owner, and anxious no time should be lost, he told the Squire there was a matter of some private importance he wished to communicate, and suggested a quiet ride together, and it was this led to their traversing the lonely little lane, in which they discovered Andy, whose name was so principal in the revelations of that day.

To the Squire, those revelations were of the dearest importance; for they relieved his mind from a weight which had been oppressing it for some time, and set his heart at rest. Egan, it must be remarked, was an odd mixture of courage and cowardice: undaunted by personal danger, but strangely timorous where moral courage was required. A remarkable shyness, too, made him hesitate constantly in the utterance of a word which might explain away any difficulty in which he chanced to find himself: and this helped to keep his tongue tied in the matter where Larry Hogan had continued to make himself a bugbear. He had a horror too of being thought capable of doing a dishonourable thing, and the shame he felt at having peeped into a letter was so stinging, that the idea of asking any one's advice in the dilemma in which he was placed made him recoil from the thought of such aid. Now, Father Phil had relieved him from the difficulties his own weakness imposed; the subject had been forced upon him; and once forced to speak, he made a full acknowledgment of all that had taken place; and when he found Andy had not borne witness against him, and that Larry Hogan only *inferred* his participation in the transaction, he saw on Father Phil's showing, that he was not really in Larry Hogan's power, for though he admitted he had given Larry a trifle of money from time to time, when Larry asked for it, under the influence of certain inuendoes, yet that was no proof against him and Father Phil's advice was to get Andy out of the way as soon as possible, and then to set Larry quietly at defiance—that is to say, in Father Phil's own words, "to keep never minding him."

Now Andy not being encumbered with a wife (as fate had so ordained it) made the matter easier, and the Squire and the Father, as they rode towards Merryvale together to dinner, agreed to pack off Andy without delay, and thus place him beyond Hogan's power; and as Dick Dawson was going to London with Murphy, to push the petition against Scatterbrain's return, it was looked upon as a lucky chance, and Andy was at once named to bear them company.

"But you must not let Hogan know that Andy is sent away under your patronage, Squire," said the father, "for that would be presumptive evidence you had an interest in his absence—and that Hogan is the very blackguard would see it fast enough, for he's a knowing rascal."

"He's the deepest scoundrel I ever met," said the Squire.

"As knowing as a jailor, sir," said Father Phil; "a jailor, did I say—by dad, he bates any jailor I ever heard of—for that fellow is so cute, sir, *he could keep Newgate with a hook and eye.*"

"By-the-bye, there's one thing I forgot to tell you, respecting those letters I threw into the fire; for remember, father, I only peeped into *one* and destroyed the others—but one of the letters, I must tell you, was directed to yourself."

"Faith, then, I forgive you that, Squire," said Father Phil; "for I hate letters; but if you have any scruple of conscience on the subject, write me one yourself, and that will do as well."

The Squire could not help thinking the father's mode of settling the difficulty worthy of Handy Andy himself; but he did not tell the father so.

They had now reached the house where the good humoured priest was heartily welcomed, and where Doctor Growling, Dick Dawson, and Murphy, were also guests at dinner. Great was the delight of the party at the history they heard, when the cloth was drawn, of Andy's wedding, so much in keeping with his former life and adventures, and Father Phil had another opportunity of venting his rage against the "couple-beggar."

"That was but a slip-knot you tied, father," said the doctor.

"Aye, aye! joke away, doctor."

"Do you think, Father Phil," said Murphy, "that *that* marriage was made in Heaven, where we are told marriages *are* made?

"I don't suppose it was, Mr. Murphy; for if it had been, it would have held upon earth."

"Very well answered, father," said the Squire. "I don't know what other people think about matches being made in heaven," said Growling, "but I have my suspicions they are sometimes made in another place."

"O, fie, doctor!" said Mrs. Egan.

"The doctor, ma'am, is an old bachelor," said Father Phil, "or he wouldn't say so."

"Thank you, Father Phil, for so polite a speech." The doctor took his pencil from his pocket, and began to write on a small bit of paper, which the priest observing, asked him what he was about, "or is it writing a prescription you are," said he, "for compounding better marriages than I can?"

"Something very naughty, I dare say the doctor is doing," said Fanny Dawson.

"Judge for yourself, lady fair," said the doctor, hand ing Fanny the slip of paper.

Fanny looked at it for a moment, and smiled, but declared it was very wicked indeed.

"Then read it for the company, and condemn me out of your own pretty mouth, Miss Dawson," said the doctor.

"It is too wicked."

"If it is ever so wicked," said Father Phil, "the wickedness will be neutralized by being read by an angel."

"Well done, St. Omer's!" cried Murphy.

"Really, father!" said Fanny, blushing, "you are desperately gallant to-day, and just to shame you, and show how little of an angel I am, I *will* read the doctor's epigram;—

> "'Though matches are all made in Heaven, they say,
>   Yet Hymen, who mischief oft hatches,
> Sometimes deals with the house *t'other side of the way,*
>   And *there* they make *Lucifer* matches.'"

"Oh doctor, I am afraid you are a woman-hater," said Mrs. Egan. "Come away, Fanny, I am sure they want to get rid of us."

"Yes," said Fanny, rising and joining her sister, who was leaving the room, "and now, after abusing poor Hymen, gentlemen, we leave you to your favourite worship of Bacchus."

The departure of the ladies changed the conversation, and after the gentlemen had resumed their seats, the doctor asked Dick Dawson how soon he intended going to London.

"I start immediately," said Dick. "Don't forget to give me that letter of introduction to your friend in Dublin, whom I long to know."

"Who is he?" asked the Squire.

"One Tom Loftus—or, as his friends call him, 'Piping Tom,' from his vocal powers; or as some nickname him, *Organ* Loftus, from his imitation of that instrument, which is an excessively comical piece of caricature."

"Oh! I know him well," said Father Phil.

"How did you manage to become acquainted with him?" inquired the doctor, "for I did not think he lay much in your way."

"Oh, it was he became acquainted with me," said Father Phil,—"and this was the way of it: he was down on a visit betimes in the parish I was in before this, and his behaviour was so wild that I was obliged to make an allusion in the chapel to his indiscretions, and threaten to make his conduct a subject of severe public censure, if he did not mind his manners a little better. Well, my dear, to my surprise, who should call on me on the Monday morning after, but Misther Tom, all smiles and graces, and protesting he was sorry he fell under my displeasure, and hoping I would never have cause to find fault with him again.—Sure I thought he was repenting of his misdeeds, and I said I was glad to hear such good words from him.—'A'then, father,' says he, 'I hear you have got a great curiosity from Dublin—a shower-bath, I hear.' So I said I had, and indeed to be candid, I was as proud as a peacock of the same bath, which tickled my fancy when I was once in town, and so I bought it.—'Would you show it to me,' says he. 'To be sure,' says I, and off I went like a fool and put the wather on the top, and showed him how, when a string was pulled, (down it came—and he pretended not clearly to understand the thing, and at last he said, 'Sure it's not into that sentry box, you get?' says he. 'Oh yis,' says I, getting into it, quite innocent;—when, my dear, he slaps the door and fastens it on me, and pulls the string, and souses me with the water, and I with my best suit of black on me. I roared and shouted inside while Misther Tom Loftus was screechin' laughing outside, and dancing round the room with delight. At last, when he could speak, he said, 'Now, Father, we're even,' says he, 'for the abuse you gave me yesterday,' and off he ran."

"That's just like him," said Old Growling, chuckling; "he's a queer divil. I remember on one occasion a poor dandy puppy, who was in the same office with him—for Tom is in the Ordnance department, you must know—this puppy, sir, wanted to go to the Ashbourne races, and cut a figure in the eyes of a rich grocer's daughter he was sweet upon."

"Being sweet upon a grocer's daughter," said Murphy, "is like bringing coals to Newcastle."

"Faith! it was coals to Newcastle, with a vengeance, in the present case, for the girl would have nothing to say to him, and Tom had great delight, whenever he could annoy this poor fool in his love-making plots. So, when he came to Tom to ask for the loan of his horse, Tom said he should have him *if he could make the smallest use of him*—'but I don't think you can,' said Tom.

"'Leave that to me,' said the youth.

"'I don't think you could make him go,' said Tom.

"'I'll buy a new pair of spurs,' said the puppy.

"'Let them be handsome ones,' said Tom.

"'I was looking at a very handsome pair at Lamprey's, yesterday,' said the young gentleman.

"'Then you can buy them on your way to my stables,' said Tom; and sure enough, sir, the youth laid out his money on a very costly pair of persuaders, and then proceeded homewards with Tom.

"'Now with all your spurs,' said Tom, 'I don't think you'll be able to make him go.'

"'Is he so very vicious, then?' inquired the youth, who began to think of his neck.

"'On the contrary,' said Tom, 'he's perfectly quiet, but won't go for *you*, I'll bet a pound.'

"'Done!' said the youth.

"'Well, try him!' said Tom, as he threw open the stable door.

"'He's lazy, I see,' said the youth; 'for he's lying down.'

"'Faith, he is,' said Tom; 'and hasn't got up these two days!'

"'Get up, you brute!' said the innocent youth, giving a smart cut of his whip on the horse's flank—but the horse did not budge.—'*Why, he's dead!*' says he.

"'Yes,' says Tom, 'since Monday last. So I don't think you can make him go, and you've lost your bet.'"

"That was hardly a fair joke," said the Squire.

"Tom never stops to think of that," returned the doctor; "he's the oddest fellow I ever knew. The last time I was in Dublin, I called on Tom, and found him one bitther cold and stormy morning, standing at an open window, nearly quite undressed. On asking him what he was about, he said, he was '*getting up a bass voice*, that Mrs. Somebody, who gave good dinners and bad concerts, was disappointed of her bass singer, and I think,' said Tom, 'I'll be hoarse enough in the evening to take double B flat. Systems are the fashion now,' said he, 'there is the Logierian system and other systems, and mine is the Coldairian system, and the best in the world for getting up a bass voice.'"

"That was very original, certainly," said the Squire.

"But did you ever hear of his adventure with the Duke of Wellington?" said the doctor.

"The Duke!" they all exclaimed.

"Yes—that is, when he was only Sir Arthur Wellesley.—Well, I'll tell you."

"Stop," said the Squire, "a fresh story requires a fresh bottle. Let me ring for some claret."

XXXII

THE SERVANT WHO BROUGHT IN the claret announced at the same time the arrival of a fresh guest, in the person of "Captain Moriarty," who was welcomed by most of the party by the name of Randal. The Squire regretted he was too late for dinner, inquiring, at the same time, if he would like to have something to eat at the side-table; but Randal declined the offer, assuring the Squire he had got some refreshment during the day while he had been out shooting; but as the sport led him near Merryvale, and "he had a great thirst upon him," he did not know a better house in the county wherein to have "that same" satisfied.

"Then you're just in time for some cool claret," said the Squire; "so sit down beside the Doctor, for he must have the first glass, and broach the bottle, before he broaches the story he's going to tell us,—that's only fair."

The Doctor filled his glass, and tasted. "What a nice '*chateau*' that '*Margaux*' must be," said he, as he laid down his glass. "I should like to be a tenant at will there, at a small rent."

"And no taxes," said Dick.

"Except my duty to the claret," replied the Doctor.

> "My favourite chateau
> Is that of Margaux."

"By the bye, talking of *chateau*, there's the big brewer over at the town, who is anxious to affect gentility, and he heard some one use the word chapeau, and having found out it was the French for *hat,* he determined to show off on the earliest possible occasion, and selected a public meeting of some sort to display his accomplishment. Taking some cause of objection to the proceedings as an excuse for leaving the meeting, he said, 'Gentlemen, the fact is, I can't agree with you, so I may as well take my *chateau* under my arm at once, and walk.'"

"Is not that an invention of your own, Doctor?" said the Squire.

"I heard it for fact," said Growling.

"And 'tis true," added Murphy, "for I was present when he said it. And at an earlier part of the proceedings, he suggested that the parish clerk should read the resolutions, because he had 'a good *laudable* voice.'"

"A parish clerk ought to have," said the Doctor,—"eh, Father Phil?—'*Laudamus!*'"

"What's that you say about d—n us?" said Dick.

"'Twould be fitter for you to tell us that story you promised about the Duke and Tom Loftus."

"True for you, Misther Dick," said Father Phil.

"The story, Doctor," said the Squire.

"Oh, don't make such bones about it," said Growling; "is but a trifle, after all; only it shows you what a queer and reckless rascal Tom is."

"I told you he was called '*Organ*' Loftus by his friends, in consequence of the imitation he makes of that instrument; and it certainly is worth hearing and seeing, for your eyes have as much to do with the affair as your ears. Tom plants himself on a high office stool, before one of those lofty desks, with long rows of drawers down each side, and a hole between to put your legs under. Well, sir, Tom pulls out the top drawers, like the stops of an organ, and the lower ones by way of pedals; and then he begins thrashing the desk like the finger-board of an organ, with his hands, while his feet kick away at the lower drawers as if he were the greatest pedal performer out of Germany, and he emits a rapid succession of grunts and squeaks, producing a ludicrous reminiscence of the instrument; and I defy any one to hear him without laughing. Several sows and an indefinite number of sucking pigs could not make a greater noise, and Tom himself declares he studied the instrument in a pigsty, which he maintains gave the first notion of an organ. Well, sir, the youths of the office assist in 'doing the service,' as they call it, that is, making an imitation of the chanting and so forth in St. Patrick's cathedral."

"Oh, the haythens!" said Father Phil.

"One does Spray, and another Weyman, and another Sir John Stevenson, and so on; and they go on responsing and singing 'Amen' till the Ordnance Office rings again."

"Have they nothing better to do?" asked the Squire.

"Very little but reading the papers," said the Doctor. "Well, Tom, you must know, sir, was transferred some time ago, by the interest of many influential friends, to the London department; and there the fame of his musical powers had gone before him from some of the English clerks in Ireland, who had been advanced to the higher posts in Dublin, and kept up correspondence with their old friends in London; and it was not long until Tom was requested to go through an anthem on the great office-desk. Tom was only too glad to be asked, and he kept the whole office in a roar for an hour, with all the varieties of the instrument, from the diapason to the flute-stop; and the divil a more business was done in the office that day, and Tom before long made the sober English fellows as great idlers as the chaps in Dublin. Well, it was not long until a sudden flush of business came upon the department, in consequence of the urgent preparations making for supplies to Spain, at the time the Duke was going there to take the command of the army, and organ-playing was set aside for some days; but the fellows, after a week's abstinence, began to yearn for it, and Tom was requested to 'do the service.' Tom, nothing loth, threw aside his official papers, set up a big ledger before him, and commenced his legerdemain, as he called it, pulled out his stops, and began to work away like a weaver, while every now and then he d——d the bellows-blower for not giving him wind enough, whereupon the choristers would kick the bellows-blower to accelerate his flatulency. Well, sir, they were in the middle of the service and all the blackguards making the responses in due season, when, just as Tom was quivering under a portentous grunt, which might have shamed the principal diapason of Harlaem, and the subs were drawing out a resplendent A——a—a——men, the door opened, and in walked a smart-looking gentleman, with rather a large nose and quick eye, which glanced round the office, where a sudden endeavour was made by everybody to get back to his place. The smart gentleman seemed rather surprised to see a little fat man blowing at a desk instead of the fire, and long Tom kicking, grunting, and squeeling like mad. The bellows-blower was so taken by surprise he couldn't stir, and Tom, having his back to the door, did not see what had taken place, and went on as if nothing had happened, till the smart gentleman went up to him, and tapping on Tom's desk with a little riding whip, he said, 'I'm sorry to disturb you, sir, but I wish to know what you're about.'

"'We're doing the service, sir,' said Tom, no ways abashed at the sight of the stranger, for he did not know it was Sir Arthur Wellesley was talking to him.

"'Not the *public* service, sir,' said Sir Arthur.

"'Yes, sir,' said Tom, 'as by law, established in the second year of the reign of King. Edward the Sixth,' and he favoured the future hero of Waterloo with another touch of the organ.

"'Who is the head of this office?' inquired Sir Arthur.

"Tom, with a very gracious bow replied, 'I am principal organist, sir, and allow me to introduce you to the principal bellows-blower,' and he pointed to the poor little man, who let the bellows fall from his hand as Sir Arthur fixed his eyes on him.

"Tom did not perceive till now that all the clerks were taken with a sudden fit of industry, and were writing away for the bare life; and he cast a look of surprise round the office while Sir Arthur was looking at the bellows-blower.

"One of the clerks made a wry face at Tom, which showed him all was not right.

"'Is this the way His Majesty's service generally goes on here?' said Sir Arthur, sharply.

"No one answered; but Tom saw, by the long faces of the clerks and the short question of the visitor, that he was *somebody.*

"'Some transports are waiting for ordnance stores, and I am referred to this office,' said Sir Arthur; 'can any one give me a satisfactory answer?'

"The senior clerk present (for the head of the office was absent) came forward, and said, 'I believe, sir,'—

372   SAMUEL LOVER

"'You *believe*, but you don't *know*,' said Sir Arthur; 'so I must wait for stores while you are playing tom-foolery here. I'll report this.' Then producing a little tablet and a pencil, he turned to Tom, and said, 'Favour me with your name, sir.'

"'I give you my honour, sir,' said Tom—

"'I'd rather you'd give me the stores, sir.—I'll trouble you for your name.'

"'Upon my *honour*, sir,' said Tom again.

"'You seem to have a great deal of that article on your hands, sir,' said Sir Arthur; 'You're an Irishman, I suppose.'

"'Yes, sir,' said Tom.

"'I thought so. Your name.'

"'Loftus, sir.'

"'Ely family?'

"'No, sir.'

"'Glad of it.' He put up his tablet, after writing the name.

"'May I beg the favour to know, sir,' said Tom, 'to whom I have the honour of addressing myself?'

"'Sir Arthur Wellesley, sir.'

"'Oh, J—s!' cried Tom, 'I'm done!'

"Sir Arthur could not help laughing at the extraordinary change in Tom's countenance; and Tom, taking advantage of this relaxation in his iron manner, said, in a most penitent tone,

"'Oh, Sir Arthur Wellesley, only forgive me this time, and 'pon my *sowl*,' says he, with the richest brogue, 'I'll play a *Te Deum* for the first licking you give the French.'

"Sir Arthur smiled, and left the office."

"Did he report, as he threatened?" asked the Squire.

"Faith, he did."

"And Tom?" inquired Dick.

"Was sent back to Ireland, sir."

"That was hard, after the Duke smiled at him," said Murphy.

"Ah, he did not let him suffer in pocket; he was transferred at as good a salary to a less important department; but you know the Duke has been celebrated all his life for never overlooking a breach of duty."

"And who can blame him?" said Moriarty.

"One great advantage of the practice has been," said the Squire, "that no man has been better served. I remember hearing a striking instance of what, perhaps, might be called severe justice, which he exercised on a young and distinguished officer of artillery in Spain; and though one cannot help pitying the case of the gallant young fellow who was the sacrifice, yet the question of strict duty, to the very word, was set at rest for ever under the Duke's command, and it saved much *after* trouble, by making every officer satisfied, however fiery his courage or tender his sense of being suspected of the white feather, that implicit obedience was the course he *must* pursue. The case was this:—the army was going into action"—"What action was it?" inquired Father Phil, with that remarkable alacrity which men of peace evince in hearing the fullest particulars about war, perhaps because it is forbidden to their cloth; one of the many instances of things acquiring a fictitious value by being interdicted,—just as Father Phil himself might have been a protestant only for the penal laws.

"I don't know what action it was," said the Squire, "nor the officer's name, for I don't set up for a military chronicler; but it was, as I have been telling you, going into action that the Duke posted an officer, with his six guns, at a certain point, telling him to remain there until he had orders from *him*. Away went the rest of the army, and the officer was left doing nothing at all, which he didn't like; for he was one of those high-blooded gentlemen who are never so happy as when they are making other people miserable, and he was longing for the head of a French column to be hammering away at. In half an hour or so he heard the distant sound of action, and it approached nearer and nearer, until he heard it close beside him; and he wondered rather that he was not invited to take a share in it, when, pat to his thought, up came an *aide-de-camp* at full speed, telling him that General somebody ordered him to bring up his guns. The officer asked, did not the order come from Lord Wellington? The *aide-de-camp* said no, but from the General, whoever he was. The officer explained that he was placed there by Lord Wellington, under command not to move, unless by *an order from himself*. The *aide-de-camp* stated that the General's entire brigade was being driven in, and must be annihilated without the aid of the guns, and asked, 'would he let a whole brigade be slaughtered?' in a tone which wounded the young soldier's pride, savouring, as he thought it did, of an imputation on his courage. He immediately ordered his guns to move, and joined battle with the General; but while he was away, an *aide-de-camp* from Lord Wellington rode up to where the guns *had been posted*, and, of course, no gun was to be had for the service which Lord Wellington required. Well, the French were repulsed, as it happened; but the want of those six guns seriously marred a preconcerted movement of the Duke's, and the officer in command of them was immediately brought to a court-martial, and would have lost his commission but for the universal interest made in his favour by the general officers, in consideration of his former meritorious conduct and distinguished gallantry, and under the peculiar circumstances of the case. They did not break him, but he was suspended, and Lord Wellington sent him home to England. Almost every general officer in the army endeavoured to get this sentence revoked, lamenting the fate of a gallant fellow being sent away for a slight error in judgment, while the army was in full action; but Lord Wellington was inexorable, saying he must make an example to secure himself in the perfect obedience of officers to their orders; and it had the effect."

"Well, that's what I call hard," said Dick.

"My dear Dick," said the Squire, "war is altogether a hard thing, and a man has no business to be a General who isn't as hard as his own round shot."

"And what became of the *dear* young man?" said Father Phil, who seemed much touched by the readiness with which the *dear* young man set off to mow down the French.

"I can tell you," said Moriarty, "for I served with him afterwards in the Peninsula. He was let back after a year or so, and became so thorough a disciplinarian, that he swore, when once he was at his post, 'They might kill *his father* before his face, and he wouldn't budge until he had orders.'"

"A most christian resolution," said the Doctor.

"Well, I can tell you," said Moriarty, "of a Frenchman, who made a greater breach of discipline; and it was treated more leniently. I heard the story from the man's own lips, and if I could only give you his voice and gesture and manner, it would amuse you. What fellows those Frenchmen are, to be sure, for telling a story! they make a shrug or a wink have twenty different meanings, and their claws are most eloquent,—one might say they talk on their fingers,—and their broken English, I think, helps them."

"Then give the story, Randal, in his manner," said Dick. "I have heard you imitate a Frenchman capitally."

"Well, here goes," said Moriarty; "but let me wet my whistle with a glass of claret before I begin,—a French story should hate French wine." Randal tossed off one glass, and filled a second by way of reserve, and then began the French officer's story.

"You see, sare, it vos ven in *Espagne* de bivouac vos vairy ard indeet 'pon us, vor ye coot naut get into de town at all, nevair, becos you dam English keep all de town to yoursefs—vor ye fall back at dat time becos we get not support—no *corps de re*serve, you perceive—so ye mek *retrograde* movement—not *retreat*—no, no—but *retrograde* movement. Vell—von night I was wit my picket guart, and it was raining like de devil, and de vind vos vinding up de vally, so cold as noting at all, and de dark vos vot you coot not see—no—not your nose bevore your face. Well, I hear de tramp of horse, and I look into de dark—for ye vere very moche on de *qui vive*, because ye expec de Ingelish to attaque de next day—but I see noting; but de tramp of horse come closer and closer, and at last I ask, 'Who is dere?' and de tramp of de horse stop. I run forward, and den I see Ingelish offisair of cavallerie. I address him, and tell him he is in our lines, but I do not vant to mek him prisonair—for you must know dat he *vos* prisonair, if I like, ven he vos vithin our line. He is very polite—he say, '*Bien obligé—bon enfant;*' and ye tek off our hat to each ozer. 'I aff lost my roat,' he say and I say, 'Yais'—bote I vill put him into his roat and so I ask for a moment, pardon, and go back to my *caporal,* and tell him to be on de qui vive till I come back. De Ingilish offisair and me talk very plaisant vile ve go togezer down de leetel roat, and ven ve come to de turn, I say, '*Bon soir*, Monsieur le Capitaine—dat is your vay.'—He den tank me, vera moche like gentilman, and vish he coot mek me some return for my *générosité*, as he please to say—and I say, '*Bah!* Ingilish gentilman vood do de same to French offisair who lose his vay.'—'Den come here,' he say, 'bon enfant, can you leave your post for aff an hour?'—'Leave my post?' I say.—'Yais,' said he, 'I know your army has not moche provision lately, and maybe you are ongrie?'—'Ma foi, yais,' said I; 'I aff naut slips to my eyes, nor meat to my stomach, for more dan fife days.'—'Vell, *bon enfant*,' he say, 'come vis me, and I vill gif you goot supper, goot vine, and goot velcome.'—'Coot I leave my post?' I say.—He say, '*Bah!*—*Caporal* take care till you come back.' By gar, I coot naut resist—*he* vos so *vairy* moche gentilman, and *I* vos so ongrie—I go vis him—not fife hunder yarts—ah! *bon Dieu*—how nice! In de corner of a leetel ruin chappel, dere is nice bit of fire, and hang on a string before it, de half of a kid—*oh ciel!* de smell of de *ros-bif* was so nice—I rub my hands to de fire—I sniff de *cuisine*—I see in anozer corner a couple bottels of wine—*sacre!* it vos all watair in my mouts! Ve sit down to suppair—I nevair did ate so moche in my life. Ve did finish de bones, and vosh down all mid ver good wine—*excellent!* Ve drink de toast—*à la gloire*—and ve talk of de campaign.—Ve drink *à la Patrie*, and den *I* tink of *la belle France* and *ma douce amie*—and he fissel. 'Got safe de king.' Ve den drink *à l'amitié*, and shek hands over dat fire in goot frainship,—dem two hands dat might cross de swords in de morning. Yais, sair, dat was fine—'twas *galliard*—'twas *le vrai chivalrie*; two soldier ennemi to share de same kid, drink de same wine, and talk like two friends. Vell, I got den so sleepy, dat my eyes go blink, blink, and my goot friend says to me, 'Sleep, old fellow; I know you aff got hard fare of late, and you are tired; sleep, all is quiet for to-night, and I will call you before dawn.' Sair, I vos so tired, I forgot my duty, and fall down fast asleep. Vell, sair, in de night de pickets of de two armie get so close, and mix up, dat same shot gets fired, and in von moment all in confusion. I am shake by the shoulder—I wake like from dream—I heard sharp *fusillade*—my friend cry, 'Fly to your post, it is attack!'—We exchange one shek of de hand, and I run off to my post. *Oh ciel!*—it is driven in—I see dem fly. *Oh, mon desespor à ce moment-là* I am ruin—*deshonoré*— rush to de front—I rally *mes braves*—ve stand! —ve advance!!—ve regain de post!!! I am safe!!! De *fusillade* cease—it is only an affair of outposts. I tink I am safe—I tink I am very fine fellow—but Monsieur *l'Aide Major* send for me and he speak—

"'Vere vos you last night, sair?'

"'I mount guard by de mill.'

"'Are you sure?'

"'*Oui monsieur.*'

"'Vere vos you when your post vos attack?'

"I saw it vos no use to deny any longer, so I confess to him everything. 'Sair,' said he, 'you rally your men very good, *or you should be shot.* Young man, remember,' said he—I will never forget his vorts—'young man, *vine is goot—slip is goot—goat is goot,—but honners is betters!*'"

"A capital story, Randal," cried Dick; "but how much of it did you invent?"

"'Pon my soul, it is as near the original as possible."

"Besides, that is not a fair way of using a story," said the Doctor. "You should take a story as you get it, and not play the dissector upon it, mangling its poor body to discover the bit of embellishment upon it; and as long as a *raconteur* maintains *vraisemblance,* I contend you are bound to receive the whole as true."

"A most author-like creed, Doctor," said Dick; "you are a story-teller yourself, and enter upon the defence of your craft with great spirit."

"And justice, too," said the Squire; "the Doctor is quite right."

"Don't suppose I can't see the little touches of the artist," said the Doctor; "but so long as they are in keeping with the picture I enjoy them; for instance, my friend Randal's touch of the Englishman '*fissling God safe de King*' is very happy—quite in character."

"Well, good or bad, the story in substance is true,' said Randal, "and puts the Englishman in a fine point of view—a generous fellow, sharing his supper with his enemy, whose sword may be through his body in the next morning's 'affair.'"

"But the Frenchman was generous to him first," remarked the Squire.

"Certainly—I admit it," said Randal. " In short, they were both fine fellows."

"Oh, sir," said Father Phil, "the French are not deficient in a chivalrous spirit. I heard once a very pretty little bit of anecdote about the way they behaved to one of our regiments on a retreat in Spain."

"*Your* regiments!" said Moriarty, who was rather fond of hitting hard at a priest when he could; "a regiment of friars, is it?"

"No, Captain, but of soldiers; and its going through a river they were, and the French, taking advantage of their helpless condition, were peppering away at them hard and fast."

"Very generous, indeed!" said Moriarty, laughing.

"Let me finish my story, Captain, before you quiz it. I say they were peppering them sorely while they were crossing the river, until some women, the followers of the camp, ran down, poor creatures, to the shore, and the stream was so deep in the middle, they could scarcely ford it; so some dragoons, who were galloping as hard as they could out of the fire, pulled up on seeing the condition of the womenkind, and each horseman took up a woman behind him, though it diminished his own power of speeding from the danger. The moment the French saw this act of manly courtesy they ceased firing, and gave a cheer for the dragoons; and as long as the women were within gun-shot, not a trigger was pulled in the French line, but volleys of cheers, instead of ball cartridge, were sent after the brigade, till all the women were over. Now wasn't that generous?"

"'Twas a handsome thing!" was the universal remark. "And faith, I can tell you, Captain Moriarty, the army took advantage of it; for there was a great struggle to have the pleasure of the ladies' company over the river."

"I dare say, Father Phil," said the Squire, laughing—

"Throth, Squire," said the padre, "fond of the girls as the soldiers have the reputation of being, they never liked them better than that same day."

"Yes, yes," said Moriarty, a little piqued, for he rather affected the "dare-devil," "I see you mean to insinuate that we soldiers fear fire."

"I did not say, fear, Captain; but they'd like to get out of it, for all that, and small blame to them—aren't they flesh and blood, like ourselves?"

"Not a bit like you," said Moriarty. "You sleek and smooth gentlemen who live in luxurious peace, know little of a soldier's dangers or feelings."

"Captain, we all have our dangers to go through; and maybe a priest has as many as a soldier; and we only show a difference of taste, after all, in the selection."

"Well, Father Blake, all I know is, that a true soldier fears nothing!" said Moriarty, with energy.

"Maybe so," answered Father Phil, quietly.

"It is quite clear, however," said Murphy, "that war, with all its horrors, can call out occasionally the finer feelings of our natures; but it is only such redeeming traits as those we have heard which can reconcile us to it. I remember having heard an incident of war, myself, which affected me much," said Murphy, who caught the infection of military anecdote which circled the table; and indeed there is no more catching theme can be started among men, for it may be remarked that whenever it is broached it flows on until it is rather more than time to go to the ladies.

"It was in the earlier portion of the memorable day of Waterloo," said Murphy, "that a young officer of the Guards received a wound which brought him to the ground. His companions rushed on to the occupation of some point their desperate valour was called on to carry, and he was left, utterly unable to rise, for the wound was in his foot. He lay for some hours with the thunder of that terrible day ringing around him, and many a rush of horse and foot had passed close beside him. Towards the close of the day he saw one of the Black Brunswick dragoons approaching, who drew rein as his eye caught the young Guardsman, pale and almost fainting, on the ground. He alighted, and finding the officer was not mortally wounded, he assisted him to rise, lifted him into his saddle, and helped to support him there while he walked beside him to the English rear. The Brunswicker was an old man; his brow and moustache were grey; despair was in his sunken eye, and from time to time he looked up with an expression of the deepest yearning into the face of the young soldier, who saw big tears rolling down the veteran's cheek while he gazed upon him.

"'You seem in bitter sorrow, my kind friend,' said the stripling.

"'No wonder,' answered the old man, with a hollow groan. 'I and my three boys were in the same regiment—they were alive the morning of Ligny—I am childless to-day. But I have revenged them!' he said fiercely, and as he spoke he held out his sword, which was literally red with blood. 'But, oh! that will not bring me back my boys!' he exclaimed, relapsing into his sorrow. 'My three gallant boys!'—and again he wept bitterly, till clearing his eyes from the tears, and looking up in the young soldier's handsome face, he said tenderly, 'You are like my youngest one, and I could not let you lie on the field.'

Even the rollicking Murphy's eyes were moist as he recited this anecdote; and as for Father Phil, he was quite melted, ejaculating in an undertone, "Oh, my poor fellow! my poor fellow!"

"So there," said Murphy, "is an example of a man, with revenge in his heart, and his right arm tired with slaughter, suddenly melted into gentleness by a resemblance to his child."

"'Tis very touching, but very sad," said the Squire.

"My dear sir," said the Doctor, with his peculiar dryness, "sadness is the principal fruit which warfare must ever produce. You may talk of glory as long as you like, but you cannot have your laurel without your cypress; and though you may select certain bits of sentiment out of a mass of horrors, if you allow me, I will give you one little story which sha'n't keep you long, and will serve as a commentary upon war and glory in general.

"At the peace of 1803, I happened to be travelling through a town in France, where a certain Count I knew resided. I waited upon him, and he received me most cordially, and invited me to dinner. I made the excuse that I was only *en route,* and supplied with but travelling costume, and therefore not fit to present myself amongst the guests of such a house as his. He assured me I should only meet his own family, and pledged himself for Madame la Comtesse being willing to waive the ceremony of a *grande toilette.* I went to the *hotel* at the appointed hour, and as I passed through the hall I caught a glance at the dining-room, and saw a very long table laid. On arriving at the reception-room, I taxed the Count with having broken faith with me, and was about making my excuses to the Countess, when she assured me the Count had dealt honestly by me, for that I was the only guest to join the family party. Well, we sat down to dinner, three-and-twenty persons; myself, the Count and Countess, and their *twenty children,* and a more lovely family I never saw; he a man in the vigour of life, she a still attractive woman, and these their offspring lining the table, where the happy eyes of father and mother glanced with pride and affection from one side to the other on these future staffs of their old age. Well, the peace of Amiens was of short duration, and I saw no more of the Count till Napoleon's abdication. Then I visited France again, and saw my old friend. But it was a sad sight, sir, in that same house, where little more than ten years before I had seen the bloom and beauty of twenty children, to sit down with *three*—all he had left him. His sons had fallen in battle—his daughters had died widowed, leaving but orphans. And thus it was all over France. While the public voice shouted 'Glory,' wailing was in her homes. Her temple of victory was filled with trophies, but her hearths were made desolate."

"Still, sir, a true soldier fears nothing," repeated Moriarty.

"*Baithershin*," said Father Phil. "Faith, I have been in places of danger you'd be glad to get out of, I can tell you, as bowld as you are, Captain."

"You'll pardon me for doubting you, Father Blake," said Moriarty, rather huffed.

"Faith, then, you wouldn't like to be where I was before I came here; that is, in a mud cabin, where I was giving the last rites to six people dying in the typhus fever."

"Typhus!" exclaimed Moriarty, growing pale, and instinctively withdrawing his chair as far as he could from the padre beside whom he sat.

"Ay, typhus, sir; most inveterate typhus."

"Gracious Heaven!" said Moriarty, rising, "how can you do such a dreadful thing as run the risk of bearing infection into society?"

"I thought soldiers were not afraid of anything," said Father Phil, laughing at him; and the rest of the party joined in the merriment.

"Fairly hit, Moriarty," said Dick.

"Nonsense!" said Moriarty, "when I spoke of danger, I meant such open danger as—in short, not such insidious, lurking abomination, as infection; for I contend that—"

"Say no more, Randal," said Growling, "you're done!—Father Phil has floored you."

"I deny it," said Moriarty, warmly; but the more he denied it the more every one laughed at him.

"You're more frightened than hurt, Moriarty," said the Squire; "for the best of the joke is, Father Phil wasn't in contact with typhus at all, but was riding with me,—and 'tis but a joke."

Here they all roared at Moriarty, who was excessively angry, but felt himself in such a ridiculous position that he could not quarrel with anybody.

"Pardon me, my dear Captain," said the Father. "I only wanted to show you that a poor priest has to run the risk of his life just as much as the boldest soldier of them all. But don't you think now, Squire, we ought to join the ladies? I'm sure the tay will be tired waiting for us."

XXXIII

MRS. EGAN WAS ENGAGED WITH some needle-work, and Fanny turning over the leaves of a music-book, and occasionally humming some bars of her favourite songs, as the gentlemen came into the drawing-room. Fanny rose from the piano-forte as they entered.

"Oh, Miss Dawson," exclaimed Moriarty, "why tantalize us so much as to let us see you seated in that place where you can render so much delight, only to leave it as we enter?"

Fanny turned off the Captain's flourishing speech with a few lively words and a smile, and took her seat at the tea-table to do the honours.

"The Captain," said Father Phil to the Doctor, "is equally great in love or war."

"And knows about as little of one as the other," said the Doctor; "his attacks are too open."

"And therefore easily foiled," said Father Phil. "How that pretty creature, with the turn of a word and a curl of her lip, upset him that time! Oh, what a powerful thing a woman's smile is, Doctor! I often congratulate myself that my calling puts all such mundane follies and attractions out of my way, when I see and know what fools wise men are sometimes made by silly girls. Oh, it is fearful, Doctor; though, of course, part of the mysterious dispensation of an allwise Providence."

"Is it that fools should have the mastery?" inquired the Doctor, drily, with a mischievous query in his eye as well.

"Tut, tut, tut, Doctoer," replied Father Phil, impatiently; "you know well enough what I mean, and I won't allow you to engage me in one of your ingenious battles of words. I speak of that wonderful influence of the weaker sex over the stronger, and how the word of a rosy lip outweighs sometimes the resolves of a furrowed brow; and how the— pooh! pooh! I'm making a fool of myself talking to you;—but to make a long story short, I would rather *wrastle* out a logical dispute any day, or a tough argument of one of the Fathers, than refute some absurdity which fell from a pretty mouth with a smile on it."

"Oh, I quite agree with you," said the Doctor, grinning, "that the fathers are not half such dangerous customers as the daughters."

"Ah, go along with you, Doctor!" said Father Phil, with a good-humoured laugh. "I see you are in one of your mischievous moods, and so I'll have nothing more to say to you."

The Father turned away to join the Squire, while the Doctor took a seat near Fanny Dawson, and enjoyed a quiet little bit of conversation with her, while Moriarty was turning over the leaves of her album; but the brow of the Captain, who affected a taste in poetry, became knit, and his lip assumed a contemptuous curl as he perused some lines, and asked Fanny whose was the composition.

"I forget," was Fanny's answer.

"I don't wonder," said Moriarty; "the author is not worth remembering, for they are very rough."

Fanny did not seem pleased with the criticism, and said, that when sung to the measure of the air written down on the opposite page, they were very flowing.

"But the principal phrase, the '*refrain,*' I may say, is so vulgar," added Moriarty, returning to the charge. "The gentleman says, 'What would you do?' and the lady answers, 'That's what I'd do.' Do you call that poetry?"

"I don't call *that* poetry," said Fanny, with some emphasis on the word; "but if you connect those two phrases with what is intermediately written, and read all in the spirit of the entire of the verses, I think there *is* poetry in them,—but if not *poetry*, certainly *feeling*."

"Can you tolerate '*That's what I'd do?*'—the pert answer of a housemaid."

"A phrase in itself homely," answered Fanny, "may become elevated by the use to which it is applied."

"Quite true, Miss Dawson," said the Doctor, joining in the discussion; "but what are these lines which excite Randal's ire?"

"Here they are," said Moriarty. "I will read them, if you allow me, and then judge between Miss Dawson and me.

> 'What will you do, love, when I am going,
>   With white sail flowing,
>   The seas beyond
>   What will you do, love, when——'

"Stop, thief!—stop, thief!" cried the Doctor. "Why you are robbing the poet of his reputation as fast as you can. You don't attend to the rhythm of those lines,—you don't give the *ringing* of the verse."

"That's just what I have said, in other words," said Fanny. "When sung to the melody they are smooth."

"But a good reader, Miss Dawson," said the Doctor, "will read verse with the proper accent, just as a musician would divide it into bars; but my friend Randal there, though he can tell a good story, and hit off prose very well, has no more notion of rhythm or poetry than new beer has of a holiday."

"And why, pray, has not new beer a notion of a holiday?"

"Because, sir, it works of a Sunday."

"Your *beer* may be new, Doctor, but your *joke* is not,—I have seen it before, in some old form."

"Well, sir, if I found it in its old form, like a hare, and started it fresh, it may do for folks to run after as well as anything else. But you sha'n't escape your misdemeanour in mauling those verses as you have done, by finding fault with my joke *redivivus*. You read those lines, sir, like a bellman, without any attention to metre."

"To be sure," said Father Phil, who had been listening for some time; "they have a ring in them—"

"Like a pig's nose," said the Doctor.

"Ah, be aisy," said Father Phil. "I say they a ring in them like an owld Latin canticle,—

'What *will* you *do,* love, when I am *go*-ing,
  With white sail *flow*-ing,
      The says be-*yond?'*
That's it!"

"To be sure," said the Doctor. " I vote for the Father's reading them out on the spot."

"Pray do, Mister Blake," said Fanny.

"Ah, Miss Dawson, what have I to do with reading love verses?"

"Take the book, sir," said Growling, "and show me you have some faith in your own sayings, by obeying a lady directly."

"Pooh! pooh!" said the priest.

"You won't refuse me?" said Fanny, in a coaxing tone.

"My dear Miss Dawson," said the *padre.*

"*Father Phil!*" said Fanny, with one of her rosy smiles.

"Oh, wow! wow! wow!" ejaculated the priest in an amusing embarrassment,—"I see you *will* make me do whatever you like." So Father Phil gave the rare example of a man acting up to his own theory, and could not resist the demand that came from a pretty mouth. He took the book, and read the lines with much feeling, but with an observance of rhythm so grotesque, that it must be given in his own manner.

WHAT WILL YOU DO, LOVE?

I

"What *will* you *do,* love, when I am *go*-ing,
  With white sail *flow*-ing
      The seas be-*yond?*
What *will* you *do,* love, when waves di-*vide* us,
  And friends may *chide* us,
      For being *fond?'*
"Though waves di-*vide* us, and friends be *chi*-ding,
  In faith a-*bi*-ding,
      I'll still be *true;*
And I'll pray for *thee* on the stormy *o*-cean,

In deep de-*vo*-tion;—
    That's *what* I'll do!"

II

"What *would* you *do,* love, if distant *ti*-dings
    Thy fond con-*fi*-dings
      Should under-*mine,*
And I, a-*bi*-ding 'neath sultry *skies,*
    Should think other *eyes*
      Were as bright as *thine?*
"Oh, name it *not*; though guilt and *shame*
    Were on thy *name,*
      I'd still be *true;*
But that heart of *thine,* should another *share* it,
    I could not *bear* it;—
      What *would* I do?"

III

What *would* you *do,* love, when, home re-*turn*-ing,
    With hopes high *burn*-ing
      With wealth for *you,*—
If my *bark,* that *bound*-ed o'er foreign *foam,*
    Should be lost near *home,*—
      Ah, what *would* you do?"
"So thou wert *spar*-ed, I'd bless the *mor*-row,
    In want and *sor*-row,
      That left me *you;*
And I'd welcome *thee* from the wasting *bil*-low,
    My heart thy *pil*-low!—
      THAT's what I'd do!"

"Well done, *padre!*" said the Doctor,—"with good emphasis and discretion."

"And now, my dear Miss Dawson," said Father Phil, "since I've read the lines at your high bidding, will you sing them for me at my humble asking?"

"Very antithetically put, indeed," said Fanny; "but you must excuse me."

"You said there was a tune to it."

"Yes; but I promised Captain Moriarty to sing him *this,*" said Fanny, going over to the pianoforte, and laying her hand on an open music-book.

"Thanks, Miss Dawson," said Moriarty, following fast.

Now, it was not that Fanny Dawson liked the Captain that she was going to sing the song; but she thought he had been rather "*mobbed*" by the doctor and *padre* about the reading of the verses, and it was her good breeding which made her pay this little attention to the worsted party. She poured forth her sweet voice in a simple melody to the following words:—

SAY NOT MY HEART IS COLD

I

"Say not my heart is cold,
　　Because of a silent-tongue;
The lute of faultless mould
　　In silence oft hath hung.
The fountain soonest spent
　　Doth babble down the steep;
But the stream that *ever* went
　　Is silent, strong, and deep.

II

"The charm of a secret life
　　Is given to choicest things
Of flowers, the fragrance rife
　　Is wafted on viewless wings;

We see not the charmed air
   Bearing some witching sound;
And ocean deep is where
   The pearl of price is found.

III

"Where are the stars by day?
   They burn, though all unseen;
And love of purest ray
   Is like the stars, I ween:
Unmark'd is the gentle light
   When the sunshine of joy appears,
But, ever, in sorrow's night,
   'Twill glitter upon thy tears!"

"Well, Randal, does that poem satisfy your critical taste?—of the singing there can be but one opinion."

"Yes, I think it pretty," said Moriarty, "but there is one word in the last verse I object to."

"Which is that?" inquired Growling.

"*Ween*," said the other; "'the stars, I ween,' I object to."

"Don't you see the meaning of that?" inquired the Doctor. "I think it a very happy allusion."

"I don't see any allusion whatever," said the critic.

"Don't you see the poet alluded to the stars in the *milky* way, and says, therefore, 'the stars I *wean*'."

"Bah! bah! Doctor," exclaimed the critical captain; "you are in one of your quizzing moods to-night, and 'tis in vain to expect a serious answer from you." He turned on his heel as he spoke, and went away.

"Moriarty, you know, Miss Dawson, is a man who affects a horror of puns, and therefore I always punish him with as many as I can," said the Doctor, who was left by Moriarty's sudden pique to the enjoyment of a pleasant chat with Fanny, and he was sorry when the hour arrived which disturbed it by the breaking up of the party and the departure of the guests.

XXXIV

WHEN THE WIDOW ROONEY WAS forcibly ejected from the house of Mrs. James Casey, and found that Andy was not the possessor of that lady's charms, she posted off to Neck-or-Nothing Hall, to hear the full and true account of the transaction from Andy himself. On arriving at the old iron gate, and pulling the loud bell, the savage old janitor spoke to her between the bars, and told her to "go out o' that." Mrs. Rooney thought Fate was using her hard in decreeing she was to receive denial at every door, and endeavoured to obtain a parley with the gate-keeper, to which he seemed no way inclined.

"My name's Rooney, sir."

"There's plenty bad o' the name," was the civil rejoinder.

"And my son's in Squire O'Grady's sarvice, sir."

"Oh—you're the mother of the beauty we call Handy—eh?"

"Yis, sir."

"Well, he left the sarvice yistherday."

"Is it lost the place?"

"Yis."

"Oh dear!—Ah, sir, let me up to the house and spake to his honor, and maybe he'll take back the boy."

"He doesn't want any more servants at all—for he's dead."

"Is it Squire O'Grady dead?"

"Ay—did you never hear of a dead Squire before?"

"What did he die of, sir?"

"Find out," said the sulky brute, walking back into his den.

It was true—the renowned O'Grady was no more. The fever which had set in from his "broiled bones," which he *would* have in spite of anybody, was found difficult of abatement; and the impossibility of keeping him quiet, and his fits of passion, and consequent fresh supplies of "broiled bones," rendered the malady unmanageable; and the very day after Andy had left the house, the fever took a bad turn, and in four-and- twenty hours the stormy O'Grady was at peace.

What a sudden change fell upon the house! All the wedding paraphernalia which had been brought down, lay neglected in the rooms where it had been the object of the preceding day's admiration. The deep, absorbing, silent grief of the wife—the more audible sorrow of the girls—the subdued wildness of the reckless boys, as they trod silently past the chamber where they no longer might dread reproof for their noise,—all this was less touching than the effect the event had upon the old dowager mother. While the senses of others were stunned by the blow, hers became awakened by the shock; all her absurd aberration passed away, and she sat, in intellectual self-possession, by the side of her son's death-bed, which she never left until he was laid in his coffin. He was the first and the last of her sons. She had now none but grandchildren to look upon—the intermediate generation had passed away, and the gap yawned fearfully before her. It restored her, for the time, perfectly to her senses; and she gave the necessary directions on the melancholy occasion, and superintendt'd all the sad ceremonials befitting the time, with a calm and dignified resignation, which impressed all around her with wonder and respect.

Superadded to the dismay which the death of the head of a family produces, was the terrible fear which existed that O'Grady's body would be seized for debt—a barbarous practice, which, shame to say, is still permitted. This fear made great precaution necessary, to prevent persons approaching the house, and accounts for the extra gruffness of the gate porter. The wild body-guard of the wild chief was on doubly active duty; and after four-and-twenty hours had passed over the reckless boys, the interest they took in sharing and directing this watch and ward seemed to outweigh all sorrowful consideration for the death of their father. As for Gustavus, the consciousness of being now the master of Neck-or-Nothing Hall was apparent in a boy not yet fifteen; and not only in himself, but in the grey-headed retainers

SAMUEL LOVER

about him, this might be seen: there was a shade more of deference—
the boy was merged in "*the young master.*" But we must leave the house
of mourning for the present, and follow the widow Rooney, who,
as she tramped her way homeward, was increasing in hideousness of
visage every hour. Her nose was twice its usual dimensions, and one
eye was perfectly useless in showing her the road. At last, however,
as evening was closing, she reached her cabin, and there was Andy,
arrived before her, and telling Oonah, his cousin, all his misadventures
of the preceding day.

The history was stopped for a while by their mutual explanations
and condolences with Mrs. Rooney, on the "cruel way her poor face
was used."

"And who done it at all?" said Oonah.

"Who, but that born divil, Matty Dwyer—and sure they towld me
you were married to her," said she to Andy.

"So I was—" said Andy, beginning the account of his misfortunes
afresh to his mother, who from time to time would break in with
indiscriminate maledictions on Andy, as well as his forsworn damsel;
and when the account was ended, she poured out a torrent of abuse
upon her unfortunate forsaken son, whch rivetted him to the floor in
utter amazement.

"I thought I'd get pity here, at all events," said poor Andy; "but instead
o' that it's the worst word, and the hardest name in your jaw, you have
for me."

"And sarve you right, you dirty cur," said his mother. "I ran off like
a fool when I heerd of your good fortune, and see the condition that
baggage left me in—my teeth knocked in, and my eye knocked out, and
all for your foolery, because you couldn't keep what you got."

"Sure, mother, I tell you—"

"Howld your tongue, you *omadhawn!*—And then I go to Squire
O'Grady's to look for you, and there I hear you lost *that* place, too."

"Faix, it's little loss," said Andy.

"That's all you know about it, you goose—you lose the place just
when the man's dead, and you'd have had a shuit o' mournin'. Oh, you
are the most misfortunate divil, Andy Rooney, this day in Ireland—why
did I rear you at all?"

"Squire O'Grady dead!" said Andy in surprise, and also with regret for his late master.

"Yis—you've lost the mournin'—augh!"

"Oh the poor Squire!" said Andy.

"The iligant new clothes!" grumbled Mrs. Rooney. "And then luck tumbles into your way, such as man never had; without a place, or a rap to bless yourself with, you get a rich man's daughter for your wife, and you let her slip through your fingers."

"How could I help it?" said Andy.

"Augh!—you bothered the job just the way you do every thing," said his mother.

"Sure I was civil spoken to her."

"Augh!" said his mother.

"And took no liberty."

"You goose!"

"And called her Miss."

"Oh indeed, you missed it altogether."

"And said I wasn't desarvin' of her."

"That was thrue—*but you should not have towld her so*. Make a woman think you're betther than her, and she'll like you."

"And sure, when I endayvoured to make myself agreeable to her—"

"*Endayvoured!*" repeated the old woman, contemptuously—"*Endayvoured*, indeed!—Why didn't you *make* yourself agreeable at once, you poor dirty goose?—no, but you went sneaking about it—I know as well as if I was looking at you—you went sneaking and snivelin' until the girl took a disgust to you; for there's nothing a woman despises so much as shilly-shallying."

"Sure, you won't hear my defince," said Andy.

"Oh, indeed, you're betther at defince than attack," said his mother.

"Sure the first little civility I wanted to pay her, she took up the three-legged stool to me."

"The divil mend you!—And what civility did you offer her?"

"I made a grab at her cap, and I thought she'd have brained me!"

Oonah set up such a shout of laughter at Andy's notion of a civility to a girl, that the conversation was stopped for some time, and her aunt remonstrated with her at her want of common sense, or, as she said, hadn't she "more decency than to laugh at the poor fool's nonsense?"

"What could I do agen the three-legged stool?" said Andy.

"Where was your *own* legs, and your own arms, and your own eyes, and your own tongue—eh?"

"And sure I tell you it was all ready conthrived, and James Casey was sent for, and came."

"Yis," said the mother, "but not for a long time, you towld me yourself; and what were you doing all that time?—Sure, supposing, you wor only a new acquaintance, any man worth a day's mate would have discoorsed her over in the time, and made her sinsible he was the best of husbands."

"I tell you she wouldn't let me have her ear at all," said Andy.

"Nor her cap either," said Oonah, laughing.

"And then Jim Casey kem."

"And why did you let him in?"

"It was *she* let him in, I tell you."

"And why did you let her? He was on the wrong side of the door— that's the *outside;* and you on the right—that's the *inside*; and it was *your* house, and she was *your* wife, and you were her masther, and you had the rights of the church, and the rights of the law, and all the rights on your side; barrin' right rayson—that you never had; and sure without *that*, what's the use of all the other rights in the world?"

"Sure, hadn't he his friends, *sthrong,* outside?"

"No matther, if the door wasn't opened to them, for *then* YOU would have had a stronger friend than any o' them present among them."

"Who?" inquired Andy.

"The *hangman,*" answered his mother; "for breaking doors is hanging matther; and I say the presence of the hangman's always before people when they have such a job to do, and makes them think twice sometimes, before they smash once; and so you had only to keep one woman's hands quiet."

"Faix, some of them would smash a door as soon as not," said Andy.

"Well, then, you'd have the satisfaction of hanging them," said the mother, "and that would be some consolation.—But even as it is, I'll have law for it—I will—for the property is yours, any how, though the girl is gone—and indeed a brazen baggage she is, and is mighty heavy in the hand:—oh, my poor eye!—it's like a coal of fire—but sure it was worth the risk living with her, for the sake of the purty property. And sure I was thinkin' what a pleasure it would be living with you, and taachin' your wife housekeepin', and bringing up the young turkeys and the childhre—but, och hone, you'll never do a bit o' good, you that got sitch careful bringin' up, Andy Rooney! Didn't I tache you manners, you dirty hanginbone blackguard—Didn't I tache you your blessed religion?—may the divil sweep you!—Did I ever prevent you from sharing the lavings of the pratees with the pig? and didn't you often dane out the pot with him? and you're no good afther all. I've turned my honest penny by the pig, but I'll never make my money of *you,* Andy Rooney!"

There were some minutes' silence after this eloquent outbreak of Andy's mother, which was broken at last by Andy uttering a long sigh and an ejaculation.

"Och!—it's a fine thing to be a gintleman," said Andy.

"Cock you up!" said his mother. "Maybe it's a gintleman you want to be;—what puts that in your head, you *omadhawn?*"

"Why, because a gintleman has no hardships compared with one of uz. Sure, if a gintleman was marri'd, his wife wouldn't be tuk off from him the way mine was."

"Not so soon, maybe," said the mother, drily. "And if a gintleman breaks a horse's heart, he's only a '*bowld rider,*' while a poor sarvant is a 'careless blackguard,' for only taking a sweat out of him. If a gintleman dhrinks till he can't see a hole in a laddher, he's only '*fresh,*'—but '*dhrunk*' is the word for a poor man. And if a gintleman kicks up a row, he's a '*fine sperited fellow,*' while a poor man is a 'disorderly vagabone' for the same; and the Justice axes the one to dinner, and sends th'other to jail. Oh, faix, the law is a dainty lady; she takes people by the hand who can afford to wear gloves, but people with brown fists must keep their distance."

"I often remark," said his mother, "that fools spake mighty sinsible betimes; but their wisdom all goes with their gab. Why didn't you take a betther grip of your luck when you had it? You're wishing you wor a gintleman, and yet when you had the best part of a gintleman (the property, I mane) put into your way, you let it slip through your fingers; and afther lettin' a fellow take a rich wife from you, and turn you out of your own house, you sit down on a stool there, and begin to *wish,* indeed!—you sneaking fool—wish, indeed!—Och! if you wish with one hand, and wash with th' other, which will be clane first—eh?"

"What could I do agen eight?" asked Andy.

"Why did you let them in, I say again?" said the mother, quickly.

"Sure the blame wasn't with me," said Andy, "but with—"

"Whisht, whisht, you goose!" said his mother. "An coorse you'll blame every one, and everything but yourself—'*The losing horse blames the saddle.*'

"Well, maybe it's all for the best," said Andy, "after all."

"Augh, howld your tongue!"

"And if it *wasn't* to be, how could it be?"

"Listen to him!"

"And Providence is over us all."

"Oh, yis," said the mother. "When fools make mistakes they lay the blame on Providence. How have you the impidence to talk o' Providence in that manner?—*I'll* tell you where the Providence was.—Providence sent you to Jack Dwyer's, and kep Jim Casey away, and put the anger into owld Jack's heart, and made the opening for you to spake up, and gave you a wife—a wife with *property!*—Ah, *there's* where the Providence was!—and you were the masther of a snug house—that was Providence! And wouldn't myself have been the one to be helping you in the farm—rearing the powlts, milkin' the cow, makin' the iligant butther, with lavings of butthermilk for the pigs—the sow thriving, and the cocks and hens cheering your heart with their cacklin'—the hank o' yarn on the wheel, and a hank of ingins up the chimbley—oh! that's what the Providence would have been—that *would have been Providence indeed!*—but never tell me that Providence turned you out of the house; that was your own *goostherumfoodle.*"

"Can't he take the law o' them, aunt?" inquired Oonah.

"To be sure he can—and shall, too," said the mother. "I'll be off to 'torney Murphy, to-morrow.—I'll pursue her for my eye, and Andy for the property, and I'll put them all in Chancery, the villains!"

"It's Newgate they ought to be put in," said Andy.

"Tut, you fool, Chancery is worse than Newgate; for people sometimes get out of Newgate, but they never get out of Chancery, I hear."

As Mrs. Rooney spoke, the latch of the door was raised, and a miserably clad woman entered, closed the door immediately after, and placed the bar against it. The action attracted the attention of all the inmates of the house, for the doors of the peasantry are universally left "on the latch," and never secured against intrusion until the family go to bed.

"God save all here!" said the woman, as she approached the fire.

"Oh, is that you, Ragged Nance?" said Mrs. Rooney; for that was the unenviable but descriptive title the newcomer was known by; and though she knew it for her *sobriquet,* yet she also knew Mrs. Rooney would not call her by it if she were not in an ill temper, so she began humbly to explain the cause of her visit, when Mrs. Rooney broke in gruffly:

"Oh, you always make out a good rayson for coming; but we have nothing for you to-night."

"Throth, you do me wrong," said the beggar, "if you think I came *shooling.*[1] It's only to keep harm from the innocent girl here."

"Arrah, what harm would happen her, woman?" returned the widow, savagely, rendered more morose by the humble bearing of her against whom she directed her severity; as if she got more angry the less the poor creature would give her cause to justify her harshness. "Isn't she undher my roof, here?"

"But how long may she be left there?" asked the woman, significantly.

"What do you mane, woman?"

"I mane, there's a plan to carry her off from you to-night."

Oonah grew pale with true terror, and the widow screeched, after the more approved manner of elderly ladies, making believe they are very much shocked, till Nance reminded her that crying would do no good, and that it was requisite to make some preparation against the approaching danger. Various plans were hastily suggested, and as hastily relinquished, till Nance advised a measure which was deemed the best. It was to dress Andy in female attire, and let him be carried off in place of the girl. Andy roared with laughter at the notion of being made a girl of, and said the trick would instantly be seen through

"Not if you act your part well; just keep down the giggle, jewel, and put on a moderate *phillelew,* and do the thing nice and steady, and you'll be the saving of your cousin here."

"*You* may deceive them with the dhress; and *I* may do a bit of a small *shilloo,* like a *colleen* in disthress, and that's all very well," said Andy, "as far as seeing and hearing goes; but when they come to grip me, sure they'll find out in a minute."

"We'll stuff you out well with rags and sthraw, and they'll never know the differ—besides, remember the fellow that wants a girl never comes for her himself,[2] but sends his friends for her, and they won't know the differ—besides, they're all dhrunk."

"How do you know?"

"Because they're always dhrunk—that same crew; and if they're not dhrunk to-night, it's the first time in their lives they ever were sober. So make haste, now, and put off your coat till we make a purty young colleen out o' you."

It occurred now to the widow that it was a service of great danger Andy was called on to perform; and with all her abuse of her "*omadhawn,*" she did not like the notion of putting him in the way of losing his life, perhaps.

"They'll murdher the boy, maybe, when they find out the chate," said the widow.

"Not a bit," said Nance.

"And suppose they did," said Andy, "I'd rather die, sure, than disgrace should fall upon Oonah, there."

"God bless you, Andy, dear!" said Oonah. "Sure, you have the kind heart, anyhow; but I wouldn't for the world hurt or harm should come to you on my account."

"Oh, don't be afeard!" said Andy, cheerily; "divil a hair I value all they can do; so dhress me up at once."

After some more objections on the part of his mother, which Andy overruled, the women all joined in makmg up Andy into as tempting an imitation of feminality as they could contrive; but to bestow the roundness of outline on the angular forms of Andy, was no easy matter, and required more rags than the house afforded; so some straw was indispensable, which the pig's bed only could supply. In the midst of their fears, the women could not help laughing as they effected some likeness to their own forms, with their stuffing and padding; but to carry off the width of Andy's shoulders, required a very ample and voluptuous outline indeed; and Andy could not help wishing the straw was a little sweeter which they were packing under his nose. At last, however, after soaping down his straggling hair on his forehead, and tying a bonnet upon his head to shade his face as much as possible, the disguise was completed, and the next move was to put Oonah in a place of safety.

"Get up on the hurdle in the corner, under the thatch," said Nance.

"Oh, I'd be afeard o' my life to stay in the house at all."

"You'd be safe enough, I tell you," said Nance; "for once they see that fine young woman there," pointing to Andy, and laughing, "they'll be satisfied with the lob we've made for them."

Oonah still expressed her fear of remaining in the cabin.

"Then hide in the pratee thrench, behind the house."

"That's better," said Oonah.

"And now I must be going," said Nance; "for they must not see me when they come."

"Oh, don't leave me, Nance, dear," cried Oonah, "for I'm sure I'll faint with the fright when I hear them coming, if some one is not with me."

Nance yielded to Oonah's fears and entreaties; and with many a blessing and boundless thanks for the beggar-woman's kindness, Oonah led the way to the little potato garden at the back of the house, and there the women squatted themselves in one of the trenches, and awaited the impending event.

It was not long in arriving. The tramp of approaching horses at a sharp pace rang through the stillness of the night, and the women, crouching flat beneath the overspreading branches of the potato tops, lay breathless in the bottom of the trench, as the riders came up to the widow's cottage, and entered. There they found the widow and her pseudo niece sitting at the fire; and three drunken vagabonds, for the fourth was holding the horses outside, cut some fantastic capers round

the cabin, and making a mock obeisance to the widow, the spokesman
addressed her with,—

"Your sarvant, ma'am!"

"Who are yiz at all, gintlemin, that comes to my place at this time o'
night, and what's your business?"

"We want the loan o' that young woman there, ma'am," said the
ruffian.

Andy and his mother both uttered small squalls. "And as for who we
are, ma'am, we are the blessed society of Saint Joseph, ma'am,—our coat
of arms is two heads upon one pillow, and our motty, 'Who's afraid?—
hurroo!'" shouted the savage, and he twirled his stick, and cut another
caper. Then coming up to Andy, he addressed him as "young woman,"
and said there was a fine strapping fellow, whose heart was breaking till
he "rowled her in his arms."

Andy and the mother both acted their parts very well. He rushed to
the arms of the old woman for protection, and screeched small, while
the widow shouted "*millia murther!*" at the top of her voice, and did not
give up her hold of the make-believe young woman until her cap was
torn half off, and her hair streamed about her face. She called on all
the saints in the calendar, as she knelt in the middle of the floor, and
rocked to and fro, with her clasped hands raised to heaven, calling down
curses on the "villains and robbers," that were tearing her child from
her, while they threatened to stop her breath altogether if she did not
make less noise; and in the midst of the uproar dragged off Andy, whose
struggles and despair might have excited the suspicion of soberer men.
They lifted him up on a stout horse, in front of the most powerful man
of the party, who gripped Andy hard round the middle, and pushed his
horse to a hand gallop, followed by the rest of the party. The proximity
of Andy to his *cavaliero* made the latter sensible of the bad odour of
the pig's bed, which formed Andy's luxurious bust and bustle; but he
attributed the unsavoury scent to a bad breath on the lady's part, and
would sometimes address his charge thus:—

"Young woman, if you plaze, would you turn your face th'other way;"
then in a side soliloquy,—"By Jaker, I wondher at Jack's taste—she's a
fine lump of a girl, but her breath is murdher intirely—phew!—young
woman, turn away your face, or by this and that I'll fall off the horse.

I've heerd of a bad breath that might knock a man down, but I never met it till now.—Oh, murdher! it's worse it's growin'—I suppose 'tis the bumpin' she's gettin' that shakes the breath out of her sthrong—oh, there it is again!—phew!"

It was as well, perhaps, for the prosecution of the deceit, that the distaste the fellow conceived for his charge prevented any closer approaches to Andy's visage, which might have dispelled the illusion under which he still pushed forward to the hills, and bumped poor Andy towards the termination of his ride. Keeping a sharp look out as they went along, Andy soon was able to perceive they were making for that wild part of the hills where he had discovered the private still on the night of his temporary fright and imaginary rencontre with the giants, and the conversation he partly overheard all recurred to him, and he saw at once that Oonah was the person alluded to, whose name he could not catch; a circumstance that had cost him many a conjecture in the interim. This gave him a clue to the persons into whose power he was about to fall, after having so far defeated their scheme, and he saw he should have to deal with very desperate and lawless parties. Remembering, moreover, the herculean frame of the *innamorato*, he calculated on an awful thrashing as the smallest penalty he should have to pay for deceiving him, but was nevertheless determined to go through the adventure with a good heart, to make deceit serve his turn as long as he might, and at the last, if necessary, make the best fight he could.

As it happened, luck favoured Andy in his adventure, for the hero of the blunderbuss (and he, it will be remembered, was the love-sick gentleman), drank profusely on the night in question, quaffing deep potations to the health of his Oonah, wishing luck to his friends and speed to their horses, and every now and then ascending the ladder from the cave, and looking out for the approach of the party. On one of these occasions, from the unsteadiness of the ladder, or himself, or perhaps both, his foot slipped, and he came to the ground with a heavy fall, in which his head received so severe a blow, that he became insensible, and it was some time before his sister, who was an inhabitant of this den, could restore him to consciousness. This she did, however, and the savage recovered all the senses the whisky had left him, but still the stunning effect of the fall cooled his courage considerably, and, as it were, "bothered" him, so that he felt much less of the "gallant gay Lothario" than he had done before the accident.

The tramp of horses was heard overhead ere long, and *Shan More*, or Big John, as the Hercules was called, told Bridget to go up to "the darlin'," and help her down.

"For that's a blackguard laddher," said he; "it turned undher me like an eel, bad luck to it!—tell her, I'd go up myself, only the ground is slippin' from undher me,—and the laddher—"

Bridget went off, leaving Jack growling forth anathemas against the ground and the ladder, and returned speedily with the mock-lady and her attendant squires.

"Oh, my jewel!" roared Jack, as he caught sight of his prize. He scrambled up on his legs, and made a rush at Andy, who imitated a woman's scream and fright at the expected embrace, but it was with much greater difficulty he suppressed his laughter at the headlong fall with which Big Jack plunged his head into a heap of turf,[3] and hugged a sack of malt which lay beside it.

Andy endeavoured to overcome the provocation to merriment by screeching; and as Bridget caught the sound of this tendency towards laughter between the screams, she thought it was the commencement of a fit of hysterics, and it accounted all the better for Andy's extravagant antics.

"Oh, the craythur is frightened out of her life!" said Bridget. "Leave her to me," said she to the men.

"There, jewel machree!" she continued to Andy, soothingly,—"don't take on you that way,—don't be afeerd,—you're among friends,—Jack is only dhrunk dhrinking your health, darlin', but he adores you."

Andy screeched.

"But don't be afeerd,—you'll be thrated tender, and he'll marry you, darlin', like an honest woman!"

Andy squalled.

"But not to-night, jewel,—don't be frightened."

Andy gave a heavy sob at the respite.

"Boys, will you lift Jack out o' the turf, and carry him up into the air, 'twill be good for him, and this dacent girl will sleep with me to-night."

Andy couldn't resist a laugh at this, and Bridget feared the girl was going off into hysterics again.

"Aisy, dear—aisy,—sure you'll be safe with me."

"Ow! ow! ow!" shouted Andy.

"Oh, murther!" cried Bridget,—"the sterricks will be the death of her;—you blackguards, you frightened her, coming up here, I'm sure."

The men swore they behaved in the genteelest manner.

"Well, take away Jack, and the girl shall have share of my bed for this night."

Andy shook internally with laughter.

"Dear, dear, how she thrimbles," cried Bridget. "Don't be so frightful, *lanna machree*,—there, now,—they're taking Jack away, and you're alone with myself, and will have a nice sleep."

The men all the time were removing *Shan More* to upper air; and the last sounds they heard as they left the cave were the coaxing tones of Bridget's voice, inviting Andy, in the softest words, to go to bed.

1. Going on chance here and there, to pick up what one can.
2. This is mostly the case.
3. Peat.

XXXV

THE WORKSHOPS OF NECK-OR-NOTHING Hall rang with the sounds of occupation for two days after the demise of its former master. The hoarse grating sound of the saw, the whistling of the plane, and the stroke of the mallet, denoted the presence of the carpenter; and the sharper clink of a hammer told of old Fogy the family "milliner" being at work;—but it was not on millinery Fogy was now employed, though neither was it legitimate tinker's work. He was scrolling out with his shears, and beating into form, a plate of tin to serve for the shield on O'Grady's coffin, which was to record his name, age, and day of departure; and this was the second plate on which the old man worked, for one was already finished in the corner. Why are there two coffin-plates? Enter the carpenter's shop, and you will see the answer in two coffins the carpenter has nearly completed. But why two coffins for one death? Listen, reader, to a bit of Irish strategy.

It has been stated that an apprehension was entertained of a seizure of the inanimate body of O'Grady for the debts it had contracted in life, and the Harpy nature of the money from whom this movement was dreaded, warranted the fear. Had O'Grady been popular, such a measure on the part of a cruel creditor might have been defied, as the surrounding peasantry would have risen *en masse* to prevent it; but the hostile position in which he had placed himself towards the people, alienated the natural affection they are born with for their chiefs, and any partial defence the few fierce retainers whom individual interest had attached to him could have made, might have been insufficient; therefore, to save his father's remains from the pollution (as the son considered) of a bailiff's touch, Gustavus determined to achieve by stratagem what he could not accomplish by force, and had two coffins constructed, the one to be filled with stones and straw, and sent out by the front entrance, with all the demonstration of a real funeral, and be given up to the attack it was feared would be made upon it; while the other, put to its legitimate use, should be placed on a raft, and floated down the river to an ancient burial-ground, which lay some miles below on the opposite bank. A facility for this was offered by a branch of the river running up into the domain, as it will be remembered; and the scene of the bearish freaks played upon Furlong was to witness a trick of a more serious nature.

While all these preparations were going forward, the "waking" was kept up in all the barbarous style of old times, and drinking in profusion went on in the house, and the kitchen of the hall rang with joviality. The feats of sports and arms of the man who had passed away were lauded, and his comparative achievements with those of his progenitors gave rise to many a stirring anecdote; and bursts of barbarous exultation, or more barbarous merriment, rang in the house of death. There was no lack of whisky to fire the brains of these revellers, for the standard of the measurement of family grandeur was too often a liquid one in Ireland, even so recently as the time we speak of; and the dozens of wine wasted during the life it helped to shorten, and the posthumous gallons consumed in toasting to the memory of the departed, were among the cherished remembrances of hereditary honour. "There were two hogsheads of whisky drank at my father's wake!" would have been but a moderate boast of a true Irish squire, fifty years ago.

And now the last night of the wake approached, and the retainers thronged to honour the obsequies of their departed chief with an increased enthusiasm, which rose in proportion as the whisky got low; and songs in praise of their present occupation (that is, getting drunk), rang merrily round, and the sports of the field, and the sorrows and joys of love resounded; in short, the ruling passions of life figured in rhyme and music in honour of this occasion of death; and as death is the maker of widows, a very animated discussion on the subject of widowhood arose, which afforded great scope for the rustic wits, and was crowned by the song of "Widow Machree" being universally called for by the company; and a fine looking fellow, with a merry eye and large white teeth, which he amply displayed by a wide mouth, poured forth in cheery tones a pretty lively air, which suited well the humorous spirit of the words:—

WIDOW MACHREE

I

"Widow *machree*, it's no wonder you frown,
　　Och hone! widow machree;
Faith, it ruins your looks, that same dirty black gown,
　　Och hone! widow machree.
How altered your air,
With that close cap you wear—
'Tis destroying your hair
　　Which should be flowing free:
Be no longer a churl
Of its black silken curl,
　　Och hone! widow machree!

II

"Widow machree, now the summer is come,
　　Och hone! widow machree;
When every thing smiles, should a beauty look glum?
　　Och hone! widow machree.
See the birds go in pairs,
And the rabbits and hares—
Why even the bears
　　Now in couples agree;
And the mute little fish,
Though they can't spake, they wish,
　　Och hone! widow machree.

III

"Widow machree, and when winter comes in,
   Och hone! widow machree,
To be poking the fire all alone is a sin,
   Och hone! widow machree.
Why the shovel and tongs
To each other belongs,
And the kittle sings songs
   Full of family glee:
While alone with your cup,
Like a hermit *you* sup,
   Och hone! widow machree.

IV

"And how do you know, with the comforts I've towld,
   Och hone! widow machree,
But you're keeping some poor fellow out in the cowld,
   Och hone I widow machree.
With such sins on your head,
Sure your peace would be fled,
Could you sleep in your bed,
   Without thinking to see
Some ghost or some sprite,
That would wake you each night,
   Crying, 'Och hone! widow machree.

V

"Then take my advice, darling widow machree.
   Och hone! widow machree.
And with my advice, faith I wish you'd take me,
   Och hone! widow machree,
You'd have me to desire
Then to stir up the fire;

And sure Hope is no liar
    In whispering to me
That the ghosts would depart,
When you'd me near your heart,
    Och hone! widow machree."

The singer was honoured with a round of applause, and his challenge
for another lay was readily answered, and mirth and music filled the
night and ushered in the dawn of the day which was to witness the
melancholy sight of the master of an ample mansion being made the
tenant of the "narrow house."

In the evening of that day, however, the wail rose loud and long; the mirth
which "the waking" permits had passed away, and the *ulican*, or funeral cry,
told that the lifeless chief was being borne from his hall. That wild cry was
heard even by the party who were waiting to make their horrid seizure, and
for *that* party, the stone-laden coffin was sent with a retinue of mourners
through the old iron gate of the principal entrance, while the mortal
remains were borne by a smaller party to the river inlet, and placed on the
raft. Half-an-hour had witnessed a sham fight on the part of O'Grady's
people with the bailiffs and their followers, who made the seizure they
intended, and locked up their prize in an old barn to which it had been
conveyed, until some engagement on the part of the heir should liberate it;
while the aforesaid heir, as soon as the shadows of evening had shrouded
the river in obscurity, conveyed the remains, which the myrmidons of the
law fancied they possessed, to its quiet and lonely resting-place. The raft
was taken in tow by a boat carrying two of the boys, and pulled by four
lusty retainers of the departed chief; while Gustavus himself stood on the
raft, astride above the coffin, and with an eel spear, which had afforded him
many a day's sport, performed the melancholy task of guiding it. It was a
strangely painful yet beautiful sight, to behold the graceful figure of the
fine boy engaged in this last, sad duty: with dexterous energy he plied his
spear, now on this side and now on that, directing the course of the raft,
or clearing it from the flaggers which interrupted its passage through the
narrow inlet. This duty he had to attend to for some time, even after leaving
the little inlet, for the river was much overgrown with flaggers at this point,
and the increasing darkness made the task more difficult.

In the midst of all this action not one word was spoken; even the sturdy boatmen were mute, and the fall of the oar in the rowlock, the plash of the water, and the crushing sound of the yielding rushes, as the "watery bier" made its way through them, were the only sounds which broke the silence. Still Gustavus betrayed no emotion; but by the time they reached the open stream, and that his personal exertion was longer required, a change came over him. It was night,—the measured beat of the oars sounded like a knell to him,—there was darkness above him, and death below, and he sank down upon the coffin, and, plunging his face passionately between his hands, he wept bitterly.

Sad were the thoughts that oppressed the brain and wrung the heart of the high-spirited boy. He felt that his dead father was *escaping*, as it were, to the grave,—that even death did not terminate the consequences of an ill-spent life. He felt like a thief in the night, even in the execution of his own stratagem, and the bitter thoughts of that sad and solemn time wrought a potent spell over after years,—that one hour of misery and disgrace influenced the entire of a future life.

On a small hill overhanging the river was the ruin of an ancient early temple of Christianity, and to its surrounding burial-ground a few of the retainers had been despatched to prepare a grave. They were engaged in this task by the light of a torch made of bog pine, when the flicker of the flame attracted the eye of a horseman who was riding slowly along the neighbouring road. Wondering what could be the cause of light in such a place, he leaped the adjoining fence, and rode up to the grave yard.

"What are you doing here?" he said to the labourers. They paused and looked up, and the flash of the torch fell upon the features of Edward O'Connor.

"We're finishing your work!" said one of the men, with malicious earnestness.

"My work?" repeated Edward.

"Yis," returned the man, more sternly than before,—"this is the grave of O'Grady."

The words went like an ice-bolt through Edward's heart; and even by the torch-light the tormentor could see his victim grew livid.

The fellow who wounded so deeply one so generally beloved as Edward O'Connor was a thorough ruffian. His answer to Edward's query sprang not from love of O'Grady, nor abhorrence of taking human life, but from the opportunity of retort which the occasion offered upon one who had once checked him in an act of brutality.

Yet Edward O'Connor could not reply,—it was a home-thrust. The death of O'Grady had weighed heavily upon him; for though O'Grady's wound had been given in honourable combat, provoked by his own fury, and not producing immediate death; though that death had supervened upon the subsequent intractability of the patient; yet the fact that O'Grady had never been "up and doing" since the duel, tended to give the impression that his wound was the remote if not the immediate cause of his death, and this circumstance weighed heavily on Edward's spirits. His friends told him he felt over-keenly on the subject, and that no one but himself could entertain a question of his total innocence of O'Grady's death; but when from the lips of a common peasant he got the answer he did, and *that* beside the grave of his adversary, it will not be wondered at that he reeled in his saddle. A cold shivering sickness came over him, and to avoid falling he alighted, and leaned for support against his horse, which stooped, when freed from the restraint of the rein, to browse on the rank verdure; and for the moment Edward envied the unconsciousness of the animal against which he leaned. He pressed his forehead against the saddle, and from the depth of a bleeding heart came up the agonized exclamation of "O God! O God!"

A gentle hand was laid on his shoulder as he spoke, and turning round, he beheld Mr. Bermingham.

"What brings you here?" said the clergyman.

"Accident," answered Edward. "But why should I say accident?—It is by a higher authority and a better—it is the will of Heaven. It is meant as a bitter lesson to human pride:—we make for ourselves laws of *honour*, and forget the laws of God!"

"Be calm, my young friend," said the worthy pastor; "I cannot wonder you feel deeply,—but command yourself." He pressed Edward's hand as he spoke, and left him, for he knew that an agony so keen is not benefited by companionship.

Mr. Bermingham was there by appointment, to perform the burial service, and he had not left Edward's side many minutes when a long, wild whistle from the waters announced the arrival of the boat and raft, and the retainers ran down to the river, leaving the pine-torch stuck in the upturned earth, waving its warm blaze over the cold grave. During the interval which ensued between the departure of the men and their reappearance, bearing the body to its last resting-place, Mr. Bermingham spoke with Edward O'Connor, and soothed him into a more tranquil bearing. When the coffin came within view, he advanced to meet it, and began the sublime burial-service, which he repeated most impressively.

When it was over, the men commenced filling up the grave.

As the clods fell heavily upon the coffin, they smote the hearts of the dead man's children; yet the boys stood upon the verge of the grave as long as a vestige of the tenement of their lost father could be seen; but as soon as the coffin was hidden, they withdrew from the brink, and the younger boys, each taking hold of the hand of the eldest, seemed to imply the need of mutual dependence:—as if death had drawn closer the bond of brotherhood.

There was no sincerer mourner at that place than Edward O'Connor, who stood aloof, in respect for the feelings of the children of the departed man, till the grave was quite filled up, and all were about to leave the spot; but then his feelings overmastered him, and, impelled by a torrent of contending emotions, he rushed forward, and throwing himself on his knees before Gustavus, he held up his hands imploringly, and sobbed forth, "Forgive me!"

The astonished boy drew back.

"Oh, forgive me!" repeated Edward,—"I could not help it—it was forced on me—it was—"

As he struggled for utterance, even the rough retainers were touched, and one of them exclaimed, "Oh, Mr. O'Connor, it was a fair fight!"

"There!" exclaimed Edward,—"you hear it!—Oh, give me your hand in forgiveness!"

"I forgive you," said the boy, "but do not ask me to give you my hand to-night."

"You are right," said Edward, springing to his feet,—"you are right,—you are a noble fellow; and now, remember, Gustavus, by the side of your father's grave, I pledge you my soul, that through life and till death, in all extremity, Edward O'Connor is your sworn and trusty friend."

XXXVI

WHILE THE FOREGOING SCENE OF sadness took place in the lone church-yard, unholy watch was kept over the second coffin by the myrmidons of the law. The usurer who made the seizure, had brought down from Dublin three of the most determined bailiffs from amongst the tribe, and to their care was committed the keeping of the supposed body in the old barn. Associated with these worthies were a couple of ill-conditioned country blackguards, who, for the sake of a bottle of whisky, would keep company with old Nick himself, and who expected, moreover, to hear "a power o'news" from the "gentlemen" from Dublin, who in their turn did not object to have their guard strengthened, as their notions of a rescue in the country parts of Ireland were anything but agreeable. The night was cold, so, clearing away the sheaves of corn, with which the barn was stored, from one of its extremities, they made a turf fire, and stretched themselves on a good shake-down of straw before the cheering blaze, and circulated among them a bottle of whisky, of which they had good store. A tap at the door announced a new comer; but the Dublin bailiffs, fearing a surprise, hesitated to open to the knock, until their country allies assured them it was a friend, whose voice they recognised. The door was opened, and in walked Larry Hogan, to pick up his share of what was going, whatever it might be.

"I thought you wor for keepin' me out altogether," said Larry.

"The gintlemin from Dublin was afeard of what they call a riskya," (rescue) said the peasant, "till I tould them 'twas a friend."

"Divil a riskya will come near you to-night," said Larry, "you may make your minds aisy about that, for the people doesn't care enough about *his* bones to get their own broke in savin' him; and no wondher. It's a lantherumswash bully he always was, quiet as he is now. And there you are, my bowld squire," said he, apostrophizing the coffin, which had been thrown on a heap of sheaves. "Faix, it's a good kitchen you kep' any how, whenever you had it to spind, and indeed, when you *hadn't*, you spint it all the same, for the divil a much you cared how you got it; but death has made you pay the reckoning at last—that thing that filly-officers call the debt o' nature must be paid, whatever else you may owe."

"Why, it's as good as a sarmon to hear you," said one of the bailiffs.

"O Larry, Sir, discourses iligant," answered the peasant.

"Tut, tut, tut," said Larry, with affected modesty; "it's not what I say, but I can tell you a thing that Docthor Growlin' put out an him more nor a year ago, which was mighty cute. Scholars calls it an 'epithet of dissipation,' which means getting a man's tombstone ready for him before he dies; and divil a more cutting thing was ever cut on a tombstone than the doctor's rhyme; this is it:—

> 'Here lies O'Grady, that cantankerous creature,
> Who paid, as all must pay, the debt of nature;
> But, keeping to his general maxim still,
> Paid it—like other debts—against his will.'"[1]

"What do you think o' that, Goggins?" inquired one of the bailiffs from, the other; "you are a judge o' po'thry."

"It's *sevare*," answered Goggins, authoritatively; "but *coorse*.—I wish you'd brile the rashers, I begin to feel the calls o' nature, as the poet says."

This Mister Goggins was a character in his way. He had the greatest longing to be thought a poet, put execrable couplets together sometimes, and always talked as fine as he could; and his mixture of sentimentality, with a large stock of blackguardism, produced a strange jumble.

"The people here thought it *nate*, Sir," said Larry.

"Oh, very well for the country!" said Goggins; "but 'twouldn't do for town."

"Misther Goggins knows best," said the bailiff who first spoke, "for he's a pote himself, and writes in the newspapers."

"Oh, indeed!" said Larry.

"Yes," said Goggins, "sometimes I throw off little things for the newspapers. There's a friend of mine, you see, a gentleman connected with the press, who is often in defficulties, and I give him a hint to keep out o' the way when he's in trouble, and he swares I have a genus for the muses, and encourages me—"

"Humph!" says Larry.

"And puts in my things in the paper, when he gets the editor's back turned, for the editor is a consaited chap, that likes no one's po'thry but his own; but never mind—if I ever get a writ against that chap, *won't* I sarve it!"

"And I dar say some day you will have it agen him, Sir," said Larry.

"Sure of it, a'most," said Goggins, "them litherary men is always in defficulties."

"I wondher you'd be like them, then, and write at all," said Larry.

"Oh, as for me, it's only by way of amusement; attached as I am to the legal profession, my time wouldn't permit; but I have been infected by the company I kept. The living images that creeps over a man sometimes is irresitible, and you have no pace till you get them out o' your head."

"Oh, indeed, they are very throublesome," says Larry, "and are the latherary gintlemen, Sir, as you call them, mostly that way?"

"To be sure; it is *that* which makes a litherary man—his head is full—teems with creation, Sir."

"Dear, dear!" said Larry.

"And when once the itch of litherature comes over a man, nothing can cure it but the scratching of a pen."

"But if you have not a pen, I suppose you must scratch any other way you can."

"To be sure," said Goggins, "I have seen a litherary gentleman in a sponging house do crack things on the wall, with a bit of burnt stick, rather than be idle—they must execute."

"Ha!" says Larry.

"Sometimes, in all their poverty and defficulty, I envy the 'fatal fatality,' as the poet says, of such men in catching ideas."

"That's the genteel name, for it, I suppose," says Larry.

"Oh!" exclaimed Goggins, enthusiastically. "I know the satisfaction of catching a man, but it's nothing at all compared to catching an idea. For the man, you see, can give bail, and get off, but the idea is your own for ever. And then a rhyme—when it has puzzled you all day, the pleasure you have in *nabbing* it at last!"

"Oh, then it's po'thry you're spakin' about," said Larry.

"To be sure," said Goggins; "do you think I'd throw away my time on prose?"—"You're burning that bacon, Tim," said he to his *sub*.

"Poethry agen the world!" continued he to Larry, "the Castilian sthraime for me!—Hand us that whisky"—he put the bottle to his lips and took a swig—"That's good—you do a bit of private here, I suspect," said he, with a wink at Larry, and pointing to the bottle.

Larry returned a significant grin, but said nothing. "Oh, don't be afraid o' me—I wouldn't 'peach"—"Sure it's agen the law, and you're a gintleman o' the law," said Larry.

"That's no rule," said Goggins, "the lord chief justice always goes to bed, they say, with six tumblers o' potteen under his belt; and I always dhrink it myself."

"Arrah, how do you get it?" said Larry. "From a gentleman, a friend o' mine, in the custom house."

"A-dad, that's quare," said Larry, laughing.

"Oh, we see queer things, I tell you," said Goggins, "we gentlemen of the law."

"To be sure you must," returned Larry, "and mighty improvin' it must be. Did you ever catch a thief, Sir?

"My good man, you mistake my profession," said Goggins, proudly; "we never have any thing to do in the *criminal* line—that's much beneath *us*."

"I ax your pardon, Sir."—

"No offence, no offence."

"But it must be mighty improvin', I think, ketching of thieves, and finding out their thricks and hidin' places, and the like?"

"Yes, yes," said Goggins, "good fun; though I don't do it, I know all about it, and could tell queer things too."

"Arrah, maybe you would, Sir?" said Larry.

"Maybe I will, after we nibble some rashers—will you take share?"

"Musha, long life to you," said Larry, always willing to get whatever he could. A repast was now made, more resembling a feast of savages round their war-fire, than any civilized meal; slices of bacon broiled in the fire, and eggs roasted in the turf-ashes. The viands were not objectionable; but the cooking!—Oh!—There was neither gridiron nor frying-pan, fork nor spoon; a couple of clasp-knives served the whole party. Nevertheless, they satisfied their hunger, and then sent the bottle on its exhilarating round. Soon after that many a story of burglary, robbery, swindling, petty larceny, and every conceivable crime, was related for the amusement of the circle; and the plots and counter-plots of thieves and thief-takers raised the wonder of the peasants.

Larry Hogan was especially delighted: more particularly when some trick of either villany or cunning came out.

"Now, women are troublesome cattle to deal with mostly," said Goggins. "They are remarkably cute first, and then they are spiteful after; and for circumventin' *either* way, are sharp hands. You see they do it quieter than men; a man will make a noise about it, but a woman does it all on the sly. There was Bill Morgan, and a sharp fellow too, and he had set his heart on some silver spoons he used to see down in a kitchen windy, but the servant maid, somehow or other, suspected there was designs about the place, and was on the watch.—Well, one night when she was all alone, she heard a noise outside the windy, so she kept as quiet as a mouse. By an' by the sash was attempted to be raised from the outside, so she laid hold of a kettle of boiling wather, and stood hid behind the shutter. The windy was now raised a little, and a hand and arm thrust in to throw up the sash altogether, when the girl poured the boiling water down the sleeve of Bill's coat. Bill roared with the pain, when the girl said to him, laughing, through the windy—'I thought you came for something.'"

"That was a cute girl," said Larry, chuckling.

"Well, now, that's an instance of a woman's cleverness in preventing. I'll tell you one of her determinations to discover, and prosecute to conviction; and in this case, what makes it curious is, that Jack Tate had done the bowldest things, and run the greatest risks, 'the eminent deadly,' as the poet says, when he was done up at last by a feather-bed."

"A feather-bed," repeated Larry, wondering how a feather-bed could influence the fate of a bold burglar, while Goggins mistook his exclamation of surprise to signify the paltriness of the prize, and therefore chimed in with him.

"Quite true—no wonder you wonder—quite below a man of his pluck; but the fact was, a sweetheart of his was longing for a feather-bed, and Jack determined to get it. Well, he marched into a house, the, door of which he found open, and went up stairs and took the best feather-bed in the house, tied it up in the best quilt, crammed some caps and ribbons he saw lying about into the bundle, and marched down stairs again; but you see, in carrying off even the small thing of a feather-bed, Jack showed the skill of a high practitioner, for he descendhered the stairs backwards."

"Backwards," said Larry, "what was that for?"

"You'll see, by and by," said Goggins; "he descendhered backwards, when suddenly he heerd a door opening, and a faymale voice exclaim, 'Where are you going with that bed?'

"'I am going up stairs with it, ma'am,' said Jack, whose backward position favoured his lie; and he began to walk up again.

"'Come down here,' said the lady, 'we want no beds here, man.'

"'Mr. Sullivan, ma'am, sent me home with it himself,' said Jack, still mounting the stairs.

"'Come down, I tell you,' said the lady, in a great rage. 'There's no Mr. Sullivan lives here,—go out of this with your bed, you stupid fellow.'

"'I beg your pardon, ma'am,' says Jack, turning round, and marching off with the bed fair and aisy.

"Well, there was a regular shilloo in the house when the thing was found out, and cart ropes wouldn't howld the lady for the rage she was in at being diddled; so she offered rewards, and the dickens knows all; and what do you think at last discovered our poor Jack?"

"The sweetheart, maybe," said Larry, grinning in ecstasy at the thought of human perfidy.

"No," said Goggins, "honour even among sweethearts, though they do the trick sometimes, I confess; but no woman of any honour would betray a great man like Jack. No—'twas one of the paltry ribbons that brought conviction home to him; the woman never lost sight of hunting up evidence about her feather-bed, and, in the end, a ribbon out of one of her caps settled the hash of Jack Tate."

From robbings they went on to tell of murders, and at last that uncomfortable sensation which people experience after a feast of horrors, began to pervade the party; and whenever, they looked round, there was the coffin in the background.

"Throw some turf on the fire," said Goggins, "'tis burning low, and change the subject; the tragic muse has reigned sufficiently long—Aenough of the dagger and the bowl—sink the socks, and put on the buckskins.—Leather away, Jim—sing us a song."

"What is it to be?" asked Jim.

"Oh—that last song of the Solicitor-General's," said Goggins, with an air as if the Solicitor-General were his particular friend.

"About the robbery?" inquired Jim.

"To be sure," returned Goggins.

"Dear me," said Larry, "and would so grate a man as the Solicithor-Giniral demane himself by writin' about robbers?"

"Oh!" said Goggins, "those in the heavy professi n of the law must have their little private moments of rollickzatio 1; and them high men, you see, like to do a bit of low by way of ariety. 'The Night before Larry was stretched,' was done by a bishop, they say; and 'Lord Altamont's Bull' by the Lord Chief Justice; and the Solicitor-General is as up to fun as any bishop of them all.—Come, Jim, tip us the stave!"

Jim cleared his throat and obeyed his chief.

THE QUAKER'S MEETING

I

"A traveller wended the wilds among,
With a purse of gold and a silver tongue;
His hat it was broad, and all drab were his clothes,
For he hated high colours—except on his nose,
And he met with a lady, the story goes.
  Heigho! *yea* thee and *nay* thee.

II

"The damsel she cast him a merry blink,
And the traveller nothing was loth, I think;
Her merry black eye beamed her bonnet beneath,
And the quaker he grinned, for he'd very good teeth,
And he ask'd, 'Art thee going to ride on the heath?'
    Heigho! *yea* thee and *nay* thee.

II

"'I hope you'll protect me, kind sir,' said the maid,
'As to ride this heath over I'm sadly afraid;
For robbers, they say, here in numbers abound,
And I wouldn't 'for anything' I should be found,
For—between you and me—I have five hundred pound.'
    Heigho! *yea* thee and *nay* thee.

IV

"'If that is thee² own, dear,' the quaker he said,
'I ne'er saw a maiden I sooner would wed;
And I have another five hundred just now,
In the padding that's under my saddle bow,
And I'll settle it all upon thee, I vow!'
    Heigho! *yea* thee and *nay* thee.

V

"The maiden she smil'd, and her rein she drew,
'Your offer I'll take—though I'll not take you;'
A pistol she held at the quaker's head—
'Now give me your gold—or I'll give you my lead—
'Tis under the saddle, I think you said.'
    Heigho! *yea* thee and *nay* thee.

VI

"The damsel she ripp'd up the saddle-bow,
And the quaker was never a quaker till now;
And he saw by the fair one he wish'd for a bride
His purse borne away with a swaggering stride,
And the eye that look'd tender, now only defied.
   Heigho! *yea* thee and *nay* thee.

VII

"'The spirit doth move me, friend Broad-brim,' quoth she,
'To take all this filthy temptation from thee,
For Mammon deceiveth—and beauty is fleeting;
Accept from thy *maai-d'n* a right loving greeting,
For much doth she profit by this quaker's meeting.
   Heigho! *yea* thee and *nay* thee,

VIII

"'And hark! jolly quaker, so rosy and sly,
Have righteousness more than a wench in thine eye,
Don't go again peeping girls' bonnets beneath,
Remember the one that you met on the heath,
Her name's *Jimmy* Barlow—I tell to your teeth!'
   Heigho! *yea* thee and *nay* thee.

IX

"'*Friend* James,' quoth the quaker, 'pray listen to me,
For thou canst confer a great favour, d'ye see;
The gold thou hast taken is not mine, my friend,
But my master's—and truly on thee I depend
To make it appear I my trust did defend.
   Heigho! *yea* thee and *nay* thee.

X

"'So fire a few shots through my clothes, here and there,
To make it appear 'twas a desp'rate affair.'
So Jim he popped first through the skirt of his coat,
And then through his collar—quite close to his throat;
'Now once through my broad brim,' quoth Ephraim, 'I
vote.'
    Heigho! *yea* thee and *nay* thee.

XI

"I have but a brace,' said bold Jim, 'and they're spent,
And I won't load again for a make-believe rent.'—
'Then'—said Ephraim—producing *his* pistols—'just give
My five hundred pounds back—or as sure as you live
I'll make of your body a riddle or sieve.'
    Heigho! *yea* thee and *nay* thee.'

XII

"Jim Barlow was diddled—and though he was game,
He saw Ephaim's pistol so deadly in aim,
That he gave up the gold, and he took to his scrapers,
And when the whole story got into the papers,
They said that '*the thieves were no match for the quakers.*'
    Heigho! *yea* thee and *nay* thee."

"Well, it's a quare thing you should be singin' a song here," said Larry
Hogan, "about Jim Barlow, and it's not over half a mile out o' this very
place he was hanged."

"Indeed!" exclaimed all the men at once, looking with great interest
at Larry.

"It's truth I'm telling you. He made a very bowld robbery up by the
long hill there, on two gentlemin, for he was mighty stout."

"Pluck to the backbone," said Goggins.

"Well, he tuk the purses aff both o' them; and just as he was goin' on afther doin' that same, what should appear on the road before him, but two other thravellers coming up forninst him. With that the men that was robbed cried out 'Stop thief!' and so Jim, seein' himself hemmed in betune the four o' them, faced his horse to the ditch, and took across the counthry; but the thravellers was well mounted as well as himself, and powdhered afther him like mad. Well, it was equal to a steeple chase a'most; and Jim, seein' he could not shake them off, thought the best thing he could do was to cut out some throublesome work for them; so he led off where he knew there was the divil's own leap to take, and he intended to 'pound³ them there, and be off in the mane time; but as ill luck would have it, his own horse, that was as bowld as himself, and would jump at the moon if he was faced to it, missed his foot in takin' off, and fell short o' the leap and slipped his shouldher, and Jim himself had a bad fall of it too, and, av coorse, it was all over wid him—and up came the four gintlemen.—Well, Jim had his pistols yet, and he pulled them out, and swore he'd shoot the first man that attempted to take him; but the gintlemen had pistols as well as he, and were so hot on the chase they determined to have him, and closed on him. Jim fired and killed one o' them; but he got a ball in the shouldher himself from another, and he was taken. Jim sthruv to shoot himself with his second pistol, but it missed fire. 'The curse o' the road is on me,' said Jim; "my pistol missed fire, and my horse slipped his shouldher, and now I'll be scragged,' says he, 'but it's not for nothing—I've killed one o' ye,' says he."

"He was all pluck," said Goggins.

"Desperate bowld," said Larry.—"Well, he was thried and condimned, *av coorse*; and was hanged, as I tell you, half a mile out o' this very place where we are sittin', and his appearance walks, they say, ever since."

"You don't say so!" said Goggins.

"Faith, it's thrue!" answered Larry.

"You never saw it," said Goggins.

"The Lord forbid! " returned Larry; "but it's thrue, for all that. For you see the big house near this barn, that is all in ruin, was desarted because Jim's ghost used to walk."

"That was foolish," 'said Goggins; "stir up the fire, Jim, and hand me the whisky."

"Oh, if it was only walkin', they might have got over that; but at last, one night, as the story goes, when there was a thremendious storm o' wind and rain—"

"Whisht!" said one of the peasants, "what's that?"

As they listened they heard the beating of heavy rain against the door, and the wind howled through its chinks.

"Well," said Goggins, "what are you stopping for?"

"Oh, I'm not stoppin'," said Larry; "I was sayin' that it was a bad wild night, and Jimmy Barlow's appearance came into the house, and asked them for a glass o' sper'ts, and that he'd be obleeged to them if they'd help him with his horse that slipped his shouldher and, faith, afther *that* they'd stay in the place no longer; and, signs on it, the house is gone to rack and ruin, and it's only this barn that is kept up at all, because it's convaynient for owld Skinflint on the farm."

"That's all nonsense," said Goggins, who wished, nevertheless, that he had not heard the 'nonsense.'

"Come, sing another song, Jim."

Jim said he did not remember one.

"Then you sing, Ralph."

Ralph said every one knew he never did more than join in a chorus.

"Then join me in a chorus," said Goggins, "for I'll sing, if Jim's afraid."

"I'm not afraid," said Jim.

"Then why won't you sing?"

"Because I don't like."

"Ah!" exclaimed Goggins.

"Well, maybe you're afraid yourself," said Jim, "if you told truth."

"Just to show you how little I'm afraid," said Goggins, with a swaggering air, "I'll sing another song about Jimmy Barlow."

"You'd better not," said Larry Hogan; "let him rest in pace!"

"Fudge!" said Goggins.

"Jim?"

"I will," said Jim, fiercely.

"We'll all join," said the men, (except Larry,) who felt it would be a sort of relief to bully away the supernatural terror which hung round their hearts after the ghost story, by the sound of their own voices.

"Then here goes!" said Goggins, who started another long ballad about Jimmy Barlow, in the opening of which all joined. It ran as follow:—

> "My name it is Jimmy Barlow,
> I was born in the town of Carlow,
> And here I lie in Maryborough jail,
> All for the robbing of the Wicklow mail,
>   Fol de rol de riddle i-do!"

As it would be tiresome to follow this ballad through all its length, breadth, and thickness, we shall leave the singers engaged in their chorus, while we call the reader's attention to a more interesting person than Mister Goggins or Jimmy Barlow.

1. These bitter lines were really written by a medical man against a bad pay.
2. The inferior class of quakers make *thee* serve not only its own grammatical use but also do the duty of *thy* and *thine*.
3. Impound.

XXXVII

WHEN EDWARD O'CONNOR HAD HURRIED from the burial-place, he threw himself into his saddle, and urged his horse to speed, anxious to fly the spot where his feelings had been so harrowed; and as he swept along through the cold night wind which began to rise in gusty fits, and howled past him, there was, in the violence of his rapid motion, something congenial to the fierce career of painful thoughts which chased each other through his heated brain. He continued to travel at this rapid pace, so absorbed in bitter reflection as to be quite insensible to external impressions, and he knew not how far nor how fast he was going, though the heavy breathing of his horse at any other time would have been signal sufficient to draw the rein; but still he pressed onward, and still the storm increased, and each acclivity was topped but to sweep down the succeeding slope at the same desperate pace. Hitherto the road over which he pursued his fleet career lay through an open country, and though the shades a stormy night hung above it, the horse could make his way in safety through the gloom; but now they approached an old road which skirted an ancient domain, whose venerable trees threw their arms across the old causeway, and added their shadows to the darkness of the night.

Many and many a time had Edward ridden in the soft summer under the green shade of these very trees, in company with Fanny Dawson, his guiltless heart full of hope and love;—perhaps it was this very thought crossing his mind at the moment which made his present circumstances the more oppressive. He was guiltless no longer,—he rode not in happiness with the woman he adored under the soft shade of summer trees, but heard the wintry wind howl through their leafless boughs as he hurried in maddened speed beneath them, and heard in the dismal sound but an echo of the voice of remorse which was ringing through his heart. The darkness was intense from the canopy of old oaks which overhung the road, but still the horse was urged through the dark ravine at speed, though one might not see an arm's length before them. Fearlessly it was performed, though ever and anon, as the trees swung about their heavy branches in the storm, smaller portions of the boughs were snapped off and flung in the faces of the horse and the rider, who still spurred and plashed his headlong way through the heavy road beneath. Emerging at length from the deep and overshadowed valley, a steep hill raised its crest in advance, but still up the stony acclivity the feet of the mettled steed rattled rapidly, and flashed fire from the flinty path. As they approached the top of the hill the force of the storm became more apparent, and on reaching its crest, the fierce pelting of the mingled rain and hail made the horse impatient of the storm of which his rider was heedless,—almost unconscious. The spent animal with short snortings betokened his labour, and shook his head passionately as the fierce hail shower struck him in the eyes and nostrils. Still, however, was he urged downward, but he was no longer safe. Quite blown, and pressed over a rough descent, the generous creature, that would die rather than refuse, made a false step, and came heavily to the ground. Edward was stunned by the fall, though not seriously hurt; and, after the lapse of a few seconds, recovered his feet, but found the horse still prostrate. Taking the animal by the head, he assisted him to rise, which he was not enabled to do till after several efforts; and when he regained his legs, it was manifest he was seriously lamed; and as he limped along with difficulty beside his master, who led him gently, it became evident that it was beyond the animal's power to reach his own stable that night. Edward for the first time was now aware of how much he had punished his horse; he felt ashamed of using the noble brute with such severity, and became conscious that he had been acting under something little short of frenzy. The consciousness at once tended to restore him somewhat to himself, and he began to look around on every side in search of some house where he could find rest and shelter for his disabled horse. As he proceeded thus, the care

necessarily bestowed on his dumb companion partially called off his
thoughts from the painful theme with which they had been exclusively
occupied, and the effect was most beneficial. The first violent burst of
feeling was past, and a calmer train of thought succeeded; he for the
first time remembered the boy had forgiven him,—and that was a
great consolation to him: he recalled, too, his own words, pledging to
Gustavus his friendship, and in this pleasing hope of the future he saw
much to redeem what he regretted of the past. Still, however, the wild
flare of the pine-torch over the lone grave of his adversary, and the
horrid answer of the grave that he was but "finishing *his* work," would
recur to his memory, and awake an internal groan.

From this painful reminiscence he sought to escape, by looking
forward to all he would do for Gustavus, and had become much calmer,
when the glimmer of a light not far ahead attracted him, and he soon
was enabled to perceive it proceeded from some buildings that lay on
his right, not far from the road. He turned up the rough path which
formed the approach, and the light escaped through the chinks of a
large door, which indicated the place to be a coach-house, or some
such office, belonging to the general pile, which seemed in a ruinous
condition.

As he approached, Edward heard rude sounds of merriment, amongst
which the joining of many voices, in a "ree-raw" chorus, indicated that
a carouse was going forward within.

On reaching the door, he could perceive through a wide chink a
group of men sitting round a turf fire, which was piled at the far end of
the building, which had no fire-place, and the smoke, curling upwards
to the roof, wreathed the rafters in smoke; beneath this vapoury canopy
the party sat drinking and singing, and Edward, ere he knocked for
admittance, listened to the following strange refrain.

> "For my name it is Jimmy Barlow,
> I was born in the town of Carlow,
> And here I lie in Maryboroughy
> All for the robbing of the Wicklow mail,
>   Fol de rol de riddle-iddle-ido!"

Then the principal singer took up the song, which seemed to be one of robbery, blood, and murder, for it ran thus:—

> "Then he cocked his pistol gaily,
> And stood before him bravely,
> Smoke and fire is my desire,
> So blaze away, my game squire.
> *For my name it is Jimmy Barlow,*
>   *I was born, &c."*

Edward O'Connor knocked at the door loudly; the words he had just heard about "pistols," "blazing away," and, last of all, "*squire*," fell gratingly on his ear at that moment, and seemed strangely to connect themselves with the previous adventures of the night and his own sad thoughts, and he beat against the door with violence.

The chorus ceased.

Edward repeated his knocking.

Still there was no answer; but he heard low and hurried muttering inside. Determined, however, to gain admittance, Edward laid hold of an iron hasp outside the door, which enabled him to shake the gate with violence, that there might be no excuse on the part of the inmates that they did not hear; but in thus making the old door rattle in its frame, it suddenly yielded to his touch, and creaked open on its rusty hinges; for when Larry Hogan had entered it had been forgotten to be barred.

As Edward stood in the open doorway, the first object which met his eye was the coffin,—and it is impossible to say how much at that moment the sight shocked him; he shuddered involuntarily yet could not withdraw his eyes from the revolting object; and the pallor with which his previous mental anxiety had invested his cheek, increased as he looked on this last tenement of mortality. "Am I to see nothing but the evidences of death's doings this night?" was the mental question which shot through Edward's overwrought brain, and he grew livid at the thought. He looked more like one raised from the grave than a living being, and a wild glare in his eyes rendered his appearance still more unearthly. He felt that shame which men always experience in allowing their feelings to overcome them; and by a great effort he mastered his emotion and spoke, but the voice partook of the strong, nervous excitement under which he laboured, and. was hollow and broken, and seemed more like that which one might fancy to proceed from the jaws of a sepulchre, than one of flesh and blood. Beaten by the storm, too, his hair hung in wet flakes over his face, and added to his wild appearance, so that the men all jumped to their, feet the first glimpse they caught of him, and huddled themselves together in the farthest corner of the building, from whence they eyed him with evident alarm.

Edward thought some whisky might check the feeling of faintness which overcame him; and though he deemed it probable he had broken in upon the nocturnal revel of desperate and lawless men, he nevertheless asked them to give him some; but instead of displaying that alacrity so universal in Ireland, of sharing the "creature" with a newcomer, the men only pointed to the bottle which stood beside the fire, and drew closer together.

Edward's desire for the stimulant was so great, that he scarcely noticed the singular want of courtesy on the part of the men; and seizing the bottle (for there was no glass), he put it to his lips, and quaffed a hearty dram of the spirit before he spoke.

"I must ask for shelter and assistance here," said Edward. "My horse, I fear, has slipped his shoulder—"

Before he could utter another word, a simultaneous roar of terror burst from the group—they fancied the ghost of Jimmy Barlow was before them, and made a simultaneous rush from the barn; and as they saw the horse at the door, another yell escaped them, as they fled with increased speed and terror. Edward stood in amazement as the men rushed from his presence. He followed to the gate to recall them; they were gone; he could only hear their yells in the distance. The circumstance seemed quite unaccountable; and as he stood lost in vain surmises as to the cause of the strange occurrence, a low neigh of recognition from the horse reminded him of the animal's wants, and he led him into the barn, where, from the plenty of straw which lay around, he shook down a litter where the maimed animal might rest.

He then paced up and down the barn, lost in wonder at the conduct of those whom he found there, and whom his presence had so suddenly expelled; and ever as he walked towards the fire, the coffin caught his eye. As a fitful blaze occasionally arose it flashed upon the plate, which brightly reflected the flame, and Edward was irresistibly drawn, despite his original impression of horror at the object, to approach and read the inscription. The shield bore the name of "O'Grady," and Edward recoiled from the coffin with a shudder, and inwardly asked, was he in his waking senses? He had but an hour ago seen his adversary laid in his grave, yet here was his coffin again before him, as if to harrow up his soul anew. Was it real, or a mockery? Was he the sport of a dream, or— there some dreadful curse fallen upon him, that he should be for ever haunted by the victim of his arm, and the call of vengeance for blood be ever upon his track? He breathed short and hard, and the smoky atmosphere in which he was enveloped rendered respiration still more difficult. As through this oppressive vapour, which seemed only fit for the nether world, he saw the coffin-plate flash back the flame, his imagination accumulated horror on horror; and when the blaze sank, and but the bright red of the fire was reflected, it seemed to him to burn, as it were, with a spot of blood, and he could support the scene no longer, but rushed from the barn in a state of mind bordering on frenzy.

It was about an hour afterwards, near midnight, that the old barn was in flames; most likely some of the straw near the fire, in the confusion of the breaking up of the party, had been scattered within range of ignition, and caused the accident. The flames were seen for miles round the country; and the shattered walls of the ruined mansion-house were illuminated brightly by the glare of the consuming barn, which, in the morning, added its own blackened and reeking ruin to the desolation, and crowds of persons congregated to the spot for many days after. The charred planks of the coffin were dragged from amongst the ruin; and as the roof in falling in had dragged a large portion of the wall along with it, the stones which had filled the coffin could not be distinguished from those of the fallen building, therefore much wonder arose that no vestige of the bones of the corpse it was supposed to contain could be discovered. Wonder increased to horror as the strange fact was promulgated; and in the ready credulity of a superstitious people, the terrible belief became general, that his sable majesty had made off with O'Grady and the party watching him; for as the Dublin bailiffs never stopped till they got back to town, and were never seen again in the country, it was most natural to suppose that the devil had made a haul of *them* at the same time. In a few days rumour added the spectral appearance of Jim Barlow to the tale, which only deepened its mysterious horror; and though, after some time, the true story was promulgated by those who knew the real state of the case, yet the truth never gained ground, and was considered but a clever sham, attempted by the family to prevent so dreadful a story from attaching to their house; and tradition perpetuates to this hour the belief that *the devil flew away with O'Grady.*

Lone and shunned as the hill was where the ruined house stood, it became more lone and shunned than ever; and the boldest heart in the whole countryside would quail to be in its vicinity, even in the day-time. To such a pitch the panic rose, that an extensive farm which encircled it, and belonged to the old usurer who made the seizure, fell into a profitless state, from the impossibility of men being found to work upon it. It was useless even as pasture, for no one could be found to herd cattle upon it; altogether, it was a serious loss to the money-grubber; and so far the incident of the burnt barn, and the tradition it gave rise to, acted beneficially, in making the inhuman act of warring with the dead recoil upon the merciless old usurer.

XXXVIII

WE LEFT ANDY IN WHAT may be called a delicate situation, and though Andy's perceptions of the refined were not very acute, he himself began to wonder how he should get out of the dilemma into which circumstances had thrown him; and even to his dull comprehension, various terminations to his adventure suggested themselves, till he became quite confused in the chaos which his own thoughts created. One good idea, however, Andy contrived to lay hold of out of the bundle which perplexed him; he felt that to gain time would be an advantage, and if evil must come of his adventure, the longer he could keep it off the better; so he kept up his affectation of timidity, and put in his sobs and lamentations, like so many commas and colons, as it were, to prevent Bridget from arriving at her climax of going to bed.

Bridget insisted bed was the finest thing in the world for a young woman in distress of mind.

Andy protested he never could get a wink of sleep when his mind was uneasy.

Bridget promised the most sisterly tenderness. Andy answered by a lament for his mother.

"Come to bed, I tell you," said Bridget.

"Are the sheets aired?" sobbed Andy.

"What!" exclaimed Bridget in amazement.

"If you are not sure of the sheets bein' aired," said Andy, "I'd be afeard of catchin' cowld."

"Sheets, indeed!" said Bridget, "faith, it's a dainty lady you are, if you can't sleep without sheets."

"What!" returned Andy, "no sheets."

"Divil a sheet."

"Oh, mother, mother," exclaimed Andy, "what would you say to your innocent child being tuk away to a place there was no sheets."

"Well! I never heerd the like," says Bridget.

"Oh, the villians! to bring me where I wouldn't have a bit o' clane linen to lie in."

"Sure, there's blankets, I tell you."

"Oh, don't talk to me!" roared Andy, "sure, you know, sheets is only dacent."

"Bother, girl! Isn't a snug woolly blanket a fine thing?"

"Oh, don't brake my heart that-a-way," sobbed Andy, "sure, there's wool on any dirty sheep's back, but linen is decency!—Oh, mother, mother, if you thought your poor girl was without a sheet this night!"

And so Andy went on, spinning his bit of "linen manufacture" as long as he could, and raising Bridget's wonder, that instead of the lament which abducted ladies generally raise about their "vartue," that this young woman's principal complaint arose on the scarcity of flax. Bridget appealed to common sense if blankets were not good enough in these bad times; insisting moreover, that, as "love was warmer than friendship, so wool was warmer than flax," the beauty of which parallel case nevertheless failed to reconcile the disconsolate abducted. Now Andy had pushed his plea of the want of linen as far as he thought it would go, and when Bridget returned to the charge, and reiterated the oft-repeated "Come to bed, I tell you," Andy had recourse to twiddling about his toes, and chattering his teeth, and exclaimed in a tremulous voice, "Oh, I've a thrimblin' all over me!"

"Loosen the sthrings o' you, then," said Bridget, about to suit the action to the word.

"Ow! ow!" cried Andy, "don't touch me—I'm ticklish."

"Then open the throat o' your gown yourself, dear," said Bridget.

"I've a cowld on my chest, and dar'n't," said Andy, "but I, think a dhrop of hot punch would do me good, if I had it."

"And plenty of it," said Bridget, "if that'll plaze you:" she rose as she spoke, and set about getting 'the materials' for making punch.

Andy hoped, by means of this last idea, to drink Bridget into a state of unconsciousness, and then make his escape; but he had no notion until he tried, what a capacity the gentle Bridget had for carrying tumblers of punch steadily; he proceeded as cunningly as possible, and on the score of "the thrimblin' over him," repeated the doses of punch, which, nevertheless, he protested he couldn't touch, unless Bridget kept him in countenance, glass for glass; and Bridget—genial soul—was no way loth; for living in a still, and among smugglers, as she did, it was not a trifle of stingo could bring her to a halt. Andy, even with the advantage of the stronger organization of a man, found this mountain lass nearly a match for him; and before the potations operated as he hoped upon her, his own senses began to feel the influence of the liquor, and his caution became considerably undermined.

Still, however, he resisted the repeated offers of the couch proposed to him, declaring he would sleep in his clothes, and leave to Bridget the full possession of her lair.

The fire began to burn low, and Andy thought he might facilitate his escape by counterfeiting sleep; so feigning slumber, as well as he could, he seemed to sink into insensibility, and Bridget unrobed herself, and retired behind a rough screen.

It was by a great effort that Andy kept himself awake, for his potation, added to his nocturnal excursion, tended towards somnolency; but the desire of escape, and fear of a discovery and its consequences, prevailed over the ordinary tendency of nature, and he remained awake, watching every sound. The silence at last became painful,—so still was it, that he could hear the small crumbling sound of the dying embers as they decomposed and shifted their position on the hearth, and yet he could not be satisfied from the breathing of the woman that she slept. After the lapse of half an hour, however, he ventured to make some movement. He had well observed the quarter in which the outlet from the cave lay, and there was still a faint glimmer from the fire to assist him in crawling towards the trap. It was a relief when after some minutes of cautious creeping, he felt the fresh air breathing from above, and a moment or two more brought him in contact with the ladder. With the stealth of a cat he began to climb the rungs—he could hear the men snoring on the outside of the cave: step by step as he arose he felt his heart beat faster at the thought of escape, and became more cautious. At length his head emerged from the cave, and he saw the men lying about its mouth; they lay close around it—he must step over them to escape—the chance is fearful, but he determines to attempt it—he ascends still higher—his foot is on the last rung of the ladder—the next step puts him on the heather—when he feels a hand lay hold of him from below!

His heart died within him at the touch, and he could not resist an exclamation.

"Who's that!" exclaimed one of the men outside. Andy crouched.

"Come down," said the voice softly from below, "if Jack wakes, it will be worse for you."

It was the voice of Bridget, and Andy felt it was better to be with her than exposed to the savagery of Shan More and his myrmidons; so he descended quietly, and gave himself up to the tight hold of Bridget, who with many asseverations that "out of her arms she would not let the prisoner go till morning," led him back to the cave.

XXXIX

"Great wit to madness nearly is allied,
And thin partitions do the bounds divide."

SO SINGS THE POET: BUT whether the wit be great or little, the "thin
partition" separating madness from sanity is equally mysterious.
It is true that the excitability attendant upon genius approximates so
closely to madness, that it is sometimes difficult to distinguish between
them; but without the attendant "genius" to hold up the train of
madness, and call for our special permission and respect in any of its
fantastic excursions, the most ordinary crack-brain sometimes chooses
to sport in the regions of sanity, and, without the license which genius
is supposed to dispense to her children, poach over the preserves of
common sense. This is a well-known fact, and would not be reiterated
here, but that the circumstances about to be recorded hereafter might
seem unworthy of belief; and as the veracity of our history we would
not have for one moment questioned, we have ventured to jog the
memory of our readers as to the close neighbourhood which madness
and common sense inhabit, before we record a curious instance of
intermitting madness in the old dowager O'Grady.

Her son's death had, by the violence of the shock, dragged her from
the region of fiction in which she habitually existed; but, after the
funeral, she relapsed into all her strange aberration, and her bird-clock
and her chimney-pot head-dress were once more in requisition.

The old lady had her usual attendance from her granddaughter, and
the customary offering of flowers was rendered, but they were not

so cared for as before, and Charlotte was dismissed sooner than usual from her morning's attendance, and a new favourite received in her place. And, "of all the birds in the air," who should this favourite be but Master Ratty. Yes! Ratty—the caricaturist of his grandmama, was, "for the nonce," her closeted companion. Many a guess was given as to "what in the world" grandmama *could* want with Ratty; but the secret was kept between them, for this reason, that the old lady kept *the reward she promised* Ratty, for preserving it, in her own hands, until the duty she required on his part should be accomplished; and the shilling a day to which Ratty looked forward kept him faithful.

Now the duty Master Ratty had to perform was instructing his grandmama how to handle a pistol; the bringing up quick to the mark, and levelling by "the sight," was explained, but a difficulty arose in the old lady's shutting her left eye, which Ratty declared to be indispensable, and for some time Ratty was obliged to stand on a chair and cover his grandmama's eye with his hand while she took aim; this was found inconvenient, however, and the old lady substituted a black silk shade, to obfuscate her sinister luminary in her exercises, which now advanced to snapping the lock, and knocking sparks from the flint, which made the old lady wink with her right eye. When this second habit was overcome, the "dry" practice, that is, without powder, was given up, and a "flash in the pan" was ventured upon, but this made her shut both eyes together, and it was some time before she could prevail on herself to hold her eye fixed on her mark, and pull the trigger. This, however, at last was accomplished, and when she had conquered the fear of seeing the flash, she adopted the plan of standing before a handsome old-fashioned looking-glass, which reached from the ceiling to the floor, and levelling the pistol at her own reflection before it, as if she were engaged in mortal combat, and every time she snapped and burned priming, she would exclaim, "I hit him that time, I know—I can kill him—*tremble, villain!*"

Now, as long as this pistol practice had the charm of novelty for Ratty, it was all very well; but when, day by day, the strange mistakes and nervousness of his grandmama became less piquant, from repetition, it was not such good fun; and when the rantipole boy, after as much time as he wished to devote to the old woman's caprice, endeavoured to emancipate himself, and was countermanded, an outburst of "*Oh, bother!*" would take place, till the grandmother called up the prospective shillings to his view, and Ratty bowed before the altar of Mammon. But even Mammon failed to keep Ratty loyal; for that heathen god, Momus, claimed a superior allegiance; Ratty worshipped the "cap and bells" as the true crown, and "the bauble" as the sovereign sceptre. Besides, the secret became troublesome to him, and he determined to let the whole house know what "gran" and he were about in a way of his own.

The young imp, in the next day's practice, worked up the grandmama to a state of great excitement, urging her to take a cool and determined aim at the looking-glass.

"Cover him well, gran," said Ratty.

"I will," said the dowager, resolutely.

"You ought to be able to hit him at six paces."

"I stand at twelve paces."

"No—you are only six from the looking-glass."

"But the reflection, child, in the mirror, doubles the distance."

"Bother!" said Ratty. "Here, take the pistol—mind your eye, and don't wink."

"Ratty, you are singularly obtuse to the charms of science."

"What's science?" said Ratty.

"Why, gunpowder, child, for instance, is made by science."

"I never saw his name, then, on a canister," said Ratty. "Pigou, Andrew and Wilks, or Mister Dartford Mills, are the men for gunpowder. You know nothing about it, gran."

"Ratty, you are disrespectful, and will not listen to instruction. I knew Kirwan—the great Kirwan, the chemist, who always wore his hat—"

"Then he knew chemistry better than manners," said Ratty.

"Ratty, you are very troublesome. I desire you listen, sir.—Kirwan, sir, told me all about Science; and the Dublin Society have his picture, with a bottle in his hand—"

"Then he was fond of drink," said Ratty. "Ratty, don't be pert. To come back to what I was originally saying; I repeat, sir, I am at twelve paces from my object;—six from the mirror, which, doubling by reflection, makes twelve; such is the law of optics.—I suppose you know what optics are?"

"To be sure I do."

"Tell me, then."

"Our eyes," said Ratty.

"Eyes!" exclaimed the old lady, in amaze.

"To be sure," answered Ratty, boldly. "Didn't I hear the old blind man at the fair asking charity 'for the loss of his blessed optics'?"

"Oh, what lamentable ignorance, my child!" exclaimed the old lady. "Your tutor ought to be ashamed of himself."

"So he is," said Ratty. "He hasn't had a pair of new breeches for the last seven years; and he hides himself whenever he sees mama or the girls."

"Oh, you ignorant child! Indeed, Ratty, my love, you must study. I will give you the renowned Kirwan's book. Charlotte tore some of it for curl papers; but there's enough left to enlighten you with the sun's rays, and reflection and refraction—"

"I know what *that* is;" said Ratty.

"What?"

"Refraction."

"And what is it, dear?"

"Bad behaviour," said Ratty.

"Oh heavens!" exclaimed his grandmother.

"Yes it is," said Ratty stoutly; "the tutor says I'm refractory when I behave ill; and he knows Latin better than you."

"Ratty Ratty! you are hopeless!" exclaimed his grandmama.

"No, I am not," said Ratty; "I'm always *hoping*. And I hope Uncle Robert will break his neck some day and leave us his money."

The old woman turned up her eyes, and exclaimed, "You wicked boy!"

"Fudge!" said Ratty; "he's an old shaver, and we want it; and indeed, gran, you ought to give me ten shillings for ten days' teaching, now; and there's a fair next week, and I want to buy things."

"Ratty, I told you when you made me perfect in the use of my weapon I would pay you. My promise is sacred, and I will observe it with that scrupulous honour which has ever been the characteristic of the family; as soon as I hit something, and satisfy myself of mastery over the weapon, the money shall be yours, but not till then."

"Oh, very well," said Ratty; "go on then.—*Ready*—don't bring up your arm that way, like the handle of a pump, but raise it nice from the elbow—that's it.—*Ready*—*fire!* Ah! there you blink your eye, and drop the point of your pistol—try another. *Ready*—*fire!*— That's better.— Now steady the next time."

The young devil then put a charge of powder and ball into the pistol he handed his grandmother, who took steady aim at her reflection in the mirror, and at the words, "*Ready*—*fire!*" bang went the pistol—the magnificent glass was smashed—the unexpected recoil of the weapon made it drop from the hand of the dowager, who screamed with astonishment at the report and the shock, and did not see for a moment the mischief she had done; but when the shattered mirror caught her eye, she made a rush at Ratty, who was screeching with laughter in the far corner of the room, where he ran when he had achieved his trick; and he was so helpless from the excess of his cachinnation, that the old lady cuffed him without his being able to defend himself. At last he contrived to get out of her clutches, and jammed her against the wall with a table, so tightly that she roared "Murder!" The report of the pistol ringing through the house, brought all its inmates to the spot; and there the cries of murder from the old lady led them to suppose some awful tragedy, instead of a comedy, was enacting inside; the door was locked, too, which increased the alarm, and was forced in the moment of terror from the outside. When the crowd rushed in, Master Ratty rushed out, and left the astonished family to gather up the bits of the story as well as they could, from the broken looking-glass and the cracked dowager.

XL

Though it is clear the serious events in the O'Grady family had not altered Master Ratty's propensities in the least, the case was far different with Gustavus. In that one night of suffering which he had passed, the gulf was leaped that divides the boy from the man; and the extra frivolity and carelessness which clung from boyhood up to the age of fifteen, was at once, by the sudden disrupture produced by events, thrown off, and as singular a ripening into manhood commenced.

Gustavus was of a generous nature; and even his faults belonged less to his organization than to the devil-may-care sort of education he received, if education it might be called. Upon his generosity the conduct of Edward O'Connor beside the grave of the boy's father had worked strongly; and though Gustavus could not give his hand beside the grave to the man with whom his father had engaged in deadly quarrel, yet he quite exonerated Edward from any blame; and when, after a night more sleepless than Gustavus had ever known, he rose early on the ensuing morning, he determined to ride over to Edward O'Connor's house, and breakfast, and commence that friendship which Edward had so solemnly promised to him, and with which the boy was pleased; for Gustavus was quite aware in what estimation Edward was held; and though the relative circumstances in which he and the late Squire stood prevented the boy from "caring a fig" for him, as he often said himself, yet he was not beyond the influence of that thing called "reputation," which so powerfully attaches to, and elevates the man who wins it; and the price at which Edward was held in the country, influenced opinion even in Neck-or-Nothing Hall, albeit though

"against the grain." Gustavus had sometimes heard from the lips of
the idle and ignorant, Edward sneered at for being "cruel wise"—and
"too much of a schoolmaster"—and fit for nothing but books or a
boudoir—and called "a piano man," with all the rest of the hacknied
"dirt" which jealous inferiority loves to fling at the heights it cannot
occupy; for though (as it has been said) Edward, from his manly and
sensible bearing, had escaped such sneers better than most men, still
some few there were to whom his merit was offensive. Gustavus,
however, though he sometimes heard such things, saw with his own
eyes that Edward could back a horse with any man in the county. He
was always foremost in the chase, could bring down as many brace
of birds as most men in a day, had saved one or two persons from
drowning; and if he did all these things as well as other men, Gustavus
(though hitherto too idle to learn much himself) did not see why a
man should be sneered at for being an accomplished scholar as well.
Therefore, he had good foundation for being pleased at the proffered
friendship of such a man, and remembering the poignancy of Edward's
anguish on the foregoing eve, Gustavus generously resolved to see him
at once, and offer him the hand which a nice sense of feeling made him
withhold the night before. Mounting his pony, an hour's smart riding
brought him to Mount Eskar, for such was the name of Mr. O'Connor's
residence.

It was breakfast time when Gustavus arrived, but Edward had not
yet left his room, and the servant went to call him. It need scarcely be
said that Edward had passed a wretched night; reaching home, as he
did, weary in mind and body, and with feelings and imagination both
overwrought, it was long before he could sleep; and even then his slumber
was disturbed by harassing visions and frightful images. Spectral shapes,
and things unimaginable to the waking senses, danced, and crawled, and
hissed about him. The torch flared above the grave, and that horrid coffin,
with the name of the dead O'Grady upon it, "murdered sleep." It was
dawn before anything like refreshing slumber touched his feverish eyelids;
and he had not enjoyed more than a couple of hours of what might be
called sleep, when the servant called him; and then, after the brief oblivion
he had obtained, one may fancy how he started when the first words he
heard on waking were, "Mister O'Grady is below, sir."

Edward started up from his bed and stared wildly on the man, as he exclaimed, with a look of alarm, "O'Grady!—God's sake, you don't say O'Grady?"

"'Tis Mister Gustavus, sir," said the man, wondering at the wildness of Edward's manner.

"Oh—the boy!—ay, ay—the boy!" repeated Edward, drawing his hands across his eyes, and recovering his self-possession. "Say, I will be down presently."

The man retired, and Edward laid down again for some minutes to calm the heavy beating of his heart, which the sudden mention of that name had produced;—that name so linked with the mental agony of the past night;—that name which had conjured up a waking horror of such might as to shake the sway of reason for a time, and which afterwards pursued its reign of terror through his sleep. After such a night, fancy poor Edward doomed to hear the name of O'Grady again the first thing in the morning—nay, awakened, one may say, by the very sound, and it cannot be wondered at that he was startled.

A few minutes, however, served to restore his self possession and he arose, and, making his toilet in haste, descended to the breakfast parlour, where he was met by Gustavus with an open hand, which Edward clasped with fervour, and held for some time as he looked on the handsome face of the boy, and saw in its frank expression all that his heart could desire.—They spoke not a word, but they understood one another; and that moment commenced an attachment which increased with increasing intimacy; and became one of those steadfast friendships which are seldom met with.

After breakfast Edward brought Gustavus to his "den," as he called a room which was appropriated to his own particular use, occupied with books and a small collection of national relics. Some long ranges of that peculiar calf binding, with its red label, declared at once the contents to be law; and by the dry formal cut of the exterior, gave little invitation to reading. The very outside of a law library is repulsive; the continuity of that eternal buff leather gives one a surfeit by anticipation, and makes one mentally exclaim in despair, "Heavens!—how can any one hope to get all that into his head?" The only plain honest thing about law, is the outside of the books where it is laid down—there all is simple; inside all is complex. The interlacing lines of the binder's patterns find no place on the covers; but intricacies abound inside, where any line is easier found than a straight one. Nor gold leaf nor tool is employed without, but within how many fallacies are enveloped in glozing words; the gold leaf has its representative in "legal fiction;" and as for "*tooling*"—there's plenty of that!

Other books, also, bore external evidence of the nature of their contents. Some old parchment covers indicated the lore of past ages; amidst these the brightest names of Greece and Rome were to be found, as well as those who have adorned our own literature, and implied a cultivated taste on the part of the owner. But one portion of the library was particularly well stored. The works bearing on Irish history were numerous; and this might well account for the ardour of Edward's feelings in the cause of his country; for it is as impossible that a river should run backwards to its source, as that any Irishman, of a generous nature, can become acquainted with the real history of his country, and not feel that she has been an ill-used and neglected land, and not struggle in the cause of her being righted. Much *has* been done in the cause since the days of which this story treats, and Edward was amongst those who helped to achieve it; but much has still to be done, and there is glorious work in store for present and future Edward O'Connors.

Along with the books which spoke the cause of Ireland, the mute evidences, also, of her former glory and civilization were scattered through the room. Various ornaments of elegant form, and wrought in the purest gold, were tastefully arranged over the mantel piece; some, from their form, indicating their use, and others only affording matter of ingenious speculation to the antiquary, but all bearing evidence of early civilization. The frontlet of gold indicated noble estate, and the long and tapering bodkin of the same metal, with its richly enchased knob or pendant crescent, implied the robe it once fastened could have been of no mean texture, and the wearer of no mean rank. Weapons were there, too, of elegant form and exquisite workmanship, wrought in that ancient bronze, of such wondrous temper that it carries effective edge and point;—the sword was of exact Phœnician mould; the double-eyed spear-head, formed at once for strength and lightness, might have served as the model for a sculptor in arming the hand of Minerva.—Could these be the work of an uncultivated people?—Impossible!—The harp, too, was there, that unfailing mark of polish and social elegance. The bard and barbarism could never be coeval. But beyond all these, was a relic exciting deeper interest—it was an ancient crosier, of curious workmanship, wrought in the precious metals; and partly studded with jewels; but few of the latter remained, though the empty collets showed it had once been costly in such ornaments.—Could this be seen without remembering that the light of Christianity first dawned over the western isles—*in Ireland!* that *there* the gospel was first preached, *there* the work of salvation begun!

There be cold hearts to which these touching recollections do not pertain, and they heed them not; and some there are, who, with the callousness which forbids the sensibility, possess the stupid effrontery to ask, "Of what use are such recollections?" With such frigid utilitarians it would be in vain to argue; but this question, at least, may be put in return:—Why should the ancient glories of Greece and Rome form a large portion of the academic studies of our youth?—why should the evidences of *their* arts and *their* arms be held precious in museums, and similar evidences of ancient cultivation be despised because they pertain to another nation? Is it because they are Irish they are held in contempt? Alas! in many cases it is so—ay, and even (shame to say) within her own shores. But never may that day arrive when Ireland shall be without enough of true and fond hearts to cherish the memory of her ancient glories, to give to her future sons the evidences of her earliest western civilization, proving that their forefathers were not, as those say who wronged and therefore would malign them, a rabble of rude barbarians, but that brave kings, and proud princes, and wise lawgivers, and just judges, and gallant chiefs, and chaste and lovely women, were among them, and that inspired bards were there to perpetuate such memories!

Gustavus had never before seen a crosier, and asked what it was. On being informed of its name he then said—

"But what *is* a crosier?"

"A bishop's pastoral staff," said Edward.

"And why have you a bishop's staff, and swords, and spears, hung up together?"

"That is not inappropriate," said Edward. "Unfortunately, the sword and the crosier have been frequently but too intimate companions. Preaching the word of peace has been too often the pretext for war. The Spaniards, for instance, in the name of the gospel, committed the most fearful atrocities."

"Oh, I know," said Gustavus, "that was in the time of bloody Mary and the Armada."

Edward wondered at the boy's ignorance, and saw, in an instant, the source of his false application of his allusion to the Spaniards. Gustavus had been taught to vaguely couple the name of "bloody Mary" with every thing bad, and that of "good Queen Bess," with all that was glorious; and the word "Spanish," in poor Gusty's head, had been hitherto connected with two ideas, namely, "liquorice" and the "Armada."

Edward, without wounding the sensitive shame of ignorant youth, gently set him right, and made him aware he had alluded to the conduct of the Spaniards in America, under Cortes and Pizarro.

For the first time in his life Gustavus was aware that Pizarro was a real character. He had heard his grandmama speak of a play of that name, and how great Mr. Kemble was in Rolla, and how he saved a child; but as to its belonging to history, it was a new light—the utmost Gusty knew about America being that it was discovered by Columbus.

"But the crosier," said Edward, "is amongst the most interesting of Irish antiquities, and especially belongs to an Irish collection, when you remember the earliest preaching of Christianity, in the western isles, was in Ireland."

"I did not know that," said the boy.

"Then you don't know why the shamrock is our national emblem?"

"No," said Gustavus, "though I take care to mount one in my hat every Patrick's day."

"Well," said Edward, anxious to give Gustavus credit for *any* knowledge he possessed, "you know at least it is connected with the memory of St. Patrick, though you don't know why. I will tell you. When St. Patrick first preached the Christian faith in Ireland, before a powerful chief and his people, when he spoke of One God, and of the Trinity, the chief asked how one could be in three. St. Patrick, instead of attempting a theological definition of the faith, thought a simple image would best serve to enlighten a simple people, and stooping to the earth he plucked from the green sod a shamrock, and holding up the trefoil before them, he bid them there behold on in three. The chief, struck by the illustration, asked at once to be baptized, and all his sept followed his example."

"I never heard that before," said Gusty. "'Tis very beautiful."

"I will tell you something else connected with it," said Edward.

"After baptizing the chief, St. Patrick made an eloquent exhortation to the assembled multitude, and in the course of his address, while enforcing his urgent appeal with appropriate gesture, as the hand which held his crosier, after being raised towards heaven, descended again towards the earth, the point of his staff, armed with metal, was driven through the foot of the chief, who, fancying it was part of the ceremony, and but a necessary testing of the firmness of his faith, never winced."

"He was a fine fellow," said Gusty. "And is that the crosier?" he added, alluding to the one in Edward's collection, and manifestly excited by what he had heard.

"No," said Edward, "but one of early date, and belonging to some of the first preachers of the gospel amongst us."

"And have you other things here with such beautiful stories belonging to them?" inquired Gusty, eager for more of that romantic lore which youth loves so passionately.

"Not that I know of," answered Edward. "But if these objects here had only tongues; if every sword, and celt, and spear-head, and golden bodkin, and other trinket could speak, no doubt we should hear stirring stories of gallant warriors and their ladve loves."

"Ah, that would be something to hear!" exclaimed Gusty.

"Well," said Edward, " you may have many *such* stories by reading the history of your country; which, if you have not read, I can lend you books enough."

"Oh, thank you!" said Gusty; "I should like it so much."

Edward approached the book-shelf, and selected a volume he thought the most likely to interest so little practised a reader; and when he turned round he saw Gusty poising in his hand an antique Irish sword, of bronze.

"Do you know what that is?" inquired Edward.

"I can't tell the name of it," answered Gusty, "but I suppose it was *something to stick a fellow.*"

Edward smiled at the characteristic reply, and told him it was an antique Irish sword.

"A sword!" he exclaimed. "Isn't it short for a sword?"

"All the swords of that day were short," said Edward.

"When was that?" inquired the boy.

"Somewhere about two thousand years ago," said Edward.

"Two thousand years!" exclaimed Gusty, in surprise. "How is it possible you can tell this is two thousand years old?"

"Because it is made of the same metal, and of the same shape, as the swords found at Cannæ where the Carthaginians fought the Romans."

"I know the Roman history," said Gusty, eager to display his little bit of knowledge; "I know the Roman history. Romulus and Remus were educated by a wolf."

Edward could not resist a smile, which he soon suppressed, and continued, —"Such swords as you now hold in your hand are found *in quantities* in Ireland, and never anywhere else in Europe, except in Italy, particularly at Cannæ, where some thousands of Carthaginians fell; and when we find the sword of the same make and metal in places so remote, it establishes a strong connecting link between the people of Carthage and of Ireland, and at once shows their date."

"How curious that is!" exclaimed Gusty; "and how odd, I never heard it before! Are there many such curious things you know?"

"Many," said Edward.

"I wonder how people can find out such odd things," said the boy.

"My dear boy," said Edward, "after getting a certain amount of knowledge, other knowledge comes very fast; it gathers like a snow-ball, or perhaps it would be better to illustrate the fact by a mill-dam. —You know, when the water is low in the mill-dam, the miller cannot drive his wheel; but the moment the water comes up to a certain level, it has force to work the mill;—and so it is with knowledge; when once you get it up to a certain level, you can 'work your mill,' with this great advantage over the mill-dam, that the stream of knowledge, once reaching the working level, never runs dry."

"Oh, I wish I knew as much as you do!" exclaimed Gusty.

"And so you can, if you wish it," said Edward.

Gusty sighed heavily, and admitted he had been very idle.

Edward told him he had plenty of time before him to repair the damage.

A conversation then ensued, perfectly frank on the part of the boy, and kind on Edward's side to all his deficiencies, which he found to be lamentable, as far as learning went. He had some small smattering of Latin; but Gustavus vowed steady attention to his tutor and his studies for the future. Edward, however, knowing what a miserable scholar the tutor himself was, offered to put Gustavus through his Latin and Greek himself. Gustavus accepted the offer with gratitude, and rode over every day to Mount Eskar for his lesson; and, under the intelligent explanations of Edward, the difficulties which had hitherto discouraged him disappeared, and it was surprising what progress he made. At the same time, he devoured Irish history, and became rapidly tinctured with that enthusiastic love of all that belonged to his country which he found in his teacher; and Edward soon hailed in the ardent neophyte a noble and intelligent spirit, redeemed from ignorance, and rendered capable of higher enjoyments than those to be derived merely from field sports. Edward, however, did not confine his instructions to book-learning only; there is much to be learned by living with the educated, whose current conversation alone is instructive; and Edward had Gustavus with him as constantly as he could; and after some time, when the frequency of Gusty's visits to Mount Eskar ceased to excite any wonder at home, he sometimes spent several days together with Edward, to whom he became continually more and more attached. Edward showed great judgment in making his training attractive to his pupil; he did not attend merely to his head; he thought of other things as well, and joined him in the sports and exercises he knew, and taught him those in which he was uninstructed. Fencing, for instance, was one of these; Edward was a tolerable master of his foil, and in a few months Gustavus, under his tuition, could parry a thrust, and make no bad attempt at a hit himself. His improvement, in every way, was so remarkable, that it was noticed by all, and its cause did not long remain secret; and when it was known, Edward O'Connor's character stood higher than ever, and the whole country said it was a lucky day for Gusty O'Grady that he found such a friend.

As the limits of our tale would not permit the intercourse between Edward and Gustavus to be treated in detail, this general sketch of it has been given; and in stating its consequences so far, a peep into the future has been granted by the author, with a benevolence seldom belonging to his ill-natured and crafty tribe, who endeavour to hoodwink their docile patrons as much as possible, and keep them in a state of ignorance as to coming events. But now, having been so indulgent, we must beg to lay hold of the skirts of our readers, and pull them back again down the ladder into the private still, where Bridget pulled back Andy very much after the same fashion, and the results of which we must treat of in our next chapter.

XLI

WHEN BRIDGET DRAGGED ANDY BACK, and insisted on his going, to bed——

———

No—I will not be too goodnatured, and tell my story that way;—besides, it would be a very difficult matter to tell it; and why should an author, merely to oblige people, get himself involved in a labyrinth of difficulties, and rack his unfortunate brain to pick and choose words properly to tell his story, yet at the same time to lead his readers through the mazes of this very ticklish adventure, without a single thorn scratching their delicate feelings, or as much as, making the smallest rent in the white muslin robe of propriety? So, not to run unnecessary risks, the story must go on another way.

———

When Shan More and the rest of the "big blackguards" began to wake, the morning after the abduction, and gave a turn or two under their heather coverlid, and rubbed their eyes as the sun peeped through the "curtains of the east,"—for these were the only bed-curtains Shan More and his companions ever had,—they stretched themselves and yawned, and, felt very thirsty, for they had all been blind drunk the night before, be it remembered; and Shan swore, to use his own expressive and poetic imagery, that his tongue was "as rough as a rat's back," while his companions went no farther than saying theirs were as "dry as a lime-burner's wig."

We should not be so particular in these minute details, but for that desire of truth which has guided us all through this veracious history; and as in this scene, in particular, we feel ourselves sure to be held seriously responsible for every word, we are determined to be accurate to a nicety, and set down every syllable with stenographic strictness.

"Where's the girl?" cried Shan, not yet sober.

"She's asleep with your sisther," was the answer.

"Down stairs?" inquired Shan.

"Yes," said the other, who now knew Big Jack was more drunk than he at first thought him, by his using the word stairs; for Jack when he was drunk was very grand, and called *down the ladder*, "down *stairs*."

"Get me a drink o' wather," said Jack, "for I'm thundherin' thirsty, and can't deludher that girl with the soft words, till I wet my mouth."

His attendant vagabond obeyed the order, and a large pitcher full of water was handed to the master, who heaved it upwards to his head, and drank as audibly and nearly as much as a horse. Then holding his hands to receive the remaining contents of the pitcher, which his followers poured into his monstrous palms, he soused his face, which he afterwards wiped in a wisp of grass, which was the only towel of Jack's which was not then at the wash.

Having thus made his toilet, Big Jack went down stairs, and as soon as his great bull-head disappeared beneath the trap, one of the men above said, "We'll have a *shilloo* soon, boys."

And sure enough they did, after some time, hear an extraordinary row. Jack first roared for Bridget, and no answer was returned; the call was repeated with as little effect, and at last a most tremendous roar was heard above—but not from a female voice. Jack was heard below, swearing like a trooper, and in a minute or two, back he rushed "*up stairs*" again, and began cursing his myrmidons most awfully, and foaming at the mouth with rage.

"What's the matther?" cried the men.

"Matther!" roared Jack; "oh, you 'tarnal villians!—You're a purty set to carry off a girl for a man—a purty job you've made of it!"—

"Arrah, didn't we bring her to you?"

"*Her,* indeed—bring *her*—much good what you brought is to me!"

"Tare an 'ouns! what's the matther at all? We dunna what you mane!" shouted the men, returning rage for rage.

"Come down, and you'll see what's the matther," said Jack, descending the ladder; and the men hastened after him.

He led the way to the farther end of the cavern, where a small glimmering of light was permitted to enter from the top, and lifting a tattered piece of canvas, which served as a screen to the bed, he exclaimed with a curse, "Look there, you blackguards!"

The men gave a shout of surprise, for—what do you think they saw?—

An empty bed!

XLII

It may be remembered that, on Father Phil's recommendation, Andy was to be removed out of the country, to place him beyond the reach of Larry Hogan's machinations, and that the proposed journey to London afforded a good opportunity of taking him out of the way. Andy had been desired by Squire Egan to repair to Merryvale; but as some days had elapsed, and Andy had not made his appearance, the alarms of the Squire that Andy might be tampered with, began to revive, and Dick Dawson was therefore requested to call at the Widow Rooney's cabin as he was returning from the town, where some business with Murphy, about the petition against Scatterbrain's return, demanded his presence.

Dick, as it happened, had no need to call at the widow's for, on his way to the town, who should he see approaching but the renowned Andy himself. On coming up to him, Dick pulled up his horse, and Andy pulled off his hat.

"God save your honour," said Andy.

"Why didn't you come to Merryvale, as you were bid?" said Dick.

"I couldn't sir, bekase"—

"Hold your tongue, you thief; you know you never can do what you're bid—you are always wrong one way or other."

"You're hard on me, Misther Dick."

"Did you ever do anything right?—ask yourself!"

"Indeed, sir, this time it was a rale bit o' business I had to do."

"And well you did it, no doubt.—Did you marry any one lately?" said Dick, with a waggish grin, and a wink.

"Faix, then, maybe I did," said Andy, with a knowing nod.

"And I hope *Matty* is well?" said Dick.

"Ah, Misther Dick, you're always goin' on with your jokin', so you are.—So you heerd o' that job, did you?—faix, a purty lady she is—oh, it's not her at all I am married to, but another woman."—

"Another woman!" exclaimed Dick, in surprise.

"Yis, sir, another woman—a kind craythur."

"Another woman!" reiterated Dick, laughing, "married to two women in two days!—why you're worse than a Turk!"

"Ah, Misther Dick!"

"You Tarquin!"

"Sure, sir, what harm's in it?"

"You Heliogabalus!!"

"Sure, it's no fault o' mine, sir."

"Bigamy, by this and that, flat bigamy!—you'll only be hanged, as sure as your name's Andy."

"Sure, let me tell you how it was, sir, and you'll see I am quit of all harm, good or bad.—'Twas a pack o' blackguards, you see, came to take off Oonah, sir."—

"Oh, a case of abduction!"

"Yis, sir;—so the women dhressed me up as a girl, and the blackguards, instead of the seduction of Oonah, only seduced me."

"Capital!" cried Dick; "well done, Andy!—and who seduced you?"

"Shan *More*, faith—no less."

"Ho, ho! a dangerous customer to play tricks on, Andy."

"Sure enough, faith, and that's partly the rayson of what happened; but by good luck, Big Jack was blind dhrunk when I got there, and I shammed screechin' so well, that his sisther took pity on me, and said she'd keep me safe from harm in her own bed that night."

Dick gave "a view halloo," when he heard this, and shouted with laughter, delighted at the thought of Shan More, instead of carrying off a girl for himself, introducing a girl to his own sister.

"Oh, now I see how you are married," said Dick; "that was the biter bit, indeed."

"Oh, the divil a bit I'd ha' bit her, only for the cross luck with me, for I wanted to schame off out o' the place, and escape; but she wouldn't let me, and cotcht me and brought me back."—

"I should think she would, indeed," said Dick, laughing. "What next?"

"Why I drank a power o' punch, sir, and was off my guard, you see, and couldn't keep the saycret so well afther that, and by dad she found it out."

"Just what I would expect of her," said Dick.

"Well, do you know, sir, though the thrick was agen her own brother, she laughed at it a power, and said I was a great divil, but that she couldn't blame me. So then I sthruv to coax her to let me make my escape, but she towld me to wait a bit till the men above was faster asleep; but while I was waitin' for them to go to sleep, faix, I went to sleep myself, I was so tired; and when Bridget, the craythur, woke me in the morning, she was cryin' like a spout afther a thunder shower, and said her characther would be ruined when the story got abroad over the counthry and sure she darn't face the world, if I wouldn't make her an honest woman."

"The brazen baggage!" said Dick; "and what did you say?"

"Why what could any man say, sir, afther that. Sure, her karacther would be gone if—"

"Gone," said Dick; "faith it might have gone farther before it fared worse."—

"Arrah! what do you mane, Misther Dick?"

"Pooh, pooh! Andy—you don't mean to say you married that one?"

"Faix, I did," said Andy.

"Well, Andy," said Dick, grinning, "by the powers, you *have* done it this time!—good morning to you;" and Dick put spurs to his horse.

XLIII

ANDY, "KNOCKED ALL OF A heap," stood in the middle of the road, looking after Dick as he cantered down the slope. It was seldom poor Andy was angry—but he felt a strong sense of indignation choking him as Dick's parting words still rung in his ears. "What does he mane?" said Andy, talking aloud;—"What does he mane?" he repeated; anxious to doubt, and therefore question the obvious construction which Dick's words bore. "Misther Dick is fond of a joke, and maybe this is one of his making, but if it is, 'tis not a fair one, 'pon my sowl: a poor man has his feelins as well as a rich man.—How would you like your own wife to be spoke of that way, Misther Dick, as proud as you ride your horse there—humph?"

Andy, in great indignation, pursued his way towards his mother's cabin, to ask her blessing upon his marriage. On his presenting himself there, both the old woman and Oonah were in great delight at witnessing his safe return. Oonah particularly, for she, feeling that it was for her sake Andy placed himself in danger, had been in a state of great anxiety for the result of the adventure, and on seeing him, absolutely threw herself into his arms, and embraced him tenderly, impressing many a hearty kiss upon his lips, between whiles that she vowed she would never forget his generosity and courage; and ending with saying there was *nothing* she would not do for him.

Now Andy was flesh and blood, like other people, and as the showers of kisses from Oonah's ripe lips fell fast upon him, he was not insensible to the embrace of so very pretty a girl—a girl, moreover, he had always had a "sneaking kindness" for, which Oonah's distance of manner alone had hitherto made him keep to himself; but now, when he saw her eyes beam with gratitude, and her cheek flush, after her strong demonstration of regard, and heard her last words, so *very* like a hint to a shy man, it must be owned a sudden pang shot through poor Andy's heart, and he sickened at the thought of being married, which placed the tempting prize before him hopelessly beyond his reach.

He looked so blank, and seemed so unable to return Oonah's fond greeting, that she felt the pique which every pretty woman experiences who fancies her favours disregarded, and thought Andy was the stupidest lout she ever came across. Turning up her hair, which had fallen down in the excess of her friendship, she walked out of the cottage, and, biting her disdainful lip, fairly cried for spite.

In the meantime Andy popped down on his knees before the widow, and said, "Give me your blessing, mother!"

"For what, you omadhawn?" said his mother fiercely, for her woman's nature took part with Oonah's feelings, which she quite comprehended, and she was vexed with what she thought Andy's disgusting insensibility. "For what should I give you my blessin'?"

"Bekase I'm marri'd, ma'am."

"What!" exclaimed the mother. "It's not marri'd again you are?—You're jokin', sure."

"Faix, it's no joke," said Andy, sadly; "I'm marri'd, sure enough; so give us your blessin' anyhow," cried he, still kneeling.

"And who did you *dar'* for to marry, sir, if ɪ may make so bowld to ax, without *my* lave or license?"

"There was no time for axin', mother,—'twas done in a hurry, and I can't help it, so give us your blessin' at once."

"Tell me who she is, before I give you my blessin'."

"*Shan More's* sisther, ma'am."

"What!" exclaimed the widow, staggering back some paces,—"Shan More's sister, did you say?—Bridget *rhua,*[1] is it?"

"Yis, ma'am."

"Oh, wirrasthru! phillilew! millia murther!" shouted the mother, tearing her cap off her head,—"Oh, blessed Vargin, holy St. Dominick, Pether an' Paul the 'possle, what'll I do?—Oh, patther an' ave—you dirty *bosthoon*—blessed angels and holy marthyrs!—kneelin' there in the middle o' the flure as if nothing happened, down on me this day, a poor vartuous *dissolute* woman!—Oh, you disgrace to me and all belongin' to you,—and is it the impidence to ask for my blessin' you have, when it's whippin' at the cart's tail you ought to get, you shameless scapegrace!"

She then went wringing her hands, and throwing them upwards in appeals to Heaven, while Andy still kept kneeling in the middle of the cabin, lost in wonder.

The widow ran to the door, and called Oonah in.

"Who do you think that blackguard is marri'd to?" said the widow.

"Married " exclaimed Oonah, growing pale.

"Ay, marri'd, and who to, do you think?—why, to Bridget *rhua*."

Oonah screamed and clasped her hands.

Andy got up at last, and asked they were making such a rout about; he wasn't the first man who married without asking his mother's leave; and wanted to know what they had to "say agen it."

"Oh, you barefaced scandal o' the world!" cried the widow, "to ax sitch a question,—to marry a thrampin' sthreel like that,—a great read-headed Jack—"

"She can't help her hair," said Andy.

"I wish I could cut it off, and her head along with it, the sthrap!—Oh, blessed Vargin, to have my daughter-in-law a—"

"What?" said Andy, getting rather alarmed.

"That the whole county knows is—"

"What?" cried Andy.

"Not a fair nor a market-town doesn't know her as well as—Oh, wirra! wirra!"

"Why, you don't mane to say anything agen her charakther, do you?" said Andy.

"Charakther, indeed!" said his mother, with a sneer.

"By this an' that," said Andy, "if she was the child unborn she couldn't make a greater hullabaloo about her charakther than she did the mornin' afther."

"Afther what?" said his mother.

"Afther I was tuk away up to the hill beyant, and found her there, and—but I b'lieve I didn't tell you how it happened."

"No," said Oonah, coming forward, deadly pale, and listening anxiously, with a look of deep pity in her soft eyes.

Andy then related the adventure as the reader already knows it; and when it was ended, Oonah burst into tears, and in passionate exclamations blamed herself for all that had happened, saying it was in the endeavour to save her that Andy had lost himself.

"Oh, Oonah! Oonah!" said Andy, with more meaning in his voice than the girl had ever heard before, "it isn't the loss of myself I mind, but I've lost you too. Oh, if you had ever given me a tendher word or look before this day, 'twould never have happened, and that desaiver in the hills never could have *deludhered* me. And tell me, *lanna machree*, is my suspicions right in what I hear,—tell me the worst at once,—is she *non compos?*"

"Oh, I never heerd her called by that name before," sobbed Oonah, "but she has a great many others just as bad."

"Ow! ow! ow!" exclaimed Andy. "Now I know what Mr. Dick laughed at,—well, death before dishonour,—I'll go 'list for a sojer, and never live with her."

1.   Red-haired Bridget.

XLIV

It has been necessary in an earlier chapter to notice the strange freaks madness will sometimes play. It was then the object to show how strong affections of the mind will recall an erring judgment to its true balance; but the action of the counterpoise growing weaker by time, the disease returns, and reason again kicks the beam.—Such was the old dowager's case: the death of her son recalled her to herself; but a few days produced relapse, and she was as foolish as ever. Nevertheless, as Polonius remarks of Hamlet,

> "There is method in his madness,"

so in the dowager's case there was method—not of a sane intention, as the old courtier implies of the Danish prince, but of *in*sane birth— begot of a chivalrous feeling on an enfeebled mind.

To make this clearly understood, it is necessary to call attention to one other peculiarity of madness;—that, while it makes those under its influence liable to say and enact all sorts of nonsense on some subjects, it never impairs their powers of observation on those which chance to come within the reach of the undiseased portion of the mind; and moreover, they are quite as capable of arriving at just conclusions upon what they *so* see and hear as the most reasonable person, and, perhaps, in proportion as the reasoning power is limited within a smaller compass, so the capability of observation becomes stronger by being concentrated.

Such was the case with the old dowager, who, while Furlong was "doing devotion" to Augusta, and appeared the pink of faithful swains, saw very clearly that Furlong did not like it a bit, and would gladly be off his bargain. Yea, while the people in their sober senses on the same plane with the parties were taken in, the old lunatic, even from the toppling height of her own mad chimney-pot, could look down and see that Furlong would not marry Augusta if he could help it.

It *was* even so.—Furlong had acted under the influence of "terror when poor Augusta, shoved into his bed-room through the devilment of that rascally imp Ratty, and found there, through the evil destiny of Andy, was flung into his arms by her enraged father, and accepted as his wife. The immediate hurry of the election had delayed the marriage—the duel and its consequences further interrupted "the happy event"—and O'Grady's death caused a further postponement. It was delicately hinted to Furlong, that when matters had gone so far as to the wedding-dresses being ready, that the sooner the contracting parties under such circumstances were married, the better. But Furlong, with that affectation of propriety which belongs to his time-serving tribe, pleaded the "regard to appearances,"—"so soon after the ever-to-be-deplored event,"—and other such specious excuses, which were but covers to his own rascality, and used but to postpone the "wedding-day." The truth was, the moment Furlong had no longer the terrors of O'Grady's pistol before his eyes, he had resolved never to make so bad a match as that with Augusta appeared to be,—indeed, manifestly was, as far as regarded money; though Furlong should only have been too glad to be permitted to mix his plebeian blood with the daughter of a man of high family, whose crippled circumstances and consequent truckling conduct had reduced him to the wretched necessity of making *such a cur* as Furlong the inmate of his house.— But so it was.

The family began at last to suspect the real state of the case, and all were surprised except the old dowager:—she had expected what was coming, and had prepared herself for it. All her pistol practice was with a view to call Furlong to the "last arbitrement" for this slight to her house. Gusty was too young, she considered, for the duty; therefore, she, in her fantastic way of looking at the matter, looked upon *herself* as the head of the family, and, as such, determined to resent the affront put upon it.

But of her real design, the family at Neck-or-Nothing Hall had not the remotest notion. Of course, an old lady going about with a pistol, powder-flask, and bullets, and practising on the trunks of the trees in the park, could not pass without observation, and surmises there were on the subject; then her occasional exclamation of "tremble, villain!" would escape her; and sometimes in the family circle, after sitting for a while in a state of abstraction, she would lift her attenuated hand, armed with a knitting-needle or a ball of worsted, and, assuming the action of poising a pistol, execute a smart *click* with her tongue, and say, "I hit him that time."

These exclamations, indicative of vengeance, were supposed at length by the family to apply to Edward O'Connor, but excited pity rather than alarm. When, however, one morning, the dowager was nowhere to be found, and Ratty and the pistols had also disappeared, an inquiry was instituted as to the old lady's whereabouts, and Mount Eskar was one of the first places where she was sought, but without success; and all other inquiries were equally unavailing.

The old lady had contrived, with that cunning peculiar to insane people, to get away from the house at an early hour in the morning, unknown to all except Ratty, to whom she confided her intention, and he managed to get her out of the domain unobserved, and thence together they proceeded to Dublin in a post-chaise.

It was the day after this secret expedition was undertaken, that Mr. Furlong was sitting in his private apartment at the castle, doing "the state some service," by reading the morning papers, which heavy official duty he relieved occasionally by turning to some scented notes which lay near a morocco writing-case, whence they had been drawn by the lisping dandy to flatter his vanity. He had been carrying on a correspondence with an anonymous fair one, in whose heart, if her words might be believed, Furlong had made desperate havoc.

It happened, however, that these notes were all fictitious, being the work of Tom Loftus, who enjoyed playing on a puppy as much as playing on the organ; and he had the satisfaction of seeing Furlong going through his paces in certain squares he had appointed, wearing a flower of Tom's choice, and going through other antics which Tom had demanded under the signature of "Phillis," written in a delicate hand, on pink satin note-paper, with a lace border: one of the last notes suggested the possibility of a visit from the lady, and after assurances of "secrecy and honour" had been returned by Furlong, he was anxiously expecting "what would come of it," and, filled with pleasing reflections of what "a devil of a fellow" he was among the ladies, he occasionally paced the room before a handsome dressing-glass (with which his apartment was always furnished), and ran his fingers through his curls with a complacent smile. While thus occupied, and in such a frame of mind, the hall messenger entered the apartment, and said a lady wished to see him.

"A lady!" exclaimed Furlong, in delighted surprise.

"She won't give her name, sir, but—"

"Show her up! show her up!" exclaimed the Lothario, eagerly.

All anxiety, he awaited the appearance of his donna,—and quite a donna she seemed, as a commanding figure, dressed in black, and enveloped in a rich veil of the same, glided into the room.

"How vewy Spanish!" exclaimed Furlong, as he advanced to meet his incognita, who, as soon as she entered, locked the door, and withdrew the key.

"Quite pwactised in such secwet affairs," said Furlong, slily. "Fai' lady, allow me to touch you' fai' hand, and lead you to a seat."

The mysterious stranger made no answer, but lifting her long veil, turned round on the lisping dandy, who staggered back to the table, on which he leaned for support, when the dowager O'Grady appeared before him, drawn up to her full height, and anything but an agreeable expression in her eye. She stalked up towards him, something in the style of a spectre in a romance, which she was not very unlike, and as she advanced, he retreated, until he got the table between him and this most unwelcome apparition.

"I am come," said the dowager, with an ominous tone of voice.

"Vewy happy of the honou', I am sure, Mistwess O'Gwady," faltered Furlong.

"The avenger has come."

Furlong opened his eyes.

"I have come to wash the stain!" said she tapping her fingers in a theatrical manner on the table, and, as it happened, she pointed to a large blotch of ink on the table-cover. Furlong opened his eyes wider than ever, and thought this the queerest bit of madness he ever heard of; however, thinking it best to humour her, he answered, "Yes, it was a little awkwa'dness of mine upset the inkstand the othe' day."

"Do you mock me, sir?" said she, with increasing bitterness.

"La, no! Mistwess O'Gwady."

"I have come, I say, to wash out the stain you have dared to put on the name of O'Grady, in your blood."

Furlong gasped with mingled amazement and fear.

"Tremble, villain!" she said; and she pointed toward him her long attenuated finger with portentous solemnity.

"I weally am quite at a loss, Mistwess O'Gwady, to compwehend—"

Before he could finish his sentence, the dowager had drawn from the depths of her side pockets a brace of pistols, and presenting them to Furlong, said, "Be at a loss no longer—except the loss of life which *may* ensue;—take your choice of weapons, sir."

"Gwacious Heaven!" exclaimed Furlong, trembling from head to foot.

"You won't choose, then?" said the dowager. "Well, there's one for you;"—and she laid a pistol before him with as courteous a manner as if she were making him a birthday present.

Furlong stared down upon it with a look of horror.

"Now we must toss for choice of ground," said the dowager. "I have no money about me, for I paid my last half-crown to the post-boy, but this will do as well for a toss as anything else;"—and she laid her hands on the dressing-glass as she spoke. "Now the call shall be 'safe' or 'smash;' whoever calls 'safe,' if the glass comes down unbroken, has the choice, and *vice versa*. I call first—'*Smash*,'" said the dowager, as she flung up the dressing-glass which fell in shivers on the floor. "I have won," said she; "oblige me, sir, by standing in that far corner. I have the light in my back,—and you will have something else in yours before long;— take your ground, sir."

Furlong, finding himself thus cooped up with a mad woman, in an agony of terror suddenly bethought him of instances he had heard of escape, under similar circumstances, by coinciding to a certain extent with the views of the insane people, and suggested to the dowager, that he hoped she would not insist on a duel without their having "a friend" present.

"I beg your pardon, sir," said the old lady; "I quite forgot that form, in the excitement of the moment, though I have not overlooked the necessity altogether, and have come provided with one."

"Allow me to wing for him," said Furlong, rushing to the bell.

"Stop!" exclaimed the dowager, levelling her pistol at the bell-pull; "touch it, and you are a dead man."

Furlong stood riveted to the spot where his rush had been arrested.

"No interruption, sir, till this little affair is settled.—Here is my friend," she added, putting her hand into her pocket and pulling out the wooden cuckoo of her clock;—"my little bird, sir, will see all fair between us;"—and she perched the painted wooden thing, with a bit of feather grotesquely sticking up out of its nether end, on the morocco letter-case.

"Oh Lord!" said Furlong.

"He's a gentleman of the nicest honour, sir;" said the dowager, pacing back to the window.

Furlong took advantage of the opportunity of her back being turned, and rushed at the bell, which he pulled with great fury.

The dowager wheeled round with haste, "So you have rung," said she, "but it shall not avail you,—the door is locked; take your weapon, sir—quick!—what!—a coward!"

"Weally, Mistwess O'Gwady, I cannot think of deadly a'bitwetment with a lady."

"Less would you like it with a man, *poltroon!*" said she, with an exaggerated expression of contempt in her manner. "However," she added, "if you are a coward, you shall have a coward's punishment."— She went to a corner where stood a great variety of very handsome canes, and laying hold of one, began soundly to thrash Furlong, who feared to make any resistance, or attempt to disarm her of the cane, for the pistol was yet in her other hand.

The bell was answered by the servant, who, on finding the door locked, and hearing the row inside, began to knock, and inquire loudly, what was the matter. The question was more loudly answered by Furlong, who roared out, "Bweak the door! bweak the door!" interlarding his directions with cries of "mu'der!"

The door at length was forced, Furlong rescued, and the old lady separated from him. She became perfectly calm the moment other persons appeared, and was replacing the pistols in her pocket, when Furlong requested the "dweadful weapons" might be seized. The old lady gave up the pistols very quietly, but laid hold of her bird and put it back into her pocket.

"This is a dweadful violation!" said Furlong, "and my life is not safe unless she is bound ove' to keep the peace."

"Pooh! pooh!" said one of the gentlemen from the adjacent office, who came to the scene on hearing the uproar, "binding over an old lady to keep the peace—nonsense!"

"I insist upon it," said Furlong, with that stubbornness for which fools are so remarkable.

"Oh—very well!" said the sensible gentleman, who left the room.

A party, pursuant to Furlong's determination, proceeded to the head police-office, close by the Castle, and a large mob gathered as they went down Cork-hill, and followed them to Exchange-court, where they crowded before them, in front of the office, so that it was with difficulty the principals could make their way through the dense mass.

At length, however, they entered the office; and when Major Sin heard any gentleman attached to the Government wanted his assistance, of course he put any other case aside, and had the accuser and accused called up before him.

Furlong made his charge of assault and battery, with intent to murder, &c., &c.

"Some mad old rebel, I suppose," said Major Sin.—"Do you remember '98, ma'am?" said the Major.

"Indeed, I do, sir,—and I remember *you*, too.—Major Sin I have the honour to address, if I don't mistake."

"Yes, ma'am.—What then?"

"I remember well in '98, when you were searching for rebels, you thought a man was concealed in a dairy yard, in the neighbourhood of my mother's house, major, in Stephen's Green; and you thought he was hid in a hay-rick, and ordered your sergeant to ask for the loan of a spit from my mother's kitchen, to probe the hay stack."

"Oh! then, madam, your mother was *loyal,* I suppose."

"Most loyal, sir."

"Give the lady a chair," said the major.

"Thank you, I don't want it—but, major—when you asked for the spit, my mother thought you were going to practise one of your delightfully ingenious bits of punishment, and asked the sergeant *Whom you were going to roast?*"

The major grew livid on the bench where he sat, at this awkward reminiscence of one of his friends, and a dead silence reigned through the crowded office. He recovered himself, however, and addressed Mrs. O'Grady in a mumbling manner, telling her she must give security to keep the peace, herself—and find friends as sureties. On asking her had she any friend to appear for her, she declared she had.

"A gentleman of the nicest honour, sir," said the dowager, pulling her cuckoo from her pocket, and holding it up in view of the whole office.

A shout of laughter, of course, followed. The affair became at once understood in its true light;—a mad old lady—a paltry coward—&c., &c. Those who know the excitability and fun of an Irish mob, will not wonder that, when the story got circulated from the office to the crowd without, which it did with lightning rapidity, that the old lady, on being placed in a hackney-coach which was sent for, was hailed with a chorus of "Cuckoo!" by the multitude, one half of which ran after the coach as long as they could keep pace with it, shouting forth the spring-time call, and the other half followed Furlong to the Castle, with hisses and other more articulate demonstrations of their contempt.

XLV

T HE FAT AND FAIR WIDOW Flanagan had, at length, given up shilly
shallying, and, yielding to the fervent entreaties of Tom Durfy, had
consented to name the happy day. She, however, would have some little
ways of her own about it, and instead of being married in the country,
insisted on the nuptial knot being tied in Dublin. Thither the widow
repaired with her swain to complete the stipulated time of residence
within some metropolitan parish, before the wedding could take place.
In the meantime they enjoyed all the gaiety the capital presented, the
time glided swiftly by, and Tom was within a day of being made a happy
man, when, as he was hastening to the lodgings of the fair widow,
who was waiting with her bonnet and shawl on, to be escorted to the
botanical gardens of Glasneven, he was accosted by an odd-looking
person of somewhat sinister aspect.

"I believe I have the honour of addressing Mister Durfy, sir."

Tom answered in the affirmative.

"*Thomas* Durfy, Esquire, I think, sir?"

"Yes."

"This is for you, sir," he said, handing Tom a piece of dirty printed
paper, and at the same time laying his hand on Tom's shoulder, and
executing a smirking sort of grin, which he meant to be the pattern
of politeness, added—"You'll excuse me, sir, but I arrest you under a
warrant from the high sheriff of the city of Dublin—always sorry, sir,
for a gintleman in defficulties, but it's my duty."

"You're a bailiff, then?" said Tom.

"Sir," said the bum,

"'Honour and shame from no condition rise;
Act well your part—there all the honour lies"

"I meant no offence," said Tom. "I only meant—"

"I understand, sir—I understand. These little deffculties startles gintlemen at first—you've not been used to arrest, I see, sir."

"Never in my life did such a thing happen before," said Tom. "I live generally, thank God, where a bailiff daren't show his face."

"Ah, sir," said the bailiff, with a grin, "them rustic habits betrays the children of nature often when they come to town; but we are *so fisticated* here in the metropolis, that we lay our hands on strangers aisy. But you'd better not stand in the street, sir, or people will understand it's an arrest, sir; and I suppose you wouldn't like the exposure. I can simperise in a gintleman's feelings, sir. If you walk aisy on, sir, and don't attempt escape or rescue, I'll keep a gintlemanlike distance."

Tom walked on in great perplexity for a few steps, not knowing what to do. The hour of his rendezvous had struck—he knew how impatient of neglect the widow always was—he at one moment thought of asking the bailiff to allow him to proceed to her lodgings at once, there boldly to avow what had taken place, and ask her to discharge the debt; but this his pride would not allow him to do. As he came to the corner of a street, he got a tap on the elbow from the bailiff, who, with a jerking motion of his thumb and a wink, said in a confidential tone to Tom— "Down this street, sir—that's the way to the *pres'n* (prison)."

"Prison!" exclaimed Tom, halting involuntarily at the word.

"Shove on, sir—shove on," hastily repeated the sheriff's officer urging his order by a nudge or two on Tom's elbow.

"Don't shove me, sir!" said Tom rather angrily, "or by G—"

"Aisy, sir—aisy!" said the bailiff; "though I feel for the deffculties of a gintleman, the caption must be made, sir. If you don't like the pres'n, I have a nice little room o' my own, sir, where you can wait, for a small consideration, until you get bail."

"I'll go there, then," said Tom. "Go through as private streets as you can."

"Give me half-a-guinea for my trouble, sir, and I'll ambulate you through lanes every *fut* o' the way."

"Very well," said Tom.

They now struck into a shabby street, and thence wended through stable lanes, filthy alleys, up greasy broken steps through one close, and down steps in another—threaded dark passages whose debouchures were blocked up with posts to prevent all vehicular conveyance, the accumulated dirt of years sensible to the tread from its lumpy unevenness, and the stagnant air rife with pestilence. Tom felt increasing disgust at every step he proceeded, but anything to him appeared better than being seen in the public streets in such company; for, until they got into these labyrinths of nastiness, Tom thought he saw in the looks of every passer-by, as plainly told as if the words were spoken, "There goes a fellow under the care of the bailiff." In these byways, he had not any objection to speak to his companion, and for the first time asked him what he was arrested for.

"At the suit of Mr. M'Kail, sir."

"Oh!' the tailor," said Tom.

"Yes, sir," said the bailiff. "And if you would not consider it trifling with the feelings of a gintleman in defficulties, I would make the playful observation, sir, that it's quite in character to be arrested at the *suit* of a tailor. He! he! he!"

"You're a wag, I see," said Tom.

"Oh no, sir—only a poetic turn—a small affection I have certainly for Judy Mot—but my rale passion is the muses. We are not far, now, sir, from my little bower of repose—which is the name I give my humble abode—small, but snug, sir. You'll see another gintleman there, sir, before you. He is waitin' for bail these three or four days, sir—can't pay as he ought for the 'commodation, but he's a friend o' mine, I may almost say, sir—a litherary gintleman—them litherary gintlemen is always in defficulties, mostly.—I suppose you're a litherary gintleman, sir—though you're rather ginteely dhressed for one?"

"No," said Tom," I am not."

"I thought you wor, sir, by being acquainted with this other gintleman."

"An acquaintance of mine" said Tom, with surprise.

"Yis, sir. In short, it was through him I found out where you were, sir. I have had the writ agen you for some time, but couldn't make you off, till my friend says I must carry a note for him to you."

"Where is the note?" inquired Tom.

"Not ready yet, sir. It's po'thry he's writin'—something 'pithy,' he said, and 'lame' too. I dunna how a thing could be pithy and lame together, but them potes has hard words at command."

"Then you came away without the note?"

"Yes, sir. As soon as I found out where you were stopping, I ran off directly on Mr. M'Kail's little business. You'll excuse the liberty, sir; but we must all mind our professions; though, indeed, sir, if you b'lieve me, I'd rather nab a rhyme than a gintleman any day; and if I could get on the press, I'd quit the shoulder-tapping profession."

Tom cast an eye of wonder on the bailiff, which the latter comprehended at once; for, with habitual nimbleness, he could nab a man's thoughts as fast as his person.

"I know what you're thinking, sir—one of my profession purshue the muses? Don't think, sir, I mane I could write the 'laders' or the pollitik'l articles, but the creminal cases, sir—the robberies and offices—with the watchhouse cases—together with a little po'thry now and then I think I could be useful, sir, and do better than some of the chaps that pick up their ha'pence that way.—But here's my place, sir,—my little bower of repose."

He knocked at the door of a small tumble-down house in a filthy lane, the one window it presented in front being barred with iron. Some bolts were drawn inside, and though the man who opened the door was forbidding in his aspect, he did not refuse to let Tom in. The portal was hastily closed and bolted after they had entered. The smell of the house was pestilential—the entry dead dark.

"Give me your hand, sir," said the bailiff, leading Tom forward.

They ascended some creaking stairs, and the bailiff, fumbling for some time with a key at a door, unlocked it and shoved it open, and then led in his captive.

Tom saw a shabby-genteel sort of person, whose back was towards him, directing a letter.

"Ah, Goggins! " said the writer, "You're come back in the nick of time. I have finished now, and you may take the letter to Mister Durfy."

"You may give it to him yourself, sir," replied Goggins; "for here he is."

"Indeed!" said the writer, turning round.

"What!" exclaimed Tom Durfy, in surprise; "James Reddy!"

"Even so!" said James, with a sentimental air;

"'The paths of glory lead but to the grave.'

Literature is a bad trade, my dear Tom!—'tis an ungrateful world—men
of the highest aspirations may lie in gaol for all the world cares; not
that you come within the pale of the worthless one; this is d—d good-
natured of you to come to see a friend in trouble. You deserve, my dear
Tom, that, you should have been uppermost in my thoughts; for here is
a note I have just written to you, enclosing a copy of verses to you on
your marriage—in short, it is an epithalamium."

"That's what I told you, sir," said Goggins to Tom. "May the divil
burn you and your epithalamium!" said Tom Durfy, stamping round
the little room.

James Reddy stared in wonder, and Goggins roared, laughing, "A
pretty compliment you've paid me, Mister Reddy, this fine morning,"
said Tom, "you tell a bailiff where I live, that you may send your d—d
verses to me, and you get me arrested."

"Oh, murder!" exclaimed James. "I'm very sorry, my dear Tom; but,
at the same time, 'tis a capital incident! How it would work up in a
farce!"

"How funny it is!" said Tom, in a rage, eyeing James as if he could
have eaten him. "Bad luck to all poetry and poetasters! By the 'tarnal
war, I wish every poet, from Homer down, was put into a mortar and
pounded to death!"

James poured forth expressions of sorrow for the mischance; and
extremely ludicrous it was to see one man making apologies for trying
to pay his friend a compliment; his friend swearing at him for his
civility, and the bailiff grinning at them both.

In this triangular dilemma we leave them for the present.

XLVI

Edward O'Connor, on hearing from Gustavus of the old dowager's disappearance from Neck-or-Nothing Hall, joined in the eager inquiries which were made about her, and *his* being directed with more method and judgment than those of others, their result was more satisfactory. He soon "took up the trail," to use an Indian phrase; and he and Gusty were not many hours in posting after the old lady. They arrived in town early in the morning, and lost no time in casting about for information.

One of the first places Edward inquired at, was the inn where the postchaises generally drove to from the house where the old dowager had obtained her carriage in the country; but there no trace was to be had. Next, the principal hotels were referred to, but as yet without success; when, as they turned into one of the leading streets in continuance of their search, their attention was attracted by a crowd swaying to and fro in that peculiar manner which indicates that there is a fight inside of it. Great excitement prevailed on the verge of the crowd, where exclamations escaped from those who could get a peep at the fight.

"The little chap has great heart!" cried one.

"But the sweep is the biggest," said another.

"Well done, *Horish!*"[1] cried a blackguard, who enjoyed the triumph of his fellow.

"Bravo! little fellow," rejoined a genteeler person, who rejoiced in some successful hit of the other combatant.

There is an inherent love in men to see a fight, which Edward O'Connor shared with inferior men; and if he had not peeped into

the ring, most assuredly Gusty would.—What was their astonishment
when they got a glimpse of the pugilists, to perceive Ratty was one of
them,—his antagonist being a sweep, taller by a head, and no bad hand
at "the noble science."

Edward's first impulse was to separate them, but Gusty requested he
would not, saying that he saw by Ratty's eye he was able to "lick the
fellow." Ratty certainly showed great fight;—what the sweep had in
superior size, was equalized by the superior "game" of the gentleman
boy, to whom the indomitable courage of a high-blooded race had
descended, and who would sooner have died than yield. Besides, Ratty
was not deficient in the use of his "bunch of fives," hit hard for his size,
and was very agile: the sweep sometimes made a rush, grappled, and got
a fall; but he never went in without getting something from Ratty to
"remember him," and was not always uppermost. At last, both were so
far punished, and the combat not being likely to be speedily ended (for
the sweep was no craven), that the bystanders interfered, declaring that
"they ought to be separated,"—and they were.

While the crowd was dispersing, Edward called a coach; and before
Ratty could comprehend how the affair was managed, he was shoved
into it, and driven from the scene of action. Ratty had a confused sense
of hearing loud shouts—of being lifted somewhere—of directions
given—the rattle of iron steps clinking sharply—two or three fierce
bangs of a door that wouldn't shut, and then an awful shaking, which
roused him up from the corner of the vehicle into which he had fallen
in the first moment of exhaustion. Ratty "shook his feathers," dragged
his hair from out of his eyes, which were getting very black indeed, and
applied his handkerchief to his nose, which was much in need of that
delicate attention; and when the sense of perfect vision was restored
to him, which was not for some time, (all the colours of the rainbow
dancing before Ratty's eyes for many seconds after the fight,) what was
his surprise to see Edward O'Connor and Gusty sitting on the opposite
seat!

It was some time before Ratty could quite comprehend his present
situation, but as soon as he was made sensible of it, and could answer,
the first questions asked of him were about his grandmother. Ratty
fortunately remembered the name of the hotel where she put up,

though he had left it as soon as the old lady proceeded to the castle—had lost his way—and got engaged in a quarrel with a sweep in the mean time.

The coach was ordered to drive to the hotel named;—and how the fight occurred was the next question.

"The sweep was passing by, and I called him 'snow ball,'" said Ratty; "and the blackguard returned an impudent answer, and I hit him."

"You had no right to call him 'snow-ball,'" said Edward.

"I always called the sweeps 'snow-ball' down at the Hall," said Ratty, "and they never answered."

"When you are on your own territory you may say what you please to your dependants, Ratty, and they dare not answer; or, to use a vulgar saying, 'A cock may crow on his own dunghill.'"

"I'm no dunghill cock!" said Ratty fiercely.

"Indeed, you're not," said Edward, laying his hand kindly on the boy's shoulder; you have plenty of courage."

"I'd have licked him," said Ratty, "if they'd have let me have two or three rounds more."

"My dear boy, other things are needful in this world besides courage. Prudence, temper, and forbearance are required; and this may be a lesson to you, to remember, that when you get abroad in the world, you are very little cared about, however great your consequence may be at home; and I am sure you cannot be proud about your having got into a quarrel *with a sweep.*"

Ratty made no answer—his blood began to cool—he became every moment more sensible that he had received heavy blows. His eyes became more swollen, he snuffled more in his speech, and his blackened condition altogether, from gutter, soot, and thrashing, convinced him a fight with a sweep was not an enviable achievement.

The coach drew up at the hotel. Edward left Gusty to see about the dowager, and made an appointment for Gusty to meet him at their own lodgings in an hour; while he, in the interim, should call on Dick Dawson, who was in town, on his way to London.

Edward shook hands with Ratty, and bade him kindly good bye,— "You're a stout fellow, Ratty," said he, "but remember this old saying, '*Quarrelsome dogs get dirty coats.*'"

Edward now proceeded to Dick's lodgings, and found him engaged in reading a note from Tom Durfy, dated from the "Bower of Repose," and requesting Dick's aid in his present difficulty.

"Here's a pretty kettle of fish," said Dick; "Tom Durfy, who is engaged to dine with me to-day, to take leave of his bachelor life, as he is going to be married to-morrow, is arrested and now in *quod*, and wants me to bail him."

"The shortest way is to pay the money at once," said Edward; "is it much?"

"That I don't know; but I have not a great deal about me, and what I have I want for my journey to London, and my expenses there,—not but that I'd help Tom, if I could."

"He must not be allowed to remain *there*, however we manage to get him out," said Edward; "perhaps I can help you in the affair."

"You're always a good fellow, Ned," said Dick, shaking his hand warmly.

Edward escaped from hearing any praise of himself, by proposing they should repair at once to the sponging house, and see how matters stood. Dick lamented he should be called away at such a moment, for he was just going to get his wine ready for the party— particularly some champagne, which he was desirous of seeing well iced, but as he could not wait to do it himself, he called Andy, to give him directions about it, and set off with Edward to the relief of Tom Durfy.

Andy was once more in service in the Egan family; for the Squire, on finding him still more closely linked by his marriage with the desperate party whose influence over Andy was to be dreaded, took advantage of Andy's disgust against the woman who had entrapped him, and offered to take him off to London instead of enlisting; and as Andy believed he would be there sufficiently out of the way of the false Bridget, he came off at once to Dublin with Dick, who was the pioneer of the party to London.

Dick gave Andy the necessary directions for icing the champagne, which he set apart, and pointed out most particularly to our hero, lest he should make a mistake, and perchance ice the port instead.

After Edward and Dick had gone, Andy commenced operations, according to orders.—He brought a large tub up stairs containing rough ice, which excited Andy's wonder, for he never had known till now that ice was preserved for and applied to such a use, for an ice-house did not happen to be attached to any establishment in which he had served.

"Well, this is the quarest thing I ever heerd of," said Andy. "Musha! what outlandish inventions the quolity has among them.—They're not contint with wine, but they must have ice along with it,—and in a tub, too!—just like pigs!—throth, it's a dirty thrick, I think.—Well, here goes!" said he; and Andy opened a bottle of champagne, and poured it into the tub with the ice. "How it fizzes!" said Andy.— "Faix, it's almost as lively as the soda-wather, that bothered me long ago.—Well, I know more about things now—sure it's wondherful how a man improves with practice!"—and another bottle of champagne was emptied into the tub as he spoke. Thus, with several such complacent comments upon his own proficiency, Andy poured half-a-dozen of champagne into the tub of ice, and remarked, when he had finished his work, that he thought it would be "mighty cowld on their stomachs."

Dick and Edward all this time were on their way to the relief of Tom Durfy, who, though he had cooled down from the boiling pitch to which the misadventure of the morning had raised him, was still *simmering*, with his elbows planted on the rickety table in Mr. Goggins's "bower," and his chin resting on his clenched hands. It was the very state of mind in which Tom was most dangerous.

At the other side of the table sat James Reddy, intently employed in writing; his pursed mouth and knitted brows bespoke a labouring state of thought, and the various crossings, interlinings, and blottings, gave additional evidence of the same, while now and then a rush at a line which was knocked off in a hurry, with slashing dashes of the pen, and fierce after-crossings of t's, and determined dottings of i's declared some thought suddenly seized, and executed with bitter triumph.

"You seem very *happy in yourself* in what you are writing," said Tom. "What is it?—Is it another epithalamium?"

"It is a caustic article against the successful men of the day," said Reddy; "they have no merit, sir—none. 'Tis nothing but luck has placed them where they are, and they ought to be exposed." He then threw down his pen, as he spoke, and after a silence of some minutes, suddenly put this question to Tom:—

"What do you think of the world?"

"Faith, I think it so pleasant a place," said Tom, "that I'm confoundedly vexed at being kept out of it by being locked up here; and that cursed bailiff is so provokingly free-and-easy—coming in here every ten minutes, and making himself at home."

"Why, as for that matter, it is his home, you must remember,"

"But while a gentleman is here for a period," said Tom, "this room ought to be considered his, and that fellow has no business here—and then his bows and scrapes, and talking about the feelings of a gentleman, and all that—'tis enough to make a dog beat his father. Curse him! I'd like to choke him."

"Oh! that's merely his manner," said James. "Want of manners, you mean," said Tom. "Hang me, if he comes up to me with his rascally familiarity again, but I'll kick him down stairs."

"My dear fellow, you are excited," said Reddy; "don't let these sublunary trifles ruffle your temper—you see how I bear it—and to recall you to yourself, I will remind you of the question we started from, 'What do you think of the world.' There's a general question—a broad question, upon which one may talk with temper, and soar above the petty grievances of life in the grand consideration of so ample a subject.—You see me here, a prisoner like yourself, but I can talk of *the world*. Come, be a calm philosopher, like me!—Answer, what do you think of the world?"

"I've told you already," said Tom; "it's a capital place, only for the bailiffs."

"I can't agree with you," said James. "I think it one vast pool of stagnant wretchedness, where the *malaria* of injustice holds her scales suspended, to poison rising talent by giving an undue weight to existing prejudices."

To this lucid and good-tempered piece of philosophy, Tom could only answer, "You know I am no poet, and I cannot argue with you;

but, 'pon my soul, I *have* known, and *do* know, some uncommon good fellows in the world."

"You're wrong, you're wrong, my unsuspecting friend. 'Tis a bad world, and no place for susceptible minds. Jealousy pursues talent like its shadow—superiority only wins for you the hatred of inferior men.— For instance, why am *I* here? the editor of *my* paper will not allow *my* articles always to appear;—prevents their insertion, lest the effect they would make would cause inquiry, and tend to *my* distinction; and the consequence is, that the paper *I* came to *uphold* in Dublin, is deprived of my articles, and I don't get paid; while *I* see *inferior* men, without asking for it, loaded with favour; *they* are abroad in affluence, and *I* in captivity and poverty. But one comfort is, even in disgrace I can write, and they shall get a slashing."

Thus spoke the calm philosopher, who gave Tom a lecture on patience.

Tom was no great conjuror, but at that moment, like Audrey, "he thanked the gods he was not poetical." If there be any one thing more than another to make an "every-day man" content with his average lot, it is the exhibition of ambitious inferiority, striving for distinction it can never attain; just given sufficient perception to desire the glory of success, without power to measure the strength that can achieve it; like some poor fly, which beats its head against a pane of glass, seeing the sunshine beyond, but incapable of perceiving the subtle medium which intervenes—too delicate for its limited sense to comprehend, but too strong for its limited power to pass.

But though Tom felt satisfaction at that moment, he had too good feeling to wound the self-love of the vain creature before him; so, instead of speaking what he thought, *viz.*— "What business have you to attempt literature, you conceited fool?" he tried to wean him civilly from his folly by saying, "Then come back to the country, James; if you find jealous rivals *here,* you know you were always admired *there.*"

"No, sir!" said James, "even there my merit was unacknowledged."

"No! no!" said Tom.

"Well, underrated at least. Even there, *that* Edward O'Connor, somehow or other, I never could tell why—I never saw his great talents—but somehow or other; people got it into their heads that he was clever."

"I tell you what it is," said Tom, earnestly, "Ned-of-the-Hill has got into a better place than people's *heads*—he has got into their *hearts!*"

"There it is!" exclaimed James, indignantly; "you have caught up the cuckoo-cry—the heart! why, sir, what merit is there in writing about feelings which any common labourer can comprehend—there's no poetry in that;—true poetry lies in a higher sphere, where you have difficulty in following the flight of the poet and, possibly may not be fortunate enough to understand him—that's poetry, sir."

"I told you I am no poet," said Tom; "but all I know is, I have felt my heart warm to some of Edward's songs, and, by jingo! I have seen the women's eyes glisten, and their cheeks flush or grow pale, as they have heard them—and that's poetry enough for me."

"Well, let Mister O'Connor enjoy his popularity, sir—if popularity it may be called, in a small country circle—let him enjoy it—I don't envy him *his*, though I think he was rather jealous about mine."

"Ned jealous!" exclaimed Tom, in surprise.

"Yes, jealous; I never heard him say a kind word of any verses I ever wrote in my life; and I am certain, he has most unkind feelings towards me."

"I tell you what it is," said Tom, "getting up" a bit; "I told you I don't understand poetry, but I do understand what's a d—d deal better thing, and that's fine, generous, manly feeling; and if there's a human being in the world incapable of wronging another in his mind or heart, or readier to help his fellow-man, it is Edward O'Connor—so say no more, James, if you please."

Tom had scarcely uttered the last word, when the key was turned in the door.

"Here's that infernal bailiff again!" said Tom, whose irritability, increased by Reddy's paltry egotism and injustice, was at its boiling pitch once more. He planted himself firmly in his chair, and putting on his fiercest frown, was determined to confront Mister Goggins with an aspect that should astonish him.

The door opened, and Mister Goggins made his appearance, presenting to the gentlemen in the room the hinder portion of his person, which made several indications of courtesy performed by the other half of his body, while he uttered the words, "Don't be astonished, gentlemen; you'll be used to it by and by." And with these words he kept backing towards Tom, making these nether demonstrations of civility, till Tom could plainly see the seams in the back of Mister Goggins's pantaloons.

Tom thought this was some new touch of the "free and-easy" on Mister Goggins's part, and losing all command of himself, he jumped from his chair, and with a vigorous kick gave Mister Goggins such a lively impression of his desire that he should leave the room, that Mister Goggins went head foremost down the stairs, pitching his whole weight upon Dick Dawson and Edward O'Connor, who were ascending the dark stairs, and to whom all his bows had been addressed. Overwhelmed with astonishment and twelve stone of bailiff, they were thrown back into the hall, and an immense uproar in the passage ensued.

Edward and Dick were near coming in for some hard usage from Goggins, conceiving it might be a preconcerted attempt on the part of his prisoners and their newly arrived friends to achieve a rescue; and while he was rolling about on the ground, he roared to his evil-visaged janitor to look to the door first, and keep him from being "murthered" after.

Fortunately no evil consequences ensued, until matters could be explained in the hall, and Edward and Dick were introduced to the upper room from which Goggins had been so suddenly ejected.

There the bailiff demanded in a very angry tone the cause of Tom's conduct; and when it was found to be *only* a mutual misunder-standing—that Goggins wouldn't take a liberty with a gentleman "in defficulties" for the world, and that Tom wouldn't hurt a fly, only "under a mistake," matters were cleared up to the satisfaction of all parties, and the real business of the meeting commenced:—that was, to pay Tom's debt out of hand; and when the bailiff saw all demands, fees included, cleared off, the clouds from his brow cleared off also, he was the most amiable of sheriffs' officers, and all his sentimentality returned.

"Ah, sir!" said he to Edward O'Connor, whose look of disgust at the wretched den caught the bailiff's attention, "don't entertain an antithafy from first imprissions, which is often desaivin'. I do pledge you my honour, sir, there is no place in the 'varsal world where human nature is visible in more attractive colours than in this humble retrait."

Edward did not seem quite to agree with him, so Goggins returned
to the charge, while Tom and Dick were exchanging a few words with
James Reddy.

"You see, sir," said Goggins, "in the first place, it is quite beautiful to see
the mind in adversity bearing up against the little antedliuvan afflictions
that will happen occasionally;—and then how fine it is to remark the
spark of generosity that kindles in the noble heart, and rushes to the
assistance of the destitute! I do assure you, sir, it is a most beautiful sight to
see the gentlemen in defficulties, waitin' here for their friends to come to
their relief, like the last scene in Blue Beard, where sister Ann waives her
han'kecher from the tower—the tyrant is slain—and virtue rewarded!"

Edward could not conceal a smile at the fellow's absurdity, though
his sense of the ridiculous could not overcome the disgust with which
the place inspired him. He gave an admonitory touch to the elbow of
Dick Dawson, who, with his friend Tom Durfy, followed Edward from
the room, the bailiff bringing up the rear, and relocking the door on the
unfortunate James Reddy, who was left "alone in his glory," to finish his
slashing article against the successful men of the day.

Nothing more than words of recognition had passed between Reddy
and Edward. In the first place, Edward's appearance at the very moment
the other was indulging in illiberal observations upon him, rendered
the ill-tempered poetaster dumb; and Edward attributed this distance of
manner to a feeling of shyness which Reddy might entertain at being
seen in such a place, and therefore had too much good breeding to
thrust his civility on a man who seemed to shrink from it; but when
he left the house, he expressed his regret to his companions at the poor
fellow's unfortunate situation.

It touched Tom Durfy's heart to hear these expressions of compassion
coming from the lips of the man he had heard maligned a few minutes
before by the very person commiserated, and it raised his opinion
higher of Edward, whose hand he now shook with warm expressions
of thankfulness on his own account, for the prompt service rendered to
him. Edward made as light of his own kindness as he could, and begged
Tom to think nothing of such a trifle.

"One word I will say to you, Durfy, and I'm sure you'll pardon me
for it."

HANDY ANDY 485

"Could you say a thing to offend me?" was the answer.

"You are to be married soon, I understand."

"To-morrow," said Tom.

"Well, my dear Durfy, if you owe any more money, take a real friend's advice, and tell your pretty good-hearted widow the whole amount of your debts before you marry her."

"My dear O'Connor," said Tom, "the money you've lent me now is all I owe in the world—'twas a tailor's bill, and I quite forgot it.—You know no one ever thinks of a tailor's bill. Debts, indeed!" added Tom with surprise; "My dear fellow, I never could be much in debt, for the devil a one would trust me."

"An excellent reason for your unencumbered state," said Edward, "and I hope you pardon me."

"Pardon!" exclaimed Tom, "I esteem you for your kind and manly frankness."

In the course of their progress towards Dick's lodgings, Edward reverted to James Reddy's wretched condition, and found it was but some petty debt for which he was arrested. He lamented, in common with Dick and Tom, the infatuation which made him desert a duty he could profitably perform by assisting his father in his farming concerns, to pursue a literary path, which could never be any other to him than one of thorns.

As Edward had engaged to meet Gusty in an hour, he parted from his companions and pursued his course alone. But instead of proceeding immediately homeward, he retraced his steps to the den of the bailiff, and gave a quiet tap at the door. Mister Goggins himself answered to the knock, and was making a loud and florid welcome to Edward, who stopped his career of eloquence by laying a finger on his lip in token of silence. A few words sufficed to explain the motive of his visit.—He wished to ascertain the sum for which the gentlethan up stairs was detained. The bailiff informed him; and the money necessary to procure the captive's liberty was placed in his hand.

The bailiff cast one of his melodramatic glances at Edward, and said "Didn't I tell you, sir, this was the place for calling out the noblest feelings of human nature?"

"Can you oblige me with writing materials?" said Edward.

"I can, sir," said Goggins, proudly, "and with other *materials*[2] too, if you like—and, 'pon my honour, I'd be proud to drink your health, for you're a rale gintleman."

Edward, in the civillest manner, declined the offer, and wrote, or rather tried to write the following note, with a pen like a skewer, ink something thicker than mud, and on whity-brown paper:—

> "Dear Sir,
>   "I hope you will pardon the liberty I have taken in your temporary want of money. You can repay me at your convenience.
>   "Yours,
>   "E. O'C."

Edward left the den, and so did James Reddy soon after—a better man. Though weak, his heart was not shut to the humanities of life—and Edward's kindness in opening his eyes to the wrong he had done one man, induced in his heart a kinder feeling towards all. He tore up his slashing article against successful men.—Would that every disappointed man would do the same!

The bailiff was right:—even so low a den as his becomes ennobled by the presence of active benevolence and prejudice reclaimed.

1.   The name of a celebrated sweep in Ireland, whose name is applied to the whole tribe.
2.   The name given in Ireland to the necessary ingredients for the making of whisky-punch.

XLVII

EDWARD, ON RETURNING TO HIS hotel, found Gusty there before him in great delight at having seen a "splendid" horse, as he said, which had been brought for Edward's inspection, he having written a note on his arrival in town to a dealer, stating his want of a first-rate hunter.

"He's in the stable now," said Gusty; "for I desired the man to wait, knowing you would be here soon."

"I cannot see him now, Gusty," said Edward; "will you have the kindness to tell the groom that I can look at the horse in his own stables, when I wish to purchase."

Gusty departed to do the message, somewhat in wonder, for Edward loved a fine horse. But the truth was, that Edward's disposable money, which he had intended for the purchase of a hunter, had a serious inroad made upon it by the debts he had discharged for other men, and he was forced to forego the pleasure he had proposed to himself in the next hunting season; and he did not like to consume any one's time, or raise false expectations, by affecting to look at disposable property with the eye of a purchaser, when he knew it was beyond his reach; and the flimsy common-places of "I'll think of it," or "If I don't see something better," or any other of the twenty hacknied excuses which idle people make, after consuming busy men's time, Edward held to be unworthy. He could ride a hack, and deny himself hunting for a whole season, but he would not unnecessarily consume the useful time of any man for ten minutes.

This may be sneered at by the idle and thoughtless, nevertheless, it is part of the minor morality which is ever present in the conduct of a true gentleman.

Edward had promised to join Dick's dinner party on an impromptu invitation, and the clock striking the appointed hour warned Edward it was time to be off; so jumping up on a jaunting car, he rattled off to Dick's lodgings, where a jolly party was assembled, rife for fun.

Amongst the guests was rather a remarkable man, a Colonel Crammer, who had seen a monstrous deal of service—one of Tom Durfy's friends, whom he had asked leave to bring with him to dinner. Of course, Dick's card and a note of invitation for the gallant colonel were immediately despatched, and he had but just arrived before Edward, who found a bustling sensation in the room as the colonel was presented to those already assembled, and Tom Durfy giving whispers, aside, to each person touching his friend; such as—"Very remarkable man;" "Seen great service;"—"A little odd or so;"—"A fund of most extraordinary anecdote," &c., &c.

Now this Colonel Crammer was no other than Tom Loftus, whose acquaintance Dick wished to make, and who had been invited to the dinner after a preliminary visit; but Tom sent an excuse in his own name, and preferred being present under a fictitious one—this being one of the odd ways in which his humour broke out;—desirous of giving people a "touch of his quality" before they knew him. He was in the habit of assuming various characters—a methodist missionary—the patentee of some unheard-of invention—the director of some new joint-stock company—in short, any thing which would give him an opportunity of telling tremendous bouncers, was equally good for Tom. His reason for assuming a military guise on this occasion was to bother Moriarty, whom he knew he should meet, and had a special reason for tormenting; and he knew he could achieve this, by throwing all the stories Moriarty was fond of telling about his own service into the shade, by extravagant inventions of "hair-breadth 'scapes," and feats by "flood and field." Indeed, the dinner would not be worth mentioning, but for the extraordinary capers Tom cut on the occasion, and the unheard-of lies he squandered.

Dinner was announced by Andy, and with good appetite soup and fish were soon despatched; sherry followed as a matter of necessity. The second course appeared, and was not long under discussion when Dick called for the "champagne."

Andy began to drag the tub towards the table, and Dick, impatient of delay, again called "Champagne."

"I'm bringing it to you, sir," said Andy, tugging at the tub.

"Hand it round the table," said Dick.

Andy tried to lift the tub, "to hand it round the table;" but finding he could not manage it, he whispered Dick, "I can't get it up, sir."

Dick, fancying Andy meant he had got a flask not in a sufficient state of effervescence to expel its own cork, whispered in return, "Draw it, then."

"I was dhrawin' it to you, sir, when you stopped me."

"Well, make haste with it," said Dick.

"Mister Dawson, I'll trouble you for a small slice of the turkey," said the colonel.

"With pleasure, colonel; but first do me the honour to take champagne.— Andy—champagne!"

"Here it is, sir!" said Andy, who had drawn the tub close to Dick's chair.

"Where's the wine, sir?" said Dick, looking first at the tub and then at Andy.

"There, sir," said Andy, pointing down to the ice. "I put the wine into it, as you towld me."

Dick looked again at the tub, and said, "There is not a single bottle there—what do you mean, you stupid rascal?"

"To be sure, there's no bottle there, sir. The bottles is all on the side-board, but every dhrop o' the wine is in the ice, as you towld me, sir; if you put your hand down into it, you'll feel it, sir."

The conversation between master and man growing louder as it proceeded, attracted the attention of the whole company, and those near the head of the table became acquainted as soon as Dick with the mistake Andy had made, and could not resist laughter; and as the cause of their merriment was told from man to man, and passed round the board, a roar of laughter uprose, not a little increased by Dick's look of vexation, which at length was forced to yield to the infectious merriment around him, and he laughed with the rest, and making a joke of the disappointment, which is the very best way of passing one off, he said that he had the honour of originating at his table a magnificent scale of hospitality; for though he had heard of company being entertained with a whole hogshead of claret, he was not aware of champagne being ever served in tubs before. The company were too determined to be merry to have their pleasantry put out of tune by so trifling a mishap, and it was generally voted that the joke was worth twice as much as the wine. Nevertheless, Dick could not help casting a reproachful look now and then at Andy, who had to run the gauntlet of many a joke cut at his expense, while he waited upon the wags at dinner, and caught a lowly muttered anathema whenever he passed near Dick's chair.—In short, master and man were both glad when the cloth was drawn, and the party could be left to themselves.

Then, as a matter-of course, Dick called on the gentlemen to charge their glasses, and fill high to a toast he had to propose—they would anticipate to whom he referred—a gentleman who was going to change his state of freedom for one of a happier bondage, &c., &c. Dick dashed off his speech with several mirth-moving allusions to the change that was coming over his friend Tom, and having festooned his composition with the proper quantity of "rosy wreaths," &c. &c. &c. naturally belonging to such speeches, he wound up with some few hearty words—free from *badinage*, and meaning all they conveyed, and finished with the rhyming benediction of a "long life and a good wife" to him.

Tom having returned thanks in the same laughing style that Dick proposed his health, and bade farewell to the lighter follies of bachelorship for the more serious ones of wedlock, the road was now open for any one who was vocally inclined. Dick asked one or two, who said they were not within a bottle of their singing point yet, but Tom Durfy was sure his friend the colonel would favour them.

"With pleasure," said the colonel; "and I'll sing something appropriate to the blissful situation of philandering in which you have been indulging of late, my friend. I wish I could give you any idea of the song as I heard it warbled by the voice of an Indian princess, who was attached to me once, and for whom I ran enormous risks—but no matter—that's past and gone, but the soft tones of Zulina's voice will ever haunt my heart!—The song is a favourite where I heard it—on the borders of Cashmere, and is supposed to be sung by a fond woman in the valley of the nightingales,—'tis so in the original, but as we have no nightingales in Ireland, I have substituted the dove in the little translation I have made, which, if you'll allow me, I'll attempt."

Loud cries of " Hear, hear," and tapping of applauding hands on the table followed, while the colonel gave a few preliminary hems; and after some little pilot tones from his throat to show the way, his voice ascended in all the glory of song.

THE DOVE-SONG

I

"*Coo! Coo! Coo! Coo!*
  Thus did I hear the turtle-dove,
Coo! Coo! Coo!
    Murmuring forth her love;
And as she flew from tree to tree,
How melting seemed the notes to me—
    Coo! Coo! Coo!—
So like the voice of lovers,
   'Twas passing sweet to hear,
The birds within the covers,
  In the spring-time of the year.

II

"*Coo! Coo! Coo!*
  Thus the song's returned again—
Coo! Coo! Coo!
    Through the shady glen;
But there I wandered lone and sad,
    While every bird around was glad.
     Coo! Coo! Coo!
    Thus so fondly murmured they,
     Coo! Coo! Coo!
  While *my* love was away.

And yet the song to lovers,
    Though sad, is sweet to hear,
From birds within the covers,
    In the spring-time of the year."

The colonel's song, given with Tom Loftus's good voice, was received with great applause, and the fellows all voted it catching, and began "cooing" round the table like a parcel of pigeons.

"A translation from an Eastern poet, you say?"

"Yes," said Tom.

"'Tis not very Eastern in its character," said Moriarty.

"I mean a *free* translation, of course," added the mock colonel.

"Would you favour us with the song again, in the original?" added Moriarty.

Tom Loftus did not know one syllable of any other language than his own, and it would not have been convenient to talk gibberish to Moriarty, who had a smattering of some of the Eastern tongues; so he declined giving his Cashmerian song in its native purity, because, as he said, he never could manage to speak their dialect, though he understood it reasonably well.

"But *there's* a gentleman I am sure will sing some other song— and a better one, I have no doubt," said Tom, with a very humble prostration of his head on the table, and anxious by a fresh song to get out of the dilemma in which Moriarty's question was near placing him.

"Not a better, colonel," said the gentleman who was addressed; "but I cannot refuse your call, and I will do my best;—hand me the port wine, pray; I always take a glass of port before I sing—I think 'tis good for the throat—what do you say, colonel?"

"When I want to sing particularly well," said Tom, "I drink canary."

The gentleman smiled at the whimsical off his glass of port and began.

LADY MINE

I

"LADY mine! lady mine!
Take the rosy wreath I twine;
All its sweets are less than thine,
Lady, lady mine!
The blush that on thy cheek is found
Bloometh fresh the *whole* year round;
Thy sweet *breath* as sweet gives *sound,*
Lady, lady mine!

II

"Lady mine! lady mine!
How I love the graceful vine,
Whose tendrils mock thy ringlets' twine,
Lady, lady mine!
How I love that gen'rous tree,
Whose ripe clusters promise me
Bumpers bright,—to pledge to *thee,*
Lady, lady mine.

III

"Lady mine! lady mine!
Like the stars that nightly shine,
Thy sweet eyes shed light divine,
Lady, lady mine!
And as sages wise, of old,
From the stars could fate unfold,
Thy bright eyes *my* fortune told,
Lady, lady mine!"

The song was just in the style to catch gentlemen after dinner,—the second verse particularly, and many a glass was emptied of a "bumper bright," and pledged to the particular "*thee,*" which each individual had selected for his devotion. Edward at that moment certainly thought of Fanny Dawson.

Let teetotallers say what they please, there is a genial influence inspired by wine and song,—not in excess, but in that wholesome degree which stirs the blood and warms the fancy; and as one raises the glass to the lip, over which some sweet name is just breathed from the depth of the heart, what libation so fit to pour to absent friends as wine? What *is* wine? It is the grape, present in another form;—its essence is there, though the fruit which produced it grew thousands of miles away, and perished years ago. So the object of many a tender thought may be spiritually present, in defiance of space, and fond recollections cherished, in defiance of time.

As the party became more convivial, the mirth began to assume a broader form. Tom Durfy drew out Moriarty on the subject of his services, that the mock colonel might throw every new achievement into the shade; and this he did in the most barefaced manner, but mixing so much of probability with his audacious fiction, that those who were not up to the joke only supposed him to be *a very great romancer*; while those friends who were in Loftus's confidence exhibited a most capacious stomach for the marvellous, and backed up his lies with a ready credence. If Moriarty told some fearful incident of a tiger hunt, the colonel capped it with some thing more wonderful, of slaughtering lions in a wholesale way, like rabbits. When Moriarty expatiated on the intensity of tropical heat, the colonel would upset him with something more appalling.

"Now, sir," said Loftus; "let me ask you what is the greatest amount of heat, you have ever experienced—I say *experienced,* not *heard* of—for that goes for nothing. I always speak from experience."

"Well, sir!" said Moriarty, "I have known it to be so hot in India, that I have had a hole dug in the ground under my tent, and sat in it, and put a table standing over the hole, to try and guard me from the intolerable fervour of the eastern sun, and even *then* I was hot.—What do you say to that, colonel?" asked Moriarty, triumphantly.

"Have you ever been in the West Indies?" inquired Loftus.

"Never," said Moriarty, who, once entrapped into this admission, was directly at the "colonel's" mercy, and the colonel launched out fearlessly.

"Then, my good sir, you know nothing of heat. I have seen in the West Indies an umbrella burned over a man's head."

"Wonderful!" cried Loftus's backers.

"'Tis strange, sir," said Moriarty, "that we have never seen that mentioned by any writer."

"Easily accounted for, sir," said Loftus.—"'Tis so common a circumstance that it ceases to be worthy of observation. An author writing of this country might as well remark that apple-women are to be seen sitting at the corners of the streets.—That's nothing, sir, but there are two things of which I have personal knowledge, *rather* remarkable. One day of intense heat, (even for that climate,) I was on a visit at the plantation of a friend of mine, and it was so out-o'-the-way scorching, that our lips were like cinders, and we were obliged to have black slaves pouring sangaree down our throats by gallons—I don't hesitate to say gallons—and we thought we could not have survived through the day; but what could we think of our sufferings, when we heard that several negroes, who had gone to sleep under the shade of some cocoa-nut trees, had been scalded to death."

"Scalded!" said his friends; "burnt, you mean."

"No, scalded; and *how* do you think? The intensity of the heat had cracked the cocoa-nuts, and the boiling milk inside dropped down and produced the fatal result. The same day a remarkable accident occurred at the battery—the French were hovering round the island at the time and the governor, being a timid man, ordered the guns to be always kept loaded."

"I never heard of such a thing in a battery in my life, sir," said Moriarty.

"Nor I either," said Loftus, "till then."

"What was the governor's name, sir?" inquired Moriarty, pursuing his train of doubt.

"You must excuse me, captain, from naming him," said Loftus, with readiness, "after *incautiously* saying he was *timid*."

"Hear, hear!" said all the friends.

"But to pursue my story, sir;—the guns were loaded, and with the intensity of the heat went off, one after after another, and quite *riddled* one of his Majesty's frigates that was lying in the harbour."

"That's one of the most difficult riddles to comprehend I ever heard," said Moriarty.

"The frigate answered the riddle with her guns, sir, I promise you."

"What!" exclaimed Moriarty, "fire on the fort of her own king?"

"There is an honest principle exists amongst sailors, sir, to return fire under all circumstances, wherever it comes from—friend or foe. Fire, of which they know the value so well, they won't take from anybody."

"And what was the consequence?" said Moriarty.

"Sir, it was the most harmless broadside ever delivered from the ports of a British frigate; not a single house or human being was injured—the day was so hot that every sentinel had sunk on the ground in utter exhaustion—the whole population were asleep; the only loss of life which occurred, was that of a blue macaw, which belonged to the commandant's daughter."

"Where was the macaw, may I beg to know?" said Moriarty, cross-questioning the colonel in the spirit of a counsel for the defence on a capital indictment.

"In the drawing-room window, sir."

"Then, surely the ball must have done some damage in the house?"

"Not the least, sir," said Loftus, sipping his wine.

"Surely, colonel!" returned Moriarty, warming, "the ball could not have killed the macaw without injuring the house?"

"My dear sir," said Tom, "I did not say the *ball* killed the macaw, I said the macaw was killed; but *that* was in consequence of a splinter from an *épaulement* of the south-east angle of the fort which the shot struck, and glanced off harmlessly,—except for the casualty of the macaw."

Moriarty returned a sort of grunt, which implied, that, though he could not further *question,* he did not *believe.* Under such circumstances, taking snuff is a great relief to a man; and, as it happened, Moriarty, in taking snuff, could gratify his nose and his vanity at the same time, for he sported a silver-gilt snuff-box which was presented to him in some extraordinary way, and bore a grand inscription.

On this "piece of plate" being produced, of course it went round the table, and Moriarty could scarcely conceal the satisfaction he felt as each person read the engraven testimonial of his worth. When it had gone the circuit of the board, Tom Loftus put his hand into his pocket, and pulled out the butt end of a rifle, which is always furnished with a small box, cut out of the solid part of the wood, and covered with a plate of brass, acting on a hinge. This box, intended to carry small implements for the use of the rifleman, to keep his piece in order, was filled with snuff, and Tom said, as he laid it down on the table, "This is my snuff-box, gentlemen; not as handsome as my gallant friend's at the opposite side of the table, but extremely interesting to me. It was previous to one of our dashing affairs in Spain, that our riflemen were thrown out in front and on the flanks. The rifles were supported by the light companies of the regiments in advance, and it was in the latter duty I was engaged. We had to feel our way through a wood, and had cleared it of the enemy, when, as we debouched from the wood on the opposite side, we were charged by an overwhelming force of Polish lancers and cuirassiers. Retreat was impossible—resistance almost hopeless. 'My lads,' said I, 'we must do something *novel* here, or we are lost—startle them by fresh practice—the bayonet will no longer avail you—club your muskets, and hit the horses over the noses, and they'll smell danger.' They took my advice; of course we first delivered a withering volley, and then to it we went in flail fashion, thrashing away with the butt-ends of our muskets,—and sure enough the French were astonished, and driven back in amazement. So tremendous, sir, was the hitting on our side, that in many instances the butt-ends of the muskets snapped off like tobacco pipes, and the field was quite strewn with them after the affair: I picked one of them up as a little memento of the day, and have used it ever since as a snuff-box."

Every one was amused by the outrageous romancing of the colonel but Moriarty, who looked rather disgusted, because he could not edge in a word of his own at all: he gave up the thing now in despair, for the colonel had it all his own way, like the bull in the china shop;—the more startling the bouncers he told, the more successful were his anecdotes, and he kept pouring them out with the most astounding rapidity; and though all voted him the greatest liar they ever met, none suspected he was not a military man.

Dick wanted Edward O'Connor, who sat beside him, to sing; but Edward whispered, "For heaven's sake, don't stop the flow of the lava from that mighty irruption of lies—he's a perfect Vesuvius of mendacity.—You'll never meet his like again, so make the most of him while you have him. Pray, sir," said Edward to the colonel, "have you ever been in any of the cold climates. I am induced to ask you, from the very wonderful anecdotes you have told of the hot ones."

"Bless you, sir, I know every corner about the north pole."

"In which of the expeditions, may I ask, were you engaged?" inquired Moriarty.

"In none of them, sir. We knocked up a *little amateur party*, I and a few curious friends, and certainly we witnessed wonders. You talk here of a sharp wind;—but the wind is so sharp there, that it cut off our beards and whiskers. Boreas is a great barber, sir, with his north pole for a sign. Then as for frost!—I could tell you such incredible things of its intensity;—our butter, for instance, was as hard as a rock; we were obliged to knock it off with a chisel and hammer, like a mason at a piece of granite, and it was necessary to be careful of your eyes at breakfast, the splinters used to fly about so; indeed, one of the party *did* lose the use of his eye from a butter splinter.

"But the oddest thing of all was to watch two men talking to each other: you could observe the words, as they came out of their mouths, suddenly frozen and dropping down in little pellets of ice at their feet, so that, after a long conversation, you might see a man standing up to his knees in his own eloquence."

They all roared with laughter at this last touch of the marvellous, but Loftus preserved his gravity.

"I don't wonder, gentlemen, at your not receiving that as truth—I told you 'twas incredible—in short, that is the reason I have resisted all temptations to publish. Murray, Longmans, Colburn, Bentley, ALL the publishers have offered me unlimited terms, but I have always refused;—not that I am a rich man, which makes the temptation of the thousands I might realise the harder to withstand; 'tis not that the gold is not precious to me, but there is something dearer to me than gold—*it is my character for veracity, gentlemen!*—and therefore, as I am convinced the public would not believe the wonders I have witnessed, I confine the recital of my adventures to the social circle. But what profession affords such scope for varied incident as that of the soldier? Change of clime, danger, vicissitude, love, war, privation one day, profusion the next, darkling dangers and sparkling joys. Zounds! there's nothing like the life of a soldier! and by the powers, I'll give you a song in its praise."

The proposition was received with cheers, and Tom rattled away these ringing rhymes:—

THE BOWLD SOJER BOY

I

"Oh there's not a trade that's going,
Worth showing,
Or knowing,
Like that from glory growing,
    For a bowld sojer boy
Where right or left we go,
Sure you know,
Friend or foe
Will have the hand or toe,
    From a bowld sojer boy!
There's not a town we march thro',
But the ladies, looking arch thro'
The window will search thro'
    The ranks to find their joy;
While up the Street,
Each girl you meet,
Will look so sly,
Will cry,
'My eye!
Oh, isn't he a darling, the bowld sojer boy!

II

"But when we get the route,
How they pout
And they shout,
While to the right about
    Goes the bowld sojer boy.
Oh, 'tis then that ladies fair
In despair
Tear their hair,
But 'the divil-a-one I care,'
    Says the bowld sojer boy!
For the world is all before us,
Where the landladies adore us
And ne'er refuse to score us,
    But chalk us up with joy;
We taste her tap,
We tear her cap—
'Oh, that's the chap
For me!'
Says she;
'Oh, isn't he a darling, the bowld sojer boy

III

"'Then come along with me,
Gramachree,
And you'll see,
How happy you will be
    With your bowld sojer boy:
Faith! if you're up to fun,
With me run
'Twill be done
In the snapping of a gun,'
    Says the bowld sojer boy;
'And 'tis then that, without scandal,

Myself will proudly dandle
The little farthing candle
    Of our mutual flame, my joy!
May his light shine,
As bright as mine,
Till in the line
He'll blaze,
And raise
The glory of his corps, like a bowld sojer boy!"

Andy entered the room while the song was in progress, and handed a letter to Dick, which, after the song was over, and he had asked pardon of his guests, he opened.

"By Jove! you sing right well, colonel," said one of the party.

"I think the gallant colonel's song's nothing in comparison with his *wonderful* stories," said Moriarty.

"Gentlemen," said Dick, "wonderful as the colonel's recitals have been, this letter conveys a piece of information more surprising than any thing we have heard this evening. That stupid fellow, who has spoiled our champagne, has come in for the inheritance of a large property."

"What!—Handy Andy?" exclaimed those who knew his name, in wonder.

"Handy Andy," said Dick, "is now a man of fortune!"

XLVIII

IT WAS A NOTE FROM Squire Egan, which conveyed the news to Dick, that caused so much surprise;—the details of the case were not even hinted at; the bare fact alone was mentioned, with a caution to preserve it still a secret from Andy, and appointing an hour for dinner at "Morisson's" next day, at which hotel the Squire expected to arrive from the country, with his lady and Fanny Dawson, en route for London. Till dinner time, then, the day following, Dick was obliged to lay by his impatience as to the "why and wherefore" of Andy's sudden advancement; but, as the morning was to be occupied with Tom Durfy's wedding, Dick had enough to keep him engaged in the meantime.

At the appointed hour a few of Tom's particular friends were in attendance to witness the ceremony, or, to use their own phrase, "to see him turned off," and among them was Tom Loftus. Dick was holding out his hand to "the colonel," when Tom Durfy stepped between, and introduced him under his real name. The masquerading trick of the night before was laughed at, with an assurance from Dick that it only fulfilled all he had ever heard of the Protean powers of a gentleman whom he so much wished to know. A few minutes' conversation in the recess of a window put Tom Loftus and Dick the Divil on perfectly good terms, and Loftus proposed to Dick that they should execute the old established trick on a bridegroom, of snatching the first kiss from the bride.

"You must get in Tom's way," said Loftus, "and I'll kiss her."

"Why, the fact is," said Dick, "I had proposed that pleasure to myself; and if it's all the same to you, *you* can jostle Tom, and *I'll* do the remainder in good style, I promise you."

"That I can't agree to," said Loftus; "but as it appears we have both set our heart on cheating the bridegroom, let us both start fair, and 'tis odd, if between us Tom Durfy is not *done*."

This was agreed upon, and many minutes did not elapse till the bride made her appearance and "hostilities were about to commence." The mutual enemy of the "high contracting parties" first opened his book, and then his mouth, and in such solemn tones, that it was enough to frighten *even* a widow, much less a bachelor. As the ceremony verged to a conclusion, Tom Durfy and Dick the Divil edged up towards their vantage-ground on either side of the blooming widow, now nearly finished into a wife, and stood like greyhounds in the slip, ready to start after puss (only puss ought to be spelt here with a B). The widow, having been married before, was less nervous than Durfy, and suspecting the intended game, determined to foil both the brigands,   who intended to rob the bridegroom of his right; so, when the last word of the ceremony was spoken, and Loftus and Dick made a simultaneous dart upon her, she very adroitly ducked, and allowed the two "ruggers and rievers" to rush into each other's arms, and bob their noses together, while Tom Durfy and his blooming bride sealed their contract very agreeably without their noses getting in each other's way.

Loftus and Dick had only a laugh at *their own* expense, instead of a kiss at *Tom's*, upon the failure of their plot; but Loftus, in a whisper to Dick, vowed he would execute a trick upon "the pair of them" before the day was over,

There was a breakfast, as usual, and chicken and tongue, and wine, which, taken in the morning, are singularly provocative of eloquence; and, of course, the proper quantity of healths and toasts were executed *selon la règle*, until it was time for the bride and bridegroom to bow and blush and curtsey out of the room, and make themselves food for a paragraph in the morning papers, under the title of "the happy pair," who set off in a handsome chariot, &c. &c.

Tom Durfy had engaged a pretty cottage in the neighbourhood of Clontarf to pass the honeymoon. Tom Loftus knew this, and knew, moreover, that the sitting-room looked out on a small lawn which lay before the house, screened by a hedge from the road, but with a circular sweep leading up to the house, and a gate of ingress and egress at either end of the hedge. In this sitting-room Tom, after lunch, was pressing his lady fair to take a glass of champagne, when the entrance-gate was thrown open, and a hackney jaunting-car, with Tom Loftus and a friend or two upon it, driven by a special ragamuffin blowing a tin horn, rolled up the skimping avenue, and as it scoured past the windows of the sitting-room, Tom Loftus and the other passengers kissed hands to the astonished bride and bridegroom, and shouted "Wish you joy."

The thing was so sudden that Durfy and the widow, not seeing Loftus, could hardly comprehend what it meant, and both ran to the window; but, just as they reached it, up drove another car, freighted with two or three more wild rascals, who followed the lead which had been given them; and as a long train of cars were seen in the distance all driving up to the avenue, the widow, with a timid little scream, threw her handkerchief over her face and ran into the corner. Tom did not know whether to laugh or be angry, but, being a good-humoured fellow, he satisfied himself with a few oaths against the incorrigible Loftus, and, when the *cortège* had passed, endeavoured to restore the startled fair one to her serenity.

Squire Egan and party arrived at the appointed hour at their hotel, where Dick was waiting to receive them, and, of course, his inquiries were immediately directed to the extraordinary circumstance of Andy's elevation, the details of which he desired to know. These we shall not give in the expanded form in which Dick heard them, but endeavour to condense, as much as possible, within the limits to which we are prescribed.

The title of Scatterbrain had never been inherited directly from father to son; it had descended in a zigzag fashion, most appropriate to the name, nephews and cousins having come in for the coronet and the property for some generations. The late lord had led a *roué* bachelor life up to the age of sixty, and then thought it not worth while to marry, though many mammas and daughters spread their nets and arrayed their charms to entrap the sexagenarian.

The truth was, he had quaffed the cup of licentious pleasure all his life, after which he thought matrimony would prove insipid. The mere novelty indues some men, under similar circumstances, to try the holy estate; but matrimony could not offer to Lord Scatterbrain the charm of novelty, for *he had been* once married, though no one but himself was cognizant of the fact.

The reader will certainly say, "Here's an Irish bull; how could a man be married without, at least, a woman and a priest being joint possessors of the secret?"

Listen, gentle reader, and you shall hear how none but Lord Scatterbrain knew Lord Scatterbrain was married.

There was nothing at which he ever stopped for the gratification of his passions,—no wealth he would not squander, no deceit he would not practise,—no disguise he would not assume. Therefore, gold and falsehood and masquerading were extensively employed by this reckless *roué* in the service of Venus, in which service, combined with that of Bacchus, his life was entirely passed.

Often he assumed the guise of a man in humble life, to approximate some object of his desire, whom fine clothes and bribery would have instantly warned; and in too many cases his artifices were successful. It was in one of these adventures he cast his eyes upon the woman hitherto known in this story under the name of the widow Rooney; but all his practices against her virtue were unavailing, and nothing but a marriage could accomplish what he had set his fancy upon; but even *this* would not stop him, *for he married her.*

The widow Rooney has appeared no very inviting personage through these pages, and the reader may wonder that a man of rank could proceed to such desperate lengths upon such slight temptation; but gentle reader, she was young and attractive when she was married, never to say *handsome,* but goodlooking decidedly, and with that sort of figure which is comprehended in the phrase "a fine girl."

And has that fine girl altered into the widow Rooney? Ah! poverty and hardship are sore trials to the body as well as to the mind. Too little is it considered, while we gaze on aristocratic beauty, how much good food, soft lying, warm wrapping, ease of mind, have to do with the attractions which command our admiration.—Many a hand moulded by nature to give elegance of form to a kid glove, is "stinted of its fair proportion" by grubbing toil. The foot which might have excited the admiration of a ball room, peeping under a flounce of lace, in a satin shoe, and treading the mazy dance, *will* grow coarse and broad by tramping in its native state over toilsome miles, bearing perchance to a market-town some few eggs, whose whole produce would not purchase the sandal-tie of my lady's slipper; will grow red and rough by standing in wet trenches, and feeling the winter's frost. The neck on which diamonds might have worthily sparkled, will look less tempting when the biting winter has hung icicles there for gems. Cheeks formed as fresh for dimpling blushes, eyes as well to sparkle, and lips to smile, as those which shed their brightness and their witchery in the tapestried saloon, will grow pale with want, and fox their dimples, when smiles are not there to wake them;—lips become compressed and drawn with anxious thought, and eyes the brightest are quenched of their fires by many tears.

Of all these trials poor widow Rooney had enough. Her husband, after living with her a month, in the character of steward to some great man in a distant part of the country, left her one day for the purpose of transacting business at a fair, which, he said, would require his absence for some time. At the end of a week a letter was sent to her, stating that the make-believe steward had robbed his master extensively, and had fled to America, whence he promised to write to her, and send her means to follow him,—requesting, in the mean time, her silence, in case any inquiries should be made about him. This villanous trick was played off the more readily, from the fact that a steward had absconded at the time, and the difference in name the cruel profligate accounted for by saying that, as he was hiding at the moment he married her, he had assumed another name.

The poor deserted girl, fully believing this trumped-up tale, obeyed with unflinching fidelity the injunctions of her betrayer, and while reports were flying abroad of the absconded steward, she never breathed a word of what had been confided to her, and accounted for the absence of "Rooney" in various ways of her own so that all trace of the profligate was lost by her remaining inactive in making the smallest inquiry about him, and her very fidelity to her betrayer became the means of her losing all power of procuring his discovery. For months she trusted all was right; but when moon followed moon, and she gave birth to a boy without hearing one word of his father, misgivings came upon her, and the only consolation left her was, that, though she was deserted, and a child left on her hands, still she was *an honest woman.* That child was the hero of our tale. The neighbours passed some ill-natured remarks about her, when it began to be suspected that her husband would never let her know more about him; for she had been rather a saucy lady, holding up her nose at poor men, and triumphing in her catching of the "steward," a man well to do in the world; and it may be remembered, that this same spirit existed in her when Andy's rumoured marriage with Matty gave the prospect of her affairs being retrieved, for she displayed her love of pre-eminence to the very first person who gave her the good news. The ill-nature of her neighbours, however, after the birth of her child, and the desertion of her husband, inducing her to leave the scene of her unmerited wrongs and annoyances, she suddenly decamped, and, removing to another part of Ireland, the poor woman began a life of hardship, to support herself and rear the offspring of her unfortunate marriage. In this task she was worthily assisted by one of her brothers, who pitied her condition, and joined her in her retreat. He married in course of time, and his wife died in giving birth to Oonah, who was soon deprived of her other parent by typhus fever,—that terrible scourge of the poor; so that the praiseworthy desire of the brother to befriend his sister, only involved her, as it happened, in the deeper difficulty of supporting two children instead of one. This she did heroically, and the orphan girl rewarded her, by proving a greater comfort than her own child; for Andy had inherited in all its raciness the blood of the Scatterbrains, and his deeds, as recorded in this history, prove he was no unworthy representative of that illustrious title.

To return to his father—he who had done the grievous wrong to the poor peasant girl;—he lived his life of profligacy through, and in a foreign country died at last; but on his death-bed the scourge of conscience rendered every helpless hour an age of woe. Bitterest of all was the thought of the wife deceived, deserted, and unacknowledged. To face his last account with such fearful crime upon his head he dared not, and made all the reparation now in his power, by avowing his marriage in his last will and testament, and giving all the information in his power to trace his wife, if living, or his heir, if such existed. He enjoined, by the most sacred injunctions upon him to whom the charge was committed, that neither cost nor trouble should be spared in the search, leaving a large sum in ready money besides, to establish the right, in case his nephew disputed the will. By his own order his death was kept secret, and secretly his agent set to work to discover any trace of the heir. This, in consequence of the woman changing her place of abode, became more difficult; and it was not until after very minute inquiry that some trace was picked up, and a letter written to the parish priest of the district to where she had removed, making certain general inquiries. It was found, on comparing dates some time after, that it was this very letter to Father Blake which Andy had purloined from the post office and the Squire had thrown into the fire, so that our hero was very near, by his blundering, destroying his own fortune. Luckily for him, however, an untiring and intelligent agent was engaged in his cause, and a subsequent inquiry, and finally, a personal visit to Father Blake, cleared the matter up satisfactorily, and the widow was enabled to produce such proof of her identity, and that of her son, that Handy Andy was indisputably Lord Scatterbrain; and the whole affair was managed so secretly, that the death of the late lord, and the claim of title and estates, in the name of the rightful heir, were announced at the same moment; and the "Honourable Sackville," instead of coming into possession of the peerage and property, and fighting his adversary at the great advantage of possession, could only commence a suit to drive him out, if he sued at all.

Our limits compel us to this brief sketch of the circumstances through which Handy Andy was entitled to and became possessed of a property and a title, and we must now say something of the effects produced by the intelligence on the parties most concerned.

The Honourable Sackville Scatterbrain, on the advice of high legal authority, did not attempt to dispute a succession of which such satisfactory proofs existed, and, fortunately for himself, had knocked up a watering-place match, while he was yet in the bloom of his heirship *presumptive* to a peerage, with the daughter of an English *millionaire.*

When the widow Rooney heard the extraordinary turn affairs had taken, her emotions, after the first few hours of pleasurable surprise, partook of regret rather than satisfaction. She looked upon her past life of suffering, and felt as if Fate had cheated her. She, a peeress, had passed her life in poverty and suffering, with contempt from those over whom she had superior rights; and the few years of the prosperous future before her offered her poor compensation for the pinching past. But after such selfish considerations, the maternal feeling came to her relief, and she rejoiced that *her son* was a lord. But then came the terrible thought of his marriage to dash her joy and triumph.

This was a source of grief to Oonah as well. "If he wasn't married," she would say to herself, "I might be *Lady* Scatterbrain;" and the tears would burst through poor Oonah's fingers as she held them up to her eyes, and sobbed heavily, till the poor girl would try to gather consolation from the thought that, maybe, Andy's altered circumstances would make *her* disregarded. "There would be plenty to have him now," thought she, "and he wouldn't think of me, may be—so 'tis as well as it is."

When Andy heard that he was a lord—a real lord—and, after the first shock of astonishment, could comprehend that wealth and power were in his possession, he, though the most interested person, never thought, as the two women had done, of the desperate strait in which his marriage placed him, but broke out into short peals of laughter, and exclaimed, in the intervals, that "it was mighty quare;" and when, after much questioning, any intelligible desire he had could be understood, the first one he clearly expressed was "*to have a goold watch.*"

He was made, however, to understand that other things than "goold watches" were of more importance; and the Squire, with his characteristic good nature, endeavoured to open Andy's comprehension to the nature of his altered situation. This, it may be supposed, was rather a complicated piece of work, and too difficult to be set down in black and white; the most intelligible portions to Andy were his immediate removal from servitude, and a ready-made suit of gentlemanly apparel, which made Andy pay several visits to the looking-glass. Good-natured

as the Squire was, it would have been equally awkward to him as to
Andy for the new-fledged lord, though a lord, to have a seat at his
table, neither could he remain in an inferior position in his house; so
Dick, who loved fun, volunteered to take Andy under his especial care
to London, and let him share his lodgings, as a bachelor may do many
things which a man surrounded by his family cannot. Besides, in a
place distant from the scene of such extraordinary chances and changes
as those which befel our hero, the sudden and startling difference
of position of the parties, not being known, renders it possible for
a gentleman to do the good-natured thing which Dick undertook,
without compromising himself. In Dublin it would not have done for
Dick Dawson to allow the man who would have held his horse the day
before to share the same board with him merely because Fortune had
played one of her frolics, and made Andy a lord; but in London the case
was different.

To London, therefore, they proceeded. The incidents of the journey,
sea-sickness included, which so astonished the new traveller, we pass
over, as well as the numberless mistakes in the great metropolis, which
afforded Dick plentiful amusement, though, in truth, Dick had better
objects in view than laughing at Andy's embarrassments in his new
position. He really wished to help him in the difficult path into which
the new lord had been thrust, and did this in a merry sort of way
more successfully than by serious drilling. It was hard to break Andy of
the habit of saying "Misther Dick," when addressing him, but, at last,
"Misther Dawson" was established. Eating with his knife, drinking as
loudly as a horse, and other like accomplishments, were not so easily got
under, yet it was wonderful how much he improved, as his shyness grew
less, and his consciousness of being a lord grew stronger.

But if the good nature of Dick had not prompted him to take
Andy into training, the newly discovered nobleman would not have
long been in want of society. It was wonderful how many persons
were eager to show civility to his lordship, and some amongst them
even went so far as to discover relationship. Plenty were soon ready
to take Lord Scatterbrain here, and escort him there, accompany him
to exhibitions and other public places, and charmed all the time with
his lordship's remarks—"they were so original;"—"quite delightful to

meet something so fresh;"—"how remarkably clever the Irish were!" Such were among the observations his ignorant blunders produced; and he who, as Handy Andy had been anathematized all his life as a "stupid rascal,"—"a blundering thief,"—"a thick-headed brute," &c. &c., under the title of Lord Scatterbrain all of a sudden was voted "vastly amusing—a little eccentric, perhaps, but *so* droll—in fact, so witty!"

This was all very delightful for Andy—so delightful that he quite forgot Bridget *rhua*. But that lady did not leave him long in his happy obliviousness. One day, while Dick was absent, and Andy rocking on a chair before the fire, twirling the massive gold chain of his gold watch round his forefinger, and uncoiling it again, his repose was suddenly disturbed by the appearance of Bridget herself, accompanied by *Shan More*, and a shrimp of a man in rusty black, who turned out to be a shabby attorney, who advanced money to convey his lady client and her brother to London for the purpose of making a dash at the lord at once, and securing a handsome sum by a *coup de main*.

Andy, though taken by surprise, was resolute. Bitter words were exchanged; and as they seemed likely to lead to blows, Andy prudently laid hold of the poker, and, in language not quite suited to a noble lord, swore he would see what the inside of *Shan More's* head was made of, if he attempted to advance upon him. Bridget screamed and scolded, while the attorney endeavoured to keep the peace, and beyond every thing, urged Lord Scatterbrain to enter at once into written engagements for a handsome settlement upon his "lady."

"Lady!" exclaimed Andy; "oh!—a pretty *lady* she is!"

"I'm as good a lady as you are a lord, any how," cried Bridget.

"Altercation will do no good, my lord and my lady," said the attorney; "let me suggest the propriety of your writing an engagement at once;" and the little man pushed pen, ink, and paper towards Andy.

"I can't, I tell you!" cried Andy.

"You must!" roared *Shan More*.

"Bad luck to you, how can I write when I never larned?" cried Andy.

"Your lordship can make your mark," said the attorney.

"Faith I can—with a poker," cried Andy; "and you'd better take care, masther parchment. Make my mark, indeed!—do you think I'd disgrace the House o' Peers by lettin' on that a lord couldn't write?—Quit the buildin', I tell you!"

In the midst of the row, which now rose to a tremendous pitch, Dick returned; and after a severe reprimand to the pettifogger for his sinister attempt on Andy, referred him to Lord Scatterbrain's solicitor. It was not such an easy matter to silence Bridget, who extended her claws towards her lord and master in a very menacing manner, calling down bitter imprecations on her own head if she wouldn't "have her rights."

Every now and then between the bursts of the storm, Andy would exclaim "Get out!

"My lord," said Dick, "remember your dignity."

"Av course!" said Andy—"but still she must get out!"

The house was at last cleared of the uproarious party; but though Andy got rid of their presence, they left their sting behind. Lord Scatterbrain felt, for the first time, that a lord can be very unhappy.

Dick hurried him away at once to the chambers of the law agent, but he, being closeted on some very important business with another client on their arrival, returned an answer to their application for a conference, which they forwarded through the double doors of his sanctum by a hard-looking man with a pen behind his ear, that he could not have the pleasure of seeing them till the next morning. Lord Scatterbrain passed a more unhappy night than he had ever done in his life,—even than that when he tied up to the old tree—croaked at by ravens, and the despised of rats.

Negotiations were opened next day between the pettifogger on Bridget's side and the law agent, of the noble lord, and the arguments, pro and con, lay thus:—

In the first place, the opening declaration was—Lord Scatterbrain never would live with the aforesaid Bridget.

Answered—that nevertheless, as she was his lawful wife, a provision suitable to her rank must be made.

They (the claimants) were asked to name a sum.

The sum was considered exorbitant; it being argued, that, inasmuch as, when her husband had determined never to live with her, he was in a far different condition, it was unfair to seek so large a separate maintenance now.

The pettifogger threatened that Lady Scatterbrain would run in debt, which Lord Scatterbrain must discharge.

My Lord's agent suggested that my lady would be advertised in the public papers, and the public cautioned from giving her credit.

A sum could not be agreed upon, though a fair one was offered on Andy's part; for the greediness of the pettifogger, who was to have a share of the plunder, made him hold out for more, and negotiations were broken off for some days.

Poor Andy was in a wretched state of vexation. It was bad enough that he was married to this abominable woman, without the additional plague of being persecuted by her. To such an amount this rose at last, that she and her big brother dodged him every time he left the house, so that in self-defence he was obliged to become a close prisoner in his own lodgings.

All this, at last, became so intolerable to the captive, that he urged a speedy settlement of the vexatious question, and a larger separate maintenance was granted to the detestable woman than would otherwise have been ceded, the only stipulation of a stringent nature made, being, that Lord Scatterbrain should be free from the persecutions of his hateful wife for the future.

XLIX

SQUIRE EGAN, WITH HIS LADY, and Fanny Dawson, had now arrived in London; Murtough Murphy, too, had joined them, his services being requisite in working the petition against the return of the sitting member for the county. This had so much promise of success about it, that the opposite party, who had the sheriff for the county in their interest, bethought of a novel expedient to frustrate the petition, when a reference to the poll was required.

They declared the principal poll book was lost.

This seemed not very satisfactory to one side of the committee, and the question was asked, "how could it be lost?"

The answer was one which Irish contrivance alone could have invented: "*It fell into a pot of broth, and the dog ate it.*"[1]

This protracted the contest for some time; but, eventually, in despite of the dog's devouring knowledge so greedily, the Squire was declared duly elected, and took the oaths and his seat for the county.

It was hard on Sackville Scatterbrain to lose his seat in the house, and a peerage, nearly at once; but the latter loss threw the former so far into the shade, that he scarcely felt it. Besides, he could console himself with having buttered his crumbs pretty well in the marriage market, and, with a rich wife, retired from senatorial drudgery to private repose, which was much more congenial to his easy temper.

But while the Squire's happy family circle was rejoicing in his triumph; while he was invited to the Speaker's dinners, and the ladies were looking forward to tickets for "the lantern," their pleasure was suddenly dashed by fatal news from Ireland.

A serious accident had befallen Major Dawson—so serious, that his life was despaired of; and an immediate return to Ireland by all who were interested in his life, was the consequence.

Though the suddenness of this painful event shocked his family, the act which caused it did not surprise them; for it was one against which Major Dawson had been repeatedly cautioned, and affectionately requested not to tempt; but the habitual obstinacy of his nature prevailed, and he persisted in doing that which his son, and his daughters, and friends, prophesied *would* kill him some time or other, and *did,* at last. The Major had three little iron guns, mounted on carriages, on a terrace in front of his house; and it was his wont to fire a salute on certain festival days from these guns, which, from age and exposure to weather, became dangerous to use. It was in vain that this danger was represented to him. He would reply, with his accustomed "pooh! pooh!"—"I have been firing these guns for forty years, an they won't do me any harm now."

This was the prime fault of the Major's character. Time and circumstances were never taken into account by him; what was done once, might be done *always—ought* to be done always. The bare thought of change of any sort, to him, was unbearable; and whether it was a rotten old law, or a rotten old gun, he would charge both up to the muzzle, and fire away, regardless of consequences.

The result was, that on a certain festival, his *favourite* gun burst in the act of exploding; and the last mortal act of which the Major was conscious, was that of putting the port-fire to the touchhole, for a heavy splinter of the iron struck him on the head, and though he lived for some days afterwards, he was insensible.

Before his children arrived, he was no more; and the only duty left them to perform, was the melancholy one of ordering his funeral.

The obsequies of the old Major were honoured by a large and distinguished attendance from all parts of the country; and amongst those who bore the pall, was Edward O'Connor, who had the melancholy gratification of testifying his respect beside the grave of Fanny's father, though the severe old man had banished him from his presence during his lifetime.

But now all obstacle to the union of Edward and Fanny was removed; and after the lapse of a few days had softened the bitter grief, which this sudden bereavement of her father had produced, Edward received a note from Dick, inviting him to the manor house, where *all* would be glad to see him.

In a few minutes after the receipt of that note, Edward was in his saddle, and swiftly leaving the miles behind him, till, from the top of a rising ground, the roof of the manor house appeared above the trees in which it was embosomed. He had not till then slackened his speed, but now drawing rein, he proceeded at a slower pace towards the house he had not entered for some years, and the sight of which awakened such varied emotions.

To return after long years of painful absence to some place which has been the scene of our former joys, and whence the force of circumstance, and not choice, has driven us, is oppressive to the heart. There is a mixed sense of regret and rejoicing, which struggle for pre-dominance; we rejoice that our term of exile has expired, but we regret the years which that exile has deducted from the brief amount of human life, never to be recalled, and therefore as so much *lost* to us. We think of the wrong or the caprice of which we have been the victims, and thoughts will stray across the most confiding heart, if friends shall meet as fondly as they parted, or if time, while impressing deeper marks upon the *outward* form, may have obliterated, some impressions *within*. Who has returned, after years of absence, however assured of the unflinching fidelity of love he left behind, without saying to himself, in the pardonable yearning of affection, "Shall I meet smiles as bright as those that used to welcome me? Shall I be pressed as fondly within the arms, whose encompassment were to me the pale of all earthly enjoyment?"

Such thoughts crowded on Edward as he approached the house. There was not a lane, or tree, or hedge, by the way, that had not for him its association. He reached the avenue gate; as he flung it open, he remembered the last time he passed it, Fanny leaned on his arm. He felt himself so much excited, that, instead of riding up to the house, he took the private path to the stables, and throwing the reins of his horse to a boy, he turned into a shrubbery, and endeavoured to recover his self-command before he should present himself. As he emerged from the sheltered path, and turned into a walk which led to the a small conservatory was opened to his view, awaking fresh sensations. It was in that very place he had first ventured to declare his love to Fanny. There she heard and frowned not;—there where nature's choicest sweets were exhaling, he had first pressed her to his heart, and thought the balmy sweetness of her lips beyond them all. He hurried forward in the enthusiasm the recollection recalled, to enter that spot consecrated in his memory; but, on arriving at the door, he suddenly stopped, for he saw Fanny within. She was plucking a geranium—the flower she had been plucking some years before, when Edward said he loved her. She, all that morning, had been under the influence of feelings similar to Edward's; had felt the same yearnings—the same tender doubts—the same fond solicitude that he should be the same Edward from whom she parted. But she thought of *more* than this; with the exquisitely delicate contrivance belonging to woman's nature, she wished to give him a signal of her fond recollection, and was plucking the flower she gathered, when he declared his love, to place on her bosom when they should meet. Edward felt the meaning of her action, as the graceful hand broke the flower from its stem. He would have rushed towards her at once, but that the deep mourning in which she was arrived seemed to command a gentler approach; for grief commands respect. He advanced softly—she heard a gentle step behind her, and turned—uttered a faint exclamation of joy, and sank into his arms!

In a few moments she was restored to consciousness, and opening her sweet eyes upon him, breathed softly, "dear Edward!"—and the lips which, in two words, had expressed so much, were impressed with a fervent kiss, in the blessed consciousness of possession, on that very spot where the first timid and doubting word of love had been spoken.

In that moment he was rewarded for all his years of absence and anxiety. His heart was satisfied;—he felt he was as dear as ever to the woman he idolized, and the short and hurried beating of *both* their hearts told more than words could express. Words!—what were words to them?—thought was too swift for their use, and feeling too strong for their utterance; but they drank from each other's eyes large draughts of delight, and, in the silent pressure of each other's welcoming embrace, felt how truly they loved each other.

He led her gently from the conservatory, and they exchanged words of affection "soft and low," as they sauntered through the wooded paths

which surrounded the house. That live-long day they wandered up and
down together, repeating again and again the anxious yearnings which
occupied their years of separation, yet asking each other, was not all
more than repaid by the gladness of the present—

"Yet *how* painful has been the past!" exclaimed Edward.

"But *now!*" said Fanny, with a gentle pressure of her tiny hand on
Edward's arm, and looking up at him with her bright eyes—"but
now!"

"True, darling!" he cried; "'tis ungrateful to think of the past, while
enjoying such a present, and with such future before me. Bless that
cheerful heart, and those hope-inspiring glances! Oh, Fanny! in the
wilderness there are springs and palm-trees—you are both to me! and
Heaven has set its own mark upon you, in laughing blue eyes, which
might set despair at defiance."

"Poetical as ever, Edward!" said Fanny, laughing.

"Sit down, dearest, for a moment, on this old tree, beside me; 'tis not
the first time I have strung rhymes in your presence, and your praise."

He took a small note-book from his pocket, and Fanny looked on
smilingly, as Edward's pencil rapidly ran over the leaf, and traced the
lover's tribute to his mistress.

THE SUNSHINE IN YOU

I

It is sweet when we look round the wide world's waste,
  To know that the desert bestows
The palms where the weary heart may rest,
  The spring that in purity flows.
    And where have I found
    In this wilderness round
  That spring and that shelter so true;
    Unfailing in need,
    And my own, indeed?—
  Oh! dearest, I've found it in you!

II

And, oh when the cloud of some darkening hour
   O'ershadows the soul with its gloom,
Then where is the light of the vestal pow'r,
   The lamp of pale Hope to illume?
     Oh! the light ever lies
     In those bright fond eyes,
  Where Heaven has impress'd its own blue,
     As a seal from the skies
     And my heart relies
On that gift of its sunshine in you!

Fanny liked the lines, of course. "Dearest," she said, "may I always prove sunshine to you! Is it not a strange coincidence that these lines exactly fit a little air which occurred to me some time ago?"

"'Tis odd," said Edward;—"sing it to me, darling."

Fanny took the verses from his hand, and sung them to her own measure. Oh, happy triumph of the poet! To hear his verses wedded to sweet sounds, and warmbled by the woman he loves!

Edward caught up the strain, and added his voice to hers in harmony, and they sauntered homewards, trolling their ready-made duet together.

There were not two happier hearts in the world that day, than those of Fanny Dawson and Edward O'Connor.

1.   If not this identical answer, something very like it was given on a disputed Irish election, before a Committee of the House of Commons.

L

RESPECT FOR THE MEMORY OF Major Dawson of course prevented the immediate marriage of Edward and Fanny but the winter months passed cheerfully away in looking forward to the following autumn, which should witness the completion of their happiness. Though Edward was thus tempted by the society of the one he loved best in the world, it did not make him neglect the duties he had undertaken in behalf of Gustavus. Not only did he prosecute his reading with him regularly, but took no small pains in looking after the involved affairs of the family, and strove to make satisfactory arrangements with those whose claims were gnawing away the estate to nothing. Though the years of Gusty's minority were but few, still they would give the estate some breathing time; and creditors, seeing the minor backed by a man of character, and convinced a sincere desire existed to relieve the estate of its encumbrances and pay all just claims, presented a less threatening front than hitherto, and listened readily to such terms of accommodation as were proposed to them. Uncle Robert (for the breaking of whose neck Ratty's pious aspirations had been raised) behaved very well on the occasion. A loan from him, and a partial sale of some of the acres, stopped the mouths of the greedy wolves who fatten on men's ruin, and time and economy were looked forward to for the discharge of all other debts. Uncle Robert, having so far acted the friend, was considered entitled to have a partial voice in the ordering of things at the Hall; and having a notion that an English accent was genteel, he desired that Gusty and Ratty should pass a year under the roof of a clergyman in England, who received a limited number of young gentlemen for the completion of their education. Gustavus would much rather have remained near Edward O'Connor, who had already done so much for him; but Edward, though he regretted parting with Gustavus, recommended him to accede to his uncle's wishes, though he did not see the necessity of an Irish gentleman being ashamed of his accent.

The visit to England, however, was postponed till the spring, and the winter months were used by Gustavus in availing himself as much as he could of Edward's assistance in putting him through his classics, his pride prompting him to present himself creditably to the English clergyman.

It was in vain to plead *such* pride to Ratty, who paid more attention to shooting than his lessons.

His mother strove to persuade—Ratty was deaf.

His "gran" strove to bribe—Ratty was incorruptible.

Gusty argued—Ratty answered after his own fashion.

"Why won't you learn even a little?"

"I'm to go to that 'English fellow' in spring, and I shall have no fun then, so I'm making good use of my time now."

"Do you call it 'good use' to be so dreadfully idle and shamefully ignorant?"

"Bother!—the less I know, the more the English fellow will have to teach me, and uncle Bob will have more worth for his money;" and then Ratty would whistle a jig, fling a fowling-piece over his shoulder, shout "Ponto! Ponto! Ponto!" as he traversed the stable-yard; the delighted pointer would come bounding at the call, and after circling round his young master with agile grace and yelps of glee at the sight of the gun, dash forward to the well-known "bottoms" in eager expectancy of ducks and snipe.

How fared it all this time with the lord of Scatterbrain?

He became established, for the present, in a house that had been a long time to let in the neighbourhood, and his mother was placed at the head of it, and Oonah still remained under his protection, though the daily sight of the girl added to Andy's grief at the desperate plight in which his ill-starred marriage placed him, to say nothing of the constant annoyance of his mother's growling at him for his making "such a judy"

of himself; for the dowager lady Scatterbrain could not get rid of her
vocabulary at once. Andy's only resource under these circumstances was
to mount his horse, and fly.

As for the dowager lady, she had a carriage with "a picture" on it, as
she called the coat of arms, and was fond of driving past the houses of
people who had been uncivil to her. Against Mrs. Casey (the renowned
Matty Dwyer) she entertained an especial spite, in consideration of her
treatment of her beautiful boy and her own pair of black eyes; so she
determined to "pay her off" in her own way, and stopping one day at
the hole in the hedge which served for entrance to the estate of the
"three-cornered field," she sent the footman in to say the *doujer* Lady
Scatter*breen* wanted to speak with "Casey's wife."

When the servant, according to instructions, delivered this message,
he was sent back with the answer, that if any lady wanted to see Casey's
wife, "Casey's wife" was at home.

"Oh, go back, and tell the poor woman I don't want to bring her
to the door of my carriage, if it's inconvaynient. I only wished to give
her a little help; and tell her if she sends up eggs to the big house, Lady
Scatterbreen will pay her for them."

When the servant delivered this message, Matty grew outrageous at
the means "my lady" took of crowing over her, and rushing to the door,
with her face flushed with rage, roared out, "Tell the old baggage I want
none of her custom; let her lay eggs for herself!"

The servant staggered back in amaze; and Matty, feeling he would not
deliver her message, ran to the hole in the hedge, and repeated her answer
to my lady herself, with a great deal more which need not be recorded.
Suffice it to say, my lady thought it necessary to pull up the glass, against
which Matty threw a handful of mud; the servant jumped up on his
perch behind the carriage, which was rapidly driven away by the coach
man, but not so fast that Matty could not, by dint of running, keep it
"within range" for some seconds, during which time she contrived to
pelt both coachman and footman with mud, and leave her mark on their
new livery. This was a salutary warning to the old woman, who was more
cautious in her demonstrations of grandeur for the future.

If she was stinted in the enjoyment of her new-born dignity abroad,
she could indulge it at home without let or hindrance, and to this end

asked Andy to let her have a hundred pounds, in one pound notes, for a particular purpose. What this purpose was no one was told or could guess, but for a good while after she used to be closeted by herself for several hours during the day. Andy had his hours of retirement also, for with praiseworthy industry he strove hard, poor fellow, to lift himself above the state of ignorance, and had daily attendance from the parish schoolmaster. The mysteries of "pothooks and hangers" and A B C weighed heavily on the nobleman's mind, which must have sunk under the burden of scholarship and penmanship, but for the other "ship,"—the horsemanship, was Andy's daily self-established reward for his perseverance in his lessons. Besides, he really *could* ride; and as it was the only accomplishment of which he was master, it was no wonder he enjoyed the display of it; and to say the truth, he did, and that on a first-rate horse, too. Having appointed Murtough Murphy his law-agent, he often rode over to the town to talk with him, and as Murtough could have some fun and thirteen and four-pence also per visit, he was always glad to see his "noble friend." The high road did not suit Andy's notion of things; he preferred the variety, shortness, and diversion of going across the country on these occasions; and in one of these excursions, in the most secluded portion of his ride, which unavoidably lay through some quarries and deep broken ground, he met "Ragged Nance," who held up her finger as he approached the gorge of this lonely dell, in token that she would speak with him. Andy pulled up.

"Long life to you, my lord," said Nance, dropping a deep curtsey, "and sure I always liked you since the night you was so bowld for the sake of the poor girl,—the young lady, I mane, now, God bless her,—and I just wish to tell you, my lord, that I think you might as well not be going these lonely ways, for I see *them* hanging about here betimes, that may be it would not be good for your health to meet; and sure, my lord, it would be a hard case if you were killed now, havin' the luck o' the sick calf that lived all the winter and died in the sumther."

"Is it that big blackguard *Shan More* you mane?" said Andy.

"No less," said Nance—growing deadly pale as she cast a piercing glance into the dell, and cried in a low hurried tone—"Talk o' the divil—there he is—I see him peep out from behind a rock."

"He's running this way," said Andy.

"Then you run the other way," said Nance—"look there—I seen him strive to hide a blunderbuss under his coat—gallop off, for the love o' God! or there'll be murther."

"Maybe there will be that same," said Andy, "if I leave you here, and he suspects you gave me the hard word" (a caution).

"Never mind me," said Nance, "save yourself—see, he's moving fast, he'll be near enough to you soon to fire."

"Get up behind me," said Andy—"I won't leave you here."

"Run, I tell you."

"I won't."

"God bless you, then," said the woman, as Andy held out his hand and gripped hers firmly.

"Put your foot on mine," said Andy.

The woman obeyed, and was soon seated behind our hero, gripping him fast by the waist, while he pushed his horse to a fast canter.

"Hold hard, now," said Andy, "for there's a stiff jump here." As he approached the ditch of which he spoke, two men sprang up from it, and one fired, as Andy cleared the leap in good style, Nance holding on gallantly. The horse was not many strokes on the opposite side, when another shot was fired in their rear, followed by a scream from the woman. To Andy's inquiry if she was "kilt" she replied in the negative, but said "they hurt her sore," and she was "bleeding a power"—but that she could still hold on however, and urged him to speed. The clearance of one or two more leaps gave her grievous pain; but a large common soon opened before them, which was skirted by a road leading directly to a farm house, where Andy left the wounded woman, and then galloped for medical aid: this soon arrived, and the wound was found not to be dangerous, though painful. The bullet had struck and pierced a tin vessel of a bottle form, in which Nance carried the liquid gratuities of the charitable, and this not only deadened the force of the ball, but glanced it also; and the escapement of the buttermilk which the vessel contained, Nance had mistaken for the effusion of her own blood. It was a clear case, however, that if Nance had not been sitting behind Andy, Lord Scatterbrain would have been a dead man, so that his gratitude and gallantry towards the poor beggarwoman proved the means of preserving his own life.

LI

THE NEWS OF THE ATTACK on Lord Scatterbrain ran over the country like wildfire, and his conduct throughout the affair raised his character wonderfully in the opinion of all classes. Many who had hitherto held aloof from the mushroom lord, came forward to recognise the manly fellow, and cards were left at "the big house," which were never seen there before. The magistrates were active in the affair, and a reward immediately offered for the apprehension of the offenders; but before any active steps could be taken by the authorities, Andy, immediately after the attack, collected a few stout fellows himself, and knowing where the den of Shan and his miscreants lay, he set off at the head of his party to try if he could not secure them himself;—but before he did this, he despatched a vehicle to the farm house, where poor Nance lay wounded, with orders that she should be removed to his own house, the doctor having said the transit would not be injurious.

A short time served to bring Andy and his followers to the private still, where a little looking about enabled them to discover the entrance, which was covered by some large stones, and a bunch of furze placed as a mask to the opening. It was clear that it was impossible for any persons inside to have thus covered the entrance, and it suggested the possibility that some of its usual inmates were then absent. Nevertheless, having such desperate characters to deal with, it was a service of danger to be leader in the descent to the cavern when the opening was cleared; but Andy was the first to enter, which he did boldly, only desiring his attendants to follow him quickly, and give him support in case of resistance. A lantern had been provided, Andy knowing the darkness of the den; and the party was thereby enabled to explore with celerity and certainty the hidden haunt of the desperadoes. The ashes of the fire were yet warm, but no one was to be seen, till Andy, drawing the screen of the bed, discovered a man lying in a seemingly helpless state, breathing with difficulty, and the straw about him dabbled with blood. On attempting to lift him, the wretch groaned heavily and muttered, "D— you, let me alone—you've done for me—I'm dying."

The man was gently carried from the cave to the open air, which seemed slightly to revive him—his eyes opened heavily, but closed again—yet still he breathed. His wound was stanched as well as the limited means and knowledge of the parties present allowed; and the ladder, drawn up from the cave and overlaid with tufts of heather, served to bear the sufferer to the nearest house, whence Andy ordered a mounted messenger to hurry for a doctor. The man seemed to hear what was going forward, for he faintly muttered "the priest, the priest."

Andy, anxious to procure this most essential comfort to the dying man, went himself in search of Father Blake, whom he found at home, and who suggested that a magistrate might be also useful on the occasion; and as Merryvale lay not much out of the way, Andy made a detour to obtain the presence of Squire Egan, while Father Blake pushed directly onward upon his ghostly mission.

Andy and the Squire arrived soon after the priest had administered spiritual comfort to the sufferer, who still retained sufficient strength to make his depositions before the Squire, the purport of which turned out to be of the utmost importance to Andy.

This man, it appeared, *was the husband of Bridget*, who had returned from transportation, and sought his wife and her dear brother and his former lawless associates, on reaching Ireland. On finding Bridget had married again, his anger at her infidelity was endeavoured to be appeased by the representations made to him that it was a "good job," inasmuch as "the lord" had been screwed out of a good sum of money by way of separate maintenance and that he would share the advantage of that. When matters were more explained, however, and the convict found this money was divided among so many, who all claimed right

of share in the plunder, his discontent returned. In the first place, the
pettifogger made a large haul for his services. Shan More swore it was
hard if a woman's own brother was not to be the better for her luck;
and Larry Hogan claimed hush-money, for he could prove Bridget's
marriage, and so upset their scheme of plunder. The convict maintained,
his claim as husband was stronger than any; but this, all the others
declared, was an outlandish notion he brought back with him from
foreign parts, and did not prevail in their code of laws by any manner
of means; and even went so far as to say, they thought it hard, after they
had "done the job," that he was to come in and lessen their profit, which
he would, as they were willing to give an even share of the spoil; and
after that he must be the most discontented villain in the world if he
was not pleased.

The convict feigned contentment, but meditated at once revenge
against his wife and the gang, and separate profit for himself. He thought
he might stipulate for a good round sum from Lord Scatterbrain, as he
could prove him free of his supposed matrimonial engagement, and
inwardly resolved he would soon pay a visit to his lordship. But his
intentions were suspected by the gang, and a strict watch set upon
him; and though his dissimulation and contrivance were of no inferior
order, Larry Hogan was his overmatch, and the convict was detected in
having been so near Lord Scatterbrain's dwelling, that they feared their
secret, if not already revealed, was no longer to be trusted to their new
confederate's keeping; and it was deemed advisable to knock him on the
head and shoot my Lord, which they thought would prevent all chance
of the invalidity of the marriage being discovered, and secure the future
payment of the maintenance.

How promptly the murderous determination was acted upon the
preceding events prove. Andy's courage in the first part of the affair
saved his life; his promptness in afterwards seeking to secure the
offenders, led to the important discovery he had just made; and as the
convict's depositions could be satisfactorily backed by proofs which he
showed the means of obtaining, Andy was congratulated heartily by
the Squire and Father Blake, and rode home in almost delirious delight
at the prospect of making Oonah his wife. On reaching the stables
he threw himself from his saddle, let the horse make his own way to

his stall, dashed through the back hall, and nearly broke his neck in tumbling up stairs, burst open the drawing-room door, and made a rush upon Oonah, whom he hugged and kissed most outrageously, amidst exclamations of the wildest affection.

Oonah, half strangled and struggling for breath, at last freed herself from his embraces, and asked him angrily what he was about—in which inquiry she was backed by his mother.

Andy answered by capering round the room, shouting "Hurroo! I'm not married at all—Hurroo!" He turned over the chairs, upset the tables, threw the mantelpiece ornaments into the fire, seized the poker and tongs and banged them together as he continued dancing and shouting.

Oonah and his mother stood gazing at his antics in trembling amazement, till at last the old woman exclaimed, "Holy Vargin, he's gone mad!" whereupon she and her niece set up a violent screaming, which called Andy back to his propriety, and, as well as his excitement would permit, he told them the cause of his extravagant joy.

His wonder and delight were shared by his mother and the blushing Oonah, who did not struggle so hard in Andy's embrace on his making a second vehement demonstration of his love for her.

"Let me send for Father Blake, my jewel," said Andy, "and I'll marry you at once."

His mother reminded him he must first have his present marriage proved invalid.

Andy uttered several pieces of *original* eloquence on "the law's delay."

"Well, any how," said he, "I'll drink your health, my darling girl, this day, as Lady Scatterbrain—for you must consider yourself as sitch."

"Behave yourself, my lord," said Oonah, archly.

"Bother!" cried Andy, snatching another kiss.

"Hillo!" cried Dick Dawson, entering at the moment, and seeing the romping match—"You're losing no time I see, Andy."

Oonah was running from the room, laughing and blushing, when Dick interposed, and cried, "Ah, don't go, 'my lady,' that *is to be.*"

Oonah slapped down the hand that barred her progress, exclaiming, "You're just as bad as he is, Mister Dawson!" and ran away.

Dick had ridden over, on hearing the news, to congratulate Andy, and consented to remain and dine with him. Oonah had rather, after what had taken place, he had not been there, for Dick backed Andy in his tormenting the girl, and joined heartily in drinking to Andy's toast, which, according to promise, he gave to the health of the future Lady Scatterbrain.

It was impossible to repress Andy's wild delight; and in the excitement of the hour he tossed off bumper after bumper to all sorts of love-making toasts, till he was quite overcome by his potations, and fit for no place but bed. To this last retreat of "the glorious" he was requested to retire, and, after much coaxing, consented. He staggered over to the window curtain, which he mistook for that of the bed; in vain they wanted to lead him elsewhere—he would sleep in no other bed but *that*—and, backing out at the window pane, he made a smash, of which he seemed sensible, for he said it wasn't a fair trick to put pins in his bed.

"I know it was Oonah did that!—hip!—ha ha! Lady Scatterbrain!—never mind!—hip!—I'll have my revenge on you yet."

They could not get him up-stairs, so his mother suggested he should sleep in her room, which was on the same floor, for that night, and at last he was got into the apartment. There he was assisted to disrobe, as he stood swaying about at a dressing-table. Chancing to lay his hands on a pill-box, he mistook it for his watch—"Stop—stop!" he stammered forth—"I must wind my watch;" and, suiting the action to the word, he began twisting about the pill-box, the lid of which came off and the pills fell about the floor. "Oh murder!" said Lord Scatterbrain, "the works of my watch are fallin' about the flure—pick them up—pick them up—pick them up—" He could speak no more, and becoming quite incapable of all voluntary action, was undressed and put to bed, the last sounds which escaped him being a faint muttering of—"pick them up!"

LII

THE DAY FOLLOWING THE EVENTFUL one just recorded, the miserable convict breathed his last. A printed notice was posted in all the adjacent villages, offering a reward for the apprehension of *Shan More* and "other persons unknown," for their murderous assault; and a small reward was promised for such "private information as might lead to the apprehension of the aforesaid," &c. &c. Larry Hogan at once came forward and put the authorities on the scent, but still Shan and his accomplices remained undiscovered. Larry's information on another subject, however, was more effective. He gave his own testimony to the previous marriage of Bridget, and pointed out the means of obtaining more, so that, ere long, Lord Scatterbrain was a "free man." Though the depositions of the murdered man did not directly implicate Larry in the murderous attack, still it showed that he had participated in much of their villainy; but as, in difficult cases, we must put up with bad instruments to reach the ends of justice, so this rascal was useful for his evidence and private information, and got his reward.

But he got his reward in more ways than one. He knew that he dare not longer remain in the country after what had taken place, and set off directly for Dublin by the mail, intending to proceed to England;—but England he never reached. As he was proceeding down the Custom House Quay in the dusk of the evening, to get on ship-board, his arms, were suddenly seized and drawn behind him by a powerful grasp, while a woman in front drew a handkerchief across his mouth, and stifled his attempted cries. His bundle was dragged from him, and the woman ransacked his pockets; but they contained but a few shillings,

Larry having hidden the wages of his treachery to his confederates in the folds of his neck-cloth. To pluck this from his throat many a fierce wrench was made by the woman, when her attempt on the pockets proved worthless; but the handkerchief was knotted so tightly that she could not disengage it. The approach of some passengers along the quay alarmed the assailants of Larry, who, ere the iron grip released him, heard a deep curse in his ear growled by a voice he well knew, and then felt himself hurled with gigantic force from the quay wall. Before the base, cheating, faithless scoundrel could make one exclamation, he was plunged into the Liffey—before one mental aspiration for mercy, he was in the throes of suffocation! The heavy splash in the water caught the attention of those whose approach had alarmed the murderers, and seeing a man and woman running, a pursuit commenced, which ended by Newgate having two fresh tenants the next day.

And so farewell to the entire of the abominable crew, whose evil doings and merited fates have only been recorded when it became necessary to our story. It is better to leave the debased and the profligate in oblivion than drag their doings before the day; and it is with happy consciousness an Irishman may assert, that there is plenty of subject afforded by Irish character and Irish life honourable to the land, pleasing to the narrator, and sufficiently attractive to the reader, without the unwhole some exaggerations of crime, which too often disfigure the fictions which pass under the title of "Irish," alike offensive to truth as to taste—alike injurious both for private and public considerations.

It was in the following autumn that a particular chariot drove up to the door of the Victoria Hotel, on the shore of Killarney lake. A young man of elegant bearing handed a very charming young lady from that chariot; and that kindest and most accommodating of hostesses, Mrs. F— , welcomed the fresh arrival with her good humoured and smiling face.

Why, amidst the crowd of arrivals at the Victoria, one chariot should be remarkable beyond another, arose from its quiet elegance, which might strike even 'a casual observer; but the intelligent Mrs.

F—— saw with half an eye the owners must be high-bred people. To the apartments already engaged for them they were shown; but few minutes were lost within doors where such matchless natural beauty tempted them without. A boat was immediately ordered, and then the newly-arrived visitors were soon on the lake. The boatmen had already worked hard that day, having pulled one party completely round the lakes—no trifling task; but the hardy fellows again bent to their oars, and made the sleeping waters wake in golden flashes to the sunset, till told they need not pull so hard.

Faith, then, we'll *plaze* you, sir," said the stroke oarsman, with a grin, "for we have had quite enough of it to-day."

"Do you not think, Fanny," said Edward O'Connor, for it was he who spoke to his bride, "Do you not think 'tis more in unison with the tranquil hour and the coming shadows, to glide softly over the lulled waters?"

"Yes," she replied, "it seems almost sacrilege to disturb this heavenly repose by the slightest dip of the oar—see how perfectly that lovely island is reflected."

"That is Innisfallin, my lady," said the boatman, hearing her allude to the island, "where the hermitage is."

As he spoke, a gleam of light sparkled on the island, and was reflected on the water.

"One might think the hermit was there, too," said, Fanny, "and had just lighted a lamp for his vigils."

"That's the light of the guide that shows the place to the quality, my lady, and lives on the island always in a corner of the ould ruin. And indeed if you'd like to see the island this evening, there's time enough, and 'twould be so much saved out of to-morrow."

The boatman's advice was acted upon, and as they glided towards the island, Fanny and Edward gazed delightedly on the towering summits of Magillicuddy's reeks, whose spiral pinnacles and graceful declivities told out sharply against the golden sky behind them, which, being perfectly reflected in the calm lake, gave the grand chain of mountain the appearance of being suspended in glowing there, for the lake was one bright amber sheet of light below, and the mountains one massive barrier of shade, till they cut against the light above. The boat touched the shore of Innisfallin, and the delighted pair of visitants hurried to its western point to catch the sunset, lighting with its glory the matchless foliage of this enchanting spot, where every form of grace exhaustless nature can display is lavished on the arborial richness of the scene, which, in its unequalled luxuriance, gives to a fanciful beholder the idea that *the trees themselves have a conscious pleasure in growing there*. Oh! what a witching spot is Innisfallin!

Edward had never seen any thing so beautiful in his life; and with the woman he adored resting on his arm, he quoted the lines which Moore has applied to the Vale of Cashmere, as he asked Fanny would she not like to live there.

"Would you?" said Fanny.

Edward answered—

> "If woman can make the worst wilderness dear,
> Think—think what a heaven she must make of
> Cashmere!"

They lingered on the island till the moon arose, and then re-embarked. The silvery light exhibited the lake under another aspect, and as the dimly-discovered forms of the lofty hills rose one above another, tier upon tier, circling the waters in their shadowy frame, the beauty of the scene reached a point of sublimity which might be called holy. As they returned towards the shelving strand, a long row of peeled branches, standing upright in the water, attracted Fanny's attention, and she asked their use— "All the use in life, my lady," said the boatman, "for without the same branches, maybe it's not home to-night you'd get."

On Fanny inquiring further the meaning of the boatman's answer, she learned that the sticks were placed there to indicate the only channel which permitted a boat to approach the shore on that side of the lake, where the water was shoal, while in other parts the depth had never been fathomed.

An early excursion on the water was planned for the next morning, and Edward and Fanny were awakened from their slumbers by the tones of the bugle; a soft Irish melody being breathed by Spillan, followed by a more sportive one from the other minstrel of the lake, Ganzy.

The lake now appeared under another aspect,—the morning sun and morning breeze were upon it, and the sublimity with which the shades of evening had invested the mountains was changed to that of the most varied richness; for Autumn hung out his gaudy banner on the lofty hills, crowned to their summits with all variety of wood, which, though tinged by the declining year, had scarcely shed one leafy honour.

The day was glorious, and the favouring breeze enabled the boat to career across the sparkling lake under canvas, till the overhanging hills of the opposite side robbed them of their aerial wings, and the sail being struck, the boatmen bent to their oars. As they passed under a promontory, clothed from the water's edge to its topmost ridge with the most luxuriant vegetation, it was pointed out to the lady as "the minister's back."

"'Tis a strange name," said Fanny.—"Do you know why it is called so?"

"Faix I dunna, my lady—barrin, that it is the best covered back in the country. But here we come to the *aichos*," said he—resting on his oars. The example was followed by his fellows, and the bugler lifting his instrument to his lips, gave one long well-sustained blast. It rang across the waters gallantly. It returned in a few seconds, with such unearthly sweetness, as though the spirit of the departed sound had become heavenly and revisited the place where it had expired.

Fanny and Edward listened breathlessly.

The bugle gave out its notes again in the well known 'call,' and as sweetly as before the notes were returned distinctly.

And now a soft and slow and simple melody stole from the exquisitely played bugle, and phrase after phrase was echoed from the responding hills. How many an emotion stirred within Edward's breast, as the melting music fell upon his ear! In the midst of matchless beauties he heard the matchless strains of his native land, and the echoes of her old hills responding to the triumphs of her old bards. The air, too, bore with it historic association;—it told a tale of wrong and of suffering. The wrong has ceased, the suffering is past, but the air which records them still lives.

"Oh! triumph of the minstrel!" exclaimed Edward in delight.—"The tyrant crumbles in his coffin, while the song of the bard survives! The memory of a sceptred ruffian is endlessly branded by a simple strain, while many of the elaborate chronicles of his evil life have passed away and are mouldering like himself."

Scarcely had the echoes of this exquisite air died away, when the entrancement it carried was rudely broken by one of the lowest tunes being braved from a bugle in a boat which was seen rounding the headland of the wooded promontory.

Edward and Fanny writhed, and put their hands to their ears. "Give way, boys!" said Edward—"for pity's sake get away from these barbarians.—Give way."

Away sprang the boat. To the boatman's inquiry whether they should stop at "Lady Kenmare's Cottage," Fanny said, no—when she found on inquiry it was a particularly "show-place," being certain the vulgar party following, *would* stop there, and therefore time might be gained in getting ahead from such disagreeable followers.

Dinas Island, fringed with its lovely woods, excited their admiration as they passed underneath its shadows, and turned into Turk Lake;— here the labyrinthine nature of the channels through which they had been winding was changed for a circular expanse of water, over which the lofty mountain, whence it takes its name, towers in all its wild beauty of wood, and rock, and heath.

At a certain part of the lake the boatmen, without any visible cause, rested on their oars. On Edward asking them why they did not pull, he received this touching answer—

"Sure your honour would not have us disturb Ned Macarthy's grave!"

"Then a boatman was drowned here, I suppose," said Edward.

"Yes, your honour." The boatman then told how the accident occurred one day when there was a stag-hunt on the lake; but as the anecdote struck Edward so forcibly, that he afterwards recorded it in verse, we will give the story after his fashion.

MACARTHY'S GRAVE.

I

The breeze was fresh, the morn was fair,
The stag had left his dewy lair;
To cheering horn and baying tongue,
Killarney's echoes sweetly rung.
With sweeping oar and bending mast,
The eager chase was following fast;
When one light skiff a maiden steer'd
Beneath the deep wave disappear'd:
While shouts of terror wildly ring,
A boatman brave, with gallant spring
And dauntless arm, the lady bore—
But he who saved—was seen no more!

II

Where weeping birches wildly wave,
There boatmen show their brother's grave;
And while they tell the name he bore,
Suspended hangs the lifted oar:
The silent drops they idly shed,
Seem like tears to gallant Ned;
And while gently gliding by,
The tale is told with moistened eye.
No ripple on the slumb'ring lake
Unhallowed oar doth ever make
All undisturb'd, the placid wave
Flows gently o'er Macarthy's grave.

Winding backwards through the channels which lead the explorers
of this scene of nature's enchantment from the lower to the upper
lake, the surpassing beauty of the "Eagle's nest" burst on their view,
and as they hovered under its stupendous crags, clustering with all

variety of verdure, the bugle and the cannon awoke the almost endless reverberation of sound which is engendered here.—Passing onward, a sudden change is wrought;—the soft beauty melts gradually away, and the scene hardens into frowning rocks and steep acclivities, making a befitting vestibule to the bold and bleak precipices of "The Reeks," which form the western barrier of this upper lake, whose savage grandeur is rendered more striking by the scenes of fairy-like beauty left behind. But even here, in the midst of the mightiest desolation, the vegetative vigour of the numerous islands proves the wondrous productiveness of the soil in these regions.

On their return, a great commotion was observable as they approached the rapids formed by the descending waters of the upper lake to the lower, and they were hailed and warned by some of the peasants from the shore, that they must not attempt the rapids at present, as a boat, which had been upset, lay athwart the passage. On hearing this, Edward and Fanny were landed above the falls, and walked towards the old bridge, where all was bustle and confusion, as the dripping passengers were dragged safely to shore from the capsized boat, which had been upset by the principal gentleman of the party, whose vulgar trumpetings had so disturbed the delight of Edward and Fanny, who soon recognised the renowned Andy as the instigator of the bad music and the cause of the accident. Yes, Lord Scatterbrain, true to his original practice, was author of all.

Nevertheless, he and his party, soused over head and ears as they were, took the thing in good humour, which was unbroken even by the irrepressible laughter which escaped from Edward and Fanny, as they approached and kindly offered assistance. An immediate removal to the neighbouring cottage on Dinas Island was recommended, particularly as Lady Scatterbrain was in a delicate situation, as well, indeed, as Mrs. Durfy, who, with her dear Tom, had joined Lord Scatterbrain's party of pleasure.

On reaching the cottage, sufficient change of clothes was obtained to prevent evil consequences from the ducking. This, under ordinary circumstances, might not have been easy for so many; but fortunately Lord Scatterbrain had ordered a complete dinner from the hotel to be served in the cottage, and some of the assistants from the Victoria, who were necessarily present, helped to dress more than the dinner. What between cookmaids and waiters, the care-taker of the cottage and the boatmen, bodies and skirts, jackets and other conveniences, enabled the party to sit down to dinner in company, until fire could mend the mistake of his lordship. Edward and Fanny courteously joined the party; and the honour of their company was sensibly felt by Andy and Oonah, who would have borne a ducking a day for the honour of having Fanny and Edward as their guests. Oonah was by nature a nice creature, and adapted herself to her elevated position with a modest ease that was surprising. Even Andy was by this time able to conduct himself tolerably well at table, only on that particular day he did make a mistake; for when salmon (which is served at Killarney in all sorts of variety) made its appearance for the first time before the noble lord in the novel form "*en papillote*," Andy ate paper and all. He refused a second cutlet, however, saying he *thought the skin tough*. The party, however, passed off mirthfully, the very accident helping the fun; for instead of any one being called by name, the "lady in the jacket," or the "gentleman in the bedgown," were the terms of address; and, after a merrily spent evening, the beds of the Victoria gave sleep and pleasing dreams to the sojourners at Killarney.

Kind reader! the shortening space we have prescribed to our volume, warns us we must draw our story to an end. Nine months after this Killarney excursion, Lord Scatterbrain met Dick Dawson near Mount Eskar, where Lord Scatterbrain had ridden to make certain inquiries about Mrs. O'Connor's health. Dick wore a smiling countenance, and to Andy's inquiry, answered, "All right, and doing as well as can be expected."

Lord Scatterbrain, wishing to know whether it was a boy or a girl, made the inquiry in the true spirit of Andyism,—"Tell me, Mister Dawson, *are you an uncle or an aunt?*"

Andy's mother died soon after, of the cold caught by her ducking. On her death-bed she called Oonah to her, and said, "I leave you this quilt, *alanna*,—'tis worth more than it appears. The hundred pound notes Andy gave me I quilted into the lining, so that if I lived poor all my life till lately, I died under a quilt of bank-notes, any how."

Uncle Bob was gathered to his fathers also, and left the bulk of his property to Augusta, so that Furlong had to regret his contemptible conduct in rejecting her hand. Augusta indulged in a spite to all mankind for the future, enjoying her dogs and her independence, and defying Hymen and hydrophobia for the rest of her life.

Gusty went on profiting by the early care of Edward O'Connor, whose friendship was ever his dearest possession; and Ratty, always wild, expressed a desire for leading a life of enterprise. As they are both "Irish heirs" as well as Lord Scatterbrain, and heirs under very different circumstances, it is not improbable that in our future "accounts" something may yet be heard of them, and the grateful author once more meet his kind readers, for whose generous support he begs to tender his genuine thanks while offering a respectful, adieu till next year.

THE END

ALSO AVAILABLE IN THE NONSUCH CLASSICS SERIES

John Halifax, Gentleman	Dinah Craik	1 84588 027 7
The Clockmaker	Thomas Chandler Haliburton	1 84588 050 1
Three Courses and a Dessert	William Clarke	1 84588 072 2
For the Term of His Natural Life	Marcus Clarke	1 84588 082 X
Three Diggers	Percy Clarke	1 84588 084 6
The Slave Son	Mrs William Noy Wilkins	1 84588 086 2
Tales	Edgar Allan Poe	1 84588 036 6
The Rise of Silas Lapham	William Dean Howells	1 84588 041 2
The Attaché	Thomas Chandler Haliburton	1 84588 049 8
The Romance of the Forest	Ann Radcliffe	1 84588 073 0
"Ask Mamma"	Robert S. Surtees	1 84588 002 1
Vathek	William Beckford	1 84588 060 9
Suburban Sketches	William Dean Howells	1 84588 083 8
The Apple Tree	John Galsworthy	1 84588 013 7
A Long-Ago Affair	John Galsworthy	1 84588 105 2
Father and Son	Edmund Gosse	1 84588 018 8
At the Sign of the Cat and Racket	Honoré de Balzac	1 84588 051 X
The Seamy Side of History	Honoré de Balzac	1 84588 052 8
The Spy	James Fenimore Cooper	1 84588 055 2
The White Monkey	John Galsworthy	1 84588 058 7
Chronicles of Dartmoor	Anne Marsh Caldwell	1 84588 071 4
Two Old Men's Tales	Anne Marsh Caldwell	1 84588 081 1
The Vicar of Bullhampton	Anthony Trollope	1 84588 097 8
Desperate Remedies	Thomas Hardy	1 84588 099 4
Christmas Books	Charles Dickens	1 84588 195 8
Christmas Stories	Charles Dickens	1 84588 196 6

For forthcoming titles and sales information see

www.nonsuch-publishing.com